Best

Bob

# BUZZARD BAY

# White Powder

There's a sayin in the islands an that sayin say
If you want to go on livin, stay away from Buzzard Bay
But if you be tired of what livin's givin an you want to make your play
Then that's where you be goin boy, down on Buzzard Bay

Chorus
White cocaine like acid rain
In the nose down to your toes an settles in your brain

I's just the boy who loads the boat and set it afloat
So the coke can go explore some foreign shore
Where it begins by creepin in under your neighbor's door
Even on to the New York tradin floor where the man knows he has to score
So tonight he can buy some more of the yeah, you got it, white powder

Chorus
There's a storm of white sand movin north across the Rio Grande
Where the man tried to make a stand but that didn't even slow the flow
Of that blow comin up from Mexico
Ran right over the Alamo, turned to snow when it hit Idaho
Decided to give the west coast a tease, got caught up in an L.A. breeze
An went across the seas to visit the Chinese
Left a smog in the air over Tiananmen Square, then went to see the Russian bear
Jumped right over the Kremlin gate, spent the night on a fashionable English estate
An at daybreak ended up on some Arab's breakfast plate

Chorus
Yeah, that white powder it don't discriminate, it don't care how much you make
It don't give, it just take everything that man can create
White cocaine like acid rain, I got a woman on the brain
I's the man who loads the boat but that don't keep me afloat
My woman wants to be a star when she walks into the bar, even wants a new car
So I do a little stealin, do a little dealin, just to keep her by my side
Now the man's comin to take me for a ride, that woman of mine never even cried
When they found me washed up in the mornin tide
She never missed a beat, wasn't even discreet
When she asked that man on the next barstool seat
If she could give him a little treat
For some of that, yeah, you know, white powder

Chorus
It don't pick, it don't choose
It don't care if you win or lose
It's just there for you to use
Yeah, you know, the white powder

BOB FERGUSON

| Library of Congress Control Number: | | 2012909843 |
|---|---|---|
| ISBN: | Hardcover | 978-1-4771-2209-9 |
| | Softcover | 978-1-4771-2208-2 |
| | Ebook | 978-1-4771-2210-5 |



This is a work of fiction. Names, characters, places and incidents either are the product of the author's imagination or are used fictitiously, and any resemblance to any actual persons, living or dead, events, or locales is entirely coincidental.

This book was printed in the United States of America.

**To order additional copies of this book, contact:**
Xlibris Corporation
1-888-795-4274
www.Xlibris.com
Orders@Xlibris.com

I dedicate this book to my wife Irene, who is
my editor, mentor and love of my life.
Without her this book would never have been written.

# One

## 1997

LIKE THE SHOCK of an electrical wire, my every sense becomes alert. Instantly, I'm awake, searching to understand what it was that startled me from that deep sleep. Someone's in the house, or is it just the house cracking and shrinking from the intense cold outside? Silence. Only the ticking of Mom's old mantle clock breaks the intensity of the moment. A feeling of fear begins to invade my senses; something's not right.

I quickly scramble from the old feather tick. Panic grips, my heart's in my mouth, and I feel like running. But where? How? Deep breaths; get a hold of yourself. Maybe it's nothing, yet something's not right. What? Slow now, think… you know you've been worried about something, and you know what that is, so confirm your suspicions. I don't think what's troubling me is in the house, at least not yet, so check out the house.

The panic is subsiding; cold calculation is setting in as I throw on my pants and shirt. I know downstairs, Dad's gun case is hanging on the living room wall. What am I saying? It's probably nothing. Much more confident, I slip downstairs.

The moonlight shining off the snow illuminates the living room, giving me no problems finding my way around as I quietly check out the house. It's out the back kitchen window that I see them. Christ! There they are, right outside the window, three of them. I'm so scared I start to cry.

"They're going to kill me," is all I can think of. My first instinct is to crawl up into a ball and pretend that this isn't happening, and then anger clears my brain. I'm still alive. I know they're there. Let's move! By the front door of the kitchen hung the coats. I grab one and put on some boots, then run into the living room where I take Dad's old .270 Winchester off the wall. In the drawer, on the bottom of the gun case, there is a box of shells, not a full box; but I'm not taking time to count them. I glance out the front window, there are two more of them, just standing there.

George. What about George, Mom's old dog? He must have got a bark off before they got him. Must be what woke me up and probably why they were standing there, waiting to see if he had woken anyone up… waiting to see if a light came on so they would know my room.

I had to have a plan. Maybe if I wait for them… no! I remember as a child that by opening the spare bedroom window, you could reach the kitchen roof. The kitchen was built onto the original two stories as an addition. The kitchen roof's eaves run almost to the edge of the bedroom window. As a child, I had been able to step over to it from the windowsill—why not now?

Fear propels me up the stairs to the bedroom window, and then doubt takes over. The window—how to quietly open the window. Would it open at all? Strangely, sweat drips in my eyes.

"You have to try. It's the only chance you've got," I hear my mind say. It opens effortlessly—must be because of the cold. Now when to make my move… If they hear me, I will be dead. I didn't have a rifle with me when I was a kid either. A crash downstairs tells me to move; they are coming in. I look down; one of them is below me.

He breaks the living room window and climbs in. I climb out. About a foot of snow covers the roof, hopefully muffling my footsteps. I am on the run now, crossing the kitchen roof, then leaping into the snow below. The snow is deep, and I flounder desperately, scrambling my way toward the tree line, which is not that far, yet an eternity away. I stiffen my back as if this would fend off the bullets about to hit my back at any second, then plunge headfirst into the underbrush.

I made it! For the first time in the last few minutes, I knew I had a chance. This newfound energy drives me down through the trees, into the valley below.

The old farmhouse was built on the edge of a deep wooded valley about half a mile wide. The valley bottom was fertile farmland with a small river meandering through the middle of it. My idea now was to keep moving until I reached the other side. There were no roads over there, and I would be able to see anyone following me. Fear propelled me, but my mind wouldn't focus.

Why? We'd been sent back to Canada without any passports. How could we be of any danger to anyone? Yet I had this nagging fear that someone might come looking for us.

"Guess that's what kept me alive so far," I think as I reach the thin row of trees along the river's edge. For the first time, I look back to see if anyone's behind me. There's no one in sight. I try to listen over my heavy breathing but can hear nothing. Quickly I crossed the ice on the river. Not until reaching the other side of the open flat would I feel secure enough to rest before ascending the far hill.

Other thoughts race through my mind. "What about the others? Bill and Hania, Dale and Pearl—had they already killed them, or was I the first?" I must try to warn them.

The hill is steep, but finally, I clear the trees at the top and come out onto open farmland, which stretches for miles on this side of the valley. For anyone who's never been in the north, it's hard to imagine how the moon lights up the terrain like a city under streetlights, creating shadows at the least indentation. Unlike the city, there are no people—only yourself and, except for the occasional wild animal, the unending world of snow and trees. It's eerie, so quiet you can hear your heartbeat, so cold you can see your own breath. Not only are you being hunted by humans, you know that nature can kill you too.

Along the top of the valley at its crest are huge mounds of snow, not unlike sand dunes. These sand like dunes were created by the wind blowing the snow off the flatlands and piling up against the trees that bordered the valley, creating hills of snow twelve feet high in places. This snow was packed hard, and it was one of these that I ascended to survey the valley below. There they were, crossing the first flat between the far hill and the river. I had done better than I thought; although they had found my trail, it had taken a while. The moon washed the valley with light, making them vulnerable, but I guess they have no idea I am armed.

My problem is that I hate guns. Although my father was a crack shot and an excellent hunter, he had never encouraged me to use a rifle. However, he had shown me how to use one, which is right now coming in handy. Pulling the box of shells from my coat pocket, I inserted three shells into the rifle, thinking I should conserve my ammunition. Then I lay in the snow, focusing on the black objects with the scope, which turn them into humans obviously laboring in the deep snow. Remembering what I had read about when shooting downhill, one intended to shoot high. I aim at one of the figures legs, not breathing, and pull the trigger. My first sensation was that my shoulder hurt. The black object in the scope seemed to leap, and snow flew; as the sound of my rifle broke the silence.

"Roll, they'll see the flash from my rifle. Get away from it."

I lay face down in the snow, expecting a barrage of gunfire; although there is noise from below, nothing is being disturbed anywhere around me. I peer over the edge. Uzis. I can see the wink of gunfire in all directions; it almost makes me giddy. Hell, they have small close-range machine guns, Uzis or whatever they are called, and it's having no effect on me whatsoever.

As my senses clear, I can see one of them thrashing in the snow. The two others are running for the tree line along the opposite side of the valley. To the west, there is a graveled road with a bridge to cross the river. Although there are no roads running toward me, this road did run north to a small village about four miles away. Just below the farmhouse, the lights of a vehicle come on and start to descend the hill toward the bridge. In my estimation, this is where the killers had left their vehicle out of sight and gone the rest of the way to the house by foot.

My thoughts went back to George.

"Should have put him away," Mom had said. "But Dad would have never stood for it, so I guess we'll let him die in his own time."

I was pretty sure that George had saved my life.

In cold fury, I turn the rifle on the descending car lights and fire, ejecting the spent casing, then aim again. The sharp crack is still in my ears as I watch the lights turn slowly to the right and then fall down the steep embankment along the side of the road. The lights bury themselves in the deep snow at the bottom, leaving only the taillights sticking straight up like beacons. I feel a deep hatred inside me; I feel like shooting some more. I have turned from a man who couldn't kill his own injured dog to a man who wants to kill anyone around him... These thoughts and the cold air bring me back to what was going on below.

The two men in the flat had now reached the trees, and the third was crawling through the snow ever so slowly in the same direction.

To my right, a figure is moving beside the ditched vehicle, and then another one appears. I guess they had dug themselves out. I loaded another cartridge into the rifle. The figures began scampering up the side of the ditch. I fire and through the scope, I watch them dive back toward the vehicle.

Actually, I couldn't believe how well I'd done. I had hit one of them with the first shot and caused their car to run off the road with one of my others. Not bad for a guy who had not fired a gun for a while—probably just damn lucky.

Now reality begins to set in. It must be at least thirty degrees below zero. The sweat I had worked up has now turned to ice. Maybe this is what they call shock. I don't know, but I'm starting to feel very cold. These guys are not going anywhere for a while, so what do I do? I have no mitts, no hat… better start to walk, but where? To the east, there's a farmhouse about one and a half miles away. It's only used in the summer months by the people who farm the land. Probably some kind of heat, still a mile and a half through three-foot deep snow, in my condition, can I make it? The lights are on in Mom's house. It looks so safe, beckoning.

Down below in the flat, the two shadows run out and grab their downed partner. I could fire at them, but I'm too tired emotionally and physically. They're going to end up in that house, and it seems so unfair. Determination sets in, and I sling the rifle over my shoulder. If I stay along the very edge of the valley, maybe the snow will be hard enough on top of the dunes to carry me.

I begin to walk. A mile and a half… well, I sure hope there's some way to heat that shack if I can ever get to it. My mind begins to wander back to a time of turmoil in my life, but I had never, never thought it would lead to this.

"Just an ordinary guy," I think. The going is good, and I begin to run a bit. I'm coming for you, July. I've dragged you through pure hell, but we'll make it. I strode on with new resolve.

# Two

## 1984

PRIDE WAS MY biggest problem. Failure was never an option, you put your head down and kept going, no matter what. I remember that bright September afternoon when reality hit - there was a time to quit before you destroyed everyone around you. If it hadn't been for July slowly getting this into my head, I was headed in that direction. It had been a beautiful fall day. The sun was shining; I was sitting in the cab of my harvester, harvesting one of the best crops in years. I should have been happy, but I was brooding. The prices were the shits; even this crop would nowhere begin to cover the debts I owed. A car pulled into the end of the field. It was my banker's car.

Well, maybe if he had come out to see me, he had good news. We had been negotiating for months, but things had bogged down lately, perhaps explaining why I had been so miserable. I knew I was taking it out on my family, lashing out at them over the most trivial of things. It was not a happy home. I reached the end of the field, unloaded the hopper into the truck, and then climbed down from my machine to walk over to the car. We didn't shake hands; things had gone beyond that. Barry got right to the point.

"Bob, we've decided to foreclose. We expect you to have your machinery lined up for an auction in the spring and be off of here by then."

It was a slap in the face. My first instinct was to strike him. No, don't show him you're scared. "I've got a good crop here," I said.

"Look, we've got a pretty good handle on what you've got, but this has been going on too long, Bob. Quit beating your head against the wall."

"Fuck you, Barry." Instantly, I knew that was a mistake. I could see the resolve set in his eyes.

"We've put a lien on your grain. The sheriff will be out to put seals on your granaries."

"How am I supposed to feed my family, Barry?"

"That's your problem, Bob. You created it—you look after it."

Don't show him you're starting to panic, Bob. Don't whine.

"I guess we'll see you in court, Barry."

"Don't be a fool, Bob. It's over. You'll only spend more money that you don't have. Give it up." His face almost showed remorse.

"You've done the best you can. Get on with your life."

Deep down, I knew he was right. He'd known July, my wife, for years; he knew what I'd been putting my family through, so did I. With that, he got into his car and drove off, his ultimatum delivered.

You can take anything from a man but his land. There's a bond; it's part of you. I stood looking at my land, and tears came to my eyes. I had nurtured it; this was my living, my way of life. My father had farmed it before me; he had broken the land, prospered on it. I had lost it; I was a failure. I had failed my father, myself, my family. I climbed back into the harvester. At least here I felt at peace, doing what I liked best, maybe for the last time.

It was after midnight by the time I had put everything away and got home that night. July had been sleeping but got up when she heard me come in. Even though I was in a rotten mood, I realized how beautiful she was, her blonde hair all tousled.

"How was your day?" she asked innocently.

I reached for a bottle under the bar. Just the way she said it was enough to get me off.

"Who gives a fuck?" I replied.

July was like my right arm, a part of me. Instead of being insulted, she instinctively knew there was something wrong. She took two glasses from the cupboard and brought the mix from the fridge to the bar. Her eyes were genuinely emotional.

"What happened, Bob?" She said it in such a way that it melted me.

"Barry was out to see me," I said.

"Yes," she said as she poured herself a drink, "I saw him go by. I thought maybe he was just by to see how you were making out."

"No," I sighed. "Actually, he stopped to tell me the bank is foreclosing and want us out of here." Somehow, I didn't want to hurt her, didn't want to tell her; but now that I had, I felt better.

"Well, that prick!" she said.

I started to laugh, and so did she; she had that effect on me. I could be so damn hard on her, yet she always got my head straight, supporting me all the way. That's why I loved her so much. Now that she had changed my mood and we had a common enemy, our conversation became much more constructive.

"Can he do that?" she said.

"Yes, you know exactly where we stand," I said, pouring myself a drink.

She was a very independent girl. She poured her own drink, but be damned if she'd pour mine. I also knew she could drink me under the table if she wanted to.

"So now what?" She spoke with no remorse, but matter-of-factly.

"Well," I said, "I guess we'll finish the harvest, salvage what we can, and move on."

She put her hand on my shoulder. "My father can still help, you know."

I flinched. "It's too late even for that. I pissed Barry off, and even then, what's the point in pouring money into a sinking ship?"

"Yes, but I know how much it means to you," she said.

"It's you and the kids that mean everything to me July, as long as I have you guys the rest will sort itself out."

She tossed off her drink then came and sat on my lap.

"What about this friend of Dad's that's trying to promote this Bahamas project? You know we've always loved that island."

"Yeah," I said, "that's starting to have a little more merit all the time."

"I know you and Dad don't get along," July said. "You're both too damned much alike, independent and stubborn."

I hated being compared to my father-in-law, although I grudgingly admired him.

"Okay," I said, "I'll give this Tom guy a call in the morning and tell him that I'm still interested. We'll see what he has to say."

"Bill and Hania Shonavon have signed on to go," July said. "I don't know Dale, but I have met Pearl Drinkwater. They seem like nice people. I think they're going too."

"Dale talks too much," I retorted, finishing my drink.

"Well, it's definitely something to think about," July said. "Now that you're finally finished that drink, let me take you to bed."

She grabbed me by the hand. I had no problem being led to bed by a beautiful big blonde; I was in the mood to give it to someone. My clothes were almost completely off by the time we reached the bedroom. I'm sure the kids would wonder why my pants were lying in the middle of the hall come morning. She closed the door while I took off my socks.

I looked up to see her stretch and pull the short nightshirt over her head. My cock became instantly hard; she had that effect on me, and she knew it.

I walked over to her, grabbing her ass and pulling her tight to me. She moaned and reached for my cock, then slid slowly down on me, dragging her tongue until she found what she was looking for. I shut my eyes, and all the stress left my body as she squeezed my balls and began to suck my cock.

"Beautiful," I groaned, almost losing my feet as she turned my legs to butter. Enough of this; I grabbed her and wrangled her onto the bed. Still standing, I lifted her long legs over my shoulders and gave her all the cock I had. Her eyes opened wide, and she caught her breath. I power-stroked her cuming far quicker than I wanted. Then I collapsed on top of her, burying my face in her breasts, totally played out and content. We fell asleep that way.

Later that night, I woke up cold and began pulling up the covers when I felt her hand on my cock. Guess I won't be getting much sleep tonight.

# Three

## 1969

JULY HANSON DID indeed live up to the image of a blonde bomber. Her five-feet-eleven-inch frame and shocking long blonde hair probably came from her father's Swedish ancestry, but it was her mother's natural grace and beauty that made her really outstanding. Coming from an aristocratic French Canadian family, her mother's charm and classic features were passed on to July, and she used them well. Her parents were going to call her June, but she refused to appear until the first of July, thus a double celebration and perhaps an omen, so the name stuck.

July's father, a tough old Swede, came from a logging background to running one of Minnesota's largest pulp mills. Her mother's family had been in the same business in Quebec for years. She was a St. Laurent, one of the oldest and very upper-crust families in Canadian history. Her brother was a minister in the government in Canada's capital, Ottawa, so it was no wonder they were not warm when Ole was invited to a reception at their home. He was at the time selling logs to a subsidiary of the St. Laurent Company. He was a big bulk of a man, standing six feet two, with blue eyes, blond hair, and a build that left Mademoiselle

Irène totally speechless. Not knowing any better, he headed straight for the best-looking girl in the room. Despite her family's reservations, the rest is history. They now lived in Minnesota and, six kids later, still have the old flame going.

July was born right in the middle of the pack. All the rest were boys; still, she was the biggest baby at birth and could fight with the best of them. Her mother feared that she would grow up a tomboy, but all that seemed to happen was that she liked men and preferred their company.

She loved sports, even excelled at them, but she grew up a lady and as she grew older an exceedingly more beautiful one. She developed early—not only in body, but in mind, finding boys were good for things besides roughhousing. If she had a weakness, it was sex. By the age of twelve, she had blown her first boyfriend; and at the age of fourteen, she had the scare of her life. She missed her period and assumed she was pregnant.

On finding out July's problem, her mother guided her through a very difficult time. It was a false alarm but taught July that life was much more complex than she had anticipated, and she began to concentrate a lot more on her future and a little less on boys. There was a time and place for everything.

There were few secrets in a small town; people loved to gossip, and there was little pity for anyone who stepped out of line, especially the daughter of the most prominent family in town. Sex still held a good deal of her attention. (Her father had said that she got this from her mother, but he said it with a smile and a faraway look in his eye. His wife too considered it a priority, and he never complained.)

July became much more focused on day-to-day issues. She was very popular, never using her natural attributes or position to manipulate others, but could damn well tell you where to go if need be.

She entered a small beauty contest, leading her to become crowned

Miss Minnesota. She didn't win Miss Teen America but gained some notoriety in the papers as the girl who "utterly represents the Dairy State." This experience made her much more worldly and expanded her knowledge not only toward life but toward men. She learned that they came in different colors, sizes, and mentalities; and that most of them were motivated between their legs. More importantly, she learned that she could manipulate them if she so wished either by being intelligent or provocative, whatever the situation required.

An intelligent woman is nice, a beautiful one is nice, but an intelligent beautiful woman is downright dangerous. Most people assumed that this title she had received would lead to a modeling career, not realizing she was much too voluptuous for the likes of Chanel and Dior, whose emaciated beauties patrolled their runways. July didn't really have time for this dream world anyway. She hated the manipulations and politics that surrounded this scene, preferring to use her wits and intelligence to be her own woman.

July could almost laugh when she saw the lust in a man's eye or when they became patronizing. She used them as she needed, sympathized with them if they deserved it. It was a man's world, they say. Well, July would have none of it. The world was her oyster, and she was ready to go for it.

In her first year of college, July flourished. She wasn't sure what she wanted to be.

"There are so many ways to go. I'll just find it as I go along," she thought. No one would ever imagine where this would lead her.

Success is measured in many ways, mostly by the money we make and people believe that money will lead to all the other things that make life desirable. Character is built by adventure, failures, and achievements; a good quality of life can be achieved without becoming rich, but it is the search for riches that creates all of these ingredients.

It's good to be alive, isn't it? July certainly believed it was. So why is it that just when one thinks that they've got it made, something or someone comes along to throw a twist into everything?

July first met Bob Green in 1969, her last year of college. He was a Canadian boy brought in on a scholarship to play goalie for the hockey team. She had heard the other girls talking about the hot new boy, but every new boy was hot to the girls. Still, she was curious to see how he did look, maybe because he was Canadian. She was in the stands nearly at ice level as the team lined up for the national anthem. Bob lined up right next to them on the blue line. He removed his helmet, and she could see that he was a very good-looking boy indeed.

A good friend of hers, Gaylene, who said she had met him in class, shouted, "Have a good game, Bobby!"

He looked over with the most amazing smile July had ever seen. Their eyes locked for just a second; there was no expression on his face as he waved to Gaylene.

"Hi Gaylene," he said. "I hope we win for you tonight!"

Gaylene was ecstatic. July was almost jealous; he'd hardly even paid any attention to her at all. That usually did not happen because if she made it known that she wanted someone's attention, she usually got it. She had caught his eye all right, but only for an instant. She began to fume so she cuddled up to her date that night, Charlie Parrs, a varsity man with tremendous credentials. Bob, or Bobby as they called him on campus, had a terrible game that night and was pulled in the third period.

"That will teach you," she thought; she felt vindicated.

Bobby's popularity in the ice rink carried over onto campus. The girls liked him, although he didn't take many of them out, but any that he did came back with glowing reports. The guys liked him too. He had none of the assuming airs that jocks often had; he liked to drink and carouse, often breaking curfew, and had been rumored to be involved with some of the older women downtown. All this added to his mystique. However, he did not work hard at school, only excelling at what he was interested in and to the frustration of his teachers, seldom reached his potential.

July loved ice hockey and had even played it with her brothers before it was in vogue. After all, they were half French Canadian, they must learn how to play 'Le hockey'. Bob's play improved tremendously in the next few weeks, and this was the only time she saw him until they met in the hall one day. He smiled at her, and she felt compelled to stop.

"Hi," she said. He came back with a hello but kept on walking.

"What the hell did I do that for?" July thought. Somewhere in her subconscious, she knew this guy attracted her, but she'd be damned if she'd let him know.

It was the start of the second semester and July was late for class. When she did arrive, there was only one seat left, and guess who was in the seat beside her. Yeah, it was Bobby Green. For a second, her heart raced but when he didn't even look up to see who it was, she became quite nervous. The classroom was made with tables for two, and just as the class ended, the professor made a statement which really agitated her.

"Your partner at your table will be your partner for the year," he stated. "Many of your assignments during the semester will be carried out between the two of you." She immediately put up her hand.

"Yes?" the professor responded.

"May I move?" she asked. This certainly made Bobby pay attention to her. Some of the class laughed, and she realized how foolish she sounded.

"What? So you can go sit with your friend," the professor said. "If I let you move, I must let everyone move. The answer is no."

Now she had not only made a fool of herself, she had to face Bob. Offensively, July turned to look at him. He sat there with his head in his hands.

"Guess you're stuck with me," he said.

"Yeah, stuck with you is right!" she retorted. "I don't suppose you know anything about this class?" she asked with a bit of sarcasm.

"Not a damn thing," he responded, "and I expect you to do all the work."

With that, she picked up her books and left.

"To hell with you, Bobby Green," she thought.

That night, she and Charlie Parrs had a damn good screw.

July felt terrible as she headed into the classroom. She had been at a party the night before and well, she'd overdone it a bit. She'd been overstressed of late and not herself at all. She would not admit to herself the reason might be Bobby Green. He'd hardly spoken to her at all and because of his hockey, he was seldom there. July began to appreciate how hard it was for these athletes to obtain a decent grade while under the obligation of a scholarship. This time, she noticed he was there. He looked up and then looked up again.

"You look like hell," he said. "You must have been over at Bill Jensen's little shaker last night."

"Yes," was all an annoyed July could respond.

"I'm surprised actually," he said, smiling. "I think you're the only one that was there last night to make it this morning." July just growled but knew by the tone of his voice that it was a compliment. July's head hurt, so she wasn't paying much attention, when through the fog she heard the professor call her and Bob's names. The prof had been randomly asking the groups questions on the assignment he had given last week. If there was one thing July didn't do, it was come to class unprepared. She worked hard at her classes and got her work done. Today she was caught. Hell, she didn't even hear the question he had asked, let alone know where to find the answer.

Through her muddle, she realized there was a voice beside her. It was Bob, giving a very solid, analytical answer. Her first sense was relief, then one of being pissed off. He didn't even have a smug look on his face. In fact, it was like she wasn't even there at all. She had to admit that she really wasn't, but she made a vow to never let this happen again, not in this class anyway. At the end of the class, she stormed out feeling worse than when she had come in. It became common knowledge around campus that the two of them were feuding. The general population loved it and did all they could to add fuel to the fire.

July waited until one morning when Bob came to class late. He looked very tired; he hadn't even shaved. "Partying," she thought and remembered the rumors about his escapades with, as some people said, the 'wives' downtown. She knew this might be her chance to get him if the prof called their names to quiz them, which he did. July immediately spoke up, saying that they had cut the assignment in half for research purposes, that this area of the question was in Bob's section, and she had not read his material yet. She knew that she had him; he hasn't done a damn thing, she thought.

He looked straight at the professor. "You'll remember our conversation from last week, sir."

"Yes," the prof said. "Our star jock requested more time because his team was on a three-game road trip. Let me remind you, Mr. Green, that we expect a certain standard to be kept in our class." The prof was showing little sympathy. "Just because you're in the Athletic Scholarship Program doesn't mean you don't have to complete your assignments. I expect both of you to have this handed in by tomorrow morning."

The prof was a nerd, probably envious of jocks for their popularity and so-called easy way through college, while he had achieved high grades and worked for everything he got. July knew the professor hated jocks, and she could almost cry. She'd been so determined in her vendetta against this man that she'd forgotten the team was away. He just sat there not even looking at her.

"Couldn't you show something toward me," she thought with tears in her eyes. She was so ashamed of herself.

"Pull yourself together, July," she thought. "You owe this man something."

When class was over, she put her hand on his shoulder. "I'm sorry, Bob. The bitch in me came out; you must think I'm awful."

He actually laughed. "That," he said, "and you're so damn beautiful that it scares me." For a moment, there was a silence between them; no one spoke.

Bob finally broke the spell. "I'm going to need some help with this assignment if we are going to have it done by morning. I know you're a busy girl, but if you could give me some time…"

"Yes," she said, "I can give you all the time you want."

Actually July was a busy girl and couldn't give him all the time she wanted, still she looked forward to their meeting all day. She arrived at the library late; she had run all the way to get there and when she did get there, she thought he'd be furious; instead, he was sitting at a table with three girls, three of her friends actually.

"Sorry I'm late," she said.

"We knew you'd be late," one of her friends said, "so we came to help him."

July knew why they were there; they knew that she and Bob hated each other, as they put it. They wanted to be in on the rumble that was sure to erupt. She almost started, almost said something to get it going, but smiled and sat down instead. The girls, realizing that nothing was going to happen, soon found the work boring and went away.

After they had completed their work, which had gone very well, Bob surprised her with "I think they were disappointed."

"Who?" July asked, knowing full well what he meant but surprised at his perceptiveness.

"The girls," he said. "I think they expected you to be a little nastier tonight."

"Me?" she said, then laughed.

"Yeah, I guess I am pretty mellow tonight. Lucky for you." He chuckled and then got up. "Well, I thank you for your time. It was really good of you to help me."

July was beginning to understand this very complex man a little better now. He was actually, in a naive way, a gentleman and would never impose on her, unless she encouraged him, not by saying, "Come here boy, I want you," but by being straightforward and honest.

"Would you walk me back to my dorm?" she asked, quickly adding, "I hate walking by myself in the dark," which was true. There were still lots of people in the library, Charlie Parrs being one of them, that's why he hadn't asked; she knew that now.

For the first time, a look of genuine interest came to his face. Not a look of lust that some gave, not the look of, "Hey, July Hansen just asked me to take her home. I'm somebody!" It was just a look a friend might give you.

Her heart was racing. "Well, a friend's a long way from being enemies," she thought.

"Yes, I will," he said. "In fact, I want to."

Their relationship continued like this through the rest of winter, warming even more as spring approached, and then exploding. Every year just before final exams, it was a tradition to party at Red Lake, about one hour's drive north of the city. The lake waters were still icy cold, but the students didn't mind building huge bonfires, many of them bringing tents to spend the night. July had arrived early and by midnight, was feeling no pain. It was about this time that Bob arrived with some buddies from the hockey team. As they approached the fire, she could see that he too had been drinking and was in a jovial mood. Like so long ago, their eyes locked, only this time, he did not look away.

From across the fire, she beckoned him with her finger. He came, never taking his eyes off her.

"Come with me," she said.

He could taste the sex in her voice as she grabbed his hand heading into the trees where her father's car was parked. They stood beside her father's car; it was pitch black, the leaping flames from the bonfire creating the only light. It would for an instant light up their skin, their hair, their eyes, and then just as quickly fade away, giving them a vanishing look. They stood this way for what seemed a long time, just drinking each other in, then she reached up and pulled his T-shirt over his head. He responded by grabbing hers and doing the same. He had only an instant to notice that she wore nothing underneath before she grabbed him and brought his mouth to hers. It was as if two lost souls had at last found each other, their tongues exploring. Her hand dropped to the front of his pants, undoing the button and unzipping the fly. His pants slid to his ankles never letting go of her lips. He kicked his runners off with his pants, and then proceeded to get rid of her pants. This was not as easy as hers were much tighter. He dropped his head to reach lower when he ran into her breasts. He had admired them before from afar, of course. He had also noticed a lot of other guys noticed them too, especially in the gym. There seemed to be guys there when she was playing who never went to the gym any other time.

Her breasts were magnificent. His head seemed stuck there, but July didn't mind. She wanted him to see all of her, to be part of her. She reached down and pulled her pants off and as she did, his head went with her and he nuzzled her nipple.

"God, that feels good," she thought.

His tongue began to stroke her other nipple and she grabbed his head and pulled his face to her chest. He placed his face between her breasts, his tongue exploring and making her groan with pleasure. Suddenly, she stepped back and as brazen as any woman he had ever seen, she pulled down his jockey shorts with one motion and grabbed his cock. He had been so engrossed with this woman that he had forgotten to get hard, but this action certainly took care of that. He felt himself growing harder as he stood there and looked at her. He had never seen anything so beautiful; her body was hard and well-muscled yet voluptuous. The flickering light teased, never clearly revealing, yet tantalizing. He'd never felt himself get so big before.

July was engrossed with what she held in her hand. She had been with enough men before to know that this was something sensational! It wasn't that it was so long, but the head was huge. Her legs shook with excitement as she could think of nothing else now. Leading him by the cock, she opened the back door of the Caddy and literally fell in pulling his cock, and luckily him too, on top of her. She guided him in; she was a woman on a mission now, her passion so high her mind failed to function. She came on his first stroke, feeling him inside her farther than any man had ever been before. His strokes driving her crazy, she couldn't stop cuming. Slowly, as she started calming down, she realized that his hand was over her mouth.

"You were screaming," he said with a beautiful smile. "I was scared someone would hear you." She didn't answer, she just grabbed his hair and pulled his mouth to hers; her eyes were full of tears, her body was full of him. Her senses cleared enough to realize that he hadn't come yet. He was still hard and stroking her very hard. She hung on for dear life; he was driving her now. She lost complete control, her legs kicking, her body convulsing under him. She heard an explosion and her mind left her body, entering his. She was now a part of him. July Hanson, Queen of the Campus, Miss Minnesota, in the throes of passion, had just kicked the window out of her father's Cadillac.

When she woke, there was twilight in the sky and it was almost morning. They had a sleeping bag thrown over top of them which he must have gone and got during the night. The scent of sex aroused her, and she nibbled at his nipple then bit it, getting no reaction the first time. This brought a "Hey..." and his face came into view. He expected a kiss but was surprised with a question.

"Why did you make me wait so long for you?"

"Because I didn't trust you and I still don't," he said. "You're a rich bitch who could have me and throw me away any time you want. The first time I saw you in the rink, your eyes told me that you could have me at any time, and I vowed that you wouldn't have me. Well, now you have me, heart and soul. You can always throw me away, but you'll always have my heart and soul."

"Yes, I will, Bobby Green," July said. "I want your heart, your soul, and your cock, so don't you ever fuck me around, Mr. Green, or I will throw your heart and soul away and hang your cock on my mantelpiece."

"Maybe that's what you've already done," he said.

"Maybe," July said. She reached up to rough up his hair, her big boob bouncing up to his face as she did so. He immediately began to suck on it.

"I think you love them more than you love me," she said pouting.

"Well, maybe it's because I can trust them to always stand up and respond to me," Bob said.

"Look at this," she said, "One night and we're already talking like old lovers!" Her breast was stimulating more than his mind, and she felt his cock begin to stir beside her leg. The thought of it made her gasp. She felt the wetness between her legs and took his hand and placed it between her thighs. He quickly found her wet spot and went to work on it. She lifted his head, her blue eyes full of passion. "Give it to me, please." So he did, this time letting her go until her screams seemed to bounce off the hills, roll off the trees, and fill his ears with beautiful music.

Bob was to go back to Canada to work on his father's farm that summer, but he could not bring himself to leave his golden vixen, as he called her.

"If you're going, I'm going with you," she said.

He knew his mother would not approve if he came home dragging a girl to live with him, so he called and told his parents that he was going to stay, telling them he was going to study and that he had a job for the summer. His father had said that this was fine as the farm was okay and if he could work, all the better, as there wasn't much to do around the town from where he came.

He did have a job; July saw to that and he worked driving a truck at one of her father's plants half an hour from the university and about an hour's drive from July's home. He rented a small cabin up by Red Lake and for the first week of summer, they commuted. By the end of the second week, July had moved in.

It didn't take long for her parents to get wind of what was going on and the first time she was home, her mother asked her to sit down for a moment and talk. "I'm hearing stories, July. It's not like you to keep things from me."

July sighed and decided to tell it the way it was. "I'm in love, Mother, and I'm going to get married."

"July, you and I have been together for nineteen years now, and I've learned to trust you to know what you're doing, but you haven't even brought this boy home yet. Are you ashamed of him?"

"No, Mother," she hesitated. "It's just that he's shy and, oh well, what the hell. I've only been going with him for a month, and I just haven't gotten around to it!"

"This just doesn't sound like the July I know," her mother said.

She took her mother's hand. "This isn't something that happens every day," she said. "This is a once-in-a-lifetime thing, and I have to grab it. It's not perfect timing… it's definitely not the way I planned it, but I do know that he's my man, so whatever happens, I've got to stick with him."

July's mother remembered making a similar speech to her parents many years ago. "Your father will not be happy. I don't think that your young man quite lives up to his expectations, but I'm sure that between the two of us, we can handle him."

A couple of nights later, July brought Bob down to her parent's house for supper. Bob was very nervous at first, but anyone who came to Ole and Irène Hanson's house was soon made to feel welcome. They found him to be a very pleasant young man, very respectful, and very hard not to like. He told them of his growing up on a small farm in Northern Saskatchewan, a province to their northwest in Canada.

"We live on the tree line," Bob said. "We are as far north as you can go and still farm. We farm in the summer and work in the bush cutting logs in the winter." This gave him and July's dad something in common to talk about; they compared logging in their respective areas.

Time flew and July was very pleased at how things had gone. Then July dropped the bomb.

"We're getting married, Dad," she stated. Even Bob seemed taken aback by this.

Ole had been in some tough situations in his time, but this was something he was not prepared for. He looked over at his wife. "Why didn't you warn me?" he seemed to say.

"What have you got to say about this, Bob?" Ole asked.

Bob took his time answering. "This is a surprise to me too, sir, but as you know, July sort of knows what she wants and goes and gets it. I have no idea why she wants me but I do love her, so as long as she wants me, I'm hers." This honesty made Mr. Hanson sit back in his chair.

"Good for you, July," her mother thought. He may not have much but he has potential; he's honest and he loves you very much; the rest is up to you.

The wedding in '73 was a gala affair, with dignitaries and friends from all over attending. Once Mr. Hanson knew his little 'Minou' was sure of what she was doing, he wanted nothing but the best for his only daughter. The occasion was held in Minneapolis, being that it was the only place with a church and ballroom big enough to hold everyone. Bob was a little overwhelmed by all this but with July at his side, he felt like a king. They made a beautiful couple. Bob's mother had never ever in her wildest dreams seen anything like this. His father had not attended; his harvest was underway and with the short northern season he dared not leave.

In a way his mother was relieved; he would have been totally out of place. He hated crowds and too much attention. She, on the other hand, loved it. She was so proud of her son and July she adored. They had become very good friends, first meeting when Bob and July had visited last summer and again now at the wedding. They all rode together in a horse-drawn carriage from the church to the hotel ballroom.

Bob shook hands at the reception until his hand ached. His head literally spun from all the people he met. There was many an envious glance thrown his way. "Well, I've got her," he thought. I don't know for how long but right now she's mine. He still had trouble understanding why a girl who could have anyone she wanted would want him. He also realized that a girl like July did not move around the world unnoticed. As long as he was with her, he now knew that neither would he.

# FOUR

JULY'S FATHER GAVE the newlyweds a two-week vacation in the Bahamas as a wedding gift. Bob was worried about his work, but strings had been pulled. "Just phone in when you get back," they had said. It was as if he didn't even exist.

Things will definitely have to change when I get back," he thought. He was too much in love right now to dwell on it, so off they went, landing in Nassau and whisked off to Paradise Island. It was the air that he first noticed, the soft breeze that blew off the ocean. For a farm boy who had spent much of his life in snow, the ocean had always had a special place for him. As a youngster, he had been on several trips to visit relatives in Vancouver. He had developed a special bond with the coast. On the other hand, he had hated the desert. "Might as well be in a snow bank as a sand bank," he had once told his parents on a winter vacation in Arizona.

For the first few days, they didn't leave the huge hotel much except for a swim in the pool. Actually, they spent a lot of time in the room, rising late, sometimes not at all. After a while, they ventured over to Nassau town, seeing the sights and sounds of the busy tourist port. Bob was feeling more and more at home with this place all the time, and he wanted to see more.

"July," he said one morning, "let's fly out to one of the outer islands today."

July thought it would be a great adventure. They hired a small plane at the airport. Everything was cash on the barrel, Bob had learned, and he instantly knew that if this was the case, you could barter on the price. The excursion was already becoming fun! Their first trip was to Abaco. They found it quiet, much more quiet and laid back than Nassau. The people were friendly, helping them find their way around, the men definitely admiring July.

For her, traveling had been to big hotels or trendy tourist spots. This was the first time she'd ever done something like this, and she was having the time of her life. They flew back to Nassau that night. The next morning, they woke up bright and early, wondering which island to visit next. They decided to ask their pilot, who was waiting by his plane.

"About half an hour from Nassau, there is Andros Island," he explained. "It's the biggest island of the Bahamas with miles and miles of beaches and no one around. The north island is built up enough to have an airport and there's a decent hotel there. It will take you a while to see it all. Why don't you stay over?"

Bob and July thought this was a good idea. They not only spent the night on Andros Island, they spent the rest of their holiday there. The second day, they found a small hotel on the beach. They spent the day exploring and cavorting, coming back to the hotel only to eat and join in on the entertainment that the local people put on each night. They found a secluded beach where they spent their days. Any clothing they did wear was put on only to and from the hotel. Their last day, they lay on the beach, their skin black from the sun. July's hair lay spilled over his belly while she gently sucked on his erect phallus. The sun had turned her hair almost the same color as the sand. She pulled her head back with a mock frown.

"You have tan lines on your dick," she said alluding to the fact that he had never been circumcised.

"I'm surprised at that," he said, shading his eyes. "You've had it standing at attention so much lately, I can tell time by its shadow."

"I guess I'd better shade it then." She stood up and mounted him, her smile turning to pleasure and agony. He lay watching her huge breasts bouncing, shedding the sand from them like a dog sheds water. He closed his eyes, his body going limp as she drained his very soul. He felt her move and opened his eyes.

"I'm lucky to be alive," he said.

"You feel pretty dead to me," she answered, referring to his limp dick. "I'm going for a swim." She climbed off him, being sure to slap his face with her boob as she did so. He smiled and watched her disappear into the water.

"What would happen if we just stayed here for the rest of our lives," he thought. Many people have thought that on a tropical holiday, never to return again. This was not the way it was to be with Bob and July; they would return to their island, as they liked to call it. They had no idea at the time how entwined it would become in their lives.

The next morning they watched their island disappear, sparkling on the horizon as their plane headed for Miami. They'd stayed as long as they possibly could, missing their connecting flight to Minnesota and had to travel standby the rest of the way home.

They decided to rent a house in the university town where they had met. It was about half an hour's drive for Bob to get to work. July soon had a job managing a large lady's fashion store in the mall downtown. July had never had a job before, finding it much more difficult than she thought. This motivated her, she always needed a challenge. She found herself enjoying work much more than she thought she would.

Upon returning from their honeymoon, Mr. Hanson offered Bob an executive job in his company. Bob thanked him but refused. "I'll never get any respect unless I earn my own way," he said.

Ole was angry but July told him, "Leave Bob alone. If he needs help, he'll ask for it."

Bob quit his job at the Hanson mill, and a few weeks later took up a job with a small competitive plant just on the outside of town. Within a year, he became a foreman and within two years he was in management. They both worked very hard, having less and less time for each other. In their second year of marriage, July came across an ad in the paper; a real estate company was selling lots on their island. The company had bought up an old estate and was subdividing the property into lots. That night she talked with Bob.

"They fly us down," she said. "If we don't like the property, we don't buy it."

"We don't have much money," Bob answered, "but we really do need a break, don't we…"

His mind was wandering back to those carefree days on the beach. Oh, I expect you to do a little work while we're there," she said, a glint in her eye.

A week later, they were gone. They found that the island had not changed at all in the two years they had been away. Even some of the hotel staff were still there, instantly remembering July and her blonde hair. This time, they saw much more of the island. The real estate agent not only showed them the property, he escorted them around the island, showing them its many attributes.

On the south end of the island, they discovered a large military base run jointly by the U.S., Canadian, and British governments.

"It's a naval base and used for training submarine technology and surveillance," they were told by the proprietor of Skinny's bar. Skinny was a tall black man who ran the main bar in the little town surrounding the air base. "The rest of the time they spent trying to stop the drug runners from flying their stuff into the islands."

This was the first Bob and July had heard of this and were quite interested.

"Yes," Skinny said, enjoying being the center of attraction, "a lot of the drugs come from South America and are flown in here and then hauled by boat to the U.S. mainland." He brought them another beer. "It's very big business in the islands, very bad for the people."

It was the people that made these islands for Bob and July; they were so friendly and happy. In a couple of days, the stress oozed out of them and they found themselves slowing down and relaxing. If any problems showed up, they became like the people on the island. "No problem," they would say to each other.

The lots were far inland and covered with trees, so they decided to wait before they bought any land. They spent most of their time on their secluded beach; July became pregnant.

The next few years were very stable and secure for the Greens. The coming of a baby girl, Mindy, only strengthened the bond between them. They worked hard and prospered. However, their lives were not meant to be lived this way; fate would keep throwing a twist into it.

It was Sunday evening and July's mom and dad had come over for supper. They did this often, Ole grudgingly admiring Bob for what he had done. To Irène Hanson, Bob was her favorite. If she had a problem in the family, it was Bob she went to. And of course they loved to see their little granddaughter, the biggest brat you ever saw.

The phone rang and Bob picked it up. It was his mother, nothing strange about that, she quite often phoned on Sunday evenings, but what she said was not the usual.

"Bob," she always came right to the point, "your dad has cancer."

A deadly chill passed through him. "How bad is it?" he finally said.

"He's in no pain yet," she said, fighting to keep her voice steady. "They give him a year at most, probably less."

"Isn't there anything they can do?" Bob asked in desperation.

July came over and stood beside Bob and put her head on his shoulder. "What is it?" she asked. There were tears in her eyes when he told her.

Bob took time from work and headed north. When he returned three weeks later, he had made up his mind what he was going to do. He had never really thought July would stay with him. He thought she'd get tired of him and move on. They'd been together almost three years now; he'd become so used to her being around and wasn't sure what he'd do if she said no. This would be the big test. As soon as he saw her, he told her. She never batted an eye.

"Okay," she said, "I think it's time we had another child."

They went right to work at it. The transition took about six months. There were many trips back and forth. Their assets were sold, and a new house was built on the farm. July was just nicely moved in when their son was born. They had wanted a boy and were rewarded. Bob was happy, July noted, the only sore spot being that his father was very sick now.

Bob had invested heavily in new machinery for the farm. His father's equipment, though in good shape, was getting older. His father didn't like to interfere, but reminded Bob that he had been away from farming a long time. "There's not much money in it anymore," he warned. His father knew the storm clouds were gathering for a full-fledged subsidy war. He had been through a few wars before and still bore the scars; the scars being memory of the depression in the thirties and World War II. But Bob had helped run a company that found it needed good equipment to be efficient in today's market. With that and hard work, there would be no problem.

Bob's dad died that winter. He had been very sick, but he always stayed happy, never letting anyone know how bad he was until he just laid down at home one day and died. He died with dignity, always a gentleman to the end. July now saw where Bob got his determination. If something had to be done, then you squared your shoulders and did it; even when you face death, you dealt with it.

July was busier now than when she had worked for a living. She laughed at this; the only difference was that she wasn't getting a paycheck. There were two children and a big yard to look after. She helped in the fields; all in all, she loved it.

The years slid by, and she hadn't even noticed how stressed Bob had been, but now the years had rolled off him. He loved working on the farm and the freedom it gave him. There was one area that bothered July; it was the books. No matter how hard they worked, the farm was losing money.

"Don't worry," Bob had said, "things can't get any worse. They have to get better." His attitude was he'd handled things before, he'd handle them now. A cold breeze made July shiver.

Things did get worse, much worse. Commodity prices fell through the floor. Bob worked like a man possessed; he mortgaged more and more of his dad's land. The bank became more and more demanding. July noticed a change in Bob that alarmed her. He became scruffy, never caring about his looks. He snarled at the kids a lot, having no time or patience for them. She tried to talk to him, reason with him, but he was a man caught up in a situation he could not control. He was like an alcoholic, there was no use helping him until he admitted that he had a problem. One of his biggest problems was that he didn't listen or ask for help. If he got out now, he could still salvage something.

The bank was now like a vulture, ready to take everything to save their own ass. They had lent far too much to too many farmers and were now after all the assets they could take to keep from going under themselves. The wolves were gathering. Bob, with his back to the wall, was doing the only thing he knew how: go down swinging.

They had been on the farm ten years when July finally talked Bob into visiting their island again. Once more, it had a magical effect on him. He mellowed out, and she was able to talk to him slowly, explaining to him what he was doing to his family, making him realize how much he had changed. Most importantly, he had to assess himself and his situation. Maybe, just maybe, they could negotiate some kind of settlement and salvage something.

They also caught wind of a new development which might be taking place on the island. "It would be nice to be involved in that," he thought fleetingly.

The island cleared his mind enough that when he returned, he and July sat down and set out a course of action. He found wounds were hard to heal, especially between himself and his daughter who had completely rebelled. Mindy felt he had abandoned her when she needed him most. It would take years before they understood each other again.

"Patience," July told him. "Things don't happen overnight."

He tried approaching the bank with a plan of attack for his debt, but they weren't very receptive, knowing that they had the noose around his neck. They just kept pulling it a little tighter.

July went without Bob's knowledge to see the bank too. Barry was the man in charge of Accounts in Arrears at the bank. The recession in the farm economy had hardened him, and he had little sympathy left for people who were stupid enough to try and stay on their land, starving themselves and their families. "Get them off and get on with life," was what he thought best for them. He had always admired July, such a beautiful woman wasting her time with a man like Bob Green was his opinion. There were a lot of things going through his mind, a lot of them not on business, as she sat across from him.

She still had the ability to turn men into jelly and used it if the need arose. "Barry looked very nervous," she thought as he explained that unless Bob could come up with more collateral or some type of security... he left it open for her to respond.

"You mean a cash injection from my father," she said. "Well, I think Bob's made it pretty clear that that won't be happening. Do you have any other suggestions, Barry?" she asked. She saw the lust come into his face.

"No, Bob," she said to herself, "you're going to have to get yourself out of this mess." There's no way I'm going to bed with this man. She stood up, gave him a provocative look, and walked out the door, never saying a word. Barry had broken into a sweat, and he felt his cock slide down his leg. Never in his life had he dealt with a women like this before, but somehow he felt that he had been gotten the best of.

Bob walked up to his mother; she was working in the garden. "Mom," he said, "I think we should have a talk." Once he started, everything poured out of him.

When he was done, it was his mother's turn to speak.

"I know exactly what's happening," she said. "July and I talk about it all the time! I'm glad you've come to your senses. This thing has been killing you a little at a time. Your father warned me that this might happen, but he wanted me to let you control your own destiny. If we had held you back, you would have always resented it. It's not your fault."

She went on, "You did everything you could to make it work, but there were too many things against you, too many things you had no control over. Your father would be very bitter against the system but never against you." She went on to say that his father, although not good at investing money, was good at saving it.

"He was downright cheap," she laughed.

"He left me comfortable," she said. "That, and he made sure some of the land is still in my name and secure so don't worry about me. I am worried about you, though."

Her tone changed. "You have your father's silly pride. I know what people are like around here. They can't wait for someone to fail, especially someone that they're envious of. Learn to live within your means, they say. Well, there's nothing wrong with living within your means, but people who do usually have very limited imagination and never go very far in life. It's the people who stick their heads out in life that motivate this earth!"

Bob was surprised to hear her say this. He felt so much better. He'd never known his mother to have so much insight.

"That's why I hate the soaps," she said smiling, referring to the afternoon shows on TV. "They're watched by people with no life of their own. This is a very limited world here, Bob. Don't be scared to move on."

It was a year later that Barry showed up in the field to tell me that it was over. No one likes to fail, and it takes a long time to get over it. The important thing was that July and I were still together. We had survived it, and now we would continue on together. It was 1988, the beginning of our interest in the Bahamian project.

# Five

## 1997

I REALIZE AS I break through the bluff that surrounds the little farmhouse that my mind has wandered. It is a shack actually, a small one-story structure with an addition built on the side. The building is reminiscent of the many abandoned farm sites in the area. Settlers had built them and then moved on as farms got larger, or people just left, tired of tough times. This one is still used in the summer months, so hopefully there is some form of heat inside.

"I'll burn it if I have to," I think, and then remember that I have no matches. I notice that] I am staggering a bit as I approach the door.

"I have to get warmed up," I warn myself. The door is locked.

"Now what do I do?" I kick myself. Here you are freezing to death, and you're worried about other people's property,

I take the rifle from my shoulder and walk around the side of the building. With the butt of the rifle, I break a window and climb through. The moon is still bright but gives little light inside. Vaguely, I make out the outline of a stove. It seems colder inside the house than it is outside. Heat, I badly need heat! I head for the stove; my knee striking something hard. The rifle goes flying, and I end up face down on the floor. I'm having trouble getting up; don't seem to have any strength.

I'm in worse condition that I thought but the all-consuming need of warmth motivates me to get up. I reach the stove; it's electric. I turn it on. Nothing! Nothing's happening! I feel drained. "Maybe if I just go to sleep," I think.

The breaker; where in the hell is the breaker box? I begin following my way along the wall looking for it.

My eyes are becoming more used to the darkness, and I see a doorway heading to another room. I follow the wall until I reach it. The room is actually a porch, a storage room by what I can see of it. I go in and continue following along the wall. That's it! I see it!. It's the old fuse type, but the fuse has been removed. I panic and start to feel desperately around for a fuse. Ah, there it is on the ledge next to the panel box. My fingers are so cold that I can't seem to screw it in, Finally I get it.

I feel like I just won the World Series, all those little successes keeping me going. I grope my way back to the stove. This time it's easier. I can already see the little red light on the panel. I crank the burners and oven on full blast.

I now see it's a chair I fell over on my way to the stove. I pick it up and set it in front of the oven door. I open the oven door, and already I can feel some heat. I sit in the chair, putting my feet right inside the oven. I place my hands over the burners. I feel like falling asleep, but my hands begin to sting, then my feet. The cold coming out, I realize.

I have frozen some parts of my body. I smell something, smells like burned rubber. I pull my feet from the oven. I must have dozed off, because my boots are smoking. They're so hot I can hardly touch them to pull them off. I'm warmer now; the air in the house is still cold but with my feet warm, I feel warmer all over. I find a small stool to prop up the over door, place a chair at each end of the open door, and lay across the front of the oven.

"What if they come after me?" I start to think, but I'm just too tired to cope with it. I fall asleep.

It was a fitful sleep. I remember getting up to look out the window and listen for any movement. I pull the blind over the broken window. At least this might hold some heat inside the building. It's hard to be comfortable with one side of you freezing and the other side too hot. By morning the place begins to warm up some, making it more bearable. The winter sun rose late, but I was way ahead of it. I first check for frostbite on my hands and feet. The pain has gone away, and there is an odd white spot on my foot, but not as bad as I had first feared.

I can now see the little shack consists of the main room I am in, one bedroom to one side and the porch where I had found the breaker box. I explore a bit, finding in one of the cupboards above the stove a can of beans, in a drawer, a can opener and a pot. It is a shame I had to turn down one of the burners to cook my beans.

Having no water, I step outside with another old pot. I fill it with snow to melt it on the stove. As I come back in the door, I notice a thermometer hanging on the door frame. It's registering -15; it's warming up, I think, that usually means a storm or at least snow. After eating my gourmet meal, I begin looking for any treasures I might find around the shack. There isn't much, but I do find a pair of coveralls that will help to keep my legs warm and a pair of work gloves. By the porch door hung a couple of hats. One even had fold down ear flaps. Dressed to kill, I smiled. My smile quickly faded as I realize this might be true.

I go outside and begin to check around the yard. There are three old buildings in the yard besides the shack. The first one I check contains a small tractor.

"Not much good to me," I think.

The second shed provides something interesting, an old Ski-Doo. It is covered in dust, indicating that it hasn't been used for a long time. I lift the cowling to inspect the engine. It appears intact. I pull the starting rope, and it turns over. Now I'm really interested. I pull the starting rope until I'm out of wind, but it won't fire. Well, I'm not going to give up yet. I know that old fuel usually makes these small engines hard to start. They must have oil mixed right with the gas if they are to run and I have no oil. I turn the machine on its side, dumping most of the old fuel out of its tank into a pail. Then I go over to the tractor with another can and drain some gas from it.

Next, I mix some of the fresh gas with the old gas/oil mix from the snow toboggan. I put this new mixture into the snow toboggan's tank, hoping I didn't dilute the mix too much. On the third try, it fires, and on the fourth pull, it starts. I get more gas from the tractor and mix it down with transmission fluid I find in the shed until I have a full tank.

Now I have transportation, but where do I go? Better warn Bill and Hania, I decide. They live about a quarter of a mile on the other side of town. It consists of about five thousand people and is the main town in this area. I'm looking at about a six-mile ride or a good hour away with this old machine considering some of the terrain I have to go through. I'd stay away from the main roads until I hit town... should be safe there. I am not sure in my mind if I should go to the police.

"There'll be time for that," I think.

By this time, I had talked myself into believing that the people trying to kill me would not follow me. They'll wait for me to show up some place. I'm sure they think I'll go to the police. Then they'll try to get me on the way there or they'll watch the neighbors. I really didn't know what they would do or what I would do in their case.

I go back into the shack to get my rifle. It is too damned heavy to carry around all the time. I check the box of shells in my pocket, five left. Well, the gun will hold five with one in the breach. I load the gun and walk back out into the early morning light. Snowmobiles! They were close, and I instantly know it is them.

Damn it! Instead of screwing around, I should have been moving.

They have followed my trail, I figure as I climb on my machine and take off. They are very close, just on the other side of the bluff. Maybe they will think I am still in the shack. That would hold them up for a minute.

I still have it in my mind to head for town. The first three miles are across open fields broken only by what we call runs. These are natural ditches that were formed by the snow melting and running down these depressions. The land gently slopes toward the river valley. These runs had never been broken, so they were lined with trees, the banks being too steep to farm. They are usually about one hundred yards across, sometimes less, snaking across the terrain for miles. The first field I come to is about one mile across until I hit one of these runs. I figure if I can make it across the field and through the run, they could not see me. They would find my track all right, but would be worried that I might wait for them in the run. They would be cautious, giving me time.

My heart sinks; I am only halfway across the open field when I look back and see them. There are three toboggans gaining fast. My old machine will only do about fifty miles per hour at the best of times. If their machines are new, they could do eighty or better. I am in serious trouble. The trees are getting closer now and so are they; if they catch me here out in the open, I'm a dead man. Anyways, I'm too damn scared to turn and fight now. I just put my head down and keep going.

I see an opening in the trees and head for it thinking, "I'm going to die. July, I'm going to die in the snow. You know how I hate the snow. God, what I'd give to see you one more time."

I hit the opening in the trees full blast; the bank of the run is almost straight down. I bail off, landing in the snow, rolling. My mouth and face are full of snow; I come up spitting. I pull the rifle off my shoulder just as the first machine hits the edge of the ditch and comes flying in. I just point the rifle in its general direction and fire. A pain goes up my arm as I watch the cowling explode on the machine. There are pieces of metal flying everywhere, and I feel tiny pieces embedding themselves in my face. The machine seems to twist in the air. The rider disappears then the machine lands and starts to roll, rolling right over the driver and continuing to roll until it piles into some trees, hardly recognizable. I lay there stunned; I am sure the man lying in the snow will get up, but he just lays there half buried. There is a pain in my hand,the rifle must have broken my finger.

"Where are the others?" I think. My legs are shaking so badly I hardly have the strength to climb the bank of the run and peer over. The other two machines are sitting back about one hundred yards, facing me. They are apparently waiting to see what happened.

"I know I can get them," I think, bringing the rifle to my shoulder and not thinking about anything else until I look through the scope. Nothing shows up. Full of snow, I quickly realize trying to clean it. I fumble around for what seems like forever; my finger's so sore I have trouble using my hand. I am amazed that by the time I line up again, they are still there. Using my middle finger, I pull the trigger. I can't believe it! Through the scope, I can see nothing happens. I missed! How could I miss? Must have screwed up the scope, I think, not believing that I could just miss.

What's that? Get down! Roll! A barrage of bullets fly all around me, one of them pings into a tree right beside my head.

"They definitely have rifles now," I think.

No more gunshots. I hear the machines start to move. I scramble back up the bank to watch the two snowmobiles head for the trees along the run farther up. They weren't wasting any time, the riders staying low. I can see however that one machine has two riders.

"No use shooting," I think, "only three bullets left." More important is what we all do now. Do what they don't expect you to do. I instantly had a plan.

Don't even think about it not working, just do it. "They'll hunt you like an animal," I think "just like the guys talk about pushing deer." They'll split up, each coming down opposite sides of the run waiting for me to make my move. Well, I'm making it now. My old Ski-Doo is still running. It had smashed into some trees; the cowling had popped off, and one ski was bent straight sideways, but it was still running.

I rev up the engine a couple of times, like I'm taking off and then jamb a stick into the throttle, letting it roar at full blast, and then I start running as fast as I can back in the same direction the men on their snow machine's had gone. I have it in my mind that they'll position themselves and then start back toward me. If they don't hear a machine they may even walk, but if they hear my machine take off, they'll follow me in a hurry, and that's what I'm hoping. I run as far as I think I dare and then crawl into a thick bunch of willows just at the edge of the run. I don't wait long; he is on me quicker than I thought.

Another few seconds and I would not have been ready for him. He is coming along the edge of the trees in a hurry, coming right at me, never suspecting that he is only fifteen to twenty feet away when I fire. The windshield disappears, and his helmet seems to explode. He goes flying back almost as if someone kicked him. The machine has so much momentum that it sails by me coming to a stop, purring quietly in the open field. I watch a few seconds but do not see anyone else coming.

"Get on that machine and get the hell out of here," is all I can think of. I start to move, but my legs buckle underneath me and I go down. I start to vomit.

Got to keep moving. I get the rifle over my shoulder and crawl to the running machine. I just sort of lay on it and take off, fearing I'd be gunned down by the other riders. The wind blowing in my face is terribly cold, helping me to clear my head and settle my stomach. This machine is a beauty: independent suspension, hand warmers, all the bells and whistles.

For the first time I look back, they're following me all right. I remember there are two of them on that machine.

"I should be able to lose them," I think as I open my machine up to all it will do. I have to put my gloved hand in front of my face as the air is freezing my skin. I gain for a little bit, but the cold air is forcing me to slow down. The windshield is completely shot away, no way to protect my face. They're gaining fast with their face masks and snowmobile suits protecting them. I pull my hat down low and pull my coat up as far as I can over my face.

"Head for town," I think, "I can lose them there; they won't follow me into town." I cut across the countryside and then for the last half mile, I follow the highway ditch into town. At this speed, it doesn't take me long.

The town mainly consists of a long main street with the residential parts surrounding it. The highway turns into Main Street for about two miles through the town and then turns into highway again on the other side. Most of the main street has a divider about five feet wide running down the center. This is banked with snow from cleaning the street.

The peak of my cap is right down over my eyes, and I only look up once in a while to see where I am going. The main street is full of cars. I slow down as I approach it and for the first time in a while, check behind me.

"Holy shit! They're almost right beside me!"

I had been so sure they wouldn't follow me into town. Instinctively, I gun my machine. The skis leave the ground, and I almost run into the pile of snow dividing the street. Swerving to the right, fighting for control, and then wide open, I continue down the street, passing cars and people as if they are a blur. I hit the first intersection full blast, no cars crossing, just lucky, I think. Then out of the corner of my eye, I see them. They're in the intersection too, about forty feet behind me but on the wrong side of the street.

The intersection flashes by, and I can't see them anymore. They're on the other side of the divider, hidden by the snow, but I know they are there. The next intersection is coming up faster than I can think. There are people! A car pulls in front of me. No place to go but into the divider. The machine goes up and over. I'm flying in the air. I go right over the other guys, and their machine disappears on the other side of me. I land very hard, spinning, with no control. A building is coming at me. I hit the corner of it and then spin off, taking a stop sign with me. I slide backward across the side street into a snow bank, surrounding a used car lot. The machine upsets; I bounce in the snow and then slide on the hard packed snow, coming to rest against one of the car's tires, sending the hub cap flying.

I hurt; God, do I hurt.

"Have I lost an arm or a leg? Did I break anything?"

I'm scared and probably in shock. My coat and coveralls are literally torn to pieces. There's blood on my hands, I can feel it running down my face. The two men chasing me start running back toward me. My rifle, it's gone! Torn right off my shoulder. I can't see it anywhere. A police car slides into the intersection, its lights flashing. I don't think the cop even sees me. He looks very surprised to see two men with guns running toward him on the street. He opens the door of his car and pulls out his revolver. The glass in the car door window in front of him explodes. I see his face turn red with blood from the glass shards blinding him.

Three men come out of the car dealership pointing at me, and then they dive back inside as the windows around them shatter. The two men continue up the street toward me. Another cop car pulls up behind the first one. The cop opens his car door with his gun drawn. I can see he's on the radio. When he sees the men running toward him, he steps out and fires his revolver at them. The men slip and slide to a stop then turn around and run back toward their machine. I lay there as if watching a movie, my own problem forgotten as I watch fascinated. The second cop is too busy looking after his fallen comrade to even see me.

"Get the hell out of here," my mind tells me.

My machine is sitting only a few feet away. It had landed on its feet, still running.

I feel a great sadness come over me as I look at it. The seat is almost completely torn off, the handbars are bent. I remember how the cowling had shone in the sun, now it is smashed to bits. My mind is numb, and I just want to leave.

"Got to go see July," I think as I climb onto the machine and drive away as if nothing had happened.

The cold air again brings back some sensibility. "Better get up to Bill and Hania's," I think, "they can help me. Got to warn them."

I know the town well, so it's no problem for me to follow the back streets out of town and then skirt around the edge until I reach Bill and Hania's place. They have a beautiful big house overlooking a hill. Bill is a contractor by trade; his yard is full of equipment. I park the snowmobile among them. I see Bill's pickup and snowmobile trailer parked behind the shop. Good, my spirits lift. That usually means he's home.

I don't feel good; I hurt all over, and it's all I can do to climb the stairs and knock on the door. Maybe they don't hear me. I look for the door buzzer and push it. No one comes to the door. I try the doorknob; it turns and the door opens.

"Hello!" My voice sounds strange. "Hello," I try to holler as I enter the house. There's only silence.

I brace myself for what I might find and begin to search the house. I find nothing. I am sure that I will find them dead, but nothing even seems out of place except for the unlocked door and Bill's pickup outside.

I pick up the phone; it's working, and I get a dial tone. The first number I call is Dale and Pearl's. There's no answer. The two couples spend a lot of time together; I was hoping Bill and Hania would be there.

I phone Hania's sister in town and ask her if she knew where they were. She tells me they were planning to go to the city; maybe they went early. I thank her and hang up. Next, I phone Dale's dad. He lives close to Dale on the farm.

"No," he says. "I haven't seen either of them for a couple of days," he replies. "Usually they're over if they are home, but you know how they are, probably just got up and went to the States for a couple of weeks." Obviously he didn't know about the government taking our passports. He did sound a little worried though, so I agreed with him and hung up.

Darkness is closing in now; I go to the cupboard where Bill keeps his booze. I find a half-full bottle of rum and take a drink straight. It burns all the way down, not sitting well on my stomach. Suddenly, a light flashes in the window. It's a bluish light. The cops, they must know I'm here. I really don't care anymore. I ease myself over to the window and look out. The irony of it all, they've just set up a roadblock right where the gate leads on to the highway. I do feel safer with a security guard at the gate. I'm pretty sure no one's going to come looking for me now.

Bill and Fran have a Jacuzzi in their bathroom. I go in and begin running water in the tub. I laugh to myself. I haven't even taken off my coat yet, and I'm taking a bath. It takes me a long time to get my clothes off; my wrists and fingers are swollen and painfully sore. Slowly, I begin to realize how badly I really am hurt. My whole body is black and blue.

I turn on the Jacuzzi pump and slide painfully into the water. My eyes are almost stuck closed from the blood that has dried on them. I feel a gash in my forehead as I try and wash the blood away. I find more and more cuts here and there, but mostly my body is just terribly bruised. Slowly the water begins to soothe my muscles, and I lay back in the tub, sipping on the bottle of rum. My mind drifts back to that first day I had phoned Tom Newman. That was really the start of it all.

# Six

## 1988

IT HAD BEEN a long time since Bob had applied for a job, much more traumatic than July had realized. But once he had made the initial contact with Tom Newman, he settled down, seemingly becoming more interested in this new project every day. He and July talked about other things as well. Moving their family away from friends to an island with none of the facilities they were used to existed. Schools were primitive, roads were poor, TV was poor, and the people were generally poor. Maybe that's good; they had both laughed. Their son Rikker's hockey would disappear. Bob loved his hockey, coaching one of the local boys' teams on which his son played. They had told the kids immediately what their plans were.

Their daughter Mindy rebelled instantly making them wonder if they should have been so open. Mindy was a pretty girl and was coming into the age of boys. She and Bob had not gotten along at all. Mindy's marks at school were not good. She resented the fact that they were poor, saying that some of her friends at school laughed at them for being stupid. She generally made their lives hell.

All of this broke Bob's heart, blaming himself for making her feel this way, but July was much more perceptive, gently trying to persuade him that she would have to cope with life like everyone else.

July had said, "If she wants to stay, she can. She can stay with her grandmother; by the time we're gone, she will not have much time for us anyway. It's up to her. We have our own lives to lead."

More and more, they began to realize how big a move they were contemplating. It would be a big upheaval for them and their family. Still, they were looking forward to their interview with Tom. They had moved before and were ready to meet a new challenge. The harvest was over before they could meet with Tom. Bob had sent him a résumé as had July, indicating she would like to work on this project, too. Tom asked to meet with them in a city about two hundred miles from where they lived.

Tom was passing through, and this was the closest major airport. He was a small man with reddish hair, a very likable person as Bob and July found out that morning in the airport restaurant. He told them he had about twenty families hired up to go, the only position he had left to fill would be in the actual processing and selling of their products. He explained this would be making sure the produce was delivered to clients in Nassau and Miami, or wherever they might be, on time and in good condition. They already knew from talking to Bill and Hania Shonavon and Dale and Pearl Drinkwater that this project was a large farm to be located on Andros Island.

The location was on a remote part of the island that had been farmed long ago by an American company.

"The land has since grown over so it must be broken and reclaimed," Tom told them.

Bob would work on the farm, helping set it up if he accepted this job. It would mean the families being away from each other until the crews had the residences ready for the wives and children.

Tom then turned to July. "You said you would like to work on this project, and we have something definite in mind. On seeing you, I would say we definitely will be offering you a position, even if Bob rejects his," Tom smiled. When July questioned him further, Tom would only say it was in the public relations field.

Bob asked him what kind of budget the project required. Tom responded by handing him a prospectus. "We're looking at approximately four million, most of which is in position." When asked how the money was being raised, Tom became even vaguer.

"It's mostly offshore money," he claimed. "That's all I can tell you, except that there is no government money involved. I don't want them sticking their nose in our business."

Then of course, he went on, "there's up-front money that investors have put in to get this thing going. That's where people like July's father come in. If this project is successful, they will be rewarded handsomely. Well, I have to catch my plane," Tom informed them.

"Sorry I don't have much time to spend with you, but I've read your résumés, and I'm confident you can handle the job," he said, shaking Bob's hand.

He turned to July. " I'm positive you'll be hearing from us shortly." And then he was gone.

Bob and July went through the prospectus that evening. They decided it was very ambitious and raised certain doubts about its viability. The project consisted of housing for the management people, housing for the locals who would be supplying the labor, farm buildings, and administration buildings. Cattle and dairy operation were to be set up as well as a hog barn; five thousand acres were to be cleared or logged off and put into vegetables, hay, and grain production. The farm was projected to be in limited production in six months' time. By this time, the cattle were to be in place with the dairy and hog operations close behind. This was a very remote area; Bob and July wondered about the scheduling. Actually they realized they worried about a lot of things.

"It's natural to worry about things that are new and different," July summarized. "There are a lot of positive things in this project. I think it has potential."

Actually Bob thought so too, but he felt he should remain reserved, giving July the opportunity to reject the whole idea if she so wished. They were extremely impressed with the people Tom had recruited. With his prospectus, he had supplied a résumé of all the people he had signed on. They were very qualified, each in their own field. Bob and July decided they weren't entirely sure what they were getting into, but they wanted in. Bob faxed his application form the next day.

A week later, Tom phoned saying Bob's application had been accepted.

"Welcome aboard," Tom said, and then he laid out what was expected. "Most of our work now will be to source out equipment needed for the project. This can be done on the phone for now. As our money is not yet in place, there will be no wages until it is in place. At that time, you will be reimbursed for your time and expenses. In March, I am organizing a trip for the people I want on the project," Tom went on.

"You and July will be asked to go. At this time we will get a hands-on view of the area and what has to be done."

Then Tom asked to speak to July. "How are you?" she heard his amicable voice say as she came on the phone.

"Just fine and excited!" she added.

"Well, good, July, because what I have to say to you I hope you will find exciting. We are auditioning for a person to represent our company both as a logo on our product and as a roving ambassador. We would be honored if you would accept our invitation to attend," Tom said.

July did find this exciting but tried not to show it. She asked where the audition was. Tom replied they were doing a shoot in Nassau next month. The applicants would be required to do a photo session as well as an oral presentation. If she was accepted, she would begin work immediately. This was all happening way too fast for July. Inwardly, she was filled with excitement; outwardly, she was filled with dread.

"Think about it," Tom said. "I have to know by Friday next week." With that, he signed off.

July immediately told Bob what Tom had asked of her, and to her surprise, he was supportive.

"Look," he said, "this is the chance of a lifetime. If you get the job, great. If you don't, it will be fun. You need some fun, July. I've kept you cooped up on this farm for far too long. Go have some fun. Besides, it looks like I'll be here for a while. I can look after the kids while you're gone." July was surprised and pleased, yet deep down she knew this man; it was what she loved about him.

"You're trying to get rid of me," she teased. Only few women could say it the way she did. Bob felt himself getting hard.

"I don't know why you hang around with me anyway," he said. She knew exactly what she was doing to him.

"Because you've got a big dick," she told him.

"Yes," he said, "but will you still respect me in the morning?"

"Listen, baby," her voice dripping with sex, "with a weapon like that, I'll respect you tonight and hopefully again in the morning."

They never made it to the bed; they had sex right there in the chair. It was like the rest of their life, unpredictable. She tried to control her emotions; "I'll wake the kids," she thought, and then she lost it, not knowing what they heard.

# SEVEN

## 1997

I LAY IN THE tub, too sore to move. The only light is from the heat lamp keeping the small bathroom warm. I realize my water in the tub is cold, probably bringing my mind back to the present. Painfully, I reach down and pull the plug, draining the cold water from the tub.

Christ, I've got a hard-on! My body's black and blue. I'm mentally and physically exhausted and I've got a hard-on. Damn I miss my July. Just thinking about her makes me hard.

I turn on the hot water warming up the tub. There's no way I can move. I just lie there wondering what's happened to the guys chasing me. Well, there's nothing I can do if they do find me. I can't fight back anyway. I just want to rest. I wonder what time it is.

For the first time, I hear the howl from the wind and through the small bathroom window, I see snow swirling around. A storm, well, I'm as snug as a bug in a rug. I wonder about the guys chasing me, hoping the storm was throwing a fuck into their plans.

Ten miles from town, sitting in Mrs. Green's old farm house, a man named Henekie reflected over what had gone wrong. Up until last night, it had all gone so well. Now Ginter, his mentor, his boss, and his best friend was dead, leaving him to figure how to get out of this mess. This wasn't the first mistake made on this trip, and Henekie had already put in question the men Ginter had selected. They'd had two jobs to do.

One was to blow up a house in Bowling Green, Kentucky, getting rid of a suspected CIA informant. While they were rigging the natural gas furnace in the basement to make it look like an accident, his helper had whispered, "Henekie?" The house was probably bugged; this was not good.

The second job was this one in Canada. Ginter was a meticulous planner. He was also a born hunter and right from the start seemed to treat this job more as fun than work. As they traveled north, Ginter explained what was to be done. Their client wanted five potential problems eliminated in a remote part of Canada.

They had all been mercenaries at one time. That's how they all got to know one another. Ginter was the contact man; if they got a job, he would phone who he needed. Henekie and Ginter had done lots of these contracts, but this one was a big one. They recruited three comrades living in the United States. They weren't the best of men but made for less false IDs and less traveling time than if they'd brought in their usual team. Both Henekie and Ginter traveled under German passports, but both could speak fluent English and had no problem getting the documents they needed to become American citizens, just part of the job.

They crossed the Canadian border passing themselves off as hunters, thus bringing their own firepower with no questions asked. They planned to go out the same way. They rented a van at the airport and drove four hours north to the hotel the outfitter had rented for them. It was on the edge of town, so every morning the outfitter came to the hotel to pick them up, and every day there were never more than three hunters that went with him. The explanation was that the other men had contacted a severe illness.

The outfitter didn't complain; it was less hunters for him to look after, and the money was the same. Ginter and Henekie spent the first week acquainting themselves with the area and spying on their targets. Bill Shonavon and his wife lived just on the outside of town. They learned that he did welding in the winter to supplement his income. They deliberately broke the trailer hitch on their van, taking it to Bill to fix. They found out that he lived there with his wife, no kids left at home. They discovered that he did not have a dog and just about anything else they wanted to know.

He charged them an exorbitant price to repair the hitch, but they didn't complain; the information was well worth every penny. They found out that Dale and Pearl Drinkwater lived twenty miles to the east. He did custom work, mainly crop spraying. Learning he had bought his equipment in the States, they went to visit Dale, Ginter pretending to represent the company. The rest were clients wanting to see Dale's equipment. Dale was so happy they picked him; he never even thought to check with the company. He treated them royally, bringing them in for supper. Dale loved to talk, so they let him, making it all the easier to carry off the charade and learn what they wanted to know.

But this Green guy proved more difficult. The information on each client they had originally been supplied with gave no indication he was any less naive than the others. This dossier also told them that his wife was in the Bahamas with their son. The daughter was away at college. They learned he was staying alone in his mother's farm house. Ginter and Henekie went looking for the place and found it to be remote and situated on the edge of a deep valley. Green wasn't home so they stopped at a neighbor's house about a mile down the road. He was a rough-looking sort who told them he didn't see much of this young Green.

"Moved in here a few years ago and blew all his mother's money then moved on. Just like a lot of them young fellas, he come in here setting the world on fire and then pulled out with his tail between his legs. Now he's back sucking on his mother's tit. Heard he lost his wife." The old man's eyes lit up, "Damn fine-looking woman."

"When's the best time to catch him home?" Ginter asked.

"He don't go out much at night. Some people say he just sits there and drinks himself to sleep." Ginter thanked the old man, and they drove away.

Ginter didn't seem to pay much attention to Green after that; he even went hunting a few days. "I think we should do it tonight," Ginter told the men his plan, "we'll end up at Greens' and burn the house with all the bodies in it. That gives us all day tomorrow to say goodbye to our outfitter friend, check out of the hotel, and head for the city just as we normally would."

"There's a storm coming in here," Henekie warned them. "That doesn't give us much time if Green's not home."

"You worry too much, Henekie," Ginter waved his hand. "It's too goddamn cold to go anywhere. He'll be home."

The Drinkwaters were first; they came to the door smiling, letting them in. It had been quick and merciful; they were not cruel, they just had a job to do. There was no blood, no mess, the bodies were placed in body bags they had brought with them and thrown in the back of the van. It was about midnight when they got to Bill and Hania Shonavon's place. They shut out the van's lights and idled around to the back of his yard. The only light on in the house was from one of the bedroom windows. Henekie got the spare key out of Bill's shop, and they let themselves into the house.

It was quite a surprise when they got to the bedroom. Bill was on top of Hania, their passion left no room for what was going on around them. Bill didn't know what hit him. Hania saw them and let out a short scream, but then she was kind of doing that anyway.

"Get them in the body bags and let's get to hell out of here," Ginter told them.

"Nice tits," one of the men named Alf said running his hands over Hania's dead body.

Henekie had watched Alf around dead people before and knew it didn't have to be a woman to get him excited. "Don't you touch her, Alf, or I'll personally cut out your balls."

Alf laughed, "Trouble with you, Henekie, is you don't know how to have fun."

Henekie just shook his head and left the room. Alf helped the other guys put the bodies in the bags. He was zipping up the woman when he saw the gold necklace. He looked around to make sure no one was watching, took it off her, and then put it in his vest pocket.

It was colder than hell; none of them were used to this, and they all wanted it done so they could get out of this damn country. They hadn't been worried about a thing, all five of them just walked up to Green's house.

"He's probably upstairs," Ginter said. "Either that or he's on the couch." Ginter pointed to the two men on his left. "You go around front when you're ready to go in, just tell me on the radio. We'll go through the windows, hit the lights, check the downstairs, and then we'll go up." It was about thirty seconds later that they heard the bark. They all froze. Ginter quickly whispering into the radio, "What was that?"

"Albert got him," was the reply. "We saw the doghouse and went to check it out, but the dog wasn't in it. He was on the doorstep. We didn't see him in time."

"Okay," Ginter replied. "If a light comes on, we'll know where he is." They had never seen the moon so bright; it was like working under stadium lights. Nothing appeared to move, and no lights came on in the house. "Let's go," Ginter gave the order, and they went in. It took only seconds to gain the upstairs landing. There were four rooms heading off the landing. Two had their doors closed. Ginter turned on the landing light; there was no noise coming from any of the rooms. He moved to one of the closed doors, opened it, and went in. Henekie went to the other, opened it, and went in. It was empty.

"Anything?" he heard Ginter say.

"No," he shouted back. They quickly checked the other two rooms then began to turn on lights thinking Green was hiding somewhere. They could hear the others searching the downstairs as they searched upstairs.

Ginter turned on the light in the room Bob had been in and saw the open window. He quickly saw the tracks on the edge on the kitchen roof.

"He's outside," he yelled.

"Probably on the kitchen roof! He climbed out onto the roof."

Henekie followed him. They followed the tracks across the roof and in the moonlight could easily see where Green had jumped off. Albert came scrambling around the corner below. Everybody was pretty tense, and they almost shot him.

"He's gone over the hill." Ginter called to Albert as the other two joined him.

"He won't last long in this cold. He'll run until he sweats up, and then he'll freeze." Ginter ordered Albert to go get their parkas from the van.

"No use us freezing too," he said. By the time Albert came back with the coats, he had decided what to do.

"Henekie and Albert are coming with me," Ginter said. "Alf, you take Metro and sit in the van. If he tries to cross the road, you'll be able to see him from there."

There was no trouble following Green's trail in the moonlight. They were almost across a large open flat when they heard a familiar noise. When a bullet hits something solid, it had a distinct sound, and the noise from the rifle was right behind it. They turned to look at the sound of the plop and saw Albert go flying into the snow, and then they heard his screams. They had no idea where the shot had come from; they had been concentrating on following the tracks. Ginter began backing up firing in all directions, so did Henekie. They were caught in the open having no idea that Green had a rifle. They left Albert to fend for himself and began running back to the trees.

Alf and Metro were sitting in the van with the motor running, trying to warm up. They didn't hear or see Green's first shot that hit Albert. Alf did see the muzzle fire from Ginter and Henekie.

"They got him!" he shouted. "Turn the lights on so they can see where we are. Pull down the hill a bit. It's probably easier to drag the body here than all the way back up the hill."

Metro pulled on the lights and started to move down the hill when Alf saw the wink of Green's shot.

"What the fuck..." was all he got out before the windshield exploded.

Metro's face was cut, he let go of the wheel. The van turned then went over the edge of the road, sliding headfirst down the steep embankment, burying its front wheels into the six-foot deep pile of snow at the bottom. With no windshield, the snow came in almost smothering the both of them. When they abruptly stopped at the bottom, something hit Alf hard in the back. He dug desperately to clear the snow away. He poked his head out, only to come face-to-face with one of their victims.

When they had landed, everything had come forward, including the body bags; one had broken open on impact. Alf screamed and dug faster. Metro was right behind him. They both left the van and began scrambling up the steep embankment. A bullet whined over their heads forcing them to slide back down and try to hide where they could around the van. Alf had seen where the rifle fire was coming from.

"He's up on the hill," he told Metro.

Ginter and Henekie also saw the wink of gunfire and now knew they had screwed up badly. Albert had managed to crawl quite a ways toward them. They hadn't seen any gunfire for a while. They decided to go out and get him. It didn't take long; they'd done it before on the battlefield, grabbing an arm and on the run pulling Albert into cover. It took them close to an hour to get him up the hill to the old farmhouse.

By then Alf and Metro had joined them. Metro's face wasn't as badly cut as he had first thought; the windshield had been shatterproof. However, it looked bad enough for Ginter to send him inside with Alf to clean it up. Ginter knew when he saw the wound there was little use bringing Albert up, but he hadn't decided what to do with him yet, so they brought him up to the house.

The house was cold with no windows left in it, so they set to work covering them with newspapers or whatever they could find. Alf had gone outside to look around. They didn't think Green would be crazy enough to come back, but then they hadn't expected him to do what he had done either.

Albert was in bad shape; he would probably live if they got him medical attention immediately, but that was out of the question. The bullet had hit Albert square in the hip bone, making one hell of a mess. Ginter told Henekie and Metro to give him a hand. They carried the unconscious body outside; there, Ginter put his pistol to Albert's head and put him out of his misery. They all knew it was for the best.

Alf came up to see what was going on. "There's a tractor in the shop," he reported. The shop is heated, so it would start. Ginter told Alf and Metro to take the tractor down to the van and pull it out.

"If it's too badly damaged to run, pull it up to the shop," he told them. "Make sure you get all the bodies and all our equipment."

Ginter sat down to plan his next move. He didn't think for one moment they wouldn't get Green; in fact, it was the hunt that Ginter enjoyed. It had been a long time since he had been on a good hunt. He sent Henekie outside to look around, then stripped Albert's body. He didn't want any way for them to figure out who he was or where he came from.

Alf and Metro came back towing the van. They reported it immobile; the front end smashed and the radiator broken. Ginter told them to park it in the shop where it would be out of sight. "Henekie and I are going to get those three snow machines we saw on Bill Shonavon's trailer. Keep your eyes open around here till we get back. I don't trust that crazy bastard out there."

They jumped into Green's pickup and drove over to Bill's yard. The snowmobiles were already hooked up to the back of Bill's pickup truck. Henekie traded vehicles putting Green's truck in the shop, and they took off with Bill's truck and trailer. They stopped at the hotel and while Henekie emptied out their rooms, Ginter went in and told the lone night clerk they were checking out.

"Tell the outfitter we hear there's a storm coming, so we're leaving early," he told the girl. Now with their tracks covered, they headed back to Green's place.

By the time they got the machines unloaded, there was a streak of red to the east. Ginter tied a rope to Albert's ankle and to the back of his snowmobile then took off over the hill finding a place far enough from the house to leave him.

"Let's go guys," he shouted when he returned.

Henekie could tell Ginter was enjoying this; he didn't mind it so much either now that it had warmed up. Not that it mattered; these machines had all the gear with them including fancy suits and face masks. They started out going around on the road that crossed the bridge and then climbed the hill on the other side of the valley. This way, they were able to come in behind where Green had fired at them. They found no tracks until they reached the edge of the valley. There they found shell casings and then tracks following the hard snow along the top of the valley. It was frustratingly slow going. Sometimes they couldn't see his tracks at all and had to watch to see that he hadn't taken off down into the valley.

Soon, they saw a bluff of trees ahead. "Looks like an old farmyard," Ginter told them. They could see the road leading to it wasn't snow plowed so they assumed it to be abandoned. They came to a row of trees with a cut through them that looked like a road or entry to the farmyard. Alf was behind Henekie, so Ginter sent them around to see if they could find a way to come in from the back. Ginter and Metro drove up the cut line through the trees until they could see some buildings. Ginter's heartbeat quickened.

"We have him," he thought. He could hear Henekie's machine behind the buildings. He watched in anticipation as he saw Henekie and Alf come around the edge of the closest shed.

"I don't think he's here!" yelled Henekie.

"There are fresh snowmobile tracks here. Better check the shack anyway!" Ginter yelled back. "Can you get to it?"

There are no windows on this side," Henekie said. "I think I can get there. Alf, cover me." Ginter watched Henekie cautiously approach the shack. When they heard him kick open the door, they all rushed the shack. It didn't take long to search the place.

"He was here all right. Left in a hurry, must have heard us coming. I don't think he's far ahead of us," Ginter said, climbing on his machine and finding Green's snowmobile tracks. He felt almost happy that Green hadn't been in the shack. It would have been too easy. Even the others seemed to be enjoying the hunt. Well, this Green had made the trip worthwhile. Ginter wished he had met him earlier in the week as he had the others. He liked to talk to his victims before he killed them.

They broke out of the trees onto an open field; they all knew the black spot they saw crossing the field ahead of them was whom they were after. Now they could open up these machines and have some fun. They gained on Green pretty fast, thinking for a while they could catch him before he made the bush on the other side of the field; but at the last minute, Ginter realized Green's luck held. He was about one hundred yards ahead of them when he disappeared into the trees.

Ginter put his hand up, holding Henekie back; but Metro, who was slightly ahead of them, didn't see this. He went right on in after Green. They watched as he disappeared into the trees right behind Green. Instantly, there was a rifle shot, some cracking noise like trees breaking. Henekie couldn't understand why Ginter had held them back. It was as if he wanted to kill this man in hand-to-hand combat. Suddenly, they heard a bullet buzz by followed by the sound of a rifle shot. Instantly, they were all down behind their machines returning the fire. Ginter took off for the trees while they covered him.

Once he reached the cover of the trees, he began throwing lead toward Green covering Henekie and Alf until they got into the trees behind him. From there, they could see it wasn't that far through the trees to the other side of what seemed to be a creek with no water in it.

"Henekie, you and Alf get your machine onto the other side of the trees," Ginter told them. "Sooner or later we'll flush him out, but be careful. We'll go on foot if we have to."

They had hesitated to use their radios. One never knows who might be listening on the channel. Now that they split up, they would have to. Henekie and Alf had just made the other side when they heard Ginter on the radio.

"I can hear him. He's making a run for it on his machine." Henekie and Alf had just begun to hustle up their side of the trees when they heard the shot.

"Did you get him?" Henekie asked into the radio. He called again, still there was no reply. Alf swore under his breath, and then they heard a machine heading away from them.

"Let's go," Alf said.

Ginter sat on his machine waiting for Henekie and Alf to get into position when he heard the machine somewhere in the bush taking off. He quickly told Henekie what was happening and took off. He could smell the kill now. The end of the hunt was near. He hurried along the edge of the trees. At the last second, he saw Green in the bushes. He'd met his victim; it was the last one he'd ever meet on this earth. Henekie and Alf's fears were confirmed as they crossed the run. They came upon Ginter's headless body immediately.

"There he goes!" shouted Alf, pointing toward Green who was moving fast across the open field. "Let's get him! I want to kill him with my own hands."

Henekie would have liked to check on Metro; he could hear the sound of a motor running in the trees, but if they did, they would lose Green. Henekie took off in pursuit. He didn't think he could catch Green with two of them on the machine, but to his surprise they started to gain. It took only a few minutes for them to realize they were going toward town.

"If he thinks he's safe there, he's in for a surprise," thought Henekie. Ginter's death had agitated him so badly; there was no common sense left in him. He wanted Green dead, nothing else mattered. Just on the edge of town, Henekie thought they had him. They were right beside him when he saw Green look back. The front of Green's machine lifted in the air as he tried to gain speed.

"Shoot him, Alf. Shoot him!" Henekie shouted, but Alf was busy hanging on with one hand and trying to shoot with the other.

He fired his rifle, almost taking Henekie's head off. The distraction caused Henekie to narrowly miss the snow piled up on the divider separating the lanes on Main Street. Green had narrowly cleared it to the right. Henekie had no time to correct but kept going although on the wrong side of the street. This didn't matter much at his current speed of close to 75 mph. Things were happening too quickly to worry about traffic direction.

At this speed, Henekie knew Green had no option but to go straight ahead. This was confirmed at the first intersection they came to. He was just ahead of them to their right, but there was too much traffic, and at this speed too dangerous to change lanes. The intersection flashed by; Green was hidden by the divider again.

They were almost to the second intersection when an object came at them from over the divider. It was Green's machine, missing them by inches and disappearing behind them. Henekie applied the brakes, and they skidded through the intersection, the machine slowing down drastically, but the street was icy. They started to spin then hit the snowbank against the divider, spilling both of them into the snow. Henekie shook the snow off and stood up. He noticed Alf doing the same. Neither of them appeared hurt.

"There he is," Alf pointed in among some cars in a car lot. Henekie couldn't see him but took Alf's word for it. He too pulled off his rifle and started to run toward Green. The cop car seemed to appear from nowhere. It skidded to a stop in the intersection almost directly between them and Green. Both of them started firing, dropping the cop and scattering some people coming out of the building behind him. Another cop car pulled up behind the first one. This cop didn't fool around; he started shooting at them.

On reflecting back, Henekie thought they could probably have killed the cop and then got Green, but who knew how many more cops were on the way. Henekie wasn't ready to die just yet. Both he and Alf tried to change directions at the same time; Alf slipped and fell, but Henekie grabbed him, helping him up. They headed back toward their machine, got on, and took off.

A car was coming right at them. The driver slammed on the brakes, apparently oblivious to what was happening farther up the street. Henekie managed to climb the divider high enough to avoid him, and then another car hit the first one from behind snarling traffic all the way down the street. Henekie turned around and took the first cross street he came to and headed out of town. Soon they were in open country.

"Where we goin'?" Alf wanted to know.

Henekie's problem was that Ginter had always done the thinking, but Ginter wasn't here.

"We'll head for the farm and burn the bodies in the house," he told Alf. This had been Ginter's plan so far, as he was concerned this was what should be done. Green would have to be dealt with later.

# Eight

ROYAL CANADIAN MOUNTED Police Constable Larry Reich was twenty-three years old and had been on the force for just over a year. This was his first posting, a quiet little town on the tree line in Northern Saskatchewan. Their territory was thinly populated but huge. It consisted of native reservations to the north to small farm towns in the southern parts.

Larry had always wanted to be a cop and knew he would be a good one, but already he found the tedious work of handing out speeding tickets and spending time in court boring. He had applied for a transfer, hoping to get a position in the city where there might be a little more action. Hell, there weren't even any women in this one-horse town. Since this office covered such a large area, the detachment consisted of fourteen officers plus support staff in the office. This was a fair-sized detachment for a reasonably quiet area, but because of the vast distance to police in such a remote region, the officers were often overworked and forced to patrol in single rather than two-man teams.

Larry came in to the office a little early for his three o'clock shift. He planned on having a coffee and going over some desk work before he took over the patrol car. He was on rural patrol this week; as he checked his desk, he saw a report that someone had stolen some gas from some farmer's fuel tank. He'd check that out first, he thought as the sergeant appeared beside him. He looked agitated.

"Larry," he said, "there's been a hunting accident out in the Cherry Ridge area. You'd better go out and see what's happened. The phone call came from Gus Helek's farm. He claims they were out hunting, heard some shots, went to see what was going on, and found a body that had obviously been shot." The sergeant reiterated. "Do you know where the Helek farm is?"

"Yes," Larry said, happy to have something out of the ordinary to do.

"I've phoned the homicide boys to come down," the sergeant went on. "It will probably take them three or four hours to get out here. It'll be dark by then. You make sure nothing's touched and see if you can piece anything together as to what's happened."

Just then the dispatcher called out. "Sergeant! Officer Jennings has two men on Main Street with rifles!" The sergeant immediately turned his attention to the radio, listening to Officer Jennings's excited voice telling them there was an officer down. The sergeant told all patrol cars to converge on the area with care. Larry asked him if he should go to the scene.

"No," the sergeant replied, "you'd better go out and investigate the shooting."

"How should I get there?" Larry asked. It was obvious that his patrol car would not be in as it was after three. The sergeant told him to take the four-wheel drive.

"It's already hooked up to the snowmobile. Just take the unit to Helek's yard and unload it, but leave the snowmobile for the homicide unit. They get upset if everything isn't ready for them when they get there."

“There’s no way we can drive out to the scene?” Larry asked, thinking of the four-wheel drive.

“No,” the sergeant told him, “they say you have to go by snowmobile. They have to show you where the body is anyway. They’ll take you out there. I know the Heleks have at least two machines on the farm.”

With that, the sergeant turned back to the radio, leaving Larry to make out on his own. It was only a twenty minute drive out to the Helek farm. There were five men waiting outside for him when he arrived. They gave him a hand unloading the snowmobile off the trailer, and then they all went inside where, over a coffee, the men told him what they knew. The five men had been out hunting when they heard some shots, they told the constable. The shots had sounded close and seeing the Heleks hadn’t given anyone permission to hunt on their land, they went to see who it was. They had come upon a man lying in the snow with his head shot off. A couple of the men were very pale. Mr. Helek stated it was a very gruesome sight. Two of the men, including his son, had been sick to the stomach.

Mr. Helek concluded by saying there had been no one around that they could see, but there were two snowmobile tracks. They hadn’t wanted to disturb anything, so they had all headed back to the yard.

They all wanted to go with Constable Reich to show him the body, but he told them he would prefer that just the two Heleks went with him; too many people wandering around might cover up evidence.

“Besides,” he said, “the rest of you guys can show the homicide people how to get there when they come.”

One of the guys asked him why they had sent only one officer. “There’s a problem in town,” he told them. “Two guys with rifles wounded an officer on Main Street.” He went on to recap what he had learned on the radio scanner coming out to the farm. “Apparently now they’re looking for a third man on a snowmobile who was badly hurt. They all seem to have gotten away. It’s a real muddle. All the officers are looking for these men, and no one even knows what they look like. They apparently took the officer who was injured to the hospital. They think he'll be all right."

Larry jumped on behind the younger Helek, and the three of them headed out to find the body. It was a gruesome sight all right; Larry had trouble keeping his stomach down when he saw the headless body.

"This guy definitely shouldn't have been hunting," Larry said to the Heleks. "He's not dressed in whites, which is mandatory for hunters here. Also, they have to wear a red hat. This man must have been out snowmobiling when someone shot him by mistake and ran."

The older Helek spoke up. "Then if that's the case, why did the man have a rifle?" It was barely visible in the snow beside the body. Constable Reich walked closer and saw indeed that there was a rifle.

"Could be the gun that shot him," Larry stated.

The three of them walked farther down the tree line to where they could see more snowmobile tracks. Young Helek was the first to see the wrecked snowmobile piled in the trees. As they came to the bank of the run, all three stood in shock; another body lay in the snow. Larry went on down into the run to check the body. His helmet was still on. Larry pulled it off; the helmet was full of frozen blood, and the man had a huge hole in his throat. Larry heard the young Helek getting sick and realized how traumatic this must be for a sixteen-year-old boy. Then he got sick too.

"Sorry," he said to the older Helek. Larry was down on all fours, puking his guts out. "I know I'm a RCMP officer and shouldn't be doing this, Mr. Helek," Larry managed to gasp out.

"Gus, call me Gus," the older Helek told him. "Get it out of your system then you'll be okay."

Gus helped Larry up then guided him to the lip of the run where the younger Helek was sitting. They all sat for a few minutes; Gus spoke first. "They sure made a mess of that machine. Looks like it was pretty near new."

"I can't figure this out at all," Larry answered. "That other machine over there is smashed too, but the strangest thing of all is that the body is wearing a bulletproof vest."

Gus looked over at Larry. "Only one reason for a man to wear one of those," he stated. "They plan to get shot at."

The younger Helek got up and went for a walk. When he came back, he was carrying a spent shell casing. "Back in the field," he pointed, "there must be twenty or thirty of these." He showed them the 30.08 shell casing.

"That's why we came here in the first place. We were curious about all the shots," Gus said as he went over and picked up a spent casing he saw along the bank, a .270 Winchester.

Looks like these guys were shooting at each other all right. Constable Reich decided it was time he started to conduct his investigation the way he had been taught. Four machines had come here and only two left, which made sense because there were two machines in the bush.

"That means," Larry deduced, "that two men have fled the scene."

Young Helek disagreed. "I can see two sets of tracks beside one of the machines," he said. "I think by the way the spent cartridges are spread that there were two men on the one snowmobile."

All three men were getting into it now, trying to piece together what happened here only hours before. Constable Reich radioed the office and gave the dispatcher all the information he had gathered. The dispatcher told him the homicide unit would be a while, when Reich asked to talk to the sergeant. The dispatcher told him he was out supervising the search for the suspects uptown.

"They've set up roadblocks, and there are more constables on their way," the dispatcher told him. "Just hold down the fort, the coroner and homicide will be with you in about an hour." Larry figured it would be dark by then; the wind had picked up, and it looked like snow. Well, there was nothing he could do about that. If it did snow, a lot of the tracks would be erased, he thought.

"Gus," Larry said, "I'd like to take one of your machines and follow these tracks back a ways." Gus said they would go with him. Larry said, "No, I don't think that's a good idea. I think you should stay and wait for the coroner to get here in case I don't get back in time."

Just then they heard the sound of other machines coming. Larry hoped it was the Homicide guys, but it was locals. Word had spread, and people were coming to see what had happened. Larry was worried that something would get touched, but he also was afraid that if too many snow machines got running around, they could obliterate the trail the suspects had left.

"Can you keep them back away from here," he asked the Heleks.

"Don't worry," Gus told him, "we know these guys. We'll keep them away."

Larry waited as five snowmobiles came to a stop a few yards from him and the Heleks. The snowmobilers were full of questions, but before anything else, Larry asked them to help the Heleks keep people away, and especially try to make sure they didn't cover the trail. It made them all feel important to help; none of them wanted to go any closer to the body anyway.

Larry pulled his helmet down over his face as he started Gus's machine and took off. He made good time. The tracks were easy to follow across the open field and then through the wooded area until he came to a shack where it was obvious someone had spent the night. Here, the constable found tracks going in all directions.

The shack was surrounded with footprints; the front door was left open so he walked in, finding the inside a shambles. The stove was turned on, an empty can of beans and dirty pot sat on the cupboard. The constable guessed by the open oven door that someone had tried to heat the place and had eaten here, but other than that, he could see no other clues as to what had happened.

He checked the shed, finding some gas cans and spilled gas in one, suggesting someone had needed fuel for something. Someone had hidden a snowmobile in here, he guessed, and had gassed it up. He took his radio out to call in what he had found in to the office. There was a constant chatter among the officers in town; one of them had found a snowmobile abandoned in a back alley fitting the description of the one the two suspects were riding. They were all converging on the area. He decided not to interfere.

"Really," he thought, "I still don't know what's happened here."

Constable Reich nearly turned back before he found a trail that actually seemed to go somewhere. The tracks seemed to lead along the top edge of the valley, sticking to the hard snow. As he went along, he began to notice footprints. These didn't mean much to him until he came to the spot where shots had been fired. Here, there were obviously many footprints, and he found empty .270 shell casings in the snow. From here, the footprints went straight over the high pile of snow he was standing on and down into the valley.

On the other side of the valley, he could see a farmyard. It was starting to get dark. The wind was blowing, now sifting the snow around. He knew he should be getting back, except that he felt that he was very close to something. It was snowing harder all the time; these tracks would be gone forever if he didn't follow them now. Besides, these tracks pointed directly to that farmhouse and somehow he felt they were connected. Starting over the edge of the valley was the tricky part. He got stuck in the soft snow and had to get off and push his way through, but once he started downhill there was no stopping. All he could do was to try and avoid the bigger trees. He picked up the set of footprints once he was in the flat at the bottom. He crossed a river following the tracks across the ice into another flat; he didn't go much farther when he found the blood.

Henekie and Alf had both worked up a sweat. Henekie figured the police would have Green. He'd have told them about the farm, and they would be checking it out shortly. They were busy carrying the bodies from behind the shop to the house. They would burn the shop, the van and any evidence they might find in it.

He had left Alf to dump the bodies out of the bags while he stripped the van of its license plates and serial number. Alf didn't see why the bodies should be taken out of the body bags, but Henekie told him the plastic would stick to the bodies as they burned. This would be detected by the forensic people.

Henekie was walking back to the house from the shop when he heard the sound of a snowmobile motor. It took him a second to locate where the sound was coming from, and then he raced to the edge of the valley and looked over. Through the trees, he could see a lone machine stopped where Albert had been shot. Quickly he ran to the house.

"Alf," he called, "there's a snowmobile in the valley bottom. We'd better go down and seen who it is."

"I'm all done here," answered Alf. "Do you want me to burn the house?"

"No," Henekie told him. "Let's see to this first." They both headed down into the valley on the run, hoping the snowmobile wouldn't leave before they got there.

Constable Reich could see that something or someone had been shot here. It's someone, he thought, as he could see where the person had crawled in the snow from that point. He pulled out his radio and called in to his detachment office. He couldn't hear anyone on the radio now, just a bunch of static. No one answered his calls; must be the high banks of the valley, he thought.

I'm going to have to get back up top to get any reception. He decided to continue following the tracks. It was pretty dark now; even in the machines' lights, he could barely see across the flat, but it looked like the tracks led to the far side where they disappeared into the trees along the bank. As the constable approached the trees, he felt a shiver go up his spine. There was something foreboding about them.

His mind told him to go back, but he knew the snow was coming down harder now, and that the tracks might be completely gone by morning. He started into the trees. Suddenly, there were two men beside him, one swung something at him. The blow caught him on the side of the head, knocking him from the machine. He tried to reach his revolver, but something hit him again and everything went black. Henekie stood over the fallen man. He could see he was a police officer. He reached down and took his revolver and on further search found his radio. They had no idea what the Mountie had told his people or how far away they were.

"Let's kill him and get the hell out of here," Alf said.

"Just a minute," Henekie replied. "We need some information. Let's see if we can bring him around." He grabbed the Mountie by the front of his coat and swung him around so that his head rested on the side of the machine. He began slapping the constable's face until he saw a response.

"So what brings you out on a night like this?"

Constable Reich's head hurt. It hurt so bad he had ringing in his ears. He could hear a voice talking to him, but he couldn't understand; he could see a face in front of him, but he just couldn't make it out. Then he passed out again. Then he felt another sting in his face. He opened his eyes, this time things were clearer. He heard, "Green, where is Green? What did he tell you?"

Constable Reich groaned. "Green, who is Green?"

A blow hit his mouth. He heard the voice ask him again, "The man on the snow machine in town. Where is he?"

The constable's mind began to put two and two together. These were the gunmen in town, "I think the man in town got away, and they haven't found him." He answered.

Henekie was surprised at this answer. He had been hoping Green was in the hospital or at least detained, that way they would have known where he was and done something about him. He didn't think the man was lying. This made everything more complicated.

Why hadn't Green gone to the police, Henekie couldn't understand it.

"Where are the rest of your guys?" Henekie asked the constable.

"They're right behind me," Constable Reich told him. "They just stopped to check that old farmhouse back there, and I came on ahead."

That could have been the truth, Henekie thought, walking around to talk to Alf. If it was true, they would see the lights coming a long way off; it was dark now. Constable Reich heard the two men talking to each other, but he couldn't make out what they were saying. He was feeling much better now. He felt around; they had taken his gun and radio. His mind raced. They would kill him, of that he had no doubt. It would do no good to run, but if he could jump them, grab a gun. He slowly rolled over and leaned on the machine to gain his feet. The two men were talking intently, not paying attention to him at all.

He sprang, knocking both men from their feet. He grabbed Alf's rifle; he almost got it, but Alf was very wiry. He grabbed Reich's coat, pulling himself up, staying so close to the constable that he had no room to use the rifle. He wrestled with Alf, trying to put Alf between himself and Henekie, but Henekie was a professional and had rolled clear of the two men. Now he got up out of the snow, pulled out the constable's pistol, walked up to the constable, and shot him in the back.

The bullet hit Constable Reich like a sledgehammer; it took all the fight out of him. As he slid down Alf's body, his hand grabbed a pocket.

He tried to hold himself up, but the pocket tore. Something came into his hand, and then he felt it come loose. He clamped it tightly in his hand as Alf gave him a shove, sending him backward into the snow.

"Let's go," Henekie shouted, knowing the Mountie was still alive, but not for long. He had shot enough men before to know the wound had been fatal.

Alf saw the gold chain hanging half out of his pocket. He shoved it into his other pocket as he climbed on the Mountie's machine behind Henekie. "Lucky for me, Henekie hadn't seen that," Alf thought.

They headed up the hill out of the valley into the Greens' farmyard. Henekie set fire to the shop while Alf set fire to the house. It was snowing hard now; the wind had picked up spreading the flames quickly.

Henekie had spent any spare time he had plotting a course to the airport four hours south of them. Four hours in perfect conditions, that is. They had twelve hours to make their plane, but the roundabout way Henekie thought they would have to take made the timeline look hopeless. He looked out the windshield of the four-wheel drive, and all he could see was a whiteout of blowing snow. Still, this storm might be a godsend in disguise. If he could make it through the closest city around one hundred miles to the south east of them, they had a chance. He was sure there'd be a gas station open there even in this weather. If he was lucky, that would give them enough fuel to make it to the airport.

At first the going wasn't too bad; they could see the grass along the side of the road, but by the time they got to the main highway everything was white, and forward progress became agonizingly slow. They took turns walking in front of the truck, just so they could stay on the road and then Henekie decided to try something. They had loaded their snow machine on the four wheel drive before they left the farm. They pushed it off the truck, and Alf rode it ahead of the truck. Alf was able to see the edges of the road much better from the snow machine, and they made a lot better time.

As they got closer to the city, there were a lot more trees and yard sites along the road. They parked the machine in a clump of trees and continued on, even getting the four-by-four stuck and having to shovel it out of a snowdrift before they got to the city. On the outskirts of the city, Henekie had a scare as they came upon a roadblock marked with flares and barricades but luckily no cops.

"Looks like they are trying to keep people from leaving the city, not who's coming in," Alf commented as they moved the barricades. It didn't take them long to find the only gas station open; it was on the only recently plowed road in the city. Alf filled the truck, while Henekie went in to talk to the young man behind the till.

"Any problem getting out of the city to the south?" he asked.

"The cops are sitting out there. No one's allowed to go south." The man must have seen the look on Henekie's face. "Where you headed?"

"Regina airport," Henekie told the truth.

"Hell, that big four-by-four will make it. I live on a back road that takes you out to the highway down past where the cops have their road block. I'm leaving here in about ten minutes, you can follow me." Henekie didn't have to be asked twice.

The young man had a big four-wheel drive too and had no trouble breaking trail for them. He stopped at his farmyard gate and came back to talk with Henekie. "The highway's half a mile up, you'll have no trouble. The highway's nice and high, except for the odd big snowdrift, and your truck will handle that."

"Thanks, buddy," Henekie handed him a hundred-dollar bill. "You saved my life."

"Thanks, mister. My friend just called, he says if you go straight south on number two, you'll run out of the storm in about an hour."

The young man's information had been right. They did indeed run out of the storm about an hour out and made their way to the airport with an hour to spare. The next thing was to get through customs.

Neither Henekie nor Alf had slept for over thirty hours, and both looked pretty rough.

The customs officer looked at their rifles and then went through their bags. "There were supposed to be five of you guys, weren't there?" he asked.

"Yep, the other guys thought they could get that last day of hunting in. We left early yesterday afternoon and still just made it," Henekie explained. "I don't expect them to make it for quite a while, that's a bad storm."

The officer seemed to be less suspicious. "Yes, we hear that's a bad one. There are a few people missing the flight this morning. Looks like you guys had a tough time of it. Have a good flight."

As Henekie got on the plane, he wondered what was going on up north. Those weren't the kind of people we usually dealt with, except for Green; Ginter had certainly been careless with him, and it had cost him his life. Once he got to his seat, he fell asleep.

The Heleks helped the ambulance attendant load the bodies onto sleds. The sleds would be pulled by snowmobiles to an ambulance waiting in the Helek yard. There were a lot of people on the scene now. There were probably forty snowmobiles in a row, all shining their lights on the area where the team of Mounties and the coroner were working. It was dark by the time the forensic team had arrived with the coroner. The wind had picked up and it was beginning to snow. They had worked as quickly as possible, picking everything up. The local people who had come to see what had happened were put to work fetching toboggans and sleds. The two wrecked snowmobiles were loaded up and hauled away. By the time an hour had passed, everything was gone over and cleaned up. The last to go were the two bodies.

It was snowing hard by this time; the wind was starting to whistle. Helek asked one of the Mounties if they had heard anything from Constable Reich. The Mounties radioed into headquarters. Gus Helek heard the person at headquarters tell the Mountie over the radio that no, they hadn't heard anything; they had assumed he was with them.

Corporal Novak looked worried. "Well, either he's back at your yard, Gus, or he's holed up someplace for the night. It's really getting nasty out here. We'd better get back."

"He should have radioed," Gus commented.

"The radios don't always work well in this weather," Novak told him. "We'll check when we get back to the yard. He's probably there waiting for us."

Gus climbed on behind his son, and they started back to his yard. He took one last look in the way Reich had gone. He had a very bad feeling that not all was well.

Constable Reich lay dying in the snow. He didn't hurt anymore; in fact, he was very much at peace. He had a floating sensation, almost as though he was looking down at himself. "Why had God put me on this earth?" he wondered. I wasn't here long; I never loved or had a family. I didn't even contribute to society the way I planned. I always wanted to be a policeman, but I didn't get a chance to show how good I could be.

The snow began to cover his face. He didn't mind; it gave him a heavenly, almost angelic look. He felt the object in his hand; his fist closed in a death grip, and he was gone. He would never know how involved and how intricate a part he would play in people's lives because of that little piece of evidence he had guarded with his life.

# NINE

I HEAR A BUZZING sound: the front doorbell. I lay very still, hardly breathing. If it's the guys after me, I'm totally helpless. The water in the tub is cold again. I must have dozed off. Fear does wonders to a person. I pull myself from the tub. I know where Bill keeps his guns. They're in the closet across the hall.

The doorbell rings again. As quietly as possible I reach the hallway, the closet door is locked. I'm about to break it in when I hear the sound of a vehicle start up the driveway. My breath comes in deep gasps; I'm sweating profusely, almost blacking out. The hallway starts to spin. I grab the wall, trying to make it stop. Gradually, the sensation subsides. I'm starved, I realize, not having eaten for a long time, even threw up my beans. The kitchen is to the right at the end of the hall. There I find a can of soup in the cupboard along with a pot. I'm in business.

While the soup is cooking, I return down the hall and break into the gun closet. No wonder Bill kept them under lock and key; he has quite an arsenal. On the top shelf, I find a pistol. It takes me a minute to figure out how the clip works but when I do, I find the gun is already loaded. Maybe Bill was worried about something happening too, I think. Going back to the kitchen, I turn on the radio and sit down to eat my soup. I lay the revolver down on the table within easy reach. Nobody is going to take me now, not after all I have been through. I eat the soup slowly; at first it makes me woozy, but gradually my stomach settles down, and I begin to feel better.

Looking toward the kitchen window, I realize it is snowing outside. In fact, the way the trees are waving, I can tell the wind is blowing. I get up and go to the window. There is probably a foot of fresh snow on the ground. The wind is whipping the snow around; I can hardly see the road out front; realizing the roadblock is no longer in place. Pretty hard for anyone to come looking for me now. For a moment I feel secure; on the other hand, I think, excellent cover for them to get me. I'm paranoid; there's no way they could know where I am. I pick up the revolver and take it to the couch with me.

I lie down on the couch listening to the radio, and eventually the news come on. It tells me that two bodies have been found shot to death near town, but the details are still sketchy. The police had moved much quicker than I anticipated. I wonder how much they know. It was quite possible that my hunters had become the hunted. Perhaps the police were looking for me too.

As I lay on the couch my mind drifts back to the first time I had met the man responsible for all this. Those were boring days, that first winter waiting for the Bahamas project to take shape, not knowing what was going on. We were not to see the site until March. The only bright spot was July. She had flown to the Bahamas in late November for her first photo shoot. It was the first time she had been away from the family for any length of time, and it was making her feel guilty, yet the sense of adventure which lay ahead of her was the most exhilarating feeling she had felt in a long time.

Her personality literally glowed with anticipation as she stepped from the plane into the afternoon Nassau heat. She had no idea what she was getting into, actually treating it as a lark.

"Who would want an old broad like me?" she thought, but what the heck, it would be fun. A short holiday would do her good. She saw Tom Newman standing at the baggage check out. He waved to her, and she waved back making her way through customs, then over to where Tom stood. Tom shook hands with her and introduced her to a stout black man standing beside him.

"July, this is Arthur. He will take you to your hotel and escort you while you are here."

Arthur shook her hand. He had a big grin on his face, and she liked him immediately. Arthur picked up her bags and led them outside to a battered old station wagon. On the way to the hotel, Tom and July caught up on what each other had been doing. Arthur was pleased to find that July had been in Nassau before and even more pleased to find she knew his home island of Andros. The hotel was a modest affair which was just fine with July. She was glad to get out of the oppressive heat. Not that she didn't like the heat, but it had just been a matter of hours since she had left minus twenty-degree weather and was a little overdressed for the occasion.

Tom saw to it that she was checked in and then told her, "We'll start work at six in the morning, and Arthur will be here to pick you up at five a.m. Don't worry about clothes. They'll be supplied on-site. Most of the photography and orientation will be outside in the courtyard back of the Crystal Palace Casino. Any questions?" he asked.

"Yes," July said, "but I'm too tired to think of what they are now. Besides, I imagine I'll find out in the morning."

Tom laughed, "Get a good night's sleep, July. I'll see you bright and early." With that, he left.

"Thank God," she thought, climbing out of her heavy clothing and into a sundress. She unpacked and then went down to the hotel courtyard. The breeze from the ocean reminded her of earlier times when she and Bob had frolicked on the beach. "Well, Bob, the memories stir my loins; it won't be long before we'll be able to do that again."

She sat out savoring the beauty and smell of the ocean until a waiter asked her if she was dining outside. She thanked him, ordering a chicken sandwich and a beer. Darkness came quickly as she finished her meal. She returned to her room, phoned the family; yes, they were happy to hear from her, all excited and asking what had happened with her day. She laughed and told them to give her a little time, she had just gotten here. After they said their goodbyes, she immediately went to bed, 5:00 a.m. comes early.

Arthur was indeed there at five o'clock sharp to pick her up. "Good morning. You're looking fine this morning, Mrs. Green," he said in a singsong voice.

She checked his eyes; they were full of admiration, not lust. "I can trust this man," she thought. "Good morning Arthur, I've been apprehensive all morning, not knowing what to expect. It's nice to see your smile. It makes me feel good."

Arthur's smile widened; she knew she had just made a friend. Traffic was light at this time of the morning, and it only took them about ten minutes to reach the Crystal Palace. Arthur escorted her through the building into the large courtyard, where July noted a camera on a tripod with three men and a woman standing nearby. On the far side of the courtyard, two tents had been erected. July guessed these would be the change rooms.

Tom waved to her; he was standing near the tents, talking to a tall black man. The black man wore sunglasses, but July could feel him watching her intently as she approached Tom. They exchanged greetings, and Tom took her over to the woman standing near the camera. The woman was older than she had looked from farther away but still had an attractive face. "I don't think we expected someone quite your size," she commented looking through a bag which looked to be full of an assortment of clothes. She pulled out a very tiny-looking bikini, "One size fits all," the woman winked as she handed July the two pieces.

July was about to protest when a noisy entourage erupted onto the scene. Five girls, three white and two black, followed by what looked to July to be at least ten men, came bursting across the courtyard. They were all young and beautiful, not much older than my daughter, July thought. She could picture her daughter walking across the courtyard buoyed by the confidence that only the young can portray. Oh well, she thought, I told myself I was only here on a holiday.

These young girls were beautiful; she felt very old and a little out of place, standing there with a string bikini in her hands. Tom had tried to greet the girls, but they ignored him, heading straight for the bag lady, as they called her, picking through the assortment of swimsuits, modeling them in the air to the approval of the men with them. Although they had ignored Tom, July noticed the girls had all waved to the tall black man who had not moved from the corner of the courtyard. July also noted the bag lady, as the girls had called her, was not amused, nor the three men around the camera. One of these men came over to July.

"Hello," he said, "my name is Ozzie. I will be in charge of the photography. I suggest you use the tent before our illustrious guests turn them into pigpens. There are dressing robes inside if you prefer. I suggest you use one, your skin is very white." He smiled and turned away, immediately trying to gain some semblance among the crowd of young people.

The bikini was very skimpy.

"I guess it covers the essentials," she thought, but she knew she looked damn good for an old lady. She slipped on the robe and left the tent. Ozzie had succeeded in separating the men, moving them to the wall surrounding the courtyard. The girls were all over around July.

One of the girls looked at July then said, "Fucking near time," and entered the tent.

Tom beckoned her to sit with him at a table under a sun cover. At first, the session went fairly well; they broke for lunch and then continued into the afternoon. The girls became bored. July could smell marijuana drifting in the afternoon breeze. She began to realize this was not being done very professionally. Tom knew it too and finally confessed that he didn't have much money, so he left the photography to be done by people that Manly Waddell, his friend, had recommended. She asked him if Mr. Waddell was the black man he had been standing beside when she entered.

"Yes," Tom said. "Manly told him he knew some models, and the photography crew did some work for the government."

One of the girls had now taken her bikini top off and was trying to pose for the camera crew, much to the enjoyment of the males she had come with, plus a few of the guests at the casino who had stopped to watch.

Ozzie approached July with a red face; he was very angry. "I apologize for making you wait so long," he said to July. "But as you can see, we wanted to get the others out of the way before they became too hard to handle."

July went into the tent to freshen up. Ozzie had been right; the tent was a pigpen and reeked of marijuana, not that July saw anything wrong with a toke or two, but there was a time and place for everything. Well, here she goes, she walked out of the tent and dropped her robe. There was a deadly silence; she looked around, no one moved.

She almost ran back into the tent when she heard a low whistle then, "Holy shit!" The boys at the back began to applaud, and even Tom had stood up and was applauding. July was not a shy girl, but this enthusiasm had her very embarrassed. The girl without a bikini top brushed by her, heading into the tent.

"Wait till they see you up close, big tits. You've got wrinkles as big as they are!" she scathed.

July smiled. That didn't bother her; in fact, it even encouraged her. She began posing for Ozzie in a way that even had him excited. This type of work was not entirely new to July, although she hadn't done much of it for years. She was naturally graceful and beautiful, yet she could be provocative and sinful.

It didn't take long for word to get around. Gamblers and waiters alike came out to watch. July was in another world. She let herself go, one minute a tramp, the next a saint. She grabbed one of the men helping Ozzie with the set, took his hat, and set it on her head. She leaned against him, and then grabbed him from behind and ran her hands over him. She'd never seen a black man blush before, but she could tell he was now.

Ozzie was loving it; there was no tripod being used now. He followed July everywhere she went, encouraging and suggesting. He was having as much fun as she was. Finally, July asked if he'd had enough. Ozzie ran and hugged her.

"You've made my day," he said. "Usually these are so boring. It's been a great pleasure to work with you."

This time a great round of applause broke out to July's amazement. She had been so wrapped up in what she was doing that she hadn't noticed the huge crowd that had congregated. Not bad for an old broad with wrinkles, she thought as she went back for her robe.

She noticed the tall black man Tom had referred to as Manly Waddell, again talking to Tom as she entered the tent. She soon found her sundress to be missing; one of the girls had taken it, she surmised. July left the tent and went back to Tom's table. The black man had left. Tom jumped up with a smile on his face.

"Terrific, July. I'm very impressed. I didn't realize you were a professional."

July smiled. "Thank you, Tom. Actually, I really enjoyed it."

"Mr. Waddell is having a small reception in the hotel later this evening, and he wishes you to attend." Without waiting for her to answer, he went on. "I'll have Arthur pick up you up at nine. There will be people there I want you to meet. Casual dress required."

With that, he kissed her and left. The words "Fuck you" were at the tip of her tongue, but she held her breath. She'd let him get away with it this time. He'd have to learn to be more careful how he handled July Green, she thought. No man made her do something she didn't want to do, at least not without getting into a lot of hot water.

July went over to the so-called bag lady that was packing up the bags and trying to disassemble the tents. "Is there somewhere I can buy a dress?" July asked. "Someone seemed to need mine more than I did."

"I'm sorry." the bag lady said, "I should have warned you not to leave anything lying around." She looked up, "With a body like yours, honey, I wouldn't cover any of it, ever." She winked and went on. "There are some small shops in the casino, just follow the wall around the back. No one uses it much. It will take you right to them. On the other hand, if you take that robe off and go through the casino, I can guarantee you will not have to buy your own dress by the time you get to the shops."

July laughed. "No thanks, I'll take the back way. I prefer to pick out my own dresses."

"Have it your way, honey," the bag lady said, grinning as she went back to attacking the tents.

July followed the steps along the wall that ran around the back of the casino. The wall overlooked the ocean. The view was breathtaking. July walked over to the edge of the wall; she stood looking out at the ocean she loved so much but had seen so little of. She heard a moan below her; someone's hurt, she thought. She heard the moan again as she went closer and looked over the wall.

On the sand about ten feet below her, she saw that Mr. Manly had one of the models pinned up against the wall. She was naked, and her legs were wrapped around his waist. He was fully clothed, but it was quite obvious he was into her a long way by the pained expression on her face. July stood fascinated at the powerful thrusts that matched the girl's moans, and then he looked up and saw July. He smiled and seemed to thrust harder. July's legs felt like jelly; she felt the heat come to her face as she managed to pull herself back. Her breath came in gasps as she started along the path again.

"Whew," she thought, "I've only been away from Bob a couple of days and already I'm horny." She and Bob had a very active sex life. They didn't miss many nights and often it was twice a night, unless she was away visiting her family or he was on a business trip. They hadn't been apart much for years. She visualized Bob's big cock and how she'd like to turn it on right now.

"Maybe I turned Mr. Waddell on too," she laughed and entered the shop where she bought a sundress for now and an evening dress for the affair tonight. She returned through the casino in her new dress to find the bag lady, but she and the others had all left. She shoved the bikini into her handbag. "A souvenir," she thought and made her way to the front of the hotel. She was relieved to see Arthur waiting patiently, sitting on the tailgate of his station wagon.

"How are you doing today, Mrs. Green?" he said with his big smile. He just made her feel so much better. On the way back to her hotel, she asked Arthur if he knew a Mr. Waddell.

"Yes, ma'am," he said. "I don't know him personally, but everyone knows about everyone in the islands."

"What does he do?" she asked.

He answered, "He is the ancestral chief of the tribe that ruled the island before the white man came. His power runs deep in the voodoo and tribal traditions that still run deep in some societies in the islands. He's very well-connected in the government," Arthur answered. "I don't know exactly what he does nor do I want to know, except that he's probably a very good man to stay away from," he said, looking at her.

"Thank you, Arthur," she said, knowing not to push any further. "Our Mr. Waddell is a very interesting fellow," she thought.

Arthur picked her up at nine o'clock and headed back toward the hotel. July had decided what she was going to do. "Arthur," she said, "what were you told to do tonight?"

"I was told to take you to the Crystal Palace and then go home for the night," Arthur told her.

"That's what I thought. Arthur, would you wait for me? I'll pay you." Arthur looked at her.

"You're a smart woman, Mrs. Green. I'll wait for you. Just leave the doorman $5, and he'll let me park out front until you decide to leave."

"I shouldn't be long, Arthur. Maybe two hours at the most. Thank you. I know you have a family at home. This is very nice."

"No problem, Mrs. Green," he grinned as she left the car, giving the doorman $10 just to make sure Arthur could indeed park out front. The doorman escorted her to the elevator and punched in the code to take her to the penthouse.

She stepped from the elevator right into the party. A small affair, she thought. There must be three hundred people here. She recognized the reggae music from her kids' tapes at home. A live band was playing loudly right beside her. She kind of liked the music, she thought as she saw Tom rushing toward her. He took her arm, intending to lead her around the room. The room was elegant; it could be very intimidating, but not to July. People came to her; she didn't need to go to them. She held the room in awe with her natural grace and beauty. She was as used to affluence as she was to reality. Not everything was as it looked; once you tore the affluence aside, you saw corruption as well as decay. She could tell the phonies from the real thing. She respected people for what they were; it never took her long to sort them out.

Tom soon found himself a hanger-on; not only was this woman beautiful, she was a mystery. No one knew where she came from, and they clamored to meet her. There were some legitimate people here, she decided, but I can tell who they are just by watching them leave here early. Her suspicions were confirmed about an hour after she had arrived. People began to leave, she was thinking about leaving too, when she looked to see Manly Waddell standing by her side. Her heart skipped a beat; he terrified her, yet there was something about him that was magnetic.

Tom jumped between them, "I don't think I introduced you two today," Tom said. "July, this is Manly Waddell." July looked Manly straight in the eye.

"I guess we didn't meet formally, but we did see each other in action, didn't we?"

A puzzled look came over Tom's face; a look of surprise came over Manly's; he hadn't expected her to be so straightforward. "Yes, I suppose we have," he said.

"I'm having a much smaller gathering later," he went on. "I want you to be there. I won't take no for an answer." He smiled and walked away.

Tom seemed very pleased. "Even I didn't get invited to that," he told her. "I'm glad you're going. It will be very good for our project." Neither man had any idea who they were dealing with. If they were used to having women at their beck and call, July was not impressed. She left Tom and went to the elevator.

A man by the door stopped her. "Mr. Waddell asked us to tell you to wait for him to escort you home," the man told her. "It's not safe to go alone." July realized she was politely trapped.

She went back to the bar and ordered a drink. She watched the people in the room as it slowly emptied out. She could make a scene, and probably Mr. Waddell would be forced to take her home. She didn't want that. Soon she saw what she was looking for. He had been introduced to her as Sir someone or another, definitely British, from their consulate most likely. He was slightly intoxicated and looking for company, definitely perfect for what she had planned. It wasn't hard; she simply went over to him and struck up a conversation.

Soon they were dancing. She steered him toward the elevator, bringing up the fact that she had brought all this money to gamble in the casino, and here she was stuck up here. Immediately, Sir so and so picked up on her plight. That's not a problem; he was more than ready to help.

"Let's go down and spend some of that money," he said.

She giggled delightedly, "I'd love it!" Grabbing him a little tighter than necessary, they headed into the elevator.

"Take us down, old boy. We're casino bound," he told the man at the elevator door. The man looked perplexed but had no choice but to code them down. When they reached the casino, July wasted no time.

"I must go to the washroom," she told him. "All this gambling makes me so excited," she explained. July gave him a provocative look and left him with a look of expectation on his face. She had no idea how long he would stand there, nor did she care.

In no time, she was out the front door, past the doorman with a quick good night, and into Arthur's car. She blew a sigh of relief, yet she was exhilarated, "You're a sight for sore eyes, Arthur," she said as they drove away. She reiterated to Arthur the events of the night. "I'm going home!" she stated at the end of her story.

"You're a brave lady, Mrs. Green," Arthur told her. "I'm sorry your stay here had to be an unhappy one, but I have an idea. My brother has a fishing boat. He's taking me to see my family on Andros tonight. Why don't you come?"

"Are you trying to kidnap me, Arthur?" she said jokingly.

Arthur smiled back. “God help the man who tries to kidnap you, Mrs. Green.”

She was giddy from the day’s events. “What the hell, another adventure is just what I need. I’ve never felt so alive,” she thought. They stopped at her hotel, picked up a few things, and the next thing she knew, she was on a boat headed for the island she loved so much.

The weekend flew by on the island; this was the Bahamas that July knew. Arthur’s family, while very poor money-wise, was very rich in sharing what little they had. When you walked into their humble home, it felt like a home, something that many people never experience. She was totally relaxed and reassured that the Bahamas were still the islands she had learned to love as she headed back to Nassau Sunday night.

She had talked to Bob; he wanted her to come right home, and she had agreed. Arthur dropped her off at her hotel. The desk was swamped with messages, which she took with her to her room to sort out. On her bed, she found a box with her sundress on it and next to the box lay a dozen red roses. The message read “Sorry for the inconvenience, Mr. W.”

Most of the other messages were from Tom, but one was from the Bahamas Board of Tourism. They wished her to phone them when she came in. For now, she’d phone Tom; the rest could wait until morning. Tom answered on the first ring. He sounded relieved that she was okay but didn’t ask her where she’d been. It came to her pretty quickly that Tom and probably everyone at the party thought she had spent the weekend with Sir what’s his name. Well, she wouldn’t tell them any different. Maybe if they thought she was involved with someone, they’d leave her alone. Her mind came back to Tom who was telling her the nature of the call from the Board of Tourism.

“They want you to do some work for them, July. It will be very good for the project,” Tom said.

“I’m going home,” July told him. Tom immediately began pleading with her. “They won’t start until after Christmas, just stay and see what they have to say. It will probably only take one more day.”

“All right, Tom,” she told him. “We’ll go and see them. Are you going to pick me up?”

“Great,” he answered. “I’ll be in the courtyard.” With this, she hung up.

Next, she phoned Bob, telling him what she was doing. Bob told her to do what she thought she should; he would come down if she needed him.

“Thanks darling,” she said. “I’ll be home in a couple of days. Miss you.”

She didn’t sleep well. What if Mr. Waddell was behind this, she thought. Tom hadn’t exactly been sterling either. Then she thought about what her mother had told her during her Miss Teen pageant days. “Keep your head up and your mind open,” she had told her. “There are leeches in that business, but there are good people too. Learn to sort them out and above all, gain their respect, and then the rotten ones will leave you alone.” Well, that still applies, she thought. With this in mind, she slept better.

Tom was there to pick her up at nine thirty. She was amazed! It was his way of saving face. When they entered the Tourism offices, Tom again tried to take control, but July paid him little mind. She saw Ozzie standing in an office doorway and headed for him. It didn’t take her long to find out it was Ozzie who had recommended and promoted her to the board for the job. Mr. Waddell was in no way involved.

“I look after the board’s photography,” Ozzie told her. “That job I did for Tom was a favor to Mr. Waddell. He’s a hard man to refuse.”

Ozzie’s expression darkened as he told her this. July got the impression that Ozzie didn’t like him much. Ozzie introduced her to the other people in the room. Lisa, a big black woman, was the person in charge. She told July how impressed they had been with the pictures

Ozzie had taken, and that they would like to use her in a new video. They were to promote tourism in the Bahamas.

She would be featured in a brochure and shoot some commercials throughout the United States and Canada. They talked well past lunch. She learned the work would be mostly in Nassau and Freeport, but the final product would be done in Miami.

Finally, she asked, "How am I to be paid?"

Ozzie and Lisa both looked at Tom. "We thought since you were working for Tom, he would be paying you..."

July spoke to Ozzie, "Ozzie, did Tom suggest you recommend me to do this work?"

"No," Ozzie answered. "I did that on my own."

July turned to Tom. "We have nothing in writing, nor have I received any money from you to confirm I am working for you, is that right, Tom?"

Tom was furious; he had lost control of the situation a long time ago, trying to break in but getting nowhere with July.

"What about your hotel room?" he managed to get out, "and Arthur,I've got to look after him"

I'll pay for my own hotel room, Tom. As for Arthur, he told me you hadn't paid him anything, so I looked after that too." Tom sputtered but kept his mouth shut.

July turned back to Lisa. "The fee Tom negotiated, was it a good one?"

"Standard," Lisa stated, "the amount we usually pay, plus expenses."

"What does an agent usually get for negotiating a price?" July asked.

This time Ozzie responded, "Fifteen to twenty percent is the usual fee," he told her.

"All right," July told them, "draw up a contract. Have it say that Tom is to receive a 20 percent agent's fee, the rest is to be paid to me." Tom, thinking he was going to be left out altogether, felt relieved; he almost seemed happy.

They went for lunch and when they returned, the contract was drawn up. July read it and found it to be fairly straightforward, until the last paragraph. "Who put this in here?" she demanded.

"I did," Ozzie said, looking her straight in the eye.

This time, it was July's turn to fume. "I've never been overweight in my life," she retorted, always having prided herself on the way she kept her body.

"All the same," Ozzie told her, "we want you to lose at least five pounds and in the right places. That means a rigorous training session in the next month before we start work. If you don't, our contract becomes null and void."

"Oh well," she thought, "this had been all too easy. I guess no pain, no gain. At Christmastime, this will not be easy." She tried to look as indignant as possible, but she agreed to his terms; now it was her turn to gain respect for Ozzie, she realized.

The next morning, Tom drove her to the airport. He seemed to have forgotten all about their differences and talked the whole time about the project.

"I'm expecting our funding any day now," he told her, "so tell Bob to stay on the alert. We could be headed down here before March if everything works out."

July had lost respect for Tom and told this to Bob shortly after she returned home. "You mean he's lined up all these people, changed their lives completely, and he doesn't have any money?"

Bob couldn't believe it. July also told Bob that Tom had little credibility in the Bahamas. "They think he's just another quick buck artist, out to look after himself," she explained. She knew that Bob wanted to see this project go ahead more than anything.

"I will say one thing. Tom's got a lot of guts, maybe he can pull it off," July said, but deep down, she didn't think so. It was one of the hardest things she'd had to tell Bob in a long time.

Whether it was vanity or just plain stubbornness, she worked out every day. Christmas was the hardest; Bob's mother was a tremendous cook, but she persevered. By the time she had to go back, she was close to 5 lbs. lighter and in tremendous shape; she knew she looked good. Bob knew it too; he was very proud of her. He hated to see her go but was happy for her. It had been a long time since he'd seen her so excited. "I kept her tied down on this damned farm too long," Bob thought. It's time she went out and had some fun.

"I hate leaving," she told him, "I'll miss you all so much." But Bob assured her it wouldn't be long until they were together again.

Bob thought March would never come, and then when it did, Tom informed them that his money had not yet come through, but he wanted them to pay their own way down to see the site.

Bob met with the Drinkwaters and the Shonavons. They decided to go. "If nothing else, we'll have a holiday," they said.

They met in Toronto; there were ten couples in all who had decided to make the trip. They met four more couples in Miami that Tom had recruited from Ohio, and the rest came from all over Canada. They spent two days in Nassau where they got to know each other. One thing Bob had to admit, Tom had picked very good people; not only did they get along well together, they were all professionals. July had met them at the airport. She and Bob were very interested to see how the others would like Andros Island. It was a far cry from what most of these people were accustomed to, very primitive with few services.

The hotel on North Andros was decent. The area around it was filled with flowers and shade trees. It was built right beside the airport, about five miles inland from the ocean. Tom found an old bus to use for touring and a car for his own personal use. The first morning, the bus pulled up to take everyone on tour. They were surprised to find Bill going around collecting money for the bus driver. However, the tour went well; they visited the beach and ate in the only other hotel on North Andros. It was a beautiful seaside setting, mostly catering to Europeans.

That night, the main topic was Tom's inability to pay for anything. "It's like he's the tour guide and we pay," Dale Drinkwater explained, summing up the situation.

The next day was the same ritual; no one got on the bus until they all paid. Since there was no other way of getting around, everyone grumbled and paid. This time Tom took everyone to the south end of the island. Along the way, they stopped at several small villages. Bob and July noticed that several of the people were appalled at the poverty and squalor. Many of the Bahamians were not ready for the disposable age. Some of the yards were littered with baby diapers and garbage. The houses were small and very shabby looking.

"They're in for a culture shock," July said to Bob very quietly.

They knew the Bahamians to be a very warm, happy-go-lucky people, and their needs were few; the next day would be the same as today. Their answer to difficult problems was "no problem." By the end of their stay, this would be everyone's favorite saying.

A big naval base was situated at the south end of the island. Tom explained it was really a submarine base used to test new technology because of the tremendously deep water just offshore, making it very suitable for these operations. Being fairly close to Cuba also made it even more strategically important.

. He added that a lot of local people worked on the base, so there were some signs of affluence here, but still pockets of poverty showed up as they toured the small town and stopped at Skinny's bar for a beer and a meal if they desired. That night, back at the hotel, Tom told everyone that the next day they would be touring the project site.

"It's a long way from anywhere," he told them. "It was a research center at one time, run by the Americans. The farm was built around a freshwater lake. The farmland has since grown up and will have to be rebroken. The road there is very poor, so we'll have to start out early. Let's get a good night's sleep.

Some of the people asked him about the poverty and poor living conditions. Tom responded by telling them a bit about the Bahamian culture. "The people are fun-loving, they don't have a lot of money, and they look after their families very well. They are personally very clean and like to dress well. I took you to these places today to show you what to expect. Anyone who came here to work on my project might as well know all the facts and what they are up against. I don't want people to come here to work and then leave because it's not the exotic place they thought it would be in their minds."

July and Bob agreed with him on this part. "He's doing a good job," Bob told July when they returned to their room. July had to return to Nassau to work early the next day; Bob would stay longer than the rest and would take July to the site later in the week when she returned.

It was just after sunup as Bob walked July down the paved path to the airport. It had rained overnight, leaving a fresh smell in the quiet morning breeze. A plane sat on the runway, its doors open. It had brought someone to the island very early and was now waiting for a load to go back. There were always people waiting around the airport, waiting for a ride to Nassau. Now they would negotiate a price and pile in as many as possible. July went up to the pilot and spoke with him for a moment. Then she came back to Bob.

"Yes," she said, "he was expecting me. This is the plane I'm to take. My fare's been taken care of." She grabbed both of Bob's hands.

"I don't want to let you go," Bob told her.

"Hang in there," July looked at him; there were tears in her eyes. "Soon we'll be together."

"I guess our lives were meant to be filled with turmoil," Bob told her. Sorry, I have to be so unstable, always looking for something or wanting something I can't have. I've been very hard on you and the kids. This little adventure could end up being a dud too, and even if it isn't, it will be quite a change for all of us."

July laughed. "You may not be rich, darling, but at least you're not boring," she reached down and gave his nuts a little squeeze. They heard the pilot call. July gave him a kiss and headed for the plane.

He heard her shout, "Good morning, boys," as she went in the door. He stood watching the plane go down the runway and then disappear into the cloudless sky. Bob's mind was elsewhere as he returned up the walk to the hotel, not realizing where he was until Dale hollered at him to pay up for the bus.

"Where's Bill?" Bob asked, handing the bus money to Dale.

"Tom's taking some people out to the site in his car," Dale told him. "Bill's going out with them."

It was almost impossible to tell how far the site was from the hotel. The road was so bad; they could only travel at a crawl. It had once been a main road. They could tell by the ditches and grade that it hadn't been maintained for years. They could tell it was still used to some extent because it was an easily followed trail; otherwise it would have grown over. The driver told them the road was still used by wild boar hunters traveling out to the old farm. Finally, the bus stopped in a wide opening.

"We walk from here," the driver told them. "This is the only place I can turn around."

They walked along a poorly marked trail until all at once there were buildings on each side of them. They were in all kinds of disarray, having been abandoned for many years. At the end of the yard was the lake, discernible through the trees. All this gave for an eerie yet beautiful setting.

Bob left the others gazing out over the lake. He walked along the shore following an old trail, passing several old buildings and a wooden water tower until he came to the airstrip. There he caught up with Tom and Bill who were with two black men he didn't know. They were all standing looking out over the landing strip; as he approached them, he realized the runway had been blocked off every few feet with rows of pushed-up dirt.

"Why did they do that?" Bob asked.

The black man closest to him answered, "To keep the drug runners out." He was a big man, very impressively built; his sunglasses looked almost too small for his wide head.

Just then Bill called him to come and see the famous Charlie's Blue Hole situated just a ways off the runway. Bob had heard of the blue holes but had never seen one. This one was the most famous; it was, they claimed, bottomless yet filled with freshwater. The rest of the group caught up with them there. Though awed by the Blue Hole, most of the group were overwhelmed by what they had encountered at the supposed farm. Even Bill wasn't as enthusiastic as he had been.

Bill and Tom had looked over more of the farmland than what the rest of them had. "There's a tremendous amount of work to do, Bob," he said, "I'm not sure Tom is allowing enough time or has the resources to reclaim it."

Bob, Bill, and Dale discussed what Bill had seen until it was time for the bus to leave. "I know it doesn't look like much," Bob tried to reassure him, "but you have to admit there's potential here."

Bill, who would be in charge of restoring and getting the farmland going, didn't seem totally reassured but more like dazed; he had no idea there would be so much work here. He told them he would have some hard questions for Tom on the way back to the hotel.

"By the way, Bob, Tom asked me to tell you to ride back in the car with us."

But Bob's mind was made up. "No," he said, "the people on the bus are rather overwhelmed right now by what they saw here. I'll try to talk to them on the way back. They saw the beauty of the place, but the site of the old farm and the remoteness of the place were pretty scary. They need some reassurance right now."

On the way back, Bob had the driver take a detour through the government experimental farm. Here, people saw what could be made out of this raw coral. That indeed, it would break down into productive soil. They saw fields of vegetables and cattle roaming on grassland. By the time they arrived back at the hotel, the group was in a more confident mood, but Bob was sure there were some of them who would not return.

They had a party at the hotel that night. Tomorrow, all except for Bob, were returning to Nassau for one final day before returning home. They had all become fast friends; Bob actually hated to see them go.

"I hope to see you all back here soon," he said.

The next morning, July arrived on the plane that the group was to fly out on. The group exchanged goodbyes with her and Bob, and when they were gone, Bob told her about their trip to the project and what he thought of it.

A car pulled up to the front of the hotel that afternoon; the driver found Bob and July inside having lunch. It was Arthur, July had asked him to come and meet Bob.

"This is the man who saved my life," July told Bob. Arthur had gone out of his way to look after July while she was working in Nassau. Bob was extremely happy to meet Arthur.

"I can't thank you enough for looking after her," Bob told him. "This lady doesn't need much protecting," Arthur responded. Bob laughed; he knew exactly what he meant.

The next day, Arthur drove them out to the project site; they spent the day roaming around the old farm. On the way back, he talked about what the black man had said about the airstrip. July asked what the man looked like, and Bob described him to her.

Both Arthur and July responded at the same time, "That's Manly Waddell."

July had told Bob about what had happened between her and this man in Nassau. Again his shadow had been cast upon them. They tried to put Waddell to the back of their minds for the rest of the time they were on Andros.

They spent their time meeting Arthur's family and at their private little beach doing as they'd done every time they'd come to Andros. But as the sun sets every day, their time came to an end, and they had to part again.

On the plane home, Bob's mind once again turned to Manly Waddell. "I've got to find out more about this man," Bob thought. "In fact, I'd better find out more about Tom too; no one had ever thought to find out about him."

# TEN

## 1997

I'D BEEN AWAKE for a while thinking about Manly Waddell, "You didn't get me yet, you prick. Now, I'm going to get you."

My anger brought me back to reality. "Where am I? Oh yes, Bill and Hania's." Slowly, it all comes back to me. What day is it, I wonder turning toward the window. I see light outside; the snow has stopped, and the sun is shining. It's in the east, "Morning." Now I'm really confused. How long have I slept? My body is stiff, but a lot of the pain is gone. I feel a lot better. I realize I'm hungry.

Hania's cupboards are well stocked, so I have no trouble making breakfast. It is the first coffee I have tasted in quite a while. The radio solves my dilemma for me. It soon tells me that it is Tuesday. I had escaped from my home on Friday night.

That means that I have been here since Saturday afternoon. I still don't think I realize how traumatic my ordeal has been on my mind and body.

Going into the bathroom, I look at myself in the mirror. Except for the cut on my forehead, my face is no worse for wear. My clothes are still lying on the floor; they're covered with blood and in tatters. My body is still black and blue in places, but the main concern is a long nasty gash on my right leg. The edge of the wound has turned white, and pieces of flesh are protruding from the center, and it has started to bleed again. I find some gauze and a large bandage in Hania's bathroom closet. I do the best I can with the wound, and then I go to the bedroom and borrow some of Bill's clothes.

Suddenly, the radio has my full attention. It tells me the Mounties have no new information on the bodies they'd found, and then tells of a farmyard that has been burned to the ground west of town. It goes on to say that the storm has hampered the police investigation, but it looks like some lives were lost in the blaze. The skin crawls up the back of my neck.

I take Bill's coat from the rack by the door and go outside. The temperature is nice considering it's northern Saskatchewan in the middle of winter. There is a shovel and a broom beside the door. My muscles protest as I begin clearing the snow from around the step and then dig my way over to Bill's shop. I clear the snow away from the big drive-in door. Bill would be mad if he found out I made a mess in his shop. It must have been a big storm. The walk-in door is half buried in snow. Once the snow is cleaned away, I open the door, and there is my truck sitting there. Now I'm totally confused. I was pretty sure I didn't leave it here and, "Where is Bill's truck?"

I guess it's time I go and find out what is going on. I have to shovel a bit to get my truck out of the driveway, but once I reach the highway I notice the snowplows have been out, making for easy going. I was pretty sure the farmyard the radio had been talking about was Mom's place. My suspicions are confirmed when I find the road to her place already plowed. As I pull into the yard, my heart is torn in two; the old farmhouse lies in a blackened hole in the snow. The shop is also burned, leaving nothing but the blackened skeleton of a vehicle and my tractor.

With tears in my eyes, I hardly notice there is a 4x4 and a neighbor's vehicle in the yard. The neighbor comes running toward me.

"God, Bob," he said, "I thought you were dead." We'd been good friends for years, one of my old drinking buddies.

He put his hand on my shoulder, "I know how you feel, Bob, and I tried to get hold of you. When we couldn't, well, we just assumed you were in the house when it burned."

I stand there and look at what had once been the house I was raised in.

"Why?" I just can't comprehend how someone could do this. They hadn't killed me, but this was the next best thing.

Jim, my buddy, must have seen the look on my face.

"Take it easy, Bob," he said, "I know your Mom's away, so at least your family is all right."

"Little do you know, Jim," I thought, "My wife and son are in mortal danger, or maybe they're already dead. I have to get the hell out of here, that's all I know, and I have to do it quickly before the police put two and two together."

My mind begins to work overtime; I'd have to concoct a story, and a good one, if I am to get out of here without the police holding me. Right now, I may be under suspicion; I have to keep my wits about me.

Jim follows me as I walk over to what had been the farmhouse. Three RCMP officers are working among the rubble; I ask them what they are doing.

One of the officers inquires as to who I am. Before I can answer, one of the other officers looks over; we had met each other before.

"This is Bob Green," he said, walking over to me. "We thought it was your remains we found in the house, but I see it's not you."

The other officer comes over too. He asks, "Any idea whose bodies we found here, Mr. Green?"

"No," I answer. "You mean there are more than one?"

"Yes," he answers, "There are at least three bodies in here, possibly more."

"Where were you that we couldn't reach you, Bob?" the officer I knew asks.

Now I have to make up a story, and it better be a good one. My main concern is for July and my son to be protected. The best way to do that I figure is to get at the source of what is threatening them. This means I have to leave the country and do it quickly. If I tell the cops what really happened, they'll hold me here. No, I'd have to lie my way out and do it convincingly enough to be above suspicion.

"I was up snowmobiling at Candle Lake," I tell the Mountie.

"Is that your truck over there?" he asks.

"Yes, I drove it down this morning."

This seems to pacify him, but then Jim butts in, "Whose van is burned in the shop, Bob?"

This startles me; I had seen a burned vehicle in the shop but thought nothing of it, being so upset about the house.

"Oh, a friend of Bill's went snowmobiling with us, and he left his van in the shop so that it would start when he got back."

I look at both of them, and they seem to accept my story. Well, I have built my nest now; I would have to live in it, hoping it didn't come unraveled.

"We'd appreciate it if you would follow Corporal Novak into our office in town," the officer Bob didn't know said to him, "he'll have you make out a statement."

I figured this was coming; well, might as well get it over with.

"Okay," I answer "I'll follow him in."

I had met the department's staff sergeant two weeks ago when we were forced back to Canada and had to report to the nearest police telling them that we were living here, our passports were being held; and we were under investigation.

I am sure he had a military background before he became a Mountie. I come by this impression of the man by the way he presents himself, reminding me more of an officer in the army than a cop.

Bob was right in his assessment of Staff Sergeant Anderson. He had spent three years in the army before being accepted for training in the Mounties. He had spent twenty-nine years in their service. He came from the old school; his image of the Mounties was what the people saw in the movies from the fifties, and he lived up to this image.

This posting was to be his last; one more year, and he could retire. He hated computers and the new image was demoralizing the force. The spit and polish, the discipline, all this had disappeared. He was ready for retirement, so he had accepted this quiet posting.

"Maybe I'll retire here," the sergeant had thought. He loved to hunt and fish, and he also loved the north. There was little crime, a perfect place to spend his remaining years.

Now, all hell was breaking loose; just when you thought you had it made this had to happen.

His service record had been impeccable; this time however, he realized, he had made some vital errors. This incompetence may have cost one of his officer's lives, which made him sick to his stomach.

This is the first thing Bob notices about the sergeant as he shakes hands and sits down at the desk across from him. The sergeant's hair is disheveled; he hasn't shaved for a while, his eyes show lack of sleep.

I hadn't expected to see him look like this. This shit must be really getting to him. I have to be very careful, just follow along and let him lead. Looking at him made me realize just how bad I must look. I had put on Bill's big winter hat to cover the scar on my forehead as much as to keep warm. Now it is hot in the office; I'll have to take it off. I would look rather stupid sitting here with sweat running down my face, with a big fur lined cap on my head. I hadn't taken time to shave either.

"Shit, I look worse than he does."

"Well, my story better be damn good," I think as I remove my hat. Sergeant Anderson is so preoccupied that he doesn't seem to notice, but I am sure Corporal Novak did.

The sergeant excused himself for a moment while he and Novak went into another room. Novak would bring the sergeant up to date on what they had found and how they had met me.

I am angry at myself for not cleaning up a little better before I left Bill's. Sergeant Anderson comes back and sits down at his desk. Corporal Novak brings a chair from across the room; he also sits down at the desk, a pen and paper in hand.

"Here goes," I think, "be alert."

"Constable Novak tells me you were up north snowmobiling this weekend, Bob, is this right?" The sergeant seems much more focused now, his eyes on mine.

"Yes, Candle Lake," I answered.

"When did you leave?"

"Last Thursday," I answer, giving myself lots of leeway.

"There were other people with you who can confirm this?" he asks.

"Yes," I answer. "I went with Bill and Hania, and the Drinkwaters, and another couple from down south," I add, covering for the van in the shop.

Novak takes up on this immediately.

"They're the ones whose van was burned in the fire?"

"Yes," I answer.

"And where are they now?"

"They're still up at Bill's cabin," I answer. "With the snowstorm this weekend, they didn't get much fishing done so they decided to stay a day or two longer."

"So why did you come back, Bob?" the sergeant asks.

"Well, I was worried about Mom's house. I didn't know if the snowstorm had knocked out the power or not. I didn't want it to freeze up. Also," I go on, "I fell off my snowmobile up there." I point to my forehead, "Bill thought maybe I should get it looked at, so I came home. I was going to clean up at the farm, but I guess that's sort of out of the question now."

Both the sergeant and Novak grunt in agreement with me.

"Yes, that's a nasty looking cut you have there," the sergeant says. "I suggest you have a doctor look at that."

But Novak isn't done with me yet.

"So you have no idea whose bodies we found in the house?"

"No," I answer truthfully, "unless someone got caught in the storm and stayed there is the only thing I can think of," I suggest.

"We'll know better after we get some dental work done," the sergeant interjects. "The bodies were burned so bad that's the only way we'll be able to get any identification."

I decide it is time to do a little detective work of my own.

"I hear you guys found a couple of people shot," I query. "You've had a busy weekend."

The sergeant becomes very agitated.

"Yes," he answers. Then he begins to spill out what he knows; it is as if he has to talk to somebody. I don't discourage him.

"Saturday afternoon we got a call from Gus Helek. I guess you know him, he lives out your way."

I knew him very well, but I just nod my head.

"Well, apparently, he and some guys were out hunting when they heard some shots, a lot of shots actually. Anyway, they went over to see what was going on. What they found was a guy with his head shot off. They figure it only took them about twenty minutes to get over there, but no one else was around, not that they saw anyway. So they headed back to his farm and phoned us. I was going to send a couple of guys out, but just then Constable Novak here called in from downtown that two guys with rifles were running down Main Street.

I thought the way Helek spoke it was a hunting accident, so I sent one guy to check it out and hold down the fort until the forensic people got there. Then we started getting reports of another guy riding around town on a snowmobile all covered with blood. So we set up roadblocks. The two guys with rifles on Main Street jumped on a snowmobile, and they were gone by the time we got the roadblocks set up. We couldn't find the man covered with blood either. Oh, we had lots of calls from scared people, but they all turned out to be false leads.

The forensic boys were held up so they got here late. I was out checking on one of the leads. Everyone else was busy when they did get here, so they decided to check out what was going on uptown. Meanwhile, Constable Reich called in saying that they had found another body not far from the first one. I finally got out there, but it was pretty well dark by then, and it had started to snow. The forensic people could only do the best they could under these conditions. Then we loaded the bodies and headed back to town. Now there's a reason I'm telling you this, Bob, and I'll get to it in a moment."

So far the sergeant hasn't told me anything I don't know, except for his problems, but I feel things are going to get dicey.

The sergeant rubs his forehead and continues his story.

"My problem is that I was careless. I sent a green officer to look after this situation and then forgot about him.

Before we got there, Constable Reich decided to follow the snowmobile tracks to see where they came from. He was right, in a way, he was worried that the snow would hide the tracks and as usual, news travels fast. The scene attracted a lot of people. He was scared they'd obliterate the trail, making it impossible to follow. Anyway, he has disappeared."

"You mean you don't know where he is at all?" I ask.

"We thought you might be able to tell us," Corporal Novak broke in.

"How in the hell would I know?" I tell them truthfully, although I have my suspicions. They both sit looking at me.

"Some of the people who saw the guy covered in blood thought it was you," the sergeant tells me, watching my face. I look them square in the eye.

"I think you guys are full of shit," I tell them.

"I was a hundred miles north of here, and I can prove it. I've lost the house I was born in; and you guys are trying to implicate me in this. I think you're grasping at straws and totally unjustified. Christ Almighty, can't you could do better than that?"

They are both taken aback by my outburst, and Novak tries to justify what they were saying. "Somehow, we think all these events are tied together. We are looking for the string. These events stretch from your place to where you were thought to be seen in town. This makes you a possible suspect." The corporal is being very careful about how he says this, telling me they weren't very sure of their facts.

"I think you guys are guessing," I tell them, "and I think there's some things you're not telling me."

"No, Bob," the sergeant answers. "We've been pretty up-front with you about everything so far, but I'll tell you what we know if you're interested."

I nod my head, and the sergeant continues, "We know that Constable Reich was following the tracks back to an old farmhouse. Apparently some of the people who were at the place where two men were shot on Helek's farm followed him. They got as far as the old farmhouse then they turned back, because it had started to snow hard. Another group tells us they followed the other set of tracks right to town.

Of course, these tracks are no longer visible because of the storm. We know Reich was still alive around dark. He called on his radio, but we could not make out what he said, so what happened to him after that we don't know. At first, we thought he had decided the storm was too bad and had stayed someplace until it was over. We had snowmobiles out early as we could Sunday morning, but as you know that was a vicious storm. The guys almost got themselves lost, let alone find anyone."

"Where's the old farmhouse?" I ask defensively.

"It's apparently the old Scarf place, maybe two miles from your mother's house, isn't it, Bob?" Novak asks.

"About that," I answer.

The sergeant took off on a different tact.

"I understand your wife is in the Bahamas, Bob."

"No," I lie. "She's in Quebec right now. Her mother's family comes from there."

"Oh," the sergeant says. "We saw her on that TV commercial about the Bahamas. I thought she was still there."

"No," I lie again, hoping to convince him I wouldn't be headed that way. "We haven't been getting along that well since what happened in Germany. I guess she's a little upset with me," I tell them. As far as I'm concerned, the less they know about July and me and the Bahamas, the better.

"Sorry to hear that, Bob," the sergeant replies then continues on, "So what we have here is your mother's house burned to the ground with bodies in it, identity unknown. Two men dead in a field, identity unknown. Then there's the guy who piled his snow machine into the ford garage downtown, who people said looked like you but wasn't, so he's unknown. We did our usual checking around town to see if there were any strangers in town. Out at Motel 35, we found that there were five hunters here from the states that checked out very early Saturday morning. Only two of them flew out on their Sunday morning flight from Regina. We're checking with the outfitter that they we're assigned to as we speak. What we wonder, Bob, is what were they hunting?"

I mull over what the sergeant had just told me. What a perfect disguise, I think; the two officers are sitting there obviously waiting for me to respond.

"Maybe," I say hoping to sound convincing, "they started fighting among themselves."

"We thought of that too, but the fact that both the John Does found in the field were wearing bulletproof jackets tells us otherwise. No, they came looking for someone, the question is who and why?"

The office girl came to the door and stuck her head in. "Sir, the helicopter pilot is on the radio. I think you should talk to him."

Novak pulls out his portable and hands it to the sergeant.

"This is Sergeant Anderson, Jack. What's going on?"

The radio crackles; you can hear the helicopter blades in the background.

"We've found a body the wolves dug out of the snow," the pilot tells them.

"Where exactly are you?" The sergeant wants to know.

"We are about a half mile west of that burned farmyard, right on the south bank of the White Fox valley."

"We see you," another voice says.

"We'll be there in about ten minutes. That's some of our search crew on snowmobiles," the sergeant explains. I can feel the tension in the room as we wait to see if they can tell who it is.

Finally, a voice comes back on the radio.

"What we have here is the frozen body of a naked male Caucasian, probably in his thirties. The wolves have badly mutilated the body, but we can see a bullet wound to the head. It's definitely not Reich."

The sergeant let out a sigh, "Any idea how long it's been there?"

"Not long," the officer on the ground tells them. "It looks pretty fresh to me."

"Damn, that's another body," Novak sounds overwhelmed.

"Bob," the sergeant looks at me, "if you're involved in this, you'd better tell us. No one else can help you. There's no doubt about it, these guys are professional killers."

If it were just me, I would tell them, but there's no way they can help July. I have to do that myself.

"Look, you guys, there's no way I could kill anyone, let alone be a part of all this. Looks to me like you've got some kind of a war on your hands."

The radio, sitting on the desk, crackles again, but there is too much static to make out what is being said.

"This is Sergeant Anderson, can anyone pick that up?"

"Ten four, this is Jack. Apparently one of the snowmobiles hit something in the deep snow. They think it's Reich."

"Where is he?" the sergeant asks. His voice sounds shaky.

"They're down in the valley, probably why you can't hear them," the pilot tells us, "not far from the other body. I'm coming in to get you. Be there in ten minutes."

"I'll be ready," the sergeant answers. He just sits there holding the radio in his hand.

"If you don't mind," I say quietly, "I'd like to go up to the hospital and get this looked after." I point to the cut on my head.

He doesn't answer me but says instead, "Do you own a .270 Winchester, Bob?"

"No," I answer, "I don't own any guns."

"That's what they tell us," Corporal Novak speaks up, "but they tell us your Dad did."

"Well, whoever they are, they were right. That rifle could have been stolen, or it could have burned in the fire, I have no fucking idea."

They can hear the frustration in my voice. The sergeant becomes noticeably upset. For a minute, I think he is going to lock me up.

I hold my breath, finally he turns to me and says, "All right, go get yourself looked after, but stop in again after supper. We will want to get your fingerprints and talk to you some more."

With that, he gets up and grabs his coat, and then he goes to the door.

"Around seven thirty will be fine, Bob," Corporal Novak tells me.

I stand up and leave the building. As I walk toward my truck, I hear the chopper coming in. "Should I make a run for it now?" I ask myself.

It is all I can do to keep myself from limping, as I walk out to the truck, but there is no way I want the cops to know I 'm hurt in other areas. I drive around a bit trying to get my thoughts in order. There's no use getting out now, I decide, I have no plan and no place to go.

One thing I do know, if I'm not healthy, I won't be able to help anyone, let alone myself. I'm pretty concerned about the wound on my leg, so better get it looked after. I head for the hospital. As I sit in emergency, I hear the chopper coming in. Bringing the bodies in for autopsies, I guess.

I don't want the doctor to see the bruises on my body, but he insists. I take off my pants; thankfully, the bruises are not near as evident as they were.

"You took quite a tumble!" the doctor shakes his head.

"Yes," I tell him, "the snowmobile rolled right over top of me."

"This is a deep wound on your leg, but it looks like you took care of it."

I tell him I was up north and couldn't get out because of the storm.

"Just kept it soaking in hot water," I tell him.

"I don't think we'll stitch it," he tells me as he scrapes gently at the wound.

"I'll just clean it up and put a dressing on it. You'll have to stay in the hospital for a bit. I want to keep an eye on this."

I had to think fast. "Look," I tell him, "you say I've looked after it well so far. My mother's house just got burned, I've got people phoning me and things to look after, and I'd really appreciate it if you would let me go home."

"Well, seeing as you have looked after it, I guess you can go, but you'll have to come in and get the dressing changed in the morning. The wound is bleeding quite a bit now, and by morning the dressing will be saturated." With that, the doctor leaves.

A nurse comes in to put the dressing on my leg. She doesn't seem to feel that I had been inflicted enough pain, I guess, because she then pulls out a needle that looks to be a foot long and gives me a shot in the ass. I don't thank her, I just pull up my pants, and leave.

The day is fast disappearing; it's four o'clock before I get out of the hospital. Time is against me; I feel the noose tightening around my throat.

"Now what?"

I decide to go back up to Bill's and clean up any mess I had made there, just in case someone checks the house out. I clean the tub and dishes then put the pistol back in the closet. I take the clothes I had arrived in and bury them in the snow outside.

My daughter Mindy is the only one I can think of who can help me now.

I had to give her credit; she'd gone on her own very young and had done really well. She hadn't liked the Bahamas, too isolated. She had left us to live with her grandmother in Minnesota.

I need her help. It's strange, but I feel I can trust her. I'm thinking of phoning her from Bill's, but they'll get a record of the call. I don't want to implicate her.

I head downtown stopping at a corner store and load up on all the loonies the lady behind the till will give me, and then I go and place a call to Quebec from the pay phone. July's grandmother cemes on the line. She's a grand old lady; I love her French Canadian accent.

"Grandmamma, this is Bob. How are you?" We exchange pleasantries, and then I ask her if she would phone Mindy for me and tell her to phone me at this number. I have to repeat the number to make sure she has it right.

"This is my cellular number," I tell her to ease her suspicions, but she's good; she asks no questions.

"She won't be home until after six," Grandmamma tells me. "She's not home from work until then."

This makes me feel good; I know I'm not the only one who's been talking to Mindy.

"Tell her she must phone before seven o'clock, otherwise I'll be out, and Grandmamma, I cannot explain why, but please ask her not to use her own phone." With that, I hang up, almost out of loonies.

Gradually, I am putting a plan together, but I have to deal my cards right or my deck will come crumbling down. This is the only payphone I can find still in operation. It's inside a small corner store. I busy myself in the magazine section nearby waiting for it to ring.

About six fifteen, a lady uses the phone. I'm apprehensive, but she just asks someone to pick her up, and she's not on it long. I'm sitting pondering my next move when suddenly the phone rings. It is exactly six thirty.

"Hello," I say.

"Hello, Dad. How are you? Are you okay?"

"Yes," I tell her. "Mindy, I'm in a lot of trouble, but more important, Mom's in danger. I've got to get to her. I need your help."

"Oh my god, Dad. What's the matter?" It sounds like she is about to cry.

"Keep a hold of yourself, Mindy," I tell her. "Here's what I want you to do. I need someone to pick me up south of the border. Can you make it?"

"Well, when?" she asks.

"I think around midnight tomorrow, and then I'm living on borrowed time," I tell her. I can hear her crying now. I know I've scared her; I'd better go a little slower.

"It's not a matter of life or death, it's just that the Mounties might not let me go after that time, and I want to be with your mother."

"What do you want me to do?" I can hear resolve in her voice now.

"Okay," I say, "it's a ten-hour drive to a place near Rugby, North Dakota. Will your car make it?"

"Ya," she says, "it's running really well."

"I'm out of time on this phone, Dad. We're only good for one more minute."

"Okay," I tell her, "Go to Grand Forks then north on 29 to Highway 5. Follow it till you see a sign saying 'Antler'. Go north until you see a crossroad saying 'Antler, one mile'. Turn right on that crossroad for about a mile and then wait. Try not to get there before ten p.m. It's pretty remote, there won't be much traffic then. I will try to phone if I need to, but watch for a light flashing in the field. If you see the light, flash your lights and for god's sake don't phone me. If I'm not there by two in the morning, go back home. Oh," I add, "bring all the cash you can get your hands on."

I think I hear an "Okay," and then the phone is dead.

It's time to head for the cop shop. I brace myself. This could be the last big hurdle before I made my getaway.

Novak comes into the office and takes off his coat. "You going to hold Green here, or do you want me to take him up to Prince Albert?" he asks the sergeant.

"Neither," was the answer to Novak's surprise.

"I got the call," the sergeant tells him, "I'm to hand in my resignation in the morning."

"Why?" Novak sits down across from him.

"You don't have all these bodies lying around and let the main suspects get away without some repercussions," the sergeant laments.

"But you've still got Green," Novak tells him.

"He'll break the case wide open for you. We have to hold him tonight though, he's ready to run," Novak tries to sound positive.

"The call was more than just about my resignation," the sergeant tells him. "Ottawa wants us to let him go."

"Are they out of their minds? They don't even know what's going on out here. What do you mean let him go?" Novak is upset.

"They want him to run. Our friends from the south, as our illustrious commander put it, want Green to make a run for it. They are scared we can't protect him, and if we put him through diplomatic channels, the Americans claim it will take too long for Green to be any good to them. Ottawa thinks the simplest way would be to let him run, the Americans will pick him up at the border."

Novak sits back. "How in hell do they know he'll head for the border? His wife's in Quebec."

"No, they say she's still in the Bahamas, and Bob knows it. Look, this is all cloak-and-dagger stuff from our intelligence arm. All I know is that they told me I was to let him run, and basically I'm the fall guy. One more fuckup one way or the other isn't going to make any difference, I'm finished."

"Jeez," Novak says. "Well, I guess that's it for me too. I'm next in command."

"No, I asked about you. Headquarters said you're too good a man to lose. They're going to send you to the Bahamas for a while, 'out of sight, out of mind' sort of thing. The Americans will release Bob back to Canada through the Bahamian embassy. You're to wait there for him to make sure he's being looked after and then escort him back."

Novak tries to assess what he'd just been told. "So all this has something to do with the time Bob spent in the Bahamas? He must have been mixed up in some pretty serious shit."

"Well, he was deported back to Canada on that drug charge in Germany," the sergeant reminds him.

"So were the Drinkwaters and Shonavons, which only confirms our suspicions that it's their bodies in the burned out Green's house," Novak answers.

"Well, we don't have to worry about any of that now," the sergeant tells him. "It's out of our hands."

The sergeant slowly stands up. "I'm going to let you handle the interview with Mr. Green. I'm going home to give the news to my wife and then, if she'll let me, get some sleep."

Novak watches a broken man leave the office. His wife is a snob who thinks her husband should be in Ottawa with some of the guys he graduated with and never let him forget it.

Novak hopes the sergeant won't tell her before he got some sleep; otherwise, it would be a long night for him.

Corporal Novak meets me at the front desk. He guides me down into the basement where he takes my fingerprints. From there, we go upstairs into the sergeant's office, where he looks at my statement as to where I had been the last few days and whom I'd been with. He hands me the statement to read, and I sign it. I am hoping he will let me go; but instead, he sits back, apparently wanting to talk.

"I've got something to show you, Bob." He leaves the room and returns almost immediately.

"Have you ever seen this before?" he asks, handing me a small gold medallion in the shape of a lion with a crown. The crown is embedded with what looks like tiny diamonds. My heart sinks.

Hania Shonavon had shown this to July and me one night. We had stopped at Bill and Hania's after a party. It was after midnight, and they had been in bed. Bill got up and poured us a drink before Hania got up.

She came out of the bedroom, giggling that we had picked a bad time to come. Bill looked sheepish enough that we knew what she was talking about. Then July had noticed the beautiful piece of jewelry around her neck. Hania showed it to us.

It consisted of a gold band from which hung a gold medallion. The band around her neck was at least two inches wide, encrusted with gold and diamonds just like the medallion.

"It's been in the family for centuries," Hania told us. "It was made in Austria. The gold and diamonds are real. No one outside of our family but you knows that I have it. I only wear it at night," Hania laughingly told us. "The sight of money turns Bill on."

"No," I lie to Corporal Novak. "It's very beautiful. What is it?"

"We don't know," Novak responds. "But it was attached to something by this gold chain, probably a necklace. The doctor found this clenched in Reich's hand. He had a real death grip on it. We stopped by the jewelers uptown. He says it's the real Mccoy."

"You mean the gold and jewels are real?" I ask.

"Yes, even this little piece is very valuable. We think he took it off whoever killed him," Novak says, looking up at me.

"They'd never have found that bracelet unless Hania was wearing it when they killed her." It pretty well confirmed to me who the bodies were in Mom's house.

"Intriguing, isn't it, trying to piece all this together?" Novak comments.

"Here's what I think, Bob. I think you're involved in this up to your eyeballs. These guys came looking for you, and you somehow got away. If you killed anyone, it was in self-defense. When these guys didn't fulfill their contract, it was probably every man for himself. Two of them got away. They'll be back for you, Bob. If I were you, I'd get the hell out of here."

"I can't really go anywhere. Immigration has my passport, remember," I sound frustrated.

"Speaking of passports," Novak opens a desk drawer and pulls one out. "Immigration sent this out to us at the beginning of the week, but we thought we had better hang on to it until we knew how involved you were in all this. Apparently the Germans decided there wasn't enough evidence to back up their allegations and dropped all charges. You are clear to fly from any airport or cross any border. I just suggest you get yourself lost someplace."

He hands me my passport. I am almost speechless, this is the best piece of luck I'd had in a long time.

"Thank you," is all I can say. We shake hands. "I'm free to go?"

"Yup. Good luck, Bob." Novak watches out the window until Bob drives away, and then goes out to the patrol car and follows him.

Funny how this old world revolves. I'm worried about the police locking me up, and now they're telling me to run. I'll take their advice and get out before they change their minds. Then there's my friends, the Shonavons and the Drinkwaters. We had fought tooth and nail through the Bahamas ordeal, and now it had cost them their lives, and I had to face facts, maybe July's too.

The question keeps going through my mind: "Why?" Well, maybe I can find that out if I get back to the Bahamas.

I stop at an ATM and take out my remaining cash. Five hundred bucks and whatever is left on my credit card from the German trip, maybe enough for a plane ticket to the Bahamas.

I guess it was all the shit I had been through that made me suspicious, but it did seem very convenient, my passport showing up that way. I begin to twig on to something else that was irregular. Before, there had always been someone else in the room when I was interviewed; there was no witness to what Novak had told me and no way to verify what he had told me was true.

I already have a plan in mind, although a risky one; maybe I will stick to it for now.

My cell phone doesn't work here, so I'm back to the corner store pay phone. This time it's a local call to a travel agent who operates from his home. He tells me there's a nonstop flight leaving Winnipeg to Nassau tomorrow night. I give him my passport number and credit card hoping for the best. A few minutes later, he comes back on the line saying I'm set to go. I thank him and hang up thinking I've got a long drive ahead of me tonight.

It's now after ten at night, and there's little traffic on the road, but as I leave town, I see a set of lights following me from a distance. I resist the temptation to speed; that's all I need is to give the police a reason to pick me up. Another thought scares me even more: what if it's the guys hunting me? The lights follow me for several miles, and then to my relief they turn off leaving me to continue on my own.

Novak stopped his patrol car and phoned the sergeant, "He's run, sir. He also booked a direct flight from Winnipeg to the Bahamas."

"All right, I'll phone Ottawa and tell them it's in their hands now. You better get some sleep, Novak. There's a guy I don't know coming in from Ottawa tomorrow morning. You're to leave with him for Ottawa when he leaves tomorrow night, so get your sunglasses and suntan oil packed because I'm sure you won't be back here for a while."

Novak admires the sergeant's attempt at humor. "Talk to you tomorrow," he tells the sarg.

I make good time crossing the Saskatchewan/Manitoba border and travel for another hour before I turn off the highway to Winnipeg and head south toward the American border. It's around six thirty in the morning when I arrive at the last small town north of the border and find the pickup I'm looking for: a 1956 red GMC; it still looks as good as I remember.

My old friend Curt from university days is as predictable as ever, and he is in the coffee shop having breakfast just as he has done most of his life. I park nearby and wait for him to come out. After an hour and a half he finally shows and gets in his pickup. I pull up beside him and roll down my window.

"Bob, you old son of a gun, what are you doing here? Let's go out to the farm and we'll talk," I tell him.

His wife works at the border, so I am pretty sure she's at work and his kids will be in school, so we should be alone at the farm. We enter the house, and Curt pours us a coffee. I get right to the point.

"I need to get across the border, Curt, without anyone knowing about it."

"Shit, Bob, you know I can't do that. My wife will lose her job, and I won't be able to farm my land on that side of the border."

"I remember the time I was here before, we crossed over on your farmland."

"Yeah, that was in the summertime, and I could have been working over there. This is winter, and I have to go around by the border crossing just like everyone else."

"How will they know?" I ask him.

"I know the sheriff over there. Nothing moves without him knowing about it. You see how flat it is around here. He sees me when I leave the yard," and he added, "as you see there's not enough snow around here to take the Ski-Doo."

My heart sinks, but I am not ready to give up. I tell him the whole story hoping to get his sympathy, and by the end he'd begun pouring whiskey. Maybe Curt is bored with his life, but he certainly becomes interested in mine, and before I knew it we were plotting how to get the bad guys.

"You know Bob, sometimes I go across the border after it's closed and ride around with the sheriff just to keep him company, then we usually go to the bar for a few beers and go home. You could sneak across with me, but then what would you do? There's no place to go."

"I have someone waiting for me on that crossroad just south of town around midnight," I tell him.

"That'll work. Don't tell me anymore." Curt calls the sheriff over in Antler and turns the speakerphone on.

"Hello, Curt," Bob hears the sheriff drawl.

"Hey, I'm thinking of coming over tonight and riding for a while, but it will be after the crossing is closed. Is that all right?"

"Ya, come on over. I'll phone it in. You got time for a few beers later?" the sheriff asks.

"Yep, sounds good," Curt tells him. "See you then," and he hangs up.

Okay the die is cast, now I have to get into the details.

"Curt, I don't want your wife or your kids to know I was here. That means you'll have to hide me somewhere until we leave tonight."

"That would be in my doghouse. I have a poker room upstairs in the shop that no one goes in unless I say so. You look dead on your feet, better get some sleep." Curt tells me.

We went out to the shop, and Curt drove my pickup inside.

"I don't care what you do with my pickup truck, cut it up, do what you want with it, just don't leave it where it can tie you into helping me." With that, I go up to Curt's doghouse and fall asleep.

A hand shakes my shoulder, and then I hear Curt's voice telling me it's almost time to go. I had slept for close to eight hours.

"Have a shower and clean up, I have something to show you," Curt tells me.

I come down the steps from the doghouse to find my truck has had a complete transformation. Even I don't recognize it.

"I always wanted a truck like that," I tell him.

"Yeah, well you may have always wanted a truck like this but this one's mine. Okay, you ready?" "This is it, buddy." He threw his big arms around me.

"We probably won't be able to talk after this, so just stay down in the back of the truck. I'll knock on the back window when I want you to jump out. Get out in that field as far as you can before you start south. Hopefully, he won't see you."

I guess his wife and kids are in bed because there are no lights on in the farmhouse when we leave. I watch as he pulls up to the crossing, lifts the pole holding the chain out of the ground, and drives through. He stops, puts the chain pole back in the ground, and is about to get back in the truck when car lights come on, flooding us in light.

I am ready to bolt and run when the lights go out, and the sheriff walks up the truck. He puts his hand on the truck box about three inches from my head and has a piss. Then he starts telling Curt about how his wife caught him fooling around with some neighbor woman. This seems to go on forever, and all the time he's pacing back and forth right beside me.

Finally, he gets a call on his radio, "Might as well leave your truck here, Curt, and jump in with me while I go see what my sweet little dispatcher wants," the sheriff tells Curt.

It's not freezing but damn close. I've had to lay deadly still for over an hour; my body is frozen so stiff I'm having trouble moving, and the wound on my leg is hurting something awful, but the relief of not getting discovered motivates me to get the hell out of here. I run right up the road behind the cop car until I am completely clear of the crossing and then take Curt's advice and head out into the wide open field.

Curt had hoped to get me close to town so it would have only been a mile walk for me, but now I am at least two miles away from Mindy, if she is there at all. I am about half a mile out in the field when I see lights coming from behind me. I try to flatten myself into the ground, as I watch the lights turn off a side road shining right on me for an instant then swing away and continue toward town. That's probably Curt and the sheriff coming back to the bar, I reason, as I continue my way toward nothing but more field.

It is nearly one in the morning before I see the outline of a parked car. I come out of the ditch in front of the car and wave, but there is no reaction. When I get up to the driver's side window, I don't know what to expect, but then I see she is fast asleep.

Those big blue eyes open wide and remind me so much of her mother as she tries to comprehend who is knocking on her window, and then recognition comes into her face as she rolls it down.

"Hi, Dad."

"Hi, Mindy. Don't open the door. I'll get in the back so the light won't come on. We're going to have to drive without lights for a while, can you do that?"

"Yes," she said, "I think so."

I climb over the front seat and give Mindy a big hug as she tries to navigate the gravel road in the dark. I begin to relax; it feels good to be back in the good old US of A.

"It's good to see you, Mindy. Sorry I had to put you through this."

"Well, sometimes it would be nice to have a normal father who didn't have me sneaking around like a kid sneaking out for the night," but she smiles when she says it.

"Now, will you please tell me what's going on?"

I tell her the whole story from start to finish.

We stop in Grand Forks for breakfast, and then I take over the wheel. The last words Mindy says to me before she falls asleep are, "And I thought you were such a loser, Dad."

I mull that over in my mind, maybe she's right, but I haven't lost yet, my problem had always been that I didn't know when to quit.

We stop for gas and more coffee in Fargo and then roll into

Minneapolis right around supper time. We are parked in front of a bus depot when I wake Mindy up.

"Where are we?" she asks.

"At a bus station in Minneapolis," I answer.

"I thought we were going to my place," she sounds disappointed.

"No, Mindy, I want to be in Miami before I stop. A person can get lost there pretty easy. Right now, that's what I want to do."

Inside, I find a bus that is ready to leave for Palm Beach in half an hour. Palm Beach is close enough. "Do you have any American money," I ask Mindy.

"Around two hundred," she tells me. "I hope it's enough for the ticket."

"It is," the girl behind the counter tells me. I give Mindy a big hug.

"Don't worry about me, Dad. Please be careful, all right?"

"When this is all sorted out, we'll spend some time together," I tell her.

"I should be going with you, Dad." She hugs me tighter.

I step back and hold her at arm's length. "The best thing you can do is stay put, so I can get hold of you if I need you. Make sure you go to work tomorrow, so no one will know you helped me." I hand her a piece of paper. "Two blocks from here there's a Perkins restaurant. I stopped there on the way in. Just behind the restaurant there's a phone booth," I tell her.

"You'll have no trouble finding it." Phone booths are a rare item these days.

"That's the address and name of the restaurant on this paper. I'll try to phone you every Tuesday evening between seven and seven thirty. If I don't phone, come back the next Tuesday, okay?"

"Okay, I will, Dad."

I kiss her one last time and get on the bus.

It takes me two nights and a day to get into Palm Beach. As I get off the bus, that old fear invades me again. I walk through the bus station trying to blend in with the other passengers. I have not shaved since I left Curt's thinking it might disguise my face. Now I think it attracts attention. Every person I see in the station is out to get me. The front door opens, and I walk out into the warm night air. I'm sweating, I realize, and not because of the warm humid air. It's fear, the same fear I'd felt back in Canada. I have to learn to handle my fear better than this.

The cabs are lined up out front. I go over to one and say, "I've got about sixty-seven dollars in my pocket. Know any place you can take me where I can still afford to spend the night?"

"Yes, jail," he answers, rolling up his window.

I am getting used to rejection; it has been part of my life for a long time. The next guy is more sympathetic. "Grab the no.7 bus. It stops at that bus stop over there every few minutes." I look that way and can see a sign with some people under it.

"It'll take you to a strip with some hotels on it." He looks at me, "Good luck, buddy." I suppose I did look a little down on my luck.

The next hurdle is to find the right change. Bus drivers don't make change. After we have all that straightened out, I find the bus driver to be a pretty decent guy. I sit right behind him; we chat for a while until I see some hotel signs coming up.

"Any of these hotels reasonable and decent?" I ask him.

He laughs, "These are all reasonable, but decent is another thing. Just hold on for one more block, there's some safer ones up there." The driver pulled up to a stop and pointed to a sign that said 'Aladdin' in bright lights.

"You shouldn't get your throat cut in that one." he says. I thank him and get off. The hotel isn't too bad; the bed is clean. I fall into it without taking my clothes off. I'm about as lost as I'm going to get, I think as I fall asleep.

About this same time, there is a conversation on a secure line between Miami and the Bahamas. "What do you mean you lost him? I thought your friend up in Canada told you he was flying directly to Nassau."

"He didn't get on the plane," Ansly the CIA man in Miami answers. "Don't worry, he'll come through Miami sooner or later. It's the only way he's going to get to the Bahamas other than flying. I've got the Miami mob watching out for him. He'll show up."

"I hear you've been fucking them around," the man in the Bahamas called the Referee says. "I doubt if they're going to do much for you."

"Fuck them. All they want is good shit, and I'm the only one who can get it for them," Ansly answers

"Well, just don't underestimate this Green fellow. He's the one who took out Ginter, you remember?

That's why I want him to do this job for us. I think he just might be able to pull it off," Ansly told him.

"Have you been able to find out who sanctioned that hit anyway?" The Referee asks.

"It was either Waddell or El Presidente himself. I'm not exactly on good speaking terms with either one of them these days, so you'll have to ask them about it," Ansly says.

"Well, what in hell would possess Waddell to take on something that stupid?" the Referee asks.

"He might have a real stupid motive. He's shacked up with Green's wife." There is silence on the Bahamas end of the line for a minute.

"This means you don't have Green or his wife. This whole thing depends on Green coming back for his wife and then you producing his wife and telling him he has to do this work for you or he won't see his wife again, isn't that your plan?"

"Yes. Well, at least I know where she is, and I'm pretty sure I can produce her when the time comes," Ansly answers.

"This plan of yours is getting weaker all the time. If you don't get started on it damn quick, a lot of moving parts are going to collide," the Referee tells him.

"Don't worry, don't worry, I've got it on the move. My people in Colombia say El Presidente is getting weaker by the day. If he isn't able to come out in his own territory and run off his competition, he's done. Then the other producers are ready to fall in behind us because we can offer them a secure market and not have to put up with the Mexican cartels," Ansly says.

"You realize you're on your own in this? If you want to supply the U.S. market with the same shit they're getting out of Mexico, go for it. I only deal in quality product, and you leave the Miami market alone," the Referee tells him and hangs up.

# ELEVEN

## 1988

EMILIO CHAVEZ WAS doing exactly what he loved best. "Skimming over the Atlantic Ocean at 450 miles per hour pumped him like nothing else, even better than sex," he thought. Too bad Zeze wasn't here right now; he'd screw her within an inch of her life. A frown came over his face; "don't bother with her right now," he thought, he'd deal with that when he got back. Right now his hat was turned backward, the tape deck was rappin', and he was rockin'. He was amused at his partner sitting beside him. Paulo wanted to come with him.

"I want to make the big bucks too," he told Emilio. He'd sounded so brave in front of the chiquitas in the bar. Now Emilio could smell the acrid smell of marijuana drifting through the cockpit, and Paulo was very quiet.

"Scared shitless," Emilio thought. He didn't like Paulo smoking on his plane. Well, if it keeps him calm and quiet and out of my hair, so what. All he had to do was help unload when they got there. Outside he could see the moonlight reflecting off the ocean swell. That the moon was so bright didn't bother him; his plane was painted a dull black, a very expensive paint really. It blended into the ocean perfectly. No one was going to see him, even the cockpit instruments were altered so no light reflected outside.

"The worst thing that could happen to me is that I run into a boat doing the same thing I'm doing," Emilio thought, meaning someone doing something illegal with his lights turned off.

Actually he'd had some close calls over the years. Emilio thought back to his first run. Those first days weren't running drugs; they were against the British in the Falklands. How stupid they were, they took advantage of us, but we were young and for a thousand U.S. dollars a month we risked our lives. For what, so some people who were fat could get fatter? He fumed! Emilio had been a trainee then. He thought the pilots who went out to fight the British were gods. They seemed to have lots of money and could have all the women they wanted; oh sure, some didn't come back, but that was because they weren't good enough.

He got his chance quick enough; Argentina was quickly running out of experienced pilots and aircraft to fly. His first run was actually in his old trainer. How he survived that first day was strictly luck. They skimmed low over water under the radar, and then all of a sudden there was the British fleet right in front of him. The other two fighters in his group were faster than him, also more experienced. All of a sudden they split off, leaving him alone heading right at a ship the size of a mountain. He'd froze until the last second; then he pulled up, actually still lower than the top deck but over the bow of the ship. He could see the startled faces of sailors on deck as he passed by.

Now he was right in among the ships so low they had trouble firing at him for fear of hitting their own. He was petrified; sure he was going to die. He turned his old trainer and headed back the way he had come, no more than a few feet above the water at times. He drove the British gunners crazy dodging incoherently all over the place. He flew right under the bow of the same ship, heading back. There was smoke and "ack, ack" exploding all over; a row of tracer bullets were in front of him and then 'thud, thud,' he heard as the planes shuddered under the impact, but he kept on going toward the open sea.

Two British fighters were closing in on an Argentinian fighter on his left, Emilio remembered. He watched in fascination as the Argentinian fighter dove heading right for him. The fighter missed him by inches, then seconds later Emilio had felt a shake; red flames shot past him. They got him, was all Emilio could think of. What Emilio didn't know was that the fighter had been hit by a sea wolf missile aimed at him. The British didn't like flying this low to the water; sometimes it was hard to tell where the sky stopped and the water started, but for Emilio the water was like his savior, and he stuck close to it. Slowly he realized that he was away from it all.

"I'm alive;" he was elated. "I'm going to make it."

Halfway back, he realized he hadn't fired a shot; his missile was still secure. He turned back out to sea and in the general direction of the British fleet; he fired his missile then emptied his guns. He was one of the few to come back that day and one of the least expected. He now realized how stupid he'd been to go in this aircraft; it had no place in this contest. He landed his plane and climbed down from the cockpit as if he'd been on a Sunday picnic. One of the mechanics came up and pointed.

"Holy shit!" he exclaimed.

Emilio looked up; there was a row of holes right down the side of his plane. Emilio made two more runs, but he was smarter now; the pilots could see the writing on the wall. He did the same as the rest of them, letting his missiles go from far away and then getting the hell out of there. The war was soon over, and there wasn't much for him to stay for. What planes Argentina had left weren't worth flying anyway. He resigned and took a job flying a milk run from northern Argentina into Chile. Of course this was pretty boring after being in a war, so it didn't take much persuasion from his old air force buddy to try something new.

"Don't be stupid, Emilio," he had told him. "I make ten thousand U.S. a trip. Just think, Emilio, that's more than you make in a year."

His friend was very drunk. "We risked our lives for our country in that stupid war, and what did we get for it? Nothing! Here's a chance to make something of yourself. All you have to do is skim over the water under U.S. radar till you get to Miami, pick your spot, and tuck in behind a plane landing at Miami International. Follow behind him until you see a hanger with a yellow light right across the top of it, turn off the runway there, and taxi to the hanger. They'll be waiting for you and let you inside. Whatever you do, don't stay on that runway any longer than you have to. There's one plane after another landing there."

Emilio was exactly the type of pilot the drug cartels were looking for. He had experience flying at low level over water at night, and he had experience in tough flying situations such as the rough, short landing strips in the Colombian jungle. He was scared, but the ten grand was pretty tempting.

"A piece of cake," his buddy told him. "I've done it a hundred times."

He found it was a lot more complicated than his old buddy had let on. There were routes around some of the islands between Colombia and Florida. For instance, Cuba had made an agreement that they could fly in a certain corridor over the island.

"Stray out of that and you're a dead duck," they told him.

His air force training stood him in good stead. To do this kind of flying, you had to be able to use your instruments and coordinates. You had to be the best of pilots, but you had to have the training too.

Emilio soon met other pilots. They were mostly ex-air force men from all over the world, all lured by the money. Emilio soon found out that most were making more money than what they offered him. "They" were what everyone called the people who paid the money. No one seemed to care who they were as long as the money was good. Emilio's first flight was into the Florida Everglades; he rode copilot in a Conair jet aircraft, learning the route. They landed on a narrow paved road, unloaded, fueled up, and were back in the air in an hour. This flight took about ten hours round trip. Emilio was tired, but he had his first ten thousand in his jeans and never looked back.

Most of the pilots spent their money as fast as they made it. They lived for today; in this business, there might not be a tomorrow, much the same mentality as going off to war. Emilio was different. He looked after his money. Each trip he made, a good percentage of his pay was put away.

"I'll quit soon," he thought. "I'll get my own plane and fly tourists wherever they want to go."

There were two problems with this plan. They never let anyone quit, and then he met Zeze. She used her good looks, like many poor Colombian girls, to get out of her village. Many of the pilots lived near the town she was born in. Very early in life, she learned they were willing to pay for certain favors. She was one of the lucky ones, not getting pregnant or totally addicted to drugs. She loved to have fun and spend money; she had no morals or sense of the value of money, it was made to be spent, and there was no other use for it.

She'd met Emilio in the bar one night. He was a good-looking guy and all the girls liked him but didn't pay much attention to him; if he needed to be serviced, he'd use them and pay well for their time, but that was about it. Zeze hit him like a thunderbolt. She was vivacious, beautiful, and smarter than most of the other girls. He fell head over heels in love, and soon they were living together. It had been a turbulent relationship. At first he gave her anything she wanted, and she seemed insatiable. He began taking more runs, completely exhausting himself until he'd had enough. He put her on a budget. This lasted a week, and then she left him.

He became desperate, and when he got a chance to do the big run, he took it. It was the run into the Miami airport that his buddy talked about. The pay was astronomical, but failure meant death. When he arrived at the airport to leave that evening, he found not his old plane but a Lear jet sitting on the runway. He also found out his load was not only drugs but humans in the form of two men. Obviously, these men were not able to legally enter the states or they would have taken a domestic flight.

Emilio had seen men like this before; he'd bet his last dollar they were hit men. His orders were to get into the airport by usual methods and then wait for the two men until they returned to his plane, after which he would fly them home. There were a hundred questions on his lips, but he knew better than to ask. He'd be told when the time came and then only what he needed to know. It was a beautiful plane; they made good time twisting and turning through the safe routes, then skimming in over the water till they reached the Miami coastline.

Emilio listened on his radio until he picked up the flight he was going to follow in. It was a jumbo jet out of Amsterdam, big with lots of body to hide him from radar detection. He could see her landing lights as he accelerated the Lear in close and then eased off tucking in near enough that his two passengers began to murmur.

The Lear responded beautifully, and he skillfully stayed with the jumbo until he saw it was turning off for a terminal. He continued down the taxi lane to where it ended, then as instructed, taxied across the grass until he saw a truck with a flashing light on top. They were a long way from the main flow of the airport, now it was completely dark; they had made it. Emilio opened the door and unfolded the steps. The truck picked up the two men, and he was told to taxi his plane down a paved lane until he found a blue hangar. Once inside, his plane was immediately unloaded. He sat and ate the lunch he had brought, watching the men paint his plane with big corporate letters.

"Might as well get some sleep," a man came and told him. "You're not scheduled to fly out until five a.m."

"You mean I'm leaving as a scheduled flight?" Emilio asked.

"That's right," the man told him, "You're scheduled to flight no. 103 for the Dominican Republic at nine a.m." Emilio couldn't believe it.

This run taught Emilio a lot of things about the business he was in. He heard later that a well-known banker had been brutally murdered in Miami the same night he had been there. Emilio realized he knew too much; they'd never let him quit. He opened an account in the Bahamas, letting Zeze empty his account at home of whatever was in it. She complained and left him, but he found she always came back anyway, so he tolerated her little affairs.

As the years went by, he had many close calls but his extraordinary abilities at low flying and nerves of steel saw him through. He amassed a small fortune but over the years the nature of the business changed dramatically. Fly-by-nighters out for a quick buck caused a lot of traditional routes to be closed. New doors were constantly being opened and the ingenuity of the operators always amazing. There was so much money to be made that greed would consume the minds of even the most influential people, whole governments became corrupted.

Money poured out of the United States, yet they seemed to treat their drug problem as a small bunch of hoodlums smuggling drugs into the ghettos of the nation. There, it was out of sight out of mind but when the violence it created came to their own streets and the kids within their own walls began to become users, then and only then did ordinary citizens begin to complain and wake up the government to the fact that the very fiber of their nation was being torn apart. Then the proper authorities started to compare notes and realized how big a conglomerate they were dealing with.

The drug cartels were ruthless, well financed, and well organized. Above all, they were well connected. When a country is awakened this rudely, it can react with a vengeance. The FBI and CIA began by cleaning up their own houses and then their backyards. People on the take were weeded out and replaced with capable people trained to deal with this particular problem. Once these enforcement agencies had their internal problems under some semblance, the results of their work became apparent. Arrests were up, and the flow of drugs was curtailed dramatically. They also realized this was a short-term solution. It would only be a matter of time before the drug cartels adjusted their distribution methods.

The U.S. government now turned its attention externally. Emilio noticed these changes immediately. Safe routes over Cuba and some of the other islands were no longer safe. Experienced runners were being shot down without warning. The rules had changed.

Even in South America itself, countries were becoming hostile as the U.S. authorities spread their tentacles. When they went directly after Noriega in Panama, a huge arm of the cartel had been clipped off. In Colombia, the drug trade had largely been controlled by one man, but now it seemed that it was every man for himself, and a regulated business had now become deregulated.

Emilio had three planes now and hired pilots to make his runs, handling only a few exclusively himself because of a request, but mostly he had to admit he missed the excitement. Then within a month, he lost two planes. It was a devastating blow, both financially and reputation wise, but Emilio was resilient. He took this as a challenge and fought back. Money was not a problem, and he used it to discover new technology. He bought a specially designed Lear with radar deflector body and paint. He went out himself and found new drop-off points. The drugs were put in canvas bags and dropped off at sea to be picked up by boats later. Emilio became known as a reliable shipper and because of this his business flourished; "he'll deliver," and he did, for a price.

Over the years his biggest customer was a man named El Presidente who ruthlessly controlled the Colombian drug trade for years, but lately his influence had begun to slip. Most of the people in this business were entrepreneurs who didn't like to be held back, and the Mexican market gave them the opening they were looking for. Still El Presidente had the best contacts in the Caribbean, and the Bahamas had remained a safe reliable distribution center.

Emilio knew El Presidente's man in the Bahamas. He was well connected in the government and had developed a system of corruption that reached to the very top. Once he had these government people on the take, there was no turning back. A few had tried to stand up to him with disastrous results. Emilio paid this man well to keep certain points open to him. That's why he was so confident this night as he sighted the outline of North Andros Island sparkling in the moonlight.

"There it is, Paulo," he shouted over the loud music and throttled back a bit. The strip was ideally situated, very remote, and at the end of a lake. He could stay low over the mangrove swamps between the ocean and the lake then over the lake on to the landing strip. The strip wasn't so bad as strips go, the coral packed hard like asphalt, making it smooth to most of the places they had to land. It was also one of the few landing strips long enough to accommodate larger aircraft like his, but it was still touch and go. Usually as he came in over the lake, the pickup people parked along the runway turning on their lights to show him the strip. Tonight there was nothing. He looked at the clock on his dash.

"I am a bit early," he told Paulo. "We might have to unload ourselves." He was glad he had brought Paulo along.

The moonlight alone was almost bright enough to land by, but his plane was equipped with special landing lights that could light up any area he wanted without drawing too much attention. He turned them on just at the end of the lake, throttling back dropping in.

"What the fuck?" was his first reaction; he hit the throttle, the plane almost in a stall, struggling to recover.

"Someone's plowed up the fucking runway," he shouted, trying desperately to keep his machine in the air.

Most planes would never recover, and Emilio wasn't sure this one would either. Instantly, the trees appeared at the end of the runway, and then the plane all of a sudden caught some air and started to climb. Even Emilio was surprised as he saw the trees disappearing and the stars enter his vision. In fact it caught him off guard.

"I'm getting too high," he told himself, as he quickly tried to level out and then get down out of radar range.

"Shit!" He'd forgotten to shut off his landing lights. He killed the lights as he brought the plane back over the lake and out to sea. He took a deep breath, probably only few seconds from death, he thought, feeling the adrenaline flow as only a man who has faced death and survived it can feel.

"You almost killed us, man," he heard Paulo whine as he shut off the stereo and began to search the night sky.

"Did I get too high and did someone see my lights?" he asked himself. He circled the shore area for a few minutes watching for anything that might be coming his way. Nothing yet; he started to breathe easier.

"Paulo, get the door open and start dumping the stuff," Emilio told Paulo, but Paulo didn't move.

"Now," he said, pulling out a revolver and putting it to Paulo's head. Paulo got the message and scampered to the back. He heard the trap door open as he kept his vigilance.

At the American base on Andros Island, a blip appeared on the radar screen.

"I've got contact with an unidentified," the operator called on the radio, giving the coordinates.

A helicopter pilot to the south of the island responded, "I don't know how in hell he snuck in here, but I have visual contact. I can see his lights."

"I've lost him now," the Andros base operator stated an instant later.

The helicopter pilot broke in saying he had lost visual, but his radar was still showing something. "I think he's still there."

Simultaneously, two more choppers were airborne with the intention of surrounding their prey.

"Hurry up, Paulo," Emilio shouted, frustrated by the amount of time it was taking Paulo to dump the bundles. They were already tied together, all he had to do was start one bag and the rest would follow; the bags would float and look after themselves just get them off the plane, all he wanted to do was get the hell out of here.

All of a sudden, his eye caught something; a helicopter appeared out of the island trees. He saw the flash at the same time as he felt the missile slam into the side of his plane. The explosion was deafening. The plane seemed to slide sideways across the sky. Emilio could feel the heat scorching the back of his head.

"I'm in hell," he thought instinctively fighting with the controls, and then there was another explosion. This was to be the last thought he'd have in this world. Zeze never really missed him. El Presidente was moving her into one of his houses and was going to look after her personally.

Captain Horatio Norton stood watching as the men gathered up what was left of the canvas bags from Emilio's plane. It should have been the police here picking up the bags; instead the government had sent in what was described as private contractors to handle the job. Word had traveled fast around the islands; Horatio knew some of the bags were already missing. Locals had reported seeing a fishing boat and some smaller boats being here early in the morning. He shuddered; we'll have trouble now, there had been crashes before and always the island suffered from the after effects. Each time a wave of violence and crime followed, usually among the young on the island.

Horatio had grown up on this island and except for a short period of training in Nassau, he had spent his life here, starting as an officer, leading up to captain of the small island force. He remembered when the island had only one small holding cell, and often it wasn't locked. Now they had a new modern building with lots of holding cells, and quite often they were full.

"I just hope it's not my kids who got involved," he thought.

His oldest boy and daughter were in secondary school; his son would soon be off to Nassau to attend the college there. They were good kids but naive and curious, susceptible to the temptation of drugs as were most of the kids on the island. Most of the people here were poor, too poor to be a market for drugs, but now with this batch floating by for the taking, the island would be saturated with a cheap source. Horatio shook his head; most of these drugs were destined for the states. Why do they have to involve us? He also knew that when a load like this went missing, heads would roll. There were certain activities he had been ordered to overlook on this island. These orders came from very high up in the government. When something like this happened, a very dark cloud surrounded the island. A very dark cloud indeed.

# TWELVE

THE YOUNG GIRL quietly crossed the room to a bed where the man and woman lay. She threw aside the covers from the man and sat on the edge of the bed beside him. She reached for his limp member and began fondling it. Slowly, it began to respond. The man moaned and opened his eyes. He watched as Greta bent down and ran her tongue along the length of his shaft; again he moaned. The woman beside him opened her eyes.

"Good morning, Greta," she said, kissing the man and then laying back to watch.

"What are you doing up so early, Greta?" the man asked. It was one of the few times he'd seen Greta smile.

"Is it early?" she giggled.

"I should have known better than to ask," he said, seeing the glaze in her eyes and knowing by the giggle she was still high from last night's drugs. That's all Greta was good at, partying and fucking.

Although not very old, Greta had left school for the streets long ago. The man knew she wasn't very old, but how old he never asked. It was better he didn't know.

His member was at full attention now as she took a rubber from its plastic wrapper and pulled it over his erect penis. He loved the sensation it gave him when she slipped it over the head and then rolled it down over the shaft. She seemed to inspect her work and then apparently satisfied, began to mount him.

"No," he said, motioning toward the mirrored chest of drawers along the wall.

Greta looked at him, "I need a hundred marks," she told him.

It was extortion, plain and simple, but he was in no condition to argue; he grunted and nodded acceptance. She knew exactly what he wanted. She got up and went to her mother's closet, coming back wearing a pair of high-heeled shoes, and then she went to the chest of drawers and bent over it facing the mirror. Greta was not very tall; the shoes raised her high enough that the man could enter her from behind. Her body was small and firm; he felt so big and powerful inside her. He looked into the mirror hoping to see pain on her face. He was disappointed; her eyes were watching his in the mirror. There was no expression on her face at all, just a cold, blank stare.

"You bitch," he thought and tried to stroke harder.

The woman who had been watching from the bed got up and came over to the man. She was older, a bit plump but still a beautiful woman. She rubbed her nipples along the man's back and then reached down and rubbed his balls from behind. She felt them tighten and then release.

"God, I'm horny," she thought. The man was mad; he was upset because Mona had rubbed his nuts making him cum quicker than he wanted to. Deep down he knew he was upset because he couldn't make Greta squeal and ask for more. He stood there a minute, his legs too weak to move. Greta waited patiently for him to uncouple himself from her, and then she walked straight over to where his pants were folded on a chair and pulled out his wallet.

"There are more than a hundred marks there," he told her as he saw her taking it all.

"You didn't tip me last time," she answered as she kicked off the high heels and left.

Mona led him into the bathroom; she pulled the rubber off his half-limp dick and flushed it down the toilet then started the shower for him. She left him and went back to bed; soon she heard him singing in the shower. It didn't bother Mona that he had screwed Greta rather than her; in fact, she preferred it that way.

Mona knew that Greta would bring some of her friends home with her as soon as the man left; she would get one or more of the boys into her bed. Two were better anyway. Sometimes they came too quick, and she'd have to work on them to have seconds, which was hard work. If there was more than one, she could lay back and enjoy it.

The man came out of the bathroom and got dressed. As he walked through his apartment to the front door, he came across Greta's friends; a boy and a girl asleep on the couch. On his big chair sat a young man with green hair and a biker's jacket. He was smoking a cigarette and staring off into space, but he seemed to sense the man's presence.

"Hey man, how's your every little thing?" The man just grumbled, wondering if Greta had told all of them he had a small dick. He picked up his coat and went out the front door.

The man's name was Erik Grundman, but most people just called him Grundman. In fact, most people who knew him called him "asshole" or "that prick." Grundman was a deviant, and everyone knew it. He liked women all right, but he liked them kinky and the more perverse, the better. He hated anything legal or moral and did his best to bend anything to do with either of them. Grundman was a con man, racketeer, and small-time hood with big-time connections. Everyone hated him, but he was the kind of guy you needed if you wanted something done, something illegal that is.

He was born in Germany and lived in Germany, but his office was in Zurich; this was very suitable for his type of business. It made it very difficult for the authorities to do anything with Grundman, because of the different laws and jurisdictions between the two countries. His dual citizenship allowed him to travel freely using whichever passport suited him to ply his trade. There is always a demand for certain services out of the ordinary. In most cases, Grundman didn't actually handle these services, but he knew who did. If someone wanted money laundered, he could arrange it. If someone wanted someone put "out of the picture," he had the contacts. Anyone who traveled on the "shady side of the street" in the business world used guys like Grundman as a contact man when they needed something done that couldn't go through proper channels.

One of Grundman's many problems was that he screwed up a lot and was always in hot water. Why he wasn't dead no one knew, but he was resilient, recovering quickly from one disaster after another, often coming out smelling like a rose. It also helped that he knew some very influential people in the world, some of them were public figures. It was amazing who would use his services and what their needs would be.

Mona had been with him for years. She had been his secretary in the early years and became a lover somewhere along the way, mainly because she had the same basic instincts and morals that Grundman had. He gained a lot of clients by granting them Mona's sexual favors. Grundman used her sexually too and though she was game for anything, she tended to be lazy. He preferred his woman to participate a little bit.

Those were heady days for Grundman; he had lots of money, and this opened the doors to excesses he never imagined possible. It was then that he met Lena. It was impossible to pronounce her last name so she was just called Lena K., her last name's first initial. She claimed she was Austrian, but no one really knew; in fact, no one really knew much about her at all.

Her story was that her mother was a countess who fell on hard times and had made a living going from one rich man to another until her beauty began to fade. In order to live the life she was accustomed to, her mother introduced Lena to her world at a very young age, but when her mother became terminally ill, she sold Lena to a German government minister so she wouldn't fall into the wrong hands.

Lena was street smart, classy, and beautiful. The German official moved her into a residence in the city not far from where he lived, but the minister had a wife and family so he was away a lot, leaving Lena to herself. She loved throwing lavish parties in his absence. At one of these she had met Grundman. Somewhere during this time, she indicated to Grundman that she would be interested in meeting other influential men. Lena had found the right person, and Grundman had his first client for his escort service.

Unfortunately, the minister found out about Grundman, mistaking him for a lover. The minister put the police onto Grundman. They found out that he might be involved in a lot more than just trespassing and soon had him for fraud. If it hadn't been for lawyer Krugman and Mona, who covered up a lot of evidence, it would have been far worse. He hadn't been able to carry on any business while this was going on, and while he got off scot-free, the costs broke him. He couldn't afford to pay for his and Mona's apartment, and no doubt about it he needed her, and he owed her a lot so he did the only thing he could do—he brought her home to live in his apartment.

"Only till I get back on my feet," he thought. She was still there.

At this time, Grundman had no idea that Mona had a daughter. In fact, it took a while for Greta to even find out where her mother had gone. Not that she cared, except when she needed money. Greta had never known who her father was. She'd seen a progression of men pass through her mother's bedroom. It had never really bothered her; in fact, most of the men were very good to her. Mona's lifestyle suited

Greta just fine; they lived very well. What Mona didn't like was having competition in her own home. She came home one day to find Greta blowing her latest housemate on the couch, so Mona kicked her out. Greta knew her mother wasn't tough enough to nor would she take the time to discipline her anyway, but she did move in with some other kids at a commune of sorts.

It was run by some street-level drug dealers who supplied a place to hang out and do drugs in return for sex. This suited Greta's lifestyle, and Mona didn't care as long as she was out of her hair. Greta would still show up at her house with some boys and just to piss her off, she'd fuck them on the living room couch. When Mona complained and told her to get out, Greta offered her to some of the boys, Mona didn't complain any more. When Mona moved in with Grundman, she knew he wouldn't stand for this arrangement, so rather than tell Greta where she was going, she just left.

It took about a month for Greta to find her. Grundman came home to find a young blonde girl dressed in a leather miniskirt, black studded jacket, and motorcycle hat, talking to Mona in his living room. She looked Grundman up and down turning him on instantly. Mona didn't introduce her to Grundman, so Greta did, telling him who she was. She began showing up more and more, bringing her friends in the afternoon. They'd get high and in general fuck around, and Mona was able to get them out before Grundman got home.

Grundman was very busy rebuilding his business at this time. His mother had been Swiss, so he was able to obtain a Swiss passport and set up an office in Zurich away from the scrutiny of the German police. Mona, for some reason or another, was very computer literate. She did most of the office work right from his apartment in Germany.

To start with, Grundman's main income was through Lena. The minister had not been able to get rid of Lena as easily as he had Grundman. He didn't know Lena was underage, and it had cost him a lot of money and would for a long time. She knew that once she had a man by the balls, she wouldn't let go. She used this money to set up an elite escort service and hired Grundman as her go-between. She thought of Grundman as a snake but a snake with good contacts and no morals.

Grundman never thought of himself as a pimp, but he was good at it, and their business was flourishing. He was in love with Lena; he had wet dreams of fucking her over the railing of a tall building where she would be completely under his control, responding to his every command; one slip and she was gone begging him not to let her go over the edge, at the same time begging for more. He'd had her once; he'd gone off before he even got started. It had cost him a thousand marks, and she had given him a taste for very young girls. Someday, he'd be rich and she'd come to him, by then he'd have a penthouse on top of a high building. Until then, he was sure he could find a young girl he could afford.

One night, he came home to find Greta sleeping on his couch. This perturbed Grundman and he complained to Mona. What he didn't tell Mona was that Greta turned him on. He got a hard-on just thinking of that black leather. He imagined her with a whip riding him naked, lashing him on. It made him so excited he climbed on top of Mona and fucked her that night, something he didn't do much anymore. Mona knew that Grundman's sexual pleasures were on the edge of being perverted. She'd been around men a long time; none of these things bothered her as long as she lived a good life, with most everything she wanted, without having to work too hard for it.

Mona even enjoyed Grundman's little Friday night poker sessions. He would bring some friends or business associates to his apartment to play poker. The highlight of the evening would be when Mona crawled under the table and blew one of the players. If he couldn't keep a poker face, he lost the pot. Of course she never blew Grundman so he never lost, but no one complained. Then she would lie around on the couch half-naked, distracting them enough so they played poorly. If they were big winners, she would take them into the kitchen and suck them off. Sometimes while she was administering to one of his clients, Grundman would come in and fuck her from behind. He wouldn't let her fuck anyone else. She was his chattel and therefore private property. He couldn't imagine anyone else having been in her. In his mind, it was all right if she had oral sex with these guys, but Mona was the only woman he would fuck without a contraceptive. He would stick it in anyone or anything, but he was deadly afraid of being diseased and always came prepared.

One night Grundman came home early to find Greta on his bed with a young boy on top of her. He tried to pull the boy off, but the kid was strong and was having nothing to do with it until he was finished, and then he got up and left on his own. Grundman watched as Greta got up naked in front of him and stretched. Her pert little tits made his mouth water, the nipples still erect from her lovemaking. Her eyes went up and down his body, and then she left, walking into the bathroom, closing the door behind her. Grundman stood fixed to the spot. He was so turned on, he almost came in his pants.

Mona was working in the den he had turned into an office. Grundman came in raging to her at what he had seen and if he found Greta here again, Mona could pack her bags. This alarmed Mona; she had a good thing going on here, and she didn't want to lose it. On the other hand, she knew a lot about his business, and she wasn't sure he could actually kick her out. Grundman fucked her again that night. This was highly irregular, and she began to suspect it was really Greta that he was fucking, not her. Well, if she couldn't control Greta, maybe she could use Greta to control Grundman, and she knew Greta wouldn't mind in the least.

Greta stayed away for a week, but one afternoon, she showed up at the front door with two boys in tow. They were very high on drugs.

Mona smoked a joint with them, watching as one of the boys finger-fucked Greta. Then the other boy stuck his face between her legs, and Greta never missed a beat; she just sat there talking with Mona as if nothing was happening.

"Herman," Greta spoke at the other boy, "go lick Mona's pussy. Where's your manners?"

Greta had always called her Mona as long as she could remember. The boy was in pretty bad shape. It took a while for him to cipher out what Greta had told him, but after a bit he crawled over to Mona. She stood up and pulled her panties off, and then leaving her dress pulled up, she sat back down. Herman stuck his head between her legs and began to lick.

"That's more like it." Greta smiled, toking on her joint and then handing it to Mona. "We can have a much more stimulating conversation this way. If you feel like coming, let me know. They say it's good for the mother and daughter to do things together."

Before long, Greta fell asleep on the couch and the two boys left, their heads cleared somewhat from all their stimulating work. Mona was in the kitchen making something to eat when Grundman came home. He came into the kitchen, and she gave him a glass of wine.

"Come see what I have for you," she told him and led him into the living room.

He saw Greta lying on the couch wearing nothing but her leather jacket. Her legs were spread open; Mona heard his breath quicken.

"I thought you might like an appetizer before eating," she said to him, rubbing his balls.

She had never seen such a painful look on anyone's face in her life. Mona dropped his pants and shorts, watching as his manhood leaped out as if it was spring loaded. He moaned as she stroked his cock; she felt his knees buckle and had to help him stand. Mona stopped rubbing his cock for fear he would go off. The last thing she wanted to do was make him angry. She led him by the cock to where Greta lay and then spread her and guided him in.

"Easy, baby," Mona whispered in his ear. "Take your time enjoy it."

Grundman seemed to relax and get hold of himself. He began moving in and out; Mona watched with fascination as the shaft appeared and disappeared into Greta's slit. Greta's eyes opened; she put her hands behind her head, and she watched Grundman enjoy himself. Mona had seen women get fucked before but never this intimately. She heard herself moan and then explode; now her legs were weak. She came again and could feel the cum running down her legs.

Mona couldn't help herself, "Cum, baby, cum," she moaned grabbing Grundman by the nuts. He moaned, and Greta could feel him gush inside her. She laughed watching the two of them get their loads off, panting and sweating.

"You two should get out more," Greta told them. "You make a beautiful couple."

Mona and Greta pretty well had Grundman where they wanted him after that. Greta brought her friends over whenever she wanted; as long as she serviced Grundman when he wanted and the way he wanted, he'd put up with it.

Greta hadn't been into whips before, but Grundman paid very well, and she kind of enjoyed hurting him. What Grundman didn't like was that he didn't have the power over her that he so desired. He couldn't make her moan and squeal; in fact, she made him moan and squeal. He hated her for this.

"I'm her bitch," he told himself, but she was the only one who could satisfy his perverted mind.

There were other things occupying Grundman's mind these days. There were billions of dollars floating around looking for a place to land. Money is of no use to anyone unless they can make use of it. Any money that couldn't be accounted for was closely scrutinized. There were astronomical profits to be made in the drug trade, but this money had to be legitimized before it could be recirculated. Even in Switzerland with its discreet monetary laws, the pressure from foreign countries especially the United States, was taking its toll. When the most powerful country in the world asked questions, some answers were required. This not only became a big problem for drug cartels; names like Noriega and Marcos began to appear as well as other well-known leaders in the world. The countries of the world concerned with drug problems within their own borders, especially the United States, were astonished with what they found.

These countries began working together and found it wasn't only drug traders that were getting caught up in their net. It was a well-known fact that most rich people and corporations had offshore accounts. But then what? Where did this money go? It didn't make them much money laying in a bank account, but if large amounts of money went into any legitimate country or business, it would have to be reported. There were three major centers for this money: Hong Kong, and then on to China, Bombay, and last but not least, Dubai, the new pearl of the desert. There were no rules or scrutiny in these jurisdictions, and they all dealt in cash. The rewards were tremendous, and these areas of the world enjoyed a great deal of prosperity as did the investors. However, this money soon collided with the illegal drug money, and investors began blaming the drug cartels for spoiling a good thing.

There was no doubt about it; illegal money was everywhere looking for a home. People like Grundman became more and more in demand than ever. They were the dreamers, the innovators of new ways to legitimize businesses and money. Grundman's main scam was to finance new projects around the world. There were always people looking for money. Some of them had good projects, but they weren't big enough to interest the big players because it wasn't possible to launder huge sums of money off it.

Grundman wasn't a big player, but if he could just land one of these projects and have it accepted by the money people, the rewards would be astronomical. Then he'd buy a penthouse in Dubai and take Lena there to live out his life. Grundman's up-front fee usually consisted of about fifty thousand U.S. dollars, each time his agents brought him a project. This would be cash often brought by the client and investors under the pretense that this was all top secret and must be done discreetly. These people thought they were part of this scheme, and none wanted to be taxed so if they delivered the money personally, they could see where their money went. Grundman spared no expense taking his clients to an impressive building which housed a banking and brokering company. The clients were very impressed as he led them to a room in the back, which the bank let some of its customers use for private business. The clients thinking this had to be legit put their money into an account set up by Grundman.

Actually greed had just made them give a perfect stranger fifty thousand cash. One of these clients was Tom Newton. Grundman laughed when he saw this one. A farm project on a remote island in the Bahamas.

Newton had obviously stolen this plan from someone, probably someone's thesis. It was so over the top that there was no way that it could actually work, so Grundman was quite surprised when his agent in the United States, Ken Holmes, told him Newton was coming with investors in hand.

He took their money like anyone else, telling them he'd submit their project and to go home and wait for their money like all the others. With the money he received from this scam and from the business with Lena, he could have lived very well, but Grundman was no different than his clients. He wanted to score the big one. He spent large amounts of money submitting some of these projects over again, trying to make them interesting to the right people. They accepted his money, but they had no intention of getting involved in his scam.

He also began to realize that both Lena and Greta were underage, a very dangerous situation and yet one that turned him on. Maybe it was because he couldn't have Lena that he was infatuated with her, but he knew she was the dangerous one. If she got into trouble, she wouldn't hesitate to use her age to protect herself and would definitely turn on anyone she could to take the blame, one of which was himself. Grundman's lust always prevailed over sensibility.

One day, Lena would get in trouble, and the only one who could save her would be him, and then she would be his; until then, he had Greta to look after him. She was young, beautiful, and totally screwed up which suited him perfectly. The big thing he liked about Greta was that he could look after her from his petty cash, although lately she'd become more demanding. But it was through Greta that he met his most valuable asset. Someone who gave him credibility among people who were in his line of business, something that was in great demand. A problem solver.

Grundman had only been in bed for about an hour when he heard a commotion outside. He got up and looked out the bedroom window. All he could see was a row of motorcycles lined up in his driveway and down the street. Studded black jackets worn by a group of rowdy bikers were illuminated off the streetlights.

"That fucking Greta," he said out loud, putting on his housecoat as he headed out to meet the revelers at his front door. "Get the fuck out and stay out," was on the tip of his tongue as he opened the door, but Greta beat him to it.

"Look what I brought you, Herr Grundman."

She was leading the prettiest little redhead as she pushed Grundman back inside. He was too weak to resist. His mouth watered as the redhead came up face-to-face and kissed him. The others behind Greta came pouring in the door, filling up the room, and paying little attention to Grundman as they carried on with their boisterous partying.

"Isn't she cute?" Greta put her arm around the redhead and took a drink from the wine bottle she held in her other hand. She held the bottle out to Grundman.

"Her name is Cindy, and she'd love to fuck you," Greta told him. Grundman took the bottle unconsciously and began to drink.

Cindy giggled and pointed down at him. He followed the direction of her finger; he hadn't realized he had a hard-on. It looked like it was peering out through the flaps of a tent. Cindy and Greta laughed hysterically, and Grundman began to laugh too. Cindy reached over and untied his housecoat, and it fell open. Greta grabbed the wine bottle as Cindy took Grundman's hands and guided them under her tank top to her breasts. She stuck her tongue in his mouth kissing him passionately then slid her tongue down his body all the way till she reached his cock.

Grundman felt his nuts tighten as she took the shaft in her mouth and buried it right to his balls. He'd never been this deep throated before. The sensation was excruciating; he was losing it fast. He grabbed the back of her head as he moaned and threw his own head back.

"She gives good head, doesn't she," Greta said in his ear, as he held Cindy's head close and stroked himself off. He would have choked most girls, but Cindy swallowed his cum and sucked for more. He felt totally wiped out as Cindy licked the last dribbles from his shrinking member.

She stood up and said, "Come with me, baby," as she took his arm and led him to his reclining chair.

Cindy removed his dressing gown and then her own clothes before laying him down and then climbing in beside him. They lay naked, curled up together on the recliner. Cindy took Greta's bottle of wine; she placed a tablet in Grundman's mouth and had him wash it down with the wine. He kissed her, and they lay very content watching as the rest of the party heated up.

Clothing had become optional; it was soon evident that a hard cock in the room was avidly pursued by more than one female at a time. Grundman noticed that some of the participants were as old or older than he was. His mind began to float; he felt himself begin to stir. He couldn't believe himself; he had never recovered this fast. Cindy took her toe and ran it up his erect phallus. To him it stood like a beacon shining in the light. He had dreamed of orgies like this, now his dream had come true.

There was too much to see; it all became a haze of naked bodies and noise. A chubby blonde girl came over to them and grabbed Grundman's cock.

"Come for a ride," Cindy asked her.

It was all the invitation the blonde needed; she climbed aboard and impaled herself on his prick. Both he and Cindy watched as the blonde slid up and down his shaft, her big tits flopping with her motion. Grundman felt as though his mind had left his body. He could feel the woman going up and down on him, and it gave him pleasure but not the pleasure that usually made him go off before he wanted to.

It was a sensation of power that he felt; he could stay hard forever, satisfying any woman he desired. If only Lena was here, she'd be his slave. The blonde was working hard, her face showing the concentration in her desire to reach her goal. Finally, her eyes became glazed and her back arched. Cindy reached up and held her hand as she tightened and moaned then collapsed, her heavy breasts resting on Grundman's chest.

Grundman felt the power, the power to bring a woman to her knees. He kissed Cindy and ran his fingers over her erect nipples. Cindy placed another tablet in Grundman's mouth. She was a teenager but an old pro with drugs, knowing just how much to administer to keep a man on the edge or if she wanted, to plunge him over the cliff. The blonde, satisfied, climbed off giving them each a kiss then stumbled off in search of other activities.

A smaller girl came out of nowhere and climbed onto Grundman's cock. She and Cindy talked about something for a while, but Grundman was too far gone to grasp the conversation. He was pretty sure other girls climbed on and off him, but he became confused and scared. He held on to Cindy very tightly until the sensation went away.

Cindy watched him very closely; she was worried she had overdosed him. All this time, he never lost his hard-on. She held his head to her breast and let the girls have their fun. When he did come back to earth, he grabbed the first thing that men see as they enter this world, and he began sucking on Cindy's tit.

"Would you like to put some money on this, Grundman?" he heard Cindy say as she turned his head away to look at the other side of the room. His eyes immediately focused on the hugest cock he'd ever seen. On the end of it was Greta trying to get it in her mouth. The man who was fastened to the other end of it was also huge. He was not that young anymore and, although slightly fat, was powerfully built giving the impression he might have been an ex-wrestler.

On the floor next to him was a pile of money; Grundman was amazed at the amount. "Greta's taking them on that she can take all of his cock," Cindy explained. Grundman looked at the size of the man's cock and then the size of Greta; he wondered how she was going to pay all the money back.

"There it is. That as big as it gets?" Greta asked, still licking on the end of the man's phallus.

"Yeah, that's about it," the man answered, picking Greta up by the ass and then still standing, tried to impel her on it. She put her legs up and dug her heels into his hips. She hung on to his shoulders and pushed against him, but he was unable to enter her, so she reached down with her right hand and held herself open, guiding him until the head disappeared. Then she grabbed back onto his shoulders as he slowly pushed his cock into her.

"You take as much as you want," the man told her, "I don't want to hurt you."

Greta began working it into herself; little by little, she eased up his shaft burying it deeper and deeper. An older woman, apparently either the man's wife or girlfriend, was giving a blow-by-blow account of Greta's progress. Everyone's eyes were on her as Greta stuffed the huge member down inside her.

"Two inches to go, Greta," the woman shouted excitedly as if it was her in Greta's place. The man easily held Greta's slight body in position as she eased herself up and down the man's shaft slowly working her way to its end.

"There's still an inch left, Greta," the older woman said to her, but Greta seemed stuck; she had worked her way down that far but could not seem to get any farther.

Then without warning, Greta wrapped her legs around the man's ass, pulled herself back almost to the tip of his cock, and then rammed herself toward him. The man almost lost his balance from the impact. Grundman had never seen any expression on Greta's face when he fucked her, but he did now. She had a pained look of pure pleasure; her mouth was open, and she let out a scream.

"She did it," the woman yelled. "She took it all."

The man whom Greta was impaled on was sure he'd hurt her. He made a move to pull her off, but Greta wasn't done with him yet. She began sliding up and down his huge cock with big lunges burying it inside her again and again. The man had trouble holding Greta.

His woman yelled at him not to go off in her and tried to pull her off her man, but Greta was stuck like glue. Greta sounded like an animal in heat, screaming with every lunge. The man's body bucked and jerked, and then his knees began to give out; it was obvious he'd blown his load under her onslaught. Greta gave one last scream; her body convulsed, and then her body lay still, glistening in sweat. The man slowly dropped to the floor taking Greta gently with him, and then he decoupled himself from her.

"You bitch. You were supposed to use his cock, not make him come in you," the man's woman told her. "Now I'm horny, and how am I supposed to get that up."

She grabbed his limp dick and showed it to Greta. Greta stretched and smiled then began rolling in her money. Everyone laughed and began to fondle one another. Greta had turned everyone on including Grundman and Cindy. Grundman had been so busy watching Greta get fucked that he hadn't noticed that the girl on top of him had passed out. She sat on him still impaled on his prick, her head lying on her chest fast asleep.

"I think it's time I had a little of that," Cindy whispered in his ear.

She raised her leg, cocked it, and kicked the girl off Grundman's prick. The girl tumbled over the front of the recliner and disappeared out of sight. Cindy stood up, took the bottle of wine, and poured it over Grundman's dick. She ran her mouth up and down it a couple of times until it passed her inspection and then guided herself on to it. She rode for a minute and then leaned forward, her nipples brushing along his chest.

He looked across the room behind Cindy and saw some guy with a big dork pocking some woman from behind. She was half laid out on the couch with her ass raised over the armrest, her legs dangling over the edge. The thought came to his mind that it looked like Mona on the couch, but a man and woman came toward him blocking his view.

The man stood right behind Cindy. Suddenly, she gave a gasp and a look of pain crossed her face. This excited Grundman; her face was inches above his. He watched her face, his groin moving as he began to stroke into her, feeling his power as her face contorted and she asked for more.

"Please," Cindy moaned, "give it to me harder, please."

Grundman beat his hips upward against her, his passion rising. He heard the man behind her grunt, and Cindy made a crying sound; he felt her body shiver and knew she was coming. What he didn't realize was the pained expression on Cindy's face was caused by the man behind her stroking up her ass.

A woman had been standing there watching the man fuck Cindy. Now that he had blown his wad, she came around the chair, straddled it, and placed herself on Grundman's face. This only intensified Grundman's thrusts; he hung on to the woman on his face and thrust into Cindy with all his might. He could feel the juice bursting from his balls but still he thrust on, feeling Cindy's juices burst with his. The woman on his face came just watching the two of them fuck. Totally spent, he felt satisfied as he'd never felt before, and then he passed out.

When Grundman woke, everyone was gone. Except for the mess in his apartment, his slight headache, and a sore dick, it could all have been a dream, he thought. He went in to have a shower; Mona was lying naked across the bed. His mind searched vaguely remembering a woman getting screwed on the couch last night that might have been Mona. He dismissed it from his mind; there had been a lot of things going on last night, most of them very confusing. He decided he'd feel better after a shower.

Grundman's neighbors were not pleased and tried to have him evicted, but again Lawyer Krugman came to his rescue. People were scared of the motorcycle gangs and Krugman let it be known they wouldn't take kindly to any harassment toward Grundman, so they backed off. In turn he had to do some favors for Krugman, but that was a small price to pay.

A week went by and Greta had not come around.

"The bitch doesn't need my money," he thought, remembering her rolling around in a pile of money.

His mouth watered as his thoughts ran back to the party. He had to get some of Cindy's drugs and then he'd make her squeal, and he knew she'd be back when she ran out of money, but deep down he missed her badly. She was the only one who could give him what he needed, and he was desperate to be serviced.

He cleaned up the apartment after the party himself, scared about what the maid might find. Next to his recliner, he found a cigarette box with a phone number written on the flap. Grundman hoped the number was Cindy's. He decided to phone her. "I can't wait for Greta any longer," he thought. He was disappointed when a man answered. They talked for a moment and when Grundman told him who he was, the man told him his name was Ginter.

"We talked a bit at the 'little shaker' you had the other night," Ginter told him. Grundman told him he didn't remember.

"I'm not surprised," Ginter laughed, "you were a little preoccupied at the time." Ginter then told him what he had in mind. He gave Grundman a brief résumé, saying he'd trained in the German army then went to Libya and retrained as a mercenary. After that, he'd fought in small wars halfway around the world.

"I'm interested in doing some contract work," he told Grundman. "That's where the action is, but I need contacts. I guarantee my work, and I have the right people, I just need to get in touch with people who are willing to pay for my services."

"What makes you think I have the right contacts?" Grundman asked him.

"I don't," Ginter answered, "I'm just following a hunch. The bunch that was at your place the other night would not have been there if you didn't have connections." A thought flashed through Grundman's mind; he didn't have anything for Ginter, but he might know who did.

"I might have something for you, Ginter. I will phone you next week."

Grundman took this information to the one person who he felt just might have the need of such a man. Lawyer Krugman represented people who worked the shady side of the street; the only difference between Grundman and Krugman was that Krugman was reliable and respected. Lawyer Krugman did seem interested but skeptical as was everyone associated with Grundman.

He took all of the information Grundman had on Ginter and said he'd get back. Krugman had the ability to find out anyone's past, and to his surprise Grundman may have hit on something good. He knew there was an informant in Milan right now, whom the Colombian cartel would dearly like to do away with. The trouble was everyone knew they'd like to get rid of him, but how to do it without certain people becoming involved seemed impossible.

The informant apparently had pictures and documented proof that people very well placed were involved in activities that left their hands dirty. The Americans were spearheading the investigation, and the informant was being guarded by a crack Italian unit. The situation was very bleak indeed.

The cartel and Krugman decided they had nothing to lose; Grundman would be the intermediary, so if something went wrong he was expendable, and there'd be no trail. It was a long shot, but desperate men do desperate things. Krugman gave all the information to Grundman and told him to get Ginter to start as soon as possible. Krugman floated a price, and Grundman quoted Ginter half the amount. Ginter came back with a price that staggered Grundman, but to his amazement it was accepted by Krugman.

"You got your price," Grundman told him. "If you fuck up, my head's on the line, as well as yours."

“I know you stand to make good money on this job as do I, Grundman, with this goes the risk. You will not hear from me for at least three weeks. By then the job will be complete, or I will be dead,” then the phone went dead. Grundman stood looking into the receiver.

“What the fuck have I done,” he thought, as he felt the fear run down his spine. Grundman didn’t sleep well for the next couple of weeks. His mind was preoccupied.

When Greta did finally show up, even she could not take his mind off what the consequences would be if Ginter failed. By the third week, Grundman was a wreck; Greta couldn’t even get him up. Usually, Grundman didn’t let these things bother him, but this time he was sure of the outcome and knew the Colombians would kill him. By the time Ginter was to call, Grundman had already gathered up some money and was ready to run. The phone rang; Grundman’s hand shook as he picked up the receiver.

“It’s done,” was all the voice said and hung up.

Grundman collapsed in his chair; he hoped Greta would come around tonight, he needed sex. For a while, Grundman thought Ginter had lied to him. There was no news of a killing; in fact, there was no news at all. It took a week before cracks began showing in the Milan situation. First, the trial date was set back, and then rumors began to appear in the papers about problems with the prosecution’s case. When Grundman had first contacted Krugman, he seemed skeptical and asked for proof. All Grundman could tell him was what he had been told. On talking to Ginter again, he asked for proof, but all Ginter would tell him was that it would soon be evident what had happened; however, he’d wait for his money until the client was satisfied. It soon became evident that the case against the cartel was unraveling.

The newspaper began reporting that the informant was unstable, that records had become available showing that he had even been in a mental institution. Even the evidence he alleged to have of photographs and documents were now in doubt. In other words, the case was dead in the water and repercussions would be felt in Washington. Heads would roll. The U.S. government did not like to be embarrassed.

At first the cartel would not believe that Grundman's contractor was responsible for all this, but Ginter had been very thorough. He was able to prove how by getting to the right people; he had persuaded the informant to suddenly become incapacitated. The cartel found this information to be true, and both Grundman and Ginter received a bonus which was unheard of.

The cartel liked to make money; they didn't like parting with it. They did admire talent, and Grundman's stock rose considerably. He and Ginter were to have a very successful relationship. Ginter proved to be intelligent, ruthless, and thorough. He handled a lot of jobs over the years making both himself and Grundman a lot of money. Things were going pretty good for Grundman.

In fact so good that Mona told him there was only so much she could do with the books; he needed to find some legitimate business. This was what he suspected she was calling about as he picked up the phone. Instead she told him Herr Krugman was flying down to see him.

All kinds of scenarios started to go through his head, and the first thing he asked Herr Krugman after they shook hands was, "Is it good news or bad?"

Herr Krugman laughed. "Yes, I know this is unusual, but do you remember a man by the name of Tom Newton?"

"Yes," Grundman had to think back, "he submitted a project in the Bahamas to be funded, must be six or seven months ago now. Why, has he gone to the police?"

"No," Herr Krugman answered, "his project has been funded."

"What—who in hell in their right mind would finance that scheme?" Grundman laughed.

"The Colombian cartel." That answer took the smile off Grundman's face. "He wanted twenty-two million." How much is he going to get?" he asked as he mentally tried to figure out his cut.

"Five million," was Krugman's answer.

Grundman's heart sank. "What's in it for me?"

"An all-expenses paid trip to the Bahamas and then on to Cuba." Krugman pulled a check out of his suitcase.

"The five million is to be delivered to this account number at this bank in the Bahamas. After that, you're to arrange a meeting with the cartel's man there, Manly Waddell. You and Waddell are to fly to Cuba for a meeting with El Presidente himself. If Waddell refuses to go, contact me immediately for instructions," Krugman told him.

Grundman didn't like the sound of that. "I'm not a delivery boy."

"Don't be stupid, Grundman. This is a chance to meet a very important man, and you've had some dealings with Waddell who didn't have the time of day for you. Now you get to watch him squirm."

"How will I know what to do?" Grundman sounded insecure.

"You will stay in room #206 at the new Crystal Palace. It's a corporate room, the best and totally paid for. You will be paged there, go to the front desk, and ask for line number 4 to make your calls, got it?"

Grundman nodded his head. "When do I leave?"

"This afternoon. I'll drive you to the airport, and don't worry, the cartel loves you. After all, you're the man who they call when they want Ginter to do the dirty work for them."

Grundman felt better when Krugman reminded him of that; still, he'd never traveled much, and this was a whole new world for him.

It was early spring in Zurich; Grundman still had his coat over his arm when the heat hit him as he got off the plane in Nassau. He definitely felt out of place among the scantily dressed tourists he'd been on the plane with. As soon as he got out of the airport, he did his business with the bank and then headed for his hotel. He told the hotel what room he was in. They couldn't do enough for him, but all he wanted to do was get some sleep; it had been a long flight.

A phone call woke him up. It was the front desk. "Your car is here, sir."

"Are you sure you have the right room," Grundman answered half asleep.

"Yes, sir. Mr. Waddell sent it around."

Grundman was awake now. He decided not to bother with a coat and tie; it was just too hot. A big black sedan waited for him; the night air offered some relief from the heat, but he appreciated the air con inside the car. The driver refrained from entering into any kind of conversation, so Grundman watched as the car seemed to enter some kind of warehousing area and stopped behind an old dilapidated-looking building.

"This is it?" Grundman asked looking around. "Are you going to wait for me?"

"Yes, sir," the driver told him.

There was a naked light hanging over a door, so Grundman guessed that was how he was to enter the building and went inside. At the far end of the room, he could see a man sitting behind a desk.

"Come in, Grundman. One can't be too careful in this business, can they?" Grundman had his confidence back now.

"What did you bring me?" Waddell asked.

"Only directions." Grundman toyed with him.

"Directions. What do you mean directions?" Grundman knew he was in the driver's seat.

"You and I are to be on a plane to Cuba at ten a.m. tomorrow morning to have a meeting with El Presidente."

"They sent you all this way to tell me that?" Waddell seemed puzzled.

Grundman decided to turn the screws. "I guess he's not too happy with what's going on here."

This brought the black man out of his chair with a speed that startled Grundman.

"They know fucking well what's going on." Waddell raged. "The Americans got Noriega in Panama by the balls, and they've threatened to do the same to the government here in the Bahamas." The black man sat back down.

"The government's scared shitless and saving their own asses," he told Grundman.

"They told me you'd know which plane to take to Cuba." Grundman thought he had pushed things far enough.

"Yes, yes, I'll pick you up at your hotel at nine tomorrow morning," Waddell waved at Grundman as if dismissing him. The driver was waiting for him and drove him back to the hotel, leaving Grundman wondering if Waddell would indeed show up in the morning.

Grundman would not have blamed Waddell if he hadn't shown up, but he did. In fact he showed up early, taking Grundman to buy some clothes a little more suited to the Bahamian heat. He looked good in a white suit and Panama hat, something he wouldn't be caught dead in back home. Waddell didn't show any stress as they flew over the blue waters and islands between Nassau and Cuba. There they landed on a small gravel strip close to the water. It was Grundman who was feeling sick, never having flown in a small plane before. They walked over to a dock where they could see several yachts parked offshore. A speedboat came along from out of nowhere and picked them up letting them off on what Grundman thought to be the biggest of the yachts.

Waddell was good until the lift started to take them to the upper decks, and then he started to sweat and squirm around. Somehow, this turned Grundman on. The fear of death was leaving a smell that quickened his breath; his mind wondered what it would be like to screw that big black ass as he thrashed about drawing his last breath.

El Presidente came over to meet them, shaking hands and putting his arms around them, spoiling Grundman's erotic thoughts. He sat them down to lunch served by one of the most beautiful women Grundman had ever seen, taking his mind off Waddell's ass and on to hers. Latino, he thought, probably about the same age as Lena and Greta; he'd read about Latino women in smut magazines, but this was the first one he'd seen. Hot blooded, well, she made his blood boil. He was so enthralled in her he almost missed El Presidente begin to interrogate Waddell.

"We are not pleased with what's happening in Nassau. We feel you've lost control."

"Look," Waddell responded, "I can't just walk in and kill everyone in the government. The appropriate actions are being carried out, but it takes time. The Americans have everyone scared. I'd like to let things cool off for a while."

"We know all this, but of all people we thought we could count on you. With this Panama situation, all our traditional routes are under heavy scrutiny right now," El Presidente told them. "We want this route kept open. In a few months, other routes will become available, but right now you're in the hot seat."

Waddell sat silent for a moment. "What do you propose?"

"Well, for one thing, money will be no object, but we're going to demand a lot from you," El Presidente told him. "The thing we are really pissed about is you not telling us about the airstrip on Andros being plowed up. We lost our best pilot, let alone close to three million in product. We pay you well. What's going on?"

"I told you they're scared shitless," Waddell retaliated. "The people who ordered this done are at the very top. They had a secret meeting with the CIA, and the next day things began happening. I didn't have a chance to know what was decided, let alone stop it. Hell, it usually takes this government a year to decide what shoes to wear and then a year to put them on. In the last two weeks, they've plowed up runways, sunk a few boats, confiscated airplanes, and already started the foundation for a low-level surveillance radar station on Antigua." Waddell sat back shaking his head, "It's going to take more than money."

Have you heard of a man named Tom Newton?" El Presidente asked Waddell. They had Grundman's full attention now.

"Yeah, yeah," Waddell answered. "He wanted to start a farm over on Andros. His problem is he's got no money and is trying to get the Bahamian government to float him a loan. In fact, I saw him last week. He thinks I can get him a loan, but the only reason I went out there with him was to see for myself that the runway had been plowed up." Waddell turned to Grundman. "I hear he spent a lot of money trying to get funding out of you."

There was only one way Waddell could know that; his agent in Bowling Green, Mr. Holmes, must have told him. "He'd have to put a stop to that," Grundman thought.

"Forget all that," El Presidente told Waddell, "this is no time to turn this into a pissing match. The point is, Grundman has found funding for Newton to start up the project. We're supplying five million to him, but what he doesn't need to know right away is he's going to have a partner who is supplying the rest. Your job will be to fast-track the project through government."

Then El Presidente turned to Grundman. "We think Newton will do anything to get his money. He's to get down here on the next flight and told his first priority is to have the airstrip open so he can start bringing supplies in. Tell him he's to bring in ten of his so-called technicians to start on the land. He is not to bring in any heavy equipment or operators, that will be supplied as government funding. We want that airstrip ready within a week, and he is to be told that his people are to stay away from the airstrip and the work there. The only part of this project they are to be a part of is the day-to-day operation of the farm itself. Once the airstrip is functional, Waddell will tell Newton about his partner."

"It will be one of our nongovernmental organizations. El Presidente turned to his beautiful companion, "Zeze, would you bring me my book, please."

She went into a room beside them with tinted sliding doors; as she slid one of the partially opened doors to enter, they saw the outline of a man sitting inside and evidently listening to every word that was being said.

She came back out carrying a book which she handed to El Presidente. He thumbed through the book mumbling to himself until he found what he was looking for.

"Here we are. Man, someone was doing a good job of collecting donations for this one, All Peoples Care Organization, or APCO, as its better known. They've got close to ten million in the kitty. Perfect for this project. We'll start releasing funds immediately, of course we'll take their clean money and replace it with some we need to clean up, you guys know how it all works.

These NGO's work well for us, but we will need Newton and his farm to show what their money has done for Andros. So you both know your jobs. Grundman, you're to get Tom Newton and his people down here as quick as possible, so we can make this project look legit. Waddell, you're to get the government to sanction this project pro bono, explaining to them all labor and equipment will be local and supplied by the NGO."

Zeze brought them drinks and some Cubans, as the small details were ironed out. A man came to tell them their boat was ready. As they got up to leave, El Presidente came close to Grundman and said into his ear, "I don't like the way you look at Zeze."

Grundman froze in his tracks, and then El Presidente smiled and punched his arm.

"She's beautiful, isn't she, but what can I do? She's my dead pilot's grieving wife. I must look after her," he winked. They shook hands.

"Say hi to your man Ginter," El Presidente told him. Grundman nodded and left knowing he had dodged a bullet. He was Ginter's contact man, and that may just have saved his ass.

On their way back to shore, Waddell tossed his cookies over the side of the boat, but facing death had a different effect on Grundman; he got hard. The excitement of facing death and surviving it turned him on. He couldn't explain why, it just did.

"I think I need something to fuck," he told Waddell.

"All right, which do you prefer, black or white?" Waddell asked.

"Both," was Grundman's answer. On the plane ride back, both men discussed the day's events. "Who do you think the man was in the room listening to what we said?"

Waddell was slow to answer. "There's a rumor in the islands that there's a man called the Referee. He's supposed to be the one who solves problems between the cartel and the Americans. If this was true, I doubt he has much influence anymore. Myself, I doubt he ever existed, there's not much I don't know about in the islands."

Grundman woke the next morning without a hangover. Cocaine, why didn't he know about it before? You could fuck all night and wake up without a hangover. He looked at the two girls getting dressed and reached for the bag beside his bed, but one of the girls took it away.

"No way, baby. Remember we're taking you out on the town tonight." She reached over and rubbed his limp dick. "You better make sure you both get some rest."

Grundman smiled; he went back to sleep. It was afternoon when he woke up again. His mind wondered what was in store for him tonight, and then it hit him; holy shit, he had to get in touch with Newton. He was less than five minutes getting down to the main desk and getting his line.

His fear was that Holmes would be out of his office, but he got an answer right away.

"Jagwar Holdings," he recognized Holmes's voice.

"This is Grundman. Hi, how's things?" Holmes sounded happy.

"Have you talked to Tom Newton lately?" Grundman asked.

"Hell, yes, he phones every day, the son of a bitch is a real bulldog," Holmes answered.

"Well, that's good, Holmes, because you can tell him his funding's come through." Grundman listened as Holmes talked excitedly into the phone.

"Why did you tell Waddell that Newton was dealing with me, Holmes?"

Holmes stuttered into the phone, "I thought you were both working for the same people, so when he phoned me I told him you were trying to get Newton some money."

"You fuck," Grundman yelled into the phone. "You don't think there might be a conflict of interest there, do you?" Holmes didn't answer, so Grundman continued. "The next time he phones, you phone me and tell me what he wants, okay?" Then he proceeded to give Holmes the exact instructions he was to give Newman and he finished with "If I don't think you're telling me everything Waddell tells you, then you can fucking well go after him for your commission," and hung up.

Next, he phoned Mona. The phone rang beside her bed. She ignored it, paying attention to the young man working on top of her. It continued to ring, and finally she reached over and lifted the receiver.

"Hello," she said. It was Grundman asking how she was. "Fine," she told him.

"Anything new at the office?"

"No, it's pretty quiet here," Mona answered then put her hand over the receiver and moaned. The young man pulled back and rammed into her again with an evil grin on his face. His lunges were driving her crazy.

"Please stop," she gasped, trying to hear what Grundman was saying. The young man stopped just long enough for her to take her hand off the mouthpiece and then began stroking into her.

"I have to go to the bathroom, Grundman, goodbye," she gasped into the phone, feeling the orgasm start as she hung up the receiver.

"You bastard," she said affectionately to the boy on top of her. Mona was relaxed; she was sure she heard Grundman say he wouldn't be back for a few days. She looked over to see Greta passed out at the foot of the bed.

"Good," she thought, "maybe I can keep this stud to myself all day."

"Fucking bitch," Grundman thought. She sounded half-asleep, probably still in bed. He sniffed a little coke just to clear the cobwebs then went down to eat. After that, he sat on the beach watching the bikinis walk by. He took another little sniff of coke; "I could live in a place like this," he thought.

# Thirteen

I CLIMB OUT OF bed and look out the hotel window. It is another balmy beautiful Florida morning. People are walking down the street in shorts, and a light breeze fans the palm trees. It is hard to believe that just a few days ago I almost froze to death. I head into the bathroom and look in the mirror. The bruises on my body are fading fast; only the very worst of them still remain visible.

"How will I disguise myself?" I ask, looking in the mirror.

"Some hair dye?" I decide not to shave; a tan would do wonders if I have the time.

Right now, I have priorities: get money from July's account, do some shopping, and try to get hold of Arthur in Nassau. At least I hope he is in Nassau; I take a chance and phone the airport where he usually places himself early in the morning looking for a fare he'd take into town in his old car.

The lady who answers the phone tells me, "No problem," so I hold my breath but am pleased to hear Arthur's voice come onto the line. He is apprehensive at first until he is sure it is me.

"How's Rikker and July?" I ask. This is of the utmost in my mind now.

"I saw them last night," Arthur tells me. "We are trying to move them. Andros is too small to hide them for long."

"Where will they go? I want to know.

"Friends of mine are to arrange something. I had to come back last night. I'm sure I'm being watched."

"Okay," I tell him, "I'm in Miami, but I'm sure they're watching me too. Is there any way I can get there?"

Arthur said he would look into it for me, and we made arrangements to phone each other two mornings from now.

I have two days to kill. I decide to work on my tan and get some hair dye. Other than that, the salt water of the ocean should help heal my wounds. I head for the beach that afternoon. I lay in the sand, my mind floating back to the events that had brought me here.

It was always the same story from Tom Newton; the funding was imminent, just a few more days. How many days could they wait before they continued on with their own lives? This was discussed often (too often as far as Bob was concerned) among the group. Bob was fortunate in a sad sort of way. He kept busy getting ready for his farm auction which the bank had ordered, but the Shonavons and the Drinkwaters, they had placed their whole future on this project.

Bill Shonavon had sold off some of his equipment and expected to move the rest to the Bahamas. Tom had told him he would buy this equipment for the project. So Bill had not tried to land local contracts as he usually did each year.

The Drinkwaters were in a similar situation. Neither had shown much sympathy for Bob and July in their plight, but now that they were in the same boat; they seemed to seek sympathy and a shoulder to lean on from Bob.

July knew what Bob was going through in Canada and was glad she wasn't there. She had found more work in Florida.

"Bob," she told him, "After the sale, let's get away from all that. You can find something to do here, and we'll go from there."

She realized it was hard on Bob. He'd had two hard hits, one after the other. A lot of people would be down and out. She knew Bob was depressed, but he was resilient. She'd have to help him though; she planned on returning home shortly to be with him. He needed her right now, and that was the most important thing—that they saw this through together.

As the days went, by it became more and more evident that Tom had led them down the garden path. It seemed that everyone in the group wanted to unburden their problems on Bob's shoulders. With his own problems and theirs, the load was very heavy indeed.

Two days before the sale, the phone rang, waking Bob up from a troubled sleep. He looked at the clock; it was 5:00 a.m.

"Some damn fool early bird wanting to know what shape the machinery is in," he thought. He'd received hundreds of such calls at all hours the last few weeks.

"Bob, this is Tom." He didn't wait for Bob to answer. "We've been funded. I need you on-site by tomorrow."

Bob's mind instantly snapped into focus. "You say the money came to fund the project?"

"Yes," Tom answered.

"You know what we told you, Tom. We're not spending another cent of our own money on this thing."

"I know," said Tom, "there'll be airplane tickets issued in your name waiting at the airport. There will be funds available to you at your bank this morning when it opens."

Bob was stunned. "My farm auction is the day after tomorrow, Tom, can't I wait till after that?"

"I'm bringing down five people. If you can't come, I'll get someone else."

"No, no, that's all right." The excitement was beginning to show in Bob's voice.

"I can be there. I'd just as soon not be here to watch my stuff sold anyway."

"Okay, Bob, Bill's coming too. I'll meet you both at the airport in Nassau."

"Dale Drinkwater's not going?" Bob asked.

"Yes," Tom told him. "He'll be there in a few days. He's picking up some stuff we need." Tom hung up, leaving Bob sitting on the edge of the bed thinking of a hundred other questions he should have asked.

It didn't take long for the phone to get hot; everyone started phoning as soon as the word got around.

"Don't get excited yet, Bill," Bob told Bill Shonavon when he phoned. "Let's wait and see if the money's really there when the bank opens."

Both Bill and Dale were waiting at the bank when Bob arrived. Both of them expected to receive money for the preliminary work they had done for Tom. Bill even expected to be paid for his equipment which could run into the hundreds of thousands of dollars.

Bob felt happy to be getting anything. Just to get the project off the ground was a major victory, but Tom had made promises before, so he kept his emotions under control. Tom wasn't quite as quick as he had promised. It took an anxious hour before the electronically transferred funds showed up.

Bill and Dale were immediately deflated; the funds amounted ten thousand U.S. each. To Bob, it was a fortune; to Bill and Dale, it was a slap in the face. Both had expected to be rich even before they started work. They threatened not to go, but Bob remained silent. As far as he was concerned, Tom was smart. Hungry men work harder than fat men.

They had no choice really; they could yell and scream, but they were in too deep to get out. He knew they'd go.

The only downer for Bob was again telling the kids they'd be apart for a while. Good old Grandma would be stuck with them again, but the kids were happy. They'd noticed the stress on their dad and were actually relieved to see him excited for a change.

Bob was anxious to see July. He was pleased to see they had a six-hour layover in Miami because as it just so happened she was working there, it wouldn't be long, but they'd make the best of it.

July was ready for Bob when he landed in Miami. She said hi to Bill, and then they left him in the airport while she whisked Bob off to a motel room. They made love like two long-lost lovers. Time flew; they had so much to talk about.

"We're still not totally going to be together for a little while, July, but at least we'll be closer," Bob told her.

July raised her head from the pillow and kissed his lips. She lay looking down at him, her hair brushing his face.

"The French have a saying," she said, "L'Absence est à L'Amour ce que le vent est au feu, S'Allûme les grands et éteind les petits."

Smiling, Bob ran his fingertips along her face.

"It sounds beautiful. What does it mean?"

She scratched her long nails against his chest. "It loses something in the translation, but roughly it means, 'Absence is to love like wind is to fire, it lights up the big ones and puts out the little ones.'"

"Why is it only the French say it so well?" he asked.

I don't know Bobby Green," she said, rolling on top of him. "You are the wind, because I'm on fire."

Tom did meet Bob and Bill at the airport as he said he would. They noticed one thing right away: no taxi. Now they rode in a limo to a hotel on Cable Beach where Tom briefed them on their assigned tasks. Bill wanted to talk money, but Tom told him he wanted Bill to focus on his job at hand.

"I want a machine shop set up on-site," he told Bill. "I have hired a local company to start work on the airstrip. That's our priority. Once the airstrip is in operation, we can start bringing supplies in. As soon as the airstrip's in business, they'll start on the road."

"What about my equipment?" Bill asked.

"We'll use that on the farm later. Right now I'm using what's available locally," Tom told them. "The government wants me to use locals as much as possible. The company I am using wants to use our airstrip for their own business. Apparently the government is charging an arm and a leg to use the local airport, so they'll use our airstrip in exchange for doing the work."

Bill was fuming, but Bob was pleased. This didn't sound like the grand scheme Tom had at first promised. That plan was too big; maybe Tom had come to his senses and would scale things down a bit. Bob had found a lot of loopholes in Tom's plan; not everything had been feasible in such an isolated place. Maybe, just maybe, this project could make it, and Bob was determined to do his best to make it happen.

Later that day, Bob flew into the North Andros airport. The truck loading the bulldozer to start work on the airstrip was waiting for him. It was the only way he could get to the site right now, and Tom wanted him to start right away.

They worked till dark flattening out the runway that had been dug up only weeks before. A company truck picked the men up shortly after dark dropping Bob off at the Andros airport hotel where the group had stayed before.

It took three days to get the airstrip leveled out and packed good enough for the aircraft to use, and then they started on the road. Bill was on-site now with an old trailer and some tools. Tom made the maiden flight in the next day. He was beaming from ear to ear.

"Supplies are scheduled to start coming in tomorrow," he told Bob. More of the crew was coming, and he'd hired another bulldozer to start to start clearing the land.

"You and Bill concentrate on that. The rest will be taken care of by our partner company, APCO."

"What do you mean 'partner company'?" Bob wanted to know.

"It's a nongovernmental organization that's financing part of the farm. Don't worry, it's one of these do-gooder organizations who are helping the locals get jobs," was all Tom would say. Bill had complained to Tom that they were terribly understaffed and wondered when the rest of Tom's recruitments would show up.

A week later, Dale and two others showed up. That put eight men in one pickup to get to the farm from the hotel every day. One morning, they met with Tom for a progress report. It was at one of the new temporary buildings along the landing strip. It was the first time they'd seen the progress in this area. There were pickup trucks everywhere, and two new buildings were being constructed. At the end of the runway sat a large aircraft. It was pretty evident where the priorities were.

Tom was quick to explain that the area around the landing strip was APCO's responsibility, and as soon as they were done with their work, all the equipment would move over to work on the farm side.

Bill argued that the farm had to make money if the project was to survive, so Tom sent some local labor to help them out. Of course, they only got the men APCO didn't want and were pretty, well, useless. Bob soon found out a lot of the locals knew something about farming, so he began going over to the airstrip in the morning and handpicking his men. Before long, they were producing enough vegetables to supply the kitchen on the project. It was a long hot summer; three of the eight guys Tom had sent down quit after the first month. That left five supervisors to build the hog and cattle barns, clear land, and raise produce.

The supervisors talked among themselves and decided to concentrate on the produce. There wasn't enough power to supply what was needed for the barns anyway. Tom was seldom on the project, and if he did come around, it was to raise hell about how little was getting done.

One thing Tom did right was to have ten cottages built around the lake for his managers. Once they were completed, the wives moved down and brought their kids. July was home for the summer, so both Mindy and Rikker came to live with Bob and her in the new cottage. It had been months since they had lived as a family, and for a while, things went well, but then Mindy became increasingly bored. She became impossible to live with and began causing problems that embarrassed Bob and July. They finally sat down with her and asked what she'd like to do.

"I want to go back to Minnesota," she told them. July knew Mindy somehow felt tied to the place where she was born. Only there had she seemed to find peace with herself. That night, Bob and July had a long talk out on their deck. It overlooked the placid lake the cottages that had been built around. It was peaceful and quiet, a good place to talk.

"I think we should let her go," July told him.

"It's not that I want to hold her here in the middle of nowhere," Bob answered. "Sometimes I blame myself for not giving her a stable life like most kids have. Anyway, I'd like her to at least finish high school."

"That's bullshit, Bob. You've done as well as you could, you always try, that's important. Mindy's too much like you in a way. She'll do all right. She just has to find her own way to do her own thing."

"All right," Bob said to her, "I guess her grandparents are close if she needs some help."

"She won't need much help, Bob, she'll suffer along just like someone else I know," July smiled at him.

Rikker, on the other hand, fit in very well. There were three other boys on the project roughly his age. Luckily, they mixed with the Bahamians very well, in fact spending most of their time with them. When it came time to start school again, Bob and July weren't sure what to do. They had thought of sending him to a private school in Florida, but because he fit in so well, decided to send him to the local school. The only high school required a long drive down to Fresh Creek near the naval base.

The parents solved this by buying each of the high school kids a Sea-Doo. In about twenty-five minutes, they could ride down Fresh Creek, which was connected by a narrow canal to the lake at the village. Only if the weather was bad did they have to be driven to school.

This project, even with all its problems, was starting to take shape. The Shonavons and Drinkwaters had not spent much time with Bob and July the last couple of months, so it was a surprise to see the two couples appear on their deck one evening. July went to get drinks. Bob was happy to see them. They had all been working too hard lately; it was time they socialized a little more. July brought the drinks, and they all sat down before Bill dropped the bombshell.

"Bob, Tom's fired all of us."

Bob thought they had all been pretty down, but never in his wildest dreams had he anticipated this.

His response was "Hell, you guys know Tom. He's always running off at the mouth."

"Not this time," Bill said quietly. "He'll give us a letter to this effect at the morning meeting."

"So what do we do about it?" Bob asked them.

"We don't know, Bob. We tried to reason with him, but he would not listen," Dale said.

"Well, I'd say we've got a lot of work ahead of us tonight," Bob told them as he reached for the company radio phone.

They all arrived at the meeting early, but Tom was already there. Tom handed each of them a letter, but they refused to accept it.

"I've listed what I feel you're entitled to in these letters," he told them. "I don't care if you accept the letters, then you can get out with nothing."

"Are you firing us?" Bob asked.

"You know fucking well I am," Tom responded.

"On what grounds?" Bob asked calmly.

"Incompetence!" Tom yelled.

"In what way?" Bob again asked in a calm voice that seemed to agitate Tom.

"You're not getting anything done." Tom was mad now. "We're way over budget, and the project's way behind schedule."

"What is not getting done, Tom?" Bob stayed with him like a bulldog.

"The dairy barns are way behind schedule. The hog barn, the land clearing, everything," Tom ranted.

"All these projects are being done by APCO!" Bob said quietly. "Our land clearing is not up to your schedule, but it's still adequate for what we can use right now, and we've outperformed APCO there too. You're responsible to make them keep their schedule."

Tom seemed a little apprehensive now. "We've also done a little checking, Tom. APCO is not only dogging it on these projects, they're charging you an arm and a leg to use our facilities, and maybe it's not us who are incompetent."

"What the fuck's going on here?" Tom yelled as he looked around at all the managers in the room. "This is my project, and I'll do as I fucking well wish."

"No you won't, Tom, take a look outside." Tom stepped to the open doorway to find everyone who worked on the project standing out in front of the building.

One of the men out front hollered at Tom, "Don't fire them, or we'll shut the whole project down."

Tom was fuming, but he also looked a little scared. "You have me at a disadvantage Bob, but it won't change things."

"Things have to change, Tom, or we'll shut you down," Bob told him.

"We are going to start doing more work at night. APCO has to get the irrigation system in order right now, or we'll never get enough produce to start shipping. Here's a list of what we want," Bob told him, "and we want it now."

Tom knew he was in hot water. "I've got a contract to supply fresh produce to a couple of hotels next week, how in hell am I supposed to fill the order?"

"All we need is our own aircraft to haul the produce," Bob told him. "You tell APCO the irrigation wells on section five have to be working tonight. If they are, you'll have your produce."

"Okay," Tom said to them, "I'll hold you to that. APCO can haul the produce, I'll tell them to be ready."

"No," Bob was forceful. "APCO's unreliable. You get us our own plane, and it better be a good one."

Bob looked around the room, "All right, let's get back to work." There was a cheer inside the meeting room which quickly carried outside.

July watched with tears in her eyes. She'd never been as proud of Bob as she was now. "You're one of a kind," she thought, "even if you don't know it."

The APCO workers were sitting drinking coffee when Bob's crew arrived. By noon they had the irrigation system working well enough to revive the plants withering under the hot summer sun. Dale had his people picking the produce that was ready. Bill was making sure the produce barns were equipped and ready for sorting and packaging. There was a good feeling in the air.

The plane Tom got them was an old crate but a powerful one. It would haul a big payload; produce was heavy, but when the pilot told him what he could haul, Bob was pleased. He didn't want to have to make two trips in a day if he didn't have to.

Larry Collins was the pilot Tom hired. He was a likable guy, about Bob's age. He and Bob hit it off right from the start. Larry was chubby with slightly balding hair and a grin a mile wide. He seemed to sweat standing still but was a really good worker. Bob checked around; he had a reputation as a hell of a good pilot.

"At least, you still have that knack," Bob thought about Tom. "You can still find good people."

Tom did indeed have a knack for sourcing out good people or at least people who were good at what they did. Tom's own morals, however, were somewhat clouded, as were some of the people he became associated with. His intentions were good but usually motivated by greed and shortsightedness.

This project had been his dream; he'd worked very hard to promote it. Banks and investors, however, saw that his business plan had huge flaws. Ton Newton had a hard time seeing why people would not fall over backward to participate in his dream. But dreamers are not usually good business people, nor are they usually willing to give up any of their ideas to accommodate others.

In desperation, Tom went to high-risk people for financing, spending all his resources. He thought he had been successful in his attempt, but there had been strings attached. He had been elated when Ken Holmes told him his project had been funded. When he had his meeting with Waddell, the ground rules had been laid out. Their rules certainly curtailed Tom's power, but he had no intention of turning back, even if it meant riding on the backs of the people he had recruited for his dreams.

Tom went with Bob and Larry on the first trip to Nassau bringing in their produce. This was a big day; finally the fruits of all their labor would begin to pay off. Bob was in a tremendous mood, but Tom seemed remote, maybe because of our incident last week, Bob thought.

It took only about a half hour from takeoff to landing depending on how busy the airport in Nassau was. Bob could feel that the plane was heavy, but Larry brought it in perfectly than taxiing over to a corner where some trucks were waiting. Bob counted everything that was unloaded; shipments had gone missing before.

A car pulled up, and Tom got in. In a few minutes, Tom got out with a tall black man. Bob recognized the man right away. Tom seemed more relaxed and in a much better mood as he showed the black man some of the produce.

"I'd sure like to have heard the conversation that went on in that car," Bob thought to himself.

Tom had been scared shitless when he saw the car pull up to the plane. Waddell's mirrored glasses always intimidated him as they did now sitting next to him in the backseat of the limo.

"I'll get rid of them, Manly, it's just going to take a little longer that's all." Manley didn't answer, so Tom went on, "I was sure once they saw the letters, they'd take them and run."

"The way I hear it, they didn't even look at the letters or they might have," Manly said. "I think for $50,000, they would have fucked off, except maybe for Green. He's too fucking stupid to know a good thing when he sees it."

"Well, maybe we'll have to up the ante a bit for him?" Tom compromised.

"No, we've changed our minds," Manly told Tom. "We don't want to attract any attention to that project right now. Those guys are too naive to know what's happening anyway. Just keep them busy, so they don't have time to nose around. Tell them the project's running out of money. I don't want to put any more into it right now."

"They're getting suspicious about APCO," Tom told him. "They're getting pissed off that they're not getting anything done."

"Fuck them," Manly answered. "Tell them the government insisted they're there. Tell them anything, but keep the produce coming in, that makes it look legitimate and keeps the cost down."

"The books will soon show it's not profitable," Tom said. "Remember Shonavon and Drinkwater are into profit sharing, they'll want to know how we are doing."

"That's the beauty of it," laughed Manly. "The hotels have no choice but to pay a fortune for the produce, that way they actually finance the farm."

Tom was amazed at Waddell's influence. It also scared him, but he was in too deep to get out now.

"So for now it's business as usual. Let's have a look at your produce," Waddell told him as he got out of the car.

Tom felt a lot better as he got out of the car; for now, the crisis had been solved.

Bob decided to pay a lot more attention to today's operations on the project. He was suspicious that not all was right but couldn't put his finger on anything concrete. The farm had shut down any expansion for the time being except for the completion of the APCO projects. Those were terribly behind schedule, but Tom had explained that the government insisted they do the work, so Bob accepted this even though they were a terrible drain on the project's finances.

Bob had a lot more time to spend with his family now. One night he and July stopped at the Andros Hotel for a drink. Bob began to pay attention to a conversation going on behind him. The two men at the bar were black. They obviously had a few beers in them by the boisterous way they talked. Bob picked up the fact that they were loading some boats at Buzzard Bay in an hour.

It struck him funny as to why anyone would be loading boats especially at Buzzard Bay this time of night. Bob and July decided to follow the two men as they left the hotel in an APCO truck. Neither Bob nor July had been down to Buzzard Bay in a long time.

The main loading dock was just a man-made lagoon dug out of the shoreline used mainly by the mail boat and the owner of an old barge. The barge was one of the few ways the locals had to haul large items onto the island such as cars or farm machinery. In fact, Tom had hired it out from time to time to haul for the project.

Scattered along the edge of the ocean both ways from the lagoon was a fairly large Bahamian settlement. The garbage from the settlement, plus the entrails left by the village's fishing industry, made it a great place for buzzards to hang out, hence the origin of its name, Buzzard Bay.

Once you got to know the locals a little better, they would tell you there was something a little more sinister about how Buzzard Bay got its name. It was a place where you stayed away from at night, if you didn't often or not you were the one who became buzzard meat. Bob had heard this story but brushed it off as folklore, tonight it kept creeping into the back of his mind.

This was the third port in North Andros. To the very north was Georgetown, where the big water boats came in hauling fresh water from Andros to Nassau. To the south was Fresh Creek, more of a remote area where the naval base was situated. Buzzard Bay was between the two about halfway down the east side of the island.

Very little but local produce went through this port making Bob very curious as to what was going on. They didn't worry about staying too far behind the truck; they knew their way, parking as close as they dared to the lagoon and walking the rest of the way. Suddenly, through the trees they could see the lagoon. Although it was pitch black out, the lagoon was lit up by two small lights from the barge. Tonight there were two other boats in the lagoon. They were at least twenty-five footers and each had three two-hundred horse outboards mounted on the back. Two trucks were backed up to the old barge using it as a dock to load large bags onto the two boats.

"Do you think those bags are what I think they are?" July asked Bob.

"Yeah," Bob answered her, "and those are APCO trucks from the project." He felt July shiver beside him.

"You've suspected something for a long time, haven't you, Bob?"

"Yep," he said, "let's get the hell out of here before someone sees us."

The next evening they told the Shonavons and Drinkwaters what they had seen. They all talked it over, trying to decide what to do about it.

"There's no proof it's drugs," Bill said. "Until we can get some proof, there's little we can do."

"We can keep our eyes open, and we all know until we get rid of APCO off the project, it's not going to go well." Bob told them.

"But," Dale Drinkwater broke in, "we've got some good things going here. We've employed a lot of local labor and use a lot of local material. It would hurt a lot of people beside us if the project was shut down now." They decided not to confront Tom just yet.

"Let's see what we can dig up before raising too big a stink," Bob told them. "It's hard to know who we should go to. Anyway, for all we know, the government might be involved." One thing they all realized, they were mixed up in something that could be very dangerous and might be just as wise to leave alone.

It was two years to the day from when Bob had arrived on the project that he and July took their first holiday. They visited his mother and tied up some loose ends while they were there. The rest of the time, they spent with July's parents and Mindy in Minnesota. They returned fresh and relaxed, glad to have gotten away from the problems at the project, but now ready to tackle them.

Each season had created new problems for the crops and animals produced on the farm. Slowly they'd learned to overcome them. They'd had to use much more pesticides than they would have liked, and some fields didn't have enough drainage during the rainy season, but all in all they'd hung in there keeping the contracts they had supplied with fresh vegetables and now with some dairy products.

Shortly after Bob returned from holidays, Tom called them to a community meeting. There he announced that there was a new hotel opening up in Miami, and he had gotten the bid to supply them with fresh produce. This was good news; so far they had been unable to crack the competitive Florida market. Tom told them it was because the hotel liked the fact that APCO was involved in their project that they got the contract, hoping this would keep the managers off his back about keeping the inefficient agency on the project.

Of course, Tom put the onus on management to be able to fill the contract, but they were ready for him. It would mean extra work, but the spring season was here and bearing disaster; this should be their best year yet.

Tom had instructions for the managers, "This is international now. You will bring the produce to the packing house and unload it. The hotel will have their own inspector on-site, and from there on, APCO will pack the produce and load the plane. When you get to Miami, the plane will land at a small commercial airport on the edge of the city. The produce will be put through customs and into cold storage trucks to the hotel as soon as possible. Whoever goes over on the flight will not be able to stay with the plane including the pilot. Once everything clears customs, there is an inspection room at the airport where they will bring you the manifesto to check with yours and if satisfied, sign it. We should train an inspector to go to the hotel just to make sure the produce is handled properly there. The plane will be bringing back supplies, so whoever goes to the hotel will have lots of time to get back for the return flight. These are strict rules, and have to be followed if we want to keep this contract."

It was decided Bob would go on the first flight along with Maggie. She had worked in the packing plant for a long time and would be a perfect trainee.

The sky was streaked with red in the east as Bob approached the plane. The sun would soon be up, and Larry, the pilot, had the engines warmed up ready to go. The early morning rain gave a fresh smell to the morning air as Larry taxied up.

They found Larry's smile contagious this morning. They entered the plane and buckled up.

"Ready," Larry asked, looking behind him to make sure Maggie was in place.

"Here we go." He pushed the throttle down, and the aircraft began to pick up speed down the runway. The lake came into view at the end of the runway as the plane began to vibrate from the speed. Larry tightened in his seat.

"What the hell has Tom got on here?" Larry's voice sounded worried. Bob trusted Larry and wasn't really concerned until he noticed they were farther down the airstrip than usual.

"Fucking Tom," Larry shouted above the roar of the engines. "I told him not to put any more on. We're way over as it is." They were almost to the lake now.

"Lucky there's no trees between us and the lake." Larry sounded calm now, "I think she'll come up." But Bob could tell he was stressed by the way he hung on to the controls.

They cleared the end of the runway and began flying over the lake. At first they seemed to climb, the engines throbbing, and then they dropped.

"Put your heads in your laps and hang on to anything you can find!" yelled Larry. "I don't think I can hold her." The plane seemed to slide along the top of the water, and then the water splashed up onto the windshield obscuring everything.

Larry stayed with it, and they felt the plane rise then slowly lose altitude touching the water pulling the engines down. They could hear the water brushing the plane's belly. It bounced once more out of the water and then plowed in. They couldn't see a thing.

"Hang on, we're going in," was the last thing Bob heard Larry say before the plane seemed to settle into the water, the motors quiet seconds before; it seemed like they hit something hard. The plane made a terrible grinding sound, and they stopped so sudden Bob felt like he was going right on out the front. But the seat belt held; Bob passed out for a few seconds from the strain on his seat belt.

When he came to, the first thing he saw was red. The cabin was full of blood.

"Is it mine?" he almost screamed and began to feel himself sure his legs were missing. Then he noticed the vegetables piled around his legs. He looked over at Larry expecting to see his head decapitated. Larry was looking over at him, red dripping off his chin.

"Tomatoes, tomatoes," Bob shouted. "It's not blood, it's tomatoes!"

They realized the plane had stopped so sudden the cargo had come forward into the cockpit throwing a crate of tomatoes up against the instrument panel. The tomatoes had flown all over covering the cabin with tomato juice.

"Get the fuck off me." They heard a voice, both realizing it was Maggie. Her seat had been torn loose throwing her up between Larry and Bob under a pile of cucumbers. She came up out of the pile spitting, her hair and face full of debris.

Bob started to laugh more out of relief than anything funny, and Larry joined him. They started to laugh insanely, and Maggie couldn't help but join in.

"Where the fuck are we?" Bob cried, and they laughed some more.

"Under the lake, I don't know," answered Larry hysterically. "Maybe we're dead, I'll find out."

They couldn't see anything out of the glass in the cockpit, so Larry climbed up on the vegetables and crawled to the back. He dug for a minute and then opened the cargo door. Both Maggie and Bob followed him back and climbed out.

It was soon apparent they had ended upon a small island in the middle of the lake. Only a week before, they had cleaned up the island and put picnic tables on it. The island wasn't much bigger than the plane. They were very lucky.

Maggie grabbed the two of them. "You're both crazy, but I love you guys." The three of them stood watching the sun rise over the lake.

"It's good to be alive, isn't it," Bob told them.

They heard a boat and turned to see July and Rikker pulling up. July didn't wait for the boat to stop; she just ran over the front through the water and put her arms around Bob.

"I was so sure you were dead," she told him.

"You won't get rid of me that easy," he told her. "In fact, we're all okay." More boats were coming now.

"You got here quick," Bob hugged July.

"I watch you go every morning," she answered. "This morning, I thought it was for the last time."

Bill pulled up. "Are you all right?" he shouted; they hollered back that they were.

Tom showed up next. He seemed more worried about the plane than any of them.

"What the fuck happened?" he snapped. Bob and July had to hold Larry back.

"What the fuck did you put on that plane, Tom? I told you not to load any more on there. What the fuck is the matter with your head?" Tom immediately had to take the defensive.

"That's the same load you always haul." Tom decided discretion was the better part of valor. He walked around the plane once, and then got back on his boat and left.

Bob talked to Bill for a minute then got into his boat with the others and headed over to his house. All the houses had their own dock. They tied up and went inside for an early morning drink.

Bill soon joined them. "Dale's trying to scrounge up enough products from the produce barns to make another shipment," he told them, but it was pretty slim pickings.

Bob looked at his watch. "We could salvage a lot of stuff out of the plane. Let's see, we have till eight o'clock to get the plane out of here. That'll put the load in Miami by 10:00 a.m. By 11:00 a.m., it should be at the hotel. That gives an hour to get the produce onto the salad bar. Can you do it, Maggie?"

"Do I have any choice?" For a black girl, she looked very pale.

"I'll go with you," July told her, taking her hand. Maggie thanked her, and then she turned to Bob. "Well, Mr. Green, let's go get that plane unloaded."

Bill went to tell Dale what they planned to do and arranged for some boats. They handpicked the vegetables as they unloaded them from the plane and loaded them onto boats. Bill and Rikker drove the boats over to where Dale's men unloaded them. July and Maggie took Rikker's Sea-Doo back to the house where they cleaned up and got ready to leave.

Just then, a plane came in low over their head. "That's the rental," Bob said, looking at his watch. "It's going to be tight. They'll have to load in a hurry."

There wasn't too much good stuff left in the wreck now. Bob sent the men who had come to help back on one of the boats to see if they could help Dale load the plane. Dale informed them on the radio that he had enough for a load.

"Take a break," Bob told them.

Bill showed up with a case of beer, and the three of them sat down in the shade from the plane. The sun was already hot, and they were sweating profusely.

Larry finished his first beer and started on his second before he said to Bob, "Did you see the bags packed in the bottom?"

"Yes," Bob answered, "that's why I sent everybody back to the other side."

Bill looked at them. "Whatever are you guys talking about?" He had an alarmed look on his face.

"Come here, and I'll show you," Larry told him, getting up. They looked in the cargo door; a few of the bags were visible under what was left of the produce. They cleared more stuff away exposing what looked like a layer of bags covering the bottom of the cargo area.

"It's a wonder the old girl came up at all," Larry lamented.

"Whoever loaded the plane either wasn't very smart or underestimated how heavy you really were," Bob said.

Bill took his knife and cut into one of the bags. "Looks like flour," he said.

Larry knew different. "Cocaine," he said, "probably half a billion dollars sitting there."

He looked up, "There's going to be hell to pay for this."

The three men went back to the shade and opened another beer. In the distance, they heard the roar of plane engines starting up, and silently the rented plane with its load of fresh produce appeared and quickly disappeared across the lake.

"That's a Gulfstream Flyer," Larry told them as they shaded their eyes watching the silver bird climb up over the lake. "He'll make good time, should be in Miami easy by 10:00 a.m."

"I don't envy July and Maggie," Bill said. "They'll be busy girls for a while." They sat drinking their beer, until Bob asked the question they knew had to be answered.

"Well, what do we do with the shit?"

"Leave it," Larry looked at him. "They'll soon be here looking for it. No one leaves that much money lying around. If you touch it, they'll blow anyone away who they think took it or even might know about it."

"Maybe they will anyway," Bob answered. "We've got to think about all the people living here and what we have here, to tell you the truth, I'm scared."

"Well, let's see what options we've got," Bill said. "Maybe if we somehow get proof of what's going on here we can blackmail them into taking the drugs and leaving us alone. You know, some kind of evidence that comes out if they kill us."

"I don't know if we have time for those kinds of games," Bob told him. "We could just go to the police. The transport department will want to have a look at the crash pretty soon, I would think."

"We don't know who in that department is on the take either," Larry was quick to answer. "I don't think we have more than a few hours at the least before someone's here."

"There's no use fooling ourselves. We all know what APCO's doing here. I'm damned sure they've told their people what's happened already."

"Burn it," Bob sighed. "Can we get the old bitch hot enough to burn everything up?"

"I thought of that too," Larry answered him. "There's a lot of fuel on board, but it's a long time after the crash. Somebody's going to be suspicious."

"Okay," Bob said, "what if they thought someone from APCO stole it?"

"How in hell do we do that?" Bill wanted to know.

"Well," Bob looked deep in thought, "they've got a boat over there at the main dock and two trucks sitting on the runway. What if we need them to move the stuff?"

"They'd know it was us," Bill told him.

"Maybe not," Larry was thinking too. "None of them are right around here. They might see us from a distance but not close enough to know what's going on."

"Yeah, I agree," Bob said. "I think most of them are pretty careful to mind their own business. There's just the people in the office. They'll probably see the trucks leaving and wonder what's going on."

The conversation went back and forth for several minutes until a plan of attack began to form. They were pretty sure Tom was in on the drugs. The original call has to come from Tom, they decided. He had the authority to tell APCO what to do; they wouldn't question any orders if they came directly from Tom. Bob radioed Dale to find out if he knew where Tom was.

"He left on the rented plane with Maggie and July," Dale answered right away. That threw a skid into their plans before they even started.

"I bet APCO doesn't know he's gone," said Bill. "If I call them on the phone from his office, I bet I can pull it off."

The three of them jumped in a boat Rikker had brought back for them and headed for the commissary where Tom's office was located. It was only a short walk from the lake to the commissary. Tom's secretary was the only one there. Bob called her over to his office down the hall, while Bill made the call to APCO's office. Within minutes, they saw the two trucks leave the runway area heading for the crash site.

"That was brilliant getting them to load the stuff rather than us; it lets us off the hook completely." Larry told Bob.

"Well, we're in luck there too," Bob told them. "That's the same two guys that were at the Andros Hotel the night we followed them. So let's hope they load up and then spend the time in the hotel until it's time to head for Buzzard Bay."

"I told them to arrange for a pick up at Buzzard Bay by midnight," Bill said. "That should give us lots of time."

“I hope old Horatio doesn’t get in trouble over this,” Larry said.

“There’s no one else we can turn to, and we know he’s straight,” Bob told them. “I think it will be a real feather in his cap.” They went back to Bob’s house and watched the plane being unloaded through their binoculars.

Their main concern now was that someone would come to look at the crash before the APCO guys were loaded and gone. It was an eternity before the last bags were loaded on the trucks and the tarps secured. The rest of the men left to go back wherever they had been working before. The two drivers stood talking, having a smoke.

“Come on, come on,” Larry said under his breath.

Finally, the two drivers climbed in the trucks and headed out toward the main gate. From now on, things could get dirty. Bob, Bill, and Larry got in an old pickup Bill had brought over from Miami and slowly followed the trucks.

They weren’t too worried about losing the trucks; there weren’t too many places they could go. Dale stayed behind at the project to keep them informed of any people or events which might show up. The three men were relieved to see the two trucks parked at the Andros Hotel when they arrived. So far, everything had gone the way they planned.

They found it hard to believe that these men would leave trucks loaded with at least a million dollars worth of cocaine parked at a bar unattended while they went in for a beer. Darkness comes quick at this latitude; one minute the sun goes down, the next it’s dark. Larry went into the bar; he would try to mingle with the two drivers, buy them a beer, and find out what their plans were.

Meanwhile Bob and Bill went to work. They let the air out of the truck tires. Bill got the hoods open and pulled the spark plug wires off. Then he found the radiator taps and drained the radiators. Bob went into the hotel lobby and called Horatio Norton, telling him what was going down.

"They're parked at the Andros Hotel," Bob told him. "That's where we plan to make our stand."

Horatio sounded scared. "Why didn't you just leave it there?" Horatio asked.

"Because as long as the stuff is on the project, we don't know who they'd hold responsible and my conscience wouldn't let me," Bob told him.

"Okay, we'll be right there, just stay back."

Norton met them in the parking lot. Norton snuck over to one of the trucks and cut the tarp covering it and then checked the contents to make sure it did indeed contain what Bill and Bob had told him. He came back with a hand full of white powder.

"Do you fellows have any idea what you've gotten all of us into?" Norton sounded upset. "I've got five inexperienced men here who are going to have to try and hold this stuff until I get help from Nassau, and when I tell them what's going down, they probably won't come."

"There are only two drivers in there," Bob responded, "and the trucks aren't going anywhere."

You don't have a clue do you, Mr. Green?" Norton had met these men before at different functions around the island. They were good men who had no idea what they were caught up in. "The people who push the white powder do not leave this kind of money lying around. They'll be here sooner or later, and we're the guys who are going to have to deal with them."

"Damn," Bob responded, "I'd better phone Dale and see if anyone's showed up at the project."

He took off to use the phone in the hotel, while Norton consulted with his men as to what they should do.

Bob came running back. "Dale says a plane came in about an hour ago. As far as he could make out, there were four men. They met with one of the APCO managers, and now they've taken a boat out to look at the wreck."

"Well, if there are only four of them, we might be able to handle them," Norton said.

They don't know where we are," Bob said. "Maybe they won't find us."

"They'll find the trucks, remember? You disabled them," Norton replied.

Bob and Bill began to realize maybe this wasn't such a good idea.

"What do you think they'll do?" Bob asked, beginning to realize how dangerous a position they were in.

"They'll come for their shit, you can bet on that. What they have planned for after that I can only guess. They can take the stuff back to the farm or call in the boats to Buzzard Bay." Norton told them.

"You know about Buzzard Bay?" Bob asked incredulously.

"I've been told to mind my own business," Norton responded, "which is what I wish some other people I know would do. However," Norton went on, "I think they'll call in the boats. I've notified the Americans at Fresh Creek, and they got clearance from Nassau to use their choppers, and that's what we're going to do. My men don't want to get involved here, and I don't blame them."

Bill still had no idea what kind of men they were dealing with, "You should be able to handle four men," Bill said.

"We'll see," Norton answered.

It was close to ten o'clock when Larry came around by the back and found them in the darkness. "They'll be out soon. They told me they're driving down to Buzzard Bay with a load of potatoes for the barge."

"I guess you were right Horatio, we should have asked you before we dismantled the trucks," Bob lamented.

"Well, I do know for sure what's on those trucks, and the smartest thing you did was to get them off the farm. I think you're right. They'll think Tom Newman and these drivers stole the cocaine. I wouldn't want to be in their shoes when the people come for them. In fact, if you happen to see Newton, you'd better tell him to disappear. He probably will anyway."

Bill and Bob found all this hard to believe, but Larry confirmed what Norton was telling them, and that they should get the hell out of here. They all watched to see what would happen when the drivers tried to start their trucks. It all happened so quick that no one seemed to realize what was going on.

Two dark figures appeared out of the shadows; at the same time there were two quiet pops, and the drivers slumped. The dark figures caught them up and dragged them back into the shadows. Bob thought it was Norton's men who were the cause of that, until he heard Norton on his radio telling his men to get the hell away from here. More black figures ascended on the trucks; when they didn't start, it didn't take them long to know they'd been sabotaged.

They heard a shout, "Check the edges, check the edges."

That's us," Norton told them. "They suspect we're here, get moving." The rock ridge they'd been watching the hotel from wasn't very high, but it was rugged terrain, and the men just ran for their lives. Finally, out of exhaustion, Bob fell into a hole behind some rocks. To his surprise, a bunch of bodies piled in with him. They all lay breathing heavily until they caught their breath, and then they crawled back up to see what they could see. Down below they saw the lights of the two trucks leaving the hotel.

"That didn't hold them long did it," Bill said quietly.

Bob put his hand on Bill's arm and pointed to a man quickly passing through the shadows across from them. He felt Bill begin to shake as they watched the man search through the rocks and then slide away from them. They lay still for a long time then made their way back to where they'd parked their truck hoping no one had found it. They were glad to see Norton was already there with his men. It was still a few minutes before midnight. Larry went round the truck and put the tailgate down. Bill had put some beer in the cab; it was warm but who cared. "That's about as scared as I ever want to be," Bob said.

"I think that's what will save you guys," Norton told them. "They'll never think you had the ball or the brains to pull this off."

It was close to an hour later when they first saw the sky light up to the east. They were a good three or four miles away from Buzzard Bay, but the flares lit up the night sky, and then there were several flashes like fireworks just below the tree line. It was a spectacular show, fascinating and yet terrifying. They could hear a continuous sound like someone beating on a drum. Suddenly, everything stopped. It was quiet, and then it started all over again only farther away.

"Let's get out of here," Norton told them. "I hope no one's missed you at the farm. Whatever you do, don't get scared and run. That will be a dead giveaway."

They started back to the project, little was said. Each had their own thoughts about what had happened and what the future would hold.

# FOURTEEN

ALMOST TWO YEARS have passed since the plane crash and the incident at the Andros Hotel. Everything had pretty well gone downhill from there, and there was no sign of it getting any better.

I sit on a Florida beach looking over the pounding surf, toward the Bahamas only a hundred and thirty miles away. Those islands that sparkle like diamonds hold my future. Love is a strange thing. Men spend their lives in the pursuit of money and fame. The heart is the biggest motivator of all. A man in love will leave wealth and fame and all his worldly possessions in pursuit of an overwhelming passion in his heart. Some men never experience this passion, maybe they're incapable or maybe they're caught up in worldly possessions, but it's the heart that makes men great. On the other hand, love can also make a man foolish.

My impulse tells me to jump on a plane, go to her and hand in hand, face our adversaries as we have done so many times before. This time I'm not even sure who our adversaries are. I think it's Waddell, but maybe he's just a cog in the wheel that keeps running over us. Whoever it is, they have no idea of the passion that drives me to get to July, they only know I will try.

I must not be foolish if I'm to succeed, but the waiting is driving me crazy. Not knowing what's happening 130 miles across this ocean barrier consumes my mind as I sit on a crowded beach blending in with the other sun worshippers. It has been over a week since I talked to Arthur and still no answer.

My wounds have healed, the scars blending into my sun bronzed skin. I also have streaked gray hair, and a beard. My life has become similar to that of a man TV called the 'Fugitive'. I keep moving from hotel to hotel, changing my name, never staying in one place too long. Every day I stop at a newsstand looking through the papers to see if I can find anything about myself, but Canada is not high on Florida's newspaper priorities.

Eventually, I do find a headline in a world news column about the mysterious case of eight bodies being found in a remote area of Saskatchewan. Three bodies had been found shot to death and five others burned beyond recognition in a house fire. The story went on to say that a Mountie had also been found murdered in the same area, and that it was suspected the victims were tied together in a mass murder. There are no pictures and big headlines which make me feel better.

At another newsstand, I find a small Quebec newspaper written in French. Florida has a large French population drawn by the lure of warm, sunny weather replacing Quebec's cold long winters and tall snow banks.

My French is very limited, but I bought the paper to see if the story is of any interest in the rest of Canada. It doesn't take me long to find it. On the inside page in bold letters, "Meurtre en Masse" jumps out at me. Below the headline is a grainy picture of a scruffy character looking exactly like a mass murderer should look.

The problem being the picture is of me. The picture was probably taken by the Mounties or from the surveillance cameras when I was being interrogated. What scares me is that my new beard is now making me look slightly scruffy resembling the man in the picture. I look up, sure that everyone around will recognize me. I have to fight down the panic and start walking quickly back to my hotel room.

Once in my room, I head straight for the bathroom mirror, comparing myself to the picture. I realize no one could really recognize me from the poor quality photograph. Actually, my beard has grown out enough to look presentable, and my hair looks nothing like the photograph. The scar on my forehead is nearly indistinguishable, whereas the man in the picture sported a large bandage.

My confidence renewed, I again return to the street and head for the phone booth whose number I had given Arthur to call. Every night at six o'clock, I make my pilgrimage to the phone booth waiting for an hour before returning to wherever my hotel room might be that night.

On the tenth day, Arthur finally phones. "Sorry I took so long, but it takes time to arrange these things," Arthur explains. Next, he asks if I have any money, "It will cost a good deal of money to carry this out," he tells me.

"How much?" I want to know.

"For you, US $5,000," he says.

July and I have about $10 grand in our numbered account. "Okay Arthur, I can handle that. What's the scoop?"

"At Pompano Beach, there's a boat channel right beside the lighthouse," Arthur tells me. "You'll see a dredge working at the mouth of the channel. The dredge has a small barge working with it to move the pipes around. The barge will take you out to my brother's fishing boat. The weather and timing must be right, so I will phone you at the same time and place as now. You will have to be ready to leave that same night," Arthur finishes.

"Okay," I answer. "Any idea how long I'll have to wait?"

"No," Arthur tells me, "it could be a few days. Things have to be right. The cash must be up-front, $1,000 to the barge man and $4,000 to my brother. That's dirt cheap, Bob. I hope you realize they are doing this only for you and July."

"I appreciate this, Arthur," I tell him. "Speaking of July, how is she?"

Arthur lets out a sigh, "I'm not sure where she is, Bob. She and Rikker were hiding out in the old barrel shack on False Creek. When my cousin went to check on them, they were gone. We don't know whether they moved somewhere else or what happened. They didn't leave a message. Don't worry, Bob, they have lots of friends here. They'll be all right."

"Okay, Arthur," I say, the wind sucked right out of me. "Please try to get your brother to hurry. I've got to get to them."

"Don't do anything foolish, Bob, you're not worth anything to them dead." With that, he rings off.

I know he's right, but the waiting is so hard; when your loved ones are so close yet so far away, the urge to throw all caution to the wind is overwhelming. I return to my hotel room but can't sleep, my mind wandering back to those fateful days after Tom left the project. If it hadn't been for July, I would never have kept going.

# FIFTEEN

JULY SAT AND listened as Horatio Norton described the events as they evolved that night. She and Maggie had spent two days at the new APCO hotel in Miami before they returned home. The second day had gone smoothly; the fresh produce had arrived on time, and the hotel personnel were now familiar with all the handling procedures. She had sat and dozed on the dock most of the next day until the evening when Captain Norton showed up with Bob. She'd heard nothing about the hidden cocaine until Norton and Bob started talking about it. She was amazed at what she heard.

Bob was especially interested in the events that happened at Buzzard Bay. Norton told him the Americans had waited till both boats were at sea, and then with the use of flares to illuminate the boats, had managed to sink both of them. Norton's men had been in place in time to ambush the vehicle from the farm.

"They either saw us or someone warned them, because they stopped and turned around just before they got to us." Norton said. "We shot at the car, and they fired back, but I don't think we hit anyone before they got away. Dale told me that four men got on the plane. That's the same number that got off, so I think they all made their escape, Bob."

"The Americans want to give me a medal," Norton told them. "But I said no. The less people know I was involved, the better. From now on, I must live with the fear of a bullet in the back. These people don't like to have someone mess with their business. It's up to them to decide whether I'm worth killing," replied Norton. "I think I'll take my family on a long vacation."

July noticed the look of shock on Bob's face. He was never one to hurt anybody. He would rather hurt himself than someone else. Norton saw the look too. He went over to Bob and shook his hand.

"We did the right thing, Bob. We could not have lived with ourselves if we had just let it go. I've seen what the white powder does to people, maybe now they'll leave this island alone."

Bob had not really talked to July since she got back. She had been exhausted. Now he turned to her and asked, "Have you seen anything of Tom?"

"Not since he left the plane in Miami," July answered. "Why is he not here?"

"As far as I know, you were the last one to see him," Bob told her.

"Well," she said, "you know what he's like, he's all over the place. This isn't the first time he's been gone this long."

"No," Bob replied, "but he usually checks with his secretary. She hasn't heard from him since he left."

"I told you if he was smart, he would disappear," Norton responded. "It wouldn't surprise me if that's what he's done."

"Do you really think it's that bad?" July asked.

"Tom's up to his eyeballs in this," Norton told her. "He knows too much just to leave him running around. Besides, I don't have much sympathy for him. In fact, what I hope is that they blame him and leave me alone," Norton added..

July was having a hard time digesting all of this. Norton again shook hands with both of them and said goodbye. Bob and July sat far into the night discussing what had passed and what was about to come. What was about to come happened about a week later when Tom still hadn't shown up and neither had their paychecks. Bill and Dale came to discuss the situation with Bob.

"Tom always disperses the funds for the paychecks on payday," Dale told him. "We phoned the bank. There are some funds in one of our accounts, but we have no authorization to use it."

"We'll explain the situation to our people," Bob told them. "If Tom doesn't show up in a week, then we'll be forced to do something. Meanwhile, keep in touch with the bank to see what can be done. We don't want our suppliers to have our checks bounce."

Dale had taken over the office while Tom was away. By the end of the following week, Dale told them he couldn't hold off the suppliers much longer. "Someone's put out the word we're broke, and they want their money right now."

The bank, realizing the seriousness of the situation and that Tom really was missing, released the money. But to their astonishment, it was barely enough to bring their accounts up to date, leaving nothing to cover day-to-day operating expenses.

July, Hania Shonavon, and Pearl Drinkwater all went to work in the office to help Dale sort out the books, so they had something to show the bank. At the end of the month, they arranged a meeting with the bank in Nassau. They were informed there would be a third party there. It was to be Manly Waddell.

Dale fired a fax back to the bank in Nassau asking what possible reason Manly Waddell would be invited to a meeting between themselves and the bank. Dale read the fax to the others as it was received, "Manly Waddell requested this meeting. He states, as representative of the Bahamian government, they have a vested interest in the Andros project.

The bank feels it may in their best interest to hear what Mr. Waddell has to say at this meeting."

"I don't like this at all," Bob said. "We'd damn well better be prepared when we get to this meeting."

They worked feverishly in the office trying to tie up loose ends and get their books in order. They soon found a lot of unknowns; hopefully the bank could shed a light on some of them. July, Hania, and Pearl accompanied their husbands to Nassau. They now knew more about the company than their husbands and could certainly find any documents they needed faster than them.

July had seen Manly Waddell a few times over the past years but had not talked to him. His presence in the office affected her. There were not many men she had met in her lifetime that she couldn't handle or at least hold her own. There was something about Manly Waddell that scared her yet attracted her.

What was it about him that intimidated her, made her catch her breath in anticipation? He was an animal: ruthless, primitive, totally without regret. There was no way of controlling this man. July sensed this and knew this was why he could have any woman he wanted, consume her, and then spit her out leaving her to the wolves. Her mind told her all this, yet her breath quickened and she felt a wetness between her legs.

Bob got the meeting started by explaining that since the disappearance of Tom Newton, the project in Andros had no access to money or moneys earned from past revenue. He asked the bank if they knew of any other accounts that Tom had access to.

The bank manager looked through his files, "Not that we know of. The project started out with two million in its account. The account has since been closed out, the money spent on the project in its first year of development."

Bob looked at the others. "We were led to believe that there were funds in the neighborhood of $6 million allocated to the project," Bob told the banker.

"No," the banker handed some documents showing the account and the amount of money that had been drawn out.

"We'll have to check these withdrawals against our books," Bob stated. "I guess our main concern is keeping the project going. We've invested a great deal of our time toward it and feel it's a viable operation with the right amount of capital available."

"So this is what you would like to do is keep the project going," the bank manager said while jotting down notes on a piece of paper.

They all nodded their heads in agreement. "We can show in our books that we can operate the project and produce enough profit to pay back a loan," Bob spoke for everyone.

"What do you have to say about all this, Mr. Waddell?" the banker asked.

"I speak for the agricultural minister in saying that we do not think this project is viable under its present financial state or with its present management." This stunned the group.

"We've had a different indication altogether," Bob told him.

Manly paid no attention to him and went on, "We are also concerned that if the project did succeed under its present management, there's no reason Tom couldn't reappear and take control. He does still, in effect, own the project. We suspect Tom of using the project for illicit gain and taking funds for his own personal gain."

"So what do you suggest we do with the project, Mr. Waddell?" the banker asked.

"We have a company interested in taking over the project and funding it," Manly told them.

"That company wouldn't happen to be APCO, would it?" Bob asked him.

"That's really none of your business," Manly told them.

"Well, it's obviously our business," the banker told him.

"The government feels they have the right to take over this project and put it in control of whomever we feel fit," Manly told him. "This way, Tom would no longer have control. Since the bank was only responsible for dispersing funds and had no invested interest in the project, we see no reason why they should object to this proposal."

"Yes, your proposal certainly does have merit," the banker responded. "However, your facts are not totally accurate. Tom came to us, and we lent him $2 million against the $2 million he had invested in the project. In order for the bank to accept your proposal, that loan would have to be paid off."

Waddell began to fidget a bit; that fucking Tom had done this, and it threw a real screw into his plans. The government sure as hell wasn't going to put money into the project without having control. He could get the money elsewhere, but the bank wouldn't accept the money unless it was clean. His mind raced; APCO might come up with the money, but they'd be pretty pissed with him.

"I'd have to confer with the company," Manly finally said.

"Okay," the banker said. "However, as first mortgagers on this property, we have the right to hear all proposals. For the time being, we will keep the present management in place. I think the project is viable as it now stands. However, we are open to any buyout proposal submitted."

The knowledge of the loan was a definite surprise to the project people too. Bob and the others had hoped to get a loan, not to have to pay an existing one off. The banker handed Bob a document explaining the terms of the loan and interest payments due.

"Actually, this may not be too bad," Bob said to the banker. "We can find no record of interest due on the original money, so this may be partly already factored in."

"We are not prepared to put any more money into the project, however, it is in our best interest to keep it in business until we can find a buyer or you people can prove your able to keep it viable." the banker told the group. "We will pay your wages for the first two months. We consider you our employees. Hopefully you can come up with a solution to eventually buy the project or we can find a suitable owner."

Waddell came over and shook hands with all of them. "Hopefully we can work something out," he said. The banker then shook hands and wished them luck. He turned to confer some more with Waddell as the group left the room.

"Well, thank God for one thing," Bob told the others. "I thought Waddell was going to tell us APCO had lent us the money, which would have really finished us.

"I think Waddell was just as surprised as the rest of us to learn about the loan," July said. "He thought he had us out of there."

"We've got a two-month reprieve to prove ourselves," Bill stated as they left the bank and walked into the hot Bahamas sun knowing they had a tough row to hoe.

Manly Waddell hated getting that call, but he'd been expecting it. This was the third time he'd met with El Presidente off the coast of Cuba, and he now understood why. El Presidente was scared if he took his yacht out in open water, the Americans would make him disappear. He now traveled in secret to his yacht and felt safe as long as he was along the Cuban coast. This was a far cry from the days when he would sail right under the Americans' noses and meet with Bahamian government officials in Nassau. Now even Waddell had to be careful who he was seen with, above all, El Presidente. The boat was waiting at the dock when he arrived. A bikinied blonde met him at the boat lift and escorted him to where El Presidente was having breakfast. He invited Waddell to join him. He gave his order to the bikinied blonde and then turned his attention to El Presidente.

Waddell knew the man preferred to be called El Presidente or

Excellency by the people who worked for him, but he personally called him the Colombian when he wasn't around. They sat enjoying their breakfast as they headed farther out to sea. As the morning wore on, three more girls showed up to kiss El Presidente good morning. He must have seen the interest in Waddell's eyes.

"I am sorry," he told Waddell, "these are my own private girls. One cannot be too careful with the diseases of today."

Manly was disappointed; the girls were beautiful and he had thought would make a pleasant break in the day. After heading out to sea for about an hour, they dropped anchor. Manly and the Colombian sat chatting under the shade of his table umbrella, pleasantly watching as the girls took off what little clothing they did have on and dove over the edge of the boat for a swim. Manly also noticed a man on top of the captain's cabin with a rifle.

The Colombian followed his gaze. "One can never be too careful of sharks," he explained.

Or of other predators that might be around, Manly thought.

Just then another girl appeared beside the Colombian. "Ah, Zeze, how's my little girl this morning?" She wore nothing above her waist, and it was very plain to Manly that she was very pregnant. The Colombian rubbed her swollen stomach and then kissed each of the rose-colored nipples on her large breasts.

"We had an accident," the Colombian said. "My wife was very angry, so I told her it was an accident. I didn't know a girl could get pregnant standing on her head." The Colombian shrugged and smiled. "So I gave my wife US$100,000 and sent her to New York on a shopping trip. Women never stay angry if they are shopping," he laughed. "Zeze will give me a nice bambino. My wife only gave me spoiled brats. Now my man, let's get down to business," he said.

Manly watched as the pregnant girl cleaned up the breakfast dishes and waddled off.

"I want to know what you suggest we do about the Andros situation," Manly stated.

"It seems to be sorting itself out nicely," El Presidente answered.

"However, we were not pleased to lose that shipment. It was a perfect plan to start with, who would have guessed the plane would crash on the very first run," Manly said.

"We're still not sure what all took place there," replied the Colombian.

"Maybe Tom staged that too, we don't know. However, it looks like Tom gave the orders to unload the product from the wreck and tried to steal it."

"Never thought of that," said Manly. "Tom would make you think everything was lost in the crash."

"Exactly, but what happened at the Andros Hotel isn't so clear. The only information we have is from our informant in the Nassau police department who talked to the old police captain on the island. He's not on the take but knows enough to keep his nose clean. He claims he only got involved because of the shooting at the hotel. He figures Tom must have been going to ambush the truck drivers and then load the stuff on his own trucks to get it where he was going," the Colombian continued with his story. "Only we beat him to it and got the stuff down to Buzzard Bay. The police captain thinks Tom, realizing he'd lost the stuff, phoned the navy at Fresh Creek. You know what happened after that. The fucking Americans blew a million dollars into oblivion."

"So what's the score on Tom?" Manly asked.

"Tom's disappeared." When we find him he'll disappear permanently," the Colombian spat.

"What about the police captain?" Manly wanted to know.

"I think we'll leave him where he is," the Colombian told him. "He keeps his nose clean, and we don't want some hotshot coming in there to take his place."

"What about APCO's plans for the project?" Manly asked. "Are you going to give the bank their two million?"

"Fuck them! We're not going to give them anything. In fact, when we're done with them, they'll pay us to take it off their hands."

"You want to get the Canadians off the project?" Manly asked, making sure he knew exactly what the Colombian had in mind.

"Not right now, what I want you to do is reopen the contract they have with the Nassau hotels and the Miami one. We'll let them keep the contracts but at a rate that will slowly starve them to death. Meanwhile, keep shipping the vegetables into the Miami hotel. They won't care if the loads are short. The more of our product gets there, the better."

"I agree with you there," Waddell told him. "That's the perfect cover. I've got my girl Maggie looking after the vegetables on the hotel end so the Canadians won't get suspicious."

The girls came back on board and lay on the deck chairs naked, the water beads shining in the sun on their skin. They pulled anchor, and the boat headed back toward the multicolored buildings of Havana.

"Tighten the noose, it won't take long for them to pull out," the Colombian told him. "As for now, we're back to normal. The shipments are going through as if nothing happened except we had to pay the boat runners a little more. However, I might suggest you consider taking care of some of these people after they leave. I think they know too much about the farm operation and they're going to be very pissed off when they're forced to leave."

"I know," Manly told him, "I've been thinking about it, but so far they seem pretty naive."

"We'll know better when the time comes," the Colombian told him. "Just don't do anything while they're still on the project. We don't want to draw any attention that would affect us more than it already has."

Manly felt good. He looked at the girls, feeling a sensation in his loins. He couldn't wait to get back to town. He couldn't have these girls, but he knew some he could have. The thought pushed the project and July Green to the back of his mind.

The days were too short for the families working on the project. They worked from dawn till dusk trying to preserve all they had worked for. It was more than themselves now; they felt responsible for all the people working there. The Bahamians did their best for them too. All the people, except for the APCO people who kept to themselves, became very close. At first things went pretty well; they showed little or no profit, but their bills were paid.

It didn't surprise Bob when the hotels in Nassau decided to break their contract. The contract itself, when he had a lawyer look at it, was poorly written and not binding.

"The onus is actually on you," the lawyer told him, "to supply the hotels, no matter what they pay you." The lawyer advised him to find out what the other hotels were paying for their produce. "If the hotels you are contracted to don't at least pay the going rate, you can break the contract and take your chances on a rebid."

He found the contract with the Miami hotel to be much the same. This was just one of the fights.

Bill and Hania, as well as Dale and Pearl, looked after the day-to-day operations on the farm, leaving Bob and July to donate their full time trying to put out fires before they spread.

July went to the government trying to get APCO off the project. Her argument was that they had not completed their projects on time, putting the whole project in jeopardy. Her voice fell on deaf ears; the APCO company was deeply imbedded in government contracts and had a strong lobby group.

"It's like beating your head against the wall," she frustratingly told Bob one night. Bob agreed that everywhere they turned, they were being shut out. July realized just how much of a fighter Bob was. She remembered his frustrations back on his farm in Canada, and she now realized how frustrating it must have been.

Bob learned a lot from past experience and fought back a lot smarter. He continuously lobbied the government and anyone who would listen. Still the noose was getting tighter, but if nothing else, Bob was gaining respect.

No one had ever had such a strong voice for the people of Andros before. The people rallied behind him. The religious groups on Andros were among the most vocal. Bob was invited to speak to all the different denominations. He seemed oblivious to his newfound fame. What did amaze him was how he could stand up in front of a crowd without being nervous and tell them plain and simple what he would like to see happen to this island and its people.

They managed to hang on for a year before they decided something drastic had to be done. Ironically, the only reason they were still in business was that the bank and APCO were embroiled in a bitter dispute. At first, the bank had thought the project was worth at least $2 million.

No one had bid, and APCO had offered a mere US$300,000. Now the bank would probably accept that, but APCO refused to pay them anything. The bank, on principle, refused to give it to them, leaving the Greens, Shonavons, and Drinkwaters to go on managing the project until the dispute was settled.

It was at a meeting on Bob and July's deck that the decision was finally made. "I guess," Bob told them, "it's time we decide if it's worth staying here or just give up, call it quits and get out."

Dale spoke up quickly, "We think we've been here too long now, there's certainly no future here. I don't know about the rest of you, but we've managed to save a little money. Let's get out with our heads held high. We don't feel we want to live under this pressure all the time."

Bob looked at Bill; he cleared his throat. "Do we have any options, Bob?" he asked.

Bob knew he was fighting an uphill battle. "You're right, Dale. There's no use staying here under the present conditions. Either we take a chance and do something drastic, or we shut it down."

"Don't get us wrong, Bob." It was Pearl Drinkwater who surprised everyone by speaking up. "We've fought long and hard here too. If there is an option, we'd like to hear about it."

"There's only one I can think of," Bob told them, "and it's a long shot. We know the name of the man who got Tom his funding. Now we don't know the ins and outs of what was involved or what the terms were, but we could go to him and see what he says."

They were silent for a moment. Finally, Dale said, "It is a long shot, but Tom did get some money."

"I take it you mean the guy that Tom and I stopped to see in Bowling Green, Kentucky?" Bill asked. He pulled out a card, "Here it is, Jagwar Holdings. Ken Holmes is the guy's name."

"Yes," Bob answered him. "That's the guy we'd have to deal with."

"Well," July said, "it won't hurt to ask. We all know APCO's still putting drugs through here.""Unless we can outright purchase the place, there's no way any of us want to continue on here the way things are."

They made contact with Ken Holmes and arranged a meeting.

They didn't know that Holmes immediately informed Manly Waddell and Grundman of his new clients. Manly Waddell thought it over.

"Tell your buddy Grundman it's all right if he takes them on," he told Holmes. "That will put the last nail in their coffin." Holmes then phoned Grundman and told him about the potential new clients.

"What does Waddell have to say about this?" He knew fucking well that Holmes had talked to him.

"Want me to talk to him?" Ken asked.

"All right, we'll play it your way for now." Grundman thought. "Ya, see if you can find out what's going on over there." Grundman's voice sounded pleasant.

"So it's okay if I take them on?" Ken asked.

"Sure, same terms, US$100,000, up-front in cash, 20 percent to be paid to you personally before you leave."

"Okay, we'll see what happens," Ken told him and rang off.

"Whether they can come up with the money or not," Holmes thought, "I'm going to milk this for all it's worth."

Bob, Bill, and Dale met with Holmes at his home in Bowling Green. "How much are you looking for?" Holmes asked them.

"Four million," Bob told him.

"Do you have your business plan in place?" he asked. They told him they did.

"I'm just a broker," he explained. "I have contracts with people looking to invest money around the world. What I do is present your plan to them. If someone accepts the plan or at least wants to know more about it, I will take you to see them at your expense, of course." They gave Holmes a copy of their business plan, shook hands, and left. They all felt better than they had in a long while.

"Now we are back to waiting again," Bob told them on the plane back to Andros Island.

The FBI had not only bugged Holmes's phone, they had also bugged his house. They sat around a table analyzing the latest tapes, including the meeting between Holmes and three men from Andros Island.

"Well, at least this confirms what we have thought all along," one agent said. "These guys wouldn't be here looking for money if they were mixed up in the drug operation on Andros."

"Maybe we should warn them to get the hell out of there," another agent suggested.

"No," Kent Ansly, the agent in charge, said thoughtfully. "We're after kings here. Unfortunately, these guys are only pawns caught up in the game."

A few days later, Holmes received a call from Grundman requesting Holmes to set up a meeting with Waddell in the Bahamas. "Okay," Holmes said, his ideas of being a highly paid agent fast fading, "I can do that, but for Christ's sake don't tell him I give you all the information he tells me," Holmes pleaded. He then got Manly on his cellular and told him about Grundman's request.

"Tell Grundman next weekend would be fine," Waddell told him. "There'll be a room reserved for him. My car will pick him up at the airport."

"Okay, I'll tell him that and let's keep us between ourselves," Holmes pleaded

Manly didn't answer. Holmes was left hanging with a dead line. He had the impression they hated each other, never thinking they would be meeting. He made a decision that he'd better protect himself. He gathered up what he thought to be pertinent documents along with some phone numbers and a letter with names. These were put into a safety deposit box at his bank. He left the key with his girlfriend if she didn't hear from him on any given week she was to take the key to his lawyer and they were to open the box.

Grundman landed in Nassau on Saturday as arranged, and that night the same driver as before whisked him down darkened back streets to the warehouse. The room was much the same as Grundman remembered it, and Waddell was in his usual place behind a table at the far end of the room.

Grundman held out his hand; Waddell stood up and took it. Grundman was relieved; this time he didn't have the powerful backing of the drug cartel but felt he came with his hat in hand. As for Manly Waddell, he had no idea why Grundman was here, but he also had a favor in mind so each showed mutual respect.

They both proceeded slowly, each feeling the other out until the conversation turned to Holmes. Here they were on common ground. They quickly determined that neither of them trusted Holmes, and the fact of the matter was that he knew too much.

"I have a man who can look after these matters," Grundman told him.

Manly looked at him with surprise and a little more respect. "That would be appropriate," he told Grundman. "I don't want the cartel in on this. However, I need Holmes for a little while yet, and I need your help too," Waddell told Grundman.

"That's why I'm glad we're having this meeting." Now that the sparing was done, Grundman relaxed and listened as Waddell told him how he would get Holmes to set the deal up with Green and his friends, and then with Grundman's help, they would finish them off.

"I want you to set Green up. You know, maybe a little cocaine in his possession. Whatever it takes, but just enough so he gets kicked out of the country. Can you handle that, Grundman?"

"Yes, I think that can probably be arranged. I'll tell Holmes that I wish to meet with Green in Germany this next week," Grundman told him. "Now," he went on, "I have a request for you. I would like to move here to the Bahamas. I will need a visa and landed immigrant status until I'm eligible for citizenship."

Waddell indicated that this would not be a problem. "I must explain a little more," Grundman told him. "In Germany I have, and shall I say, a select group of friends."

"A while ago we were having a bit of a party when the police raided the house. I was found in a compromising position with a young woman, a very young woman. Also, a large amount of drugs were found in the house. This girl has agreed to testify against me, and also against the woman by whom she was employed. This woman Lena K. will also need the proper documents to move here. However," Grundman went on, "as you can see, this may make your task to have us accepted a little more complicated. I may add that money is not a problem."

Waddell leaned back in his chair and smiled. He remembered the two girls he had supplied to Grundman the last time he was here and what they had told him.

"Yes, that will make things a little more complicated, but there's nothing that can't be overcome. As far as the money goes, you can scratch my back, and I'll scratch yours. In other words, I think we can do business." They stood up and shook hands.

"Don't worry about Holmes," Grundman told Waddell, " he will be taken care of!"

The next morning, Grundman phoned Holmes to meet him in Nassau. They met at Grundman's hotel where he told Holmes to tell the people at the Andros project they were about to receive funding. Holmes was to bring them to Munich where he would meet them at his bank. Holmes did as he was told.

Two days later Holmes met with Green, Shonavon, and Drinkwater in the same hotel. "My contact in Germany is very interested in your project," he told them. "If we are to handle this transaction for you, we will need some up-front money."

"I will require US$10,000 up-front in cash to cover my expenses. If your project is accepted, you will require US$50,000 up-front in cash as collateral."

Bob looked crestfallen, "Where in hell are we going to get that kind of money?"

Holmes told them that because the project was good, he would see what they could come up with. "I think it would be to your advantage if you could come up with close to this, Bob. The party interested in financing your project likes your expansion idea of a golf course and is willing to invest up to $22 million in this venture."

This news excited all three, and Holmes hoped it would provide the incentive to come up with the collateral.

That night, the three men and their wives discussed the proposal. "It's the only hope we have of continuing on here," Bill Shonavon lamented. "If we get that kind of money, we can take over, lock, stock, and barrel."

"Yes, I agree," said Pearl Drinkwater. "Then we could pay our bills on time." She was fed up of working in the office and being hounded for money.

"We have US$10,000 we can put in cash," July stated. "That's all the money we have."

July knew they had a small account put away in Miami, but her instincts told her to keep that quiet. Besides, this was more than they actually had. She would probably have to borrow some of it. Maybe her family would help, she thought to herself. Still, she wanted the project to succeed. As far as she was concerned, the situation was the same for Bob here as it was when he was trying to save the farm in Canada. It was beginning to pull him down. Both the Shonavon and the Drinkwater families were grown up and gone.

With everything supplied on the project, they had been able to put away a good little nest egg the last three years. Bill's equipment was mostly still sitting in his yard back in Canada as was Dale's. They decided to borrow against their equipment to raise the rest of the cash. The ownership of the project would be divided up as to the amount of cash each of them would put up front.

They met back with Holmes in Nassau and told him they had the money and would be ready to go in a week.

"Meet me at the Nassau airport next Monday," Holmes told them. "Remember, I have to be paid in cash before we go."

July lay in bed squirming. Bob had just been on top of her, and they had made beautiful love. It had been a long time since she had seen him so excited. She'd felt the raw power as he drove into her; the thought made her shiver and wanted more of it. She could hear Bob in the shower, the image of water running down his body was too much.

She rose from the bed and tiptoed to the shower. She opened the door feeling the steamy heat hit her body as she stepped inside. She stood facing him looking him in the eye then closed her eyes letting the water run through her hair.

"July, damn it, I've got to catch a plane," she heard him say with no conviction in his voice. She put her hands behind her head and moved closer, rubbing her breasts against his chest. She opened her eyes and smiled. He was no longer looking at her face; his gaze had dropped to watch those two beautiful mounds.

He watched the water hitting her breasts then pouring down between them like a waterfall. He brought his hands to her breasts and with his fingertips gently rubbed the tips of her already erect nipples. He raised his eyes to find she was watching him. "God, I love you," he told her.

His eyes told her everything. She was so happy, tears came to her eyes. She kissed him passionately, her hands roaming over his body. She pulled back from him and deliberately placed her hands on her breasts.

"You just love me because I've got big tits," she pouted.

"I love every part of you," he told her, "and with what you're doing to me, I'm going to show you how much in a minute."

July looked down; she was surprised to see he was rock hard. Usually the second time she had to work on him a bit. His cock got her full attention now, as she dropped to her knees and held it in her hand. Bob smiled, "Sure, you just love me because I've got a big cock," he chided her.

She didn't seem to pay any attention to what he said. She seemed totally enthralled with what she had in her hand, exploring every part of it. Bob didn't mind that she was concentrating on his cock; there was no way to explain the pleasure it gave him. In fact, he was happy he'd already made love to her that morning. The second time he'd have much more control, otherwise, his balls would be pretty tight right now. He felt her hold his sack in her hand.

"You must have blown your balls pretty good this morning." She looked up at him, her eyes squinting into the falling water. "I can only feel one nut," she told him.

"If you keep that up, it won't take long to fill the other one up," he quipped.

July didn't answer; she'd returned her attention to his erect phallus. This discovery had excited her. She had felt his nuts like this before; usually it meant she was in for a long hard fuck. She put his member in her mouth and tried to deep-throat it, but she never had much luck; its head was just too big to get much more in her mouth, let alone try to shove it in farther. She sensed his body tighten; it made her feel so good to give him pleasure. She ran her tongue along its shaft then turned her attention to his sack, gently sucking on his balls.

Bob leaned back against the shower wall feeling the water pound against his body and July pound upon his very soul until he could stand it no longer. He reached down and pulled her up against the shower wall and entered her from behind. He beat against her rear, each stroke almost lifting her feet off the shower floor.

Her face was contorted with pleasure; the water made her body slippery as she fought to hold her footing on the slippery floor. She could hear the slap of their bodies coming together as he stroked into her, and then the orgasm overcame her and she felt herself sliding to the floor.

But Bob hadn't finished with her yet. It was all he could do to pull her from the shower; July was a big woman. There wasn't an ounce of fat on her anywhere; she was built like a powerful athlete, but right now she was deadweight with no strength left to help him at all. He managed to lay her headfirst onto the bed, and then he entered her from behind again, but this time he was much more gentle, stroking her back to life.

He felt the strength coming back into her legs as she began to move with him. She raised herself up onto her knees and hands being careful not to lose his penetration. Bob reached forward and caressed her hanging breasts. A moan escaped her lips. He was up in her way too far; he was touching her soul, becoming part of her. She felt orgasm after orgasm pour through her body, and she collapsed again.

Bob lay beside her and ran his hands along her body still wet from the shower; or was it sweat, he wasn't sure. Her wet hair stuck to her face; he brushed it aside as she opened her bright blue Nordic eyes and smiled at him.

"You're not done with me yet, are you?" It was more of a fact than a question.

Bob looked down at his still swollen member, "No, but I think my other ball is filling up," he told her.

"Well, climb on board," she stroked his face, "and I'll see if I can empty them."

Bob turned himself till he could put his head between her legs and began to lick her vagina, his fingers finding her "spot" bringing her back to life with a start. She grabbed his cock feeling how soft the head had become as she caressed it with her lips. This stimulation was too much for Bob.

He turned himself around and entered her, his upper body supported by his arms. He looked down upon her his face full of love, his loins almost ready to give her a part of himself. She thought back to when they were young. She had asked him if he thought she was a good fuck. He tried to avoid the question, but she persisted.

"I know you were no virgin before we met," she told him. "I'm so big and clumsy. Do you sometimes wish I was a skinny little thing that could wrap herself around you like a snake?"

He told her she was like a "747," a wide-bodied jet built for comfort. "You, my dear, are built for a beautiful, comfortable ride, and there isn't a man alive who wouldn't like to take my place."

She had pouted, but deep down she had taken it as a compliment. By the look on his face, he was enjoying the ride now. She lifted her legs and wrapped them around his rear to spur him on. She watched as the passion entered his face, his cock stroking her violently; now she could feel his balls slapping against her ass. She heard strange sounds like a wild animal screaming, and then she realized they were coming from her lips. She tried to focus on Bob's face; she wanted to watch him cum, to see his pleasure, but her body wouldn't let her. They exploded together orgasm after orgasm griped her body and stole her mind as she pumped him dry.

Bob lay on top of July for several minutes unable to move. He'd love to have fallen asleep, his face full of her unruly hair drying, cuddled there with her for the rest of the day. He pulled himself from the bed and showered. Then he returned to the bed and began to dress, all the time looking at that beautiful body sprawled on his bed.

It was late afternoon in Munich. Grundman was also excited about his upcoming conquest. It always made him horny when he knew he was about to con some suckers out of their money. Now with Waddell's request, it was doubly exciting. He and Greta had been "snorting cocaine" all afternoon, and now he was about to enjoy the ultimate experience.

Greta was mounted on his hard prick. She reached up and pulled the plastic bag down over his head, and then she slowly tightened the specially designed drawstrings on the bag around his throat. Grundman felt the blood rush to his head. His balls were on fire, the pleasure in his loins intense. Greta tightened the strings even more, and Grundman began to buck and gyrate his loins, but Greta managed to stay on top of him keeping his cock in her as far as possible.

Grundman had never felt such pleasure; he felt so powerless, so weak. He wanted Greta to let go, but his hands were helpless, and then everything went black. Greta held on tight to the bag, expecting Grundman to blow his load in her. Suddenly, she felt his body go limp and still.

She released the strings and pulled the bag from his head. "Maybe I killed him," she thought. Serves the asshole right if I did. The idea excited her. She felt Grundman's prick still hard inside her. She remembered hearing that men get a hard-on when they die. She placed her hands on his chest and began riding up and down on his cock, giving a little scream of satisfaction as she came.

Her gyrations caused Grundman to cough and begin to breathe again. Greta looked down at him with disappointment; "maybe next time," she thought as she lifted herself off Grundman. He rolled over and began puking on the bed. She looked at him in disgust and headed for the bathroom.

Bob stood at the door with his suitcase in hand. "How can I leave something as beautiful as this?" he thought. July had thrown one of his shirts on and came out of the bedroom to see him off. She had deliberately left the top buttons undone so her breasts would be on display.

"Take it easy on those frauleins over there," she said rubbing against him. "Save something for me." She ran her hand teasingly through her tousled hair.

"Quit it, July," he pleaded. "It's hard enough to leave you when you behave yourself, let alone when you're like this."

"I just want to give you something to remember me by," she pouted, knowing exactly what she was doing to him. "Good luck," she told him, "and come back with lots of money."

"That's not all I'll come back with." He kissed her passionately as he reached under her long shirt to touch between her thighs.

"Hurry back," she told him and pushed him out the door.

Both Bill and Dale were standing waiting for Bob next to the plane as he came up. Both of them were smiling knowingly. July and Bob's romantic episodes were renowned throughout the project; they called July the screamer.

"You're late," Bill told him as Bob approached them, a sheepish grin on his face.

"Yeah, well, I got held up," was all he would say as he entered the plane.

They met Holmes at the Nassau airport, gave him his money, and arrived in Germany the next morning. They caught a little sleep before noon when Holmes came and took them to lunch. He then escorted them downtown to meet Grundman.

They met at Grundman's bank. It was an impressive building with high ceilings and pillars. Along one side was a row of busy tellers. On the other side were offices, some with glass surrounding them, some more private. It was into one of these offices that Grundman and the two men with him guided Bob, Bill, and Dale.

Grundman spoke very good English, but the other two, Grundman introduced as manager and chairman of the bank, could not speak very well at all. Grundman showed them some documents lying on the office desk.

"These are documents authorizing me to lend you $22 million dollars at 2 percent interest." Grundman got right to the point. "In return, we will use the project as collateral plus the money you have presumably brought us."

First Bob, then Bill, and finally Dale read over the documents. "Is this all there is to it?" Dale asked. "We just sign this paper and you give us $22 million."

"That's about it," Grundman told them. "It will take a few days to process the papers, and then you can go to work."

They began asking Grundman about time and repayment schedules.

Grundman answered everything they could think of to ask, so they signed the documents.

Bob opened his briefcase to show Grundman and the people from the bank that they did indeed have the money. "I demand, however," Bob told them, "that this money be put in trust until the deal is finalized."

"By all means," Grundman told him, "we will take the cheque out to one of the tellers to transfer it into cash. He will then open an account and Harold here," he pointed at the bank manager, "will place it in the bank's trust account."

This suited Bob and the others fine, so it was done as described. Little did they know that Grundman rented the office from the bank. The man who signed the trust account was actually a fly-by-night lawyer who worked for Grundman from time to time. The bank suspected Grundman of perhaps being on the shady side, but he was a large depositor, so they turned a blind eye to his dealings.

"Will you need us for anything else?" they asked Grundman.

"Yes, you will have to sign the final documents in a couple of days," he told them. "You should stay till then."

It was the next day when they came back to their room that they found the police waiting for them. On the bed lay what the police told them were three small bags containing cocaine. They were taken down to the police station where they were questioned for hours and then spent the night in jail.

Everything they had done in the last twenty-four hours looked suspicious. They had come from the Bahamas, and they had immediately gone to a bank to deposit cash. They were only in Munich for a short time with no company business or signed contracts to prove why they were here. They told the truth about how they were to meet Erik Grundman with whom they were doing business here in Germany. The police seemed interested in the name Grundman but told the three men there was no one in the city doing business under that name. Bob was pretty sure they'd been done over, but Bill and Dale held out hope. "At least our money is in trust," Bill said; Bob wasn't so sure.

The next day the police told them they were to be deported out of the country. The police escorted them to the airport where they found their bags packed. They were all put on a flight to Nassau. This had all happened so fast the three men were totally devastated. The consequences could be profound. They decided to get their company lawyer on this as soon as they landed in Nassau.

At the Nassau airport, they found the Bahamian police waiting for them. The police escorted them off to an immigration office in the back of the main terminal. The immigration agent was blunt. "Your work visas have been lifted," he told them. "We are putting you on the next plane to Canada."

"What about our wives?" Bill asked.

"They'll be sent home too," the agent told them.

"Can we see them?" Dale asked. The answer was a stern no.

"You will remain in this office until your flight leaves this afternoon. You will not be allowed to talk to anyone or use the phone."

Bob had a sick feeling in the pit of his stomach; someone out there had gone to great lengths to set them up. On the other hand, he supposed that whoever it was could have had them disappear completely, at least they were still alive.

That night, they landed in Toronto where the police interviewed them and took their passports, and then sent them off to Saskatchewan. They were told to report to their local police station when they got there and then stay put until the government decided what to do with them.

It was dead in the middle of winter in Saskatchewan. Not one of them was prepared for the intense cold that greeted them. Bob's mother spent the winter in Arizona so her house was available to him. The other two had never had the confidence to sell their homes with the constant turmoil that swirled around the farm project in the Bahamas and felt fortunate they still had them. Two days later, Hania and Pearl showed up but not July.

"They just came and took us," Pearl told them. "We could only bring the clothes on our backs. July was working in the fields with the men. We didn't get a chance to see her."

Bob phoned their company lawyer in Nassau, and he told Bob he would look into it. He tried phoning the project office, but all he got was the APCO manager who told him all the women had been sent away, and that he knew nothing more. Finally, he got hold of Arthur at the Nassau airport.

"We are hearing strange stories, Mr. Green. Yesterday your son came to my brother and asked for his help. He is taking them supplies tonight. After he has seen them, I will know better," Arthur told him.

"If possible, have July or Rikker phone me. If that's not possible, you can leave me a message." Bob set up a time for the call. He told Arthur to be careful and to take care, and then hung up.

"I feel we should be very careful," he told the Shonavons and the Drinkwaters at their next meeting. "I have a feeling that we are in a lot more danger than we realize, if you need to get hold of me I'll be out at mom's house."

Grundman received Waddell's coded fax in his Swiss office. The next night, they again met at the old warehouse in Nassau.

"I've held up my end of the bargain," Grundman told Waddell. "How's things going on your end?"

"I apologize," Manly Waddell told him, "for being so slow, but I had to bypass some channels here. The wheels turn slowly. I feel it could be two weeks yet before your papers are accessed, I hope you can wait that long."

"That's not a problem," Grundman told him. "It's going to take at least that long to tie up the loose ends before I can move. However, I think we both have some other loose ends to tie up before then."

"That would be the simplest, wouldn't it?" Manly agreed.

"And the safest," Grundman stated. "They know both of us. Pretty soon they'll put two and two together and come up with us tied together with Holmes."

"Yes, Holmes phoned me," Manly told Grundman. "These guys are ringing his phone off the wall wondering what's going on."

"That link will disappear tonight," Grundman told him. "However, I think if we get rid of the rest of our problem, we're home free."

"What's my end going to cost me?" Manly asked. Grundman told him, and Manly nodded, sli- cing his finger across his throat.

Grundman had already talked to Ginter about the Holmes job. This time he told Ginter about the rest of his assignment. "It's a big job. There are five clients," Grundman said, "so take lots of help. I'll get you all the information I can about them, but it should be easy. They're naive as hell and don't suspect a thing."

They negotiated a price; it was in line, and Grundman didn't argue. "I'm in the Bahamas," he told Ginter. "I'll send you the information you need from here to your pickup point. There's not a big rush," Grundman told him, "but I'd like it cleaned up in a couple of weeks."

Ginter didn't think this was a problem. He asked that Grundman have cash deposited in a numbered account in Minneapolis. "I'll contact you in two weeks to give a progress report," Ginter told him. "Hopefully, it's all wrapped up by then."

Grundman hung up and turned his thoughts to tonight's encounter with the girls Manly had promised him. As far as he was concerned, with Ginter on the job, it was as good as done.

The FBI operator was dozing. Holmes seldom got calls after midnight, especially when he brought his girlfriend home, there was little of interest going on. That's why he woke up when he heard Holmes's doorbell ring.

"Might be interesting," the operator thought. He heard Holmes make his way to the door and ask who was there. He couldn't hear the answer, but he heard Holmes open the door.

There was no talking after this, just the sound of people milling around the room. Slowly, he became suspicious, someone searching the room, he thought. The operator immediately placed a call to his superior, Kent Ansly. Kent's voice came sleepily onto the phone.

"Someone's in Holmes's house," the operator told Ansly.

Ansly's voice became immediately clear. "Call the police, 911, anyone you can get there in a hurry. I'm on my way."

The agent did as he was told. He listened to the person or persons rummaging inside the house.

"The phone's bugged, Henekie," he heard a voice say.

"Well, she's ready to blow. We'd better get out of here," someone else said.

The house became quiet, and then the operator could hear the crackle of fire. A minute later, he grabbed his ears in pain as the house blew up.

Two days later a man impeccably dressed in a dark blue suit entered Ken Holmes's bank. He walked straight up to the reception desk and asked the girl to see the manager. She asked who he was.

He handed her a card and said, "My name is Mr. Haskins." She came back with the manager and introduced Mr. Haskins.

"What can I do for you?" the manager asked.

"A Mr. Holmes has died," Haskins told him. "I'm the lawyer in charge of his estate. I see in his will he has a safety deposit box in your branch. I would like to open it please."

"I'm sorry, Mr. Haskins, but we are not allowed to do that without a death certificate for the deceased or some kind of authorization."

Mr. Haskins produced a letter with the same letterhead as the card Mr. Haskins had given him. The banker recognized the prodigious name of the law firm; still, the manager hesitated.

"He also left this in our care," Mr. Haskins produced a key.

"Right this way," he led Haskins into the vault and showed him the deposit box. The manager waited to make sure the key was the right one then turned and left the vault. Mr. Haskins

took all the papers from the box and put them in his briefcase. Then he signed out and then, waving to the manager, left the building.

Henekie was waiting for Ginter in the car. "Any problems?" he asked.

"No," Ginter replied, "our work is completed here." They found a secluded place on the edge of town and burnt the papers.

"Now we head north to meet the others in Minneapolis," Ginter told Henekie.

"It's been a long time since we were all together," replied Henekie.

"Yes," Ginter answered. The thought of joining their old comrades in arms pleased him too.

"Can you tell me where we are going after we meet the others?" Henekie asked.

A smile came to Ginter's lips. "We're all going on a hunting trip up in Canada."

Little did Henekie think that within two weeks, he would be headed back to Minneapolis with the police hot on his tail. This would not be a problem for Ginter though, because he would be dead.

# SIXTEEN

HENEKIE AND ALF knew the Canadian Mounties would be able to trace their trail to Minneapolis, but that's where the trail had to stop. It's not hard to disappear if you have the proper documents and lots of cash. Ginter had been a very careful man; Henekie knew he had a system and followed it religiously. All Henekie had to do was use what he knew about Ginter to figure out the system.

As soon as he and Ginter had crossed the Minnesota line, they put Minnesota tags on their car. It was a plain Jane Chevrolet that blended well into the surroundings; in fact, Henekie had trouble finding it in the airport parking lot. He knew Ginter had left the keys under the driver's side fender. He quickly found them and headed down town; Henekie asked Alf to open the glove box. In there was a map and other assorted goodies, but of special interest to Henekie was a key. It definitely was a locker key; even the locker number was on it, but there were hundreds of such lockers in the area. As Henekie drove through the city, he tried to think of what Ginter would do. There had to be a clue somewhere. Without money or fresh ID, they were sitting ducks.

Suddenly, Henekie pulled into a gas station and parked. He asked

Alf to hand him the map. He scoured over it, looking for a clue, maybe coordinates, he thought. Henekie almost gave up when he saw a circle drawn around one of the legends. Henekie traced with his finger till he found the same number on the map. His heart leapt; the gym was only blocks away.

Ten minutes later, he found it. The building was old, and the neon sign out front said simply "Boxing." Henekie found the locker that matched the number on the key; it opened easily. Inside was a sports bag one might take to the gym.

"Nice touch," Henekie thought as he took the bag back to the car. He let Alf drive as he checked out the bag. Inside were five false passports with driver's licenses to match and, most importantly, twenty thousand in small bills.

Henekie decided he had to do something about Alf. He had seriously thought of leaving him dead at their hotel in Canada but decided to wait. Alf was stupid but in a tight situation he was fearless, a born killer, an ideal man for their kind of work. Now that they were clear, Alf became a liability. When Alf wasn't working, he was drunk. When he was drunk, he became violent and talked too much. Henekie wondered what Ginter had in mind for Alf when the job was finished. The quicker he got rid of Alf, the better.

Darkness had settled over the city. Henekie told Alf to pull into a small restaurant. He left Alf to go to the bathroom; instead, he went out a back door and checked out the alley. Next to the restaurant was a printing and stationary shop. "Perfect," Henekie thought. They finished their meal and left the restaurant.

Outside, Henekie turned to Alf, "Ginter had our money left here."

"What do you mean here?" Alf looked around, "In the middle of the street?"

"No," Henekie had to laugh, "in a dumpster in the alley out back."

"You're shitting me. Sounds like a stupid fucking place to me."

"Yes, well you know Ginter, he always had his reasons. Anyway, he told me it was only dumped once a month, so it would be the perfect place for his contact to leave the money." Alf still looked dubious, so Henekie added, "If it's any consolation, we get to split all five shares." That seemed to be the right motivation for Alf as he followed Henekie around the building into the alley behind.

They looked in the dumpster; a single light over the back door showed the dumpster to be half full of paper and assorted scraps. "Knowing Ginter, it's funny he didn't put it in a garbage bin behind a slaughterhouse," he grumbled and climbed in. Henekie stood in the alley screwing the silencer onto the gun Ginter had stored in the sports bag, then he climbed into the dumpster. Alf was on his hands and knees searching through the papers in the bottom when Henekie pulled Alf's jacket hood over his head and shot him. He went through Alf's clothes taking anything he could find. In one of the coat pockets, Henekie found the necklace.

It was too dark to see exactly what it was, but he put it in his pocket and went back to the car. He felt extremely tired as he drove into the Holiday Inn. It had been a long day, and he had not slept well. With the dawn would bring a new day, Henekie knew he must erase the past and ponder his future

He had always been the follower from the army to his work with Ginter; there had always been someone to give orders, now he was on his own with few resources and no one to tell him what to do. If it hadn't been for the overwhelming goal to even the score with Bob Green, Henekie might have just given up, resorting back to his old ways of life.

Henekie had been a mercenary most of his life. His contact and friends were mostly in the same business. Eventually, if they could no longer hire out their services, they turned to crime, drugs, and alcohol. This probably would have been the fate of Henekie had he not tasted the success of how he had handled the situation so far. The scary part was could he handle the future.

He opened his eyes to the new day, finding his mind full of doubt. But once he focused on Bob Green, the doubts disappeared. He had to find this man and settle matters. Why do this for nothing? His mind began to scheme. Someone else obviously wanted Green dead, and they were willing to pay for it. The police would have Green by now; these people would be desperate to have him snuffed. They'd pay a fortune to the one who did it, and Henekie worked long enough with Ginter to know there was nothing that couldn't be done if you put your mind to it. The problem now was to find the people who hired Ginter.

It had been a long drive from Bowling Green, Kentucky, to Minneapolis, Minnesota. Ginter had talked more than usual to pass the time. Henekie thought back, trying to remember just what Ginter did tell him. He remembered Ginter saying he had a woman in Munich, Germany, and spent most of his time there when he wasn't working. Henekie also remembered him telling about a little blonde girl named Greta, who belonged to a motorcycle gang that he hung around with. "She would do anything," Ginter had told him. "In fact I am seriously thinking of bringing her on some of my jobs. She can kill as well as fuck, and that could be very valuable."

It wasn't a whole lot to go on, but Henekie decided he had no choice. Until he could find out where Green was, his hands were tied anyway. He would drive to Milwaukee and fly to Germany. If he could find this Greta, maybe things would fall in place. It was then he remembered the piece of jewelry in his pocket. He had forgotten about it till now. His instincts told him to get rid of it, but on closer inspection he realized the piece might be very valuable. He put it in the sports bag Ginter had left in the locker.

"My funds are very limited," he thought. "I might have to pawn it."

He sold the car to a wrecker on the outskirts of Milwaukee taking a taxi to the airport.

Early the next morning, he landed in Munich. Henekie never knew his parents. The first person he remembered in his life said that she was his aunt. They were living in Gibraltar at the time, so his first language was English. She ran off with a man who took them to Spain and then into France. About the only thing Henekie learned through this time was the different languages and how to cope for himself.

He got himself in trouble and, as with lots of young men, was put in the army and eventually into the French Foreign Legion. This was where he got the only piece of identification that was real. He was classed as an Algerian nationalist and therefore had access to France. After putting in his time with the legion, he found his services were in demand, and he fought in several small wars in Africa before running into Ginter, who became Henekie's mentor and best friend.

Ginter insisted Henekie live in Germany so he could get a hold of him in a hurry, but they were never together there and never associated with one another in any way until they were out of the country. Henekie was immersed in German and while finding the language difficult, he was a quick learner and soon knew enough to get around with.

He found out that there were a lot more than one biker gang in Munich and they were not open to strangers. But Henekie could handle himself, and his personality fit in well with the crowd. He soon found that some of them too had been mercenaries; they exchanged war stories and other information which gradually led him to Greta. Henekie bought his new friends as many drugs as his limited budget would allow, and they rode together. The first thing Henekie had done was to buy a used bike and a leather jacket. One day, when he and his friend were riding, they met a group of bikers. Henekie told his friend the truth.

"My friend Ginter was killed last month. He asked me if anything happened to him, I was to tell a girl named Greta. She belongs to a biker gang in Munich, is all I know."

"Everybody knows Greta," his friend told him. But that's all he told him. Henekie didn't want to push too hard.

As they passed the bikers, his friend pulled over close, "There's your friend Greta," he told him.

All he saw was blond hair flying out behind a bike rider. Henekie didn't know what to do, "I wonder where they're headed?" he tried not to sound excited.

"Probably over to the Reo," his friend told him. "They hang out there."

It didn't take long for Henekie to find out the Reo was a bar, but getting close to Greta was another matter. He began to hang out at the Reo bar. It was a rough place, again making him feel right at home. He began integrating himself into the atmosphere of the bar. He thought things were going well until one day a biker he was talking to suddenly pulled a gun and put it to Henekie's head.

"I think you're a pig," the man told him. He was a big man with wild eyes. Henekie had seen his type before.

"Unpredictable," he thought, "capable of anything." He'd have to be careful.

"I like to see pigs squirm before I kill them," the man said.

The bar had become very quiet; the man cocked his gun. The sound was deafening in Henekie's ears; he held his breath and hung his head. The biker took this as a sign of submission. He pulled the gun back from Henekie's head slightly and turned to the others.

"Should I shoot him in the nuts first?" He got out before Henekie's hand hit the gun and the man's jaw in one motion. The gun went off harmlessly into the ceiling. The biker sat, stunned, on his stool. Henekie stood up, grabbed the man's head, and twisted violently. The sickening sound of bones breaking ripped through the silence of the bar as the man toppled off the stool, dead.

Henekie stood facing the others for a moment; no one moved, and then a man got up from a table and came toward him.

"Get rid of him," the man pointed at the dead biker, "I want to talk to this guy." Two bikers pulled the dead body out the back door as the bar slowly returned to normal. The man ordered a beer for himself and Henekie.

"I can tell you're a mercenary," the man said, "by the way you handle yourself." What I don't know is why you are here."

The man had long hair and a scruffy appearance, but Henekie could see he was no fool. He decided to tell the truth. "A man named Ginter told me I could find friends here," he said.

"Ginter was no fool if he told you that. He must be a very good friend," the man told him.

"I worked with Ginter," Henekie explained. "He was killed on a job. His last request was that I find a girl named Greta and tell her."

The man asked him some more questions then told Henekie that Ginter was a very good friend of his. "Greta will probably be around this evening. I will introduce you."

Greta was not at all what Henekie had built her up to be in his mind. She was short with long blonde hair; she looked much too young to be able to have all the qualities Ginter had described about her. Still, Henekie liked the way she wore her motorcycle cap at a slight angle, and her small breasts were partly on display under her half-open leather jacket. He'd been sitting at the bar when she came out of nowhere and sat down beside him.

"Hi, I'm Greta. Hear you want to talk to me," was all she said as she lit a cigarette. Henekie introduced himself.

"I hear you're a friend of Ginter's," she said.

"I was a friend," Henekie told her. "Now he's dead."

"That's too bad, he was a good fuck," Greta said, showing no remorse. "I'll have to tell Rona."

"Who's Rona?" he asked. Greta turned and looked at him.

"His wife," her gaze left Henekie and went around the room. "I guess she's not here tonight."

"I'd like to meet her," Henekie told Greta.

"Sure," Greta said, downing her beer. "If you give me a ride, I'll take you to her house."

The house Greta pointed out was a small bungalow in what looked to be an average neighborhood. Typical of Ginter, Henekie thought as he and Greta climbed off the motorcycle. Greta knocked, and a tall redhead answered the door.

Henekie thought her to be about thirty-five or maybe a bit more when he saw her up close. She had a pretty, thin face covered in freckles. She wore shorts and a low-cut blouse showing good cleavage. Henekie was immediately attracted to her.

"Ginter and I had more in common than he knew," he thought to himself.

"Hi Rona, this is Henekie, he's a friend of Ginter's," Greta told her.

They sat down and had a beer. Henekie noticed three kids in the living room watching TV. "Yours and Ginter's?" he asked.

"Not entirely," Rona told him. "The oldest one, I don't know who the father is, but the other two are Ginter's," she said. I was pregnant when he married me."

Henekie decided it was time to tell her, "Ginter's dead."

She looked at Henekie, "It's just like that prick to fuck off and leave me with nothing," she said.

Henekie was surprised, "You mean Ginter didn't leave you any money?"

"He was a real tight prick," Rona growled. "It was bad enough when he was here, but when he went away, we damned near starved."

Greta laughed, "I don't know why you stayed with him, and there are lots of guys down at the gang who would have looked after you." To Greta, life was simple.

"Most of them were scared of Ginter," Rona answered her, "and so was I."

Greta finished her beer. "I'm off," she said. "I think Rona needs a good fuck to get over her mourning. I can find my own way back."

Henekie looked a little embarrassed.

"Do you have anywhere to go?" Rona asked.

"No," he answered.

"Then you might as well stay," Rona got up to get another beer.

Henekie woke up a totally satisfied man, not only sexually but mentally. He had been so wrapped up in what he was doing he'd not had a woman in a long time. Rona had settled that problem; he was totally fucked out. He looked over at Rona lying beside him. She was sleeping with a very satisfied look on her face.

Henekie placed his hands behind his head letting what he had learned sift through his mind. After two weeks of frustration, he'd had two days of incredible luck. He was gaining more confidence every day in his ability to function on his own. He felt now that Rona was the key; he just had to find out what her mind had locked up.

Over the next couple of days, he and Rona became very close. They had both been under Ginter's thumb. The better he got to know Rona, the more he realized how much of an arrogant asshole Ginter had really been.

"I know Ginter has money," Henekie told her, "I can't believe he wouldn't confide in you as to where it was."

"I know he had money," Rona agreed. "I know he has a Swiss bank account, but that's all I know."

She was very good to her kids, Henekie realized. He became very upset with the way Ginter had treated Rona and decided he would set things right for her. In fact, Henekie was very comfortable here with Rona. He could have Ginter's business and his wife, if only he could find Ginter's contacts. Rona tried to help him in any way she could, trusting Henekie to help her find some of Ginter's money.

"He always fucked other women from the gang," she said. Even Greta, I could handle that, but when he started meeting women behind my back, I was very upset."

"Did you see him with these other women?" Henekie asked.

"Only one." Rona told him, "when he was home we usually did the bars together except every Tuesday he would go off by himself. So one day, I followed him. He went to a bar two blocks from here. At first he just sat inside, drinking, but then a woman sat down with him. I recognized the woman from a biker party Ginter and I attended. Ginter fucked her from behind on the couch that night, I thought nothing of it. He did this at parties all the time, then I found out this broad was Greta's mother, Ginter always had a soft spot for Greta, so I figured something was going on.

Something clicked in Henekie's mind. "Let's go over to that bar tonight," he told her.

Henekie was running awfully low on funds. It was time to see if he could pawn the necklace he'd found on Alf's body. "First," he thought, "I'll get it appraised and take it to a small jewelry shop not far away."

The jeweler looked bored until Henekie showed him the necklace. It was an exquisite piece of work, the best he had ever seen.

"Did you want to sell it?" the jeweler's eyes showed his exuberance.

"No," Henekie answered. "It's been in the family for years, I just want to get it valued."

"It's a very authentic piece," the jeweler told him. "There's one piece missing," He showed Henekie where the medallion had once been fastened to the main strap. "Even so, it is very valuable, I would say at least twenty thousand euros," and he looked up to see if Henekie was interested. Henekie whistled, he had no idea the value would be anywhere near that. He decided to keep it for a while longer.

That evening he and Rona went and sat in the same bar where Rona said Ginter had met Greta's mother.

"Is that the same bartender that was here when you saw Ginter talking to the woman?" Henekie asked her, "I think so." Rona didn't sound exactly sure so Henekie decided he'd have to find out on his own if the bartender knew anything about Ginter.

It was after two in the morning when the bar closed. Henekie sent Rona home and then followed the bartender. As he unlocked his door Henekie moved up behind him, "Let's go inside." The bartender was scared. "Please all I have is ten euros in my pocket, you can have it." "You'll have a hundred euros in your pocket if you give me the information I want," Henekie told him.

They stepped inside, Henekie told him and to stay where he was and not to turn around. "No one gets hurt if you tell me all you know about a man who only came to your bar on Tuesday afternoons to meet with a woman."

The bartender sounded worried, "I know the one you're talking about but I don't know anything about him."

Henekie decided he was going to have to get rough, then the bartender added, "I do know the woman."

"Okay, the woman might do," Henekie told him. "What do you know about her?"

"She lives in a swanky apartment near here. When I was younger I used to hang around with her daughter, Greta. Sometimes Greta would take a bunch of us guys over there and we'd all get high then we'd gangbang her mother, I think her name was Mona," the bartender added.

"Can you show me where this apartment is?" Henekie wanted to know.

"Sure, or I can give you her phone number and address if you want."

"That sounds very convenient," Henekie told him. "Why would you have that?"

The bartender shrugged. "My girl friend left me and I've been getting a little horny lately so the last time she was in I asked her if I could come over sometime. She gave me her number and address and told me to make sure I phoned first. The address is in my pocket here." He began to reach in his pocket but Henekie stopped him and fished it out himself.

"Okay," Henekie told the bartender, "let's hope your telling the truth." He stuck a hundred euro note in the bartenders pocket and left.

Mona was reluctant to turn the phone over to Grundman but when he heard her say the name Ginter he grabbed the phone from her.

"Ginter," it was a man's voice.

"No," Henekie answered, "I'm Ginter's friend, Henekie, he sent me to talk with you."

The voice on the other end of the phone sounded suspicious. "Where's Ginter?"

"He's dead," Henekie told the voice. "I must meet with you to tell what's happened."

"How do I know you're telling the truth?" the voice asked.

"I was in Canada with him, how else would I know this phone number?"

"Okay," the voice said, "I'll meet you at the Oka Bar tomorrow at seven. Do you know where it is?" Henekie told him he could find it.

Now that he had found Ginter's contact, things were going very well. He rode Rona hard, making love to her well into the night. Grundman had told Henekie to meet him at seven o'clock, but he was there long before that. He wanted to get a look at this person before he committed himself.

Grundman sniffed a shot of coke up his nose then walked into the bar. It was nearly empty; there was a man and a woman sitting at a table and a couple of barflies watching TV at the bar. He took a seat at the bar and began his vigilance.

Grundman did not like what he heard coming out of Canada. Something had definitely gone wrong, but then Ginter worked in mysterious ways, and he didn't know what to believe. Waddell had sent him a coded fax congratulating him on the Holmes job. Ginter had not contacted him for two weeks in a row, and now this Henekie guy had answered the phone throwing a whole new twist into the scheme of things. Waddell's next fax had not been so complimentary. He had to have heard the job had not gone well. What bothered him was that Waddell now claimed the cartel had sanctioned the Canadian job. Waddell bullshitted a lot, but still this did not look good for Grundman; the cartel did not like botched work. He hoped he could find out exactly what happened from this Henekie, if indeed he was who he said he was.

The bar began to fill up. A couple of guys came in by themselves. One of them stood in the doorway looking around before he sat down. Grundman decided he might be worth watching. Grundman had hired a man to hold the bar stool he had told Henekie he would be in. Grundman had decided to wait till his man made a contact with this Henekie before committing himself. With all the bad luck he'd had over getting caught in the crack house and now this girl going after Lena.He wasn't going to stick his neck out any further than he had to.

His man was talking to a man beside him and a woman on the other. He looked over and shook his head; Grundman looked at his watch—seven twenty. Where in hell was this guy? The couple who had been sitting at a table got up and walked toward the bar. Grundman thought the woman looked familiar but couldn't place her, as the couple sat beside him. Grundman didn't pay them much attention until the man turned to him.

"Hello, Grundman," he said, "I'm Henekie."

Grundman laughed, "That's something like Ginter would do."

Henekie didn't laugh, "Maybe that's not a very good compliment, Mr. Grundman. Ginter was careless, now he's dead."

Grundman's smile faded, "I was afraid of that, so what happened?"

Henekie told him the whole story. "We had misinformation," Henekie concluded, "especially on this Green fellow. He's a lot more dangerous than we were ever led to believe. As far as I remember our informer said he was just an ordinary schmuck like the rest of them, only he was supposed to have a hot wife," Grundman said.

"His wife wasn't with him, so I know nothing about that," Henekie said. "All I know is that I want that Green son of a bitch, and I think you do too."

Grundman said nothing. "What I have here is a diamond in the rough," he thought. After all his bad luck, finally something was going his way. "Who's your friend?" Grundman looked at the woman.

"I'm Ginter's wife," she told him and "I was at a party at your house once a long time ago."

"This man is very good," Grundman thought, "he already knows too much about me."

"I need some time to put together the information I now have," Grundman said, "I will meet you in two days. I will pick you up in my car outside the Reo at six o'clock."

Henekie nodded his head, and then he and Rona got up and left. Grundman looked over and smiled; his man was still holding his seat at the bar. Grundman faxed all his new information in code to Waddell. In effect, he warned him that Green had survived and could be coming after him.

Waddell in return faxed all the new information he had. "Our police informant tells us every police force in the world is looking for Green. However, we are sure they don't have him. It is imperative to many people that we get to him first. I have an ace in the hole. We have his wife. We are sure he is headed this way. If he gets into the Bahamas, we have him. Put your new man onto the trail. If we can get someone to chase him, it will flush him out."

Henekie got into Grundman's car, and they pulled out into the traffic. Grundman told him what he had found out about Green.

"Shit, I was sure the cops would have him," Henekie lamented, "and then at least we'd know where he is."

"We don't know where he is," Grundman told him, "but we know where he's going. The trouble is we don't know how he plans to get there."

"If you know where he's going, so does everyone else who's looking for him," Henekie said. "How in hell am I supposed to find him?"

"You found me, didn't you?" Grundman stated. Henekie just grunted. "Before we go any further, we have to get down to business, Henekie. Do you have any money?"

"No, I'm tapped out," Henekie told him.

"How about Ginter's wife?" Grundman asked. "He must have left her some, he had lots."

"That's what I thought," said Henekie, "but the bastard never left her a cent."

Grundman was surprised at this, "He had lots, I know because I deposited over a million dollars in a Swiss account for him over the years."

"Well, there's no way we can get at that unless we know the number," Henekie said, looking at Grundman hopefully.

"Ginter wasn't that stupid," Grundman said.

"I have no idea what his account number would be."

"Look," Grundman told Henekie, "before we go anywhere, I need some collateral from you. Otherwise, I could finance you to run off and have a good time with my money. I don't know you well enough to do that."

"How much do you expect me to put down?" Henekie asked.

"Oh, US$20,000 would be minimum," Grundman said.

Henekie thought about mortgaging Rona's house. "I do have something valued at that amount," he told Grundman, "but if I pawn it, I know they'll pay me far less. I wonder if you'd be interested in having a look at it."

Grundman shrugged, "Why not?"

The next day, Henekie brought him the necklace. "I will get it appraised," Grundman told him, surprised at the quality of the piece.

The goldsmith that Grundman went to was another of his friends who lived on the edge. He ran a little shop downtown, but most of his income was from fencing stolen gems to rich collectors around the world.

"Where did you get this, Grundman?" he asked.

"It's been in the family for years," Grundman said.

The goldsmith smiled knowingly; it was the only answer he ever got. "This is an exquisite piece," the goldsmith told him. "Sixteenth-century Austrian, look at the work," he showed Grundman the inset diamonds. He could have told Grundman much more but knew he was interested in only one thing, the value. "There's one problem, though," he pointed out to Grundman the broken chain link where a medallion had once hung. "Still, I know people who would give you at least $60,000 US dollars for this piece."

Grundman's mouth fell open, "No thanks," he said, "I think I will hang on to it for a while."

"Okay," he told Henekie on their next meeting, "I don't like it, but I have no choice. We need each other. I will take the jewelry as collateral." Henekie hated to part with it but knew he had no choice.

"Here's the information you asked for about Green's family and friends." Grundman handed Henekie the dossier. "I am moving to the Bahamas for good next week. Before you go after this Green, Henekie, I have a little job for you. I'll pay you well to do it, and we'll call the money you make a retirement fund for Rona."

"Good." Henekie was in agreement with this, "I'll feel better if she and the kids are looked after."

"There is a woman who lives in my house. She and I have been together for a long time, but I can't take her with me to the Bahamas, so I want you to bring her to a certain spot where I have a going-away present for her." Henekie had thought Grundman was going to tell him to kill this woman and was relieved that he hadn't.

Henekie listened as Grundman told him when and where, and then he had a question. "How do you know Green's heading for the Bahamas? It's such a stupid place for him to go."

"Because my business partner is holding his wife there, and we know he'll do anything to get to her."

Henekie just shook his head, "I'll never understand how a man can lose his head over a piece of tail," Henekie said as he opened the car door.

"Yes, well, to hear my business partner tell it, you haven't seen this piece of tail," Grundman said as Henekie shut the door.

Grundman drove over to Lena's apartment. "Are you ready to leave in the morning?" he asked her. This was very traumatic for Lena. She had it made here, or so she thought. She realized she had a lot to learn. She had thought that once her clients found out she was underage they would back off, but they had outfoxed her. Some of the girls she had hired for her escort service were younger than she was, and suddenly her age was of no consequence. She had no choice but to leave Germany as quickly as possible.

Lena had supplied consorts for too many influential people to think they would allow her to appear in court. To add to her problems, most of her money had been confiscated. Where in hell was Grundman taking her anyway, some backward island where she'd have to live in a grass shack?

"Yes," she said sounding bored, "I'm ready to leave in the morning."

Lena was more dependent on Grundman than she wanted to admit. The German police wouldn't let her leave the country, but Grundman had supplied her with false ID to get her over the Swiss border with him. They would leave for the Bahamas from there. She knew why Grundman was here, he wanted her to start paying him back now.

Besides, he had put something around her neck that she'd do anything to have. She went to work on him gradually and professionally and was quick to get a rise out of him. His mind floated away in a cocaine haze, and he thought of all the things he would be doing to Lena. He felt the juices begin to boil in his loins.

Lena sucked on the end of his cock, keeping her hand on his balls so she would know where they were at. She felt his balls move up and then eject; she quickly pulled his cock from her mouth and rubbed it against her bare chest. His cum shot out, flooding her bare skin running down between her breasts and onto her nightgown. Grundman stood with his head thrown back and his mouth open. She rose up and kissed him. "Oh! Grundman, please let me keep it." He quickly came to his senses and unclasped the necklace from her neck.

"Not yet," he told her, doing up his pants.

"Please," she pouted, putting her arms around his back and rubbing her breasts against him. Grundman laughed; he had her where he wanted her.

"It will take more than a blow job to get this," he told her and turned away walking toward the door. He stopped in the doorway, "Don't forget, we leave at six o'clock in the morning. Don't keep me waiting." He closed the door just in time to stop the ashtray aimed at his head.

That evening Rona showed up at Grundman's house. She didn't know Mona that well, but everyone knew she was a pushover when someone cried on her shoulder. She and Rona began to talk. They had a few beers and then smoked a few joints. It was still early in the evening, but the two women were in a jovial mood.

"Tell you what," said Rona, "I just met this new guy. He's not bad looking and one hell of a good fuck." They both giggled.

"Sure, phone him up," Mona told her, "and we'll try him out."

Henekie arrived on a bike half an hour later. They both met him at the door buck naked. It didn't take Henekie long to get in the mood. Rona made sure Mona got her fair share. She took hold of Henekie's hard cock and guided it into Mona then stood behind him pushing back and forth in rhythm with his strokes watching Mona squirm and heave. "Enjoy it, you bitch," she thought of the times Mona and Greta had fucked Ginter and then laughed at her. When Henekie couldn't control himself anymore, he pulled out and blew his load all over Mona.

Rona reached around from behind him and held his cock as he ejected, and then she felt herself shudder as she came herself. Henekie and Rona lay back on the couch, lighting up a joint, while Mona went into the bathroom to clean up. When she came back, Rona suggested they go for a ride on the bikes.

"You should see Henekie's new bike, Mona. He'll take you for a ride, it's brand-new."

"Look what I've got," Mona already had some white on her nose. "It's Grundman's private stash." She handed them the cocaine.

"Let's go naked," Henekie suggested. The girls were too far gone to do anything but giggle and decided it might be fun. Henekie and Mona got on Henekie's new bike while Rona followed on his old one.

It was close to midnight, but the air was still warm. There wasn't much traffic; most cars flashed by, some honked their horns, and the two girls would wave and yell back. They were having great fun. They cleared the city limits and took a narrow winding road along the river.

With no traffic for Mona to play with, she turned her attention back to Henekie, playing with his cock. He stopped, and Mona did some more coke; she was almost out of it by the time they got to the bridge. Rona pulled up beside him and watched as Henekie got off his bike and handcuffed Mona's legs and wrists to the bike leaving her straddled on top of it, tits down. Mona just lay there giggling, she was sure she was going to get fucked. Henekie and Rona got dressed with the clothes in their saddle bags and left Mona, as instructed.

Grundman took one last snort of coke and came up on Mona out of the darkness. He was already naked except for the gloves on his hands and just thinking about what he was going to do made him hard. "I'm going to give you a goodbye fuck, Mona, how's that?"

"I don't care, Grundman, I just need to get fucked," she giggled.

"I'm going to fuck you up the ass, Mona," he straddled the bike and started to work his way into her. She began to squirm, and that made him worry he would come to quick. He reached forward and pulled the bag up over her head. Now he felt her really start to jerk like a bucking horse; it was driving him mad. He came as she began to slump, and for the first time in his life he felt total satisfaction.

He lay on top of her gradually coming back to life. He pulled the bag off her head then raised the kickstand and pushed the bike over the bank of the river. The bike was stolen and had no registration. He watched as it and Mona tumbled into the water below.

Even lawyer Krugman had told him someday he was going to have to do something about that woman; she knows too much, he had warned. Well, she'd fucked around one too many times, and he'd taken the bitch out in style. He went back to his car and sniffed a little more cocaine up his nose. All he could think about was Lena.

Rona rode behind Henekie back into the city. It was around two in the morning as they stopped down the street from Grundman's apartment. Henekie walked down the street and entered the apartment. He threw the firebomb inside and walked back to where Rona was waiting with the bike. They were a long ways away when they met the first fire truck. As soon as they arrived back at Rona's house, they began making love. Henekie had never felt anything like this before. Women had always been something to get satisfaction from, good for one thing and one thing only. He'd never learned to love or be loved. Looking after himself had always been a priority.

One mistake like Ginter made, and you were gone. Maybe that was why Ginter had been so hard on Rona and the kids. He wouldn't let himself feel for them, Henekie thought, as he held his cock in Rona, looking down on her face. Rona's eyes had a look of pleasure he'd never seen before. They were partners not only in bed but in life.

"I'm not protected," Rona told him, "if you don't want to get me pregnant, you'd better pull out before you blow your load in me."

He'd never been faced with this before. "Yes, we've got enough mouths to feed," he told her. Still she'd given him the choice. And he respected her for that. Rona was out of it; her eyes shut; she bucked and twisted beneath him. He knew what he wanted to do and the shape she was in she had definitely left the decision up to him. At the last possible second, he pulled out. She held his lips to hers.

"Oh, Henekie," she moaned, "thank you." He thought she might be mad, but now for the first time he felt at peace. He fell asleep like a little baby, his mouth on Rona's nipple.

The next day when Rona went to get the kids from her sister's place, Henekie poured over the information Grundman had given him. "The daughter's the key," he thought. Henekie didn't like the idea of going back to Minnesota. But if he was going to get to Green, that was where he was going to have to go. Rona came back with the kids. They all jumped on him trying to get his attention before the other. Henekie played with the kids for a while then he went over to Rona. "I have to go away tomorrow," he told her.

"I know," she smiled, "we still have tonight." The problem, he realized, was that he didn't really want to go; distractions in his business could be deadly. Hopefully, once he was away from here, he could forget all this and concentrate on the business at hand.

The next day he was on a plane to the United States. He spent the first night in New York and went right to sleep. The next night he slept in Minneapolis. Already he was horny, wishing Rona's warm body was next to his.

# SEVENTEEN

THE WOMEN RAN the farm when the men were away. In fact, the men were so distracted that the project actually ran better when they were away. The girls knew they could get more out of the people working there than the men could. The men were too easy on them.

The girls were actually clones of the men. Pearl looked after the office, while Hania and July looked after the field work. Hania spent most of her time in the produce barns, leaving July to roam the fields, making sure the work got done. Often, she worked in the evenings when it wasn't so hot. That's when most of the picking and harvesting was done.

Today, she had gone out early. One of the irrigation pumps had broken down, and she had to make sure it was fixed. It was a terribly hot day, but now the early evening breeze had begun to cool the air.

July drove her pickup with the windows open trying to get the air to cool her sweaty body. She'd just have time for a shower and a bite to eat before she went back to the fields, she thought as she pulled up to her lane.

Down the road, she noticed two cars; one was a police car. They were parked in front of the Drinkwaters' and Shonavons' houses which were side by side. July nearly went down to see what was going on, and then she thought better of it. She was tired; they'd let her know soon enough if there was a problem. She parked the truck and went in the house, glad to be out of the hot sun. Sitting at her kitchen table was Horatio Norton.

"You startled me," July gasped, putting her hand to her sweaty chest.

"July," he said, "listen and listen carefully. You, Hania, and Pearl have all been deported. The police from Nassau are with Pearl and Hania right now. I told them I would wait for you."

"Why?" was all July could say.

"It's not totally clear," Horatio told her, "but it's got something to do with your husbands."

"Are they all right?" July asked.

"Yes, I think so," he answered. "What bothers me, July, is that Pearl and Hania are being sent back to Canada, but you're to be detained here in the Bahamas. I find that very odd. The other thing is that I cannot find out why you're being detained or where the order is coming from."

July sensed he was trying to tell her something. "What can I do?" she asked him.

"If I were you, I'd take your boat and get the hell out of here. You can meet Rikker coming back from school, that way he'll be safe too. That's all I can do for you, July, the rest is up to you."

"What about Bob?" said July, starting to panic.

"You're no good to him if they hold you somewhere, now get going."

July grabbed the keys to the boat off the wall peg and headed out to the dock. She heard voices in the house as she untied the boat and pushed off. She sat behind the steering wheel and turned the key, but the engine wouldn't start. Don't panic, she told herself. She gave it some choke and the engine coughed to life. July headed across the lake, never looking back.

When they had first come here, the channel from Fresh Creek to the lake was overgrown and too narrow to navigate. The men had gone to work clearing and widening it big enough for small boats to push through. It was a good quarter of a mile before the channel widened, and she dared look back. No one was in sight; her heart began to settle down.

There were enough kids on the project now that a school bus hauled them back and forth to school. A new road to False Creek had shortened the trip considerably. Rikker still preferred to ride his Sea-Doo if the weather was good.

She met him just as she came into the main stream. She waved him over and told him what had happened. She was proud of Rikker; he had grown into a good-looking young man, well liked by everyone, especially the girls. He had begun to remind her more and more of his dad with his smile and stubborn determination.

Last week they had taken some boys from Andros over to Nassau to play soccer. Nassau was a far superior team, but Rikker had his team full of confidence. It was Rikker's determination that had inspired the team. They hadn't won, but the other team knew they were in a game right to the end. He was the kind of man who would make something of the Bahamas someday, that was if they got to stay.

Rikker was hopping mad, but his mother cooled him down. "We'll worry about all that later," she told him. "Right now we have to find a place to hide."

"Let's go to the old barrel shack," he told her, "at least we'll have a roof over our heads."

It was just a small shed with a dock. It was used to store barrels of fuel for the bigger boats that came up Fresh Creek bringing in supplies. Here the supplies would be loaded onto smaller boats as the water became too shallow for the big boats to navigate. The big boats would refuel from the shack before heading back down the creek. Now with the better roads, the shack wasn't used anymore.

That night, Riker went back to the project to find out what was going down. When he came back, he had some sandwiches and coffee that he had stolen from the APCO kitchen. "Everybody's scared," he told her. "They don't know what's going to happen. I saw two APCO guys in our office going through the papers."

They put the top up on the boat and closed it, so they could sleep on the soft seats. Really, they had nowhere to go.

The next day, July hid their boat in a little channel near the shack. Rikker headed down to Fresh Creek town to see if he could get help.

An hour later, July heard the plane and watched from the shack as it flew low over the creek. There was no way they could see the boat, but she was worried about Rikker. He also heard the plane before he saw it.

He'd been skirting along the edge of the creek and stopped under some overgrowth to watch the plane appear and then disappear over the trees. He continued down the creek till he came within view of the bridge. He parked his Sea-Doo in some weeds.

The town itself was built at the mouth of the creek along both sides. A rusted steel bridge connected one side to the other and was the only access to the naval base. He walked along the bank until he saw a man standing on the bridge. He then skirted around the bridge going through the town and then back toward the creek where the fishing boats docked. He was in luck; Arthur's brother's boat was there. Rikker found him working on his engine.

He wiped his hands on a rag and shook hands with Rikker, a big grin on his face. Arthur's brother no longer grinned as Rikker told him what had happened. He took Rikker up to see Skinny, who had been fast friends with Bob and July since they had first started coming to Andros long ago.

They sat in Skinny's office discussing what was going down. "I'll find out what I can," Skinny told Rikker. Arthur's brother said he would bring some supplies that night. "That's as good a place to hide as any until we can move you out of there," he told Rikker.

Rikker told him there was a man watching the bridge. He headed back to his mother.

Later that night, Arthur's brought some blankets, food, and a small camp stove.

"We'll get you out of here as soon as we can find a place where you'll be safe. It's not easy to hide a woman as well-known as you," he smiled.

It was around noon the next day when they first heard the boat. July had just cooked lunch on the tiny stove. Both she and Rikker lifted their heads at the same time. Few boats came this far upstream, especially powerful-sounding ones. They both knew what it meant.

"They'll check here for sure," Rikker said, "let's get to the boat."

They jumped off the dock and ran down the little path to the hidden channel where the boat and Sea-Doo sat.

"Help me push the boat out to the creek," Rikker told his mom.

He sounded so much like his father that she didn't even question his motive. They could hear the powerboat slowing to land at the barrel shack as Riker took the mooring rope and then tied it around the outboard engine of July's boat. Then standing beside it, he started the engine and set it in gear. The boat leapt from the cover of the bushes hiding the channel and headed across the creek. Even this far upstream, the tide still affected the creek, making it a good one hundred feet wide. They heard the powerful motors of the other boat fire up to give chase.

July climbed on behind Rikker as they left their hiding place heading the Sea-Doo upstream for shallow water. It didn't take long for July's riderless boat to plow into the other bank of the creek.

The men on the powerboat quickly saw Rikker and July on the Sea-Doo and gave chase. Rikker thought the distraction would be enough of a head start to get them into where the water was too shallow for them to follow. What he didn't know was that the craft following them was a jet boat with a very shallow draft. They could go in water almost as shallow as he could.

July watched the powerboat gaining behind them. For a minute, she thought they might make the channel to the lake which was definitely too narrow for the speedboat. Now she saw that this was impossible.

"It's me they want," she hollered in Rikker's ear, "keep going, they'll stop to pick me up if I jump off."

"I'm not leaving you," Rikker hollered back, intent on making the channel.

"Someone's got to warn your dad," July told him. "You know he'll come for us, they won't hurt me, it's him they want."

With that, he felt her let go. She turned a somersault in the water behind the Sea-Doo before coming to a stop. The water was only up to her waist as she stood up sputtering. The powerboat pulled up right beside her; she tried to swim away, but they were on her. She kicked and swung at them until she was played out, and then they loaded her into the boat.

Rikker turned to watch from the mouth of the narrow lake channel. He saw one of the men point at him. The man driving the boat shook his head and turned the boat back down the creek.

July lay in the bottom of the boat completely exhausted. She saw there were five men in the boat with her. All of them were black, and all of them were armed. The boat continued down the creek for a ways and then stopped. July looked up to see them hook a tow rope to her wrecked boat and begin pulling it downstream.

They went until they found a place along the edge where there was a small inlet. Two of the men pushed the wrecked boat in as far as they could then sank it. To July's surprise, they headed back upstream stopping at the barrel shack.

Here they removed everything that she and Rikker had put in the shack, painstakingly making sure to remove every trace of anyone being there. Then except for the driver, all found some shade to sleep.

"Might as well make yourself comfortable, Mrs. Green," the driver said, throwing a tarp over the windshield of the boat to protect them from the sun. "We'll be here till sunset."

It was almost pitch black when July saw the old steel bridge at French Creek pass overhead. She could see the lights along the edge of the creek from where she was lying on the bottom of the boat.

"We're heading out to the ocean," she thought. The water was choppy, making the ride rough in the bottom of the boat. July tried to sit up, but a rough hand would quickly push her down again. It seemed to July the ride went on forever, but suddenly they slowed and then came to a stop. She struggled to get up, but two of the men grabbed her and held her down while a third stuck a needle in her arm. She fought it as long as she could, but she became very tired.

"I'm going to sleep now, Bob," she murmured.

The driver of the boat was on the radio.

"The harbor patrol is just going by now," a voice said, "wait another fifteen minutes and then come on in."

"Roger," the driver answered, looking at his watch. He waited until the time had gone by then headed into the harbor coming to the APCO warehouse along the waterfront and drove inside. They tied up the boat as the huge front door closed behind them.

"I see you had good luck hunting," Manly Waddell said to the men as they lifted July's sleeping body from the boat. He led the way, showing the men a room to put her in.

"Okay, I'll look after her from here on in," he told the men. They smiled and left him alone.

July still had the same clothes she'd worn the day she'd taken the boat from the project. Manly took them off her body, undressing her until she was naked. He bent down and kissed her nipples, and then he ran his hand along the inside of her thighs and put his finger up inside her. He felt the lust come in his loins, "Not just yet," he said to himself, "not till you come to me will I give you my seed."

He fondled her breasts, hating to leave her. He set the glass on a small table beside her cot. "This will help you understand how much you want me," he told her then left the room and locked the door. He went upstairs to where a TV screen monitored the room July was in.

The man watching the screen turned to him. "She's beautiful, isn't she?"

Manly grinned, "Better than most of the riffraff you get in here. Probably has you going off in your pants," he laughed.

He was Waddell's interrogation expert. He had learned his trade from Castro before escaping to find better-paying employers. He had shown Manly how, instead of torture, he could with the use of drugs, turn the hardest of men into blithering idiots. He had also assured Manly he could turn this woman into a totally submissive piece of flesh catering to his every command.

Waddell had no worries of this man ever bothering July. He was as gay as they came.

"How long do you think?" Manly asked him.

"A woman is always more susceptible to these drugs than a man. Their metabolism seems to break down the drugs quicker. I'd say we could have her ready in thirty-six hours."

"Perfect," Manly told him. It would nicely give him time to get ready.

When July woke up, there was a bright light in her eyes. She rolled over and sat up. She was in a white room, everything was white.

"Where am I?" she thought, "I'm so thirsty." She saw the glass on the table and reached for it. She tasted it and then drank it all. She stood up shading her eyes from the light and felt the white walls. "I'm tired," she said to herself, crawling back into the cot and falling asleep.

An hour later, something woke her up again. It was pitch black in the room except for a window high on one wall. There was just enough light for her to make out the glass on the table. "It must be night," she thought, "how long have I been sleeping?" Her thirst was overwhelming; "I emptied the glass," she thought but reached for it anyway. "Maybe I didn't drink it," she thought, finding the glass full. She drank it, and then fell back asleep.

This went on hour after hour. She didn't know if it was night or day and whether she slept all night or all day. As the time went on, she became more and more confused, breaking down at times, eyes wide open and insomniac at others.

"She's coming around much faster than I thought, Manly," the interrogation expert told him. "I think you should talk with her."

Manly sat and held her hand. She was crying. She sat up and hugged him. He could feel the heat from her bosom against his chest.

"I'll help you," he told her. "I won't let anyone hurt you." He looked up at the camera and smiled.

"I think we're peaking here too early," Manly's man told him. "I think we'd better cut back the dosage and ease up a bit. You don't want her to be a zombie, do you?"

"No," Manly answered. "I want her to know exactly what's happening."

The second day, Manly came to see her again. Then a woman came to see her. She gave her a shirt to wear and combed her hair.

"Thank you," July said.

"Manly told me to help you. He's very nice, isn't he?"

"Yes," July said, "he's very good to me

"Manly loves you very much," she told July. "He wants you to live with him so he can look after you."

"Yes," July said, "I need him to help me."

On the fourth day, Manly and the expert watched July on the TV screen. She sat with her head down very passively.

"I want her to be at her very best tonight," Manly said.

His expert smiled, "I have some different drugs to administer today, and she'll spread her legs as soon as she sees you."

Manly tried not to show it, but he was shaking with excitement.

July hadn't eaten for a long time. Now the black woman brought July some soup and made her eat it. She couldn't really taste it, but she ate it anyway. She began to feel better. Manly came to see her.

"I will take you away from all this," he told her. "You will come with me, and I will look after you."

"Thank you," was all she could say.

"Tonight you will come to me, and we will be one." Then he left.

July felt confused. "Am I going away?" she asked the black woman.

"Yes." The black woman began combing her hair, "We must make you look pretty for tonight. Many years ago, before the white man, these islands were owned by the black man. They had kings who ruled their own people and their lands. That was a long time ago, but some people still believe in witchcraft and voodoo and follow the old ways. Manly is the king of his people, and they follow him through the power of his ancestors."

July's mind somehow parted the curtain hung over her memory. She remembered the raw savagery she saw in Waddell, the primitive sexuality he exuded, and she knew what the woman was telling her.

"Who are you?" July saw this woman for the first time. She was beautiful, not young but not old.

"I am his queen," she told July.

July looked at her, "Then why is he to be with me?"

The woman looked at July; the smile disappeared from her face, "Because until now he could not have you. Now he is consumed by your beauty. He wants you to have his child."

July thought this was so beautiful. It would be so nice to be with Manly, to feel his body on hers, to feel him in her. She felt the wetness between her legs.

The black woman made her drink her medicine, and then another woman came and they bathed her. Afterward they began to rub July's body with oil.

It felt so good, July giggled. She felt the anticipation build up in her like she was sixteen again. The two women oiled her body till it shone. They fixed her face and hair. She felt beautiful.

"It's time," the black woman said, and they guided her out of the room.

She felt the fresh air hit her face as they led her out of the building. It was very dark, but she could see the glow of light ahead. July turned to the black woman beside her who said, "If you are his queen, then you should have his baby."

"I have his children" she told July. "But that doesn't matter now, he wants you."

Something tugged at July's mind. "That's not right," she heard herself say.

They came into the torch light, the fire bothered her eyes like the white light she remembered. The drums; she'd heard these drums once before a long time ago. She'd been with a man; they were on a beach, and they were listening to the drums. Her mind came back to the present.

There was Manly straight ahead. She felt her heart skip. He was standing in front of a wall that was painted with many different scenes. He was naked, but his face was painted as well as his chest. Then her eyes riveted to his huge phallus. It stood hard and strong in front of him, its ebony knob shining in the flickering light.

She stopped, the drums again pounding in her head; her mind was like a fog that was clearing. Now she heard the chanting, and she was becoming confused again, "Who was that man I was with on the beach?" She shut her eyes trying to remember.

The two women left her. She opened her eyes again seeing Manly standing there so inviting. On each side of him hung a brightly colored red and yellow rooster.

"Voodoo," the black woman had said.

She had called him a king, but if she was his queen, shouldn't she be the one to do this? July's mind tried to reason. But his beautiful body beckoned to her. She walked toward him smiling, knowing what she wanted now.

She stood in front of him, her nipples puckered in anticipation. She reached down and ran her hand up and down his hard phallus. He spread his legs slightly as she cupped his balls. She moved closer, rubbing her breasts against his chest. The sound of the drums and chanting grew louder in her ears as she suddenly brought her knee up to his balls. The air went out of him, and he dropped like a rock. On his way down, she kneed him in the face seeing blood spurt from his nose. Then she turned and ran.

Someone put their arms around her, but the oil made her slippery, and they slid off behind her. She ran and suddenly it was dark, and she felt trees slap and scratch her body as she flew by. Her mind cleared as she ran; it was like a fog lifting and then settling again, each wave a little clearer. She ran until she came to a wall. She could almost reach the top, but she didn't have the strength to pull herself over.

She leaned against the wall shivering, her breath coming in short gasps. She could see the torches coming through the trees, getting brighter, bright enough for her to see a garden fork stuck in the middle of a freshly dug flower bed. She took the fork and leaned it against the wall. July stepped up on the top of the fork and then put her toe in the handle and pushed herself up, grabbing the top of the wall and pulling herself over. She landed and rolled flat on the ground. She as much felt the asphalt as she saw it; road, she realized, and began running down it toward some lights. She didn't run far before she came to a residential area.

"I'm sure this is Nassau," she spoke to herself. It was very late at night, she decided; no one was around. It was a very rundown part of town. She heard a horn in the distance. "I'm in the harbor district," she thought.

In a backyard, she saw a huge pair of pants hanging from a clothesline. She took them and ran just as a dog came around the corner of the house and barked at her. She kept going trying to put the pants on as she ran. The pants were big enough for three of her, the only advantage being she could pull them right up under her armpits, covering more of her body.

She came to a crossroad she recognized. Two blocks up lived her friend, Sir Harry Chamberlain, from the British embassy. For a long time after she had left him standing in the Crystal Palace, he wouldn't talk to her. Then one night after a photo shoot for the Bahamian Travel Bureau, she went with some people who were invited to his house for a party. She'd taken him aside and told him the whole story. They had both laughed. He had thought it hilarious that he had unwittingly outfoxed Waddell, whom he had absolutely no use for. After that night, they had become fast friends, although she'd seen little of him.

She knocked on the door pulling her pants up expecting to have to try to explain to a servant why she wanted in. She was surprised to see Sir Harry answer it himself.

"I don't suppose I could borrow a cup of sugar," she said to him.

He tried to smile, but the look of her scared him. "Whatever happened to you?" He guided her through the doorway.

"I need a place to stay," she leaned against him.

"Well, you've come to the right place," Sir Harry told her, turning her back toward him and putting his dressing gown over her shoulders.

She thanked him. "Our mutual friend has been spinning his fan of shit again," she told him.

"You're asleep on your feet," Sir Harry told her, "you can tell me about it in the morning."

He showed July to his guest room and then came back down to his den. He picked up the phone and dialed a number. A voice answered the other end of the line.

"Guess who just came to visit me?" he said.

# EIGHTEEN

I COME FLYING OUT of bed; the dreams are getting worse instead of better. Damn it, Arthur, you have to call me soon, or I'm going to go out of my mind. The more I sit and wait, the more my memories bother me. Every night I wake up in a cold sweat. It's always the same dream; I see a face and then it explodes, pieces flying everywhere, but the face still looks at me laughing. I tell myself I have no remorse. He would have killed me given the chance. Killing a man is very traumatic. It works on my mind. If only Arthur would call then my mind would be busy again, hopefully too busy to remember.

Yesterday as I laid on the beach, two cops walked by carefully looking at all the people. I didn't see them coming, and I laid very still watching as they passed by. They were definitely looking for someone, it could well be me.

Every night I make my excursion to the phone booth. When it rings tonight, it startles me. I'm not sure I can handle much more if Arthur has bad news for me.

"Hello," I say into the phone.

"It's on for tonight," he tells me. "Be at the dredger by midnight."

"What about July and Rikker?" I ask.

"My brother will tell you when you reach his boat," then he hung up.

Something's not right, I can feel it. Maybe it's just in my mind. I have to shrug it off, get rid of my depression.

That evening I take a bus to the edge of Pompano Beach. It's a good two-mile walk to where the dredger is, but it's a cloudy night and few people are around, the walk will kill time. I stand and watch the dredger work, pumping sand out of its excursion pipes. There are no lights on the barge; it just appears out of the night. A black man jumps off and walks toward me.

"Hello," is all he says and holds out his hand. I reach out to shake it, but he pulls it back.

"Money," he says.

"I give him his money, and he waves me aboard his barge."

He heads the barge straight out to sea. The shore lights get smaller and smaller. I realize we are getting a long way out, at least two miles, maybe more. Suddenly, the moon shows its face through the clouds, and I can see the old fishing trawler that I had traveled on between Andros and Nassau many times before.

I climb on board with the help of Arthur's brother, and we leave the barge behind. The moon has gone behind the clouds again, but the sky is broken and it threatens to break out at any time.

He invites me to join him in a cup of coffee up in the wheelhouse. His helper leaves to go out on deck leaving us alone.

"It's been a long time," I tell him.

"I would have thought you'd lived long enough in the Bahamas to get the hang of waiting, Mr. Green. Waiting always makes time go slowly. I spend half of my time waiting, waiting for the fish, waiting for my boat to be fixed, and waiting for the right time to move men where they want to go. Patience is something you learn in this business," he smiles, "or you don't stay in it long."

He is right, it really hadn't been such a long time since I saw him last, not in Bahamian time anyway. Everything would get done in time, tomorrow was just another day to their way of thinking.

"I apologize, it's just that I'm worried about July and Rikker. I didn't mean to be sarcastic."

"You have a right to be worried about your wife, Mr. Green. We believe Mr. Waddell is holding her."

Somehow, this news does not surprise me. "Why would he want her?" I ask.

"I don't know," Arthur's brother shrugs. "Maybe because he knows you'll come for her, so he can kill you."

This does not totally make sense, or Waddell would not have tried to have me killed up in Canada. This is really irrelevant right now, I decide.

"Did they take Rikker too?" I ask.

"No, Rikker's been staying at Skinny's." He relates the story just as Rikker had told it to him. "After they took July, he hid out on the project for a few days then came down the creek at night. He's been at Skinny's waiting for you to show up at Buzzard Bay."

"Why there?" I ask.

"Because they're watching everywhere else like hawks, but at Buzzard Bay everyone minds their own business, if they want to stay healthy."

"That's got to stop!" I hit the table with my fist. "There's one man who is the key to all this, and he has to be stopped."

"It's much deeper than that," Arthur's brother tells me. "You can cut off an arm, but the monster will survive. You have to go deeper than that. You are the key, not the man you're after, but you can't do it alone. We will do all we can to help you because we believe in you. You know how the drugs are coming in, and you know how they go out. You know too much and the drug people want you dead. Their tentacles are everywhere. Did you ever think that they're willing to sacrifice Waddell to get you?"

I took a long drink from my coffee cup. How often we underestimate the common people of the world. From them come the words, 'common sense'.

Until now, my mind has been obsessed with one man. He is a danger to my family, but deep down I know that once I get to him I have no plan, no idea what I would do.

"It's good you're here," he tells me, "your son reminds me of you, and he's ready to go after Manly Waddell too. If you didn't get here soon, I don't think we could have controlled him much longer. That's why we wanted to get him involved, so we could get his mind off Waddell. We weren't happy with the idea that it's him meeting you at Buzzard Bay. We know it's dangerous, but he needs to feel important right now, I hope you understand."

"I'm beginning to understand a lot of things," I tell him. "Thank you."

We had caught up on a lot of things when the deck hand broke in.

"Boss," he sounds excited, "there's a boat closing in fast. It could be the Coast Guard."

Arthur's brother looks at me, "Okay, you're going to have to go over the side. On the left side of the boat under the gunnel is a handle, it's just under the water line. Hang on to it until they leave."

I am just over the side when our boat is bathed in light. First, I can hear a siren, and then a voice over a loudspeaker telling us they are coming aboard. Minutes later a boat pulls up beside ours and I hear the Coast Guard come aboard. Arthur's brother skillfully keeps the boat's other side turned toward their ship's bright light.

"What are you doing in American waters?" I can hear the officer ask.

Arthur's brother explains to him that he had found a reef with good fishing just inside the Bahamian waters. He shows the officer on his chart, "We came around from the American side and then drifted over the reef."

"You're a long way into American waters for that," the officer tells him.

Arthur's brother explains that the clouds had made it difficult to navigate, and they had lost their way, but they were back on course now. "As you can see, we are only about five miles from the reef," he shows the officer by drawing on the chart.

A flashlight beam suddenly appears in the water on my side of the boat. I watch as the beam comes toward me, submerging my head at the last second as the flashlight focuses on where I had been. Whoever is holding the flashlight has to lean way out to see in under the bow where I am hiding.

He is very thorough, taking his time; my lungs are bursting before the beam disappears.

"All right," I hear someone say, "you can continue on, we'll escort you into Bahamian waters."

Arthur's brother comes and stands over to where I am hiding. "I've got to start moving," he says in a low voice. "I'll try to go as slow as I can without raising suspicion. Hang on, it's going to be tough, but hopefully they'll tire of us soon."

The wake from the water hitting the bow makes the waves explode over my head, making it hard to breathe. I hang on to the handle for dear life, but there is tremendous pressure on my arms, and I don't know how long I can hang on.

Something black heads toward me. "A shark," I scream. It comes at me hitting my face; it feels soft and cold like plastic. I open my eyes; there are lots of black objects all around me. Garbage bags, I realize as my heart slows down and I begin to breathe again. I can't hang on any longer, I tell myself it's over. The boat is not bathed in light anymore, and I feel it slow down.

I hear a voice, "Are you still with us?"

"Just barely," I tell him, "I can't hang on any longer."

The boat doesn't stop completely, but a rope appears over the bow and I grab it. "Try to slip the loop over your body," I hear him say. Slowly, they pull me up and over the edge of the boat. I lay totally exhausted.

"Lucky for us, the Americans were interested in that garbage. They stopped to pick some up. If they can find out which cruise ship dropped it in American waters, they'll be in deep shit."Arthur's brother is grinning.

"I thought the bags were sharks," I confess. "I'm sure I pissed my pants."

He starts to laugh as he tells me to get out of my wet clothes handing me dry ones. I curl up under a tarp and fall asleep.

Arthur's brother shakes me awake. "I was hoping to get here before daylight," he tells me, "but the Coast Guard slowed us down too much."

I look up over the side of the boat. I recognize the shore line of Buzzard Bay.

"We'll go in and fuel up. Stay under the tarp until we're docked. I'll make sure it's clear before you leave."

I feel the boat hit the dock; a minute later, he tells me it's time to go.

"I hope Rikker is patient enough to have waited for you. Just stay to the trees along the road, he's supposed to be waiting for you somewhere along the way."

I shake his hand and quickly make a run for the trees, anxious to see Rikker again. I haven't gone far, when from behind me I hear a "Yo!" I turn around; in my eyes I see a young man, not the boy I remember. I'm suddenly very proud.

"How you doing?" He embraces me and tears come to my eyes. I try not to let him see.

"How's it going?" I don't know what to say.

"It's going great now that you are back." He goes into the edge of the trees and pushes out a motorbike.

"So where'd you get a bike?" I ask.

"It belongs to Peter Norton, you know, the police captain's son."

This is getting more bizarre all the time. "You just borrow it?" I ask.

"No, his dad told me to use it to pick you up," Rikker tells me as he tosses me a helmet.

"For Christ's sake, Rikker, I haven't fought my way across a continent to have myself arrested riding a local yokel cop's motorcycle."

"Settle down, Pops, the old cholesterol's getting pretty high."

"What the hell are you doing talking to him anyway? It's amazing he didn't arrest you too," I fume.

"Nope," he says, "they forgot to name me on the deportation order. As far as Captain Norton's concerned, I don't even exist. He'd have picked you up himself except he's in enough trouble for letting Mom get away."

"He knew I'd come through Andros on my way to Nassau, didn't he?"

"Well, he's not stupid, you know!" Rikker responds. "He asked me to ask you what you planned to do when you got to Nassau." I don't get a chance to answer because Rikker keeps right on talking. "I told him you were fucking well going to cut Manly Waddell's throat, or I would do it for you."

I look at him feeling the same hate he does, yet blaming myself for being so immature. Now I have to play the part of the wise old dad.

"You realize, Rikker, that if we just go and kill him, that would be the end of us. We'd rot in jail, no good to anyone especially your mother."

"Yeah, that's exactly what Captain Norton told me too, but you didn't see them take Mom," he was mad and almost in tears. "Mr. Norton told me you've got one chance. A man by the name of Sir Harry Chamberlain can help you get Waddell."

"I remember Mom talking about him," I tell Rikker, "Seems to me he works for the British embassy."

"Mr. Norton also told me that this guy knows where Mom is, but I don't know, it could be a trap," Rikker states.

"Do you think Captain Norton would lead us into a trap?" I ask Rikker.

"We'll find out riding this motorbike back to Skinny's," Rikker grins. Rikker sees I have the same idea and that I am a little hesitant.

"Put your helmet on, Dad, there are lots of tourists on the island this week. That's the nice thing about these helmets, nobody recognizes you."

I look out the sun-tinted helmet visor. "Let's hope you're right," I tell him.

It's a long ride across the island from Buzzard Bay to French Creek. My ass is pretty sore by the time we get to Skinny's, but I don't let Rikker know that. It's one thing for your kid to call you old , but it's another thing to admit it.

I have a good visit with Skinny and his family. They fill me in on a lot of things that are happening in the islands, but after a good night's sleep, I am anxious to find my way to Nassau.

"Arthur's brother says it's impossible for him to take you. They check him every time he goes to Nassau," Skinny tells me. "He didn't want me to tell you, but his boat was ransacked last night, and he was roughed up."

"By who?" I ask.

"It's pretty obvious they were looking for you, so you tell me, who isn't after you?" Skinny says, looking perturbed.

"Well, that does leave the door open," I realize. "I can't think of anyone who isn't looking for me."

"I think we are going to have to move you," Skinny tells me. "I'm sure there were eyes and ears at Buzzard Bay. It won't be long till someone shows up here nosing around."

Just then Rikker shows up with one of his friends. "Hi Pops, this is Peter Norton."

I stand up and shake hands with Rikker's young friend.

"I know your dad quite well," I tell him.

"Yes, my father speaks of you a lot, that's why we are here to help."

I smile, "We'll need lots of that. Right now I need a place to hide."

"No, you don't, Pops, you need to get to Nassau right away, and I'm going to drive you."

"What, you stole a boat?" I ask him.

"No, we're taking the Sea-Doo and don't say no, you have no choice. There's a car in town right now with four men in it. They're checking out the town, and they'll find out you're here, it's only a matter of time."

"That's a long way," I say. "Will it make it?"

"We figured it out," Peter Norton said, "enough gas for three hours flat out. It's about fifty miles, and the weather's decent. Should be no problem."

"Yeah, right." I'd seen how quick a squall could come up. "Where's the Sea-Doo?" I ask.

"I hid it in some weeds up French Creek," Rikker said.

"So how do we get it out of there?" I ask.

"Peter here is going to take it out of Fresh Creek and meet us farther up the shore."

"How do we get over there?"

"Same way we got here," Rikker tells me. "We ride the motorbike over across the bridge. There's a trail down to the beach."

It sounds simple, and simple plans often work.

"Okay," I decide, "Let's go for it. Those who hesitate are lost," is what I think of; if I wait too long, I'll probably change my mind.

Rikker and I haven't gone far when we meet a car with four men in it. We pass the car and keep going; as we turn a corner, I look back and see the car is turning around.

"Hustle," I yell to Rikker, "I think they're going to follow us."

The resulting ride scares me nearly as much as the men chasing us. We cross the bridge and almost immediately turn off onto a narrow foot path. Rikker stops. In a minute, we see the car fly by on the road.

"They'll be back," I tell him, "We'd best keep going."

We continue down the path stopping at the edge of the beach. We are pretty edgy by the time we finally see Peter riding in on the Sea-Doo through the pounding surf.

"I've got to do this alone, Rikker," I tell him.

"Fuck, Dad, the only time you even rode a Sea-Doo was the first day we got it, and then you fell off just horsing around."

I look up at the palm leaves blowing in the breeze. "I'm lucky to have you," I tell him. "I'm going to tell you the same thing I told Mindy when she helped me. I have to have you here in case I need you. I'll get a hold of you through the Nortons. I would like it if you would stay with them. They're good people, and you'll be safe there. If something happens to me, you'll have to look after Mom." I go on, "If I don't get to her, I know you'll try, just be careful and plan everything you do." I take him by the shoulders and look him straight in the eye. "Promise me you'll try to make something of these islands that your mom and I love so much." It was a lot to put on the shoulders of a young boy.

He grabs me and holds me close, and his voice is full of tears. "You get Mom for us, Dad. So we can make this our home."

My eyes fill full of tears as I feel the warm Bahamas breeze that July loves so much. "I love you, Rikker," I tell him, holding him again at arm's length. "It feels like we are always leaving each other, but someday soon we'll be a family again, and we'll always remember these moments. I'll get Mom, Rikker, and the people who took her are going to have to pay along the way."

Suddenly Peter is standing beside us. He hands Rikker a compass which he in turn hands to me.

"I'm not going," he tells Peter.

"My dad says not to forget what he told you about this Chamberlain fellow." Peter hands me the address "Dad says it's your only hope.

Now I get some instructions that make a lot of sense to me. The boys tell me the mail boat will be passing by in a half hour or so. I'm to go out and wait for it and then stay in it's wake until I see Nassau. "They might even stop and help if you fall off" Rikker tells me.

"Watch out for the guys in the car," I tell them.

"No problem," Peter says, "we're just two guys out for a ride."

I smile, "Yeah, I guess I'd better worry about myself. You guys can handle yourselves.

I impress the shit out of them by falling off the Sea-Doo twice in the surf as it hit the beach. Out farther, it's better going when I tuck in behind the mail boat. Two fishermen slip their boat beside me about half way across and together we follow the mail boat into Nassau.

The island of New Providence appears on the horizon much quicker than I thought it would. Soon, I can make out the multicolored houses running back up Spy Hill. As I come into Nassau, I worry about someone wondering who I am. My worries are soon pacified as there are other water craft running all over the place. I find a public beach where there are other Sea-Doos parked. I just pull mine in with them. I recognize the area; it's part of Cable Beach. Too far to walk downtown, but the public buses run every five minutes or so. I mix in with some tourists leaving the beach as they walk back up to their hotel.

There is always someone waiting in front of the hotels for the bus. I stand waiting trying to stay in a crowd. Once on the bus, I feel safer. I get off near the Straw Market, the major center in Nassau for tourists. I would feel better if there were more people around. I begin to realize I really don't want to go to Chamberlain's house. I don't trust anyone anymore, yet here I am in Nassau, where I had planned for weeks to get to and now that I am here, I have no idea what to do.

I wander through the market contemplating my next move, trying to get straight in my mind what Arthur's brother and old Norton know that I don't but the fact is I have to trust someone, and they'd always been straight shooters.

Just walking up to Waddell and killing him is the idea of a man obsessed with one goal in life. I now realize that that goal is unrealistic and it's not necessarily going to get July back. To get her back to the family is really my goal.

I take a deep breath and start walking in the direction of Chamberlain's address. On the way, I think, maybe I'll watch the house for a while, or I could look in the windows to see what's inside. I'd never met the man other than July pointing him out at a function we had attended once; plus her telling me that he had helped her leave one of Waddell's parties. That's all I know about the man.

The address turns out to be an apartment attached to the British embassy. I stand in front of the door, straighten my shoulders, and knock. An elderly black lady answers the door.

"Hello," I say, "I have just had an accident down the street. May I use your phone?"

"Yes, come in," she tells me. "I will get Mr. Chamberlain. He will lead you to a phone." She is back in a moment. "Follow me, please."

She leads me into a large room. I recognize Sir Harry Chamberlain sitting on a couch with another man. To my astonishment, the other man is Constable Novak from the Royal Canadian Mounted Police.

"Hello, Mr. Green," Chamberlain says, "it's about time you got here."

I feel totally dejected to have it all end like this after what I have been through.

"There are a lot of people looking for you," he smiles, "you are very lucky you were able to get to us."

"Lucky for you I walked right into your house," I retort.

"Yes, it took a lot of patience on our part, but Novak here assured us you'd be ingenious enough to get through."

"Who in the hell are you?"

"I work for British Intelligence, and you know where Novak's from. Right now, I'm part of the Interpol organization looking into the illegal drug trade. Novak's on loan to us for a while."

"So what's this got to do with me?" I ask.

"For some reason, people who we believe are involved in this business are very interested in getting rid of you. That would indicate to us that you know more about them and their business than they would like," Chamberlain tells me.

"Look!" I've seen a few things and know a few people who may be involved in some things they shouldn't be, but what I really know is shit, I can't prove any of it."

"Sometimes it's not what you actually know but what they think you know that makes you dangerous to them." Chamberlain interjects, "The fact remains that someone wants you dead."

I decide not to banter with him anymore. "There are a few things I want to know which are very important to me," I tell him. "First off, I hear you might know where July is?"

"Yes, we do. Let us relieve your mind by telling you she is safe and in very good hands."

"Whose hands?" I ask, although I do feel relieved.

"All in good time, Bob. I think we should go back and make sure we have everything straight in our minds before we go any further."

Novak is still sitting on the couch. He's been going through a folder.

"My information may be one-sided, Bob, so I'll tell you what we have here and hopefully you can fill us in," he spoke for the first time. "We presume you suspect the same person we do as to whose responsible in the attempt on your life?"

I smile, "I saw a newspaper with a picture of me in it wanted on suspicion of murder. Now you ask me if I am a victim?"

Novak looks up at me. "We always knew there were extenuating circumstances, and yes, at first, we did think you were involved in a local murder. Especially when you lied about where the Drinkwaters and the Shonavons were. You probably still don't know for sure, but yes, those were their bodies discovered in your mother's house. However, we discovered three more bodies. Two, along the run in Helek's field, another along the White Fox Valley. They had been shot to death by an unknown assailant. Then later, we found Constable Reich shot to death, but we'll get to that later. What I want to know is, did you kill any of these men we found shot?"

"I'm not even sure I know what you're talking about," I tell him.

Chamberlain quickly broke in, "Quit the bullshit, Bob. I could sit and bullshit with you all day, but I'm out of patience. So I'll put it this way, and it's no idle threat. If you want to see July again, you'd better play ball. We pretty well know what happened, we just want it confirmed."

"Okay, all right," I say meekly, knowing he means it. "No, I don't know any of those men, but I think Manly Waddell sent them to kill all of us."

"Then we're on the same wavelength," Novak nods in agreement.

I tell them the whole story as I remember it. "I felt if I didn't get down here and help July, no one would," I finish up.

Novak jots down a few notes. "Okay," he says, "it took a while, but we sent pictures of the two men to Interpol. One of them they identified as a mercenary with links to a couple of terrorist groups. This confirms both our theories that these people were hired killers." Looking at his notes, he then says, "Do you know anyone or hear these people talk about someone called Henekie?"

"Not that I can recall," I tell him.

Chamberlain turns on a tape cassette. I hear my own voice talking to Ken Holmes. We listen for some time, my face incredulous. Waddell's voice now comes on to the tape. After that Erik Grundman in Germany talks to Holmes.

"Grundman and Waddell know each other?" I can't believe my ears.

"Oh yes," Chamberlain answers me. "In fact, Grundman has now moved to the Bahamas."

I begin to feel much better about coming to Chamberlain now. Without all this knowledge, I would have been sunk.

"Listen to this," Novak tells me, "This is about a week and a half before those guys tried to kill you."

I heard Holmes go to the door and then the agent wiretapping his house calling for assistance. "Henekie, the phone is tapped," I hear a voice whisper and then the answer to get out.

"I tried to phone Holmes," I tell them, "but his phone was disconnected."

"His whole house was disconnected," Novak tells me. "We believe it may have been the same people hired to kill you."

"Why Holmes?" I ask.

"You heard the tapes, he knew too much, maybe they suspected the wiretaps too—I don't know. However, he gave us the link between Grundman and Waddell."

"Guess I can kiss our money goodbye," I say.

"You were never going to get any money out of Grundman. That's why we were investigating Holmes," Chamberlain tells me. "They were coning people out of a lot of money, especially in the United States and Canada. We couldn't do much about it though. It was always in cash."

"Tom got his money through Holmes," I tell them.

"We don't think so," Novak says. "We think Waddell financed it through the people he works for."

"Would that be the APCO Company?" I ask.

"In a roundabout way, Bob," Chamberlain answers.

"APCO is the legitimate front for a man they call El Presidente. Waddell doesn't shit without him knowing about it. He's a Colombian who controls the drug trade in this area."

"I can't believe all this," I say, sitting down. "I wanted to get at one man, now you tell me there's a whole cartel after me?"

"Not only that"—Novak frowns—"we believe the men who came after you were hired by Grundman."

"Fuck me," I sit looking off into space. "Why do you think that?"

"There is a thread through all this," Novak tells me, "thanks to a very alert CIA agent. You remember that piece of necklace Constable Reich had in his hand that I showed you?"

I nod, and he goes on. "Well, we sent a picture through Interpol to all the police forces in the world, including the FBI. There was a fundraiser for the government the other night at the Crystal Palace. Lucky for us, it was there because we have an excellent surveillance system set up in cooperation with the Cruise line, who owns the hotel. We labeled the jewelry Reich's necklace. That way people are more apt to remember it, and that may have helped. Anyway, the U.S. government is not pleased with the present government here. We had specific orders to watch who attended this affair. Manly Waddell's name was on the guest list but didn't attend."

"We think we know why, but that's another story. Grundman and an unknown lady showed up in Waddell's car, so we assumed he was taking Waddell's place.

Anyway," Chamberlain continues, "the lady Grundman was with was real knockout. Our dedicated men took some fantastic close-ups."

He flips a switch on the wall, and a huge TV screen comes into view. The picture of a dark-haired beautiful woman appears and the camera soon zooms in on her well-exposed cleavage. Chamberlain freezes the close-up.

"Do you recognize the jewelry, Bob? If you're like the rest of us, we are looking a little lower, but if you look up a bit like our observant agent did, you'll see what we're talking about."

"My God," I say, "it looks like Hania's necklace."

"You're right, Bob, we think it did indeed belong to Hania Shonavon. However, it's now identified as Reich's necklace, as you can see the missing piece found in his hand has been replaced. however this would certainly tie Grundman to the deaths up in Canada, but we need some help," Novak looks over at me.

"We know who the woman with Grundman is. Apparently, she flew in with Grundman when he first came but doesn't live with him. Her name's Lena, and she likes rich men."

"So what's that got to do with me?" I ask.

"You're going to turn into a rich man, Mr. Green, and you're going to find out how she got that necklace," Novak tells me.

"Look guys, I'm not your man, I'm no damn good with women, plus too many people know what I look like."

"You're in no position to argue, Bob. We have July, and we can arrange that you never see her again. We know that's a cruel threat, but there's too much riding on this not to go after it. Besides, we know how much of a motivation July is to you. We won't have to worry about you running out on us," Novak replies.

I'm not a happy man, and they know it. "So what all do I have to do?" I ask.

"We'll arrange for you to meet Lena. We think she's very vulnerable right now and looking for someone to get her away from Grundman."

"Yeah," adds Chamberlain, "from what we hear she hates his ass, but he's got her over a barrel. He's a real kinky bastard, likes screwing young girls up the ass while another one whips him."

"Look guys, I don't think this is going to work," I tell them.

"Got any better ideas, Bob?" Novak asks.

"Here's the scoop, Bob," Chamberlain begins. "A while back, a drug lord in the Mediterranean died mysteriously aboard his yacht with all his crew. The CIA couldn't just let his yacht drift around, so they decided maybe they could use it in this little covert operation their planning here. Nobody knows he's dead, and nobody over here knows him, but they do know his reputation as a ruthless bastard. Tomorrow we're flying over to that yacht and bringing it to the Bahamas. Bob, you're about to become the man."

"It won't work guys, they all know me."

"Our people will go over you until you don't recognize yourself. Your crew will all be CIA. A fellow by the name of Ansly will look after you from here on in."

"So I'm to get this Lena to tell me where she got the necklace, and then what?" I ask.

"Come on, Bob. We know you want to get Waddell and Grundman as much as we do," Novak says. "We figure you can turn them against each other so you can find out what they know and if they kill each other, so be it. However, the one we really want is El Presidente. You're going to turn his world upside down until he comes looking for you himself.

It's the only way, Bob," Novak tells me, "you're life is always going to be in danger until you get to the source."

I take a deep breath, "Can I at least see July?"

"Yes, she'll meet you on the yacht tomorrow, and then you won't see her again until this is over."

I walk to the window; it is dark out, already fitting my mood. "So what is happening with Waddell?" I ask.

"Someone beat the shit out of him. It seems July rearranged his nose when she escaped from where he was holding her," Chamberlain says. "Quite a woman, isn't she?"

"Yes," I agree feeling better, "she does get her kicks in."

Chamberlain and I stand looking out the window at the harbor lights. "It's such a pretty country, Bob, but drugs have fucked it up. They've corrupted the government to the core. A few get rich, the rest either have to contend with the drugs or use them. But things are changing. Next month, there's an election. The old government's going to be kicked out, Bob. The new one is going to clean it up. There'll be hard times after the drugs are gone but not for long. The Bahamas are just starting to wake up. Once the drugs are gone, the tourists will return and people will prosper, just wait and see."

We sit up late talking about things that are ahead for me. I finally get to my bedroom and stand for a long time in front of a mirror. This is one of the last times I will see the old Bob Green. The fact that these people have the ability to change my features and personality I have no doubt, but will I like the man they create. Tears come into my eyes and most importantly will July still love this new man. I shut the lights out and crawl into bed.

Novak wasn't happy with what Sir Harry had planned for Bob Green, but he didn't have any other options available either. A lot of things had changed since he'd left Canada. He was told that his job was to wait in the Bahamas until Bob Green was released to the Canadian government and then bring him back. The commander told him to enjoy himself as they thought it would only be a couple of weeks.

"Hit the beach. Find some girls because when you come back, you'll be reassigned here in Ottawa, and we've got a lot of winter to get through." They told him the embassy would put him up while he stayed in the Bahamas. He was soon to find out the embassy was really a consulate in a building shared with several other countries and businesses. The room consisted of a small cot used for staff who had to work late. Novak guessed the people in Ottawa didn't know or care about this as long as it didn't go on their expense account.

The consulate was small and had none of the communication facilities he was looking for. It was okay to go down to the beach for an hour or so, but Novak was obsessed with trying to figure out what really happened up in Canada. He needed to be able to communicate with other countries' police forces and his own constabulary to find out anything new that might have been uncovered about the case.

He tried the American embassy, but they were not very forthcoming as to sharing their facilities. It was on a visit to the British embassy that he had met Sir Harry Chamberlain. Novak explained to him what he was trying to do, and to Novak's astonishment, Sir Harry told him, "My good man, you need access to Interpol. I heard about the massacre up there, and I am aware the Americans are looking for the man who got away. Any light you can put on the subject would be greatly appreciated." Novak couldn't believe that Sir Harry had all this information and that he had stumbled on to the right man to help him.

Interpol was a whole new world to Novak, and Sir Harry gave him unlimited access. It was a world where police the world over exchanged information, and he soon began to get answers to some of the information he put out there. The Mounties up in Canada had a computer system, but it allowed the officers a very limited database. This system he had been introduced to give him access to files around the world including himself and, most interestingly data on the commander who'd sent him here and who was described as being very incompetent.

Novak found that some of the bodies found up in Saskatchewan had been identified, but not all, and one of the men who had escaped was found dead in Minneapolis. That left two known survivors, Green being one and the other still unknown. Novak pushed his necklace theory and sent pictures everywhere, but there had been no hits. Sir Harry was very impressed with Novak's work ethics and encouraged him with his work.

"I'm supposed to be the Interpol man here," he said. "But these damned machines get the best of me. You've taken to that machine like a duck takes to water. I'm going to request that the Canadians leave you here to look into some drug-related matters that may concern them, and after all, you are here to look after Bob Green."

A month went by, and there was still no sign of Green. The government requested Novak to find out what was going on. He went to Sir Harry to see if he knew anything.

"Well, I want you to keep this to yourself," Sir Harry told him. "The Americans lost him."

Novak couldn't believe his ears, "What do you mean lost him?"

"Well, they assumed that when you gave Green his passport, he'd just fly down here to the Bahamas and look for his wife."

"I told them this guy was a different cat, but as usual who pays any attention to me. Anyway, he got himself across the border, and we know he was in Miami."

"Damn," was all Novak could come up with. "Don't you think there must be people out there that would like him dead?"

"Well," Sir Harry scratched his head, "the name of the CIA man in this area is Ansly. If you'd like to talk to him I'll arrange it. He put word out to the Miami mob to bring Green in, but it seems they are not getting along with Ansly right now and let Novak slip out of Miami."

Now Novak was really confused. "Why in hell would the CIA want the Miami mob to do work for them?" He wanted to know.

"The murky world of good guys and bad guys, Novak, some people are just better at doing things than others. The more you dig into this business, the more you'll understand."

"Anyway, Green got himself out of Miami, and we know he's headed our way, it's just a matter of time."

"How in hell can you be sure he's coming here?" Novak sounded upset.

"Don't worry, he'll come for his wife. When he does, I'll let you know," Sir Harry told him. It was then he'd told him about Ansly's plans for Bob Green.

"That sounds pretty far out there." Novak was not in favor of this at all.

Sir Harry agreed with him, "But what alternative does Green have? If you take him back to Canada, chances are he's in for a long jail term. At least this way we hide him till some of this blows over."

Novak knew Sir Harry was right, either way it didn't look too good for Bob Green. He also saw firsthand how Sir Harry operated.

He'd not given Green a chance to think through what was happening to him. Green was tired and all he cared about was that his wife and family survived.

"Maybe Sir Harry is doing the same with me," Novak thought. He'd just been asked to leave the Canadian police and go to work for the Bahamian police.

"We need someone who can head up our computer training department along with a few other areas we're lacking expertise in," Sir Harry informed him. "You'll double your salary and be our Interpol guy here, I guarantee you won't be bored."

Things were moving fast maybe too fast, Novak realized, but he loved it here in the Bahamas and dreaded going back to the old grind.

He also felt he had a responsibility to see Green through what could possibly be a dead end street. Novak found it to be a little vague as to whether Green was working for the good guys or the bad guys. There seemed to be no black or white in this world he was entering into. Now he'd have sort that out because he'd handed in his resignation to the Royal Canadian Police this morning.

# NINETEEN

LENA GRITTED HER teeth; Grundman was getting worse. Maybe he was bored here in the Bahamas, but Lena knew this Green person was eating at his insides.

Grundman had been increasingly demanding of Lena, and she had done her best to satisfy his desires. She watched as he snorted up his coke and then inserted his cock into the young girl on the bed. She'd recruited several girls, all young and uninhibited, but Grundman was looking for another Greta. This was the first one he had asked back again. He was about halfway up her ass now. "Jeez, that must hurt," Lena thought to herself, glad it was the girl and not her. The girl squirmed and moaned trying not to scream as Grundman worked his way into her.

"This was nothing yet, wait till I start slapping his ass with this rod," she thought. Then he'll really ram it into her. It probably helped that the girl was high on whatever drugs she and Grundman had indulged in. Lena was sure the drugs were the reason the girl had come back to endure more of his tirades.

Lena didn't like it that Grumman had control over her. "I've got to find a man who can stand up to him," Lena thought as she stroked his ass with the rod. She knew enough to start slow building him into a fury with faster, harder strokes. She'd hoped to meet someone at the party last week in the Crystal Palace. There was some potential all right, but it took time to sort them out, and she wasn't sure how long she had. Manly Waddell, she found extremely interesting, but he was recovering from a broken nose and showed little interest in her right now. Besides, he and Grundman were buddy-buddy which was not to her benefit.

The phone rang; Lena answered it, recognizing Waddell's voice.

"I have to speak with Grundman. Please, it's important."

"Grundman, it's Manly, he says he must talk to you," Lena told him.

Grundman had no intention of stopping his fun. He just indicated for Lena to bring the phone over to him. "They got Green," Manly told him. "He was seen being loaded on to an American government plane this morning. We're not sure, but it looks like Sir Harry Chamberlain was the guy who turned him over."

"We spent all that money hiring those guys of yours, and he gets out of here right under your nose." Grundeman sounded very agitated.

"We don't know how in hell he got into Nassau, but Sir Harry got him out before we had time to act," Waddell told him.

"You'd better pull some favors Manly. If the Americans start asking him questions about us, we're fucked."

"Better get your man onto this, Grundman. The Americans don't exactly owe me any favors," Manly replied.

Grundman was plunging into the girl now, taking his anger out on her. He didn't need Lena to whip him; his anger was his passion.

"Find out where they're holding him," Grundman told him. "My man will look after him. Listen and you will hear what my man will do to Green." Grundman put the phone down by the girl's head and began stroking his cock into her with long hard thrusts. Waddell could hear her screams.

“Perverted prick,” he grumbled and hung up.

It was Sir Harry’s idea to make sure Bob Green was seen boarding the plane. What no one would know was where the plane would end up.

They didn’t even tell me until the plane was in the air. “The Canary Islands,” I am finally told. “That is where your boat is tied up right now. When we think you’re ready, we’ll sail back to Nassau. That should give you a month to get your sea legs.”

It is early evening when I first get to see the ship. Chamberlain had left us at the airport, but Novak stayed with me. We were driven to the harbor in a U.S. embassy car, and then hustled into a waiting boat to take us out to our ship.

The boat driver points out the ship; it is brightly lit like many of the other ships in the harbor and didn’t look much different from the many American warships at anchor.

“It’s an old British frigate completely converted and modernized,” the boat driver tells us.

As we pull up alongside, I can see it is painted pure white, the name Aphrodite running along its bow. A man is waiting for us as we come on board. He introduces himself as Kent Ansly.

“This is my brainstorm,” he tells me. “We’ll be seeing a lot of each other for a while.”

“This is a yacht?” I ask incredulously as he leads me into a room.

“Beautiful, isn’t it? There was no lack of money when the former owner refitted this baby. Not only was it refurbished with elegant rooms, it still carries a full arsenal of guns, and the electronic systems are way ahead of their time. It’s good to see the black market is alive and flourishing.” He then tells me to sit down. “I’m sure you were briefed about the little operation we’re attempting here?” Ansly asks.

I skim over what I have been told.

“That’s basically it,” he tells me. “We have a month to prepare you for the task ahead. By the time you get to Nassau, you'll think you are Mark Bertrand."

"Mark Bertrand," I repeat. "I hear he was a rather tough fellow."

"Probably no tougher than you, Mr. Green. The difference being is you have some morals and compassion whereas Mr. Bertrand was only interested in himself. This was, in the end, the cause of his demise."

"How did you get him anyway?" I ask.

"A woman," Ansly shrugs "Men who are selfish often underestimate the scorn of a woman. You'll meet her later. She's a member of our team."

I nod, "Do you think a month's going to teach me how to run this boat?"

"That's not necessary, Bob," Ansly goes on. "You've got to stop thinking like an ordinary man. You're rich and powerful beyond your wildest dreams now. Somebody does everything for you, but the thinking and even this, in your case, will be taken care of, you just have to play the part. What we have here, Bob, is a basic plan. The rest will just evolve."

"Sure," I think, "and if I end up dead, it's no skin off your ass."

"We'll lift anchor in the morning, Bob, but tonight is yours. I have someone for you to meet." He led me down a long hallway almost to the rear of the ship. "This is your room," he tells me. "I'll see you in the morning." He hands me a key, and I use it to open the door.

It's a huge suite, very elegantly done. Lounging on a couch in the middle of the room is July. She is absolutely beautiful, more so than I could remember. Her dressing gown hangs loosely from her shoulders showing most of her breasts, her long legs stretch across the couch; now I know why I am in love.

"Hello, sailor," she says coquettishly.

"Jeez, July," is all I can say, my eyes staring, trying to take her all in.

She laughs, "The least you can do is to come in and shut the door."

I come out of my trance and shut the door.

"Come here and hold me, Bobby Green."

I hold her tight and kiss her tenderly, "You are for real," I tell her. "I was scared you were just a mirage." There are tears in her eyes, I kiss them away. "So we meet again," I say trying to lighten the situation. Her breasts look so inviting, but I don't want to rush things.

She must have read my mind; she takes my hand and places it on her breast, "They've missed you so much," she tells me. "I want you so bad, let's fuck now and talk later." She undid my belt and felt inside my pants. When she found what she was looking for, she shut her eyes, her breath coming in sharp gasps. "I go to sleep dreaming about this big cock of yours," she whispers in my ear.

My nuts ache. It's been so long since I've been fucked that I'm scared I'll come in my pants. "Easy, July," I tell her as she unbuttons my shirt. My cock's excited, and she knows it. Somehow we get my clothes off, and I climb on top of her and she guides me in. I'm too excited to worry about foreplay or pleasuring July. My nuts are one with my brain, and I begin plunging into her quickly draining my balls in pent-up emotion. I hear a scream in my ears that spurs me on, knowing that July is coming with me.

We lay totally burned out on the couch. I can feel her body still twitching under me.

"I'm still coming," she giggles in my ear. "It's like little aftershocks from an earthquake," she exclaims. "My body's been waiting for that earthquake too long."

It feels like I just got rid of a huge pressure on my balls," I tell her, "but they still ache for more."

July rolls me off her and begins massaging my sack. "You went too long without getting fucked," she says, "you should get a service job. There are women you can hire for that."

"I really don't need anyone but you," I tell her. "Sometimes I dream about you in the morning, and I wake up covered in cum," I smile at her. "I guess you get it whether you know it or not."

"No wonder I get so wet down there when you're not around," she laughs.

It's so good to hear her laugh again; I become serious. "Do you know anything about what they have in store for me?"

"Yes," July answers. "I basically know what the plan is and what's expected of you."

"I think you and I should get up right now and walk out of here," I tell her. "Let's just go somewhere, anywhere away from here, Let's just go somewhere and live a normal life together."

July looks away and is silent for a while. "I don't think that can happen for us in the near future, Bob. Maybe our lives weren't meant to be normal. I do know if we don't do what we are asked, they will carry out their threat to never let us be together again. Besides, I don't know if you could live with yourself if you just walked away."

"I don't know, July, it just seems that I have no control over my life anymore. Look at this lame-brained scheme they've cooked up. Jeez, instead of a knight riding in on a white horse, I'm a drug dealer on a white yacht riding in to save the day. I think it's corny."

"Got any better ideas," she asks.

"No," I have to admit, "I just don't feel good about it."

"What would you say if I told you this plan was partly my idea?"

Now it's my turn to sit back. "This thing just keeps twisting and turning along, doesn't it? I mean, one minute I hear Waddell is holding you, the next you're kicking the shit out of him. Now you're telling me you're the mastermind behind a scene to clean up the drug trade in the Bahamas."July keeps massaging my balls, maybe she found it therapeutic.

"No," she says slowly picking her words. "Ansly thought up the scheme, I just sat in on a couple of meetings and gave a few suggestions. I did suggest you were the man for the job, even though it worries me about the danger you'll be in."

"So you think this might work?" I ask her.

"There's no way you could face these people alone, darling. At least, I'll feel safer knowing you have some good people with you."

"I finally get to live like a rich man, and you won't be here to enjoy it with me," I tell her.

"I'm here tonight," she purrs, turning herself so she can reach my cock with her tongue. "There's nothing like it," she says, "to watch a man's cock rise is the most gorgeous sight in the world."

"You sure know how to make it hard," I tell her, spreading her thighs and running my tongue along her slit.

July knew how to drive me crazy, she worked on my cock until I couldn't stand it anymore, "I want it in you," I tell her.

"I want you to fuck me upside down and backward," she says, pulling my cock from her mouth.

I roll onto my back, and she mounts me. I play with her breasts, my tongue circling her nipples. She rides me like this for a while and then suddenly gets off. "Fuck me from behind," she says, getting on her knees, turning her rear to me.

I stand up and enter her. She puts her head down so she can watch my cock slide in and out between her legs. Her voice sounds very much on edge. "I'm going to come, baby, can you hold on, I want to use you some more."

"I have to get a hold of myself," I think, as I feel her body begin to shudder. She becomes very still and relaxed. I pull out and roll her over, placing a pillow behind her head. Her face is flushed, her eyes are shut. I can see the glint of sweat forming between her breasts.

"Please, put it back in," she pants.

I climb on top of her, my cock finding its own way in. She put her hands behind her head watching me. I ride her with easy, soft strokes, gradually ramming harder as I feel the passion begin to boil in my loins. I'm beginning to get to her too. She wraps her long legs around me, and we begin to move in rhythm. Her hands lock in mine, and together we scorch the universe, her screams echoing off the stars.

"Damn it, July," I am the first to catch my breath, "you're going to be the end of me yet." We lay in a pile covered in sweat. I don't have the strength to climb off her.

"The end of you!" she pants. "Do you realize how many times I came? That's hard on my body, and I feel like a rag."

We doze for a while not wanting to sleep for fear of missing some of our limited time together.

"July," I ask, looking up, "what time is it in Minnesota?"

She smiles, "I don't even know what time it is here. Why?"

"Well, because I always phone Mindy at six o'clock on Wednesday evening."

"It would be nice to talk to her," July tells me. I tried to talk to her from Sir Harry's the other night, but it said her phone had been disconnected.

"Yeah, well she had a party the other night and some of her so-called friends used her phone to make some long-distance phone calls. I sent her some money to help pay the bill, but she had her phone taken out. Now she uses her friends' phone down the hall. Anyway, Mindy and I set up a system. Every Wednesday night at six o'clock I phone a number in a phone booth not far from her place," I tell July.

"Um, aren't we cloak and dagger," July smiles. "I'm so happy you've been talking to her, Bob. I've been very worried about, well, all of us, I guess."

"I know," I tell her all about how Mindy helped me get across the border and why I set up the phone booth system.

"It's good to see you two working together," she gets up and throws on her robe. "I think I have time for a shower. The phone is on the table over there. As long as we're on shore, it works just like any other phone, but you'll have to go through the operator." She bends over and kisses me. I wait a few minutes and then give the operator the Minnesota number.

Henekie had been following Mindy for two days now. He'd found out she had no phone, that she had a boyfriend who had stayed over one night, and where she worked. Not much to go on, he thought, as he followed her down the street. At first he thought she was going for dinner and was surprised to see she didn't go in the restaurant but continued on past the entrance and sat down on the parking lot retaining wall beside the phone booth. This is it; he instantly knew what she was up to. Still, he'd have to play his cards carefully. She doesn't have her own phone, maybe it's just her boyfriend.

Henekie looked at his watch; almost six o'clock; if he was to make a move, the time was now. He left the cover of the restaurant and walked toward the phone booth. Just as he was about to enter it, he heard, "Excuse me!" He stopped and looked at the girl sitting there.

"I'm very sorry, but I'm expecting a very important phone call at six," she told him.

"This is a public phone, man," he told her.

"Well, okay. I just ask you to please make your call short."

He hesitated, "Guess my call can wait a few minutes," he smiled. "It must be very important to you."

"Yes," she said, "It's my dad. I haven't seen him for a long time. It means a lot to me."

Henekie sat down and began talking to her when the phone rang. "Right on time," Henekie said to Mindy. "Your father's very prompt."

Mindy didn't answer as she turned and ran to the phone. She closed the door behind her but Henekie could still hear what she said.

He waited until he heard, "Hello, Dad," and decided to make his move.

July comes out of the bathroom toweling her hair. She smiles as she hears Bob say, "Hi, Mindy, how's things?" Then she sees Bob's face suddenly freeze.

"Who is this?" his voice becomes panicky.

"I've been waiting to talk to you for some time, Mr. Green."

Bob and July weren't the only people who were panicking right now. Ansly monitored anything and everything that went on in his ship. The agent monitoring Bob's call immediately buzzes Ansly's room.

"What's up?" Ansly answers sleepily.

"Green's on the phone to his daughter. Someone got hold of her. He's questioning Green right now."

Ansly is fully awake now. He flips a switch opening a panel in Bob and July's room. Several TV screens came on, showing Ansly the control room and Bob and July's room.

"They've been watching," July thinks, embarrassed, as she watches the screens. A speaker came on so she could hear what was said on the other end.

"It doesn't matter who I am, Mr. Green," the voice says. "We almost met up in Canada, but you kept avoiding me, now we must rectify that."

Bob immediately understands where this is coming from. "Yes," Bob answers evenly, "I'm looking forward to meeting you as we have a score to settle!"

"Yes, we do," Henekie answers, his arm securely around Mindy, "however, the meeting will be on my terms seeing as I have an ace in the hole."

"Guess that makes you the dealer," Bob tells him, sounding calm. "Name the place, I'll come to you."

July is amazed at the way Bob is handling the situation, and so is

Ansly. "This guy can keep his cool in a tight spot," he thinks to himself wondering if he could do as well if it was his own daughter's life on the line. Ansly also knew something Bob didn't. He had asked the FBI to watch Mindy, he was sure they would soon be making their move. What the outcome would be probably didn't look very good.

Henekie wasn't the only guy to be suspicious about the phone booth. Two weeks in a row, the FBI had watched Mindy answer a call from the same phone booth. Now they were sitting in a van across the street listening to every word. Both agents were bored.

"I hear they got Green, so why are we bothering with this," one agent said.

"You know how slow they are," the other agent replied. "It takes time for orders to come down through the system. Maybe they even forgot about us," he chuckled. "Besides, this is easy work. We'll be able to catch some sleep tonight."

They are relaxed when Mindy answers her call; the hair stands up on their arms when they hear the strange voice on the line. One agent crawls up to the front of the van and looks out the window. He can make out two people in the phone booth. He crawls back to his partner.

"We'll go out the back door, up the alley, and come in from the back side of the parking lot," he says.

"Where are you now?" July hears the voice over the speaker.

Bob knows by the sound of the ship to shore phone crackle, it is not a normal call. He figures the guy holding Mindy knows it too. "I'm on a cruise ship heading for the Bahamas," Bob tells him.

Ansly had been holding his breath on that one. Now he can lead Bob. He listens as the man asks Bob where he could reach him in the Bahamas. Ansly quickly jots down some words on a chalkboard and holds it up to the TV screen.

July taps Bob on the shoulder and points to the screen, "I'm staying at the Crystal Palace under the name of Savard," Bob answers, reading off the screen.

Suddenly, they all hear what sounds like a shot and a loud clatter like the phone had been dropped.

"Freeze, right where you are," Henekie hears a voice behind him. He turns and fires a shot through the booth glass. Two men stand facing him at the edge of the parking lot, twenty feet away. His shot hits one of them, sending him backward, firing as he fell. The shots go high into the glass filling Henekie's eyes with shredding fragments. He feels the girl slip away. He grabs for her blindly, but the door comes open, and she is gone.

He blinks away the glass from his eyes. Luck stays with him; the girl runs right at the other man blocking his line of fire. Henekie takes off running toward the restaurant. People are coming out of the entrance. They stand there unable to move as they watch a man run toward them with a gun pointed in their direction. He runs through the people and around the side of the restaurant out of the agents' view.

The agent runs after him cursing because with the people around, he can't get a clear shot. "FBI, get down!" he shouts, stopping at the corner of the restaurant and carefully peering around. He sees the assailant run through a hedge on the other side of the parking lot. He runs across the parking lot just in time to see a car screech away. The agent holsters his gun and runs back to the restaurant. He sees many people gathered around the crying girl. His partner is sitting up.

"Are you okay, Al?" he says to his partner.

"Yeah," he responds, "just hurts like hell, thank God for bulletproof jackets."

The agent sees that the girl is all right. "The bastard got away," he tells Al as he is walking over to the phone booth. The receiver is hanging down, and he picks it up. "Hello," he says.

"What the hell's happening there?" a voice asks.

"Well I'll be damned, I'd recognise that voice anywhere, what the hell are you up to now Ansly?"

"What the hell Smith, are you working for the FBI now?

"Since you ran me off, I just put in time working for whoever needs me," Smith answers with sarcasm in his voice.

Ansly had no time for formalities. "What the fuck's happening there?" he asks.

"The girl's all right. My partner was hit, but his bulletproof jacket saved him. The assailant got away; there were too many people around to get a good shot," the agent tells him.

I drop into a chair; July grabs me and pulls me close. I hug her tightly for a moment, and then I look up, first at July, then at Ansly's face on the screen.

"I'm ready to take these guys on," I tell him. "They've got me pissed off now."

Henekie was fully clothed under the jogging suit he was wearing. He took it off and threw it in a garbage can in a dark alley along with the gun. He decided the best thing to do was get out of town as quickly as he could. He wasn't worried; he had all the ID he needed to get through a roadblock. No one was real sure what he looked like except the girl, and it would take time for the cops to get a composite drawing from her. The best thing he could do was to get away as far he could.

"I screwed up," he cursed to himself. Those agents must have been listening to that phone too. I should have seen them, now I've got nothing that will make Green come to me, so I'll have to go to him, Henekie thought, I'll phone Grundman in the morning to see what he knows.

July and I talk with Ansly well into the morning. When it was time for July to leave, we get to spend a few moments together.

"I'm going to be helping the agents," she tells me, "I can identify people and voices for them, so I'll be able to follow what you're up to,"

July smiles. “It will be like I’m with you all the time. I’ll probably be in Miami. They’re bringing Rikker there too. I’ll be in touch, love you.” With that, her shuttle boat pulls away, parting us again.

They let me sleep till noon, by then the Canary Islands were long out of sight. Ansly took me on a tour of the boat.

“She’s fast,” he tells me, “there’s a crew of ten on board, not including us. We are all agents and trained in the navy.” He shows me a large room filled with panels and screens. “This is the nerve center of the ship. It even has sensors warning us if divers are near. It’s more sophisticated than many of the warships we were tied up in port with.”

As he shows me around, I can see that the ship is completely done up. “A floating palace,” I tell Ansly.

“That’s why they call it a yacht,” he answers.

They also show me a canon and several mounted machine guns all cleverly disguised behind portable curtains and removable covers.

That afternoon, the water becomes choppy and I get sick. The second day, I am even sicker, but they make me read some material on my new background. They also start the disguise process, in this case, plastic surgery. It takes a few days for the swelling to go down then I begin my orientation of becoming Mark Betrand... My days are filled with briefings and meetings with the crew so that I could get to know them better. Carol is the only girl on board.

“Don’t let that pretty little face of hers fool you, she’s a tough little cookie. Her job is to be your secretary and if need be, your roommate.” Ansly tells me. “If you need her to sleep with someone to get information, that’s her job. In other words, she’s yours to do with as you need.”

Carol has different ideas about that and quickly tells me so, “You can go fuck yourself, if you think I’m going to sleep with you.” I’ll do what I have to do but on my own terms.”

“Damn it,” I smile, “I was really looking forward to it too.”

She smiles back, “Just because you can satisfy that big blond doesn’t mean you can look after a redhead." She blows me a kiss and wiggles her ass at me as she walks away; we'd do just fine.

We are so busy that time flew. We stop for a few days in Trinidad to refuel and bring on supplies then one morning, I came on deck to see the checkerboard colors of Nassau in full view.

"They'll send a pilot out to take us into the harbor," Ansly tells me. "By tonight, you'll be a busy man."

We are docked near some other yachts. I realize just how impressive our boat is, as I look down on the others scattered about the harbor. I think with a ship this size that we will be staying on board.

"You're going ashore to eat tonight," Ansly tells me. "It will be a trial run to see how well you handle your new job. You'll be staying at the Atlantis tonight," he goes on. "In case you didn't know, you've booked out the penthouse suite for two weeks. Carol will be your escort for dining. What happens after that is up to you. Night dining in Nassau's finest restaurants is 'black tie' or 'tux only' affairs."

One thing I had learned about Bertrand was that he never wore a tie or tux. He considered them bourgeois and wore only polo shirts under an expensive blazer.

The European look, they call it, suits me just fine. I hadn't worn a tie in a long time and found them very constricting. As for being accepted in this attire, I feel it won't be a problem. Money, I know, looks after all the doors in this world. Acceptance is only dollars away. Besides, maybe I will start a new trend.

The face I see in the mirror is not mine anymore. Jet-black hair combed straight back, wire-rimmed glasses (still uncomfortable on my nose), a scar on my cheekbone, and capped teeth. Mark Bertrand, that's who I am now. I have to forget Bob Green, my life depends on it.

For a while now, I had taken acting lessons, learning Bertrand's quirks, likes, and dislikes. But with all this, I realize that it is up to me to pull this off, and I am determined to do it.

My people, as I now called the agents, had let it be known that I was coming to town. Word had spread fast. There are quite a few people at the dock as we come in, curious to see the man who owns this beautiful yacht. Among the first to come aboard is the harbor captain.

He looks very nervous in all this elegance. I meet him at the head of the gangplank, shake his hand, and introduce him to Mr. Ansly, my captain, who will answer any questions he may have. Our plan is to be as mysterious as possible, showing myself only when necessary. After all, my disguise will be open to scrutiny and in order to create interest, one has to remain aloof.

The rest of the day, I practice my accent. "Don't overdo it," the agent tells me, "just enough so it comes natural and they don't recognize your voice." I am dressed and ready to go ashore when I hear a knock on my door. It opens and in walks Carol.

"Hi," she says, "I'm your escort for the night."

I hardly recognize her in a dress, having only seen her in blue jeans until now. I let out a low whistle. Her dress is very short, the top consisting of two straps of cloth running from the belly button to just covering her breasts and tied behind her neck.

"I thought we were going to a nightclub, not the beach," I tell her.

"Everyone knows you like your women hot, Mark." She spins around, "Am I hot enough?"

"You're making me sweat," I tell her, which isn't far from the truth.

"Okay, let's go. First, we're off to a tourist floorshow, where we'll have diner. Later, we'll hit some clubs."

I have seen the local tourist show before, but the meal is good. After the show, we get back into the limousine. "Where now?" I ask the driver and my so-called bodyguard who is in the front seat.

"There's a private club we want you to crash," one of my bodyguards tells me. "You've got lots of money, spread whatever it takes to get in, and then make sure they all know you're there." At the door to the club, the doorman says, "I'm sorry, sir, but we're all full for the evening."

"Bullshit," I snap my fingers. My man pulls out five one-hundred American dollar bills.

The doorman's eyes get as big as saucers. "I'll see what I can do, sir," he rushes away.

Shortly after, an American couple comes out, red-faced. "That's the last time we're coming here!" the man exclaims.

I tell my bodyguards to wait outside as the maître d' escorts us to our table. The place is packed. My eyes soon became accustomed to the light, and I notice that many people here have no business being here on their incomes. I also notice that many of them are with women other than their wives.

"I've lived here quite a while in the Bahamas," I tell Carol, "but this is a part of Nassau that I didn't know existed."

She shrugs, "Every place has a nightlife of its own. You've just become part of this one."

A couple of drinks and I begin to loosen up. A few people stop by to say hello, and I can tell by the turned heads that word is getting around as to who I am.

Shortly, I see Manly Waddell following the maître d' to a secluded table back in one corner. On his arm is one of the most beautiful women I have ever seen. Carol pokes me in the ribs, "There's the woman you're going to sweep off her feet, Mr. Bertrand."

"God, she's beautiful," is all I can say.

"Well, okay," Carol says, "so she sweeps you off your feet. I don't care how it's done as long as you two get together."

"Manly looks like he got his nose put back on his face," I tell Carol, trying to change the subject.

"Okay," Carol says. "From now on, you've got to start getting some attention. Give me a kiss and run your hand inside my dress."

"What?" I say incredulously.

"Come on, it's just a tit. If you want her attention, you've got to do something to get noticed. It's considered very suave in Europe to do something daring in public. Men in the know in Germany are very good at this. It is very common there for a man to fondle or expose a woman's breast and for a woman to make a man hard under the table like this," she runs her fingers over my crotch. "No one can see what you're doing, but they can all imagine."

"Are you fucking me around?" I ask, my lips touching hers.

"No way," she says. "Actually, I think it's a good idea to have your man hot by the time you get him home."

I reach inside her dress making sure not to hide what I am doing. The soft flesh feels good in my hand. I can feel myself getting hard.

"That a boy," I hear her say, "now we get up and dance." I was never much of a dancer, but part of my training to be a well-rounded ladies' man is to be able to move around the floor. We'd actually gotten pretty good, I thought, although she was a strong partner, I had to admit. Now I know why sophisticating Bob was such a high priority. This is where I will be seen and judged. Certain things are expected of me. Now is the time to establish my reputation.

We are doing fine; the music is slow, and Carol very erotic. The night wears on. We meet more people, just fish so far. I am fishing for sharks. It still amazes me that some of these people are here. One has to know all aspects of a person before he begins to understand them, I realize.

It is getting early into the morning before Waddell and his lady get up to dance.

I've been inside Carol's dress a lot, the drinks making me braver; besides, it feels good, and Carol is not complaining.

"Pull one out, kiss my nipple, and then slowly put it back where you got it," she whispers in my ear as we sway provocatively to the music. My groping hand spreads open her top, enough so that it isn't hiding much. I hesitate; they are just hanging there waiting for me.

"Do it, damn it," she smiles through clenched teeth. "What's the matter, you're so used to playing with watermelons that you can't find my little titties?"

I laugh, knowing she is referring to July. Our crotches grind to the slow music. I reach inside her dress and pull out one tit. I admire it, then bend and nuzzle her nipple before slipping it back behind cover. I look up; her eyes are closed, her face showing the pleasure of an erotic encounter.

"Christ," she even has me excited. I am sure it showed through the crotch of my pants. Now other women are envious of the attention Carol is creating and begin trying to turn on their partners with much the same tactics.

I realize most of these people are bored. They are looking for something different, something exciting. What I consider to be exhibitionism, these people consider erotic and something to break the monotony.

"You've got her mouth watering now," Carol says breaking into my thoughts. I realize she is talking about Lena, Manly's partner.

"She hasn't taken her eyes off you since she's come to the dance floor." Carol says as she wraps herself around me. I can feel all of her. She has me hot, and everyone in the place knows it.

"Time to leave," she whispers, pulling me out of the place.

We fall all over each other out front while waiting for our limo to come around and pick us up. When we get in the back seat, I am ready to fuck her right there and then. I kiss her, but she does'nt respond.

"Remember, as long as people think they know what's happening in here, it doesn't have to happen," she tells me.

I lay my head back on the seat. "Thank you, Carol,. "I'm sorry I lost it."

Carol is sitting back in the seat with a flushed look on her face. "I hope Lena jumps on you quick," she says, "I don't think I can take much more of this."

"If you were Lena, I would have to fuck you, wouldn't I?" Beginning to face the reality of what will be expected of me.

"Don't be stupid, Mr. Bertrand. We both know what's required to pull this off."

I now understand when Ansly had told me it was a woman who had been the demise of the real Mark Bertrand. That woman is sitting beside me and expects me to perform my duties just as she executes hers.

I could have fucked Carol; it would only have been lust, the heat of passion, and it would not have made me feel less of her. However, it would have bothered me the rest of my life because of July's loyalty and my love for her. It would have hurt Carol much more; a woman's sex is much more personal and this has to be respected.

I have a million questions to ask Carol, but right now we are too close. To become lovers could only end in pain and jeopardize the goal at hand.

"Do you fall in love with every woman you play with," she looks at me.

"I don't usually play with women," I tell her, "I respect them too much, just as I respect you for what you let me do in there."

"It's never easy, you know," she begins to cry.

I bring her close. "Did you love Mark Bertrand?" I ask.

"It was so hard not to," she sobs, burying her face in my chest.

"God," I say to her, "that is all you needed, another man hitting on you."

"No," she looks up and dries her eyes. "I can tell you're a very special man. That big blonde's a very lucky woman." She immediately changes, sitting back, gaining control again. "I think we did a good job in there tonight. It won't be long now before Lena comes for your body, just don't give her your soul."

Carol went to see July the next day. July hadn't told Bob the whole truth about where she would be. The narcotic agents were shorthanded. They found July invaluable in her assistance with identifying people, keeping her on the ship with people gathering information and formulating strategies.

July laughs when Carol describes how Bob had exposed her tit to the world. She wants to keep July informed as to what is happening as well as prepare her for the future.

"You know what will be required when he gets to Lena," Carol tells July carefully.

July answers just as carefully, "I know, but that's Mark Bertrand, not Bob Green. I just hope he can separate the two and I get Bob Green back at the end of this."

Carol holds her hand. "You will, he's a very strong man, but if we think he's beginning to crack, we'll let you go to him."

July brightens up. "Let us hope that doesn't happen. I want to get this over with so we can continue on with our lives."

Things move pretty fast the rest of the week. I have meetings all day and party all night. I am popular now with lots of invitations to big parties and small; the agents try to keep me in the same circles as Waddell, scrambling to find out which places he will show, so Bertrand can be there too. I'm conveniently alone the night I first meet Waddell.

I 'm dancing with a young girl I picked at the bar. She was sitting at Waddell's table the night before and I am pretty sure the meeting was prearranged.

Waddell is dancing with Lena. They had become an item lately, showing up together at all the nightspots. The young girl introduces me to Waddell, and Waddell invites us to sit at his table.

"I hear you're looking for investments here in the islands," Waddell tells me.

"Yes" I'm looking for something interesting. So far, I haven't met the right people for what I have in mind," I answer him.

"There will be a man here later tonight who specializes in investments that you might be interested in," Waddell tells me. "I'll introduce you."

"Perfect," I tell him, "I'm looking forward to it." I turn to Lena, "You are the most beautiful woman I have ever seen, I don't believe we've been introduced."

Waddell smiles and introduces Lena to Mr. Bertrand.

"Mark is my first name," I tell Lena, "and I love to dance, would you join me?" I lead her to the floor and know instantly she is used to the European style of dancing as she fell into a familiar rhythm. She giggles and says. "You certainly don't waste any time, do you?"

"I never let beautiful women slide through my fingers. They're like a rare piece of art only appearing once in a while."

"Oh," she says, "and romantic too." The music stops, and we return to the table. Another man has joined us now; it's Grundman.

I am enjoying this; both of them would like to see me dead, now they are going out of their way to meet with me. If they had any idea how close I am to saying "Fuck it" and killing the both of them, they would shit their pants. This is even better; I want to play with them for a little while. I'd have fun fucking them around while they suck holed after my money.

Manly introduces me to Grundman, and we talk for a bit.

"Why don't you meet with me tomorrow at my office?" Grundman tells me..

Great," I tell him grabbing hold of Lena and to her squealing delight, push her toward the dance floor where we dance for a long time talking and becoming more intimate as the night wore on. When we do go back to the table, both Lena and I keep the conversation lively. There is a number of young girls around the table now. They all want a dance with me, and I oblige them all, but every once in a while I lock eyes with Lena, letting her know I am interested. By the time the place closes, I know I can take any one of the young girl's home with me, but I excuse myself.

"I have an appointment," I wink at Waddell and leave the group, making them wonder what I am up to.

The next morning I show up at Grundman's office early. His secretary is filing her nails and looks startled to see anyone come in this early. She phones him and after a while he shows up looking perturbed that I have come so early.

"You look a little bit under the weather, Grundman," I tell him. "Rough night?"

He grunts and pours himself a coffee. "You're looking for some investments?" he gets right to the point, in no mood for small talk.

"Yes, "In fact, I may have found one I'm interested in."

"Oh," he sits tapping his pencil on his desk, "and what is that?"

"The Royal Bahamas Bank is holding a mortgage on a farming operation on Andros Island. I can get it for a song, would you be interested in handling it for me?"

"What are we looking at?" he asks.

It is just as I think. He doesn't know it exists. "The bank has a mortgage of over two million owing against it. I offered them one million, they've accepted the offer," I tell Grundman . "I need you do the legal work and make sure the transaction is complete."

"A transaction such as this could take months here," Grundman tells me, taking a drink of his coffee.

"Say I give you a couple of hundred thousand American to have this done in a week.. Are you sure this couldn't be completed?"

Grundman chokes on his coffee. "I don't know, Let me make some phone calls. Come back at one, and I'll know for sure then."

I know he won't phone Waddell, Grundman is too greedy to give him a piece of the pie. We also know he will have the work done for us; all he wants to find out is how cheap he can get it done for.

When I go back at one, it is exactly as we planned.

"You'll have your title in one week and the bank will have the transaction completed tomorrow," Grundman tells me. "I will expect my money at that time."

"Perfect," I tell him. "There's one more thing maybe you can help with. I don't want to upset Waddell, but how tight is he with Lena?"

"I've known her for years," Grundman tells me. "They're just friends. She's new here and does not know many people. Why, are you interested in her?"

"Who wouldn't be?" I tell him, "She's a fuck of a lot of woman." I can see Grundman's mind ticking over. If he can get Lena in tight with me, would it be beneficial to him? Obviously, he decides it would be because he gives me her address and phone number.

"Why don't you invite her to the dinner we're throwing tomorrow for the government's election campaign? We've got a tough fight on our hands to keep our present government in power," he says. "The fucking bleeding hearts want a reform government in power here. If we let them in, nobody's going to make a living."

"Great," I tell him. "I'll be sure to bring my checkbook."

I phone Lena that afternoon. I get the impression that she is expecting my call. "I've been invited to the fund-raiser tomorrow night. I need an escort," I tell her. "How about going with me?"

"I'd love to Mark, only I don't have anything to wear."

I figured that it would be this way. Lena was used to being a kept woman. Even when she ran her own escort business, her men friends bought and paid for every favor they got from her. It was the way she had been taught from birth to do business. She loved everyone and gave nothing away. I played the game.

"It's a beautiful day, why don't we go shopping this afternoon?"

"That would be nice," she says. "Pick me up at four o'clock, I'll be waiting for you in the lobby."

I find her to be very thrifty; she could have bought a dress for US$5,000 but likes one for $4,500 better, probably because it covers less.

"Maybe we could find some jewelry to go with it," I suggest. watching as the wheels in her mind turn.

"I will wear some jewels tomorrow night. If you like them, you may buy them for me." She runs her fingers along my face.

"If they're as beautiful as the woman wearing them, then they must be made a match." It sounds corny to me but bring a shine to Lena's eyes.

Everyone wears a tux but me, which is all right now because I am not expected to. Lena is absolutely stunning, her hair piled high on her head. "I don't suppose that's to make sure I see the necklace," I think.

When I dance with her, I can feel everyone watching, Lena knows it too and glows in the attention. I drink too much and become far too brave. Lena is a beautiful dancer and actually seems to encourage me as I begin to fondle her and dance crotch to crotch. She becomes very flushed and just as Carol had shown me in the finest European fashion, she begins to fondle my crotch as we sit at our table.

As the night goes on, Lena becomes braver. I have no chance to dance with anyone else; Lena has herself wrapped me so tight, no one can tear us apart. When we sit down at our table I feel her hand undo my fly and pull out my penis. Her eyes are on my face waiting for a reaction. I give her one by running my tongue up between her breasts. Her hand is doing its job. I am becoming very hard.

"Um my," she purrs. "You are an interesting man, aren't you? No wonder women fall all over you with a weapon like that."

"You like it," I whisper in her ear.

"I love big cocks," she tells me. "I've seen lots of them, believe me. You are magnificent."

I look at her smiling, "You're telling me I'm a big prick."

She pushes at me jokingly, "You don't believe me, maybe we should get a second opinion."

Sitting on the other side of me is a bored looking black woman. She is pretty, although plump, as many Bahamian women tend to be as they get older. It gives them a voluptuousness that many men admire, and she certainly hung out over the table admirably. I know her husband. He is a junior minister in the government. I had seen him at the club the other night with a young white girl, and tonight he is paying little attention to his wife, table-hopping by himself.

"Excuse me," Lena says to her, "but I've always heard that black men are bigger than white men, is that true?"

The black woman looks at Lena in surprise and laughs, "I've never had a white man, and I haven't seen my husband's for so long, I forget what it looks like. So I'm not really an authority on men's sizes.".

"I bet your memory will come back if you feel what I've got under the table," Lena tells her.

The woman looks at me and then around the room. She reaches down groping till she finds my shaft. Her hand is cold, startling me a bit, making me even harder. Lena's hand goes to my balls as the black woman explores my erection.

"Jeez," her breath quickens, "I can hardly get my hand around its head."

So I wonder what the poor people are doing today, I think, totally enjoying myself. Lena has no intention of stopping here.

"Why don't you go down and have a closer look. You don't mind, do you, Mark?"

"I definitely think it needs looking after," I say, fighting to keep my voice even.

The black woman looks over to where her husband is talking to a couple of women. She raises her brows and then slides under the table. I'm sure the last thing I see disappear are her big tits. Lena kisses me passionately, watching the pleasure on my face as I feel the woman's tongue on my cock.

"Oh, Lena you're so good to me," I growl. "You really know what a man likes, don't you?"

"Yes," she says. "Thank you for the dress."

I feel the juices begin to build up in me. Lena feels me shiver as she holds me and nibbles on my ear; my hand is inside her dress.

"I can feel your body building up," she gasps. "You're going to blow soon. I'm going to come with you."

The woman under the table has my cock a long ways in her mouth now. She slides her lips along my shaft in short quick strokes making the top of my head feel like it is blowing up. Lena grabs me and holds me tight as my balls explode, causing my body to convulse. I hear the woman under the table choke as she swallows my cum. She has the head of my cock on fire; it throbs so much it almost hurts as the woman continues to suck on it until I feel her slump against my knees, her head resting on my lap. I put my hand under the table and stroke her hair.

Lena sits back and straightens her dress. I'm not one to recover fast. When I have sex, it always takes me a while to get my shit together. Probably this is why I don't see the black woman's husband coming until he sits down beside me.

"Have you seen my wife?" he asks.

I just stare at him stupidly, but Lena comes to my rescue. "She's on the dance floor with the cutest young man you have ever seen." He looks around trying to find her on the crowded floor. "Would you like to dance with me?" Lena asks him. "Perhaps we can find her." The husband jumps up falling all over himself to escort Lena to the dance floor already forgetting about his wife.

"Is it safe to come up now?" she asks.

"Now's the time," I answer. She has one hell of a time getting those big tits up through the narrow space between the table and the wall. I think it is only fair I help her, so I grab them and kind of wiggle them around until they pop up above the table.

"I don't think we've been introduced, my name is Mark Bertrand."

"Yes, I know," she says. "My husband told me who you are. He didn't tell me about the rest of you."

Your husband's a fool," I tell her, "I bet he has no idea you're such a dangerous woman." She leans her head against me for an instant. "Thank you for everything." She gives me the most beautiful smile.

Lena brings her husband back and quickly whispers in my ear. "Let's get out of here."

I go to follow her, but she catches my shoulder. "Put it back in your pants before all the other girls see that thing." She works on me all the way back to the hotel. By the time we get out of the elevator on the top floor, I am ready. Luckily, it is the penthouse suite because she leads me by the cock down the hallway to my door and then right into the bedroom. She undresses me, but I hardly know it. I sit on the bed as she does a striptease for me, then she comes to me and bends down to lick my cock. Its been a long time since I've had a condom installed on me, but it feels good having her fingers slide the rubber down over my shaft.

It makes me feel better, somehow that thin bit of rubber makes fucking her more of a business proposition than intimate lovemaking. She stands over me on the bed and puts my head between her legs telling me to lick her before lowering herself onto my cock; she is much smaller than July and easier to handle. She seems so small and fragile I'm scared to move in case she breaks like glass. That doesn't last long.

"I want all of you," she growls, grabbing my shoulders and pulling herself up and then driving down on my erection. Her face contorts, and

I feel her shiver way down inside. She buries her face on my chest until she is done with her orgasm.

She sits still for a moment looking into my eyes then slowly begins moving up and down again until she reaches climax. "It's been so long since I've come like this," she pants. Her nipples are standing out at least half an inch. I bend down and lick them as she moans with pleasure. Suddenly, she rises up and places her legs under herself. She puts the tip of my cock just inside her.

"I want you to come in me," she purrs, and together we began to move up and down in rhythm. I hold on to her ass for dear life as she impales herself on my phallus. I feel myself let go, all my juices pump out of me. Lena's long nails scratch my shoulders and back. Her back arches, I can feel her orgasms pound through her body. I fall over backward on the bed; we fall asleep with her still on top of me.

In the surveillance room, Carol watches as the two lovemakers go through their last throes of passion and collapse on the bed. This job is worse than watching porn movies, she thinks; damn, I'm horny. She waits an hour before she goes into Bob Green's bedroom. The dim light outlines the two naked figures on the bed as she goes through Lena's handbag and then places a small microphone to the underside of it. She looks at the bed. "You've got her body, now you have to get her mind," Carol thinks as she leaves the room. It's going to be an interesting tomorrow, she thinks, wondering what she would tell July Green when she asked her what had happened last night.

Henekie dreaded calling Grundman and telling him the Green girl had gotten away on him, but he braced himself; it had to be done. He was surprised when Grundman didn't give him a chance to tell what happened. "The U.S. feds picked Green up a few days ago," he told Henekie. "We're trying to find out where they've taken him. You might as well come down here. We might have some work for you in the meantime."

Something's terribly wrong, Henekie thought as he hung up the phone. Well, Grundman's paying the bills, so he'd do as he was told, but he was going to do a little looking on his own when he got down there. Things were getting very interesting.

# TWENTY

I WAKE UP WITH a slight headache and an arm full of flesh. "I'm home," I think, but the dream soon fades to reality. "This is not July in my arms, and this is not home."

Lena opens her eyes and smiles. "Good morning, Mark."

I caress her face; my eyes see a young woman wise far beyond her years. I wonder why such a beautiful young girl is hanging around with the likes of Grundman and Waddell, but I guess youth and beauty are everything in her business.

"She's vulnerable," I think as I drop my head and kiss her; she's looking for a man to look after her, and she needs to find him soon. I know one thing: if she stays with these characters, she won't last long. If I can convince her to turn on them, the answers to many questions will be answered.

"Let's shower," I hear her say through my thoughts.

We wash each other making sure certain areas are cleaner than others. When we get out, I have a real boner. She laughs and takes a cloth from the bathroom counter. "I don't give shoe shines," she tells me, “but it’s kind of my trademark to make sure a man’s knob is shined in the morning before he leaves.

“I’m not quite ready to leave yet,” I tell her.

While she works on my knob, I sit on the toilet and phone Carol to tell her I wouldn’t be in today.

“How’s it going?” she asks.

I look down at Lena and my shiny knob. “Yes, I’m a little under the weather,” I tell her, “but the doctor’s here now, and I’m feeling better already.”

Lena rolls the rubber down over its head and then down the shaft. “It feels so good when you do that,” I tell her.

She shrugs her shoulders. “It is my job to bring pleasure to men,” she says. “It’s what I’m good at.”

We lie on our sides in the bed; her back is to me, and I slide my cock into her. A lazy man’s fuck, but we are lazy, and it is a comfortable way to talk business.

“So do you like the necklace,” she asks me.

I hadn’t noticed she’d put it on. I push her hair to one side and look at it. “Who does it belong to?” I ask her.

“Grundman,” she answers simply, waiting to see what I would say.

“Where did that creep get something like this?”

“One of the men who works for him owed him money. It’s what he told me,” she says.

“Must have been quite a debt,” I tell her. “That jewelry’s worth a few bucks.”

“He wants $75,000 US for it.

I whistle. “That is some debt.”

“He told me something about a botched job. I don’t pay much attention to him,” she says. “He’s such an asshole.”

“Could be it’s stolen?” I ask her. “Maybe it’s hot.”

“Probably was at one time,” she answers, “but it came with

Grundman, and he got it from someone called Henekie. I think it's been through enough hands now. No one's going to trace it."

Henekie was the name we had heard in Holmes's house. This is a lot to digest, and I lie silent for a moment trying to piece everything together.

"You had better stroke that thing a bit," she giggles. "Or it is going to fall right out."

Time to sort this all out later; I come back to the present and begin stroking into her regaining my prominence and gaining a small moan of satisfaction from Lena.

"I want to talk to you about something else, Lena. If I buy this necklace, I want something in return."

"You mean I'm not enough," she sounds disappointed.

"Yes, you're enough, if I get all of you." I kiss her back. "I think you're capable of using much more than your body," I say to her. "I need someone to look after my affairs here as well as to look good on my arm." She remains silent, so I go on. "I've found over the years that it is beneficial to make a woman my partner. They're tougher, and yet men tend to underestimate their abilities."

"What is it that you have in mind, Mark?"

I can tell she is interested. "I'm going to take over these islands, Lena, and I want you to look after them for me."

"What makes you think I'm capable of all this?" she asks.

"Instinct," I tell her. "Carol's a good business head, but she doesn't have your charisma or the ability to knock a man off his feet and screw up his mind."

"I'm not sure you have the power to take these islands," Lena says. "Manly Waddell has some very influential people behind him. Both he and Grundman want me to tell them everything you tell me."

"The two of us can do it, Lena. We'll start by driving a wedge between the two of them. We'll let the best man win unless of course you prefer to stay on their side."

"Grundman's a perverted little prick," she spits out, "and Manly will dump me as soon as someone else comes along. You're making me play a dangerous game, but at least you offer a future. That is, if you can stand up to Manly."

"I'll give you the option of staying neutral for a little while," I tell her. "I understand you don't know much about me, so I'll give you time to see what I can do."

I'll have to tell Grundman and Waddell something," Lena replies.

"I want you to tell them everything," I tell her "I especially want you to tell Waddell that Grundman told me to buy a farm on Andros Island and got $300,000 for making the deal,then I'll make a deal to buy the necklace for you if you agree to my terms."

She pulls away from me and rolls onto her back. She lifts her legs and spreads herself open to me. "Let's consummate the deal," her voice is like velvet.

I climb on top and put her legs over my shoulders, power-stroking into her until our worlds explode.

I order her a sundress, sandals, and panties from her favorite dress shop to be delivered before we return to the shower. She laughs that I didn't order her a bra.

It's a shame to cover these up at all," I say, lathering her breasts with soap.

I take her shopping in the Straw Market. She buys lots of what I would call junk, but it makes her happy, and that is my main intent.

It is late in the afternoon before we get to Grundman's office. He seems happy to see us. I tell him I am happy with the expediency in which he has completed our transaction.

"I haven't been here long," he tells me, "but I know how things work here, and I know the right people to get it done. I hope we can do more business in the future."

"You can be assured of it," I tell him. "In fact, Lena tells me you might part with some jewelry," I run my hand along Lena's cheek and then down to the necklace. "I think it was made for her, and I'd like for her to have it." She pulls my head toward her and kisses me. I'm sure Grundman has the idea that I am enthralled with her.

I fold my legs and clasp my hands on my knee. I want to make sure the speakerphone in my ring picks up all that is said.

"That's an exquisite piece of work," I tell him. "Wherever did you get it?"

Grundman seems anxious to stress the fact that he is someone with authority in the Bahamas..

"I have people in my employ who have the ability to find almost anything you might desire," Grundman tells us.

"What you're saying,is that you not only handle business deals, but you have people who perform certain jobs if you so desire."

"Almost anything you desire," he says, watching me closely.

"You're a very interesting man, Mr. Grundman, I'm sure I will appreciate having you around," I tell him.

He looks very pleased with himself. "I'm sure I can give you a very good deal on that necklace, say, US$60,000." He pulls open a drawer and gives me a letter. It states basically that the necklace has been appraised at $75,000US by an approved jeweler here in Nassau.

I have no idea whether it is authentic or not but decide to dicker a bit. "US$50,000 in cash," I tell him. "Take it or leave it."

I can see the wheels turning in Grundman's head. "How badly does he want it?" he was thinking.

I know he also wants my business. I take the necklace off Lena's neck and lay it on his desk. "Good day, Mr. Grundman," I say, and begin leading Lena from the room.

"Okay, okay," Grundman shouts. "That's cash? When do you want it?" Grundman asks.

I turn to Lena, "I'm sure you are anxious to have it."

She is so excited, she'd have screwed me right there on the floor if I'd wanted, but she restrains herself. "Yes," she says, "the sooner the better."

"Tell you what," I say, "you can have the money tonight. I have a meeting, but Lena can bring you the money and collect her necklace."

"Great!" Grundman shakes my hand, and we leave the building.

"You're willing to let me do this on my own," Lena asks after we are back in the limo. She pulls down her dress and rubs her nipple across my face.

"This is the test," I tell her, putting her tit back where it came from. "If you're going to fuck me around, now's the time to do it, only make sure you get a running start because if I find out you are screwing with me, they'll find that pretty little body of yours floating tits up in the ocean."

Lena pouts, but I know she takes me seriously.

"I don't care if you fuck him when you go there tonight, but any information you can get from him about what he or Waddell are up to might prove interesting to me," I tell her.

She looks shaken; maybe she had thought I was just another John. "Well, now she knows different."

We stop in front of her apartment, and I walk her to the door. "I think we're going to have a long and profitable career ahead of us," I say, kissing her cheek.

She smiles, looking better and goes inside.

Lena lay on the couch, her mind reeling; never had she been surrounded by so many powerful and dangerous men before. It scared her, yet exhilarated her. Soon though, she knew she'd have to make a choice. Grundman was the weakest, she decided. The other two would use him to get at each other; it was just a matter of time.

Once she had the necklace, his power over her was gone, but who was the stronger of the other two? Who was powerful enough to overcome Waddell and his Colombian boss; was it Bertrand?

She wanted him to be. A shiver went down her spine. "What a team we would be," she thought, but still Waddell seemed unbeatable, and her life depended on backing the winner. She fell asleep.

A sharp pain between her legs caused her eyes to open wide. Manly was bent over her, his hand under her night dress. "I just wanted to see if Bertrand wore it out," he said to her, moving his hand and wiping it on her gown.

"How did you get in here?" she asked.

He shrugged, "There's no place in Nassau that I can't go." He unbuttoned his pants, pulling out his half-limp cock and hung it in Lena's face. "Suck on this for a while, baby, and then I'll make you forget all about that slimy fuck."

Lena was tired from the day with Bertrand, and the last thing on her mind right now was sex, but there was no refusing Manly. She opened her mouth and accepted his rapidly swelling member.

"So did he tell you anything interesting?" Manly asked.

Lena pulled his cock out of her mouth long enough to say, "Not that I remember." She put it back in her mouth and began to suck again, but Manly shoved it down her throat, choking her. She gagged, fighting for breath. Slowly, he pulled it out leaving it half an inch from her face. "You do that again, and I'll bite it off," she gasped.

His eyes became pinpricks. He flipped his cock and slapped her in the face with it. "You bite me," he snarled, "and I snap your back, leaving you paralyzed for the rest of your life. Now, what did he tell you?"

She was very frightened now. "Grundman sold him a farm on Andros," Lena told him.

"What do you mean a farm?" Manly quizzed.

"I don't know, he just told me Grundman sold him a farm for a million dollars. He said it was a real steal."

Waddell's face turned to a look of rage, "There's only one farm on Andros worth that kind of money." The reality of it all hit him, and he began to holler. "That little prick. Why didn't he tell me before he made the deal?" He began shaking Lena, "Is Grundman working for Bertrand now," he yelled. "Is he?"

Lena was terrified; she had never seen Manly like this, she was sure he would kill her. His hands closed on her throat. She tried to act calm. "Don't be a fool, Waddell, I can help you," she told him. He held his hand on her throat for a while longer, and then to her relief, he let her go.

"I want to know every move those two guys make," he told her. "If I hear one of them has a shit and you don't know about it, you'll be shark bait in the bottom of the harbor."

Lena watched as he stuffed his prick back in his pants. Then he flew into another violent rage. "That fucking little bastard, he's dead meat." Manly began throwing her furniture around the room smashing everything he touched. Lena lay silent, glad it wasn't her he was tossing around, and then he left.

Lena had a shower and dressed. "I wish Mark would get here with the money," she thought. Lena was worried that Waddell would kill Grundman before she got there, and then she'd never get her necklace. Finally, the doorbell rang, it was Mark's driver. He gave her a package and left.

She counted the money, $50,000 in U.S. bills; it was all there. She ordered a taxi and took it to Grundman's apartment. He lived near the top of a high-rise overlooking the harbor. The door was partially open. "That's strange," she thought, stepping through it. She was scared of what she might find. "Hello," she yelled, searching the rooms and finding no one.

She noticed the curtains blowing in the open patio door to the deck. Stepping out into the warm air, she saw Grundman sitting naked in a chair.

"Hello, Lena," his voice was slurred, and she could tell he was very high on something. "Did you bring the money?" he asked.

"Yes," she held up the packet.

"Good," he said, "just lay it on the deck for now, we're going to play a little game."

"Where's your little consort?" Lena asked. "She's your plaything, not me."

"You best be nice to me if you want the necklace," Grundman told her.

"Come on, Grundman, I brought the money, now where's the necklace?"

"Out there," he pointed.

She followed his direction and looked out over the balcony. Tied to a string from the balcony above was her beloved necklace. She walked over to the balcony and tried to reach it but the necklace was too far out from the railing. She looked down, which made her dizzy, and she stepped back. Grundman laughed.

She turned to plead with him, but he was standing now in the dim light; she saw a gun in his hand. Fear entered her heart. "What do you want, Grundman?" she asked.

"First, I want you to take your clothes off, and then I will hold you while you reach for the necklace."

"How do I know you won't let me go?" she asked.

"Because I'll have my cock up your ass," he told her. "That will anchor you, or I guess I'll go over with you," he told her.

Lena winced. She would be totally at his mercy which was something Grundman did not have much of. Still, the jewels sparkled from the lights below, so close yet so far. "What will Mark think if I come back without the necklace," she thought. He had said this was a test. If she came back without it, he would either think she was working with Grundman and Waddell or that she had no balls.

These men seemed to think it was very important to have balls. Lena saw no humor in this; men had always held the fact that they have balls over a woman. Well! Balls or no balls, she wasn't leaving without that necklace.

"Does it have to be up my ass, Grundman?"

"I want to hear you squeal with pain, Lena," he licked his lips in anticipation.

"All right, Grundman, I agree, but only if you get rid of the gun and tie me to the railing."

This seemed to deflate Grundman. His bargaining power was being tested, he hadn't thought this far ahead, he'd been so obsessed with his fantasy finally coming true. Now the bitch wanted to negotiate. Still, he was so close. "Okay," he agreed.

He left the balcony through the patio door and came back with one of the ropes he used to tie his girls or himself to the bed.

Lena stripped down with Grundman watching every move. She walked to the railing naked, taking only her handbag with her. She took the rope and tied it around her waist. The rope was very short. She tied the other end to the railing. It only allowed her about a foot of slack. She reached in her bag and pulled out a condom. Lena always came prepared. The condom she pulled out was especially lubricated for Grundman had in mind.

"Come here, Grundman," she said, like calling a small child. Once he saw she was tied to the railing, he threw the revolver down beside his money and moved up close to Lena. She slapped his cock, getting a sigh of pleasure from him and making him fully erect so she could properly install the rubber on him. He was drooling from the mouth now and becoming very impatient.

"Just a minute, Grundman." She took a lubricant can from her handbag and sprayed it up her anus. She turned herself and bent over the railing headfirst. "Please be careful, Grundman," she pleaded, glad he wasn't the size of Mark and Waddell. The very thought of them made her shudder.

Grundman was so excited he had no time to listen to her pleading; in fact it turned him on. He felt himself slide into her easily and went in as far as he could. Lena felt the initial pain of penetration then the lubrication took over, and she turned her attention to reaching the necklace.

She tried not to look down; fear rose in her stomach, but she swallowed keeping it down. Almost but not quite her fingers touched the necklace, but she couldn't quite reach it. She felt her toes leave the deck and the rope stretch tight as she extended herself to the limit. Her fingertips closed around the necklace; she felt herself falling forward, the string tied to the necklace snapped from her weight.

I have it; her exultation was instantly replaced with terror. Grundman was hammering into her hard from behind now. The only thing holding her was the rope cutting into her waist. She tried to scream, but her mouth filled full of vomit gagging and leaving her gasping for breath.

Her squirming only excited Grundman more. "I'm in control, you bitch. Now I can have the money and the necklace too." His mind elated with the prospect. When I'm finally done with you, Lena, we'll bargain all right, we'll bargain for your life. He felt the power of having someone's life in his hands and imagined cutting the rope and watching the fear in her eyes as she fell away from him. He rammed into her in quick hard motions feeling the tide rising in his balls as he reached over her to pull the plastic bag over her head.

Lena felt Grundman pull out of her, and then his body seemed to slide over hers and she watched, terror stricken, as his body fell away from her.

Grundman had never felt this sensation while having sex before, not even when the bag was over his head nearly choking him to death was the sensation so intense. He was floating in the air, soaring through the sky; he reached for his cock and stroked himself off. The next sensation he felt was death.

Lena felt hands pull her back inside the balcony and vaguely saw a shadowy figure disappear through the patio door. She lay on the deck crying, unable to move. The pain in her waist broke through her fear. She looked down; the rope was gone, but a red welt showed where it had been. The necklace, where was it? She panicked thinking she'd dropped it, but to her amazement the necklace was firmly grasped in her hand. She began laughing and crying at the same time then slowly it sunk in what had just happened. "What do I do now?" she thought, getting up. She looked over the balcony railing hanging on tightly. A crowd had gathered around where Grundman had fallen.

I've got to get out of here. She quickly put on her clothes fixing her face and hair in the mirror before checking the apartment for any evidence she might have left. She placed the necklace and Grundman's gun in her handbag. She looked for the money, but it was gone. "Well, whoever you are, I guess you earned it," then left the apartment.

She placed her head against the cool wall of the elevator. She thought about the figure she'd seen leaving the balcony. She wondered who he was working for; was it Mark or Manly who had sent him? Neither of them would probably admit to doing it, leaving her in the same boat, who's the strongest. The way Waddell had stormed out of her apartment, she might not have to wait too long to find out. The elevator stopped, and she went over to the doorman to order a taxi. She could see the crowd of people milling around outside the front door. "What's going on?" she asked.

"Some fool jumped off one of the balconies," he told her as he whistled for a taxi.

Lena didn't sleep very well and when she did sleep, she was woken by the dream of a man falling away from her. She was still in bed the next morning when the phone rang; she picked it up. "Grundman's dead," It was Waddell's voice. "Someone pushed Grundman off his balcony last night," he told her. "Are you going to meet your friend today?"

"You mean Mr. Bertrand? Yes, I'm to meet him this afternoon," she answered.

"Tell him I want to see him in his office as soon as possible." He hung up.

Lena sat looking at the phone. It didn't sound like Waddell had killed Grundman, but she was sure he wouldn't tell her anyway. She was sure Mark would want her in bed as soon as she arrived, but instead, he invited her to lunch on his terrace.

"I hear Grundman was killed last night. Did you get there in time to get your necklace?" I ask her.

Lena breaks down; she has to tell someone what happened. She had not realized just how shaken she was. "I couldn't see the man who pushed him over," she says between sobs, "but if he had not, I'm sure I'd be where Grundman is now." She suddenly stops crying, "Did you kill him, Mark?" She looks right into my eyes.

I evade the question, "Grundman was a prick. He had no friends and made lots of enemies, any of them are capable of getting rid of him."

Lena realizes she might never know who killed Grundman, or who had saved her life for that matter.

July played the tapes again that night in the privacy of her own room. She dreamed that Bob was on top of her and played with herself until she heard the words "July," putting her over the top and leaving her in a sweating pile. She spent the rest of the night dreaming instead of her usual nightmare.

Manly Waddell sat in front of Bertrand's desk. I can easily see he is upset even though he tries to hide it.

"That farm you bought over on Andros is our operation," he tells me. "No matter what Grundman told you, that property was not for sale."

"Is that why you killed him?" I ask.

"Don't shit me, we both know who killed Grundman," he says, looking me in the eye. "There are certain things people know enough to leave alone on the islands. Anything APCO is involved in, you leave alone if you value your life."

I shrug, "The bank held the mortgage and wanted to get rid of it, I simply took it off their hands."

"We realize Grundman may have pulled the wool over your eyes, Mr. Bertrand. The company has authorized me to pay you back your investment in return, of course, for the title."

"Plus the $200,000 it cost me to have Grundman handle the deal?" I ask.

Waddell squirmed, "That little shit did stick you good, didn't he?"

I shrug my shoulders, "If you want it back, it must be worth a lot more than I paid for it."

"I don't think you understand what I'm telling you, Bertrand. You may think you're tough because you can kill some little leech like Grundman, but you have no idea who you are fucking with here. Even the U.S. government can't handle these guys. You're lucky they decided to pay you rather than kill you, or you'd be dead by now." He is silent for a moment letting what he said sink in.

"All right, we'll pay you the $200,000 Grundman cost you, but you take your little tin ship and get the fuck out of here just as fast as you came."

"You don't have any fucking idea who I am, do you?" I say to him calmly. "You think I'm some fuck pot head who pedaled a little horse on the streets of Beirut." I'm starting to get angry now. "If it isn't for the fact that I need you alive as a messenger boy, you'd be with your buddy Grundman in hell right now. And don't shit me, we both know you killed Grundman, so don't try to pin that on me."

"You'd love to get your title and then have me thrown in jail for Grundman's murder. Well, the tables have turned, Mr. Waddell. We've let the word out on the street that you did Grundman in, and we have some tapes in our possession that makes things look pretty bad for you," I turn on the tape which includes sounds of Waddell wrecking Lena's apartment.

"I've heard enough," Waddell got up to leave.

"Sit down, Mr. Waddell. We may do some business yet."

He hesitates and then turns to me, "What do you want, Bertrand? You might as well ask for lots, you're a dead man anyway."

"Like the old gunslinger said, 'There ain't room for both of us in town'," I tell him. "It's a small island. I don't think there's a hole big enough for you to crawl into." I watch his eyes blaze.

"What I want is a billion in cash, and the farm is yours."

All Waddell could get out was, "Fuck you," before I got a chance to continue with, "Otherwise, I want half of everything you put through the farm."

Waddell looked at me in amazement.

"If you don't agree to my terms, we'll simply shut you down and put our own stuff through there."

"You've got bats in your belfry, man!" he exclaims."I can see there's no use trying to tell you fuck all. That's what I'm going to do. I'm going to hang your dick as a trophy on my wall. The epitaph will read, 'What's left of the man they couldn't tell fuck all'," Waddell expounds.

I stand up and speaking very low, "If I was you, I'd hurry and tell your friends what I just said. Maybe if you suck their cocks long enough, they'll hide you till they realize they don't need you anymore. Either way, you're fucked, Waddell. You've got no place to go and no place to hide, you're just fucked."

Waddell backs out of the room; one never knew what a manic might do.

The next night, a shipment of drugs landed at the runway on the Andros farm. Another plane followed close behind. All the APCO men had no idea what was going on until men began pouring out of the second plane; by then it was too late. The APCO men tried to fight back, but they were quickly overpowered. Then the men shot the tires out from under the APCO plane and loaded its contents onto their own plane. By the time the APCO people figured out what was going on and got reinforcements, the intruders were long gone.

The next day, two truckloads of heavily armed men suddenly arrived at the farm. There was a short firefight, but the APCO men were no match for this kind of firepower. They were told APCO no longer owned the property, and the new owner, Bertrand., was taking over. They were all put in an old boat and towed out to sea. Fortunately, there was a U.S. Coast Guard cutter waiting for them when they drifted into American waters.

Lena was a scared woman. Grundman was a weasel and always got her in trouble, but at least he had been there to help her work out her problems. Now he was gone. She had met a few other men during her stay in Nassau, but the government was in turmoil and most of them were fighting for their livelihoods, let alone being seen with a woman like her. That left her with two men who were bitter enemies. Sooner or later, one of them was going to decide she had sided with the other, and she was convinced they would kill her just like they had Grundman.

Waddell had come to her apartment last night, forcing himself on her. He had fucked her hard, hurting her, asking her if she enjoyed it when he rammed it into her, slapping her when she did not answer. He had climbed off her when he was done.

"I hope you got your rocks off listening to that," he shouted to no one in particular.

"What are you saying?" she asked.

"I know your house is bugged," he told her. "Bertrand played back a tape of us together when you told me Grundman sold him the farm on Andros."

She watched as Waddell did up his fly and headed for the door, "You picked the wrong side, baby. That might be the last fuck you ever get."

"I did not know," she tried to tell him as he went out the door, but he did not stop to listen. She searched the house but found nothing except Mark's ring.

She would give it to him when she went to see him that afternoon. She thought she would wait until after they made love. Mark was like everyone else these days, stressed out.

He was having trouble getting hard; it did not bother Lena, she had seen lots of men go through this, but to Bob it was embarrassing. He was glad Lena didn't seem to mind. She eased things a lot. He couldn't understand what was happening to him. In his mind, he should be able to get it up on demand. He loved sex, why did she have to work so hard on him before he could do it.

Lena was sure his mind was somewhere else on all his troubles. What she did not know was that his mind was subconsciously consumed with guilt. Today was not a good day, and Bob was very embarrassed.

"I'm going away for a few days," he said. "I'm worried about you, I wish you'd move in here and let me protect you, Lena."

"Maybe then you would not have to bug my apartment," she decided to say.

He smiled, "It was the only way I could protect you, Lena. If that bastard would have stayed one minute longer last night, I would have killed him."

"To say nothing about my privacy," she countered, "you left your ring at my place." She gave it to him and began to dress.

He went over to a drawer and pulled out a beautiful gold chain. He hung the ring on the chain and went over to Lena. "I want you to have this while I'm gone," he told her as he placed it around her neck.

"You know I'm used to receiving gifts, Mark. I very seldom give them back."

Mark smiled at her, "We'll see if you can earn it first."

Lena's mind wandered as she got into Mark's car for the ride back to her apartment. She sat in the back seat watching the city lights go by. "If only I could be like the people living in their secure little homes," she thought.

"You knew Grundman in Germany before you came here, didn't you, Lena?" It was the driver's voice. He sounded different somehow.

"Yes," she answered, "why do you ask?"

"Can you even remember him talk about a man named Green?"

The question instantly put her on alert. "Who are you?" she asked.

He looked at her in the rearview mirror. "I'm a man who needs some questions answered, and I'm not above using painful means to get them. You know what happened to Grundman," he told her, "the same thing could happen to you. So let us just be comfortable, and we shall chat while I take you home."

"You did not have to do it this way, Mark," she thought. "Why can't you just trust me to tell you all I know?"

Ansly came bursting into surveillance room. "What's going on?" he asked breathlessly. "Some guy is quizzing Lena, but we don't know where in hell she is," the agent told him. Ansly listened for a moment, "Jeez, he must have her in the car. Where's our driver?"

One of the agents got on the phone to see if anyone knew where he was. "We've got to tighten up around here. What the fuck does this guy want?" All they could do was listen, hoping Lena would be all right.

"I worked for Grundman when he was still in Germany," the driver told her, "but when I saw what he was doing to you and to my necklace, I lost it. I began to realize he was small fish anyway." The driver went on, "So now, I figure you owe me one. What I want to know is why did he come here? There must have been someone here to set him up."

"Are you working for Bertrand?" Lena asked.

"I'm not working for anybody right now," he told her. "Now are you going to answer some questions, or do I stop the car?"

Lena had already thought about what she would say, "All I know is that Grundman was friends with a man named Manly Waddell. I'd like to thank you for helping me the other night, whoever you are."

"The only reason you stayed alive that night is because I thought you were some bimbo Grundman was playing with. Besides, I don't kill unless there is something in it for me. I had talked with Grundman earlier that afternoon," Henekie told her. "He wanted me to kill half of Nassau, but when it came to paying me the money he owed me, he then threatened me. That necklace you almost lost your life over,is a fake," he told her. "I came back to get the real one and get rid of Grundman, then when I saw how determined he was to kill you, I started thinking maybe you were someone of interest. so I followed your taxi when you left the building."

He turned to her, "You lead a very interesting life, Lena, and you are no bimbo." Then he turned back to his driving. "I'm only telling you all this because when a woman travels in the company you do, you know she knows too much and becomes a liability. What I'm saying is that to someone, you are worth money. Whether they want you dead or alive, it does not matter to me."

Lena shivered; she had no doubts that this man could kill her without blinking, she had to think fast. " If you go to work for me,I won't tell Bertrand you took his money."

"What would you like me to do?" he asked.

"I know the right people," she told him. "You get Manly Waddell out of the way, and we can run these islands."

"You're an ambitious lady!" Henekie told her.

"Stick around," she told him, "you'll find out just how ambitious." She smiled, "Take me to my apartment, and we can talk about this over a drink." Lena heard the rain begin to pound on the roof about the same time as she heard Henekie's laugh ring through the car.

"I need better references before I make up my mind about who I work for," he told her. "Who knows, you might not be the high bidder." He pulled the car over to the sidewalk. "How much money do you have on you?" he asked.

She opened her handbag, felt the revolver, and then pulled out whatever cash she had and gave it to him. "We shall call this bond money on your bid," he told her. "Now get out. You're only a block from your home, but I'm a new boyfriend, and your father might be waiting for you."

She opened the door, "This girlfriend might not want to go out with you again after being treated like this."

"We will definitely have another date," he told her. "Whether it is our last one remains to be seen."

She shut the door and watched the car lights disappear. The rain actually felt good, cooling her skin. She began walking toward her apartment. At least she had kept herself alive for tonight. Tomorrow, she would be worth more dead than alive, and she had no place to run.

"Shit," was all Ansly could say. He'd had his men wait for Lena and her intruder at her apartment. They wouldn't get him now, but they'd certainly got an earful. They also had a dead agent. He'd been found in a parking lot; his ID and revolver were missing.

Henekie found Lena's offer more intriguing than anything else. He hadn't been in the Bahamas long, but the winds of change were on everyone's lips. Right now everything that was done on the islands had to be sanctioned by Waddell. A new reform government if elected would leave him vulnerable. Henekie knew Waddell was the drug cartel's front man here. They might soon be looking for a new man.

Then there was the new man in town, Bertrand. Henekie suspected Bertrand was much like himself, sensing a change in the islands that would leave them ripe for the picking. Bertrand apparently had money and the backing to try and solidify his position before the new government took power. Did he have the power to take out a well-organized drug cartel; that was the question. Then there was Lena, she was playing a dangerous game with both sides. Was she really working for one side or was she trying to sneak through the middle?

Henekie decided to talk to Waddell. He was the only one he could contact right now anyway or the only one who would return his call if he left the right message. Henekie got Waddell's answering service when he phoned, but it took only minutes before Waddell answered his call.

"You said you had information about a man called Green?" Waddell asked into the phone. It didn't take Henekie long to convince Waddell that he was legitimate.

"Be on the street in front of your hotel, alone," Waddell told him. "I'll pick you up in my car."

Fifteen minutes later, Henekie watched the limo pull over to the curb, and he got in. Henekie knew he had to get Waddell's attention right away, so he told him about the botched hit up in Canada and how he had found Grundman.

"I was coming to work for Grundman when he told me to come here. Now I find he's dead. I still want to get Green," Henekie told him. "But I can't do it alone."

"The American government has him somewhere," Manly told him. "Grundman was trying to find out where."

"The point is I think I know where," Henekie said.

Waddell knew without asking that to find out where would cost money.

"How did you find me?" Waddell asked.

"The night I was to meet Grundman, I saw this woman called Lena leaving his apartment. I followed her and got your name," Henekie told him.

Waddell frowned. "She talks too much."

"I decided to let her live till I talked to you," Henekie said. "Who knows, she might be valuable to us in the future."

Waddell looked straight ahead. "What's this so-called information going to cost me?"

"The information is not for sale. What I sell are my services. I have a plan that will get rid of both Bertrand and Green. My services, on completion of this contract, will cost you two million U.S."

Waddell pursed his lips and thought for a while.

"We're having a little trouble over on Andros Island right now," Waddell told him. "The Colombians are coming in to handle it themselves. I would doubt we will have to worry about Bertrand after that. If you do know where Green is, then we may require your services for that job later—that is, if we can negotiate a price."

"Yeah, well, just in case things don't work out, remember I told you what I can do and what the price will be." Both Henekie and Waddell remained silent, lost in thought as the car took Henekie back to his hotel. Henekie decided to head for Andros Island first thing in the morning. He wanted to see what was happening there firsthand.

Kent Ansly was an unassuming name. He'd worked his way up the CIA ladder quickly; and when the new Drug Enforcement Agency, or DEA, was set up, he was the first to move over. His job was to enforce the area around Miami. He did a good job, not so much by enforcing but by working with the Miami mob. The DEA didn't care how he did it, as long as they got results, and soon he was in control of the whole

Caribbean. He convinced his superiors that the way to control the drugs coming in was to find a man with the experience to liaison with all the people in the region.

They had found the perfect man. He'd been involved with the drug trade in Asia and in no time had an agreement with the main drug cartel in Colombia, run by El Presidente, and with Ansly, the DEA man in control of the southeastern area of the states. The liaison man was situated in the Bahamas, his identity known only to Ansly and El Presidente under the code name the Referee.

The agreement worked on a quota system, and it was so successful that over the years the DEA left Ansly to do basically whatever he wanted without any oversight what so ever. They didn't care that he received a huge kickback from the cartel and the Miami mob each year, as long as they looked like they were getting results.

As time went by, the suppliers in Colombia got tired of being limited in their operations and created a whole new route into the United States. The Colombians had opened up a whole can of worms. The Mexicans were as ruthless as the Colombians, and soon the drugs entering the United States were a low-grade, low-priced commodity that appealed only to the lower classes. The only people that still demanded top-grade cocaine was the Miami mob, but they looked after their own markets in Miami, New York and the west coast. This diminished Ansly's take drastically.

He complained to El Presidente, but it was evident he'd lost control of the other cartels in Colombia and was concentrating on the new markets the Referee had found him in Asia and Europe. When he complained to the Referee, he was told to get out and leave the Mexicans to fight it out.

"That's not a market we should be in anymore, Kent," he told him. "They have all the Hispanic desert storm vets they need to form an army and all the mules to haul it in cheap. Why bang your head against the wall? Ansly was still young and not ready to retire. He was convinced by his agents in Colombia that if he could get rid of El Presidente, he could bring the other major drug lords under his fold and again control the American market.

He hatched a plan to force El Presidente to come out of Colombia and have a showdown with a rival who was making him look weak and toothless in his own territory.

Ansly went to Sir Harry Chamberlain, who was the Interpol man in the Bahamas, and asked him if he knew of anyone who could carry out the part of being El Presidente's rival. Sir Harry immediately thought of Bob Greene, whom he considered to be a prime hit by the cartel because he was causing trouble on the farm over on Andros.

Ansly didn't bother to tell Sir Harry that there would be no loose ends. He just told Sir Harry to get him wherever he was.

At dawn, a turbo prop appeared out of the sun, making a low fast pass over the Andros farm project. The pilot made two more passes before strafing the trees along the runway with the high-caliber machine guns mounted in the nose of the plane. Nothing!

The pilot spoke into his radio. "It is like our reports told us, there's nothing here."

"Okay," his radio crackled, "we're coming in, cover us."

A large transport dropped in low over the lake and taxied down the runway. It stopped at the very end of the runway and the cartel's men began jumping out, securing the perimeters. They soon reported that there was no one anywhere. The pilot in the turbo prop began searching the area, "Nothing!" he repeated, and "Whoever was here has left."

"There's no sign of bodies or any damage that we can find. It is eerie, as if everyone just vanished," the ground captain reported. "The runway is secured. You might as well come in, he told Waddell.

Henekie chartered a plane into Fresh Creek, He found a car to rent and got some vague directions on how to tour the island. He soon realized that this may have been a mistake. There were few roads, and he didn't find anyone who knew what he might be looking for.

He finally made it to the Andros airport hotel that night. He sat in the bar and started buying drinks. It was usually a good way to get information. He decided to make the hotel his home for a few days. The place just felt right. Sooner or later, he would run into somebody who would tell him what he wanted to know.

"So what are we going to do with Lena?" Ansly asked at their daily morning meeting.

"We've given her every chance to work with us," Carol said."Now, by the tapes, we just heard she's in a real jam. I think we should bring her in."

July concurred that Lena was in a real jam. "But if we convince her to come and stay with us, will she help us?"

"I don't think so. We've got two agents in the room across from her, and her room is wired, maybe it's better to leave her. So far, she's been a gold mine of information, thanks to the mike Bob put around her neck," Ansly said, looking at July.

"What I'm worried about is that we shall probably need her testimony to link Waddell and this new guy to the people murdered in Canada," July told the other agents around the table.

What July didn't know was that Ansly didn't really give a shit about the necklace other than it motivated Bob and July Green to play a part in his plan. So he played along, knowing in the grand scheme of things it would be of little consequence.

"We've got her pretty well-covered ," Ansly told them. "I'm leaving today to join the ship. We got word this morning that the Colombians landed at the Andros farm. There will be a shipment coming through pretty quickly. Hopefully, we can intercept it. You all have your assignments here, just keep your eyes open and wish us luck."

For two days, the Colombians held the farm on full alert, but nothing happened. On the third night, a plane landed and was quickly unloaded onto trucks for delivery at Buzzard Bay. The Colombians knew they would have to spread themselves thin, but they didn't dare send all their men to guard the shipment.

"I can't see having any trouble anyway," their commandant told them. "We've checked out the island, whoever was here has definitely left."

The trucks and their armed guard arrived at Buzzard Bay right around midnight. At the given signal, the two high-speed motorboats began moving in. They tied up beside the old barge as usual. The Colombians set up guards, and the rest started unloading the trucks.

The light from the flares was so bright that it lit up the entire area as well as blinding the Colombians. They made a run for it, but vicious gunfire from the surrounding trees cut them down. Their guards had already been taken care of, and within seconds they were decimated. The motorboats tried to take off but were trapped by two large motorboats blocking the only way out of the bay.

The drug runners' boats were racked with machine gunfire and both quickly burst into flame and exploded sending sparks high into the sky. Armed men swarmed over the site, picking up bodies and the wounded.

This was only the first part of Ansly's plan. He was already on his way to the farm project aboard one of two helicopters from the naval base. Ansly knew exactly how many Colombians had landed there and approximately where they were located on-site.

It was still dark when the first helicopter took out the renovated fighter plane on the runway. Ansly and his men then landed and took control of the area. The other helicopter unloaded its men on the only road into the farm. Two vehicles tried to escape, but they were quickly cut down by a heavy crossfire. The farm was sealed off. The remaining Colombians had no place to go but still fought viciously. A hectic firefight ensued lasting till dawn when the last of them were surrounded and rounded up.

Ansly counted the bodies. He decided there were still two missing. These were dug out after a manhunt with help from the helicopters tracking them down in the nearby trees. The helicopters returned to base, leaving only Ansly and his men to clean up and secure the site.

Henekie was asleep in his room when he heard an explosion. He looked out the window to see the sky to the east completely red. Other people were milling about outside. He pulled on his pants and joined them.

"What's happening?" he asked one of the men he had met in the bar.

"It's Buzzard Bay," the man told him. "Very bad shit happens there."

"Can we go down and see what's happening?" he asked, finding his car keys.

"If you value your life, it would be best to stay away from there. That road will be very dangerous tonight."

Henekie decided he was right. It would be too dark to see much and if no one would show him the way, there was no use chancing it tonight.

He was early for breakfast, so were the others. In the daylight, he had no problem finding people wanting a ride down to Buzzard Bay. There was little evidence that anything had happened really. There were some pieces of wood and metal floating near the dock. The only thing Henekie could see was the top of a boat or barge sunk in the small lagoon where the fishing boats came in to load, but it was impossible to know how long it had been there. The police were there towing the burned-out remains of a truck and leaving it parked back among the trees. What did remain, ominous though, was the sight of a big white ship anchored in the bay.

Henekie listened to the rumors spreading around him. Bertrand was the name on everyone's lips. Looks like he won this round, Henekie thought. It would be interesting to see how the Colombians countered and even more interesting to see if Waddell would listen to his proposal now.

Henekie wasn't ready to rush off to Nassau just yet. "If I play my cards right", he thought, "I might just be able to bypass Waddell and go right to the top." No longer was he going to offer his services to lieutenants who took all the money and glory. If he could put together a foolproof plan, they would listen to him, and he would never have to do the dirty work again. The real money was knowing the right people wanting the work done and knowing the ones who could do it. "Soon," he thought to himself, "I'll be in that position."

His break soon came. For the next few days, he watched the activities around Buzzard Bay closely. One morning, he watched as a fuel truck pulled up beside an old fuel barge and began loading it with fuel. Two armed men watched the barge as the driver left and returned with another load. Then the old barge was towed out to Bertrand's ship by a powerful looking patrol boat. The driver watched for a while then jumped in his truck to leave.

"Any chance of a ride?" Henekie asked the driver.

"Where you going?" asked the driver.

"Andros Hotel," Henekie answered.

"Sure," the driver replied, "I'm going right by there."

As they drove away, Henekie said to the driver, "Good job," he pointed back at the ship, "I imagine it uses a lot of fuel."

"Yes, every second day, they will need two loads," the driver answered. "They've got so much electronic shit on board. They have to keep the engines working all the time."

"She's a fuel hungry bitch," Henekie said to himself as much as to the driver, his mind clicking on to something they had used once before.

Henekie made two calls from the Andros Hotel. One was to an

engineer he knew in the States, the other was to Singapore, where Bertrand's ship had been retrofitted. What he got back from these two phone calls excited him; he had his plan.

Waddell picked him up in his car again. Henekie noticed he was much friendlier this time.

"Needless to say, I can't give you a million dollars just because you tell me you have information which may or may not be of value," he told Henekie. "But if you give me something to go on, I can take your information to the right people and see what they think."

"I know how to get to Bertrand," Henekie told him, "but I want to deliver the information myself."

Waddell laughed, "That's impossible. My contacts do not wish to get personally involved in this type of work."

"Just tell them what I told you, and we shall see what happens," Henekie told Waddell.

"You realize if these people don't like you," Waddell snapped his fingers, "that's it."

"I have a feeling if you don't come up with something pretty quick," Henekie snapped his fingers, "that's it for you too."

Waddell gave him a long hard stare, "When can you leave?"

"Anytime," Henekie told him. "The sooner the better."

Waddell knew it was a long shot, but it was the only shot he had.

El Presidente was under extreme pressure from the Colombian government and the U.S. government agents. He was no longer able to sail his yacht wherever he wished for fear of attack. Now with his main supply route cut off, he was desperate. Waddell was expendable; in fact, now that Bertrand controlled the airstrip on Andros, Waddell was a dead man, unless he could come up with a way to gain control of his own backyard.

Waddell and Henekie flew into Colombia the next day, both knowing they might not come back. A car picked them up at the airport and took them out of the city. They traveled down a highway which turned into a gravel road leading to a small village. From here, a jeep with armed guards took them down a trail, through several checkpoints, finally arriving at a walled compound.

Henekie noticed the walls bristled with weapons of all kinds. Inside the compound, antiaircraft guns stood at the ready. Henekie was impressed; he hadn't seen this many weapons in one place since the Civil War in Somalia.

They were searched and then led into a small room where were told to wait until the man would see them. Henekie was surprised to meet a small man with a big smile, not at all looking like a man who would hold their lives in his hands.

He exchanged pleasantries and got to the point. "We have a serious problem on our hands, Manly," he said. "What do you propose to do about it?"

"Henekie here has some information which may help us resolve our problem," Waddell answered for the first time, showing his nervousness.

El Presidente turned his attention to Henekie and indicated for him to proceed.

"I'll start with some background," Henekie said. "A while ago, there was a man named Green who, along with some other Canadians, were running the farm on Andros Island where your airstrip is located. I was with a group who had the job of eliminating any potential risks these people might have to your operation. Green somehow slipped away from us. I was on his trail when a Mr. Grundman, who was our contact man, called me back to Nassau saying the U.S. agents had picked up Green. The problem I had with this information was that I had a telephone conversation with Mr. Green after this was to have happened. He was on a ship when I talked to him. I believe he is on the same ship Bertrand is on."

El Presidente sat digesting what Henekie had just told him. "You think Bertrand has Green?" El Presidente asked.

"I think something funny is going on all right," Henekie told him. "It was definitely U.S. agents who took Green from Nassau, yet I talked to him on a boat. For whatever reason, I think the U.S. government has Bertrand working for them, and it's actually their agents that have you tied up on Andros."

Some of this was making sense to the reports El Presidente had been receiving. "Very interesting." El Presidente told Henekie, "So what do you propose we do about it?"

"Bertrand's ship is almost impregnable from the air and sea," he said, "but I have a plan to make it vulnerable. However, I will need your help and a couple of million sent to a certain address before you can hear what I have to say."

"You demand a lot for a man in your position." El Presidente's smile was gone now.

"My plan will work," Henekie looked him right the eye. "We both know if you defeat the U.S. government here, they'll go home with their tail between their legs, and the Bahamian government may not be so hasty to change course."

"Where do you want the money sent?"

Henekie gave him an address in Munich, Germany. Rona would signal him when the money had been safely put away.

"I will need two armor-piercing rocket launchers of this type." He handed El Presidente a letter with the information he needed to get the right ones. "I will also need a ship," Henekie told him, "and some specialized electronic equipment."

"Okay," El Presidente sat back, "you've intrigued me enough to make you a deal. I'll put the funds in trust in your bank. If and when I walk back in this door and that plan of yours has worked, the funds will be released in your name. If I don't come back, you won't get the money, which won't matter because you'll be dead anyway."

"Does that mean you're coming with us?" Waddell asked.

"My men are losing faith in me," El Presidente told them. "If I go with them, it will boost their morale, plus, I think this is important enough for me to make sure it's handled properly. Besides, it's time I gained back a little respect."

Waddell felt left out as he listened to the two men haggle over how the payment was to be handled, but when he was asked to leave the room while they discussed Henekie's plan, it really made him feel left out.

# TWENTY-ONE

THINGS DIDN'T GET any better for Waddell. "Funny," he thought, "I held the upper hand when we left Nassau, now on the way back, Henekie has control." No matter what he had tried to find out, Henekie put him off, telling him that he had been told to say nothing. When they landed in Miami, Henekie told Waddell he was to continue on to Nassau alone.

"I have a message I want you to take to Lena," Henekie told him.

"Take your own fucking messages. I'm not your messenger boy," Waddell snarled back. Henekie shrugged and walked away not seeming to be at all disturbed.

When Waddell got back to his office in Nassau, he expected his desk to be covered with messages. It was, but all from the wrong people. He phoned his contacts reassuring them all he was still in control.

"There are rumors on the street that there's a new boss in town," one of his government men told him, "in fact, the word is it's a woman," the man told him sounding very nervous.

Waddell laughed, "Goes to show there's no truth in the rumor, doesn't it?"

"Yeah, you're right," the man answered sounding unconvinced. A woman, Waddell thought feeling better, that would be the day the cartel would put a woman in charge.

Little did Waddell know this was exactly what Henekie had asked El Presidente to do. As Henekie explained his plan to the cartel boss, it became clear to both of them that Waddell would not be the person they wanted in Nassau.

"We greased a lot of wheels in Nassau," El Presidente told Henekie. "There's no reason we should be in this position if Waddell had done his job."

Henekie just plain didn't like Waddell or trust him. "I know a woman there," Henekie told El Presidente, "who would be perfect for the job. She's got good contacts. She's smart, but most of all she'll do anything for money."

El Presidente didn't laugh. He'd begun to respect this little guy with the funny Spanish accent, who would ever suspect a woman to be the cartel's representative. "What about Waddell?" El Presidente asked."Do you think he's of any value to us?

We might need him as a decoy," Henekie told him. "Don't worry if he's a problem, I'll take care of it."

El Presidente smiled; this was why he had asked and exactly what he wanted to hear. "This woman, does she have a name?"

"Lena," Henekie answered. "When you meet her, you won't be disappointed."

El Presidente looked pleased. "Okay, set it up, Henekie. All you've got to lose is two million and your life." Henekie failed to see the humor, "Just get me the stuff I asked for."

"We've both got too much at stake in this thing to lose," Henekie told him, not batting an eye.

It only took a few days for Waddell to find out that Lena was the cartel's new person in Nassau. At first he wouldn't believe it, but when he got his orders to do whatever she asked of him, he was livid. He also knew if he was to go on living, he would have to do something in a hurry.

Henekie couldn't have done anything that could have affected him more. Waddell had no respect for women; they were good for one thing and one thing only. There was no way he was going to take orders from a woman, especially one who's mouth he'd had his cock in only days before.

"If she ends up dead, they'll know I won't put up with any shit here," Waddell thought. His mouth began to water; I'm going to fuck her to death, we'll see who's boss.

Waddell checked around; he was surprised to find she was still in the same building but had changed the locks. By dark that night, he had a key to fit her new locks and a scouting report on the building. He was told she still lived alone but that two men had rented a suite down the hall from her. His contact told him they were Americans, possibly CIA, but as far as he knew they hadn't had any contact with Lena. So they're on to her being boss already, he thought. It made things a little stickier, but the danger seemed to make him even more excited.

Waddell thought of all the ways he could kill her and what he would do to her first. These thoughts consumed his mind, driving him to take chances. The quicker I get to her, the less chance of her getting more security.

Lena was deadly afraid of Waddell and rightly so. When Henekie told her she was to become the new cartel boss, she had been skeptical. "Who in hell are you to appoint me the head of anything, and what if I don't want the job? It sounds like a position with a short life span."

Henekie reassured her that she'd be protected, and she had the job whether she wanted it or not. Then when two high officials in the government stopped by to confirm she was now the boss here in Nassau, she began to understand Henekie wasn't lying and realized the potential that came with the job.

The trouble was the potential could be a two-headed coin. On one side was wealth and power, on the other, the chance she might not live to enjoy it. Her love of money and the fact that Henekie told her she had no choice in the matter made her decision relatively easy. She did lay down some conditions, one being she be given more security.

Henekie balked at that telling her that for the time being, they didn't want to any attention drawn to her. "Don't worry, I will look after you," he told her.

This was the second night she'd been alone, and she hadn't slept a wink nor had she seen Henekie. Now she was sure they all wanted her dead. "I know Waddell's going to come after me," she thought, "and this time, he'll do more than screw me."

She'd taken to sleeping what little she did sleep, curled up in a blanket in the corner of the bedroom. Although she didn't know it, Henekie was watching out for her. He too figured it would be Waddell himself who would come after her and followed him everywhere he went, finding out who his contacts were that could cause him problems in the future.

It was after midnight when Henekie heard the gates to Waddell's walled estate open. He'd been dozing, dreaming Rona's body was beside him. The sight of Waddell's Porsche turning on to the street brought him back to reality instantly. Since it was Manly's sports car, it would mean he was driving it himself. When this happened, Manly was either off to meet a woman or to visit some people of great interest to Henekie.

He followed the Porsche, keeping his distance until he realized they had circled the block around Lena's apartment twice. Henekie's mind began to race; "Damn, he's going after her tonight."

This surprised Henekie; he knew two American agents had moved into the building to keep an eye on the comings and goings in Lena's suite. He didn't think Waddell would try anything with them there,but just in case he'd paid the doorman to tell him if anything out of the ordinary went on.

Waddell pulled his Porsche over and parked on the street directly behind Lena's apartment complex. Henekie turned into a parking lot a block back, totally perplexed as to how Waddell was going to get into Lena's apartment without being detected.

Henekie didn't want to find out; "I'll get him now," he thought. He hurried down the alley behind the parking lot till he was close to Waddell's car. He looked from behind a hedge row seeing that Waddell was still behind the wheel of his car. Perfect, he thought, and was about to walk up to Waddell's car when out of the corner of his eye, he saw two figures come out of the shadows and come toward him walking up the street.

Waddell got out of his car and hurriedly walked across the grass toward Lena's apartment. Henekie now saw that the figures were of two men; they stood in the middle of the street talking, making it hard for Henekie to cross the street undetected. Slowly, he dropped to his belly and slithered to the far end of the hedge, and then in the deeper shadows, he slipped from shrub to shrub heading in the same direction Waddell had.

He had almost made the first courtyard when the lights went out. The emergency lights flickered on, and then they too went out, leaving Henekie in total blackness. "Son of a bitch," Henekie said under his breath, beginning to panic.

He now realized Waddell could make Lena's apartment undetected, but the doorman should see him, and the men across from Lena had her apartment under surveillance. "How would he get out? Maybe he doesn't care," Henekie's mind raced. "I should have been better prepared." He had to take chances now and stumbled through the darkness to the front door. The power failure had locked it. He began knocking loudly, hoping to at least attract the attention of the doorman.

Henekie stepped back frustrated; no one opened the doors, and they were too heavy for him to break down. "Take a deep breath and think," he told himself; it was then that the heard the gunshots.

A cold grin set Manly's jaw as he hurried toward Lena's building. His men had told him that they'd taken care of the night security guard. They'd watch if anyone followed him back from the apartment to his car, they'd take care of it. He entered the apartment by the front door looking to make sure the security camera had been rendered useless. He smiled as he turned and climbed the stairs. The camera had been turned to face the wall.

When he reached the top of the stairs, he pulled out his cellular and spoke the word "Now" and almost instantly the lights went out, then flickered, and went out again, leaving him blinded. His ability to see, however, did not slow his forward progress down the hall. A penlight helped him locate Lena's apartment.

Other doors began to open up and down the hallway as people checked to see if it had lights or not. There was no reason to think that Waddell wasn't one of them, as he opened Lena's door and then quietly closed it behind him. He knew she was alone, but he had to remain quiet because of the men across the hall monitoring the suite. He didn't want them interfering before he was done. He shone his penlight around probing the darkness looking for any movement.

It was a large suite, very expensive. "Bertrand had good taste," Waddell thought as he walked through the room. Lena's bedroom door was closed; it was the only place she could be. Manly tried the knob, but it was locked. He felt the key in his pocket.

"No problem," he murmured under his breath, but first he opened the patio door. He took a knotted rope from the bag he carried and secured it to the balcony railing throwing the other end over. Satisfied, he returned to Lena's bedroom door, shining the light on the rumpled pile covering the bed. Somewhere among them, Lena was hiding. He felt an erection coming on just thinking of what was coming next.

Lena thought she heard her apartment door open and close. Her ears strained to hear; yes, now she could hear someone moving around in her suite. Fear caught in her throat choking back a scream. She heard her patio door being opened, and then it was quiet. Maybe they left, she began to breathe again.

"No," her brain screamed; someone was at her door.

Then like a cornered cat, her back stiffened, and her claws came out, the fear replaced by hate. The feel of cold steel in her hands gave her the ability to lash out. She pointed the revolver at the dark shape in the doorway and pulled the trigger. A strange sense of power came over her as she pulled the trigger again and again.

Manly's mind was so involved with his own intentions, it took a second for him to comprehend that something had hit the door frame just above his head. He saw the flame from the muzzle blast come toward him, and then the deafening sound filled his ears.

"The bitch has a gun," he heard himself say. He dived as he heard the gun go off again and had almost cleared the doorway when he felt a severe pain somewhere in his backside. "Fuck, she shot me." He was more astonished than anything. For some reason he could not fathom Lena doing something like that to him. He had no idea how bad he was hurt; his only intention was to get out of there. A searing pain drove up his back as he grabbed the rope and lowered himself over the balcony railing. The shots still rang in his ears; he was sure people would be swarming all over the place in minutes.

He reached the ground and turned to run, but somehow the rope was around his neck; he felt himself becoming weak as he struggled to release it. Then someone lifted his head, cold smiling eyes looked into his as everything went black.

When Henekie first heard the gunshots, he wasn't sure where they came from or why he could hear them. These were luxury apartments, very soundproof. The balcony door had to be open. He hurried around the building just in time to see Waddell coming down. Henekie calmly waited for Waddell to reach the ground and just as he let go of the rope, Henekie chopped at his neck, stunning him. As Waddell began to drop, Henekie in a flash wrapped the rope around his neck using the big man's own weight to strangle himself.

Waddell was indeed a big man; it was all Henekie could do to hold on to the loose end of the rope and keep it tight. Finally, Henekie had to kick Waddell in the nuts to calm him down and gradually Waddell began to sag more and more, his own weight attributing to his strangulation. Henekie moved in close; he lifted Waddell's head and saw exactly what he wanted to see—the fear in his eyes before he died.

So simple, Henekie surmised; he couldn't figure out why all the problems in the world weren't solved this way. It was so final; if you have a problem, eliminate it. He couldn't understand why people wasted time negotiating and arguing. He took a deep breath; he felt the air was clear.

"What was this on his hands?"

"Blood."

Curiously, he turned Waddell's hanging body around; his ass was covered in blood.

"Gunshot."

Henekie assessed the situation; until now he had assumed Lena to be dead but maybe not. As he went through Waddell's pants, he found a phone fastened to his belt. He'd heard the government had set up a tower so government officials could use these phones supposedly for government use only. Well, let's see if they work; he dialed Lena's number.

The phone in Lena's apartment rang, startling her. The first instinct was to not answer it, but she desperately needed to talk to someone. She was still huddled up in the corner of her bedroom ready to take on anyone, but everything had been quiet for a while; maybe she should go out and see if she had killed her intruder. She was disappointed there was no sign of anyone in her living room, and then she spoke quietly into the phone.

"Yes."

Henekie sounded surprised. "Lena." The answer he got back was some of the most profound German he had ever heard. When she finally stopped cursing him, Henekie told her to calm down. "Is there anyone with you?" he asked.

"No," she replied. "Someone knocked on my door, but that's all I've heard. Get me out of here," she demanded.

Henekie wasn't sure that was such a good idea. "You haven't done anything wrong, Lena, maybe you should stay there and wait for the police."

"Get me out of here now!" she told him. "I don't want to stay here, and I don't trust anyone, not even you, you bastard."

"Okay," he decided, "I'm coming up."

He climbed over Waddell's hanging body and pulled himself up the rope into Lena's apartment. The first thing he met was Lena's gun pointed at his head; he could sense the anger in her.

"I should have shot you the first time I met you," she seethed.

Henekie kept his voice calm. "I'm the only one here who can help you, Lena, it's up to you." Lena seemed to make her decision without resignation. "How do we get down from here?" she asked looking over the balcony.

"There's a rope," Henekie answered. "You'll have to climb on to my back and let me take you down." Lena hesitated and looked over the edge; just then there was another knock on the door, someone began shouting to be let in.

Henekie moved to the edge of the railing. "Put your arms around me and hang on," he told her. She didn't hesitate this time, although he noticed she didn't let go of the gun. There wasn't much to Lena; Henekie had no trouble carrying her down the rope and over Waddell's body. It was when he let her go at the bottom that she gasped and pointed the gun at Waddell's swinging body. "Easy, he's dead," he told her.

"Who is it?" she asked.

"Waddell," he said, turning to leave. He was not ready for the reaction he got from his revelation. She began kicking and beating at the body. Henekie had to pull her off and forcefully carry her away.

"Don't be stupid, Lena, Waddell has men around here," he told her as he hustled her down the alley and back around to his car.

Once he had her in the car, she seemed to calm down and become very quiet. "Where are we going?" she asked in a low voice.

Henekie was very careful. "I thought I would take you to a compound the cartel keeps here in Nassau. No one will bother you until you decide what to do."

Lena nodded her head. "Is he really dead?"

"Yes," Henekie smiled. "Did you know you shot him in the ass?" Henekie began to laugh, as did Lena. It broke the ice. "Nassau is yours, Lena. Now that Waddell is out of the way, you are the power here."

There was little traffic in the city at this time of the morning. It took only minutes to reach the compound. Lena had been quiet the rest of the way.

"This is it," he told her as she watched a gate open in front of them.

"You are the power here, Henekie. I'm just the one everyone will see," he heard her say.

He sat back in the seat looking at her intently. "No," Henekie said firmly. "I will make sure that you are secure here, but this is not where I will spend my life." It was the first time she had seen him smile. "I wish to spend time with my family. These islands have given me the ability to live comfortably the rest of my life. Other than that, they mean nothing to me."

"Maybe I should leave too," Lena said to herself as much as anyone.

"That would not be wise, Lena, you know too much."

Lena knew that Henekie could kill her here and now with no hesitation. It was the fear that made her cling to her gun as if it was her only friend. "Why me?" she asked.

"Because you are the only one I know and trust in the islands," he answered immediately. "I need someone I can set up here quickly and quietly. You fit the part perfectly: you are greedy, you have always manipulated men, and you are a survivor."

Lena laughed at his candid description of her.

"Just remember, Lena, you will still be a kept woman. As long as you do what you do well, the cartel will look after you."

"Never again will a man take advantage of me," some of Lena's anger surfaced again.

"Let me give you advice, Lena. I would be very nice to El Presidente. Sure, he is a pig. People are only valuable to him if they fill his needs. You can do that, Lena. He only gets rid of women when he tires of them. You have the perfect situation. He will not be able to spend much time here, as long as you have control of things he'll leave you alone."

Lena began to catch on to what Henekie was saying. She liked the idea. "You mean he is the boss, but I'll have control?"

"If you play your cards right, Lena. Right now, you have the best hand. Don't let anyone bluff you out of it. After what you did to Waddell, everyone will come into line."

"They will know I didn't do it myself," Lena stated.

"That's even better. They know you have the power to do it. Powerful people don't get their hands dirty. Just by coming here to the cartel's house lets the people know who is in charge. Believe me, nothing goes on in this town that someone does not know about. The word always gets around."

"How will I get in touch with you?" Lena asked.

"I will contact you from time to time. Other than that, you will probably not see me again. Come, I will let you in."

"You seem very confident, Henekie, that the cartel will have control of these islands. Right now, the way I hear it, Mark Bertrand has them on the run," Lena said.

This seemed to agitate Henekie. He stopped and turned to her. "We have a little party planed for Mr. Bertrand, a surprise party. This party will be in honor of his retirement and to pay for my retirement fund. Have no fear, Lena, no one can stand in our way. Bertrand will soon be like Waddell, an example for others who do not fall in line."

They continued up a driveway until they came to a house. They got out of the car and he led her to a door where Henekie rang the buzzer. Soon the door was opened by a sleepy looking man. "This is Quinn, Lena. He's El Presidente's right hand man, From now on, whatever you need, just talk to Quinn here. He will look after you now."

"What about my belongings in the apartment?" Lena wondered aloud. She was still dressed in her nightgown.

"Tell Quinn what you need and he will go shopping for you. Money is no object. In a few days,some people will want to question you," Henekie warned her. "Just tell them you weren't home and have no idea what happened at your apartment. Make up a story: you don't feel safe there anymore, so you are moving," he shrugged. "They will have to let you take your stuff. Make sure that if you have any problems, consult with Quinn. He will take care of it for you." He turned and walked out of the door, closing it behind him.

It was like closing a chapter in the islands. With Waddell gone, power had shifted to other hands.

Henekie started his car and drove away. Not bad for a poor boy from the ghettos. He was proud of himself remembering how he had grown up, always fending for himself. How at the age of fifteen, he got caught stealing and was forced to join the army. This had been a stroke of luck for him as it turned out. He learned all about killing and the weapons that were needed to accomplish it.

He soon found friends who hated the regimental life but loved the power that came with the feel of a gun. It wasn't long until they were deemed uncontrollable and kicked out of the army. This was a real blow to Henekie, but not for long. His friends soon invited him to join them. They were hired for good money to fight in Africa. There, he learned that people would pay him to kill. He had also learned to trust no one. From there, he had worked his way to becoming a hired assassin but always working for someone else, taking all the chances, living from job to job. Well, that was all behind him now, he thought as he drove into the Nassau airport.

He had received a message that a package was waiting for him in Miami. Henekie chartered a plane, landing in Fort Lauderdale Municipal two hours later. He immediately phoned a central registry for his messages. The one he received got his adrenaline going. The coded message told him El Presidente had purchased a freighter in Argentina, where it had been fitted with the equipment Henekie had specified.

They were now south of Cuba, staying east away from U.S. surveillance, with a rendezvous time of three days from today. Henekie picked up his package and took his charter back to Andros Island. His ingredients would have to be mixed with the next fuel delivery to Bertrand's ship. That's tomorrow afternoon, he calculated. He'd not slept in two days. He fell asleep, confident that everything was going on schedule.

Lena was not quite as confident. At least, she felt secure in her new home. Quinn showed her to her bedroom. It was huge, very elegant, making her feel important, and restoring her confidence. There was a heart-shaped tub in the corner.

She turned on the water and began undressing. Her mind skimmed over what Henekie had told her about Bertrand. She thought about trying to warn him. He had been very good to her. She had sensed something in him that she'd seen in very few men. He had genuinely cared about her. Most men were so self-centered; they had little time to care about anyone but themselves. They turned to her only for self-satisfaction, using her to fulfill their own needs, never thinking that she might have feelings also. Well, she took what they had given her, learning to stay emotionally distanced.

Tonight was the first time that she had ever fought back. Now she had respect. The power made her skin tingle as she stepped into tub, feeling the water engulf her.

"No," she thought, "I had to stand on my own two feet; now you'll have to do the same, Mark Bertrand." Her decision seemed to bring serenity over her, and she fell asleep in the soothing water.

# Twenty-Two

AGENT ANSLY WAS extremely surprised when he received El Presidente's message. After their ambush of Buzzard Bay and the ensuing attack on the Andros farm, the CIA agents had been very busy consolidating their positions, expecting a counterassault at any time.

At first, they considered the message a hoax, a diversion to catch them off guard. Ansly immediately informed the agency of El Presidente's message that he wished to meet with Bertrand to make a deal. The people at CIA headquarters were equally suspicious, putting their intelligence people in Colombia to work finding out what was going on.

Ansly returned El Presidente's message asking for more details. Again they received the same message that El Presidente would set sail tomorrow to rendezvous with Bertrand in three days' time.

"There's no use fighting each other," the message went on to say, "I'm sure something can be worked out. CIA intelligence sources confirmed that El Presidente's yacht did indeed leave Cuba."

"The agency isn't sure what he is up to," Ansly told everybody on board. "The cartel has never, to our knowledge, negotiated with anyone before. On the other hand, they have never been pushed this hard before."

Ansly showed them on an overhead projector the route El Presidente would take to come and meet them.

"The agency has decided we'll meet him right here at Buzzard Bay. El Presidente has agreed to this. We shall have surveillance on him at all times. Any tricks or suspicious actions and, Ansly drew a finger across his throat, 'No more El Presidente.' Headquarters thinks this is as good a time as any to take him. It's quite possible that as he negotiates with us," he looked at Bob, "he will tell us a lot of things we would like to know. The risk in all this is that here we are on neutral ground. The Andros base is not far away, but they cannot help us unless the request goes through the proper channels. However, I don't see much of a problem. There's not much he can do to this floating fortress short of bombing it. His yacht is not armed with anything heavy enough to be a threat, so the rest is up to us."

Ansly told Bob he'd be spending the next three days on board preparing for his meeting with El Presidente. "You'll have to convince him that you're Mark Bertrand because he will know everything there is to know about him. We will also be briefing you as to the information we want you to get out of him."

It was July who changed Ansly's mind. She wasn't alone; many of the people on board, especially Carol, backed her up. The wind was blowing hard across the deck as July and Ansly walked up and down, deep in conversation.

"Look, Ansly, we've got three days," July told him. "I want my husband back. This has been hard on him and on me," she stopped and looked out over the railing. "He needs a break and so do I. Captain Norton's house is just off to the right," she pointed toward shore. "His place is very private and runs right down to the ocean. I want Bob and I to spend the next three days together there."

Ansly did not like the idea, but he was under a lot of pressure. Bob was crucial to their plans. He told July this and how he felt. "He'd be a lot safer on board, July. Besides, he has to be briefed on his meeting with El Presidente."

Her reply was the coldest blue eyes he had ever encountered. "You owe me," she told him in a commanding voice. "Put whatever you want Bob to know on paper, we'll go over it every day. I can teach him as well as you."

Ansly had worked with July for some time now. He had come to respect her intelligence. She had a remarkable knack of sifting through whatever was put in front of her and making sense of it. This work they were doing was a dirty, dangerous job, yet she handled it with dignity. There wasn't one agent on the ship who wouldn't back July to the limit, that's how much they thought of her. He'd also taken enough courses through the agency to know she could be very manipulative, using any of her various attributes to get what she wanted.

He watched her blonde hair blow against her face. "God, she was beautiful," he thought. Ansly shook his head. "You can be very persuasive, July." He'd shaken his head as much to clear it as to tell July he was undecided.

But July was determined to have her way and continued her argument. In the end, he relented, saving as much face as he could by placing conditions on her demands. They haggled, finally coming to an agreement.

"There's one more thing," she said emphatically, "Bob is not to know that I know about him and Lena." She looked out over the water. "You can threaten us with anything you want, but you can't separate us anymore."

A small boat took July to Horatio's beach under cover of darkness. There was no way of letting him know she was coming, but when he saw her standing in the doorway, he hugged her like a long-lost friend.

The CIA had known Horatio for a long time, considering him "friendly." They knew he'd walked a fine line keeping law and order on the island while taking a blind eye to many of the activities going on there. Had he played ball with the right people, he would have had a cushy job in Nassau instead of having being left in charge of a small outpost.

On the other hand, they'd had no trouble on the island, so he became a valuable man to have here. At least, there had been no trouble until now. Horatio had no control on saying what was happening; he could at best stay out of the way.

July spent the rest of the night briefing Horatio as to what had happened since they had last met.

"Both of you just fell off the face of the earth," Horatio told her. "I assumed you were dead."

"I would like to bring Bob here and spend some time with him," July explained. "I realize it could be very dangerous for your family, so we will understand if you say no."

"I've sent my family away until this is over," Horatio told her. "Of course you may stay. There is a small house in the backyard where the kids stay when they're home. It's yours as long as you want it."

July spent the next day fixing the little house up as best she could with the limited resources available. She felt like a schoolgirl on her first date waiting for Bob to come, yet dreading what might happen when he did. She was on the beach when the small boat carrying Bob landed. Her heart was in her mouth, "What will I say?" and began to shake uncontrollably.

Ansly thought it best to tell Bob that July was waiting for him. "One false move, Bob, and you are going back on board," Ansly warned him.

A dark shape left the bow and bounded toward her. Before she knew what was happening, it had swooped her up in its arms, kissing her lips.

All the tension went out of her. She wrapped her arms around Bob's neck. "Never, never leave me alone again, you son of a bitch." He knew he was home. They spent the days in the little cabin making love, talking, and working. They set aside three hours every day studying everything the CIA wanted Bertrand to find out about the Colombian drug lord.

It was the nights they enjoyed the most. They could spend their time along the beach romping naked much the same as they had a long time ago in less troubling times. July or Bob never talked about the time they had been apart.

One night as they lay on the sand spent with passion, she sensed Bob becoming very still.

"What is it?" she asked.

"You know I've been posing as Mark Bertrand, don't you?" It was as much a statement as a question.

"Yes," she answered simply, wondering where this would lead.

"You know, I had forgotten who I really was until I saw you standing on the beach the other night. I had really begun to think that I was Mark Bertrand. Everything I did or touched was like someone else was doing it."

"So what's he like, this Bertrand?"

Bob rolled over and kissed her. "You wouldn't like him," he told her.

Time flew, the sight of the ship offshore a constant reminder that their time together was limited. It was on the third night that Ansly himself visited them.

"You'll have to come aboard tonight," he told them.

"El Presidente is docking in Nassau sometime today and wants to rendezvous the day after tomorrow. That will give us a day to get ready." It was disappointing news, but they had known it was coming.

"They have to get their things together," Horatio told Ansly. "I'll bring them over after midnight." Ansly agreed and left, leaving Bob and July to their last few hours together.

July said, "I asked Ansly how long El Presidente would be here. He thought probably a couple of days would be all he would want. After that, depending on the situation, the CIA would decide what they wanted to do with him. Bob, something is wrong about all this!"

It had been bothering her for a while; their time together was almost gone, and she felt an urgency to get it off her chest. "Ansly and his people are trusting this too lightly. They seem to have the mentality that they are the most powerful people in the world. How can they be so naive? The cartel probably has more resources than the total of the CIA. We know how ruthless they can be."

"I didn't want to worry you," Bob answered, "but I'm just as apprehensive. It doesn't make sense to me that only a few months ago this El Presidente was scared to take his yacht anywhere for fear the Americans would sink him. Now he's sailing right under their noses. It is as if he knows the CIA is waiting for him here."

July agreed with Bob's assessment, "There's no way he's going to walk into their ballpark without an ace up his sleeve," she told him. "The point is that El Presidente wanted to meet and agreed to meet here. Does he think the CIA won't do anything to him, nor does he really believe Bertrand is alone in this? I don't believe for a minute that El Presidente has any intention of negotiating in good faith with anyone."

"There are too many things going on here that we don't know about," Bob answered her.

He smiled, "We're just pawns again, July. We are being used, and we are expendable."

Captain Norton had sat quietly listening to their conversation.

"I can get you out of here," he told them, "but I doubt you would be able to hide from either of these people for long. You both know too much."

The anger on July's face softened, "Thank you, Horatio. I have a feeling Bob's going to go through with this, even though it's like walking into a minefield."

"It's the only way we'll find out how this thing ends up," Bob told them. "We've gone too far to run away now."

Horatio knew exactly how it felt to be caught in the middle. "Keep your wits about you," was all he could advise. "If you need to get out, I'll help all I can."

Tears came to July's eyes; it was Horatio that had looked after their son and taken him to safety in Florida with his family. He had shown up time and time again to help her and Bob. "You're a true friend," she told him.

"It's not all one way," Horatio told them, "matter of fact, through you two, these islands have a chance for the better."

The huge black man got up to leave. "Better get ready," he told them. "We'll have to leave soon."

Bob and July's assessment of the situation was probably closer than they knew. Both sides had everything on the line. Any failure on the cartel's part would certainly curtail their activities in this part of the world. On the flipside, the CIA had everything on the line. If they came home with their tail between their legs, the drug lords would gain confidence. America's war on drugs would lose its momentum; countries around the world working with them would abandon them like a sinking ship leaving the rats to return.

El Presidente's yacht had arrived in Nassau early in the afternoon. Now he sat watching out his stateroom window as the tugs pulled the American destroyer into its docking position across the harbor. El Presidente had not seen the destroyer before, but he knew it had shadowed him since leaving Cuban waters. He smiled, remembering that Henekie had told him it would.

What a find his little German friend had turned out to be. Very expensive, but worth it for now anyway. El Presidente turned his attention to the papers in front of him. He'd had a lot of time to think on this trip. Things had been too good; he had lost the hands on part of his business. He felt like a young man again taking chances, getting involved with the dangerous side of the business.

This was what he was good at mainly because he had no morals or conscience. He could kill without remorse and loved to torture. The affliction of pain was a particular specialty he excelled in. His innovative ways of killing were renowned.

There were two reports in front of him. One was Henekie's plan for tonight. The other was a list of people who would have to be terminated after. At the head of the list were the names Bob and July Green. The names, he remembered, had been on many lists before. Henekie had told him that Green was the luckiest man he had ever seen. Well, Green's luck would soon run out tonight, if indeed, he was on Bertrand's ship as Henekie suspected.

It made sense. It was the only way Green could hide from them for so long. The question was, "Why was he on this ship?

El Presidente read the report on Green: small time, broke, just in the wrong place at the wrong time, and he knew too much about what was none of his business, but really nothing there to indicate why Bertrand would keep him alive unless he planned to use him as a bargaining chip. This would confirm Henekie's theory that the CIA were working with Bertrand.

Now, Green's wife, that was a different story. She was reported to be very loyal to her husband. El Presidente could not understand this. "Why would a beautiful woman like this be with a loser like him?" He suspected there might be a little more to this Green than Henekie thought. Tonight should take care of this problem. As for July Green, well, he'd heard that Waddell had taken her for his own pleasure. Then there were rumors that she had escaped him. He couldn't confirm this with Waddell now that he was dead.

Wherever she is, I will find her, his eyes roaming over her photograph. But that's for later, now I must concentrate on the problem at hand. He spoke to his lieutenant who sat across from him.

"Have you heard from Henekie in the last hour?"

"Yes, Your Excellency," he answered. "He will bring the boat in for you at dark."

"So his plan to inject his goodies into their fuel supply was successful?" El Presidente asked.

"He just told us everything was going as planned," the lieutenant told him.

"Have a car brought around for me in one hour," El Presidente told him. He had some things to discuss with Lena now that she was their person here. Besides, she was to be his alibi for the night. He wanted to be seen going into her place in the daylight and not coming out till the next morning. This was all part of Henekie's plan; no one would ever know he was close to Bertrand's ship that night.

Lena was indeed everything Henekie said she would be, El Presidente thought on meeting her. I'll be spending a lot of time here after this is over. Business came first, however. As soon as he arrived at Lena's, he began briefing her as to what would be required of her. He gave her a list of people who would become expendable in the next while.

"You will be responsible for seeing that this is carried out," he told her, waiting to see if she blanched at the assignment. She showed no emotion whatsoever, reading over the list noting that most of them were Waddell's old cronies.

"To us," El Presidente held up his glass.

Lena touched her glass to his, giving the Colombian her most seductive smile. "There's something you can do for me. I see you have a small money laundering business here. Quinn drew up some papers we would like you to sign. Quinn and I will guarantee you to double your money in one year if you sign over half of the business to us."

Immediately, El Presidente's hackles were raised. He didn't like overly ambitious women, but what the hell, he didn't need to deal with this right now.

"Sure," he said, "I can do that." He quickly signed the papers and headed for the guesthouse from where he and his men took the passage down to the old warehouse to wait for Henekie. When he returned, he'd put this Lena on her back and show her you don't make deals with El Presidente, you do as you're told. Henekie would have to learn the same thing, but that would all happen when he came back as king of the Caribbean.

It wasn't long after dark that the huge door opened and Henekie's powerboat entered the building. El Presidente felt relieved when he saw it was a large boat; in fact, it hardly made it through the door. He stepped into the boat immediately as it docked and shook hands with Henekie.

"I want to show you something before we go." El Presidente beckoned with his finger for Henekie to follow him onto the dock. El Presidente unlocked a box mounted in the wall and pushed a button, almost immediately there was the unmistakable sound of rushing water and the speed boat began to drop. once the boat was completely below the dock, El Presidente pushed another button and the dock began to move until it completely closed over where the boat had been.

"Not only does it hide your boat, there's living quarters under there," El Presidente told him. "It all works on water pressure from the many caverns underground here. We think it was built by hand for the slave traders. I've modernized it but you have to admit it's an incredible feat of engineering." El Presidente opened the dock and floated the boat back up to their level.

They then went down with the boat into the underground cavern. Here he showed Henekie the way to a set of stairs. "These run all the way up to the guest house." El presidente told him. "On the inside of these stairs where you see the wooden cribbing is a shaft that has a lift to haul stuff up and down. From the top it looks like it might be an old well so anyone nosing around will not be able to detect anything. I'm showing you this because it's a perfect way to get people or other things in or out of Nassau which in the future may be useful to you."

Henekie was fascinated With the place but it put him on over load and he had to get back to the job at hand, this was no time to get distracted. Both men were decidedly nervous, which was to be suspected, everything was on the line.

"Are we ready?" Henekie asked.

"Like they say in the States, 'Let's rock and roll'," El Presidente smiled.

As soon as the boat was fueled, the doors opened and under the cover of darkness idled its way out of the harbor. About ten minutes out, the boat shuddered coming to life as its powerful engines opened soon, leaving Nassau a speck behind them. Henekie and El Presidente huddled in the small cabin going over their plan.

"Our ship is here right now," Henekie pointed at the map. "It will take us approximately two hours to catch her."

"Won't they see her on radar?" El Presidente asked.

"Yes, but she's in one of the shipping lanes. They'll think nothing of it. By the time Bertrand's radar goes down, she'll be in position to jam everything going in and out. Now there's two other ships in the same area," explained Henekie. "Only the one," he pointed to the map again, "may be close enough to notice anything. She's an old plugger, very slow. I doubt if she'll bother to investigate. Even if she did, it should be all over by the time she arrives on the scene."

"Our jamming system will prevent any radio contact with this ship, won't it?" El Presidente asked.

"Oh yes," Henekie answered. "This system is sophisticated enough to stop all the frequencies that would get help to Bertrand in time."

"He'll be able to broadcast on some of the higher frequencies. The CIA kind of screwed that up themselves. A lot of these frequencies were being used for, shall we say, illegal activities."

El Presidente chuckled at Henekie's insinuations.

"The CIA and others began monitoring these frequencies," Henekie went on explaining. "Now they're filled with jargon and coded messages. By the time Bertrand's message is ciphered out, we'll be long gone."

El Presidente looked at his watch. "Two hours, that means we'll rendezvous with our ship shortly after eleven o'clock."

"That's right," Henekie answered.

El Presidente rapped his fingers on the table nervously. "I thought you told me your chemicals were unpredictable, aren't you cutting it a little close?"

"At first, this was a real problem for me," Henekie conceded. "Then my engineer explained to me that they had improved these chemicals considerably since I was involved with them. The only obstacle in my way was in my original plan. The chemicals were to be put into the fuel truck on its way to the barge. I realized there were too many variables if I did this; variations in heat, an unpredictable time of actual delivery to Bertrand's ship, just to name a few. These chemicals are very volatile and susceptible to any change in their environment. This left me with no option but to have the chemicals installed as the fuel was pumped onto the ship itself."

El Presidente sat stunned, spellbound, listening to Henekie, "How in hell did you do that?"

Henekie shook his head, "Actually, it was easy once I figured it out, and I let them do it."

El Presidente asked incredulously, "You got them to do it?"

"Oh, unwittingly of course," Henekie responded. "I first checked the fuel filter on the barge to see what it was. Then I acquired one the same. I phoned the fuel company pretending to represent the ship and demanded a new fuel filter be installed on the barge before they would accept any more fuel. As I told you, I caught a ride with the fuel truck driver one day before. He had told me how they refueled and roughly how much fuel the ship held. So it was no problem knowing the quantity to put in the filter. On the day they delivered the fuel, I again asked the driver for a ride. The filter was on the seat beside him. I simply exchanged my filter for his. When we got down to the barge, I got out and walked away. I heard the driver tell Bertrand's men guarding the barge that he was going to change the filter. They told him to begin fueling the barge; they would look after it. So now the chemical won't get mixed with the diesel fuel until it is actually pumped into the ship directly. Under these conditions, the chemical is quite predictable. We should begin seeing results around midnight, give or take a few minutes."

"If this chemical will blow up Bertrand's ship, why did you need the missile launchers?" El Presidente asked. Technology still baffled him and usually left it to others. In this case, however, he was too close to the action not to know what was going on.

"The chemical won't necessarily blow Bertrand out of the water. Theoretically, the chemical will not explode but combust. What happens is the chemical mixes with the diesel fuel and begins to gel. This will plug the filter to their engines causing them to stop. The lights on board will go out, and auxiliary lighting will come back. This will be our signal to move in. All the equipment on board, including their radar and big guns, are hydraulically driven and will get so hot they can't be run manually.The auxiliary engine will run only minutes, and then its fuel lines will also be plugged. This will leave them with only their batteries, but all their power will be required to run the radio and emergency lighting. They will be virtually dead in the water. The engineers will immediately go to work replacing the filter and when they do, the chemicals will release deadly gas. I've been around it only in the open air," Henekie told him.

"In the confined area of the engine room, it will kill them instantly. They will have to seal off the engine room. The chemical will continue to build pressure in the fuel tank. It will soon blow the tank, but this is where it is unpredictable. The tank may just blow apart doing no immediate damage to the hull itself, or it might just blow everything to smithereens. If it only breaks the tank, the diesel fuel will flood the engine room. The chemical will combust causing a massive fire. It won't be long till Bertrand feels a living hell under his feet."

El Presidente liked this idea; a smile came to his face. "This will take a little longer than if the ship blew up, but I will enjoy it a lot more."

"We still have only so much time," Henekie warned him. "Two hours maximum and we have to be out of here."

"That's why the missile," El Presidente confirmed.

"Yes, the fire will be below deck. It will give off lots of smoke but not visible fire that will attract attention. One of the launchers is mounted up-front on this boat, but you'll be pleased to see what we have in store for you on the freighter. It is designed to breach the hull, causing a big, loud explosion. Once the hull is breached, it won't take long before they will try to abandon the ship. Their machine guns will still be dangerous, but we can stay out of range and just circle with powerboats making sure no one escapes."

The driver called down to say that their ship was in sight.

"Time has flown, Henekie," El Presidente said to him.

"Enjoy yourself," Henekie slapped him on the back, "champagne's on board. I'll be back to pick you up after our hunting is done."

A large loading ramp hung off the side of the ship with stairs running up to the deck. The powerboat's driver was able to pull up beside this while they were still on the move. Two men were standing out on the deck and pulled El Presidente and his lieutenant aboard, and then the powerboat pulled away and kept abreast of the ship waiting for their signal to move in. At five minutes after midnight, Henekie began to sweat.

He knew the chemicals would not be exactly reliable, but waiting was the hardest part of any operation. They had been ready for a long time now, El Presidente would be getting impatient. The minutes ticked by; maybe the chemicals were not working. All these thoughts were going through his mind.

"Almost twelve-thirty," his throat was getting tight. Suddenly, Bertrand's ship disappeared then appeared again, much dimmer. Henekie felt an immediate exhilaration.

"Let's go," he told the driver. They turned away from El Presidente's ship and closed in on Bertrand.

Ansly decided to stay up until Green was aboard. He was sitting in his office when the lights went out and the auxiliary cut in. He was immediately on the phone to the bridge inquiring as to the problem. The bridge told him they were in contact with the engine room, and they were looking for the problem. Ansly was still on the phone when the auxiliary lights went out, leaving only the low-voltage emergency lighting. A sense of fear went up Ansly's spine; for the first time, he felt something was not right. Get a message out to the base for help, he told the bridge and tell the men to get to their stations until we find out what's going on. He left his office and went up to the bridge.

"Anything new?" he asked his captain.

"There doesn't seem to be any answer from the engine room. I sent Lieutenant Gerard down to investigate," he added.

Ansly looked out over the ocean until he came to El Presidente's ship. "What's that?" he asked.

"It showed up on radar about noon today," the captain told him. "We took it for a freighter. He was following the shipping lane until now," he pointed as the ship seemed to be coming toward them.

The radio operator burst onto the bridge, "Sir, all channels seem to be jammed, there's no communication in or out."

Ansly began to realize their predicament. "Bring the guns to bear on that ship," he told the captain.

"We can't turn the guns sir, the men say there is hot hydralic oil shooting out evereywhere."

The phone rang; Ansly picked it up. "The engineer and two of his men are dead in the engine room," he recognized the second mates voice. "The engine room is filled with gas. We are getting some gas masks and going in, but I doubt it will do us any good. We can't even see in there."

"Stay out of there," Ansly told him. "Seal it off and come up to the bridge." Ansly looked at the captain; his face was ashen in the dim light.

"At least we are well armed," Ansly reassured him. "They'll have one hell of a time taking this ship." He had no sooner said this than they felt the deck shake beneath their feet as a rumble shook her from stern to stern.

Ansly grabbed the phone, "What's going on down there?" There was no answer. Another seaman on the bridge was sent to find out what he could, but the black smoke billowing up around them confirmed their worst fears.

"Tell the men to abandon ship," Ansly told the captain.

The captain reached over and pulled a button on the wall. The horns immediately began to blow, calling everyone to the lifeboats. They heard a machine gun off to their right begin to fire, followed by a hollow thud which knocked them off their feet.

Ansly heard the captain shout, "I've felt that before, we've been torpedoed." He quickly got to his feet, grabbing a set of binoculars from one of the men. He searched through the smoke until he spotted the two patrol boats circling like buzzards. He also saw the ship not more than half a mile away, now sitting there with lights aglow.

A howl of anguish escaped his lips, "The bastards want to kill us." In a fit of frustration, he ran from the bridge to the nearest machine gun and began firing at the ship, but the tracer bullets only disappeared into the night air. He knew the same thing was going to happen to him.

It became pretty apparent to El Presidente as he came on deck that this wasn't much of a ship. An old freighter really, but he was pleased to see a place had been made ready for him on the forward deck. There were some chairs and tables complete with umbrellas. A table ran along one side filled with food. In the middle sat a cabana complete with bartender. Soft music filled the air. In front of one table, a huge telescope was mounted so he would see the action up close.

El Presidente did not mind the ship; they were going to scuttle it in a couple of hours anyway. But he was very pleased to see a place of honor had been set aside for him, "I see you planned a party," he joked with his lieutenant.

"Wait till you see the floor show, El Presidente, it will be even better than the American movies."

El Presidente took his place, but he too was becoming very nervous when finally he saw Bertrand's lights go out. Like Henekie, once the action started, he was all right.

He watched proudly as the other powerboat was lifted from the hold. He was always fascinated by his new toys, especially if they were destructive. It gave him great satisfaction to have these instruments at his fingertips, to be able to pull the trigger himself. Hell, it was like screwing a beautiful woman.

He felt the excitement being radiated by his men as they boarded the powerboat and headed toward Bertrand's ship to perform the 'coup de grace'. He was on the phone steady trying to get the captain to get their ship closer to Bertrand. They were within a quarter of a mile when his men pulled the tarp off of what looked to El Presidente to be a long tube on a tripod.

"It is our honor that you should be the one to finish off the Americans' ship," one of the men said, showing El Presidente how to look down the sight and where the trigger was located. He was like a kid with a new toy; he found Ansly's ship in the sight and pulled the trigger a little quicker than the men around him were ready for. They all watched the missile wing its way past the target and shortly after, El Presidente saw the explosion of water along Bertrand's hull. It didn't matter that everyone knew the missile that hit was from Henekie's boat, just as long as El Presidente didn't.

A roar went up from his crew. Already they were celebrating. Usually, El Presidente didn't allow this, but word had gotten around that this was a special occasion. He had supplied all the food and booze they wanted. "Enjoy," he thought, watching them cheering on Bertrand's ship as the flames began to appear above deck, "it will be your last."

He paid little attention to what was going on around him; the spectacle of the giant ship brought to its knees was awe inspiring. To know that he possessed the power to destroy something as assuming as this ship appeared to be was almost spiritual. He sat glued to his seat, watching through the infrared telescope. He could see the men's faces on board as they desperately lowered the lifeboats, knowing like a god that it was an act of futility. There was no escaping him; they would die because he wished it to be so. Let it be a lesson for those who followed, no one could stand in his way; life meant nothing to him except his own.

Tonight he felt that the world was his; he owned it and everything in it. It was humbling in some ways too. He realized how fortunate he was to find a man like Henekie who could bring such a giant down without firing a shot. Such a man must be kept on a leash. All these things were going through El Presidente's mind as he watched his powerboat blow the small lifeboats out of the water as soon as they cleared Bertrand's ship and reached open water.

It was almost twelve-thirty when Bob and July pushed Horatio Norton's small outboard through the surf and scrambled aboard. Horatio gave them a rough time as he started the engine. "It's about time you white guys learned your place," he shouted at them and aimed the boat toward their ship.

Bob was about to answer him when he saw the lights go out and the considerably dimmer lights of the auxiliary come on.

"What's going on?" Horatio asked.

"Probably just a check to make sure everything is working," Bob answered.

They hadn't gone much farther when all the lights went out again, only this time there was only a dim glow rising from the ship. They were about halfway there when Horatio cut the motor.

"What's the matter?" Bob asked.

"If it's just a check, the lights should be back on by now," Horatio told him.

"They know we're coming," July spoke up. "Maybe they want it dark so no one will see us."

"Look out there," Horatio pointed, "that ship was headed east, now it's turned straight toward us."

They all stood up to have a better look. July saw it first. "Look, a small black object was skimming across the water."

"What the fuck's going on?" Bob was as puzzled as July.

The boat suddenly took off knocking both of them off their feet. All they heard was, "El Presidente," before the small outboard roared to life.

Horatio turned the boat and headed east away from the ship and then again cut the engine. They stood and strained to see, but the black object had disappeared on the other side of Ansly's ship. All of a sudden they heard a deep roar, and then black smoke began to appear over the ship.

"My god, they're attacking the ship," was all that July could get out as they all stood trying to comprehend what was happening.

The other ship Horatio had first spotted was much closer now.

"Why don't they do something?" Bob sounded exasperated. "Ansly's got some big guns, why isn't he firing?"

Horatio answered matter-of-factly, "They can't Bob, and without power they can't do much of anything."

Another small black object appeared, headed straight for the ship. They saw some tracer bullets come off Ansly's ship, and then the object turned away.

"They've still got some firepower left." Bob felt some sense of satisfaction, but seconds later they heard a sickening hollow thud.

"Torpedo," Horatio confirmed what they already suspected.

"I can't believe it," Bob was astonished. "I know that ship. It was a floating fortress, now she's being torn apart without hardly putting up a fight. Why?" He shook his fist in frustration.

"Must have been an inside job," Horatio reasoned. "Whatever happened, happened in a hurry by the looks of the smoke coming out of her. She's in real trouble."

July grabbed Bob's arm. "What can we do?"

They felt totally helpless watching as the scene unfolded. The other ship had pulled in close now, almost straight out from where they were sitting.

"You really think it's El Presidente?" Bob asked Horatio.

"He's the only one with enough power to pull this off, I'm sure that he's on that ship right now laughing at us."

"If I had something to fight him with, I'd go after him right now."

"We do have something," Horatio answered, opening a metal chest beside him. He pulled out two machine guns, handing one to Bob. "I found this box floating near here one day. There's more ammo in here, and the rest are flare guns. Now what I'm thinking is that everyone on that ship is watching Ansly's ship. They'll never think anyone is going to sneak up behind them."

A voice Bob had heard only a few times before came from deep down July's throat, "Let's go get that bastard. I'll cut his balls off myself."

Bob and Horatio both looked toward July; her face was white with fury. She had good friends on board that ship too.

"Let's try it." Bob was not optimistic; he'd seen enough killing, but July was determined. He knew she'd go alone if they didn't try to do something. As they got closer to the boat, they could hear machine gun fire coming from toward Ansly's ship. The flames were above deck now, casting a dancing light across the water.

"Look," Bob saw the tracer bullets from one of the powerboats shower into a lifeboat. "The fuckers are killing anyone leaving the ship."

"Maybe we should go after the patrol boats instead."

"How would we catch them?" Horatio countered, "Let's get the one responsible for all this."

July agreed with Horatio. Bob was too pissed off to care now, he just wanted to get hold of somebody and beat the shit out of them. El Presidente would do just fine.

They had made a wide arc and were coming in on El Presidente's ship from the backside. They were surprised at how dark it actually was; the ship itself was not well lit.

"There," Bob whispered, "there's a loading dock on the side of the ship."

"That solves that problem," Horatio answered. "I wasn't sure when we got here how we were going to get on board."

They quietly paddled up to the loading dock watching the ship's deck for any movements. Bob hopped out of the boat and pulled it up beside the dock. They could hear the soft sound of music drifting down from above along with some shouting.

"The pricks are having a party," Bob snarled.

Horatio climbed out onto the loading dock to join him. "Better for us," he grinned. "Let's go join him." He then turned to July as she went to leave their boat.

"July, someone has to stay in the boat. It's our only chance of getting out of here. Take the boat out a ways and wait for us. We may have to bail out over the railing, that way you can pick us up. If they follow us to the railing and start shooting, use one of these." He showed her one of the flare guns from the box. "Just shoot it at the ship. The light will blind them till we get to you." He showed her how to use the flares. "Don't be scared to keep firing them, but shield your eyes."

July was reluctant to leave but realized Horatio was right. Bob grabbed her face in his hands and kissed her hard. She looked back at him with cold blue eyes, "You've got to kill him, Bob." He nodded his head; their lives would never be at peace until El Presidente was dead.

Bob and Horatio pushed July away from the loading dock, and then cautiously proceeded to climb the steps up to the ship's main deck. There was a stack of crates near the top of the stairs; they ducked down behind them, surveying the deck. Other than some junk strewn around here and there, the deck was just a wide open surface, except for the cranes sitting over the holes to the holds below. At the front of the ship were the tower and the ship's quarters. It was on the far side of this that they could hear the music coming from. The deck was fairly well lit and along with the eerie glow from Ansly's sinking ship, they would be easy targets.

"This side is the darkest, there's stuff piled along the way. We'll stay close to the railing, that way we can jump over if we get spotted."

Horatio assessed the situation and agreed with Bob. "Let's go."

July paddled her boat back from the ship until she felt safe in the darkness. From here she could see Bob and Horatio's progress along the deck, moving from cover to cover. Then her eye caught something. There was a man standing on a platform up high near the bridge. He had been standing in the shadows before, now he'd come forward into the light.

July watched as the man took a drink from a bottle. Her heart was in her mouth; she saw the man crouch down and slip his rifle off his shoulder. "He has seen them; I've got to warn them, but how?" Her mind raced.

"Don't panic!" she told herself, reaching into the box and pulling out a flare gun. She aimed in the general direction of the man and fired. The trail of fire left her hand and arced toward the ship hitting a wall, then skipped by the man, almost hitting him before it exploded into a flash of light, nearly blinding her. The man tumbled off where he had been standing and disappeared below. This didn't stop July. She started grabbing flare gun after flare gun firing them onto the ship.

When the first flare went off, Bob's first instinct was to go over the railing; in fact, he almost did when he felt Horatio's hand on his shoulder. "I saw a man fall off from up there," he pointed. "July must have seen him." Another flare went off sending the most spectacular array of colors.

"Come on," Horatio told him, "let's make a run for the front." Bob followed him as they ran as fast as they could until they reached the enclosed part of the ship.

The whole ship was awash in color now; the light was blinding. They shielded their eyes as they peered around the corner. There they were in full view. Most of the men were standing around looking up at the exploding lights. In the center, sitting at a table in a white shirt was a man Bob took to be El Presidente.

Bob heard Horatio's gun beside him begin to fire, and he did the same. There was total chaos; men began to scramble everywhere. Bob tried to concentrate his fire on the table where El Presidente sat, but it wasn't easy to do as men were running right in front of his line of fire trying to get away. Bob's gun wasn't firing anymore.

"Empty," he said, pulling out the clip and frantically trying to put another one in. He saw the man in the white shirt slide under the table. Fucking clip wouldn't go in, he looked to see; he was trying to put it in backward.

"There," he felt it click in. "Short bursts," he remembered Horatio telling him to pull the trigger only halfway back.

He concentrated through all the shit going on around him and systematically began shooting into the table where El Presidente had sat. He saw the table splinters fly off the table, but whether he had ever hit El Presidente, he would never know. Bob was so focused on hitting his target; he didn't notice anything else happening until an electrical panel box near him blew off the wall.

His reflex was to get down behind the wall in front of him. The next second, a doorway disappeared above his head sending splinters and debris into all parts of his body.

"Holy fuck!" he screamed out in fear; he opened his eyes to see Horatio rising from the rubble. His face was covered in blood and dust.

"Let's get out of here," he shouted.

Bob took one last look around the wall. He could see a steady stream of tracer bullets flashing by disintegrating everything in their way. There was no way of standing up to this onslaught; fire was breaking out all over the place.

Bob looked over at Horatio, and they began to run across the deck staying as low as they could. They reached the top of the stairs leading down the side of the ship, only to see a powerboat docking below. They turned and ran back on deck hearing the ping of bullets hitting the steps where they had just been. They ran farther down the deck toward the back of the ship.

The last time Bob had been this scared was the night he had jumped off the roof of his mother's house and run through the snow expecting a bullet in the back any second. They caught the light of a flare drifting over them and then a flash of light somewhere behind. He could hear Horatio breathing hard. Bob knew he couldn't go much further.

"Ready," he looked at Horatio who nodded his head. They climbed the railing and jumped as another flash of light exploded behind them. Bob hit the water just ahead of Horatio. It seemed forever before he bobbed up above the surface gasping for air. He was worried about Horatio; he was a heavier man and had gone down a lot deeper than he had. Bob heard a splash and some splattering behind him. He was relieved to see Horatio gasping for air.

"Which way?" Bob asked.

"It doesn't matter," Horatio gasped. "Just get away from the ship, July will find us."

El Presidente was concentrated on his telescope; he did not notice the exploding flares until his men began shouting something about fireworks. He had no idea what his men were talking about. He turned in time to be blinded by a bright light exploding somewhere up near the smoke stacks. The next thing he heard was the sound of machine-gun fire and the sickening thud of bullets hitting bone.

There were bodies flying everywhere; his instinct told him to get down. He lay on the floor beneath his table. He put his hands over his head and stayed still, pieces of wood from the table and chairs began to sting his back, and then something hit his knee making him scream in pain. He had to get out of there. Slowly he slid on his belly; he had no idea which way he was headed.

El Presidente's lieutenant had his orders when he came on board. "Only you and I will leave this ship," El Presidente had told him. "No one must ever have seen me here." He had been briefed as to where each explosive device was to be placed. Now that his task was completed, he came on deck joining the men in celebrating their great victory. He assessed the situation; it was just as El Presidente had said it would be. Bertrand's ship was well in hand, the men suspected nothing, and most important of all, he had the signaling device to set off the charges. He felt particularly proud of this fact. El Presidente had been good to him in other ways too. Giving him his main whore was another reason he would protect El Presidente with his life.

El Presidente invited him over to look through the telescope. Pouring him a drink, El Presidente quietly asked him, "Is everything ready?"

"Yes." They spoke in English in case they were overheard.

The lieutenant mixed and drank with the men until he was as drunk as they were. His mind switched to the whore in his cabin; she needed one last screw before she went to hell. He opened the cabin door; she was lying naked on the bed, passed out as usual.He sat on the bed beside her and slapped her face hard. She moaned and opened her eyes.

"Fuck off," she mumbled and rolled away.

"Don't turn away from me, bitch." He grabbed her by the shoulders, lifting her face to his. "You think you're better than me because you were El Presidente's whore, well, he gave you to me." He saw her eyes open with hate, and then she spat in his face. He laughed at her, "You see this thing on my belt?" He showed her what looked like a telephone with red flashing numbers.

"Soon, I will push these numbers and you will be in hell," he told her.

Zeze looked at the device hanging from his belt, and then looked over and reached for a bottle near the bed.

"I'd just as soon be in hell as with you," she told him. She took a drink from the bottle as he left the bed and began removing his pants. She remembered when she thought she was on top of the world sleeping with the great El Presidente, having his baby, life had been so good back then.

El Presidente's wife hated her and wanted her out of the house. El Presidente was tired of her anyway. He took the baby away from her and gave her to this man so he would have something to do on the long voyage from Argentina on the freighter. Drugs helped her survive; she needed some now.

"Give me some of your good shit if you're going to send me to hell. I want to go on a cloud," Zeze told him.

The lieutenant went to a locked cupboard on the wall. He opened it brought out a bag, and handed it to her. She sat up on the bed, taking a spoon and filling it with the white powder, and then inhaled it up her nose.

"How you don't blow your brains out with that stuff is beyond me," he told her. She shrugged holding a spoonful out to him. He didn't often use the stuff, but this was a special occasion, a last occasion to be exact. Standing in front of her, he took the spoon and began sniffing up some of the coke. The effect hit him immediately.

The whore began playing with his cock. He could feel himself become instantly hard as she ran her tongue up and down his shaft. Neither of them heard the flares bursting outside. If they did, they assumed they were bursting in their own minds.

It was the sound of machine guns that brought the lieutenant back to reality. They were real, very real. He left the whore sitting on the bed and raced to the cabin door. What he saw on the deck outside was total chaos. His own men were shooting each other; no one seemed to know where or who was shooting. El Presidente was no longer at his table, the lieutenant noticed as he ran on deck, oblivious to the bullets flying around him. He grabbed the handles of the double-barreled fifty-caliber machine gun mounted there and began firing. He had no idea what he was shooting at; he just began raking the decks killing anything that moved. He stopped firing; everything he saw in front of him was in shambles.

The whore came to the cabin door; she began screaming and pointing, and the lieutenant saw something move. He blasted away almost blowing the man into little pieces. He stood watching, but nothing moved. He walked over to the party deck, and only then did he realize what he had done.

"My god," he thought, "I've killed El Presidente."

His mind filled with rage, he turned toward the whore standing in the cabin doorway. She was laughing at him. He could see that her nose was white with powder. She was laughing the most hideous laugh he had ever heard. In her hand was the signaling device to the explosives.

"No," he screamed, starting toward her.

By now, she was laughing uncontrollably and began pushing the buttons. He was almost to her when he heard her say, "You're going to hell without your pants on!"

Zeze pushed the last button and felt the gods rumble beneath her feet taking her away from this hell to where they would take her, she did not care.

Henekie was satisfied everything was going according to plan, as the two powerboats circled around Bertrand's ship. The missile had worked perfectly; the ship was already starting to list to one side. "Perfect execution," he thought. Now all they had to do was maintain the perimeter. Already the powerboats had rammed and sunk two of the safety boats loaded with people. Any survivors had been shot in the water. Even the bodies floating by were shot to make sure no one survived.

The flares exploding over El Presidente's ship took Henekie by surprise. At first, he thought it was probably El Presidente's men celebrating, but he decided to check it out. Unfortunately, the jamming equipment shut down their radio communications too.

This problem was solved by converting a spotlight for use with Morse Code. This had worked well between the two boats, and now

Henekie signaled the other powerboat to go back and check on the ship. This was his kill, and he wanted to stay on top of it. They circled, watching for anyone trying to swim for shore.

He heard the blast about the same time as he felt the hot air on his back. His mouth fell open; El Presidente's ship had literally blown apart. Something was dreadfully wrong; all of his plans were ruined. Someone must have been careless with the explosives. He stood watching and hoping to see the other powerboat, but there was nothing. That would mean that El Presidente was dead. Without El Presidente, he would not get paid. All his work, all his planning was for nothing.

The other four men were also standing watching El Presidente's ship wondering what was going on. Henekie realized he would have to use his head just to get out of here alive. If these guys found out that El Presidente was dead, they would kill him without a second thought.

"Okay," he told them, "Bertrand's ship is done for. Anyone left, the sharks will get. The other powerboat picked up El Presidente and took him around the north side of the island, away from anyone who happens to come to inspect what's happening here. We'll head back toward Nassau and head off any patrol boats that happen to be looking for him." The men accepted this explanation and much to Henekie's relief, they headed out to the open sea.

There was a case of booze in the cabin; Henekie brought it out. "Help yourselves," he told them, "It was a good night's work." The men were pretty well out of it by the time Henekie saw the lights of Nassau in the early morning light. He machine-gunned the men and threw their bodies overboard. He had to hurry; daylight was already on its way. He didn't bother sneaking in this time; he came in full bore stopping only for the door to open into the old warehouse. There was only one man in the warehouse. He helped Henekie dock.

"I'm going to stay for a while and get some sleep," he told the man.

Henekie was dead tired; he needed some sleep, and then he would think.

Bob and Horatio swam away from the ship. It was very dark, and they could see nothing of July until they heard the small outboard coming toward them. She cut the motor and scrambled forward to help the men into the boat.

"Let's get Horatio into the boat first," Bob told her, "He's exhausted."

It took all their strength to get him over the side; he rolled into the bottom of the boat and stayed there. July helped Bob into the boat.

"Better get life jackets on," she told them. "If they spot us, we may have to go in the water again."

July bent down to help Horatio with the jacket. Bob stood up putting his jacket on.

Ansly's ship was tipped halfway over; now flames and smoke poured from her. Bob looked around but could not see anyone near them. Something erupted in front of him; the force of it knocked him headfirst into the outboard, and then propelled him over the back of the boat into the water.

The shock went over July and Horatio in the bottom of the boat, but seconds later waves from the blast capsized the boat, throwing them both into the water. July had no idea what had happened; the first thing she remembered was floating in the water watching pieces of El Presidente's ship flying high into the air.

Explosion after explosion racked the ship; the heat was intense. There was lots of light now.

July looked around. She saw Horatio floating nearby; she began to panic, and there was no sign of Bob.

"Can you see Bob?" July screamed.

Horatio tried to calm her down; he'd seen Bob being thrown from the boat and didn't give him much hope, but he didn't tell her that.

"July," he said, "you've got no life jacket. Swim to the boat, and I'll look for him."

July didn't listen to him as she began swimming away.

"I see him," she shouted excitedly and began swimming toward a body floating in the water. Horatio went over to help her; together they pulled Bob over to the capsized boat.

"Is he dead?" she asked Horatio, the fear showing in her eyes.

"Can't tell," Horatio told her. "All we can do now is hang on to him and get to shore."

July looked toward the shore; it looked so far away.

"At least he had his lifejacket on," Horatio tried to reassure her, "or he would have drowned."

The waves from the explosion made it hard to hang on to the boat; sometimes they lost hold and had to swim back to it, but July had a death grip on Bob, she never let go of him. The waves had a good effect too. They helped push them toward shore far quicker than July realized.

The racing surf actually threw her up against the sand, beating up her already bruised body. She pulled at Bob as hard as she could, pulling him away from the pounding surf and up onto the sand as far as she could. She looked up to see Horatio being battered about in the surf, and she used the last of her energy to help him into shore then returned to Bob. She was scared to touch him for fear he was dead. To her relief, his body was still warm. She found a pulse; it was steady. She curled up beside him in the warm sand and fell asleep.

# Twenty-Three

IN THE DISTANCE, Bob could see a point of light. It tried to entice him into walking toward it, but he was happy where he was. "It's so peaceful here, and I'm so tired. I'll leave in a little while, now I want to sleep," he thought.

It pleased him that he heard July's voice from time to time. He heard other voices too. It made him feel good to have his friends with him. It made this place he was in even more comfortable. No one could hurt him here; there was no violence, no one making demands. Darkness drifted over him, and he returned to his state of unconsciousness.

It had been two weeks since the boats looking for survivors had found the three of them lying on the beach. They were the only survivors, July had been told later.

July and Horatio were, except for minor scrapes and bruises, in good shape, suffering mostly from exhaustion. But Bob was unconscious and had to be moved by stretcher into the boat where they were taken to the airport at Fresh Creek and then flown to a hospital in Nassau.

Since that time, Bob had not regained consciousness. The doctors told July there seemed to be nothing wrong with him other than that he had taken a knock to the head. "Sometimes the brain just never recovers," they told her. All they could do was wait and see. July sat with him every day. Sometimes she tried to talk to him, but there was never any response.

People they knew stopped by; both Mindy and Rikker were there. Neither could stand to see their dad like this; they didn't stay long, leaving their mother to sit with Bob alone. The hospital staff tried to get her to get out for a bit.

July had no intention of leaving Bob. He meant everything to her; she felt he knew she was there. Every day she talked to him, trying to bring his mind back to reality.

Novak came to see July at the hospital. They had a good visit. "I was hoping you could spend a day with us at our office," he told her. "There are a lot of things we would like to ask you and some things we have to show you."

"I thought you'd be back in Canada by now," she told him.

"Sir Harry talked me into staying and going to work for him or, I should say, the Bahamian government," he answered her. "As of last Thursday, I am no longer a member of the Royal Canadian Mounted Police. I now work for Interpol and as part of the Bahamian Police Department."

"Well, congratulations, Mr. Novak, I must say I'm surprised," July told him.

"I have to confess, it's a big move for me. But since coming here, I realized that I like it here, and I like working here. My old job was getting pretty boring."

July hesitated leaving Bob, but finally, they agreed to meet the next afternoon.

July sat with Bob the next morning, hating to leave him for the afternoon. Once she sat down to get ready, she realized how awful she looked. She went to work, giving herself a major overhaul from head to foot. She began to feel better about herself, vowing not to let herself get like this again.

July had not been outside for at least two weeks. She had spent the days at Bob's bedside and slept in the room with him. Novak had told her he would send a car around to pick her up, but she had insisted that she would walk even though the address he gave her was at least a half-hour away.

It was an absolutely beautiful day; the sun was hot, but the cool sea breezes felt good on July's skin. Her usually dark skin had turned white from her stay inside. She hated being pale; it did not look healthy in her estimation. As she walked, she realized a lot of things. The hospital people were right. "I have to get out more," she said to herself. She enjoyed the walk so much that she was disappointed to realize she had arrived at her destination. It was a small middle-of-the-road downtown hotel, an old place with character; she liked that.

Novak was waiting for her in the lobby.

"You are looking good today," he told her.

July laughed; he had seen her yesterday, and anything would be an improvement, but she knew he was sincere and thanked him for it.

"We have one of the small meeting rooms at the back of the hotel reserved," he told her. "Would you please follow me?" He led her to the room and sat her in a chair by itself on one side of the room. Across from her was a long table with five chairs lined up behind it. Novak sat in one of the chairs, introducing the other men as they came into the room.

July found all this very interesting; an interrogation? Well, July had spent many hours in the hospital thinking about when they would get around to this. They would wait to see if Bob came around, she had thought. Now they were impatient so she would have to do.

Upon looking at them, she thought she had them pretty well-placed. At least they weren't all CIA, she concluded, but the only one she knew was Novak. "At least I have one friend," she thought.

The young man who started the questioning was definitely CIA. He looked like a nerd with an attitude problem. After all, he worked for the most powerful country in the world. The CIA seemed to instill this fact into the minds of all their employees. She had seen this arrogance in Ansly; it had ultimately been his downfall.

"Mrs. Green, we would like to ask you a few questions," the young man said to her.

"On whose authority?" she returned.

The young man had not expected this. "I don't think that's necessary for you to know," he answered blustering.

"Are you CIA?" she asked bluntly.

The young man's face became very red, angry that his authority be questioned. "I said, that's none of your business."

July got up and stood in front of the young man. She leaned over the desk putting her face inches from his, her ice-blue eyes looking directly into his.

"Don't fuck with me!" Her voice was very husky. "You look like the type of brilliant little prick the CIA would send out to rule the world. Well, I've got news for you. I think you fucked up big-time, and now you are going to try and save your ass."

The young man's mouth fell open. She could see the rage build on his face. If he could have hit her, he would have.

"If you are here in the Bahamas, that means you are sanctioned here. It means you run their office and you look after their people. My husband and I have put our lives on the line for you, and you say it is none of my business. Who do you think you are? Where were you when that ship went down with everyone on board? How come there was no backup or contingency plan? I know why. Because conceited little bastards like you and Ansly think that because you work for the CIA, no one is as smart as you." She stood back looking at the other men sitting at the table.

"As for you gentlemen, I have a pretty fair idea who you are too. What bothers me is that you would have sat there letting him tell you what he wanted you to know. Well, get your tails out from between your legs. You had better ask the CIA what actually happened here. They fucked up, and they fucked up big-time. If you guys want to talk to me, you shall be up-front with who you are and what is happening."

She looked at Novak. "I did not come here to be interrogated. I'll tell you what I know, but there are things I want to know also. Do we understand one another?" The men looked at each other but said nothing.

"I'll be in the courtyard if you decide you would like to discuss matters further. I'll meet you there." She left them and stepped into the courtyard.

Instantly, she felt the hot sun on her already flushed skin. It is the only way, she thought to herself. You had to face them down. Once they realized they couldn't manipulate you and came down to the same level, they became humans again, probably not bad guys really.

July found a table with an umbrella shading one side. She sat down in the shade leaving the other chairs for the men sitting in the sun, just in case they wanted to negotiate a little more.

Novak smiled to himself. He had not known until today what was going on either, and when he found out, he was not pleased. He felt sorry for the men around the table. There were lots they wanted to know, and July could supply much of this information, but they now thought the CIA had not been quite up-front with them, and it was causing quite a lively discussion.

At last, they turned to Novak and asked if he would reason with her.

"No," he answered, "but I will apologize. You people got exactly what you deserve. She risked her life for you and hasn't asked for anything in return but respect. Surely you can trust her as an equal and confide in her some of the things you know."

This did not fizz on the CIA man at all. He thought they should arrest July. The man who represented the Bahamian police fired back that he thought the CIA agent should be arrested.

Novak saw that this was going nowhere. He left and joined July in the courtyard. He took a chair that afforded as much shade as possible accepting his punishment for bringing July to this meeting without first researching its intent. Novak apologized to her, and then he encouraged her.

"I'm glad to see you've still got your old spark, July. You were perfectly right to do what you did in there."

July smiled at him. "It is always nice to have friends, Mr. Novak. Right now, I need them very badly." Her face quickly changed. "I have put those men in a spot. They are going to have to save face somehow. It will be interesting to see what they come up with."

Novak laughed, "It will be more interesting to see what you come up with!"

The four men filed into the courtyard and walked to where July and Novak were sitting. One of the men looked like he wished to speak, but before he did so, July asked, "Would you please sit down, gentlemen?"

They sat down already feeling the disadvantage of sitting in the hot sun. "We understand you should have been informed as to who would be here today and that certain information would be required," the same young man told her. "However, we have already talked to Captain Horatio Norton. He has basically told us all we need to know. All we wanted you to do was verify a few facts."

"Gentlemen, what Captain Norton knows and what I know may be two different things," July told them. "If you want to talk to me, here is what we do. I suggest an informal meeting at Mr. Chamberlain's house. That should be fair because he is one of yours. I want Captain Norton to be there, and I want to be briefed by Novak here as up to date as possible. The meeting date is up to your discretion."

The hot sun was beginning to take its toll. The men looked at each other and nodded. Only the young CIA man showed any signs of having fight left in him.

"Since we already know what we need from Captain Norton, I don't think this meeting is necessary," he told her.

"That is fine," July shot back, "but whether it is from me or from the news media, you are going to hear my story."

The young man became very red in the face again.

"We can have you put where no one will ever see you again," he threatened.

"That's one of the reasons the rest of you must hear my story," July told them. "Not just the questions this young man chooses to ask, but the whole story. Believe me, gentlemen, it is worth hearing."

"Would you be ready by tomorrow night?" one of the other men asked.

"If that's convenient for Mr. Novak to bring me up to date?" She looked at Mr. Novak; he nodded his head.

"Yes, we can do that." July got up from the table. "Till tomorrow, gentlemen. Now if you'll excuse me, I have work to do." The sweating men gladly rose and watched her leave.

"That's a lot of woman," one of the men said.

"In more ways than one," one of the other men speculated. They all chuckled, but they all knew it was the truth.

The next day Novak briefed July on what had happened since the incident at Buzzard Bay. There were speculations and rumors but not much concrete evidence as to what really happened. They had only Captain Norton's testimony to go on. He was the only eyewitness they had questioned until now. Other than him telling Interpol that he and Bob Green had been on a ship they speculated El Presidente to be on minutes before it blew up, Norton had little proof to back up his story. Novak told July that this seemed to please the CIA man, and he wanted the rest of the investigation turned over to them.

"You've certainly changed that," Novak told her.

"I think everyone will get an eye opening tonight."

July asked him candidly, "You were a Canadian Mountie. Is that the reason you're still here is because they think Bob's responsible for our friends' murder in Canada?"

Novak was equally candid, "Your husband is still a suspect. Yes, there is a warrant out for his arrest, but I have told them nothing yet. This means there aren't any orders for extradition started. In fact, that is why no one has found you until now. Chamberlain and I have kept your identity a secret to Interpol, who work very slowly. Soon they will inform the RCMP that they have Bob, and then the Bahamian government will have to detain him pending an investigation. I was hoping he would recover quickly, and then Chamberlain and I could get him a cover but," he gestured, "there is no way we can help him in his current condition."

Novak went on, "As for me, I've become more and more involved with the situation here in the Bahamas. Chamberlain has given me a couple of leads that have led to the arrests of drug dealers in Canada. This has made it worthwhile leaving me here. I do now have some jurisdiction in the Bahamas. I'm hooked up with Interpol, and thanks to Chamberlain's influence in MI5, they keep me informed and in touch with the other agents in Nassau. We all know what the CIA was up to here, July. We helped them set up El Presidente. We helped supply them with information and even people like yourselves. Typical of them, they did not need us anymore. The German Embassy received rumors of a ship fitted with illegal equipment in Argentina and heading north. El Presidente would not stick his nose out of Colombia. All of a sudden, he was boarding his yacht and sailing right under the CIA's nose. As far as Ansly was concerned, bring 'El Presidente on!' There was no way they could touch him. The CIA just did not seem to realize they were dealing with a ruthless man who had a larger budget to work with than the entire CIA."

"You speak as though he's still alive," July asked him.

"We think he is dead," Novak told her, "but we are not sure."

Their meeting, at July's request, was held at Bob's bedside. There was no sign of improvement; in fact, Novak thought he looked very much like a dead man.

Novak picked July up that night to take her to Chamberlain's. "How's my July?" Sir Harry asked her in his lilting English accent that always seemed to cheer her up. He asked her if there was any change in Bob. "I'm sorry," he explained, "that I haven't been able to visit you. I've been out of the country." Then he winked at her.

"I hear this party is your idea, July. You never fail to amaze me."

"At least, I have two friends here tonight," she thought, "the odds are getting better."

The people at Chamberlain's were basically the same people that were at the first meeting, with the exception of Chamberlain himself and the young CIA man who was now accompanied by an older gentleman whom no one seemed to know. This time, each man introduced himself and the police force or organization he represented. After this was accomplished, Chamberlain asked July to tell her story, going back to day one.

It seemed so long ago to July as she remembered how excited they were to be leaving Canada to start a new life on the farm complex in the Bahamas, and then gradually how they learned the truth as to why they were really on the farm at Andros.

July started, "No one ever thought we could actually make a go of it after Tom Newton disappeared, and the cartel cut off our funding. We were too naive to know the power and money that was involved in the drug trade. We had had no idea how ruthless these people could be."

She told them how everyone but herself was extradited out of the country. "A man by the name of Waddell seemed to do what he wanted in these islands."

She looked at the Bahamian, "Waddell took me basically for his own pleasure. I was fortunate to get away and get to Mr. Chamberlain for help. Bob and the others were not so fortunate. Someone decided they knew too much and sent some people to get rid of him and the two other couples who had run the farm, but Bob managed to get away. This is where Constable Novak came in. He can tell you more about what happened than I can because he was there. However, Bob told me he wounded one and killed another of the men who were after him. There were at least seven people all told killed in Canada. The police suspected Bob, but he knew Waddell had me, so rather than staying and clearing himself, he managed to slip away trying to come to my rescue. He also ended up here at Chamberlain's. It was here that we were, let us say, persuaded into working with the CIA, in a plot to get a man we all know as El Presidente."

July went on, "My husband masqueraded as a notorious drug lord by the name of Bertrand who was trying to run El Presidente's cartel out of the Bahamas. The CIA told us that Bertrand's ship had been taken somewhere in the Mediterranean and Bertrand himself killed. This had all been done secretly so that no one knew Bertrand was actually dead. Everything seemed to be going according to plan until the night a ship attacked Ansly and his crew. I guess we all know the ship was sunk. As we were not on board, I do not know how or why, maybe you people know more than I do about what happened. I'm sure Captain Horatio told you how he and Bob went on board a ship that seemed to be responsible for the attack on Ansly. That's a brief history of all I know. Since then, I have been isolated with my husband, who is lying unconscious in the hospital. If you have any more questions, I would be happy to try my best to answer them."

Just then, Captain Norton and his wife came into the room. July gave them both a big hug. The Bahamian representative came over and shook Horatio's hand.

"I know you are very skeptical of our government's actions in the past, Mrs. Green. I think you will agree we are cleaning up our police department by putting Mr. Norton in charge. As you can well imagine, he is a very busy man, which is why he is late tonight."

July congratulated Horatio on his promotion but was still skeptical of the Bahamian government's actions. Then it was back to business. The German representative asked her the first question.

"Do you know a man by the name of Grundman?"

"Yes, I know who he is, although I have never met the man personally," July answered. "I saw him on a surveillance camera when Bob was masquerading as Bertrand. He had several dealings with Grundman. In fact, Grundman was the agent that made the deal for Bertrand to buy the farm on Andros."

The German put on his glasses and scanned a sheet in front of him. "Up until a few weeks ago, we knew him as a perverted small-time con artist. His name was mentioned a few times on our Interpol list but only as a possible go-between and a bungling one at that. In fact, our information is that he screwed up so badly that certain people would have liked to see him dead, so he ran off to the Bahamas taking with him an Austrian immigrant by the name of Lena, who went by so many last names that we won't bother to go through them. She was a courtesan to some very high-ranking people in the German government. There was eventually a scandal, and there were people who would have liked to see her put away too. So we figured Lena had paid Grundman to get her out of the country. This did not bother the German police too much.

After all, the country was rid of two problems without much fuss. Let someone else worry about them."

"However," he continued, "Interpol become very interested in these two characters after the German police picked up a young woman in a drug raid in Munich. It was a very serious charge which would result in a long-jail sentence. Realizing she was in a lot of trouble, she began offering information in return for a lighter sentence. On hearing some of this information, the German police turned her over to us at Interpol. It seems her mother was Grundman's live-in secretary. This girl figures Grundman killed her mother because she knew too much. From what she told us, we were able to identify an unknown body pulled from a river. This verified that she was telling the truth, and we began listening to what she had to say. Grundman apparently let the young woman stay in his house in return for sexual favors. Her mother did all of Grundman's books and ran errands for him. Grundman kept an office in Switzerland, which enabled him to move large amounts of money for the Colombian drug people. We now believe he supplied the money to Waddell, who in turn supplied a company here in the Bahamas by the name of APCO with funding. We have reason to believe he supplied Tom Newton with funding to start the farm on Andros through an intermediary in Bowling Green, Kentucky, by the name of Ken Holmes. It was becoming very obvious that we were onto something very big, but by the time we got to Grundman, he had fallen fourteen stories off his apartment balcony."

"Astonishingly," he continued, "Our informant also told us another story of how Grundman was the contact man for an assassin we had been looking for, for some time. This assassin did all of the drug cartel's work for them around the world. Grundman, the little weasel, believe it or not, had this assassin working for him. All the money the cartel paid for these contracts went to Grundman, and he paid the assassin. We also believe that with the help of Mr. Novak and the Canadian police, it was this assassin who went after your husband and your friends up in Canada, Mrs. Green. From the remains given to us by the Canadian RCMP, we thought we had identified this assassin, but from what we have learned since, this assassin is still out there and had something to do with the sinking of Bertrand's ship. Another thing we do not understand, Mrs. Green, is how your husband got away from him. This man was a mastermind who had fooled most of the police forces around the world."

July had not had a lot of time to spend with Bob since he'd gotten back to the Bahamas. She guessed that with what little time they had had, he had not wanted to bother her with all he'd been through. Besides, she'd had enough problems of her own that she had had no time to think that Bob too had come through hell to get back to her.

The German began talking again, tearing her mind away from Bob. "When the Canadian police sent us a picture of a necklace to keep a lookout for, we did not really pay much attention. Like all of Interpol, we in Germany had no reason to think that a necklace would show up here. However, a thread of evidence found clasped tight in a dead policeman's hand alerted the authorities. Somehow, before he died, he had gotten hold of a medallion that had hung from this necklace."

The German pointed to Novak. "Mr. Novak stayed like a bloodhound on the trail of this necklace. The Canadian Mounties loaned him to their Interpol division, sending him on the trail of Mr. Green, which led him to the Bahamas. Sure enough, both Mr. Green and the necklace showed up here, not together of course. Mr. Green showed up at this very spot, Mr. Chamberlain's house. The necklace showed up around the neck of our courtesan, Lena, in the company of a Mr. Waddell. Mr. Novak told us about the necklace and where he had seen it. By this time, we were heavily into the investigation of Mr. Grundman, so we too wondered where they could have gotten this necklace. Luckily—and there is always a little luck involved in these things—we found a jeweler, whom we knew fenced items for people from time to time. He was able to identify the necklace from the picture as one Grundman had brought him to appraise. He remembered telling Grundman that it was worth far less because of one missing medallion. Still it was worth enough to get Grundman excited. We still do not know how Grundman got it or why he gave it to Lena. Of course, we assume the assassin took it from one of his victims and gave it to Grundman, but why he would do this, we have no idea. I think Novak may have more to add to this."

"Yes, I do, as a matter of fact. Mrs. Green probably does not know it yet, but Manly Waddell was found dead strangled by a rope hanging from Lena's apartment balcony. Captain Norton and I went to question her a few days ago. She, of course, claims she was not home when this took place and knows nothing about what happened to Waddell. We know the CIA had two men in the apartment across from hers and that they had her apartment under surveillance but they say that they heard nothing until there was the unmistakable sound of gunshots. The power had gone out, leaving the whole building in darkness. They knocked on her door but got no answer.

Having no communication with their superiors because the phones were also out, they decided to watch for anyone coming out and waited for the police to arrive not wanting to blow their cover. I told Lena this, saying that as far as they were concerned, she was still in the apartment when the shots were fired. Lena still denied that she was in the apartment, so Captain Norton took a different tact.

He told Lena they knew that El Presidente had spent the night with her when the ships were sunk. El Presidente had not been seen since. There were rumors that El Presidente's family was looking for her. It would be easy to spread more rumors that she was responsible for his death. This threat seemed to bring Lena around. She asked what we wanted, so we showed her the pictures of what we now call Reich's necklace. She asked what was so important about the necklace, so we told her how it had been obtained in Canada with connection to a murder and that we wanted to know how it had come into her possession. She explained how she had a fascination with beautiful jewelry. When Grundman had first showed it to her, she knew that she must have it. Grundman knew he had a hold on her with the necklace and promised it to her in return for sexual favors that she had never granted him before. She claims she obtained it the night Grundman was killed. I won't elaborate on the circumstances."

Norton went on to ask her if she knew where Grundman had gotten the necklace. He explained to her that Mr. Green was in the hospital here, and that it was the only way of proving he did not commit the murders back in Canada. She told us that she wished she could help, but Grundman had never told her where he had obtained the necklace. Until we can find this missing link, I am afraid the thread is still broken.

"Additionally, I have something to add to this," said Norton. "I offered Lena protection but she refused, telling us that she would never be dependent on men to protect her ever again. We found this strange coming from a woman who has lived off men almost all of her life. We know the building she lives in is owned by El Presidente, and if he is dead, it now belongs to his family. We confiscated El Presidente's yacht in the harbor, but his family is fighting hard for its release. We believe Lena is working for the family now. In fact, we have reason to believe she has taken Waddell's place as the cartel's person in charge here. We must not underestimate this woman. She is smart and can manipulate people if she so chooses. We have heard rumors coming out of Colombia. Maybe our Colombian colleague can give us an update as to what is going on there."

The Colombian Interpol agent was basically a CIA man put there to watch the comings and goings of the drug trade. He looked nervous as he cleared his throat. "You all appear to be very well-informed," he told them.

"We in Colombia also believe El Presidente to be dead. There is a power struggle to take over his territory, however, his wife and two sons are fighting back. They are desperately working to keep intact the international organization their father built, but these are different times, whether they succeed or not remains to be seen. One thing we can be sure about, they will be ruthless in hunting out anyone responsible for their father's death. Right now the CIA is being blamed, and El Presidente's family has declared war on them. I guess the CIA and DEA people are the only ones left to help us fill in the pieces."

He turned to the two American agents. "Maybe you can start with why the Argentina freighter was not stopped and searched even though we warned you she had suspicious cargo on board."

The young agent looked at the older man beside him. "The man beside me is a lawyer on the CIA staff. He is an expert on international law."

"My name is Ted Heath and I've taken over this area after agent Ansly's demise." He then went on to explain that they had indeed kept track of the freighter out of Argentina. In fact, they had checked her cargo when she stopped to refuel in San Salvador.

"Our people were looking for drugs, not illegal weapons. Her point of destination was Savannah. He thought we'd wait until she got into American waters before we stopped her again. Gentlemen, the point is that we are going to treat this incident as if it never happened. The report will read that the freighter caught fire and sank with all hands on board. There will be no mention of Ansly's ship or that she even existed. As for El Presidente, he was last seen going into his place in Nassau and never came out. If he is dead, someone did him in at his own place or is holding him there."

"My god, that is preposterous," July blurted out. "How will you explain all the dead bodies that were picked up or floated to shore? I'm sure there were lots of people who saw two ships burning on the water. Word will get around, and your story will never wash."

"It has already been filed, Mrs. Green. A boat was sent out from the base on Andros to rescue the survivors. It must have gotten too close to the burning freighter and exploded. That is how we are explaining the dead Americans. There are very few people who actually know what happened at Andros, Mrs. Green. It would certainly be in the best interest for yourself and your husband to keep quiet. No one knows you were there, that is the best way to keep it. If you do tell people your story it will be the Colombians not us who will be interested. I've seen what they can do to a person before they kill them. I strongly suggest that you forget about the whole thing."

July was stunned

; she looked at Captain Norton whose eyes were drooped. "He's right, July, you'll never have a moment's peace in your life again unless you let this pass."

July's mind flashed back over all that she and Bob had been through; because of all this, Bob might never come back to her. She had to think of the family they needed to get back to a normal life. "All right," she told them, "I'm done fighting with you people or anyone else. I'm tired, gentlemen, I just want to go home." She gave Mrs. Norton a hug and left the room. A strange sensation of loneliness hit at her stomach as she realized she had no home to go to.

Lena had never seen Henekie lose his cool until she told him that Green was still alive. "All I know is that he's in the hospital," she told him.

Green was the nemesis of Henekie's life. Not only did he not get his money, now both the cartel and the CIA were after him. He had to get out of these islands quickly, but not before he took care of Mr. Green. The son of a bitch had fucked him up at every turn. How he was still alive, Henekie had no idea. Well, not for much longer, he thought and immediately went to work finding exactly where Green was located.

It took a while, but he found him. Henekie cased the section of the hospital that Green was in. He was surprised to find no guards in the hallway. During visiting hours, he walked by Green's room and peered in the door; no guards in there either. The other bed in his room was empty. Henekie was tempted to go in right then and there, but there were too many people around.

Tonight, he thought, would be better. Just before visiting hours were over, he entered the hospital and slipped into a closet he had found near Green's room earlier on.

He waited until everything was quiet then hurried down the hall to Green's room. Just as he opened the door, he ran smack into a nurse.

"What are you doing here?" said an intimidating big black woman.

Henekie thought fast as his mind raced as what to do next.

He'd seen a car pick Green's wife up early in the afternoon. Henekie decided to go with that.

"Mrs. Green won't be back tonight," he lied to the nurse. "She asked me to look in on him."

The nurse told him there was no use going in. "He's just a vegetable in there."

Bob began to grow restless; he sensed that July wasn't there with him. He tried to call her, but she did not answer. The faraway light had disappeared; he was in total darkness. Maybe this world wasn't so nice after all. "What was that?" The skin on his flesh turned to goose bumps; every nerve came alive. Listen, that voice, he had heard it before, but where. I know on the ship, he had Mindy! Bob's mind began to function.

"He's going to kill me. It's Henekie. Someone help me!" But he realized he was alone. He hated this world; it wasn't safe at all. They were talking about him; he strained his ears trying to hear.

It was a woman's voice; she was telling this Henekie that he couldn't go in the room. "I don't care who you are," she told him. "It won't do you any good anyway, he ain't gonna get no better, just gonna lie there till he die," the lady's voice explained.

A vegetable. "I'm no vegetable," Bob thought. "I've got to tell July to get me out of here. Who the hell does she think she is, calling me a vegetable?"

Bob felt relieved, but he felt the sweat running down his face as he heard Henekie's voice answer the nurse. "Okay, thank you very much, I'll come back another time."

The information seemed satisfying to Henekie. "A vegetable," he thought, "that's much more punishing than death." Why put the man out of his misery?

Henekie told the nurse, "I'll tell Mrs. Green there is no change then, thank you." He turned away and began walking down the hall. He walked out of the hospital with a lighter step. It was only fitting, he thought, that Green should suffer as he himself had. There was a charter waiting for him at the airport. By noon tomorrow, he would be in Germany, far from here.

The plane had cost him a lot of money. He knew the airport was being watched. Even his brilliant disguise and passport might not get him through this time. He waited on the runway until the charter pulled up beside him then jumped on board as the plane taxied down the runway. Not until he saw the lights of Nassau fading behind him did he let out a sigh of relief.

Henekie thought back to all the work he had done in those islands. He had been so close to reaching his goal. Just a few minutes more and El Presidente would have escaped on his speedboat as planned. Why had El Presidente's ship blown up so early? He remembered the flares exploding above the freighter at the time he thought the men on board were just celebrating. Now he wasn't so sure.

Green had survived which meant he wasn't on the ship as he had first thought. Somehow through it all Green must have been involved, because he now lay dying in a hospital bed. Henekie didn't know how, but he felt Green was responsible for El Presidente's ship blowing up.

Well, nothing he could do now, he thought. Green got what he deserved and as for himself, he had survived which was more than most of them, but he had a taste of bitterness in his mouth that he would never forget. Never!

July had not gone back to Bob's room that night. She had decided to spend the night with Mindy and Rikker who had rented a small apartment nearby. They sat up the rest of the night discussing what had taken place at the meeting. Rikker was upset that his mother had agreed to remain quiet about her involvement in the past events.

"Because of these people, Dad's lying in a hospital bed unconscious, and you're willing to say, 'That's okay, you guys fucked up.' The druggies won, let's not make any waves, go home, and keep your mouth shut."

July was impressed with Mindy's more mature grasp of the situation. "That's not going to bring Dad back, Rikker. We have to face the fact that he might not be able to be with us anymore. That's all we need is Mother running around telling stories that people may or may not believe. Even if they do believe her, so what? No one will protect her. One day, she'll just end up dead like so many others."

Rikker finally had to concede that for his mother's sake, they should let it go. He shook his head, "I just can't believe that after all we've been through, they can throw us to the wolves."

"I told them our story," July told him. "They know what happened, but we are only pieces of paper in a windstorm. If we blow away, no one will find us, but if we land in someone's yard, these people might raise a lot of shit trying to find out who is polluting their property. It is best that we blow out to sea and be forgotten."

They laughed at her quasi quote, but July became serious again. "Mindy's right, we have to contemplate our future without your father. It will be tough enough making it. We don't need someone threatening to kill us on top of it all."

July had not slept at all, but she decided to go to the hospital anyway. It was going to be a beautiful day; a rain shower overnight had freshened the air, and a soft breeze rustled through the palms. If only Bob was here with me, she thought. He loved the early morning, especially the sunrise. "It's when the whole world comes alive," he always said.

She entered the hospital to find the nurses changing shifts. The nurse gave July a hug, "Sorry, he is still the same." July was not really disappointed; she had not expected Bob to be any better; in fact, she was beginning to accept that he might not come back to her.

She entered his room and saw him lying quietly on the bed. Her intention was to get some sleep before the hospital became too busy. She went over to the other bed and took her shoes off. Just as she pulled the covers back, she heard a rasping sound. July looked around the room but saw nothing. She heard the sound again. Someone was whispering her name.

"Bob!" No, it couldn't be; she froze, afraid to believe it was him for fear she might be just tired and hearing things. "I must not get my hopes up," she said to herself, slowly walking to Bob's bed. She picked up his hand and to her amazement, he was looking at her. She began to cry uncontrollably. This time, she unmistakably heard him say "July."

"Yes, darling, I'm here." She kissed him tenderly.

He was trying to say something at first; she did not pay any attention until she felt his hand tighten on hers. "July, he was here. He was going to kill me." Bob thought he was yelling the words, but his voice was only a whisper.

"Who?" she asked, thinking he was hallucinating.

"It was the same voice, the one that had Mindy, Henekie."

Instantly, July felt a shiver run up her spine.

"How do you know he was here?" July asked him.

"He was talking to the nurse over there." His eyes looked toward the door. "I'm not a vegetable, am I, July?" His eyes looked at her pleadingly.

"Of course not, darling! I will phone Captain Norton right away and see if he can get to the bottom of this."

Bob squeezed her hand and seemed to fall back to sleep.

It was only minutes until Norton showed up in person; ten minutes after that, Novak showed up. They were a little suspicious when they saw Bob lying sleeping like usual.

"He told me he heard Henekie's voice talking to the nurse last night."

"I'll see if I can confirm it with the night nurse. I shall give her a call," Norton said, leaving the room.

"Maybe we should have a look around," Novak told July, not wanting to leave her alone. They went up and down the hallway checking every room. When they got back to Bob's room, July gave out a gasp. Bob was sitting up on the bed.

"I know they didn't believe you," Bob told her, his voice sounding stronger now.

A nurse rushed by July pushing Novak out of the way. "You are back from the dead, Mr. Green. You had better lay down, or you will be dead for good this time."

The three of them helped Bob to lie down.

"How long have I been like this?" Bob asked.

"A little over two weeks," July smiled at him.

"I'm sorry, I'm so tired," he told her. "When I heard Henekie's voice, I was scared he'd come after me. My mind was working, but nothing would move. You have no idea how hard it was to get my fingers to move. I worked until I heard you come in this morning. Now I know everything's all right. I'm not a vegetable. The nurse said I was a vegetable."

Both Novak and July assured him that he was all right. The most important thing to July was that Bob was his old fighting self. She knew he would be all right now.

Captain Norton hurried back into the room. "The nurse said there was a man here last night. He told her you had sent him around, July, to see how Mr. Green was doing."

"I certainly didn't send anyone around," July told him.

Norton nodded, "I put a call in. If he's on this island, we shall find him."

Bob recovered quickly once he had made up his mind to. An armed policeman sat outside Bob's room day and night until one day Norton came to see them.

"The airport security people reported that a car had been parked near the runway for a few days. We found out when it had been left there. A plane loaded with freight left early that morning. The pilot confessed to picking up a man and hauling him to Havana. We checked, but he seems to have vanished from there on. I don't think he'll bother you again. We have a description of him now. He's too smart to show his face around here."

A week later, Novak showed up. He came right to the point. "Tomorrow, someone from the Canadian Embassy is going to visit you. They are considering extraditing you in connection with the murders committed there. If you are at all able, I suggest you not be here. I am trying to get it through their heads that you are innocent, but it takes time. Captain Norton is living in Nassau right now. His place on Andros is empty. Arthur's brother will be in the harbor tonight." Novak gave them a smile. "I'm sure you can find him."

Arthur himself had no idea what had happened to Bob and July. He was as surprised as anyone when Norton had phoned asking him to help them. "It will be an honor," he told Norton. "Leave the rest to me."

Novak had no sooner left than Arthur showed up at the door with a big grin on his face. He embraced the both of them. "Whenever you're ready, I'll take you to my brother's boat," he told them." I have to ask this Arthur, what is your brothers real name," Bob wanted to know. Arthur smiled." Our mother died while giving birth to him. He was never given a name and I was responsible for raising him so everyone just calls him Arthur's brother."

Arthur helped Bob to the car, and then they picked up the kids and headed for the harbour. "Just like old times," Bob told him as they boarded the boat. "We're on the run again."

Arthur's brother laughed, "At least this time you have narrowed the odds. The whole world isn't after you, Mr. Green."

They waved goodbye to Arthur and headed out of the harbor. "What a beautiful view," Mindy said as they headed under the bridge to Paradise Island.

It was late in the afternoon; one of the cruise ships was pulling into dock, its load of tourists itching to get ashore for a night of chance in the Nassau casino. Most of the ships they saw were coming in for the night. They were headed out.

"The view is much better from the deck of my boat than it is from below, isn't it, Mr. Green?"

Bob explained to July and the kids how he had hung on to a handle under the bow while a U.S. Coast Guard had searched the boat and then followed them, forcing Bob to be towed along in the water. "I was so sure those garbage bags were sharks. It seems funny now."

"It was those bags that saved us in the end." Arthur's brother finished the story. "The Coast Guard wanted to look through it to see if they could find out what ship had dumped them. I wonder if they ever did."

Mindy and Rikker thought it was a wonderful adventure, but July was beginning to realize what Bob had been through trying to get to her. She wondered what he had not yet told her, but it confirmed his love for her, and right now that meant more than anything.

"These islands are full of rumors," Arthur's brother told them. "Rumors and legends. The legend is that two warring drug lords faced off at Buzzard Bay. The rumor is that one drug lord sank the other one's boat, and then Captain Norton, with the help of the Greens sank him. People here hadn't realized the drug cartel's grip on our government. It is no doubt a new government will be elected now."

Bob went to say something, but Arthur's brother put up his hand.

"It doesn't matter. The drug people still want to do business here. They're not going to show that they believe these rumors. It would make them look small and vulnerable. People of these islands love mystery and intrigue. They aren't sure they know exactly how or what you did. They know Horatio Norton is a hero for getting rid of the drug lord, El Presidente, but did you help him or is that just a rumor? You two are a mystery, and the locals love to talk about it."

Rikker and Mindy were very impressed by the revelation of Arthur's brother. They certainly had not realized how respected their parents were.

As for Bob and July, they knew how rumors could spread in these islands. They just hoped that Arthur's brother was right, that it would not affect their stay on Andros Island.

Sir Harry Chamberlain came in to Novak's office and sat on the edge of his desk. "This is a lot better than that dingy little hole you had over at the Canadian consulate, isn't it, Novak? A lot more room."

Novak rose and shook his hand, "And a lot more responsibility. Yes, I like the security guidelines you set up for the new prime minister and his cabinet," Sir Harry told him. "Now I have a new job for you. As you know, Horatio Norton's been named the new police chief. It's kind of a figurehead appointment. He's the new hero for the nation, and the government needs him to show their desire to shake the drug image the Bahamas have."

"The problem is the government's pretty vulnerable right now. If something were to happen to Horatio, it would look very bad for them, and you know there's lots of people who would like to bump him off. What I want you to do, Novak, is to make sure nothing happens to Horatio. That will include setting up his itinerary and making sure his family is safe," Sir Harry summarized.

"Sounds like a full-time job," Novak looked worried already.

"I wouldn't ask you to do this if I didn't think you could handle it, and of course, I expect you to keep up the good work with Interpol. You didn't expect to get this nice office for nothing, did you, Novak," Sir Harry slapped his back. "Now I want you to come with me and meet Lena. I think there's a few things you would like to ask her."

Novak had heard lots about the infamous Lena, but he had not expected her to be so beautiful and well-informed.

"So you're Sir Harry's new man about town and the one all the girls are talking about," Lena gave him the once-over. She made them a drink, and Sir Harry asked his questions, then Novak got his chance.

"I hear you have a necklace in your possession that you got from a man named Grundman. Would it be possible for me to see it?

It seems a lot of people are interested in that necklace." She left the room and brought it back to show him. "You may be disappointed in this necklace Mr. Novak as was I."

"It certainly looks like Hania Shonavon's necklace," Novak thought. "This looks like the one I have an original piece for," Novak told her. "Would it be possible for me to have this analyzed to see if indeed my piece is from this necklace?" He looked up at her, "Of course I'll bring it back to you."

Lena smiled, "I'll make you a deal. You escort me to the policeman's ball Saturday night, and I'll let you borrow the necklace." Novak was stunned. Why would this woman ask him to escort her, but he needed that necklace and he thought, I guess I could wear my old Mountie uniform after all, this is in the line of duty.

"Okay," he blurted out.

"Great," Lena said as she showed them out the door, "I'll pick you up."

On their way back downtown, Sir Harry didn't say much until he dropped Novak off. "That's a very dangerous woman you're dealing with there." Novak didn't know how dangerous until they were about to enter the ballroom Saturday night. Novak couldn't believe he was escorting this beautiful creature beside him.

"All eyes will be on you tonight, Lena," he told her. She turned toward him and kissed him passionately her hand rubbing the front of his tight uniform trousers. She felt him getting hard.

"There's nothing like a bulge in those tight pants to take the attention away from me," she told him as she led him through the ballroom door. They certainly got everyone's attention, she radiant in her evening gown, and Novak with his face as red as his tunic.

# TWENTY-FOUR

THE GIRL LAY naked over the pool deck. Her head rested in one man's lap, while another man stood in the pool stroking in and out between her legs.

Bob and July always got up just before dawn to get everything ready for the day ahead. The hotel was filled to capacity, and breakfast would be hectic. It was while they passed the pool on their way to the kitchen that they heard the moaning and stopped. Gradually in the dim morning light, they made out what was going at the edge of the pool.

They stood watching for a moment then July asked, "Should we put a stop to it?" They had seen the same girl flashing some men on the dance floor, and the party must have carried on till now.

"No," Bob answered, "it's none of our business. They seem to be enjoying themselves."

"Well, we'd better get to work then. They are making me horny," July rubbed against him. "I think you're a little too late to get into that fray. I'd say they're just about done."

July pushed him toward the kitchen. "Let's get out of here or there'll be another fray, and you'll be involved." July was very happy that Bob had become so laid-back, because it hadn't always been this way.

If Bob could have stayed at the hospital in Nassau, he would have been able to receive professional help, but Canada's sudden interest in a comatose patient being treated there put Novak in a tight spot.

Novak no longer worked directly for the Canadian government, but he still had close ties with their embassy, so he reported back to the authorities there that the man in question had not been identified. He explained that the patient was under intensive care and not allowed visitors. He also reminded them that Mr. Green had been reported missing after the two ships had collided off the Bahamian coast, and he had no reason to suspect that the patient and Mr. Green were one and the same. After he sent the message back to the Canadian authorities, Novak took a minute to reflect on the fact that he had lied. There was a time when that would not have happened. "Now I'm getting just as devious as Sir Harry," he said out loud. He also realized that this world was not always black and white; there were gray areas that were not covered by the code of conduct he had so rigidly adhered to.

Novak picked up the phone and contacted Horatio. "You've got to get Green out of there. I told the Canadians no one could get in to identify the patient, but they'll have someone down there pretty damn quick."

"How did they find out?" Horatio wanted to know.

"I don't know, and I don't want to know any more about anything," Novak hung up the phone.

Things were not easy after they reached Andros Island. They spend their time at Horatio's guesthouse. July knew Bob's physical condition needed to be looked after and that was not a problem. She knew that he was very resilient, and already he showed signs of improvement.

What she hadn't realized was his mental state. July was not meant to be a shrink; she had no patience for people who as she called it, had a terminal case of head fuck. She thought the location would be perfect for Bob's rehabilitation, but she was soon to find out it made no difference to Bob.

From the start, he was paranoid that someone was after them. No matter what she said, he just wouldn't relax; all day he paced the floor, and at night he'd toss and turn then wake up screaming and dripping in sweat. The first month, he showed little improvement. July was beginning to wonder how much more she could take.

Physically, he had improved to almost where he was before the head injury, but she could not seem to get into his head. Finally, one night as he sat up in bed, shaking and covered in sweat, instead of trying to comfort him she asked, "What did you see, Bob? What woke you up?"

"I killed a man, July. I shot him, and I saw his head explode. Now all I see is his face inside a helmet rolling across the snow. He's smiling at me, July, a hideous smile. No matter what I tell myself, he won't leave me alone. I'm sorry, July, but I can't shake him."

"Was this the same man who wanted to kill you, Bob? Would this man have stopped with you, or would he have killed your family?"

"Yes, I believe he would have," Bob told her.

July retorted, "We need you Bob, but we need you in the future, not dwelling in the past."

Bob slept through the rest of the night. July began to see a ray of hope. She had made a breakthrough. The next day, July sat Bob down and began asking questions, learning more about what Bob had been through. It was not his head injury that had caused his trauma; that was merely a conduit to what had happened before. The more she gleaned from Bob, the better she understood he had simply shut down. But now she had to know how to get him back.

In Horatio's yard, they'd found one of the jeeps from the farm. Bob and Rikker spent hours together getting it running again. July noticed that this was when Bob was at his best. Once they had the jeep running, Bob and she began exploring the island.

The more they looked around, the more they wanted to stay here, but how do you make a living was the question. Bob was hoping that they might salvage something at the farm. It soon became evident as they looked at the burned-out buildings and the fact that the locals were starting small farms on anywhere that had not been taken over with vegetation; this was not an option.

Their ventures always brought them back to the old San Andros Hotel at the airport. From the outside, it looked pretty good, but once they got inside, Bob's comment was "This is almost as bad as the farm."

Still they could see potential, but how to actually purchase the property could be insurmountable, let alone making a go of it. Old Man Gator owned the property; in fact, he and his family owned most of the island if the truth were to be known and certainly didn't need the money.

"We have to make up our minds. We got $261,000 from the sale of El Presidente's yacht, do you want to invest it into this sinking ship?" July asked Bob.

Sir Harry had insisted the money the Bahamian government got from the sale of El Presidente's boat went to the Greens for services rendered. The Government agreed but only if the money was to be reinvested in the Bahamas.

"I've got something more to confess to you, July. I invested fifty thousand in a necklace."

This took July by surprise. "I hope it was a good one," was all she could think to say.

"I think it was Hania Shonavon's, so I borrowed the money from Ansly to buy it. I thought it would clear up a lot of things in Canada. It was Novak who told me he thought Lena had it or one that was an exact replica."

"I think Novak mentioned something about it at one of the meetings we had, but I can't remember what he said," July answered.

"My point is that I don't have the necklace, and I don't have the fifty thousand so if I can blow that much on a necklace, why not on a broken down hotel. Besides, you said the money had to be reinvested in the Bahamas," Bob told her.

"At least we know this island. We stand just as good a chance of keeping our heads above water here as anywhere." Once July made up her mind, there was little that could detour her. She knew a lot of people and began nosing around, eventually finding a chink in Gator's armor.

July was having coffee with the Minister of Agriculture's wife one morning when she mentioned that she and Bob had been negotiating with Old Man Gator to buy the Andros Hotel, but they just couldn't get a reasonable price out of him.

"We'd love to have you and Bob there," she told July. "The government needs a place close to the airport for our people to stay, but we certainly can't put them up in a place as rundown as that. They've been putting the pressure on Gator to clean it up. I think I can convince my husband to pressure him enough that he'll be a little more cooperative. The only advice I can give you and Bob is when and if Gator comes up with something acceptable, you'd better be ready to pounce."

Bob and July took her advice heading for Nassau to see a lawyer and begin drawing up papers. While Bob went to see if they could get a loan from any of the Nassau banks for their project, July went off on her own to see her old friends at the Bureau of Tourism. There she proposed they do a feature on Andros Island and the hotel. They told her it would certainly be given some thought, which to July meant they weren't all that interested. The matter had pretty well been forgotten when July received a call proposing she feature a series of ads promoting all the outer islands and their tourist spots. In return, she would be able to highlight the old Andros Hotel.

The timing was terrible, but if the hotel was to be successful, she had no choice but to accept. July dreaded telling Bob; she felt like she'd just sold her soul for a thirty-second TV spot.

Gator was under a lot of pressure to do something with the hotel. 'If we're going to put any money into this island, you're going to have to help on your end," the government told him. Gator was too old to start running a hotel. He paid his son to run it, but the only time his son ran was to pick up his money at the end of the month. Renovations would cost a lot more than he could ever make out of operating the hotel, so he came to the conclusion that someone else should do the work. Someone who would do the work and then give it back would be best, and that someone would be the Greens.

Gator invited the Greens to lunch at the hotel, but when they got there, Gator found out there was no lunch because the cook had not been paid so she quit. Gator was not one to be detoured however, and so they all sat down to a liquid lunch from the bar. Gator was hard to pin down, but finally, it seemed that he might settle for around one million. Bob was deflated, but July kept after Gator until she had him down to around eight hundred thousand.

"Okay, here's what we'll do. The first year we'll pay you fifty thousand up-front and guarantee that another fifty thousand will be put into the hotel, and from then on we'll give you a hundred thousand every year till it's paid off," July offered.

"Sure, if you can come up with the money, stop by my shop and we'll make a deal," Gator told them as he got up to leave obviously thinking by the look on Bob's face that this was a waste of time.

Bob and July walked outside the hotel.

"What do you think, Bob?" He didn't answer her right away, instead shading his eyes, his head turned toward the sky.

"That's a government charter coming in. I think I'd better catch a ride back to Nassau on it. I'll make sure the lawyers make the appropriate changes to the papers and get them back here on the evening flight."

He smiled at her, "I'm going to stay in Nassau and get supplies ready to load on the mail boat."

July couldn't believe her ears; she'd expected to have a fight on her hands. "We haven't got him to sign the papers yet?"

"I'm not totally naive here, July. Gator knows the property alone is worth more than $800,000 so he's selling it to us betting he gets it back in one or two years. I'm leaving Gator to you, July, I don't want to be anywhere around or even know how you get him to sign, I just know he will."

July leaned over and kissed Bob."How far do you think I'll go?"

Bob kissed her back then started walking toward the airport. "I don't know, but I feel sorry for Gator," Bob said over his shoulder.

July knew exactly what she was doing when she put on her skimpy sundress that didn't hide much. She'd have to make use of everything she had to deal with Mr. Gator. It was a terribly hot day. The sundress stuck to her as she climbed out of the old jeep and walked into Gator's garage.

It was the perfect front for Gator to conduct his business, whatever that might be. Anyone could stop by to have his car serviced. Sometimes his office door was open, sometimes it was closed depending on who stopped by. Today it was closed, but July was pretty sure it wouldn't be for long. Whatever his mechanics were doing was unimportant now as they fell over each other coming to her assistance. Gator came out of his office to see what the commotion was all about. His order to get back to work was basically ignored, as the boys gathered around July bantering for her attention. Gator saw he was getting nowhere.

"Come in to my office, it's cooler in here," he beckoned to her. She said goodbye to the boys and followed Gator into his office. He sat down behind his desk, "What can I do for you, Mrs. Green?"

"I've come to consummate our deal, Mr. Gator." She watched his eyes as they lit up with interest. Many of the Bahamian men were terrible womanizers. It was well-known that Gator's many kids were from different women scattered around the island. In all fairness, he had at least given all his women a home and looked after the kids or the ones he knew about.

"You have something for me?"

"Maybe." She leaned over his desk giving him a good view of her bosom.

His mouth fell open as he watched the sweat run down between her breasts. He was totally distracted; it had been a while since he'd had a hard-on, but now he felt his prick becoming hard. He'd never had a white woman, or any woman for that matter, that could turn him on like this.

He barely heard her add, "But first we have to make sure we have a deal..."

"Damn, it's hot in here," he thought feeling himself start to sweat.

"I give you 50,000 up-front, put 50,000 into fixing up the hotel, and pay you $800,000 over eight years. Is that good for you?" she asked in a voice that would melt ice.

Gator swallowed; he'd give almost anything to have this woman. "That could be arranged," he heard himself say. She stepped back looking at him. Christ! He could see her belly button; her dress was so wet.

"Do you agree to leave us alone and let us run the hotel the way we want, if I give you what you want?"

He sat back full of confidence. He had her where he wanted her. "Certainly, Mrs. Green. If you give me what I want, you can run the hotel any way you want."

July handed him a piece of paper. "Here is a letter of agreement for the sale of the Andros Hotel property. If you get what we agreed on, will you sign it?"

Gator took the document and looked at it. It was a standard letter of agreement complete with a lawyer's seal. He sat it on the desk in front of him. "Yes, we have a deal, if you give me what I want." There was no mistaking what he meant by his voice.

July reached into her handbag and pulled out the $50,000 all in nice crisp American bills. She laid them in front of Gator on his desk. He looked at the money in shock; this was not what he expected.

July walked around the deck and stood beside him. "I believe I have kept my side of the bargain, will you keep yours?" Gator started to protest then he looked up and realized that he forgotten to shut the office door. All his employees stood looking at him through the doorway.

He'd look like a fool if he didn't sign now. He was also very aware of her presence. He could feel her body next to his; a faint smell of perfume and sweat filled the room. He picked up a pen and signed the agreement; July in turn signed it. "We need a witness." She looked toward the mechanics. Gator cursed under his breath; they were all witnesses and all on her side. He called one of them in, and he signed the document.

"There," she tousled Gator's hair, "we have an agreement." She took his hand and shook it. All the mechanics followed her out to the jeep to see her off, but Gator stayed behind his desk. He still had a hard-on and was not about to let his boys razz him about it. He was pretty confident that before long Mrs. Green would be back to see him hat in hand, then he'd show her that black and white goes very well together.

July was elated; she took the old jeep out to the main highway and opened it up letting the air cool her body. Then she passed by the airport and posted her documents on the first flight back to Nassau. She took a walk around the hotel grounds to get her mind on track then headed back to the guesthouse only to find Fauna Norton sitting on her front step.

Fauna was Horatio Norton's youngest daughter. Rikker and she knew each other since middle school. The last few years Rikker had spent most of his time with the Nortons, they had become like brother and sister.

"Fauna, have you been crying?" July asked as she walked up to her. Fauna burst into tears; July put her arms around her. "Tell me what's wrong."

"It's about Rikker," Fauna sobbed. For an instant, July's heart stopped beating, and then she heard Fauna say, "I'm so embarrassed."

July heaved a sigh of relief as she realized this was something personal. "It's okay, Fauna, tell me what happened."

"If I do, he'll be so mad at me he'll never talk to me again."

"I think you need to talk to someone about this," July tried to sound reassuring.

Fauna burst back into tears, "I have to tell you because you're the only one he'll listen to."

July remained quiet; Fauna wiped her eyes. "Rikker been seeing this girl. She's older than us, very pretty. I think she's Haitian because she's new to the island. Rikker's been following her around like a little puppy dog. All us girls are mad at him; you can tell she's had lots of men before, but he won't listen to us. He's always protecting us girls. If any of the boys do something we don't want, they have to answer to Rikker. But will he listen to us? No. Anyway, I went down to the beach last night to hang out for a while. There was a group of girls standing around talking. They said this girl had told them she didn't want Rikker to go away to college, so she was going to let him make her pregnant so he would have to stay here and look after her."

Fauna looked up at July. "Rikker doesn't want to stay on this island, Mrs. Green. We used to spend hours down on the beach talking about what we thought was on the other side of the water. I couldn't just let him throw his life away, so I walked down the beach looking for them.

There they were laying in the sand, and Rikker was on top of her. I felt I had to do something so I ran over to them and rolled Rikker off her, but then his… well, you know… his thing popped up in front of me, and then it spouted at me."

"It did what?" July asked.

"Well, I guess the proper word is it ejaculated all over the front of my shirt. I'm so embarrassed, Mrs. Green. He gave me this disgusted look, and then I just ran away."

July tried to lighten up the situation. "Well, you're going to the States to study biology, I guess that was one hell of a first lesson." But Fauna was not in the mood, so July just held her for a while. "You're a very brave girl, Fauna, and I'm very grateful. Rikker's a wild boy, reminds me of his father when I first met him. He needs an education and some direction. If you and your friends can't help him, then I guess it's time his mother did."

July was on the phone the rest of the afternoon; her jubilation on getting the hotel had worn off. Rikker was the most important thing on her mind now. When she heard his motorcycle coming up the lane, she stepped out onto the porch to meet him.

"Hi Mom, I hope you've got supper on. I'm starved."

"Sit down, Rikker. You and I have to talk."

"What's happened, Mom, is something wrong?" he said, hurrying up the steps, looking concerned.

"Fauna was here. She told me what happened last night."

"Oh jeez, Mom! That's embarrassing. What I do is none of her business." He flopped down on a chair.

"So that's embarrassing to you. Well, what's embarrassing to me and your friends is you've been screwing around with a girl who's already married to a young man whose family is supporting her. She has a baby whom her grandmother is looking after, and she hasn't seen her for a week."

July sat down beside him. "You were having unprotected sex with a woman you didn't even know and never once thought about the consequences. Her intent was to get pregnant. Then who would look after the child? She obviously won't and you can't, so who would? The answer is obvious, isn't it? So in the long run, she saved my ass."

Rikker put his face in his hands. "Is this all true, Mom?"

"You know mothers have ways of finding out these things, Rikker."

"God, I'm just like Dad, aren't I? Running off and doing something lamebrain that gets you in trouble."

July had to be careful how she handled this one. "There's a lot you don't know about your father, but yes, you are like two peas in the pod. One thing you have to understand is whatever trouble we got into, we always had each other and friends to help us out, but there were always consequences, and these are yours, Rikker. I know college doesn't start for another month, but I've been talking to Mr. Novak. I think you met him at the hospital in Nassau."

Rikker nodded his head as July continued, "He has agreed that you can go to work for him until school starts. He has a room off his villa that you can live in while you go to school, and if you want to continue working part time, you can, or you can say goodbye to all of us and go live with your woman."

Rikker asked meekly, "When do I leave?"

July gave no ground, "Tomorrow, so I suggest you go and make amends with Fauna. Mrs. Norton's going to live in Nassau, and Fauna and her brother are going to school in the States, so you won't be seeing them for a while, might as well say your goodbyes."

There were tears in Rikker's eyes. "Thank you, Mom." They stood and hugged each other for a long time. He stepped back and looked at her, "Even when we're apart, we're together, aren't we?"

"Yes, always, no matter what happens." She watched as Rikker walked toward the Norton house; she couldn't resist shouting after him, "Tell Fauna you'll buy her a new shirt." She laughed as she got the finger from Rikker.

"Don't push it," he replied.

Those two decisions—buying the Andros Hotel and sending Rikker off to college in Nassau—were the best they'd ever made, July thought as she helped get the kitchen ready for breakfast. Bob hadn't woken up in a sweat for months now. In fact, he was lucky to get any sleep at all. The early morning participants in the pool had faded away with the coming light, and Bob was out cleaning it.

The first year had been a tough one with her away so much doing the tourism gig. Then the ad hit TV's in a brutally cold North American winter. All hell broke loose; the hotel was suddenly inundated with people, and they never looked back. People seemed to love the charm of the old hotel. They had leased a beach and bought Sea-Doos and other toys to keep their guests entertained during the day then supplied them with a bar and bands at night.

There wasn't much time for sleep, but Bob and July didn't mind; the hotel was making money, and they had no problem making their second payment. Rikker had successfully completed his second year of college. His grades were okay, and he loved his job with Novak, although he couldn't actually tell them what he did because it was top secret.

Mindy had been their biggest source of inspiration. She had worked her way up becoming the manager of a large hotel in Minneapolis. Bob and July were not prepared for the influx of guests and were totally overwhelmed until Mindy came to their rescue. She spent her holidays helping them train new people and getting their house in order. She still sacrificed some of her weekends to fly down to help them; she'd been a real godsend, July thought as she went out to help Bob clean the pool.

# TWENTY-FIVE

A RED HAZE HUNG in the early morning air as Henekie walked across the field. It was covered with dead bodies, and carnage was everywhere. Around him, he saw soldiers walking; they were his friends. He saw Ginter and yelled at him, but for some reason no one could hear him. This surely must be hell, Henekie thought, as that's the only place a man like Ginter would be. Then he heard a voice, and it certainly wasn't a friend. The voice he heard was Bernard's, the police interrogator, and the man he was talking to was the prison superintendent. The prison super was obviously very agitated. "I've got Amnesty International breathing down my neck, and in three days the Americans are coming to interview this guy. If they see him like this Bernard, we're both fucked."

"Give me one more day. I know he's right there."

"Fuck! You've been telling me that for a week now, Bernard. Get this man cleaned up and down to the infirmary."

"I don't think that's a good idea," Bernard told him. "The people down there will rat us out. My man here is a medic. He knows what to do."

"No more, Bernard! We have to keep this man alive, and then we have to figure how in hell to get out of this mess."

Maybe you should talk to Krugman. He seems to want this prick."

The superintendent scratched his head. "Maybe you're right. He's the one who's behind Amnesty International getting involved, and you can bet there's an ulterior motive."

Bernard picked Henekie up by the neck and stuck his face in front of his. "So you think you've won, you murdering bastard? You think the Americans are going to be easier than me? They're going to cut your balls off." He turned to his two helpers. "Take this stinky bastard down to the showers."

What Bernard didn't know was that Henekie was screaming at him, "Please let me tell you I can't take this anymore." But somehow no one was listening; he didn't realize he could no longer talk. Bernard had grabbed him by the throat one too many times. The two guards dragged Henekie to the showers where he dropped to his knees trying to brace himself against the icy blast of water about to hit him. It took a while for his senses to realize that the water was warm. He hung his head, letting the water splash over his body, the aroma of flowers surrounding him. At first he thought he was in heaven, but he knew that couldn't be true; there was no place there for a man like him.

Henekie was aware that he had left the Bahamas by the skin of his teeth. Sir Harry would be pissed that he'd outfoxed them, and even in Cuba, he wouldn't be safe. Now that Interpol had computers and satellite communications around the world, it was becoming very dangerous for him to move around. That was why he preferred to work in backward or poor areas where communications were not so good. From Cuba, he had taken a direct flight to Liberia. There, a Cuban passport was like gold.

Liberia had been in chaos for years. The Americans pumped money in by the truckload to prop up a corrupt government. The Cubans had no money, but they supplied the local government with arms and expertise. They also supplied the many factions with expertise on how to run a revolution there; in theory playing both sides and as a result took the Americans' money out by the boatload back to Cuba. It was common for a boatload of humanitarian aid to come into harbor and overnight be unloaded onto a Cuban freighter. The Cuban freighter would in turn unload its cargo of arms onto the humanitarian ship to be unloaded onto the docks in the morning. This was where Henekie felt at home. He had been a mercenary most of his life and still would be if it hadn't been for Ginter. "This is a fool's game, Henekie. The money's not that good, and sooner or later your luck has to run out."

Well, Ginter's luck had run out but not before he'd shown Henekie there was a lot of money to be made in this business. Monrovia, the capital of Liberia, was a bustling seaport city. There he had contacts that moved mercenaries around Africa for a price. He waited a couple of days to make sure all the warlords along his route had been paid off then made his way overland to Algeria. There, Ginter had set him up as an Algerian national which gave him the right to travel to France. His work permit said he worked for a private security service and was to be employed as a bodyguard for Algerian diplomats. This enabled him to cross over the German border. He stayed in a hotel for a couple of weeks just to make sure he wasn't under surveillance and to check out Rona's house.

"The one thing you never do in this business is fall in love," Ginter had told him. "Sooner or later, she'll turn on you or someone will find out and use it against you. Either way, you're dead."

Henekie wasn't in love, he told himself, yet every time he'd pass Rona's house, he felt something inside he'd never felt before. This was something he didn't understand; she wasn't beautiful, she had no money, and she had three kids. Yet he thought about her all the time. How many times had he lain at night dreaming of sleeping on her soft breast? He told himself that maybe if she didn't have a man staying with her, he might stop in and say hello, but that's it.

The fact was that there was no place else for Henekie to go. He'd lost all his other contacts, so his options were either to go back to being a mercenary or back to Germany where he had the potential of finding new people in need of his services. Grundman, he'd found out had been nothing more than a messenger boy, but who was his boss?

Henekie racked his brains trying to remember something Ginter would have said that gave him a clue. Ginter had talked about an asshole lawyer but had never mentioned any names. A lawyer by the name of Krugman used to ride with the motorcycle gang once in a while. Henekie had dismissed him as a nobody at the time, but what a perfect way to meet with Ginter when he used to ride with the gang. Krugman was obviously not a lightweight. His office was in one of the most prestigious buildings in Munich. Over the next couple of days, he learned something else about Krugman; everywhere he went, someone was following him which meant Henekie would have to meet him somewhere else.

Henekie began frequenting the bars where his old motorcycle friends hung out. He let it be known he wanted to meet with Herr Krugman. When they asked why, he just told them he knew Ginter. His persistence paid off. One day, as they were out riding, one of the gang waved him to follow him into a rest area. When they stopped, Henekie noted that two other riders had stopped with them.

"So I understand you're looking for me?" The man who spoke wore a helmet with full-face visor which he didn't bother to lift.

"If you're Herr Krugman?" The man nodded but didn't say anything. "My name is Henekie, and I worked for Ginter."

"That means nothing to me," the man answered.

Henekie was becoming frustrated. "Does the name Grundman mean anything to you?"

The man started his machine. "I don't think I like this conversation."

Henekie had to let it all hang out. "I was part of a team that worked for Grundman. I'm the one that got away up in Canada." The man shut off his machine and lifted his visor to reveal he really was Krugman.

"How did you find me?" Krugman wanted to know.

"It wasn't easy. At first I thought Grundman was you, but it soon became obvious that he didn't have the brains. Ginter told me he used to ride with an asshole lawyer, and I remembered your name being mentioned among the gang, so I put two and two together and came up with you."

"That's funny because I cannot remember riding with a man named Ginter. The only one I knew personally was the liaison between Grundman and me," Krugman told Henekie. "He would ride with us, I would give him the assignment and negotiate a price, and then he'd take the information back to Grundman. You are right. Grundman was an idiot, but he had control over this group of men that took care of our problems without anything coming back on us so we put up with him."

"Describe this man to me would you, Herr Krugman."

As Krugman described the man, Henekie began to laugh, "That man was Ginter."

Now Krugman began to laugh too. "We knew Grundman was a weasel and wondered how long it would take Ginter to figure out he was being screwed. Ginter negotiated the deal before Grundman ever even knew what was happening."

"Yes," Henekie added, "and Grundman took all the risks because everything went through him but if he tried to take more than his cut, Ginter would make sure to get it out of him."

"Brilliant man, this Ginter, I just want you to know we didn't sanction that hit up in Canada. That came from someone in the Bahamas." Krugman sounded apologetic.

"Yes, I figured that out," Henekie told him.

"We do business with him, but it's all done through intermediaries. All we know is he controls that whole Caribbean," Krugman added.

"Someday, I'll find him. Until then, I need some work," Henekie told him.

"We always need people with your qualifications, Henekie. Ride with us next week, and we'll talk business."

Henekie started up his bike and pulled out of the rest area. He was elated; there had been a great deal of risk to his returning to Germany, but then he was in a risky business. Herr Krugman and the two other riders watched Henekie ride away. "That's a very dangerous man," one of them said.

"Yes," Krugman answered. "That's why we'd better make sure he's on our side."

Henekie's risk at returning to Germany was paying off financially, but there was something missing. He'd been too busy with other things to spend a lot of time finding out about Rona. He'd been by her house a few times and made a few observations. One was that the house was not under observation, and the other was that it seemed to be unoccupied. He couldn't blame her for finding a man and moving in with him. He certainly hadn't been much help to her, and she did have a family to feed. Still he was curious as to where she was. He asked some of the bikers if they'd seen her, but no one seemed to know anything.

After leaving Krugman, Henekie decided to make a pass by Rona's place. In North America, it would be classified as a town house he guessed, being as it was joined to the buildings on either side of it. In fact, it looked like every other building on the street except for the color of the door and the number on it." Maybe she's just away visiting someone," Henekie thought as he parked the bike on impulse and reached into his pocket. He pulled out the key to the front door. He decided to go in; maybe she had left something inside that would tell him where she had gone, he reasoned.

Henekie opened the door and went to step inside, but the barrel of a gun appeared right between his eyes impeding his forward progress. Henekie remembered what his old instructor had taught him, "If you hear the shot, you're already dead, but if you don't hear the shot, it means the man holding the gun doesn't want to shoot you, and the advantage comes back to you for the next five or six seconds." Another gun appeared behind that one.

"Come on in," he heard a voice behind the second gun say. Henekie relaxed; he'd have to wait for his next advantage.

There were three men inside the house and not much else. The interior walls had all been stripped leaving only the studding. The kitchen table and four chairs were all that was left of the furniture. One of the men frisked Henekie and then guided him to a chair. "We'd almost given up on you." The second gunman seemed to be the boss. He looked at Henekie's passport. "Why are you here?"

"I could ask you the same question," Henekie answered. "This is Rona's house, what have you done to her?"

The boss walked over and whacked Henekie in the head. "Why are you here?"

Henekie cowered a bit, "I work as a bodyguard for a French company. They gave me a few days off, so I came here to see Rona." One of the men took Henekie's passport and was immediately on the phone to see if what Henekie told them was true. Henekie had no trouble giving them information that might help him, and that's how it went; the men would beat on him a bit, and he would give them only what he thought they should know. Some more men came, and they all talked over in a corner.

Henekie overheard them say that his story checked out. "Maybe I'll get away with this yet," he thought.

There was a bit of an argument, but finally, the boss won. "Take him and put him in high security. I want fingerprints, blood work, ass search, photos, and then get everything out to Interpol. I think we have their man."

"I want a lawyer," Henekie told them as they cuffed him.

"Get him out of here." The boss man gave him another whack in the head. Henekie didn't mind; he'd like to whack himself in the head for being so stupid.

Twice they almost let Henekie go, but each time someone would come along to change the German authorities' minds. The Americans were sure they could identify him then; the Canadians were sure they had their man. There weren't too many countries in the world that Ginter and his crew hadn't in some way caused problems, and they all wanted a look at him. The autopsy on the bodies up in Canada had all been identified, but one was inconclusive.

This man and the one that got away carried Argentinean passports. They were of German descent, the sons of high-ranking Nazi officers who had escaped there after the war. The Argentinean government denied the existence of these men, and most police officials believed one of these men was still hiding there, so no one was sure which of these men was actually dead. "Could this be the missing man?" Some thought so, but no one could prove it.

Henekie's passport was legitimate as far as passports go. Many of these were issued to sons of French soldiers married to Algerian women. The records were poorly written or sketchy at best, but his seemed legit and gave him French residency.

Eight months rolled by and as Henekie had hoped, people began to lose interest in him. He passed his time reading every book about computers that he could lay his hands on. The fact that he was in isolation required that he keep his mind occupied, and his curiosity about these machines led him to be referred to as the "Geek."

The police forces of the world had not been able to pin anything on this man, so the German Secret Service decided to turn Henekie over to the local police to see if they could get him on some internal issues.

Now Henekie faced a whole new group of faces and a whole bunch of new questions. One of the questions was about a woman's body found in the river. He fended off the questions, but it concerned him that the only one who could tie him to that murder was Rona.

Then one day, he was told he had a visitor. Henekie had to take a risk; there were some things he had to find out. He was right; his visitor was Rona. He watched her eyes as he approached her, and they told him what he needed to know. He sat down to face her; they were separated by a pane of glass with a hole in it, but to Henekie there was no separation, there was only that beautiful face he'd waited all these months to see. There were tears in her eyes as she struggled with her speech.

Henekie touched the glass with his fingertips, and she put out her hands to meet his, and then he turned his hands palms up. There in plain view for her to see he'd written video, microphone in big letters on one hand and in the other, "Who talked Rona? I know it wasn't you. Write next time." Rona nodded slightly, and then Henekie began to talk, not giving her a chance to answer. It didn't matter; she had no idea what he was talking about anyway. A uniformed officer tapped Rona on the shoulder.

"Time's up," he told her.

She looked at him and said, "I hope we can meet again," then she blew him a kiss.

"I think we will," he replied, knowing his future depended on it.

Rona didn't know what to think as she left the visiting room. "Make him talk," the officers told her. They'd given her some questions to ask, but she'd not been able to say anything. The officers however were smiling as she entered the debriefing room. No one before had been able to get more than one full sentence out of this guy, and they were sure they got a wealth of information this time.

"You will come again tomorrow," the officers told her, and again she was given a list of questions to ask.

This time, Henekie played with her fingers through the holes in the glass as he read, "Greta has aids, is talking. I and kids in safe house." Rona was amazed at his concentration and in turn read his palm. "Tell Lawyer Krugman I'm here, will begin torture soon, can't last more than two weeks." They stayed that way for a while and then changed hands; she read, "Tell him I know where there's one billion dollars."

Rona slowly turned her palm toward him. In big letters, it said, "I love you."

For the first time since she had sat down, Henekie stopped talking and turned his head away. Then he turned back to her and returned to his babbling.

Now she understood what Henekie was doing; there was no way anyone could blame her for not asking questions. She could not get a word in. She just sat and looked at his face until the officer told her she had to go. Rona looked back over her shoulder as long as she could knowing she might never see Henekie again.

When she met the officers in the next room, she knew by the look on their faces that her suspicions were confirmed; either this guy had lost his marbles completely, or he was playing them for fools.

Rona was living in a heavily supervised safe house on the outside of Munich. Since she'd been taken from her own house, she'd had little contact with the outside world. Her new home was situated in a walled commune with one gate which was guarded and required permission for anyone to enter or leave. Her phone went through a switchboard, and anything she required was delivered. If deemed safe, the children were allowed to go to local schools.

Rona was not considered to be a danger to society, nor was it thought that her life might be in danger, so her kids were given the right to live as normal a life as possible. Her oldest son was fourteen now and had become very close to Henekie in the past. He too was a bit of a geek; Henekie had tweaked his curiosity and resulted in his grades improving tremendously. Rona knew she was taking a big risk, but her son was the only way she could contact Herr Krugman.

A young boy left Rona's compound one morning as did the rest of the kids on their way to school. The only difference with this young man was that he didn't go to school but rather made his way to the railway station and headed down town to the heart of Munich's business district.

Around an hour later, Rona received a call that her son was not in school today. "Yes," she told them; her son had left home that morning but since they had moved to the new neighborhood, all he could talk about was how he missed his girlfriend. She would inform the police that he was probably hanging around his old school until he could see her."

Rona then phoned the guard at the gate to inform him of where she thought her son might be. The guard seemed to be sympathetic to a young man's "affairs of the heart" and told her he would tell the police to watch for the young man.

Rona had made the gravity of the situation very plain to her son.

"You must make sure you hand this letter to Herr Krugman yourself. It's a matter of life and death for Henekie."

"Don't worry, Mother, Henekie told me what to do." Rona smiled; the boy didn't know who his father was, and Ginter had fathered two of his brothers but had always kept his distance and was away a lot. The boy was drifting and starting to get in trouble when Henekie had come along. For some reason, he cared about her family.

Henekie had spent a lot of time with her son, teaching him things she didn't understand, and his whole attitude turned around. She remembered when Henekie had brought a new computer home. He and her son had spent hours taking it apart and reassembling it; they'd created a game to play on it. None of this she understood, but her son began to excel in school and seemed to take an interest in what was going on around him.

Rona also didn't understand how a man could do what Henekie did and then show affection for her and her family, but he did. As they got to know each other better, Henekie confided in her that all this was new to him too; but this was his family now, and for the first time in his life, something mattered to him other than his army buddies. He also confided in her just how dangerous it was to be around him, and if she asked he would leave. They had formed a bond, and now they both knew the risks. If Krugman decided it was best just to get rid of them all, he could. She was pretty sure that was why Henekie had thrown in the billion-dollar kicker.

The tall buildings of downtown Munich were intimidating enough for a young boy who had never been there before, let alone finding the one he wanted. He found solace in the fact that Henekie's training was proving to be invaluable; "Always map your route there and back and have a plan when you get to where your going. Be aware of your surroundings. Is there another way out? Who are the people around you? Are they watching you? Would you know them if you saw them again? Be prepared for anything, don't panic, think your way out of any trouble you may find yourself in, remember you don't have to be the best-looking or the best-dressed person in the room, just be the smartest and you'll be all right." All this went through the young man's mind as he walked up the steps and in through the main door.

In the middle of the main concourse was a round desk that said, "Check in here."

“I have a message to deliver to Lawyer Krugman,” he told the man behind the counter.

“Okay, leave it here, and we’ll see he gets it,” the man told him.

“My orders are to deliver it in person,” the boy countered.

The man pushed a book toward him, “Very well, sign here. They occupy the entire top floor. There’s a reception area as soon as you step out of the elevator.”

There were a lot of people on the elevator when the boy got on, but by the time he reached the top floor, everyone else had gotten off. He stepped into a world of mahogany and glass, making him feel slightly out of place. Then he looked out through the glass, and he froze. The people below looked like ants; he’d never been this high up before.

“May I help you?” he heard a voice say behind him. The boy swallowed hard to keep his stomach down and turned to see a woman sitting behind a desk.

He walked toward her, but right behind her, the glass started again and fearing he would be sick, he tried to focus on something, and then he saw them. The girl behind the desk had a big beautiful set of breasts and a good part of them were on display. The funny part of it was that she knew he was staring, but she didn’t seem to mind. “We don’t often get men as young as you up here,” she smiled. He pulled an envelope out of his schoolbag.

“I have a message for Herr Krugman,” he told her.

“All right, leave it with me. I’ll make sure he gets it.”

“No!” the boy answered, “I have to deliver it in person.”

“That’s impossible, Herr Krugman has meetings all day.”

“Okay, I’ll wait.” The boy shrugged his shoulders.

“You’re very persistent, aren’t you?” the receptionist noted that he was still fixated on her chest. She pictured most of the men who came by her desk, what they’d look like naked, but this young man interested her just the way he was in his school uniform, tie, and unruly hair. She pursed her lips as if thinking for a moment, "Okay, let's see what I can do." She turned to her computer screen. The boy tore his eyes from her chest to look at what she was doing.

"That's a very new model. I haven't seen that one yet," he said.

"Yes, she told him, "we have our own mainframe here, so I'm upgrading all the time."

"I do programming if you ever need some help," the boy told her.

The girl stopped what she was doing and smiled at the boy. "I do all my own programming and for a lot of other companies too." The boy showed surprise on his face. Most of the girls who dressed like her at school were airheads. For a few moments, they discussed their theories finding they had a lot in common. None of the other men the receptionist met could give a shit about computers.

She was probably ten years older than the young man, but she found herself very attracted to him and what was so important in his message. She stood up and bent over her desk shuffling some papers, giving him a better view of her front. "Maybe if I read your message, I could be of help to you." She looked up only to find his eyes locked on hers.

"Tell Herr Krugman I have a message from Grundman, Ginter, and Henekie. He'll see me."

The receptionist looked disappointed. "Never heard of them," she pouted.

"Herr Krugman has. Don't worry, he'll be happy you let me in."

The receptionist went over and knocked on an office door then went inside. She came back out of the office acting very professional, "Herr Krugman will see you now," as she held and then closed the door behind him.

Herr Krugman smiled and shook the young man's hand. "My secretary tells me you don't trust her."

"Henekie told me never to trust a woman with big tits."

There were two other men in the room with Krugman, and they all grinned at the boy. “Did he say why?” one of them asked.

“Because men forget to look up into their eyes to see what they’re thinking.” The men burst out laughing.

“You’re pretty young to be worried about things like that,” Krugman told him. “We like to think of her as a marvelous piece of German engineering.”

“There is more to her than meets the eye,” the boy said seriously, but the men howled in laughter not understanding he was referring to her intelligence.

Krugman saw the boy wasn’t laughing. He wiped his eyes and put on his glasses. “Let me see the message.” Silence enshrouded the room as Krugman read; finally, he looked up at the boy. “Do you know what’s in the message?” Krugman asked.

“Yes, Mother and I discussed everything she told you. I also know you’re the only one we can turn to for help.”

“All right, this is very serious, so you think the torture has started?”

“She is no longer able to visit, but that’s what Henekie told her,” the boy answered.

“Okay, has your mother been charged with anything?” Krugman asked.

“No,” the boy answered.

“Then we’ll soon have you out of there. Is it safe for you to go back?”

“Yes,” the boy told Krugman about how he got to his office and how he was getting back.

“Perfect, now we’d better let you go and do what you need to while we get to work.” The boy shook hands with the three men and left the office.

He stopped on his way past the receptionist. "I think you're a marvelous piece of German engineering," he told her.

"Thank you. Maybe you can come and help me fix my computer some time?"

"Sure," he answered, and away he went. She wasn't sure he understood what she was insinuating and probably just as well he didn't. The boy took the train across town and got off near his old school. He sat on the stone wall out front until the police came and took him home. They scolded both the boy and his mother, telling them both not to let it happen again.

The two men with Krugman were heads of local biker gangs and pretty well controlled everything illegal in Munich. "I thought this guy was either dead or had gone off on some job. We're very lucky we found out where he is. Do you think he's talked?" one of the men asked.

"No, Krugman told them. Otherwise, he'd be asking the police to protect him, not us."

If he knows as much as you say he does, we'd better get rid of him," they both told Krugman.

"That may be easier said than done. I suspect they'll use that army dude, Bernard," Krugman told them."We've run into him before, only his men will be allowed to get close to Henekie."

"No, we have to get him out of there." The two men could almost see the wheels turning in Krugman's head.

"Okay, what I need from you is to have a small crowd of protesters in front of the prison tomorrow morning. I also need an article in as many newspapers as you can influence to write about this guy being held for a year without being charged. Have them allude to the possibility of torture. Amnesty International owes me a favor. I did some work for them, now it's time for payback. If I can get Amnesty to demand as their representative that I see Henekie, that should put a crimp into how far they go with the torture." The two men left to go about their business leaving Krugman to go about his.

It was obvious his partners wanted Henekie dead as soon as possible, but he hadn't told them about the money. Somehow, if he could get Henekie out and everyone thought he was dead… It was a long shot, but if he could lay his hands on that kind of money, he wouldn't be working for these people anymore; they'd be working for him. Krugman looked at his watch; money or the thought of it always made him horny. He took off his clothes and carefully hung them in his closet.

"Are we done for the day, Karla?" he spoke into the intercom.

"Yes," came a sultry answer.

"Then come in and take some dictation," he said, settling down in his office chair. His receptionist had no illusions as to what Krugman had in mind. She lived very well; in order to maintain her lifestyle, certain things were understood. She entered his office and locked the door. He felt his cock stiffen as he watched her undress.

"You must have had a very productive day, Herr Krugman," she speculated, running her fingers up and down his erection. Usually she had to use a little stimulation, but not today.

"I had a very stressful day, sweetheart. Right now, I need some relaxation." She straddled the office chair facing him and pulled his face into her big tits, and then began moving up and down on his cock. He never looked up to see her eyes; it was just as well, or he might have realized it wasn't him she was fucking. She was far away riding on a young boy wearing only his school tie, and teaching him everything she knew.

"Stand up when I talk to you," the man in the military khakis barked at Henekie as he entered the room.

Instinct told Henekie to stand up and salute, but he controlled himself and casually rose to his feet. The man continued over until his face was inches from Henekie's. Neither said a word, they just stood there eyeing each other. Henekie's body language was submissive, but his eyes held the other man's.

Suddenly, the man grabbed Henekie's throat. "You're a murdering bastard, aren't you? I've seen lots like you before. Those cold eyes tell me all I need to know." The man released Henekie's throat but didn't back away. "You know you're going to talk. I can tell you've been around enough to know what's going to happen here. Why not just tell us what we want to know and make it easy on yourself."

Henekie's eyes never left the other man's, but he kept quiet.

"All right, if that's the way you want it. Looks like we're going to get to know each other a lot better. My name's Bernard, what's yours?"

"It's the same as on my passport," Henekie told him.

"Ya, that's what your soldier buddies tell me, but they also tell me you haven't been in the field for a while, so where have you been these last few years? I guess that's what we're going to find out, isn't it? Okay guys, take him down to the penthouse. This one's going to play tough, so give him his needles and tuck him in."

Bernard watched as his helpers escorted the prisoner away. He took no pleasure in what he did. These characters he worked on we're usually either battle hardened or had a cause. They'd kill him as easy as look at him, but in the end they all talked. And usually their information was very valuable.

Bernard was Israeli and had been trained by the Mossad. When he had retired, he found his services to be in demand; the German army was the high bidder, and he'd been here ever since. No man could take what he did to them for long, but this one was going to be a challenge.

So then it began, bright lights would wake him, and then it was black. He'd wake up sweating; then they'd pull him from his bed and hose him down with ice-cold water, the blast so strong it would knock him off his feet. Again and again the bright light would wake him up until Henekie found himself lying on the cement floor.

Bernard picked him up off the floor by the throat."I'm listening," he told Henekie, and then he left him leaning against the wall and hosed him down with cold water again. It was the end of the third day when the warden came to Bernard.

"Somehow the media's got wind that we're holding this guy without charging him. I couldn't get to work this morning because protesters were blocking the road."

"Somebody is behind that," Bernard responded. "People just don't show up like that unless someone is instigating it."

"That lawyer Krugman seems to be behind it. He's representing Amnesty and wants to see our man right away."

"He's close," Bernard told him. "You know if he talks we're in the clear, and once he opens up I'm sure everyone will be appreciative."

"You've got tonight, Bernard. Tomorrow I'm expecting Krugman to show up with a court order." The warden looked over at the prisoner and shook his head; "Why would anyone endure that?"

Bernard kept up his tactics till about four a.m., and then he got desperate. "Booster cables," he sounded like a doctor ready to operate.

"You sure he can take it?" His helper sounded skeptical.

"Fuck him. We're running out of time. He's close, we just have to put him over the edge is all." Bernard picked Henekie up by the throat and dragged him into a chair.

"No, not the battery," Bernard instructed. "Plug it into the wall." He stood in front of Henekie, touching the cables together making the sparks fly. "Damn, this is going to hurt. In fact, it just might blow your nuts right off." He raised Henekie's head. "You don't want to lose your balls, do you, Henekie?"

For the first time, Henekie squirmed; his lips trembled, but nothing came out, and then Bernard saw those cold blue eyes stare into his.

Bernard lost it, "You son of a bitch." He clamped one cable to Henekie's dick and held the other to the top of his head. Henekie's body began to buck and bounce around in the chair; there was the unmistakable smell of burning flesh.

One of Bernard's helpers pulled him away, then took Henekie's arm, feeling for a pulse. "Jeez, I thought you'd killed him, Bernard. What the fuck's the matter with you? He's no good to us dead."

"Give him an hour and then douse him with cold water. If he won't talk then, I'll give him another shot." Luckily for Henekie, the warden showed up, putting an end to it.

The warm shower put Henekie to sleep, or maybe he passed out, but the next thing he remembered was lying in a comfortable bed. What had he done to deserve this? Had he talked? It didn't matter; he was too tired to care.

The warden and Bernard sat talking to Krugman. "I know you have a court order, but there's paperwork to do. Why don't you come back tomorrow?" the warden told him, trying to buy time.

"He's no good to you now anyway." Bernard spoke up. "He's been singing like a little Birdie."

"I don't think so, or you wouldn't be willing to let him go. Anyway, that's not a concern of my clients," Krugman told them. "I think the only reason you won't let me see him is so you can get more time to make him talk, and that's not going to happen."

"He's been very sick the last few days. He's sleeping now," Bernard explained.

Krugman was having none of it.

The three men stood looking at Henekie sleeping on the cot. "This is not good." Krugman looked at the other two men. "Has anyone else seen him?"

"Just us and my two men," Bernard answered.

"Jesus, what were you two thinking? It's a little late now. How did you plan on explaining this?"

The warden hung his head. "I'm fucked. All the people that wanted this done have left me out to dry."

"Yes," Krugman nodded his head, "fair-weather friends. I've had a few of them, so that means you can authorize anyone to take him out of here if you want."

"I guess, but I can't just have him disappear. The Americans are coming in two days. I'll have to sign him over to them," the warden stated.

"How about signing him over to me?"

The two men looked surprised. "Why, so you can show the world what we've done?"

"Here's the deal. My clients are the Israelis. They think this guy's the one who assassinated that diplomat in Korea last year. They want him bad, and they're willing to pay me big-time if I can deliver him before the Americans get him. If I can get a little cooperation from you guys, I think we can come up with a solution to our problem."

Both men looked interested, so Krugman continued. "Suppose I made a statement saying that I was this man's lawyer right from the start, but he wasn't charged because other countries thought he might be someone of interest and asked us to hold him until he was properly identified."

Krugman turned to the warden. "Anything international would have to come down from someone far higher than you. That should turn everything back on to your fair-weather friends, shouldn't it?"

"I guess the thing is, can we really do this and get away with it?" the warden pondered.

"I'll make a statement in the papers, and tomorrow morning we'll appear on the front steps to show everyone that this man's been released into my custody, and that he's suffered no harm."

"Tomorrow morning. How in hell are we going to get that man on to the front steps tomorrow morning?" Bernard wanted to know.

"That's all the time we have. You're the professional here, just rev him up because people have to see him. They're not going to take our word that he's all right."

"You know, I think legally we can do this, but what are you going to want from us?" the warden wanted to know.

"If you sign him over to me and keep your mouth shut, you and I are even. As for Bernard here, I need him to deliver our man to the Israelis."

Henekie had been briefed as to what would be required of him. They had put a hat on him and a big coat, now he knew why. The cold winter air that hit his face revived him to an extent. Bernard and Krugman walked on each side of him supporting him as they entered the top landing of the front steps.

He heard Krugman start talking, and then the crowd below cheered as Bernard prompted him to raise his arm. Then as Krugman continued to speak, Bernard steered him back inside the building and dropped him into a wheelchair. Henekie was wheeled into the underground parking lot beneath the prison where Bernard loaded him into a car, and they drove away.

Henekie tried to remember what Krugman had told him as he drifted in and out of consciousness. "He's to take you to a building where he drives in one end, drops you off, and drives out the other end. If this doesn't happen, you'll know something's wrong." They continued through the streets of Munich, reaching the suburbs and then into the countryside; all the time not a word was spoken between the two men.

Henekie saw a car ahead with its hood up. Bernard pulled in beside the car and walked around to Henekie's side, opened the door, and reached in to pull him out; that's when Henekie shot him. He heard Bernard grunt then come back at him. "You son of a bitch," was all he heard before he fired again and then passed out.

The pain between Henekie's legs brought him around rather quickly.

He clenched his teeth in pain as he looked up to see Krugman and a woman dressed in white. “I thought that might bring you around,” the woman in white said.

“What do you think? Did they fry his balls?” Krugman wanted to know.

Henekie realized they were talking about him, and he too suddenly became very interested.

“Is there anything left?” he whispered in obvious pain.

“That’s a good sign, he can talk,” Krugman smiled.

“I’m afraid he’s going to do a little more than talk before I’m done with him,” the lady in white was more apathetic. “It’s not as bad as it looks,” she went on describing what she saw. “All the hair is burned off your balls, but other than that, they seem okay. It’s your penis that needs a bit of attention. If you had a foreskin, you don’t now. I’m going to have to graft some skin, but in time you’ll be back poking it in places you shouldn’t just like all men. For now, I’d try not to get a hard-on. It might be quite painful.”

“This is the doctor who does all our cosmetic surgery, Henekie. She knows all about pain. She’ll be doing a little alteration on your face as well as on your fingers and thumb. That should neutralize the pain between your legs, but long-term gain for short-term pain,” Krugman shrugged. “Of course this is all costing me money, so I think we should get down to business. Our deal was that for your freedom you would tell me how to lay my hands on a billion dollars, right?”

Henekie nodded his head. “You need to get me back into the Bahamas.”

“I think we can work that out,” Krugman said, scratching his chin. “We have a small import/export business in Nassau. I would guess we could get you in there.”

“What I need from you is someone who has experience hacking into computer systems,” Henekie whispered.

"Okay," Krugman answered. "I have someone in mind that can handle that. We can work out the details later."

"Have you taken care of Greta?" Henekie asked.

"How in hell did you know she was the one to turn you in?" Krugman seemed surprised. He went on, "She was her own worst enemy, and in the end she self-destructed. The story is they were keeping her in a high-security prison, making it virtually impossible for anyone to get near her, but she screwed two of her guards failing to tell them she was infected with the HIV virus. Seems she was found hanging in her cell, suicide they called it. You can draw your own conclusions."

"And Bernard?" Henekie whispered.

"Ah, Bernard, what a fool. He thought he was going to take things into his own hands and rid the world of you. Of course that's why I gave you the revolver. You put him in a lot of pain, and our guys finished him off. He was ex-Israeli, and that played right into our hands. The consensus is the Israelis kidnapped you and Bernard helped them. Of course the Israelis have denied this, but no one believes them. If the Israelis have you, then it's assumed they'll get what they want out of you and finish you off. Bernard will just vanish, which is exactly what will happen to him. This is a big industrial complex one of our companies own. We do a lot of recycling here. Right now Bernard is soaking in our acid pit. When we get a truckload of acid, we ship it to Poland. Everything toxic in Germany is shipped over to Poland. They don't really care about pollution, and it's a cheap way to get rid of our waste. No one wants to get too close to our trucks, so they cross the border virtuously without scrutiny. We have a compartment built into the tanks for shipping toxic people such as yourself. Bernard may well be floating in the acid tank behind you. Whatever is left of him will probably be flushed down a sewer drain or end up spread on some Polack's field." Krugman smiled, "I'm telling you this because it will be your fate if you've been lying about the money."

Henekie nodded. "I know the score," he whispered.

"You'll be taken to our doctors' clinic in Poland for your operations and then put on a freighter with our tractor parts to Argentina. That will give you time to heal up. From there, you'll end up in charge of our Nassau shop. Or is time a factor here?" Krugman wanted to know.

Henekie laid back totally exhausted. "Don't worry, the longer we wait, the more money there'll be."

# Twenty-Six

Jon SMYSKIN SAT in his father's office wondering what he was doing there. He'd spent four years at Harvard and was about to graduate with a business degree when his mother phoned him in a panic. "We think something has happened to your father, Jon. There's no money for you or us either, you must come home and straighten out his affairs."

His dreams of sitting in a plush office overlooking Manhattan were dashed. His father's office consisted of a small room overlooking some kind of boat building yard which had been obsolete for years. His father had an obsession with boats, and this yard had been a cover for his real business, Jon supposed. He'd arrived home expecting to take over or at least salvage something, but there was nothing here.

The office had been vandalized leaving no records if there ever had been. His father had run his business with an iron hand keeping track of everything in his head. Jon knew all this, yet he expected there would be something left of his father's business; after all, when he'd left Bogotá, his father was called El Presidente, and the family was treated like royalty. Now the whole organization that his father had spent years setting up was gone, and his mother survived, shacked up with a man who sold body parts for a living.

Jon asked his mother why his younger brother Julio hadn't taken over, but she told him that her Julio was a young sensitive boy who had tried to protect his father's reputation, but everyone had turned against him. Jon knew Julio to be a big strapping boy, and upon further investigation found out he liked girls and drugs, and that was about it.

Julio had treated everyone like shit, and as long as he had his father's protection, he was king of the shit hill. Now he was scared to walk in the streets and never left the house. Jon also learned that his father had lost interest in his mother years ago, basically giving her money to stay away. He condoned the fact that she had a man living with her, and that she had developed a devouring appetite for young men and money. It was Julio who told Jon the stark truth about their mother.

"She's crazy, just like the man who lives with her. He can't get it up until he butchers someone then they go at it for hours," he told Jon. "She gets these young guys to come to the house and make love to her, and when she's tired of them, they kill them for the body parts, and I have to help get rid of what's left of the body."

Jon wasn't sure he believed Julio, but on talking to some of his old friends, he found out that indeed the so-called doctor his mother lived with made his living selling body parts. He also found out that when rival families found out that El Presidente was dead, they considered his properties up for grabs. The only reason his mother and Julio survived was because of this doctor.

One of the families had attempted a raid on the main house where Julio and his mother lived. From then on, the home became known as the house of the devil, and they left it alone. Jon was sick of all this; there was no business and no money to start one. His family members were all crazy, and all he wanted to do was get the hell out of there and back to the States. He'd gotten a call from a man who said it would be very beneficial for them to meet that afternoon; otherwise, he'd have been out of there. "Stupid of me to be sitting here." He thought of what this man could possibly have that would be of benefit to him.

"I guess I'm about to find out," as he saw a man walk in the door.

The man walked over to him and held out his hand, "Hello, they call me the Referee. You must be Jon Smyskin, El Presidente's son."

Jon shook his hand as the man calling himself the Referee looked around. "You're rather a brave young man, aren't you, no security of any kind?"

Jon laughed, "There's nothing in here worth stealing."

"Except you, young man, you're very valuable."

"Well," Jon gestured, "this building is the extent of my wealth. Take it for what it's worth."

"You know, that's exactly what I thought the first time I met your father here. There was no way a man who ran the biggest drug cartel in Colombia would have an office like this. I guess it fooled a lot of other people too because the authorities left him alone until the last few years."

The Referee sat down on the edge of Jon's desk. "We had a very tight organization. Your father supplied the product, my people delivered it to the marketing people in the States and Europe, and they sold it. We sold only the best product to high-end users and even had an agreement with the U.S. government that we would stay within a quota set every year. In return, we allowed a certain amount of high-profile arrests and confiscations. This lasted for a while, but as usual people got greedy, and suppliers found they could make more money cutting the product and dumping it into Mexico. We had no intention in getting mixed up in that fiasco, so our shipments were less and less into the States and more oriented toward Europe and new markets in the Middle East. That pissed off the DEA man who was looking after the enforcement of their quota in our area because his cut was getting smaller. He decided to get rid of your father and get someone here he could control. Your father had no choice. He had to go after him to show who was boss. We're not entirely sure what happened, but they killed each other off. That's why we want you to take over here, Jon. We've done some background on you, and we think you can handle the job."

"So you want me to go to work for you?" Jon concluded.

"Oh no, Jon, this is your business. Of course if you can't supply our needs, we will not be pleased, but that goes for any company. Now here's what you don't know, Jon, you are half owner of a multibillion-dollar company, but you need us to get control."

Jon's eyes got very big. "I don't follow you."

"This company was set up by your father to primarily launder his money. We have no idea why, but he gave half of the company to a woman named Lena. She was a former high-class call girl who got caught up in some kind of trouble in Germany and ended up in your father's house in Nassau. Maybe he knew what she was capable of. Anyway, she's turned the business into a holding company that controls a number of umbrella companies, but mainly she launders most of the dirty money roaming around the world, and believe me, it's substantial."

"How do you know all this?" Jon wanted to know.

"That's part of my job," the Referee told him. "You have to know what's going on in this business. Now the proper succession of this company would be that it goes to your mother, but you know what would happen if she got a hold of it. We have people in the right places that can legally have this company put in your name. Lena will certainly work with you. She knows it was only a matter of time before someone came forward to claim their half of the company, and I have seen the books, everything that belongs to you is there down to the penny. "So," the referee went on, "it's up to you. You can go back to New York broke or become a wealthy man and start a new empire here."

Jon scratched his head, "Wait till my friends hear I've become a drug pusher. That should get the old water cooler buzzing."

"For God's sake, Jon, don't be so naive. Your so-called friends will end up crooks and thieves using the stock market to take money from little old ladies. A license to steal money is what we laughingly call a Harvard business degree. Their motto is 'Do anyone you can and the easy ones twice.' There aren't any of them that will end up doing anything better or worse than you, and I might add that most of them will be envious of you. If you're smart, your good businesses will cover up the bad ones."

"Any suggestions where I start?" Jon asked.

"Yes, get some security. I can imagine how you feel about the man living with your mother, but I think he might be very beneficial in bringing your suppliers around." The Referee walked around the desk; Jon stood up and shook his hand. "You have all the money you need now, Jon, you now have the power to get what you want. Don't be scared to use it. We need product, and we need it now, but it must be the best, don't settle for anything less. Here is the code to call me if you need to. I can get you in touch with anyone or anything you need. There is one more thing. I plan to retire soon. The Bahamas will become too small for an operation like yours. I think you should build your own bank and operate the business from here. Remember, the worst thing you can think from now on is small." The Referee turned and left the way he came in.

Jon sat reflecting on what had just happened; he squared his shoulders. "This is what you always wanted," he thought, "now let's see how you handle it."

He went to his mother's house and asked to see the doctor. Jon didn't find him quite so intimidating anymore. They called him the thin man; now Jon could see why. He stood well over six feet tall and was as thin as a rail, but it was his penetrating blue eyes that caught Jon's attention.

"I need you to do some work for me," Jon told him.

"That takes money, my dear man."

"Just name your price, and from now on I'll be looking after Mother financially."

"Your ship come in?" the thin man asked.

"For all of us, as long as we give the pope his cut," Jon held his gaze; he watched as the blue in the thin man's eyes turned warm.

"I'm sure we can work something out."

It was two years later that Jon met with the President of Colombia. He had absolutely no problem getting an appointment. "I'm going to move my company headquarters from Nassau to Bogotá, and start my own bank, this will require that I build the tallest building in the downtown area. We will employ well over a thousand people and bring in millions of dollars into the Colombian economy. In return, I need the best location, the best communications systems, and no taxes," Jon told him.

"They told me you didn't waste time with formalities," the president smiled. "Now may we sit down and get to know each other better?"

Jon's face was flushed, "I'm sorry, I guess I'm not much of a conversationalist."

"That's okay, I like to talk," the president told him. "We've watched you operate the last two years, and we like what we see. You've settled down the turf wars out in the countryside, and a lot less addicts are getting poisoned on the streets." He stopped to take a puff from his cigar then looked directly at Jon.

"We all have skeletons in our closets, but I've never heard a whiff of scandal or wrongdoing about you. You do an excellent job of keeping everyone in line except for one. Families are the hardest to keep in line. It seems they think they can throw their weight around just because they're related. Your brother's been causing some problems for the police, but we've condoned it till now." The president stopped and took another drag on his cigar. “Two nights ago, he assaulted a U.S. diplomat’s daughter. Her parents want blood. I would appreciate you making your brother disappear. It is better you handle this situation yourself because if we have to deal with him, it will be very difficult to keep your name out of this.”

Jon’s eyes wandered off into the distance. “I’m embarrassed that you, of all people, are the one to come to me with this. Of course, this matter will be rectified immediately. Whatever costs or remediation required is available with my deepest appreciation to you, your government, and the police force.”

“See! Who said you weren’t a good conversationalist, Jon? I will arrange a meeting between you and the diplomat in question,” the president told him. “If this matter is handled discreetly and without incident, I will say yes to all your demands. We are honored to have you with us, Jon. Colombia needs more young people like you.” Jon took his cue, standing up and shaking hands with the president. He was a lot less cocky leaving than he was going in, he also had a lot more respect for the president.

Jon didn’t go anywhere without bodyguards anymore. He knew they would protect him with their lives and would do anything he asked of them, but there was a little thing called respect. This meant he would have to deal with Julio himself. Jon knew a bullet to the head was the best solution, but as he neared his mother’s home, his resolve weakened. His mother was waiting for him. She knew why he was here and began to rant at how it couldn’t be her baby’s fault.

“If you kill him, you kill me,” she screamed.

The thin man came to Jon’s rescue. “We both know what should be done here, Jon. I’d do it for you, but maybe under the circumstances we should look at alternatives.” So it was decided that Julio would be sent to the Bahamas.

Jon then had a little chat with Julio. “We have property there, and a lady by the name of Lena who runs a very important part of our business also lives on this property. She supplies security for the property. Now we want you to take that over. As soon as we have our building ready, we plan on moving that part of our business here, so maybe you can put that big cock of yours to good use and convince Lena that she should move with us."

Julio didn't want to leave, but he didn't like the alternative either. As far as the woman was concerned, this was no problem; all the women loved him, especially the older ones. Once their legs were in the air, they all begged for more. "You never ask a woman what she wants, you tell her," was Julio's motto.

# TWENTY-SEVEN

WILBUR SMITH'S LIFE was a mess. In the last year, he'd had an affair, his wife had divorced him, his kids hated him, and now he'd been called into the head office in Houston. His job as a special agent for the CIA was coming to an end three years before retirement. What the hell; the last few years he'd been shuffled back and forth between the CIA and The FBI doing odd jobs .

Perhaps that's why he had the affair he reflected, boredom. It had started innocent enough; his neighbor had run his lawnmower into the fence dividing their property. The lady next door came to see him saying they would pay for the repairs. She was a very attractive lady, and something about her piqued his interest. He told her he would repair the fence himself.

He and his wife had been drifting apart without really noticing it. Once the kids were gone, there was really no glue left. She painted and worked in the garden; he went to work and spent his time with the guys, so it really hadn't taken much to seduce him. When he went to repair her side of the fence, she met him at the door in her bikini. "It's so hot out, have a drink by the pool with me before you start your work."

After three drinks, he was on top of her on the lounge chair fucking her with a hard-on he hadn't been able to obtain in years. The fence never did get fixed properly; he left the bottom of the boards unnailed so he could swing them aside and sneak over to see his neighbor whenever he wanted.

Maybe it was because he had a spring in his step and a new outlook on life that led his wife and family to find out about his affair. Deep down, Wilbur knew it was bound to happen, and he guessed that deep down he didn't care. What really hurt him was the next day when he went through the fence, he found the house empty; his neighbor had left him to fend for himself. Since then, his life had been in a downward spiral and his work had suffered, so he wasn't really surprised to be in his boss's office this morning.

"Good morning, Wilbur." His boss sounded cordial. Wilbur shook his hand.

"Jeez, couldn't he be a little more condescending?" Wilbur thought as he sat down across from him bracing for what was to come.

"You worked for Ansly down in Miami for a few years before he went over to the DEA, didn't you, Wilbur?"

"Aha!" Wilbur thought; "the rogue agent Ansly, they're going to hold that against me too."

"Yes, I spent quite a few years with him down there," Wilbur answered.

"We're looking for someone to take over that area, someone who knows the lay of the land so to speak. We have a young man in charge there right now, but he's a little too gung ho. Everything's black and white, good guy bad guy, and as you know, Wilbur, in this business, there is a lot of gray areas."

His boss went on, "That area has been one of our most successful programs. We were able to set quotas. It's all high-end product, so you don't have hop heads on every corner. In other words, we had a controlled substance being handled by sensible people, not like this fiasco happening on the Mexican border. I don't know what you thought of Ansly and I know most of the CIA community thinks he was a rogue agent, but a few of us know what he was up to."

His boss got from behind his desk and began to pace. "You are aware of who El Presidente was, aren't you?"

Wilbur nodded, wondering where this was leading.

"El Presidente was losing control of the Colombian market. Our people on this end knew this and figured if they could replace him with someone more powerful, then we could maintain some kind of control at the source. This in turn would help control what was going into Mexico. Ansly accomplished getting rid of El Presidente but unfortunately got rid of himself in the process. However, Ansly isn't the only man we had in that area. There is a man there called the Referee. His job is to keep all the parties working together and to settle any disputes that crop up. He has successfully installed El Presidente's son into Colombia and has made big inroads toward controlling things there. The only component missing is someone to represent us. We'd like you to be that component."

The adrenaline level in Wilbur's veins was surging. "Guess I have to ask, why me?"

"Well, that wasn't just my decision. The Referee requested you. According to him, you have experience, and both he and you will retire about the same time. He thinks by then both of you will be redundant in that area as everything is getting bigger and faster. The Bahamas area will simply be passed over. I have to warn you, Wilbur, this is a dangerous place to be in. If anything goes wrong, we don't know you. The young man you are replacing is going to be breathing down your neck every step of the way, and the people you are going to be working with are ruthless, which means you have to be too. You're three years from retirement, Wilbur, you can walk away, and I will understand."

"That's exactly why I have to do this," Wilbur said, shaking his boss's hand. "I'm not dead yet."

"Okay, Wilbur, get yourself down to Miami. The first thing you'll have to do is meet the Referee. Very few of us know who he is. Once you meet him, there's no turning back."

Wilbur walked into a café off a busy Nassau street and looked for the second table in. "You," was all he could say.

"Yes, me," the Referee answered, shaking hands with Wilbur. "Perfect, isn't it? People expect we will meet from time to time just as we are now." The two men sat down at the table.

"I know we know each other," Wilbur told him, "but why me?"

"You are a good man, Wilbur. I know Ansly wouldn't give you a piece of the action and sent you elsewhere. However, we're both about to retire, so I think that should be incentive for both of us to get things done here. By the way, there's someone I'd like you to meet, and here she comes now."

Wilbur looked up to see his neighbor standing beside the table. "Hello, Wilbur. I hope you're not angry at me," she said softly.

The Referee answered the question on Wilbur's face. "She works for us, Wilbur. We knew you wouldn't have been any good to us under your old circumstances. We put this girl onto you to get you the hell out of there and to find out if you still had it." The Referee looked at the woman. "She says you still do."

Wilbur spread his hands. "I've been fucked, sucked, and seduced to get me here, so it's my turn to dick you around. What's in it for me?"

"That's the old Wilbur I wanted to see," the Referee told him. "Ansly left very suddenly with a lot of money in his account. In case of death, that account reverts back to us and ironically to you, if you're successful the next few years."

"How much are we talking here?" Wilbur wanted to know.

"Millions. I don't know the exact amount," was the answer.

"And what's required of me?"

"That young agent, Ted Heath's his name, is not very happy you're being sent here. You'll soon make it plain to him that he has run of the place. You are just here to finish out your pension and don't want to shake the boat. We have inside knowledge of everything that is coming out of Colombia, so anything we don't sanction Ted will get a shot at. We'll give him enough to make him look really good, but once in a while he'll get his nose into something he shouldn't, and you'll have to diffuse it. Don't get the wrong idea here, Wilbur. You, me, and Jon Smyskin are running this show."

The woman who had been his neighbor smiled, "I work in your office, Wilbur." He smiled back; she was there to watch him, but what the hell.

Herr Krugman had been right; the pain in having Henekie's face redone had at least taken some of the pain away from his dick. Both had healed on the long boat ride from Poland to Argentina where he spent two months learning about the machinery parts business and getting his papers in order. Henekie no longer recognized himself when he looked in the mirror which was good. He'd still been apprehensive upon entering the Bahamas where a couple of years ago he'd been the most wanted man there, but there'd been no problems.

He took over as manager of the parts depot which consisted of a small front office with counter space and a shop and storage room in the back. Some of the training he'd taken in Argentina was business oriented, but most of it was how to dismantle and assemble the many castings and parts going through the Nassau depot. Each piece was loaded on the inside with as much contraband as possible, mostly cocaine for consumption in the local domestic market, but the animal parts were the most fascinating to Henekie.

The Asian market was huge; there was great demand in China and Korea where these parts were considered to be an aphrodisiac for male consumption and brought big prices. Everything going out of Argentina was checked for exotic animal parts except for machinery headed for the Bahamas. There were no animals in the Bahamas that fit this description, so shipping was easy from here. Most of his customers ordered parts by phone, leaving Henekie time alone to clean out the parts and ship everything as required. Of course that was not the main reason he was here, as Herr Krugman was constantly pointing out.

Henekie had to remind him there was work to do here before they made their move."You have a fair idea who we are taking this money from and the consequences if we don't do it right."

"Don't forget who's been financing you and who you owe your life to," was Krugman's reply.

Henekie had by no means been idle, but experience had taught him the hard way not to rush into projects. Many of the characters were the same. Horatio Norton now headed the police force, and Sir Harry Chamberlain still had his nose stuck in everything. The new part of the equation was that one of El Presidente's sons was living with Lena in the guesthouse and the other was running the show in Colombia. So he concentrated a lot of his time on researching these men whose money they would be stealing.

He still heard rumors about a man El Presidente had called the Referee, but Henekie could get nothing concrete on him, and this bothered him. He didn't like unknowns. "I'm sure this robbery we are about to pull off will smoke him out, but how big a problem would that create?" Henekie wondered.

His most important character was Lena, and she got all his spare time. He didn't recognize any of her guards, so he couldn't get any insider information there. She didn't go out much, but when she did, Henekie followed her. This time she went to the Atlantis with her driver, a big strapping young man, the kind Lena liked to bed once in a while. Only this driver acted a little strange. As soon as she left him, he was be on his phone then he followed her, appearing to be reporting her every move. Herr Krugman had made it plain he wanted things to move along, so Henekie decided it was time he tipped his hand.

Henekie stood up on the high breaker wall that protected the Atlantis complex from the wind and sea. Down below he watched Lena's driver take a place leaning on the rail of one of the many bridges crossing the channel that floated people on rubber dinghies around the property. Henekie made his way down to the bridge and in behind the driver, who was supposed to be watching Lena, but was much more engrossed in watching the bikinis floating down the channel.

He waited till no one was coming then stepped up behind the driver and paralyzed him with a punch to the kidneys, and almost instantaneously he pulled the driver's jacket down, turning it into a straitjacket, taking his hat, keys, wallet then flipped him over the railing, the whole procedure taking no more than five seconds. He heard the splash, and then a commotion erupted among the floaters below as he walked away giving the driver a 25 percent chance of surviving.

Lena was sitting close by at one of the outdoor tables talking to a man whom Henekie recognized as a government official. The man began looking over at the commotion and decided to go have a look for himself leaving Lena alone.

As Henekie approached, he took the man's place. "Hello, Lena."

"Who in hell are you?" Lena was indignant.

"It's Henekie."

"Henekie?" She looked at him intently now.

He removed his sunglasses. "This is the new Henekie, but I think you recognize the voice."

"My god, Henekie, what are you doing here?"

"Oh, some people owe me money here," he answered vaguely. "I hear you have a new partner in Colombia."

Lena flicked her cigarette at the ashtray. "What have you heard?" she asked.

"I hear Jon Smyskin's brother is living in the guesthouse, and I see you've changed your security guards. He must be looking after you very well."

Now it was Lena's turn to take of her sunglasses, showing Henekie a black eye.

"I see, we'd better go somewhere and talk before your friend comes back," he told her. They got up and walked toward one of the inside bars.

"He's really not a friend," she told him. I'm trying to find someone in the government with enough balls to get Julio Smyskin deported, but none of them seem to have the guts to stand up to him." They sat down and ordered a drink.

"You know it's funny, but there's someone pulling strings here in the islands. I have my fingers into everything, but I'll be damned if I can find out who it is," Lena lamented.

"So this Julio is the one who did this to you?" Henekie asked.

"Yes, perhaps some of it is my fault. He's a good-looking boy, and you know I have a soft spot for them, so I invited him to my bed, but as always it's on my terms. He told me his terms were he could have me when and wherever he wanted to. Of course I refused and he beat me, and still does, but that's not the worst of it, Henekie." For the first time, he saw tears in Lena's eyes. "He killed Quinn."

"What?" was all Henekie could say.

"Julio was slapping me around, and he came to help me. Julio hit him, and he died," Lena said through her tears.

Henekie couldn't believe it. "He must be crazy, Quinn was El Presidente's right-hand man. He kept things going."

Lena pulled herself together. "I'm sorry, Quinn was like the father I never had."

"Have you talked to anyone about this?" Henekie wanted to know.

"They kept me locked up in my bedroom for a week," Lena told him. "Then Julio raped and beat the shit out of me, telling me to keep my mouth shut." Henekie noticed Lena shake as she lit her cigarette.

"I had no intention of keeping this quiet and phoned Jon telling him he had better get his brother out of here or I would go to the police. He said that he would look after it, but a few days later he phoned me saying I was a liar, that he had a copy of Quinn's passport, an airline ticket, and a letter proving that Quinn did not want to work for me anymore and left. When I first met Jon Smyskin, I thought he would be thankful that we had kept the business in order here. Instead, he was much more interested in what I had done with my half of the money and why he was not a partner. It was made clear to him that I did not invest his money because it was not mine, and what I did with my money was none of his business."

Lena shook a bit as she lit another cigarette and continued, "We didn't part on good terms. I didn't hear much from him for a while. He was too occupied in getting his own house in order. Then out of the blue he tells me he is sending his brother to take over security at his compound. Of course, I asked him to clarify what he meant by that. In the meantime, his brother moved into the guesthouse, and suddenly my security disappeared. When I went to go out of the compound, I was told that I would need permission to do so. I was a prisoner in my own house."

Lena stopped talking for a moment and concentrated on her cigarette before continuing on. "I fought back the only way I knew how. I thought if I could bed Julio, maybe he would come over to my side or at least find out what Jon was up to. That was a mistake that resulted in my getting raped and Quinn getting killed." Lena's voice began to quake again. "Throughout all this, I complained to Jon, but all he would say was, 'I'll take care of it,' and I guess he has because all of a sudden, I feel very alone."

"You must have gone to Sir Harry or someone who could help you with Quinn?" Henekie asked her.

"This is the first time I've been allowed out on my own since it happened. Smyskin did tell me he was sending Julio a Venezuelan beauty queen so he would leave me alone, but as you can see, that hasn't happened yet. I've had no phone or way of communicating with anybody until today and I know that meeting got me nowhere."

You must be doing very well with your business end of things," Henekie surmised. "I also think he still needs you or you would have disappeared by now."

"Oh, he needs me all right. I'm the only one who can understand how my business works and how to run my computers. I think his plan is to move me to Colombia where he can study my operation and that could happen at any time. As for my business, yes, I have been incredibly successful. That island I told you about in Dubai, it's a playground for only the very rich, and Dubai itself will double or quadruple our money on everything we built there. I did everything right but cover my ass, Henekie. I still have my little pistol, and when they come for me, that will be the end, but I shall make sure to take that prick Julio with me."

"This is serious," Henekie thought to himself. If I don't have access to her computers, I'm dead too.

"How come they're letting you go out now?" Henekie asked.

Lena shrugged, "They know that I'm powerless. All the people that I thought were in my pocket are scared to talk to me. My driver watches my every move. I guess they want to see who I talk to. He's probably watching us right now."

"Don't think so," Henekie smiled. "He fell off a bridge. That's what the commotion was about out there a while ago."

Lena smiled, "Are you trying to get me in trouble?"

"I think you are doing a good job of that all by yourself," he told her. "How many men does Julio have with him?"

"Five, but I saw three go out this morning. So unless they are back, he has just two. Why? What are you thinking, Henekie?"

"How close do they check your car when it comes in?"

"There is a camera at the gate. My driver honks twice, and they let us in," Lena answered.

"Good, you and I are going to pay Julio a visit," Henekie told her. "I'm your new driver."

The gate was not a problem. Once they entered Lena's house, Henekie told Lena to get her pistol and put some pants on since they might have to do some crawling around. Lena did as she was told, and Henekie noticed a spring in her step. He felt a sense of guilt that he was doing this more for himself than he was for Lena.

"We're all after her money," he thought, it was by no means clear who would get it.

"There are security camera's covering the grounds. We'll have to wait till dark before we have any chance of getting over to the guest house," Lena told him.

"You don't have to come with me, Lena. I'm going to kill them you know." He picked up a butcher knife to emphasize what he had in mind.

She turned and looked Henekie straight in the eye. "I know. All I ask is that you let me do Julio."

"Okay, but we aren't waiting until dark. We're taking the tunnel."

"Tunnel? What tunnel?" Lena wanted to know.

El Presidente took time to show me how he got in and out of Nassau without anyone knowing he was here. Henekie led her to an old door in the garage with a flashlight in hand. "It's damp. There are cobwebs and bats down there, but it does come out in the guesthouse."

"So this is where you hid when you used to show up in my house unannounced," Lena exclaimed.

"Only when I had to. It's pretty nasty down here. Most of the time, I just hid out in your house." He lied, not telling her about his lair down in the old warehouse. They went down some steps and began making their way through the tunnel. It certainly had not improved with age; the ceiling was low, and in places it was only wide enough for one person to squeeze through.

Henekie walked ahead, breaking through the cobwebs, waiting for Lena to start complaining; but instead, he heard her ask, "So, you saw me walking around the house naked?"

"Yup," was his answer.

"Did I turn you on?"

He stopped and shone the flashlight on her. "Because I have never come on to you, you are wondering if I'm gay, aren't you?"

"You know everything about me," Lena answered, "I know nothing about you."

Henekie looked at her. "In my business, it is not wise to get too close to people or them to me.Your next question would be why am I helping you. My services are very expensive, Lena, and my loyalty goes to the highest bidder. If I can get you through this rough spot, you may have a future, and that means I have a future. Now be quiet and let me concentrate on the job at hand." He turned, and they continued up the tunnel.

Finally, they came to another set of steps leading up to a heavy wooden door. Henekie found a key. "I hope they aren't in the garage."

He had to push hard to open the door enough to get them through. Henekie immediately saw that he was lucky he got the door to open at all; someone had put a stack of bags against it. He whistled. "These are the old-style canvas bags they used to ship cocaine in." He bent over and opened one, "Holy shit! They're full."

"I heard Julio talk about an old barge on Andros, and then the other night some men worked most of the night pulling something up over the cliff," Lena told him.

"Interesting. Show me where the surveillance cameras are, and we shall see if anyone is manning them." Quietly, they went from room to room until Lena motioned to a door. They looked in to see a fat man with his head thrown back over a chair snoring. Henekie pointed at Lena and put his hands over his eyes, and then he carefully walked up behind the man and slit his throat. Henekie went back out of the room to see how Lena was, but she wasn't there. This puzzled him, but only for a second, as he saw her tiptoeing toward him.

"They are out on the patio," she whispered. "I checked the rest of the house. There is no one else here."

Henekie nodded, "Here, take your gun and if anything happens to me, make sure you get anyone who is left. Just don't panic and shoot me."

Lena waved toward the patio door. "Let's go. I've taken shooting lessons since the last time you saw me."

Henekie looked around the doorway just as the phone rang. He listened as Julio told someone on the other end to stay in the safe house.

"There will be a boat at Buzzard Bay between eleven and one o'clock to pick you up. Just make sure you're there." Julio hung up the phone.

The man across from him said, "What are the guys in Miami going to say when they find out our guys didn't find any shit?"

"Fuck them," Julio responded. " Now they'll believe me when I tell them the guy who owns the hotel stole it all."

The man across from Julio shook his head, "That's a dangerous game, Julio." He put his head down to snort a line of coke.

Henekie was instantly behind Julio, putting the butcher knife to his throat. "I suggest you both stay very still," he told them.

Henekie could feel Julio go stiff with fear, but the man across from him slowly raised his head and stared at him. "You're thinking that if I go for my gun, what's he going to do. I think I can put this knife through you as quick as you can blink, but there's only one way to find out, isn't there?"

The man was shifty eyed, making it hard to know which way he was going to go. Then suddenly, he upset the table and went for his gun. Henekie braced himself behind Julio, letting him take the full brunt of the table. The butcher knife's blade was quite blunt, which meant it might bounce off a rib, so he had to pick somewhere soft.

It was at times like this that Henekie seemed to go into a surreal state. Everything slowed down; he was totally focused on what he was doing, but in reality it all happened in a split second. Henekie threw the knife and watched the knife enter the man's throat, and they both knew whose luck had run out. The man turned and took a few steps before crashing headfirst through the patio railing onto the ground below. Henekie expected Julio to resist; but instead, he slumped, taking everything Henekie had to hold him up. Lena appeared in front of them.

"I'm going to blow his balls off," she screamed.

"No, no. Settle down, Lena. My balls are right behind his. Just push that chair over here, and I'll sit him in it," Henekie gasped.

Lena did as he asked. "My, my, our big tough guy has pissed his pants."

"He did more than that by the smell of him," Henekie added sliding him down into the chair.

Julio began to sob, "I love you, Lena. How can you do this to me?"

"Poor little boy, I think you and I will get along fine once I cut off your balls," she stated.

Henekie took a towel and blindfolded Julio. "You know, I think she really wants to cut off your balls. I think if you tell the truth about some questions I'm going to ask you, maybe we can keep you in one piece."

"Okay," Julio said between sobs.

"Where did you find the bags piled in the garage?"

"They were on an old barge that sank in the marina at Buzzard Bay."

"Who told you they were there?" Henekie wanted to know.

"The Miami boys figured they might be there, but they didn't know how to get at them."

"So how did you do it?"

Julio was talking about himself now and began to buck up. "One of our companies has a barge with a crane, so I had them tell the government that we would need the marina for a project on Andros. They told us to go ahead and get the barge out of there as long as it did not cost them anything."

Henekie was curious. "How did you get the bags out of there without someone seeing something?"

"We floated the barge then waited until dark and dragged the barge out to sea, only it broke apart, but we were able to gather up the bags," Julio told him.

"There are rumors that you didn't find any bags on the barge. Now Andros and Nassau are flooded with drugs. How in hell are you going to explain that?" Lena wanted to know.

"Hey, there's some coke in that cabinet over there. Do you think I could have a hit? I could sure use one."

"Maybe, we'll see how well you do in the next few minutes," Henekie told him. "So how come the cops haven't nailed this guy over on Andros?"

Julio laughed, "You see, that's the beauty of things. I needed quick money, so it was me who flooded the market. We heard there was some kid on Andros who had found some bags, so we put the word out he was flooding the market. You've got to give me a hit for telling you all this, man."

"So far you've just told us how smart you are. I asked you what's with the cops?" Henekie repeated, taking the knife from Lena and holding it where Julio could see it.

"They are stupid," Julio answered. "We heard they'd been to see this guy but didn't find much, so I guess they figure it was just a rumor."

"So why did you send your guys in there?" Henekie asked.

"How did you know about that shit? You got my place bugged?"

"Just answer the question," Henekie replied.

Julio gave them a sheepish look. "I didn't tell the Miami guys I've got the stuff. They heard about this kid on Andros and think maybe he's got all of it, so they tell me to go in and find out what's there. It was risky because we think the DEA was watching him, but we figured if we went in quick, found out what he knew, popped him, and got the hell out, no one would be the wiser."

"But something went wrong," Henekie quizzed.

"Yeah, stupid fucks for some reason couldn't get back to the plane, so we had to hide them in a safe house and pick them up tonight by boat."

"I think you're fucked, Julio. The Miami guys aren't going to believe this story for a minute."

"Give me a hit, and I'll tell you why they already have," Julio whined.

Henekie reached into the cabinet and took out a bag, and then he sat the table upright and put everything in front of Julio and shoved his face in it. Julio poured some powder on the table and began snorting it.

"Hey, slow down," Henekie said, pulling Julio's head up by the scruff of the neck. "You can kill yourself later. I'm not done with you yet, so tell me why anyone's going to believe you."

The hit made Julio belligerent, "Because I'm a fucking genius, and you're both going to be dead soon."

"You may be right, Julio, but you saw what I can do with a knife. I can pop your balls out of your sack as quick as I killed your buddy, so whether I'm dead or not, your voice is going to be a lot higher."

Julio definitely did not like that idea, "Okay, okay." Then he began laughing uncontrollably. "The plan is fucking brilliant, you gotta hear this."

Henekie put the knife to Julio's throat and cut the skin just enough to get his attention. "So tell me this brilliant plan of yours."

Julio stopped laughing. "I've been running with a guy from Andros. His father owns most of the island. In fact, he owns a good chunk of Nassau, but his old man's like my brother. He won't give him nothing either. One night my brother phones me and says I have to go downtown and entertain some business people from Miami, so me and my friend go and meet these guys. They invite us to Miami, take us, you know, gambling, we do lots of shit, fuck some women, the usual, and then they send us a fucking bill. I complained to my brother Jon, and he says nothing's free in this world, and I'd better come up with the cash. The Miami guys know fucking well I've got no cash, so they come up with this proposition. They tell me they think there's a whole shitload of coke on board a barge sunk in the marina at Buzzard Bay, but they don't know how to go about getting to it without everyone knowing what's going on. So my buddy and I go and get the shit, but then we start to think why in hell should we give it all to the Miami fucks. At first we were going to cut just a little bit, then we found a market in Mexico, and my friend's old man came up with a plan that made it possible for us to sell all of it. We set up a lab right here in the garage, and we're selling everything we can produce to a dealer in Mexico. Fuck, we're making millions," Julio announced proudly.

"I still don't understand how you plan to get away with this," Henekie told him.

"A few years ago the government forced my friend's old man to sell a hotel over on Andros. Now it's worth a bloody fortune, and he wants it back. We told the Miami guys that we didn't find any coke on the old barge, but we found out that it had been there. We told them that this Green guy who owns the hotel has been stealing it a little bit at a time. He hired a young guy over there to set up a lab, and they've been quietly selling the shit off until lately, when the kid running the lab decided he wanted more of the action and flooded the local market."

The name Green instantly grabbed Henekie's attention. "Have you seen this Green?" Henekie wanted to know.

"Yeah, my friend took me over to the hotel one night last week. It's the place to be in the Bahamas."

"Did he look like he had anything wrong with him?"

"Hell no," was Julio's response. "You don't keep a wife like his around if you're fucked up. She's a movie star here in the islands. My friend was going off in his pants just looking at her."

"I think that might be another reason your friend wants the hotel. She comes with it," Henekie suggested.

"Could be. I know they're only after Green. He pretty well cut his own throat when he helped hide the rest of the shit the kid stole from us."

"So you sent your guys over to Andros to pop this Green?" Henekie asked.

"Nope, they went over to pop the kid who stole our shit. We got rid of him and then told the Miami guys we found the lab and what was left of their coke. We told them it's had the shit cut out of it, but we have what's left."

"So then you give up Green for the Miami guys to hack up?"

Julio pointed at his head. "You're not too smart, man. We don't want him talking too much. We'll set him up to get caught with the shit. The DEA boys will take care of him."

"Sounds like you've got it all figured out, Julio, so where's the millions you're making?" Henekie wanted to know.

"You think I'm stupid enough to leave it where you can get it. My friend's old man invested it for me."

Henekie looked at Lena; they both shook their heads. "No doubt about it, Julio, you're a brilliant strategist."

"Wait till my man Benito gets back to see what I've got planned for you," Julio blurted out.

"Well, maybe we better clean you up before he gets here," Henekie told Julio as he lifted him from the chair and guided him into the garage. Henekie pulled his shirt up over his nose and put on sunglasses before he undid Julio's blindfold. "Okay, Julio, get in there." He pointed to the huge shower built into the garage.

Julio immediately began to blubber, "What are you going to do to me?"

"You know what that shower is for, don't you, Julio? You've probably enjoyed hanging some poor bastard up in there and gutting him, you perverted little prick. Get your clothes off and wash the shit off your ass before I change my mind and hang you up in there."

Julio did as he was told then turned on the shower and began cleaning himself up.

"I just thought that was a party shower," Lena said to Henekie. "Is that really for torturing people?"

"Yep, what did you think the hooks built into the tiles were for?"

Lena looked very pale.

"I'm going after Julio's men," he told her. "My best chance is to surprise them before they get back. Do you want me to hang Julio up in the shower? He'll be easy to look after in there."

Lena thought for a moment. “No, I want you to take him over to my garage and spread-eagle him over the hood of my car.”

“Jeez, Lena, it makes me kind of queasy thinking of what you have in mind for him, but I think you’re right. If his men come back, that means I probably won’t. You’ll have a better chance of getting away from over there.”

“I’ll get away all right. If I see his men come back, I’ll drive my car right down Nassau’s high street with Julio spread out on the hood. They can follow me if they want,” she told Henekie as they herded Julio across the yard to her garage.

Henekie whacked Julio on the head with Lena’s gun, stunning him and then laid him over the hood of Lena’s car. She brought him some straps which he used to fasten Julio down and then tied his ankles to each end of the bumper.

“Okay,” Henekie told her, “he’s all yours, just don’t kill him. You’re in enough trouble already.”

“Don’t worry, Henekie, you go do what you have to do. I’ll be all right, just get out of here. Men seem to get a little squeamish when they see what I’m about to do.”

Henekie didn’t have to be asked twice. He went across to Julio’s house to enter the tunnel. He didn’t want Lena to know where he was going.

Lena had already turned her attention on Julio. She took a broom from a corner of the garage and showed the handle to Julio. “You remember how much you enjoyed hearing me scream when you shoved that big thing of yours up my ass? Let’s see how much of this you can take before you start screaming, Julio.”

“You bitch, Lena.”

“You’re my bitch now,” Lena told him as she rammed the broom handle up his ass.

# TWENTY-EIGHT

TOMMY'S SKIFF WAS pretty small so he had to keep it close to shore out of the rough water. This was a long trip for such a small boat. He'd taken his brother down to the south end of Andros to sell some weed to his friends. As usual his brother's friends had no money, so they smoked the weed, and Tommy ended up borrowing enough petrol to get back home. His brother sat sullenly in the front of the boat not caring that it was pitch black out. Tommy had been hauling him around for a long time now, and he knew that Tommy knew these islands like the back of his hand.

Tommy's brother was a throwback to the heady days when Andros was the port of choice for drugs to enter the United States, and there was money to be made. He was one of the best boatmen around, and his services were in demand, but even back then he had one major flaw. His nickname 'Sniff' told it all; his nose was always stuck in a bag of coke.

He had built a house on a hill overlooking the sea; he had two sports cars and the fastest boat in the islands. Then as quickly as they came, the good times faded away. Sniff had never left the good old days; his habit quickly burned through whatever money he had. Now his house was falling down around his ears, the cars lay rusting in the front yard, no one knew why he hadn't sold them except for the fact that while he had been going through his withdrawal period, he'd go out and sit in them for hours at a time. The only thing he had of value was this small boat which he'd taken in trade when he'd sold his speedboat. Thanks to Tommy, it was still running, and this was now their only source of income.

Tommy was only ten when he first moved in with his brother. His father had too many kids and too small a house. Some of his brothers slept outside, but Tommy could see no future in that. Sniff was at least ten years older than Tommy, but it was pretty obvious that he needed looking after and he had an empty house, so Tommy moved in and did his best to keep things going. He only went to school because the government made him, but most of the time Tommy snuck away, spending his time fishing or working in the small garden in the backyard. This was the only place where his brother would come out and help him, mainly because of the weed he grew among the vegetables. Tommy had been looking after his brother for at least five years now, and he was tired of it. Tonight was just about all he could take; Sniff was getting worse instead of better. He'd been working with his father down at the hotel, and Mr. Green had offered him a full-time job with a place to stay.

"Maybe it was time his brother looked after himself," Tommy thought. The shoreline disappeared in front of them, and Tommy turned the boat into Buzzard Bay.

Suddenly, they found themselves surrounded by bright lights. Just to their left was a large ship which was throwing off most of the light, but there were also two smaller spotlights floating over the water. Tommy had never seen his brother so animated. He crouched in the front of the boat and began waving Tommy ahead.

"I'm getting out of here," Tommy shouted at him.

His brother turned and pointed a pistol at him. "Are you coming or not?" For the first time, Tommy realized just how unstable his brother was. He followed his brother's directions as he pointed him to what seemed right into the light.

Then Tommy saw what his brother was after; two black objects appeared beside their boat.

"Help me load these, Tommy."

They rolled the two bags on board; Tommy was scared skinny, but his brother seemed to be loving it.

"Over there," he pointed, "we'll get that one." Tommy's heart was in his mouth as they loaded the third bag. Their boat lit up as one of the spotlights pointed directly at them.

"Head back to the shoreline," Sniff told him. "We'll blend in there."

Their boat was so overloaded that Tommy couldn't get any speed out of it. He looked back to see the light closing in on them at an alarming rate. He was ready to go over the side when all of a sudden the light stopped and turned the other way.

His brother laughed in glee. "They found some more bags. They're more important than us."

Tommy saw his brother put the pistol in his belt; there was no way he would have given up the bags without a fight.

They continued around the edge of the bay until they arrived at the dock below their house. Tommy was amazed at the energy his brother displayed as they spent the rest of the night dragging the bags up the hill. Tommy had no idea what they were going to do with these big bags, but Sniff had this under control too. He showed Tommy an old cellar buried along the edge of the rock bluff not far from the house which was almost impossible to find.

"This is our secret, Tommy, I'll know who talked if anyone finds this place."

Tommy nodded; he knew exactly what would happen if Sniff was separated from his stash.

For a while, everything went all right. Sniff sold a little bit, and for a change they had some money. He even talked about fixing up the old house and maybe getting the cars running again. Thing began to go wrong when Sniff moved his old girlfriend into the house. She was a bad influence, wanting to lie around all day smoking dope, and now she had coke to add to her diet. Her friends started showing up from all over, and then Sniff's old buddies began hanging around. The allure of free coke brought the dregs of society to their door; soon, no one left. It was just one big party every day. Then what Tommy feared happened.

A girl came running up the hill. "They're coming, the police are coming."

The eyes and ears of the island made it almost impossible for the local police to keep anything secret. By the time they got there, everyone had scattered, and Sniff was waiting quietly for them in the front door. There was nothing to be found, so the police left, but not before they gave Sniff a stern warning to clean up his act.

Tommy pleaded with his brother to get rid of his so-called friends, but he told Tommy that his girlfriend liked to party, and she wanted them to stay. He did tell Tommy that he was going to start charging for the coke they used, but Tommy never saw that threat materialize.

It was the next week that all hell broke loose. Out of the blue, choppers appeared overhead. This was a DEA raid, and it happened so fast no one escaped. Tommy was out working in the garden. He was happy now that there were no marijuana plants left growing; people had tried to smoke them green. He wasn't entirely innocent though. There were two naked girls sitting smoking grass watching him work. They were both in their late twenties, and their main goal in life was to party. Tommy had been pretty innocent until this last month; he didn't touch the white powder, but the girls, well that was another story. These two looked after him most of the time probably because they thought he had an inside track on the coke.

"I think I'd get rid of the grass," he told the girls as they watched the cops round everyone up.

"Fuck that," one of the girls stated. "I'm not going to waste anything."

Two cops walked over to them. One had a camera and smiled when the girls posed for the picture. "Are you Tommy?" one asked.

"Yes, he's Tommy," one of the girls told them. "If I suck your cock, will you let us go?"

"I don't think I want my cock anywhere near either of you," the cop smiled back. "I suggest you both get some clothes on and get to fuck out of here."

He nodded toward Tommy, "It's him we want."

They grilled Tommy for a long time by himself and then took him into the house where he saw Sniff and his girlfriend naked on the bed surrounded by cops. "Tommy here told us everything, Sniff, so you might as well tell us what you did with the coke."

Tommy was amazed; somehow Sniff must have known the police were coming because obviously they hadn't found anything. The cops looked for two days but found nothing. Finally, they gave up and left, but Sniff knew it wouldn't take much to get them back. The next day people started to return; Sniff made it quite plain that the party was over, but no one believed him.

It wasn't long though, and everyone realized there was no more coke floating around. Some people left, but a lot of them decided to find the coke for themselves and began rooting through everything. Sniff seemed to be oblivious to this for a while; he and his girlfriend never left the bed. They just stayed there snorting coke and fucking. It wasn't until he looked out the window and saw some guys tearing the inside out of his cars that he became violent. He came out of the house yelling and firing his pistol at them. People scattered running for their lives; this time they didn't come back. Sniff walked back to Tommy and held the gun to his head. "I thought I told you to look after my stuff."

"Come back inside here, Sniff, and leave Tommy alone. He ain't done nothin'," Tommy heard Sniff's girlfriend say. Sniff uncocked his gun and went inside, leaving Tommy knowing he had to do something.

How the logical mind of a fifteen-year-old works is unpredictable at the best of times, but Tommy came up with the idea that if he hid the bags, then Sniff wouldn't kill him. "He would have to depend on me," Tommy rationalized. He would have control of Sniff's supply, and that way maybe he could wean his brother off the coke. He couldn't do it by himself, so he went to his father for help.

At first, Old Joe was dead against it. He had lived and worked on the island since he'd been born. Some people had done very well back when the drug trade was the main industry on Andros, but all he saw was the devastation it caused to ordinary families including his own. He also understood the predicament Tommy was in and finally agreed to help him.

It was hard work, especially when it had to be done at night, but they managed to get the bags down the hill and into Tommy's boat. Then they traveled around to the east side of the island which consisted of mangrove trees and mud. This was also the side of the island that most of the hurricanes passed by, never giving anything a chance to get established for any length of time. Old Joe knew the hiding place, but even he couldn't find his way in there till daybreak. They waited offshore until he could find the small stream that took them into the mangrove swamps and eventually to a small hummock with a grove of larger-than-normal trees growing on it. There under a bunch of exposed roots, they hid the bags. Old Joe knew no one would find them there, and he hoped he didn't have to find them again either.

Old Joe's main concern now was for Tommy. "We've got to get you off this island," he told Tommy.

"No, I don't think that will work right now. If I run and Sniff finds out the coke's gone, he'll come after you and the family. I kept some of the coke back in the cellar. If I can stash it in the house and then have the cops make another raid, they'll put him away for a while. It's the only way I can see us saving Sniff and keep him from hurting us."

"Okay," Old Joe told him, "but don't hang around there too long. There's no telling when he might fly off the handle."

Tommy's main fear was that Sniff had checked on the cellar while he was away. He was relieved to find him and his girlfriend sleeping on the bed.

Sniff lifted his head, "Where you been, man?"

Tommy told him he'd been working at the hotel.

"You don't have to work," Sniff told him. "You're rich."

Sniff sat up on the bed. "I saw some more people nosing around here. If you see them, bring them in here, and I'll blow them away." He picked up his pistol and waved it around in the air then pointed it at Tommy, "You haven't been stealing from me have you, Tommy?"

"Nope," was Tommy's answer, hoping he sounded convincing. Sniff looked over at his girlfriend sleeping on the bed.

"You been fucking her?"

"Jeez, Sniff, she's your girl," Tommy was starting to panic.

"Okay," he put the gun down and started to play with the girl's tits.

"I think you better hang around the house here for a few days," Sniff told him. "I'm thinking we're going to have company, and I may need your help." His brother turned his attention back to playing with his girlfriend, and Tommy didn't ask what he meant, but he was sure Sniff was on to him.

The two customs agents hardly looked up when they saw the small aircraft land on the runway. They knew who it was; he came in all the time hauling people back and forth to the hotel. The daily flight from Nassau had just come in, and they were busy processing people, so they didn't see the three men get out of the plane and head into the trees at the far end of the runway. The pilot taxied back and parked near the small customs building. He waved to the agents as he passed through.

"Just here to pick up some people at the hotel."

"That's what we figured," one of the agents answered him. "The hotel's moving everyone out because of the hurricane coming our way. We're going to have a busy day."

The three men made their way through the trees and into a waiting car. The driver knew them and where they were going. He took them up the road to Sniff's as far as he could.

"This is as close as I can get," he told them. "The house is just a ways up that path. I'll wait here for you."

"What, you want to miss out on all the fun?" Benito, the big one, laughed as they got out of the car.

"We won't be long. It's too fucking hot out here." All three men were sweating profusely by the time they found their way up to the house.

"Won't be any air con in that dump," Benito mumbled, gesturing to the other guys with his hand to move in around the trees and check out the house. The man who reached the house first looked in the window then waved to Benito. They all met at the doorway.

"Doesn't seem to be anyone outside," one of the men whispered. "What's going on inside?"

The man looking in the window laughed, "He's on the bed fucking with his lady." Benito pulled out his gun and entered the house followed by the other two. They checked out the house; all they saw was a black man and woman lying naked on a bed, neither of them seemed to pay any attention to the men as they approached the bed.

"Damn, it stinks in here."

"Yeah, smells like rotten pussy," one of the men remarked.

Benito was more to the point, "You Sniff?"

The black man on the bed acknowledged them for the first time. "Welcome gentlemen, I've been expecting you. Now if you'll all mind your own business for a little while, I've got something I have to look after." The men looked at each other with amusement as Sniff turned back to his woman. "Look at it," he said to her. "Limp as shit, I been snortin' and strokin', but it just won't get hard."

"Don't worry, baby," the girl told him, "bring it here, I'll fix it for you."

The men watched as Sniff stood up on the bed; the girl began rubbing his balls then stuck his limp dick in her mouth and went to work on him.

One of the men grabbed the front of his pants. "Bring it over here, baby, I got something hard for you to suck on."

It was Benito who got Sniff's attention. "Hey Sniff, how about throwing that bag of coke over here then we can all get hard together?"

The men all laughed but Sniff didn't. "Nobody touches my coke," he growled.

The girl grabbed the machete from the headboard and was on them before they could react. She sliced Benito's arm to the bone then cut a red ribbon across another man's chest before the third man was able to grab her arm as they wrestled over the blade. She continued to attack him, but he managed to slice open her neck before all the blood made the handle so slippery neither of them could hang on to it. Everything stopped for a second as she watched the blood spurt from her neck, and then she attacked them again scratching at them with her fingernails, covering all the men with her blood. Finally, the blood stopped spurting, and she slid down the men to the floor, dead.

The men looked at each other not believing what had just happened, and then they looked up to see Sniff jumping up and down on the bed.

In one hand, he had a big hard-on; in the other, he held a pistol pointed at them.

"Look what you did," he yelled at them. "Now what am I going to stick this into." He pulled the trigger, but there was no bang. He pulled the trigger again, but there was only a click. "What the fuck—is this a toy gun?"

Sniff looked stupidly down the barrel and pulled the trigger; again there was only a click. Benito began looking around desperately for his gun when he heard Sniff scream, "Tommy, you little bastard, you stole all my bullets." Then he heard a loud bang followed by the sound of bone bouncing off the ceiling. Sniff had blown his brains out.

Benito, winced, and turned his head away from the pieces of bone showering down on him. "Where's my gun?" It was his security blanket, and that's what his mind told him he needed right now.

"Here it is," one of the men picked the gun off the floor, wiped it on the bed covers, and handed it to him. Benito was no stranger when it came to inflicting pain, but being on the receiving end was another matter. It had definitely rattled him and was the catalyst in his decision to head for the sack of cocaine beside the bed. One snort brought everything into perspective immediately. One of his men was standing by the bed trying to hold the skin on his chest together with his bare hands.

"Take a shot of this," Benito said as he handed the coke to him. "It'll make you feel better." His other man, except for being scratched and covered with blood, seemed to be all right.

"You'd better do something with that arm," one of the men said.

Benito looked down and saw the blood dripping from his sleeve. He tried to raise his arm, but that only resulted in pain shooting up through his shoulder. "Let's get out of here. I saw some clothes hanging on a line outside. Maybe there's something out there that's clean enough to use on these wounds."

Once outside, the man who wasn't hurt wrapped up their wounds. He made a sling for Benito's arm, while Benito stuck his head in a rain barrel trying to wash some of the blood off his face.

"You take a quick look inside," Benito told his man. "I'll look outside. There must be some more coke and money here somewhere."

That's when the man who went inside found Tommy laying on the floor in a little back room. Tommy had watched the whole thing through a crack in the wall. His mind told him to run but instead, his body just curled up in a ball, frozen with fear. He didn't change position as the man dragged him outside.

"Look what I found," the man showed Benito. They asked Tommy a bunch of questions kicking him a few times for encouragement, but it was obvious the kid was too scared to talk.

"Someone must have heard the shot," Benito said, looking around. "Grab that burlap bag covering the door. We'll put the kid in it and drag him along."

The driver saw the three men coming down the hill dragging a bag behind them. He jumped out yelling, "You guys can't get in my car looking like that."

Benito pointed his gun at the driver's head. "Shut up, and help us get this bag in the trunk." They all got in the car. "As you can see, getting back to the plane is out of the question. You're going to have to hide us until we can find a way off this island."

The driver looked disgusted.

"Here, have a shot of this," Benito told him holding up the sack of cocaine, "It'll make you feel better."

The driver took them to a house where an old woman crudely sewed up their wounds. After a barrage of phone calls, it was decided a boat would pick them up between eleven and one in the morning at the little marina on Buzzard Bay. Then they brought Tommy in and with a little coaxing gleaned whatever he could or would tell them.

“That’s the one good thing you guys did was to bring the boy along. It fits into our plans perfectly, just make sure the first thing you do when you get on the water is get rid of him,” the driver told them.

Henekie made good time after he left Lena. There was only a small chop on the water allowing him to make the crossing between Nassau and Andros in good time. The boat performed beautifully, something Henekie had worried about, but he was a meticulous mechanic and had done a good job of dry docking the boat before he’d left over two years ago.

Every chance he got, he brought fresh fuel back to the old warehouse in the little fishing boat. Now all that planning and hard work was paying off. There was no use going into the marina early. He didn’t want to get trapped in there by the other boat in case he had to wait for the men he was to pick up. He sat out in the bay until his watch said eleven then headed into the marina. He was pretty sure the men would want to get off the island as soon as they could and would be there early. There was only a small yard light at one end of the marina leaving everything dark and casting long shadows more than anything else. It wasn’t until he pulled up to the small dock that he saw the man standing there with a gun pointed at him.

“Julio sent me to pick you up,” he told the man. Immediately, he saw two other men appear on the dock carrying a big bag. The first man seemed impressed with Henekie’s boat. “I thought that cheap bastard Julio would get us some old fishing scow,” he said as they piled in.

Henekie kind of laughed. “This is a cartel boat. Julio probably has no idea yet what this is going to cost him.” Once the men were in the boat and he began navigating his way out of the marina, Henekie saw the state of repairs these men were in. “Jeez, you guys look like you were put through a meat grinder.”

“Yeah,” Benito answered, “they knew we were coming and ambushed us.”

Henekie nodded his head toward the bag, "What's in there?"

"Shark bait!" was growled back at him, giving Henekie the impression the men were in no mood to talk. He started out across the bay keeping his eye out for other boats. "There's rum in the cooler if you're interested?" He didn't have to ask twice; the men each grabbed a bottle and drank it straight. Henekie got out on the main water and relaxed a bit; the rum had loosened up the men and soon turned their attention to the bag. Henekie saw a boy come out of the bag swinging at the men, but he was quickly subdued with a kick to the head.

The men found a mooring rope hanging on the side of the boat and tied one end of it around the boy's ankle. "Hey," one of them shouted up at Henekie, "slow down a bit. We want to do a little trolling." Two of the men were standing at the back of the boat; the other big man with only one good arm was sitting just back and across from him. "Guess this is as good a time as any," Henekie thought to himself as he threw the throttle wide open. He turned and shot both men as they went over the back. He didn't care whether he killed them or not; nature would take of that. He turned his gun toward the big guy only to see a rum bottle coming at his head. Henekie managed to get his arm up in time to deflect the bottle, but Benito was right behind it attacking him. They were eye to eye when Henekie got his arm down and got two shots off as Benito's full weight came crashing down on him pinning him between the two captain's chairs.

Henekie sensed it was three hundred and fifty or more pounds of dead weight that was compressing his chest. The fact that he was pinned between the seats with no way of getting out and the boat going at full speed put him in a real predicament. He was on the verge of blacking out when he felt the boat come to a stop, and then the weight on top of him being transferred from his chest to his legs.

A black face appeared above him. "Are you alive?" it asked.

Henekie sat up gasping for air.

"Are you going to kill me?" The boy looked at him with big eyes. Henekie shook his head.

"If I was going to kill you, I'd have let them do it." There had been a fleeting moment when Henekie had thought of letting the men throw the boy in. After all, what was he going to do with a boy, but he couldn't do it. He was getting soft and in this business that could be lethal or as in this case, it had saved his life. It made some of the rules Ginter had beat into him a little confusing.

"What's your name?"

"Tommy," the boy answered.

"Well, Tommy, let's see if we can get this guy off me." Between the two of them, they were able to move Benito's body off his legs.

Henekie stood up and looked around, "Now if I could figure out where we are."

"That's the light at the end of South Andros," Tommy pointed. "If you're headed for Nassau, it's that way," he gestured with his hand.

"Okay," Henekie sensed he was right. "Now what I want you to do is help me lift this guy over the side of the boat."

When they managed to get the body's head and shoulders over the side, Henekie told him that was good enough for now. He took Tommy up front. "Can you operate a boat?"

Tommy nodded.

"Show me." Henekie watched as Tommy started the motor and smoothly got under way. "All right, this is fast enough for now. Be careful with all this weight to the one side. Now I've got some work to do back here, Tommy. No matter what you hear, I want you to concentrate on driving the boat and not look back, okay?"

Tommy nodded his head. Tommy could hear a hacking sound behind him, but he concentrated on the boat. What a beauty; all he ever dreamed about was owning a boat like this someday. He heard a splash and felt the boat level out. He knew the body had gone in the water.

Henekie came up beside him. "You all right?"

"Nice boat," Tommy answered.

"Okay, you can open it up to about half throttle. When you see the lights of Nassau, let me know. I'll be back here cleaning up."

Tommy was in heaven; here he was skimming across the water on the boat he'd always dreamed about owning, but how could this be real when only an hour ago he was in hell. Religion was part of life on the islands and so was belief in the devil. Tommy was beginning to think he had just met him.

The lights of Nassau town came into view, and Henekie took over the boat. As they got closer, Tommy soon realized they weren't headed into Nassau itself but rather into an area considered by most boaters as quite dangerous. He was even more concerned as Henekie entered a bay at a high rate of speed.

"I don't think you should go in there," Tommy told him. "There are some really bad reefs and rocks in there just under the water."

"You seem to know this water pretty well," Henekie observed.

"My brother was one of the best boatmen around, but he stayed out of there. They call it Devil's Bay."

Henekie didn't answer, seemingly concentrating on steering the boat. Tommy clenched his teeth waiting for the sound of the bottom being torn out of the boat. Instead Henekie seemed able to zigzag his way through the maze of rocks until suddenly they were right in front of a warehouse that Tommy had sometimes caught a glimpse of when he and his brother had passed by the bay. To his amazement, they continued right in under the structure. A wall came down leaving them in what looked like a swimming pool. The water in the pool began to drop, and they went down with it, and then they stopped going down. Another huge wall on the inside opened up revealing a cavelike room with a dock and what looked like a place to live in. Henekie docked the boat while the wall behind them closed. Tommy could hear the sound of water bubbling on the other side of it. Henekie took the cooler from the boat and set it in front of a door.

"Okay Tommy, I have to leave you for a while. Make yourself something to eat. There's lots of food in the cupboard over there. Then get some sleep. You have to be dead on your feet. If I'm not back by the time you wake up, I want the boat cleaned to perfection." He pointed to another cupboard. "You'll find everything you need in there. Any questions?"

Tommy was pretty direct in what he thought. "You are the devil, aren't you? And my brother was right, this is where you live."

"Some people may well call me the devil," Henekie told him. "But we are not in heaven or hell. We're right here on earth, and you have survived what you've just been through." Henekie smiled, "Don't worry, Tommy, no one's going to hurt you here. We'll talk about it tomorrow." Henekie picked up the cooler and disappeared through a door.

Tommy found his new friend exciting yet terrifying. He ate a little bit and then laid down on the bed thinking of his brother; he cried himself to sleep.

Henekie climbed the long steep set of steps leading up from the old warehouse to the tunnel connecting the main house to the guesthouse, better defined now as Lena's house and Julio's house, Henekie thought. He checked out Julio's house to make sure no one was there and then leaving the cooler on the kitchen table, he crossed the lawn to Lena's garage.

He found Julio snoring on top of Lena's car. There were signs of dried blood around his asshole. Lena was asleep on a chair in one corner; she jumped up when he came in.

"Well, at least you didn't kill him."

Lena walked over to where Henekie stood. "No, and I didn't find out much about what his brother is up to either." Lena told him. "I did get out of him where he hid his money. There's about two hundred thousand in that paper bag over there. I'm sure you can use that."

Henekie nodded, "Thanks, Lena."

"I guess that's about all he'll ever see of the millions he made selling the coke," Lena told him. "I'm sure his friends thought they were being generous giving him that much, and now you're taking that on him. You are such a nasty man, Henekie."

"Mere pocket money to a high roller like Julio," Henekie answered, cutting the ties and slapping Julio to wake him up. He sat up and looked at them.

"Are you going to kill me?"

"We're going over to your place and talk to your brother. Guess it will depend on him," Henekie said.

"Don't worry, he'll pay you whatever you want," Julio answered.

Henekie pushed him out the door. "You're walking a little funny, Julio, kind of like you got butt fucked last night," Henekie said as they entered Julio's place.

"Nobody does that to me and gets away with it, Jon will see to that."

"Okay, I dare you to tell him what she did to you," Henekie handed him the phone.

Jon Smyskin's voice came over the speakerphone, "Damn, Julio, I thought you told me you laid off that stuff. Do you have any idea what time it is here?"

"There's a man here who wants to kill me, Jon," Julio blubbered.

"Tell him to go ahead so I can get some sleep."

"I'd be careful what you wish for," Henekie interjected.

"Who's that?" Jon suddenly sounded interested.

"That's the man who wants to kill me," Julio told him.

"Where's Benito?" Jon had handpicked Benito to take care of Julio.

He was as tough as they came and totally loyal; something was very wrong here.

"I sent him to take care of some business, when he gets back, he'll gut this fuck, but until then I need your help," Julio pleaded.

"Okay, what is it you want?" Jon asked.

"I want you to leave Lena alone."

"Okay, that's not a problem," Jon answered.

"I don't think you understand. It is a problem, a big problem for you if you don't leave her alone." Henekie told him. "You see, I work for a company that used to work for your father. We do odd jobs: put out fires, things like that. No one's immune to us, not even you. If you don't believe me, ask the Referee. He'll confirm what I say is true."

"Are you threatening me?" Jon sounded perturbed.

"I don't threaten." Henekie took Julio by the hair and led him over to the table with the cooler on it. He opened the lid and held Julio's head over it.

"It's Benito, Jon," he screamed, "It's his head. They cut off his head."

"That's what will happen to you if you ever touch Lena again, you little prick," Henekie kicked him in the nuts then walked away leaving Julio squirming on the floor.

"I don't threaten, Jon. What Julio just told you is proof of that. Lena's building a fence right down the middle of this property. Your people stay on their own side of the fence, Lena stays on hers, and from now on she'll supply her own security." With that, Henekie hung up the phone.

They left Julio to his misery and walked back to Lena's house just as the sun came up, spreading its morning heat.

"That's a great idea dividing the property with a fence," Lena told him.

"I want you to start on that--- now," Henekie answered, "and get yourself some security--- now."

"I like it when you get bossy, Henekie. Why don't you come to work for me so you can tell me what to do all the time?"

"That wouldn't work, Lena. We're too good of friends for that, and you know very well that sooner or later someone like Sir Harry would come nosing around wondering who I am."

"Then why are you going out of your way to protect me? There has to be something in it for you, but I'll be damned If I can figure out what it is."

"I need you to be where you are, Lena," replied Henekie. "I introduced you to El Presidente because I needed someone close to him that could tell me what he was thinking. I bet all my cards on him and lost everything except for one thing. That one thing is you. Quinn saw the potential in you I guess, and turned you from bouncing from man to man, into men and their money bouncing off you. You took a little seed money off El Presidente and turned it into a bloody fortune, but you still think you can stroke a man's cock and keep him satisfied. From now on, you're going to have to squeeze some balls."

They walked into the kitchen, and Henekie poured a cup of coffee. To his amazement, Lena took a frying pan out of a cupboard and began cooking some eggs. "You told me to be honest with the Smyskins. I'm making them lots of money which seemed to stroke them the right way when they needed it. I don't think they need their balls squeezed. I think it's a case of head fuck," Lena lamented.

Henekie moved up beside her and began making some toast.

"So you think I'm a good friend," Henekie told her. "El Presidente was fighting for his life when I told him you would be perfect to run things here in the Bahamas. He agreed, thinking it would be a real slap in the face to the people who were trying to get rid of him here, to have to take orders from a woman. He signed your little agreement because he wanted you to fall in bed with him when he got back and had absolutely no intention of honoring the agreement. He'd have done much the same as Julio did to you except he always went one step farther. He'd have gotten you pregnant. It was an obsession with him, especially any woman who thought she might have some standing or authority. Once you began to show, everyone would know you were El Presidente's woman, and you would have no trouble with anyone. You would however be a figurehead and expendable at any time he chose."

Henekie put some eggs and toast on a plate and sat down at the table. "I knew all this before I brought you here, but as I told you, I needed someone on the inside."

Lena sat down across from him and began to eat. "But El Presidente didn't come back. Good for me, but not so good for you," she said between mouthfuls.

"Temporarily, but you see, you did have El Presidente's baby. It's in the form of a company you nurtured and conceived. It was the seed money of Jon's father that started it. As far as Jon's concerned, it belongs to his family, and his honor is on the line until he shows that you're his woman and he's the boss."

"Is he so stupid and vain that he thinks he can just walk in and take over my baby?" Lena stabbed at her eggs.

"You see, he knows this is your baby and no matter what, you can't let it go," Henekie replied. "You're not the only one who can run this company. He'll keep you around somewhere until he can wean the company off you. When you realize your baby doesn't need you anymore, you'll turn to drugs or alcohol and eventually kill yourself. That's what happened to El Presidente's other women."

"That's a wonderful prognosis, but I'm not one of El Presidente's other women," Lena told him.

Henekie took his and Lena's plate to the sink and began washing them. "If I were you, I'd walk out of here right now with the clothes on your back and go to Dubai. You have good security there. We've bought some time, but I don't know how much. Whatever you do, Lena, do it quick."

Henekie could see by the look on her face that his words were falling on deaf ears.

"Come with me," she told him. "I want to show you my baby." Lena led him into where he remembered the computer to be. To his astonishment, instead of a machine that took up the entire wall, there were three smaller computer screens, and the room was full of metal boxes with wires running everywhere.

"Quite a change since the last time you were here," Lena said proudly. "It pretty well runs itself now. I still have to make some decisions and tweak it once in a while, but nothing I can't handle. Quinn and I customized and built the whole system ourselves. There's no other baby in the world like this one."

She looked at Henekie, "I'm not leaving it, but I can corrupt the program enough so that no one can use it."

"You die, it dies, an accessory after the fact, a lot of good that does you when you're dead," Henekie told her.

"Then I guess I'll have to squeeze your balls until you come to work for me," Lena told him.

"You're already squeezing my balls, Lena. I have to keep you alive so I can steal your money." Henekie was dead serious, but Lena thought he was joking with her.

"You don't have to steal my money, Henekie. I can pay you more than you will ever need."

She turned away, "I'm going to bed, make yourself at home."

Henekie wasn't sure what to make of this new machine. Would it allow them to get into Lena's accounts, this was the question. It was on her desk that he found the book. He remembered what Krugman had told him. If you can find the codes, you'll make our lives much easier. He looked in the book and instinctively knew what was in there. "The man saved my life," he thought, "I've got to do this." He wrote down the codes then borrowed Lena's car and drove down to his shop.There he faxed all the information to Krugman's office. It was already late afternoon in Munich; Henekie thought they might have left for the day.

The phone call he received told him differently. "These codes should make our job quick and simple," he told Henekie. "Book a room for us at the Atlantis. We'll be arriving at the airport at ten tomorrow morning. Pick us up."

You know there's a hurricane headed our way," Henekie warned him.

"No, don't worry. They say that's going south into Mexico somewhere."

Henekie did as he was told, meeting Krugman and a woman he introduced as Karla at the airport. "Look, I want you to take Karla to the hotel. I have to fly to the Caymans and set up an account there. My banker in Zurich says it's best to put a transaction of this size through there first. You and Karla can set things up here. I'll be back day after tomorrow. Isn't this exciting?"

Somehow that wasn't Henekie's sentiment at all. He took Karla by the shop to show her where they would be working, but she wasn't the least bit interested.

"Take me to the hotel," she told him, "and maybe tonight you could show me around town," she said, looking him up and down.

"I'm sorry, but I'm not into that," he told her.

She pouted, "At least you could drop me off at one of your hot spots." That evening he did as she asked, dropping her off at Johnny Canoe's. "I'll find my own way home," she told him.

What he didn't know was that it took her ten minutes to find Julio, fifteen minutes to get him on the dance floor, and an hour later she was getting fucked. Karla didn't show up at the hotel at all that night or the next day. Then the hurricane turned farther north flooding Nassau, cutting off all communications and closing the airport.

As if this wasn't bad enough, just before the storm hit, Henekie tried to take Lena's car back, only to find two men dressed in military uniforms guarding the gate. He tried to ask questions, but they sent him on his way without answering them. He tried to stay positive; he had the codes, a nice car to drive, some money, and he hadn't got caught up in whatever was going down at Lena's. Henekie managed to rent a small fishing boat and get to the warehouse where Tommy and he waited out the storm.

# Twenty-Nine

JULY GREEN SAT in the new sunroom they'd just built onto the side of the main hotel. The sun had been shining a minute ago, but now it had begun to rain, probably a band of cloud from the hurricane headed their way, she surmised. She watched as Bob ran for cover; he'd been surprised by the suddenness of the shower too. She was enjoying the fact it was so nice and quiet; all the guests had been sent home early. There were no taking chances on Andros. The terrain was very low; a direct hit could wipe it out. The weather forecast was now swinging the hurricane closer to them, but they felt they had everything battened down and were prepared to ride out the storm.

She saw Old Joe coming in the door; she was perturbed with him for not showing up to work today. Old Joe, as everyone called him, came with the hotel. At first, Bob was going to fire him until it became apparent that Joe knew where everything was and how it worked. The added bonus was his repertoire with the guests. His stories were legendary, whether fact or bullshit, people loved to hear them. She was about to scold him, but the look on his face changed her mind.

"Joe, what's the matter?"

"They killed my boy, Mrs. Green, they killed my boy."

July took Joe's arm, "Oh no, Joe, what happened?" Bob heard the conversation and came up beside them.

"They killed Sniff," Joe sobbed. "He stole some white powder from the drug lords. They wanted it back so they killed him." Joe picked his head up, "I know we talked about this before, Mrs. Green. We said this could happen, but it's my fault because Tommy and I hid the shit."

It was a well-known fact that Sniff had flooded the island with cocaine causing problems everywhere. The police couldn't seem to catch him at it, so it was assumed he was just a distributor, but the rumors persisted that he had stumbled on to an aborted drop and had stolen whole canvas bags of the stuff.

"Sniff gave his soul to the white powder. If the drug people didn't kill him, the drugs would have. I can live with that." Joe began to cry again, "But they took Tommy. They know I hid the drugs," he sobbed. "They told me if I didn't give the drugs back, they'd kill Tommy and then come after me and you, Mr. Green."

Bob and July looked at each other. "Why us?" They both asked at the same time.

"I don't know, Mr. Green, that's just what the voice told me over the phone."

July sat down, "What the hell is it about the white powder, Joe? It's the same as an addiction. You don't use the stuff, but it follows you around, never letting go until it consumes you."

"I guess you're right, Mrs. Green. It's been around me all my life. It just keeps picking away at me, first my daughter, now my boys, and in the end my family."

July sat down, "Joe, you've got to tell whoever it was on the phone we have nothing to do with this," she said forcefully.

"I know everyone on this island, Mrs. Green, and that voice sounded like one of the Gator's."

"You think the Gators are mixed up in this?" Bob interjected.

"There ain't nothin on this island they aren't mixed up in, but phonin' them is just goin' to get you more mixed up," Joe told them. "I lost a daughter and now a son, I can't lose no more. I got to gets them their drugs."

Bob and July knew the story well, how Joe had lost his daughter. It was before they had come to the island. Apparently, there were two brothers who were drug runners on the island. They each had an airplane, and one day, they took some of the local girls for a ride. They started playing chicken, clipped wings, and crashed into the sea. Joe's daughter was one of the girls. They never found the bodies; the funeral was held in small boats on the water above where the planes were thought to have gone down. Joe had told them one time that he always remembered his little boy Tommy sitting beside him in the boat saying he would never use the white powder.

"Maybe he hadn't used the white powder, but he had stolen it and probably now it had taken him," July thought to herself.

"So do you think the Gators are responsible for Sniff's death?" Bob quizzed.

Joe looked very uncomfortable. "I had to go up to the house to identify Sniff's body. There's no one on this island capable of doin' what I saw there, Mr. Green. That was a message from the cartel itself not to mess with them."

"Well, I guess you'd better take the drugs back and explain we weren't involved," Bob told Joe.

"Mr. Green, that's what I intend to do. But there's three canvas bags at least five feet long, two of them full. I can't handle them by myself."

Bob whistled. "I would guess that's worth a lot of money."

"Yes," Joe answered. "I don't know how much, a million for sure. You're the only man I trust on this island to help me get those drugs,

Mr. Green. Even my own boys wouldn't be able to resist taking some of it, and then we'd start the cycle all over again."

July was adamant, "He's not going with you, Joe. If he does, he can forget about coming back here."

"I'm sorry, Mrs. Green, you and Mr. Green mean the world to me. I never thought you'd make a go of this hotel and neither did anyone else on this island. Now you're the biggest employer here next to the government. You've also made some powerful enemies. I think they're the ones who want you involved in this."

"Okay, Joe. Let's not let that happen. After the storm, there's no reason you can't go unload the bags, and arrange to trade it for Tommy," Bob told him.

"If you won't help me, Mr. Green, that's what I intend to do. The storm is going to take the same path most of them take, hitting South Andros, then pass by the east side of our island. That means the mangrove swamps where I hid the bags are going to flood. I hid the bags on a high piece of ground. It's all mud, but I'll get what I can before I have to get out."

Joe turned to go, but Bob stopped him, "Is there any way you can get there by land?"

Bob walked over to a map of the old farm he had hung on the wall. "The farmland here"—he pointed to an area on the map—"runs down almost to the mangrove swamps."

"Any idea how far from there you hid the bags?"

"Somewhere in here." Joe showed him. "I'd say about two miles from where the farmland starts. It's all mud and water, Mr. Green. Besides, I ain't never come in from that side. I be lost and never find my way out."

"Okay, so it has to be by boat. How much time do you think we have before the hurricane hits?" Bob wanted to know.

"Hard to know exactly. The first rain bands of clouds are just starting.

I'd say we have eight hours or more before we get the big winds," Joe told him.

"How long to get the stuff out and put somewhere safe?"

Old Joe's eyes lit up; he knew Bob was coming with him. "We might be quicker if we took one of your boats. They're bigger."

"Okay, Joe, there's one I left on the trailer. Go hook your truck up to it while I get ready." Joe knew Bob meant he needed time to make this right with his wife.

July was extremely angry. "Are you ready to throw everything away that we've built here, Bob? This is my home."

"July, the bottom line here is I can't have that boy on my conscience."

"Shit, Bob, you know that boy's probably already dead. What about our family? What's going to happen to us if you get mixed up in this?"

"Somebody has got us mixed up in this already, July. I want you to find every document of every transaction we've ever had with Gator, and I want you to hide them." Bob went into the office and came back with a pistol; he checked it for bullets and stuck it in his belt. "I want you to go and stay with one of your friends." Bob stopped; he could see July had no intention of leaving her home.

"All right then, you know there's a rifle in the closet, keep it close. I don't think anyone will come sneaking around before the storm, but don't trust anyone if they do." Bob took his rain jacket and headed for the door. He stopped and smiled, "If I don't get back before the storm hits, maybe when it's safe, you could take a ride down the old logging road, you know the one that goes by Charlie's Blue Hole. We might have to come out that way." Tears came to her eyes as she watched him go out and jump in Joe's truck.

Bob and Joe were good boatmen; it didn't take them long to launch the boat and head down toward the mangrove swamps. It was easy to see why no one lived on this side of the island. Hurricane Alley, some called it. They followed up the channel of water separating Andros and Cuba causing a lot of damage every few years. The farm had lost crops on the land closest to the swamps, but it was good land down there and well worth the risk.

Joe pointed toward the swamps; Bob followed his direction finding the mouth of a small stream. Once in the swamps, the stream became wider but branched off in many directions. Bob had no way of knowing how Joe navigated his way through the twists and turns, but once he saw the island covered with trees other than mangroves, he was pretty sure this was their destination.

Joe had been right; they had to pull the boat through knee-deep mud to get it close to the island. Then they slipped and slid up to where the roots of a tree were exposed. To make matters worse, it started to pour as Joe dug under the roots to expose the bags. They slid the bags down to the boat and managed to load them. The rain stopped, and the sun came out making for good going; they'd be home in good time before the wind picked up.

It was just as they came to the mouth of the stream that Bob saw the helicopters. They were flying out over open water, one about a quarter of a mile behind the other. He knew immediately what they were looking for and quickly turned the boat around back into the stream hoping they hadn't seen him. He parked the boat in under a tree that hung out over the water and waited. They didn't have to wait long. They could hear the choppers getting closer, but it wasn't until Bob saw the shadow of the chopper hovering right over them that he knew they'd been spotted.

"Go, go," Joe yelled. "Head for where we got the bags. It's the only place with enough trees to hide us."

Bob opened up the boat; Joe stood beside him hanging on to the windshield, pointing the way through the maze of waterways and mangrove trees. Bob was late turning into a channel, and they almost got hung up in the mud. As they sped up again, he caught out of the corner of his eye two plumes of water just off to their left, but it didn't register what might have caused them. He saw the high piece of ground straight ahead of them and rammed the boat into the mud as far as it would go. They scrambled over the front of the boat and in under the trees.

Looking up, they could no longer see the choppers, but they could hear them. There was the sound of something bouncing around in the tree branches, and then before their eyes the boat leapt into the air, pieces flying everywhere.

Joe jumped into the hole where the bags had been, and Bob rolled in beside him. They covered their heads as the grenades bounced through the trees then exploded covering them with mud. Then as quickly as it started, it stopped, and they could hear the choppers fading away.

Bob got up and climbed out of the hole. He saw a lump of mud sit up beside him.

"Kind of fucked up our boat, didn't they?" Bob said.

"Kind of fucked us up too." Joe didn't swear very often telling Bob this was a bad situation. It started raining again, and for the first time they could hear the wind in the treetops.

"Lucky for us, I guess the rain chased the choppers away," Bob lamented.

"No need for them to stay," Joe answered. "If they didn't get us, they know the storm will."

"Sorry Joe, I guess I should have pulled out onto open water and gave ourselves up."

"No, Mr. Green. There was no time to process us before the storm. They would have made sure we were who they were looking for and then dropped a grenade on us. That's a risk drug runners take if they get caught, the police make an example of them."

Bob hadn't thought of himself as a drug runner but obviously the police did.

"I don't want to just sit here, Joe. I think we should start walking."

"Where you gonna go, Mr. Green? This is a mangrove swamp. Soon it will start raining hard enough that we can't see where we are. This is the highest piece of ground around here. We'll just have to hope the water doesn't get this high."

Bob walked out into the water; Joe was right, the mud was up to his knees. He washed the mud off his face; it was then he noticed the three canvas bags floating in the water.

"Look at that shit, Joe, it won't leave us alone."

It didn't stop raining; now the sky had turned gray, and the wind was getting a lot stronger. Bob needed something to do, so he began emptying the bags. "Never had much in my life," he thought, "maybe someday I can tell the kids how I threw away millions, but right now the bags are worth more to me than what's in them."

Joe seemed kind of depressed and stayed on high ground sitting up against a tree. Bob brought him one of the bags. "Put this over you, it will help keep off the rain."

As night set in the wind began to bend the trees, and the rain was coming in sideways. At first they could lie in under the tree roots, but as the hollow filled with water, they were forced farther and farther out into the open.

Bob and Joe had talked about their options including climbing the trees if the water got too high. Somewhere along the line, Bob knew this would be impossible as the wind snapped the tops of the trees off. The wind wasn't their only problem. The water was surging up around them.

Joe turned his head and yelled in Bob's ear, "I know you have a pistol, Mr. Green. Please shoot me I can't take any more of this."

Bob knew he couldn't do it; besides, he wasn't quite ready to give up just yet. They were already lying in the bags for protection.

He yelled in Joe's ear, "I'm going to close the zipper on your bag, Joe.

I'll leave a small hole for air. I'm tying us together. If these bags will float that shit, they should float us, if not, they'll make good coffins."

Joe didn't argue; he put his head down inside the bag, and Bob zipped it up. Bob slid down, finding the lashings, he tied the bags together then lay back in his own bag and pulled the zipper shut just as the wind pushed them off the little bit of land left and into the water. Bob was elated the bags were floating, maybe they could beat this yet. Then a wall of water from the main storm surge hit them. Bob knew they were under water; he rolled over and over, and he was having trouble breathing. Then the bag seemed to pop up out of the water, and he had the sensation of moving very fast then they hit something very hard; after that, he couldn't remember anything.

July had watched Bob walk out the door. He pissed her off, but she knew his mind was made up; there was no use arguing with him. She made her way into the office and began making sure she had all the documents pertaining to their dealings with Gator. The phone startled her, and she picked it up.

"Hello," she answered.

"Is Mr. Green in?" a voice said.

"No," she answered. "This is Mrs. Green, may I help you?"

"Yes, tell him he has something that belongs to us, and we expect him to deliver it to us here in Nassau."

"What does he have that belongs to you?" she asked into a dead phone. July was immediately shaken; the first thing she did was to get the rifle out of the closet and kept it close to her as she finished looking for documents. The lawyers in Nassau had copies, but things had a way of getting lost, and Bob was right, there was no use taking chances. Once she was satisfied that she had all the documents, she went outside and inspected the property. As far as she could see, everything seemed in order. It began to rain again, and this time it didn't let up. July looked at her watch; five hours had passed and still no sign of the men. By nightfall, it was raining so hard she couldn't see anything except into the courtyard where the trees were bent in half and the pool had overflowed. Sometime during the night, she fell asleep.

Maybe it was the quiet that woke her up. There was no wind or rain, streaks of red poked through the clouds telling her daylight wasn't far away. She checked the bedroom to see if Bob had snuck in not wanting to wake her up, but there was no one there. July busied herself making coffee and sandwiches and trying to think of anything else she might need. As soon as there was enough light, she went out to get the jeep. The top was half torn off, and the inside was full of water. She tore off the rest of the top and bailed out most of the water. The most important thing was that it started. July drove up to their living quarters and picked up what she thought she needed. Having no top on the jeep made keeping things dry a bit of a problem, but most everything fit in the toolbox. She threw on some rain gear and put a plastic bag over the rifle. As she was walking out the door, she saw Bob's baseball cap hanging on a peg. July put it on her head. "Bet you wish you'd taken this with you," she thought as she got in the jeep putting the rifle on the seat beside her and took off.

It was light enough to see that other than a lot of tree branches strewn around, this had been mostly a rain event. The main highway presented no problems at all; it wasn't until she came to the turnoff to the farm that an obstacle appeared. A huge pool of water had obliterated the farm road entirely. She could see where it started again on the other side of the pool, so aiming the jeep for that she edged into the water. Somewhere about halfway through, she felt her feet getting wet and realized the water was running over the floor of the jeep. Then just as she came out on the other side, the motor began to sputter. July revved the motor over a few times until it seemed to clear itself and continued on.

She made her way along the road trusting the jeep more and more as it seemed to make its way through and over almost anything. Finally, she made it to the old farmyard. It was a high piece of ground and had escaped the flooding. July pulled up close to where her house had overlooked the lake. She couldn't believe her eyes; there were no edges to the lake, it was just one sea of water that went on forever.

For the first time, July faced reality. No one could survive this. A squall came in, the rain mixing with her tears as if trying to blind her from reality. She sat there lost in thought until the sun broke through the clouds chasing the rain away. July sat straight up; she couldn't believe what her eyes told her. In the short time she'd been sitting there, the water had receded, the lake had edges again, and the tops of trees and high ground were poking up everywhere. "The tide is going out," she thought.

She wasn't too sure whether she could get down the road where Bob told her to meet him. The going was good until she got by Charlie's Blue Hole. The terrain dropped off down into rich black soil built up by the mangrove swamps over the centuries. This had been the best producing ground on the farm but very susceptible to flooding and hurricanes as it was now. As soon as the farm had stopped functioning, locals began producing vegetables on plots down here. Some years they did quite well. She bought a lot of the produce for the hotel, but as she could see that wouldn't be happening this year. This road, like many of the back roads on the island, had been built by a logging company who years ago had virtually logged all the trees off the island.

The only good thing that they left were the roads built of hard coral that didn't wash away. It was here that she saw the total devastation; in fact, the only thing she recognized was the road. The ditch was littered with broken buildings and farm machinery. There was no sign of the vegetable crops, instead there was only mud and water turning it back into the swamp it had originally been. July picked her way through the debris and mud on the road, eventually making her way onto higher ground that held the trees the logging company had been after. Here they had built a big turnabout for the trucks, and July knew this was as far as she could go.

Her father had told her a story about how he and a friend had gone hunting. They built a camp and in the morning decided to hunt in different directions. When her father came back to camp that evening, his partner didn't show up. He was pretty sure his friend was lost, so he shot twice into the air; soon he heard an answering shot, and after that was able to guide his friend back to camp with the sound of his shots. This was July's plan. She lifted the rifle and aimed at the sky then lowered it. What if there was no answer? She had to know; she raised the rifle and fired three times into the air. Then she held her breath and waited.

It was a nightmare he couldn't wake up from; no matter how hard he squirmed and fought, it was like he was under the blankets and couldn't find his way out. There was no air, panic set in then he heard the sound of a zipper, and fresh air hit his face. "Funny," he thought, "I'm looking at a man upside down."

"Is that you, Joe?" he gasped.

"Yas, sir, I'm sorry but I couldn't open your bag because you was layin' so still. I thought you was dead."

Bob crawled out of the bag and realized one end of the bag was hooked in a tree four feet off the ground.

"Any idea where we are, Joe?" he asked.

"If this is heaven, then it sure looks a lot like Andros," was Joe's reply. "The good thing is we was washed up out of the swamps, but where we ended I don't know," he added.

All at once Bob went down on his hands and knees and began throwing up anything that was left in his stomach.

"You're full of salt water," Joe told him. "I did the same thing to get rid of it. Here, it rained a few minutes ago. I made a bowl in the bottom of this bag. When you think you can hold it down, drink some freshwater, but don't drink from the ground. It's too salty."

Bob crawled over to the bag and took a drink; slowly, he began to feel better. It was when he stood up that he saw the pained look on Joe's face. "What's the matter, Joe, you hurt?"

"I's messed up, Mr. Green. My arm's broke, and I'm havin' trouble breathin'. Think I got some broken ribs."

"Think you can walk?" Bob asked.

"Gots to, ain't gonna survive here when that sun comes out with no water. I'm thinkin' the old farm's over that way," Joe pointed with his good arm. "If I can just put my hand on your shoulder maybe we can make it."

They hadn't gone far when Bob saw a fair-sized shark flopping around in a pool of water. "You and I have the same problem?" he thought. "We survived the storm, but now what?"

A rain squall came splashing down on them; both stood there with mouths open catching what they could. Bob took his shoes off, and they collected some more before the rain quit. Right behind the rain cloud was the sun; now the humidity really set in. Bob and Joe were leaning against a tree catching their breath when they heard the shots.

"That's coming from about where I think the farm should be," Joe commented. "Must be in trouble, no way anyone could make it in there."

Bob pulled his pistol out of his belt and fired off two shots. There were two shots in return.

"That crazy woman's going to get herself killed one of these times looking after me," Bob said to himself as much as to Joe.

"Well, Joe, those shots didn't sound all that far away. Think we can make it?"

"You wouldn't shoot me back in the swamps, Mr. Green. I guess you're stuck with me now."

July was elated; she heard two distinct pops. She was so excited; her first return shot took out the windshield on the jeep. She got the second shot up in the air and heard a "pop" in return. She put her hand over her mouth and looked at the windshield. "What's he going to say about that?" she thought and then came to her senses. Who in the fuck cares; they were alive, nothing else mattered. Her first intuition was to go into the trees after them, but sanity prevailed. "That would only get us all lost," she thought. She decided she'd wait fifteen minutes before shooting again, but it was hard to stand around and wait. She took off Bob's hat, threw it on the ground, and jumped up and down on it.

"You stupid son of a bitch. Why do you always get yourself in so much trouble?" But then as if forgiving him, she put the cap back on her head. A good hour disappeared before she saw them coming through the trees.

The chest-deep water in the ditch hardly slowed her down as she rushed to meet the two men. It didn't bother her that they were struggling just to get their breath; she smothered them with kisses anyway.

"Easy on Joe," Bob gasped, "his arm is broken, and he's got some broken ribs."

July took Joe's arm that seemed to be stuck around Bob's shoulders and put it around her own. He was deadweight on her as she carried him down into the water-filled ditch, and then literally dragged him up onto the road. She heard a splash behind her and looked back. Bob had tried to follow her; he was floundering in the water. July had no choice; she told Joe to brace himself and left him standing on the road as she went back and grabbed Bob, throwing him up onto the side of the ditch.

"Don't you die on me now," she yelled at him. Then she went back to Joe, guiding him to the jeep and easing him down on the seat. July made sure he had water and a sandwich before she took the same back to Bob and sat down beside him on the edge of the ditch.

Bob was too tired to move; he just laid there struggling to catch his breath. He took the water and then reached over and put his hand in hers. "That was a stupid thing for me to do, wasn't it, July?"

There were tears in July's eyes. "Yes, I keep telling you, you are one stupid son of a bitch."

"No, that's not what I mean," Bob gasped between breaths. "I should have known you'd risk your life coming here to look for me."

"See, there you go again worrying about everyone but yourself. That's what pisses me off. I saw the water, Bob. How in hell did you get out of there alive?"

Bob didn't answer; he wasn't sure himself. The water and food soon revived him; he and July had started to head over to the jeep when they heard the whoop, whoop of helicopter blades.

# THIRTY

HORATIO NORTON LEFT the house before daybreak. He knew it bugged the shit out of Novak and his driver/bodyguard that he sometimes took off on his own, but he was the police chief and in the end, he could do what he wanted. This morning he had good reason, he thought. Nassau had basically missed the brunt of the hurricane, but his home island of Andros was much closer to the storm's path, and he wanted to have a firsthand look for himself. The main airport had been shut down overnight, so there was none of the usual hustle and bustle around as he entered the area where the Drug Enforcement Agency kept their helicopters. He went into the office and began looking at yesterday's reports. The one on top was of particular interest.

Norton picked up the phone and called the duty officer. "What do you know about the operation over on Andros yesterday afternoon?"

The officer told him he didn't know much. "A reliable informer told our men there was somebody making a big drug run using the hurricane as a cover. The guys stayed out longer than normal and sure enough, caught the drug runners in the act. They chased them into the swamp and then had to leave, but they were pretty sure they got the boat, so there's no way they survived the hurricane. They got in pretty late. I expect a full report later this morning," the officer reported.

"Is there a chopper available this morning?" Horatio asked.

"The standby's fueled and ready to go. The pilot's sitting here beside me," the officer told him.

"Okay, tell him I want to take a look and see how much damage there is over on Andros."

It took only thirty minutes of airtime to be over North Andros. The sky was still cloud covered but getting brighter all the time. Horatio was happy to see little damage on the western side of the island where the majority of the population resided. Other than a lot of water lying around, they appeared to have dodged a bullet.

He then asked the pilot to take a run up the east side of the island. Here it was a different story. That was why very few people lived along this side, and those who did generally knew enough to get out when the hurricanes came by. The land on this side was just above sea level, even a good blow could flood this ground. One of Horatio's sons farmed down next to the mangrove swamps; it was plain to see there'd be no income for him this year. It was about this time that the pilot pointed down at something they hadn't expected to see.

"Drop down and let's see if we know who those people are," Horatio told him.

The pilot did as he was told, cautiously hovering over what appeared to be three people around a jeep. "What the hell would anyone be doing out here in this mess? They look to be okay," the pilot sounded puzzled.

"That's what I'd like to know?" Horatio answered.

"Can you land?" was his next question.

"I've landed here before. The ground's good on that old turnabout where the jeep is," the pilot told him. "I'm not landing though, unless you know who these people are."

"Yeah, it's all right. They're friends, and I suspect they're in trouble."

The pilot was no stranger to landing on rough terrain. He skillfully settled the chopper down and then slowed the rotors before letting Horatio out. "Novak's on the radio," the pilot yelled at him, "wants to know where you are."

"Tell him I'm home," Horatio yelled back.

The pilot started to laugh. "He says to make sure you lock the door." Horatio laughed too; Novak knew very well he was on Andros, but at least he was being good about it.

Horatio's face changed to a very somber look as he approached his old friends. He was the last person Bob and July expected to see get out of the chopper. They didn't quite know what to say. It was old Joe that broke the ice, "Jeez, Horatio you're getting fatter every time I see you." Everyone broke out laughing including Horatio.

"You don't look so good yourself, Joe." Horatio's face grew somber again; he stood in front of them and clasped his hands behind his back. "I had a report that my officers chased some drug runners back into the swamps near here yesterday afternoon. Now that I find you here, that's a bit of a coincidence, don't you think? It would probably be a good idea if you told me the whole story about why you're here, and I don't want to hear any bullshit."

Bob felt like a little kid being scolded, but he also knew he was in trouble, and Horatio was one of the few people who could help them out. Bob told him the whole story. "That's basically what happened," Bob told him. "We're in a lot of trouble, aren't we?"

Horatio paced back and forth in front of them. "Your best option is you get in the helicopter with me, and I take you to where you can get out of the Bahamas. There's no one who will believe you survived the hurricane in the swamps. July can sell the hotel and then come and join you somewhere."

"He be right, Mr. Green," Joe nodded in agreement.

"Thank you, Joe, but what about Tommy?" It was July who asked the question.

"I got you in enough trouble, Mrs. Green, there ain't no drugs left anyway. I guess that's all over."

"They don't know that, Joe," Bob told him. "If we're alive, why can't there still be drugs?"

Horatio had stopped pacing. "You know, Novak's been trying to set something up, and this just might be the thing. The cartel sent one of their family members in here to look after things. He's a real hophead and fucks things up all the time. Novak's been waiting to nail him, this might be his chance."

"You think this guy has Tommy?" Bob asked.

"If he doesn't, he knows where he is, dead or alive."

Bob looked at July; she nodded her head. "Let's go see Novak."

First things first," Bob began lifting Joe out of the jeep. "Joe's in bad shape. He needs to get to a hospital."

"Okay, I'll take him in the chopper and drop him off, and then I'll meet you and July back at the hotel." Once they were in the air, Horatio had a question for Joe. "You sure that was a Gator on the phone who told you they knew the Greens helped you hide the drugs?"

"Yep, one of the boys, I's known them all my life."

Once Horatio had Joe safely into the hospital, he told his pilot, "Now we're going to pay a little visit to an old friend of mine."

Gator stood at the front door of his shop to welcome Horatio. "I've had all kinds of machines come to my shop, but this is the first time for a helicopter."

"A lot different from the days when I used to drag my old police car in here and you'd charge the government an arm and a leg to fix it," Horatio answered then nodded toward the office door. "Let's go inside, I need to talk to you." Horatio closed the door behind them and then continued his discussion. "For years, I've watched you run this island, and for years I looked the other way, but since then, the tables have turned. Now I want a few things coming back my way."

"Didn't I always look after you, Horatio?" Gator responded. "You remember those little envelopes I handed you."

"Oh yes, those little tokens of appreciation you handed out to the people on this island whom you needed to keep their mouth shut. I know all those people, Gator. Most of us couldn't make ends meet on what the government paid us, so you got rich, and we took whatever we could get."

"Quit your whining," Gator told him. "You could have done as well as I did if you had had the balls. You didn't earn those gold stripes on your shoulders. They were given to you because you fell into a pail of shit and came out smelling like a rose."

Horatio smiled, "Everything you say, Gator, is true, but everything isn't always roses, is it? There's always someone like me coming along to make life miserable."

"All right Horatio, put me out of my misery and tell me how much you want," Gator walked around behind his desk. "I'm sure you don't want a check, so it will take me a few days to get the money together."

"Oh, I don't want money, Gator, that's too easy. I want guarantees."

Gator sat down behind his desk. "I thought you'd got a little smarter over the last few years, Horatio. I don't handle guarantees."

"I found that out the hard way, you never guaranteed the work you did on my car," Horatio smiled. "No, I'm thinking more like along the lines of life insurance."

"Don't handle life insurance either, never found it to profitable on this island," Gator stated.

"It's about to become a very important part of your business, Gator, because you're guaranteeing this policy with your life."

Gator was all ears now; he knew Horatio just might have the power to make this happen.

"You're going to insure you and your family's life for the guarantee that nothing happens to the Greens and their family, or to me and my family."

Gator just sat and stared at Horatio, so he continued on. "You see, my wife wants to retire here. This is our home, and most of our family lives here. No one thinks it's safe for us to stay here, and that's where you come in, Gator. Nothing happens on this island without you knowing about it. You're going to protect us and the Greens. If anything happens to any of us, even remotely suspicious, all hell will let loose on you. For instance, we know you've been helping Julio sell off some of the cartel's product. What would happen if some of the boys in the DEA slipped that word out to the wrong people? We also have lots more than that on you."

Gator didn't like the way this conversation was going at all.

"You don't have the balls for this, Horatio. You know I'll take your family down with me if it comes to that."

"Maybe," Horatio told him, "or you can carry on the way you always have, and I'll make sure no one bothers you."

Gator didn't look good. "I can give you all the money you'll ever need to live somewhere else, Horatio, why don't you just take it and run?"

"I have to live with my wife, Gator, and she wants to live here." Horatio got up and headed for the door, "I've waited a long time for the tables to turn, Gator, here's to what we both hope is a long working relationship."

Gator stood and watched Horatio's helicopter disappear in the distance. He didn't like this; he didn't like it at all.

# Thirty-One

IT TOOK A long time for Bob and July to get to the hotel. The old farm road was just as formidable coming back as it was for July going in. They both thought Horatio would be waiting at the airport, but he was nowhere to be seen, so they made their way over to the hotel. Everything seemed to be in order, but July was sure someone had been into the office desk. They were walking over the grounds looking for damage when Horatio caught up with them.

"Everything look okay?" he asked them.

"No storm damage," July answered, "but someone's been in our office."

"I had a little chat with Gator," Horatio said. "I don't think you have to worry about that situation anymore. In fact, I told him he would be personally held responsible if anything happened to you."

"You think he has that kind of power, if the drug cartels are involved?" Bob asked.

Horatio sounded a little doubtful. "He knows everything that goes on here, and he knows his ass is grass if anything happens to you, so I'd say he has an invested interest in keeping you alive."

"Thanks, Horatio," July gave him a hug. "But things still have a way of happening in this country. I think we should still go over to Nassau with you and have a talk with Novak."

Both Novak and Sir Harry were there to meet the helicopter. They shook hands. "Long time no see," Novak greeted them, "come on into the office and we can talk."

Bob told them the whole story ending with "Horatio told us this might be a good time to confront this Julio and set up some kind of trap."

Novak rubbed his face with his hands. "Yes, you're right, it would be," he stopped for emphasis, "but as you know Horatio's retirement party is next week. The problem is I'm in charge of security, and I just don't have the time or manpower to concentrate on something that would require so much planning. Maybe Sir Harry could help you?"

Sir Harry shook his head, "I've already retired. The government asked me to stay on for Horatio's farewell only because I know so many of the people coming. I have another nugget of information that I don't think even Novak knows yet. Last week the Colombian government took over the compound where Lena lives. They're going to turn it into their embassy."

Novak looked rather pale. "I thought Lena had some kind of contract on that property?"

"Not anymore. She's been put under house arrest. I put a lawyer on to it to see if he can find out what the charges are, but you know how long that can take."

"Does that mean Julio has diplomatic immunity?" Novak asked.

"Don't know. That's the problem with getting involved in something with Julio right now. Best to wait till after Horatio's little affair is over," Sir Harry told them.

"Look, the first thing they're going to hear is that we didn't come out of the swamps, and that means there's no need for them to keep Joe's boy, Tommy, alive."

Novak put his hands in his pockets and looked out the window. "You always have a way of complicating things don't you, Bob?"

"I know he's probably dead, but I have to live with my conscience if I don't try," Bob answered.

"Yeah, I guess we all do," Novak agreed. "Let's see. My informants say this Julio's got himself a German girlfriend, and they're hanging out down at Johnny Canoe's most nights. Maybe you should confront him there, lots of people around, so he can't really do anything to you."

"Tell him you got the drugs here in Nassau, and if he wants them, he's to name a place and bring the boy. Then you leave, and we'll hide you for a while. We should be able to put Julio off long enough to get Horatio's party over with, and then we can concentrate on getting Tommy back."

"There he is. That's him over by the dance floor sitting with the dark-haired girl and his two bodyguards. July and I'll watch from here," Novak told Bob. "Say your piece and get out. We'll meet you outside. If there is any trouble, I've got four officers outside. They'll be in here in a flash."

Bob nodded and headed toward the dance floor. It was a Friday night, and the place was jammed to the rafters. He had to fight his way across the dance floor to where Julio was sitting. None of them saw him coming until he yelled, "Hey, Julio, you sniveling little prick. How are you?" The two bodyguards jumped up in front of Julio and began to push Bob away.

"My name is Green, and I've got some shit for you."

Now it was Julio who jumped up, "Just a minute, guys. I want to hear what this prick has to say." The bodyguards backed off, leaving Julio and Bob face-to-face on the dance floor.

Julio usually wasn't this brave, but he had a girl to impress, plus he had a great coke buzz going on. "What can I do for you, Mr. Green?"

Novak and July watched from the bar as the two men began to push each other; the dancers backed away from the two men as they came to blows and finally went down rolling around on the floor still pummeling each other. Novak immediately was on his cell phone, and a minute later the police were pulling the two men apart. July was pleasantly surprised to find herself excited and proud; Bob had certainly held his own. She wanted to go to Bob, but Novak held her back.

"What will they do with them?" July asked.

"Throw them in jail," Novak told her. "Julio will be bailed out in an hour, but that's probably the safest place for Bob to spend the night. We'll bail him out in the morning."

Julio was on top of Karla. She could tell by his strokes he was ready to come, and she wasn't ready for that yet. The fight had exited her, and she'd had to wait for over an hour for him to get out of jail. She had made the best of the time snorting a little coke and dressing down to wearing nothing but black fishnet stockings.

When he got home, he was ready for some coke and action. Karla had wanted some romance; Julio just wanted to get fucked. It wasn't that Karla didn't like her sex rough and ready; she needed to be satisfied, and his coming now just wouldn't cut it.

"Bring it up to me, baby," she moaned.

This was what he wanted to hear from her more than anything else. After the first time, he'd tried to beat her into doing it to him, but she was as big as he was, and he learned that she was stronger and tougher. If he wanted anything from her, he had better earn it.

Julio didn't like this part of the relationship, but what she did to him made him come back for more, and that more was about to happen to him now. He moved so his cock was just over her face. She raised her head and ran her tongue along his balls then up the underside of his cock. She admired the long shaft; it was disappointing the head wasn't bigger, but it was perfect for what she was about to do. She put it in her mouth, positioned it with her tongue, and then swallowed it. She could feel Julio's body stiffen, and a huge groan escaped his lips.

The sensation was so intense his body locked up. He wanted to come, but somehow that was locked up too, and the pressure seemed to back up into his body. He held it in there until the pleasure he felt became overwhelming and he had to pull it out. He felt himself breathe again; everything in his body was focused on his cock, never had he felt so hard. Gradually his muscles began to relax, and he began to settle down on top of her then she swallowed it again.

Instantly, his body turned into a board above her, his muscles screaming with pleasure. This time when he pulled it out, she gagged a little bit making him feel vindicated. "Fuck me baby, make me come," he heard her tell him. He still felt overcome, but his cock seemed to be on a mission. It needed to find a home, and he slid down her body till it surrounded itself in something wet and warm. He began ramming it into her, watching her big boobs bounce with every stroke.

It was her that was overcome now. The sensation was hers to enjoy. Wave after wave of pleasure invaded her body. She heard herself scream, making his stroke even more intense. Just as she thought she was going to pass out, he shot up into her, and both of them went limp in a pile of flesh. Julio lay on top of her completely exhausted. She ran her fingers through his hair; she was in love with her Latin stud, and she didn't want to let him go.

"Let's run away together, Julio."

Julio raised his head. "We talked about this before, what would we live on?"

She continued to play with his hair. "What if I told you I could get us more money than we could spend in a lifetime?"

"Yeah, and how are you going to get that much money?"

"Steal it," she told him.

Julio chuckled, "Who are you going to find that has that much money to steal?"

"A lady named Lena," Karla answered.

Now she had Julio's full attention. "How are you going to do that?"

Karla took Julio's sudden interest to mean he might think she was serious. "That's why I'm here, Julio. My boss has someone on the inside who has this Lena's passwords to her computers. I'm going to hack into her system tomorrow night and drain her accounts."

"Then what do you do with the money?" Julio wanted to know.

"It goes to an untraceable account through the Caymans," Karla told him. "But," she touched her fingers to his lips, "I know the account number. If my boss and his helper were to disappear, that money would become ours."

"Interesting," Julio felt himself becoming hard. "How much do you think there is?"

"Oh, a billion or more."

"That fucking Jon," Julio thought to himself, "and he wants me to live on nothing." He was filled with excitement as he climbed off the bed and stood in front of Karla showing off his hard cock. "Here's to our being rich."

"I'm jealous," Karla pouted, reaching out with her hand to admire it, "money makes you hornier than I do."

Julio left Karla sleeping and paced the floor. He had to be sure he handled this right. The one priority over everything else was to get even with Lena. He picked up the phone and dialed his brother; eventually he came on the line.

"Yes, Julio, what is it this time?"

"Look, I know you don't think I do anything here, but I've just uncovered that Lena is going to steal your money."

"Lena's not in the position to steal anything, Julio, go back and sleep it off."

"No, no, this is real, Jon. I've been sleeping with this girl, and she told me how they're going to do it." Jon didn't answer so Julio went on, "She and Lena made this plan. She's going to hack into Lena's computer system and clean out the accounts and put them into a Swiss bank account. That way she'll have something to bargain for her release."

Jon was still skeptical, "There's no way she can get into the system. We have too much security."

"Lena gave her all the passwords. This girl says it's a piece of cake."

"Well, I guess there's only one way to find out, isn't there, Julio?"

"I know where they're going to meet," Julio told him. "Once they're together, I'll look after them before they can do anything."

Jon was quiet for a moment. "No, let them take the money. I can have the Swiss make it look like they accessed the account, and then they can freeze the money. Do you have any way of knowing when they think the transaction will be complete?"

"I'll have the girl wired," Julio told him.

"Good," Jon said. "Get rid of them as soon as you know the transaction is complete. Looks like that big cock of yours might pay off yet, Julio."

Julio hung up the phone; he couldn't believe his ears. Brilliant, just brilliant. Jon would never suspect a thing. The money was going into a Cayman account, not a Swiss account, and Jon would think Lena hid it. Fuck, he was smart. Now Jon would be short of money, and he could say to him, "I have a little bit, Jon, but I think you should learn to live within your means," and see how he liked it.

Julio walked back to the bedroom. He took a big hit of coke; damn, he was getting hard again. "Wonder if she'd swallow me one last time?" He took his cock and began rubbing Karla's face with it. She turned her face away, but he just shrugged. "I guess with that much money, I can hire lots of girls to swallow this piece of meat and on my terms too," he thought as he jammed his cock up Karla's ass.

Before he could begin to enjoy himself, Karla pulled away and gave him a kick with her leg that sent him to the floor. " If you only want to satisfy yourself, then whack yourself off." She left the room.

# Thirty-Two

"Hello. Is that you, Henekie?" Yes was the answer.

"Yes, well, Krugman here. Should have listened to you about the hurricane, Henekie, but anyway, I'll be flying into Nassau tonight around ten o'clock. Can you pick me up?"

"Yes," he replied..

"Have you talked to Karla today?"

"No," was Henekie's answer.

"I couldn't get her either. Tell her we're on for tomorrow night. The Caymans are up and running."

"Okay," Henekie answered. "See you at ten o'clock then."

Henekie picked Krugman up at the airport and took him over to his hotel. "You'll be at the shop tomorrow if I need you?"

"I'll be there all day until we finish tomorrow night," Henekie told him.

"All right, I'm sure Karla's ready to go." Krugman gave him a wink. "Hot stuff, isn't she?"

"I wouldn't know," Henekie told him.

The next afternoon, Henekie got a call from Krugman saying Karla told him she was ready and they'd come down to the shop that evening. That fucker's going to steal a billion dollars and instead of paying attention to what he's doing, he's more interested in getting fucked.

Henekie was right; Krugman was pissed at Karla for not showing up at the hotel that night. But in the morning when she did finally did show up, she had some soothing coke with her, and once she began working on his cock, he was her little sugar daddy again.

When Krugman and Karla finally did show up at the shop, it was almost midnight. Karla went right to work.

"Is there anything you need?" Henekie wanted to know.

"Is your Internet access up and running?"

"Yes, this is a commercial area, so it's as good as it gets in Nassau," Henekie apologized.

"That's why we came so late." She seemed to know Henekie was agitated. "The line won't be busy, and hopefully Lena's in bed." Karla looked up at Henekie as if to reassure him. "The logistics of doing this were well-planned before we left Germany, it's just a case of going in, finding the main account, and transferring it into cyberspace, which means Lena won't be able to follow the money."

Henekie decided Karla knew what she was doing, but Krugman was another story. He just stood there with a stupid look on his face; Henekie could tell he was higher than a kite. "Where's the Krugman I knew that planned everything down to a T?" Now he's celebrating before the transaction is complete. It was pretty obvious he had committed the cardinal sin in this business; he was a puppy in love.

They stood listening to Karla as she gave them a blow-by-blow description of going through the accounts. "Aha, Lena you bitch, you're on there trying to fuck me up, aren't you? Tough titty, there's nothing you can do. I'm too close for you to stop me. This is it, I've got the account," Karla squealed.

Then her tune changed to frustration. "What? It's empty. How can that be?" She began rapidly beating on her keyboard. "I can't find the money," she screamed. "Where did it go? Julio, you bastard. You told on me, didn't you?"

Krugman was trying to calm her down, but Henekie knew it was time to get out. He opened the back exit door and ran. He didn't get far before the blast flattened him.

Julio had found the missile launcher one day when he was snooping through the main house looking to see if his father had hid any money there. He didn't find any money, but he found this piece of treasure hidden in up in the attic. He played with it all the time rubbing the barrel and dreaming he was like the guys he saw in the movies blowing away everything in sight. One of his bodyguards said he had learned how to use them in the Cuban army. "Very good, made in Russia," he had told him. Tonight they were sitting in a car across the street from the shop where Karla said she would be. They were listening to the conversation inside when Julio heard Karla start her rant.

"Give me the launcher," he excitedly told the bodyguard.

"Okay, but don't put your finger on the trigger until you're ready to fire," the bodyguard told Julio, knowing how jittery he got when he was excited.

Julio was sure Karla had finished the transaction and was putting on an act to fool the two men with her. He stuck the launcher out the window and pulled the trigger. Little did Julio know that the missile was armor piercing. It went through the front window and then through the wall separating the office from the workshop. It probably would have gone through the back wall too, but as luck would have it, the missile hit a solid steel anvil on a workbench detonating it. The blast blew out the block walls leaving only the solid concrete pillars on the corners holding up the building. Julio could have sat there all night admiring what he'd done, but the two men with him knew enough to get the hell out of there.

It was one of those cement pillars that protected Henekie from the full force of the blast. He managed to get to his feet, but the world was spinning around dropping him to his knees.

"Okay," he tried to tell himself, "am I all here?" He checked his arms and legs; they seemed to be in place.

"The one thing I can't do is stay here," he told himself. He struggled to his feet, fighting off the nausea; he began to stumble across the back alley. He'd parked the car down a side street off the alley, and in his mind that's where he had to get to. His head was like a hollow drum, and he realized he couldn't hear anything.

Where was the car? Why had he parked it so far away? His mind tried to make him stop and lay down, but somehow he knew he had to keep going. He leaned against a car as some people came rushing down the side street to see what the blast was about. They paid no attention to Henekie, probably used to seeing drunks at this time of night. There it was—Lena's car. He opened the door and got in behind the steering wheel. His intention was to drive away but instead passed out, falling across the seat.

# Thirty-Three

Bob WOKE UP to the sound of a cell door banging open.

"Time to go, Green, your wife's bailed you out." He followed the guard down the corridor to the front desk of the police station. An officer at the desk handed him his stuff. Bob looked up at a wall clock to see it was three o'clock in the morning.

"Guess she thought she'd let me cool my heels for a while," he thought. Bob looked around. "Where is she?"

The officer nodded his head, "Said she'd wait for you outside."

Bob stepped outside and saw blonde hair through the back window of a parked taxi. "Boy, she must be really pissed," he thought as he got in the taxi ready for the onslaught.

For a second, he thought he'd got in the wrong car. The next second, a man pushed him over on the seat and got in beside him. Bob felt something cold against his ear, "I have no problem using this, so either sit back and relax or end it right now." Bob just sat there; he was too scared to move.

"Welcome to my world," Lena told him. The taxi took them to a gate guarded by an armed military officer. He let them in the walled area where they got out and went into what looked to Bob to be a large house. The man who had gotten in the car with Bob followed him into a room where they stayed until another man came and stood before them.

"Are you Mr. Green?" he asked.

"Yes," Bob answered.

"May I have your passport please?"

"I don't have it with me," Bob told him. "What's this all about?"

"You are being held by the Colombian government for assaulting one of our representatives," the man told him.

"I'm a Bahamian citizen, and I demand a lawyer," Bob stated.

"We obviously don't know who you are. Until we find out, you will stay here. You will be confined to the inside of this house, and we will make you as comfortable as possible. If you cause any problems, you will be bound and confined to one room. Is that clear?" The man didn't give Bob time to respond; he turned and left the room.

The other man said to Bob, "I think you understand the rules, only I'm a little more blunt. Cause any trouble and you'll be put in a room where you'll be bound and shot… by me," he added. He opened the door to a bedroom and gestured for Bob to enter. The door closed behind him, and Bob heard the lock turn.

What the hell had he got himself into now? He had time to reflect on this for a long time. It was late the next day before he heard the lock turn in the door and Lena's head appeared.

"There's a man here to see you," she explained. Bob hoped it was a familiar face, but it was the same one who had asked for his passport the night before.

"You will dine with Miss Lena. She will look after you until your situation is resolved. Good day, Mr. Green," the man turned and left the room.

"Kind of looks like we're cell mates," Lena told him. "Come sit at the table, and we'll eat." Bob hadn't eaten in over a day and proceeded to eat everything in sight. "You do me honors, my forte is certainly not being a cook."

Bob looked at her sheepishly, "Sorry, I guess I didn't leave much for you, did I?"

"That's all right. I didn't find it quite as appetizing as you did," she hesitated then added, "Mr. Green or Bertrand or whoever you are?"

Bob sat back, "So you recognize me?"

"Oh, you don't have a beard and you're older, but it's your eyes that give you away. You don't know someone as intimate as we were and not recognize them."

"I feel very guilty about our affair, Lena. You have to understand that I was using you and was forced into doing things I normally wouldn't do."

"You can say all you want, Mr. Green, but I know there were times when you enjoyed your little masquerade as did I, and that's why you feel guilty. As for the rest of it, we used each other. Men come and go in my life, I learned a long time ago not to trust any of them. Your eyes, however, always gave you away. They were not the cruel eyes that Jacques Bertrand would have had, if he did what they say he did. Other than that, you were just another man I knew, no more, no less. You, in turn, are very fortunate, Mr. Green, in that you have a soul mate for life: a woman who takes you for what you are and looks above everything else. You don't think she knows what went on between the two of us, but we women always know, so get over it."

Bob took a deep breath, "You're right, Lena. You're an exciting woman, and I got caught up in your lifestyle, but the funny thing is, after all these years, I can still watch my wife walk across a room and get a hard-on. I've put her through pure hell, and she keeps coming back for more, and in the end she'll probably be the one to get me out of this."

Lena tried to lighten up the subject, "So I guess that means we won't be sleeping together?"

Bob just plainly changed the subject. “So why are you under arrest, Lena?”

“I made a deal with El Presidente just before he died that I would rebuild one of his businesses for him if he gave me half the business and fortunately got him to put the deal on paper. To my amazement and everyone else, the business has become very successful. In fact, that business is what pulled the Smyskin family back to its prominence. But instead of thanking me, they want my half too.”

Lena shrugged, “It’s my fault. I should have paid more attention to protecting myself, so here I am with you in a lot of trouble. To tell you the truth, Mr. Green, I don’t think there’s much chance that either of us will come out of this alive. Donating this piece of ground to the Colombian government makes it very hard for anyone to set foot here without strict permission, and in your case no one knows where you are, so that makes you a missing person, and that will probably appear on your death certificate.”

“Someone has put a lot of planning into this, haven’t they, Lena?”

“Yes, and it’s not only Jon Smyskin. There is someone here called the Referee, and I know he is behind a lot of it, but unlike me, he has covered his ass well. No one has ever found out who he is or if they did, they are not alive to tell about it. You see I thought Sir Harry or Novak would protect me but none of us thought of Smyskin donating this compound to the Columbian government as its embassy. It’s almost impossible for anyone to enter here let alone do anything without going through diplomatic channels. I’m positive this wasn’t done overnight, someone had this in the planning stages for a long time.”

Their conversation moved to the bar and continued well into the night. It was after midnight when they were interrupted by a beeping from Lena’s computer room.

Lena frowned. “That’s strange,” she said and walked swiftly away to see what was going on. Bob followed her into the room and was amazed at what he saw. "Shit, someone's broken into my system," Lena said to herself as much as to Bob.

"Is it serious?" he asked, in awe of the machinery humming around him.

"Um, they are going through my accounts, but they're not taking anything out, which means they're looking for something in particular." She began typing on her keyboard, "Nope, I can't stop them. They have my passwords. I didn't believe you, Mr. Henekie, when you told me you were going to steal my money. I guess I forgot you were so honest."

Bob's head came up when he heard that name. "What do you think he's after, if it's not the money?"

"He's after the mother lode. Someone knows Jon doesn't empty his account till the end of the month. There is close to a billion dollars in there right now, and I have no place to hide it, unless—Do you have a U.S. account, Mr. Green?"

"Yes, I do."

"How about a swift code?"

Bob reached for his wallet and gave Lena the numbers he'd written on a piece of paper. She typed in the numbers and waited.

"It's gone. They might be able to follow the money trail to the United States, but that's the end of it. A transaction of that size will be immediately frozen and scrutinized, quite possible none of us will see it again. Anyway, you look at it, Mr. Green. We just stole a billion from a Colombian cartel, and it's in your U.S. bank account."

# Thirty-Four

THE CRYSTAL PALACE was a beehive of activity. One tower was completely reserved for guests coming from all over the world to honor Horatio Norton who was credited with breaking the drug cartel's stranglehold on the Bahamas. Many countries were sending the heads of their law enforcement people, the CIA, FBI, and DEA would be represented from the very top along with Interpol officials. Mixed in with them were heads of state and their representatives. Neither Novak nor the Bahamian government had any idea that the response would be so overwhelming.

For Novak, it was a logistical nightmare. Some of the dignitaries from surrounding countries were coming on private boats and wanted their private helicopters to drop them off right at the hotel. He had the hotel shut down their pool area on the ocean side, so it could be used as a helipad. Once others learned about this, many of them wanted to use the same service; now the pool area would be so busy they would have to set up appointments and have a special air controller to handle helicopter traffic.

Every one of these people would have to be checked in by his officers before they could enter the building. Out front, there would be the usual problems. Parts of the city would be closed to traffic letting the limos get through and then unload them in an orderly fashion. The fact was that the Crystal Palace was not set up to handle an event of this size, but it was far too late to change the venue now.

The program for the night had originally been scheduled for the main ballroom but now would use all the reception and meeting rooms on the main floor. Novak would have to have twice as many security people as originally planned and had to turn to a private firm for help. Wilbur Smith said his men would look after the surveillance system which was a big help to Novak because his men were well-trained. The hotel surveillance was set up in a command post up above the casino. Extra cameras and sound systems now covered much more than that area, and his men would be Novak's eyes and ears both inside and outside the casino.

This was why Novak didn't need the distraction of July Green's call that Bob was not at the jail when she went to the bail him out nor did anyone there know where he was. When his phone calls didn't get any results, he told July he'd be right there. He sensed that the officers knew they were in trouble when he saw they had called the night clerk to come back in.

"So what happened last night?" he asked.

"A blond woman came in last night and showed me her driver's license to say she was July Green. She paid her fee and signed him out. Here's her signature." The officer showed him the book.

"Did she look like Mrs. Green?" Novak asked.

"I don't know I've only seen her on TV" the officer answered.

"Would you recognize a picture of her?"

The officer seemed unsure so Novak asked, "Was she wearing a low-cut top, and did she lean over in front of you?"

"She was quite friendly," was all the officer would admit.

"Fuck, the guy probably never looked up to see her face." Novak knew this was serious, and he immediately got on the phone to Sir Harry. About all he got from Sir Harry was a bunch of swearing on the other end of the line.

"Look, do you have somewhere safe we can put July until we get to the bottom of this?"

Sir Harry said he would look after her and have some officers bring her around to the British embassy.

"He'll pick you up there," Novak told July what Sir Harry had said.

"I'll get some detectives on this right away and track down that taxi. We have a good source of informers around the city. Something should start showing up pretty soon."

July left with the officers, but Novak could see by her face that she was scared and so was he.

"A friend of mine bought this piece of land from a Canadian family," Sir Harry told July. "They'd let it go to rack and ruin, so he got it pretty cheap and fixed it up."

July knew what she was looking at. It was probably the best piece of real estate in Lyford Cay, right down at the end surrounded with ocean views. It was one of the most beautiful spots she had ever seen. "I planned to rent it and retire here, but now I see they'd never leave me alone. Somebody would always be after me for something."

"So I guess I'll have to skip that idea and retire somewhere else," he sighed. "As you can see, July, the property is completely surrounded by a wall, and it has excellent security, so you're perfectly safe here." He showed her around the guest quarters. "Make yourself at home. I will be in and out, as you know Horatio's affair is keeping us hopping. Novak and I will be in touch about Bob. I'm sure something will turn up soon." He gave her a hug and left.

Jon Smyskin stood leaning on the railing as the helicopter silhouetted against the Cuban coast came toward him and landed on his helipad.

Wilbur Smith and the Referee got out and walked down the steps to where he was standing.

The Referee had a wide smile on his face as he shook hands. "She's a real beauty, Jon."

Wilbur seemed a little overwhelmed with the size of Jon's ship. "I've seen cruise ships not much bigger than this," he said to Jon shaking hands.

"First time we've had her out," Jon said proudly. "Come up to the lounge deck. The view is much better up there." Two bikini-clad girls brought them Cuban cigars and Cuban rum.

"Here's to your new yacht, Jon. I see you have a little of your father in you." The Referee nodded toward the girls, "only he would have had them topless."

"I suggested they meet you a little less dressed, but they complained about getting burned in this hot sun. Besides, I need your full attention for a while. We can get to that later."

Wilbur was disappointed to hear the Referee say that they wouldn't be able to stay that long.

"So everything seems to be coming along nicely," the Referee said drawing on his cigar.

"Maybe so, maybe no," Jon answered. "Something strange happened last night. Someone broke into our computer system. They seemed to be well-informed. We think Lena gave them the passwords to our accounts. Anyway, we're missing close to a billion dollars."

The Referee whistled, "That's a chunk of change."

"Yes, it is. Julio of all people got wind that it was going down and phoned me. I decided to let them go ahead with it and find out who they were when they tried to put the money in their offshore account. Everything was going fine until Lena got involved and somehow stuck the money in a U.S. account which is going to make it tricky to get the money back."

"Yeah," Wilbur agreed; they would investigate the origin of that money for sure. "If they find out it has anything to do with you, it might be gone forever."

"Thanks Wilbur for that word of encouragement, but what I need from you is how we get the money back and whose account did the money go into? This yacht cost me a lot of money and the guy who built it for me wants his payment now, if I can't pay him my reputation is ruined."

This piece of information bothered the Referee; in this business you didn't owe people, they owed you.

Jon turned towards Wilbur."There's a phone in that cabin behind us. One of the girls will help you." Wilbur understood he wasn't being asked and did as he was told.

The Referee just smiled at Jon from behind his cigar. "Sometimes he forgets who he works for. So do you think this attack on your computer system is the same person who threatened you on the phone?"

"Don't know. Do you think that guy had any credibility about once working for my father?" Jon asked.

"There was a group of people who used to handle our problems back in the old days. Most of them were killed off, but one man in particular survived and went to work for your father. Our sources say the Israelis got hold of him, and that means he is no longer on this earth," the Referee told him.

"Okay, so who is this man? It's not just anyone who can present one of my best men's head on a platter."

"I think we have that under control. If he tries to help Lena again, we're waiting for him. I hired that man I told you about, to run the security at the new embassy. No one's going to get past him and Julio says he terminated the people hacking into your accounts, so one way or the other he's nullified," the Referee reasoned.

Wilbur Smith came back sounding very officious. "All right, the account is in the name of Bob and July Green. Now the banking officer I talked to says if the bank in the Bahamas signs a paper saying it was a banking error and the Greens sign off, the money will be given back, that's the simplest way."

Both Jon and the Referee began to laugh. "Well, I'll be damned. You see, Wilbur, we moved Green in with Lena with the plan that sooner or later they would decide to take the money and use it as a bargaining chip for their lives. This gives us physical evidence Lena stole the money, committed fraud, and can no longer be an officer of the bank. She will have to turn the bank over to Jon. Green's been stealing from the Miami cartel, so we'll turn him over to them. The only one not in place is Mrs. Green. I expect the police have her hid away someplace.

"Lena doesn't have many friends. Men don't like being manipulated by a conniving bitch, but how about Sir Harry, he might have to get involved," Jon stated.

"Don't worry about Sir Harry," the Referee laughed. " He's retiring and doesn't have the clout he once had. So when are you going to drop the bomb?" the Referee wanted to know.

"The day before Horatio Norton's farewell party. That should throw a fuck into his little red wagon," Jon scowled.

"Could topple the government," the Referee added.

Jon raised his glass, "That's the plan."

# Thirty-Five

LENA THOUGHT LONG and hard about the consequences of what she had done last night. She came to the conclusion that this might work in her favor. She couldn't see any way Jon could get his money out of the United States without her help. She also thought of a way to get Bob out of here, but it was risky. Bob already had breakfast ready when she came out of her bedroom. It had been a long time since she'd had an appetite; this morning she was ravenous.

"There may be a way out of here, Bob," she told him between mouthfuls, "but it's going to require you to do things, as you said yourself, that you don't normally do."

"Anything is better than sitting here doing nothing," Bob was obviously interested.

"The Venezuelan girl Jon sent over here to keep Julio satisfied is living in the pool house," she pointed down toward the pool. "He has another girlfriend so he put her over here out of the way. Once in a while, he has one of his bodyguards come over and get her, probably for his guys to play with, I don't know. But anyway, with the new wall separating the property, they have to escort her around by the front gate. If you could disable his man, dress up like him, and escort her out the front gate, you are home free. They usually come after dark, and the soldiers at the front gate don't seem to pay much attention to this sort of going on."

"So all I have to do is wait for Julio's man to show up, whack him over the head, and take the girl out," Bob summarized what she had told him.

"Sort of," Lena answered. "A little more effort may be required on your part such as seducing the girl into wanting to go with you, which may not be too hard, considering your vast experience at seducing woman and the fact that she probably doesn't like getting gangbanged by the paid help?" Lena shrugged, "It's just a thought. Maybe it's better to sit here and see what happens."

Bob took a deep breath, "Down by the pool, hey?"

"Yes, and don't play hard to get, you don't have much time. I've got a tight little thong for you to wear, and I can help you get a hard-on if you want. Then go lay by the pool. I guarantee you won't be alone long. Honestly, Mr. Green, most men couldn't wait for a chance like this, but then if their lives were on the line, most of them couldn't get it up anyway."

"Go get me that thong, Lena, and I'll see what I can do."

Lena watched out her window seeing Bob lay himself out by the pool. Soon the Venezuelan girl came out of the pool house and lay across from him. By late afternoon, they were laying beside each other, the girl rubbing her hand on his body then they disappeared.

After dark, Lena usually went for a swim. Tonight she was curious, if anything, to find out how Bob was doing. As she entered the pool, she saw something flash among the shrubbery at the far end. She entered the pool and quietly swam toward the strange glow that appeared and then disappeared. She was quite close when she heard the moaning and realized what the light was. The girl had put one of Julio's fluorescent rubbers on Bob, and as he moved in and out of her the condom flashed in the dark. Damn, she was horny; she remembered that cock, and for an instant thought of joining them then she thought better of it. She couldn't spoil Bob's chance to get away. She quietly swam back to the end of the pool and went inside where she had a drink and went to bed. Her dreams were quite pleasant and made her sweat.

Bob and the Venezuelan girl lay naked on the bed. "I'm sure they're coming for me tonight, you've got to help me," the girl was definitely scared. Bob had already laid out his plan to her, but she seemed uncertain that she could trust him and continued to play with his cock as if it was her only way to keep a hold on him. "They're going to kill me. They don't care. They're animals," she laid her head on his chest. This seemed to be the only way he could console her, otherwise she was into the coke and became a violent, raving maniac. The knock on the door caught them off guard.

"Let me in," a voice said.

"It's them," the girl jumped up off the bed and slipped on a sundress.

"Open the fuckin' door, or I'll break it down," the voice said.

Bob scampered over behind the door and picked up the frying pan he'd left there. He nodded, and the girl opened the door. A man burst through the door pushing the girl back toward the bed. "We're going to have a little one-on-one before I have to share," was all the man got out before Bob nailed him over the head. The man stopped dead in his tracks but didn't go down, so Bob whacked him again, and the man collapsed on the floor. Quickly, Bob removed his pants and shirt and put them on. They were pretty big; he had to hold up the pants.

"Here." The girl, seeing his dilemma, took a pillow and shoved it down his pants.

"Okay, let's go," Bob told her. She showed him how to take her arm, and they headed out to the front of the house. As far as they could see, there was no one around.

“I hope we can fool the guards at the gate,” he whispered to her.

She sounded confident now, “Don’t worry about the soldiers, I can take care of them.” It was the last words he ever heard her say.

A figure came out of the shadows, and Bob recognized the feel of cold steel against his ear. The girl screamed and broke away running toward the gate, but the guards caught her up and carted her away.

“I thought I told you to be a good boy, Mr. Green.” Bob recognized the voice of the man who had put the gun to his head before. Bob felt like the wind had been kicked out of him.

“Don’t hurt the girl,” he pleaded, “I forced her into doing this.”

“Don’t bullshit me. She was as consensual about your plan as she was about the sex you had. You don’t think we’d leave you and Lena alone together without some audio and video, did you? The only guy in the place that didn’t watch you screw all day was the guy who came to get the girl. He just came back to work, and the guys didn’t like him much I guess.”

The man guided Bob out through the gate and back through on the other side of the fence. Once they were into the yard, two other men grabbed him and dragged him into the house. They sat him in a chair and held him there.

“Mrs. Smyskin put in a request for a young black man with a big cock, but on short notice you’re going to have to do. I don’t personally go for this perverted stuff, so I’ll introduce you to the doctor here and let the two of you get to know each other better.”

“Hello, Mr. Green,” the doctor smiled. “Kind of a prudish chap, wouldn’t you say? Oh well, just one of those efficient people they bring in to keep a lid on things, I suppose.”

The doctor walked toward Bob with a needle in his hand. “This is a little something to make you relax. You’ll wake up thinking you’ve gone to heaven." Bob was convinced that what the doctor was giving him was lethal. He felt the needle in his arm, and immediately felt sleepy. Not a bad way to go, he thought.

The first thing Julio's mother said when she saw him was, "My poor baby, you look so sad." Julio looked over, but there was no compassion in the doctor's eyes. In fact, what he saw made his blood run cold.

Julio needed some sympathy; the account number Karla had given him did not show any deposits, let alone one for a billion dollars. Then Jon had sent in this new guy who told Julio he was not to go anywhere until Jon himself arrived. He was supposed to be Jon's man here, now he was taking orders from some yahoo and to take the cake, the doctor showed up with his mother; even her embrace did not lessen his insecurity.

"At least they didn't poison her against me," he thought as he walked over and shook hands with the doctor. Julio knew this was Jon's right-hand man besides his mother's lover. If Jon had a problem, the doctor took care of it. No one knew if this man was a real doctor, but his surgery skills were renowned. It was said he could walk up to a man and cut out his vital organs before he hit the ground. If there was trouble or if someone threatening came around, one of the first things he would do was to bring out a stiletto-style knife and begin cleaning his nails. Julio was thankful he wasn't doing that right now, or his legs probably would have gone out from under him.

"I see my mother brought her usual amount of luggage," Julio could see cartload after cartload of luggage around them.

"Yes, be a good boy and get a van to bring this luggage up to the embassy grounds, would you?"

"Embassy?" Julio sounded confused.

"Yes, for God's sake, the property Jon donated to the government for the new embassy."

"Yes, I know," Julio answered, "but there's no room for all this in there."

"Oh, maybe they forgot to tell you. Your mother and I are staying in your place. I think they found you a hotel. We'll get your driver to take us to the embassy. You can help load the van and show him where to go."

"But I wanted to spend some time with my mother," Julio tried to sound like he wasn't whining.

"Your mother's tired right now, and we have plans for tonight. You can see her tomorrow," the doctor told him as he helped Mrs. Smyskin into the car, and they sped away.

Julio had been excited at going to the airport to pick up his mother. He was sure she'd listen to him and put him back in charge. Now here he was telling some van driver how to put luggage into a van. The only solace he got from all this was that he knew what the plan for tonight was; Mr. Green would be the entertainment; and it served the prick right, he thought as he moved farther back into the shade, leaving the driver alone to contend with the luggage. He looked around and then took a hit of coke. "It won't be long now," he thought, "and they'll know I'm the one they should be listening to."

Bob opened his eyes and gradually things came into focus, but they didn't mean anything. He looked around, "I'll be damned. I'm naked and hanging in the air." He could hear himself laughing, "and I'm surrounded by white. Now I understand, I'm an angel flying through the clouds, no wonder I feel so good." He saw in front of him two people sitting at a table covered by a long white tablecloth. The man was dressed in a tuxedo while the woman was dressed in red. They were drinking champagne and seemed to be talking about him. He tried to comprehend what they were saying, but it's hard to do when you're flying.

"Ah, it looks like our man is coming around, Mrs. Smyskin."

"I am a little disappointed dear, I thought we were going to get a young black man. I've heard they have adorable big long dongs."

"Well, it was short notice, and I've been told they saw this guy in action, and he's pretty good. He's a little old, but he does look in pretty good shape."

The woman went over to Bob and lifted his cock, "My goodness, look at the size of these balls." She held them in her hand and fondled them. "I think we may have some potential here."

Somewhere in the back of his mind, Bob thought this wasn't exactly right, but he didn't know why he would think that; it felt so good. I wonder if this lady is the devil, he thought. Well, it didn't matter; he liked what she was doing.

"Look at that big rib cage. I bet he's got a huge heart," the man said admiringly.

"Now, Doctor, you know Jon said we could use him but not kill him," the woman said.

Bob laughed at them. "You can't kill me, I'm an angel."

The woman walked to the table and brought a wand-looking thing back with her. She hooked it to Bob's penis and turned it on. "I'm anxious to see what we have here." The electrical impulses went through Bob's body, conducting on through the steel chains holding his body to the wall. His body bucked uncontrollably. The woman found this fascinating, but the doctor reached down and turned the prod off.

"You have no patience, dear. I don't want you to ruin that big heart."

"Yes, but look what I did to that thing. Isn't it marvelous? Look at the size of that knob. How would you like that shoved up your ass, darling?" She gave the doctor a hug.

"I prefer mine long and skinny, that one might make me squeal a little bit," the doctor answered.

Mrs. Smyskin reached up and kissed him. "We shall find out, won't we dear?"

The doctor smiled at her, "First, we'd better make this thing permanent."

He showed Bob a needle and was pleased to see that Bob only had a faraway look in his eyes. "Lucky for you, you're not here right now, or this would really hurt." The doctor knew Bob didn't understand him, but he talked to him anyway. "This can be taken other ways, but seeing as you're not feeling much pain right now, I want to see how you react when I inject it direct."

The doctor stuck the needle into Bob's one testicle and then the other. His body seized up and then began to spasm. Even with all the drugs in his veins, the pain was excruciating. The doctor stayed with him. "Don't worry, it will only last a second, and then you'll feel like a bull. I just hope your heart is as good as I think it is," he added. The man was right; after a minute, the pain left the rest of Bob's body to concentrate in his balls. He needed to blow his nuts in the worst way, but for some reason he couldn't.

The doctor let him down from the wall and led him into another room. He saw a woman laying on a couch beckoning him to come to her.

"It's July. Good, she'll look after me." He rushed over to her, and she put his enflamed cock to work.

Slowly Bob came out of his drug-induced sleep. He had no idea where he was nor could he remember anything about why he was here. He realized he was on a couch cuddled in behind a chubby woman who was snoring contently. He not too gently pushed her aside and stood up. The woman moaned and rolled over, still dead to the world. Damn, his cock hurt; he looked down to see it standing at half-mast, and its head looked like someone had been chewing on it.

In the next room, he could hear what sounded like water running and people talking. He went to the doorway of what looked like it might be a garage and peeked around. There standing with their backs to him were three men in white uniforms. They were standing at the edge of what looked like a big shower. It was what was in the shower that took a minute for Bob to get his mind around. The Venezuelan girl was laying on a table, her eyes looking at him, but most of her body was gone. One of the men dressed in white was helping another put something in a plastic bag. "Okay," said the tallest man, "that's it. You can get rid of the rest."

Bob couldn't believe his eyes. It was when one man took a sledgehammer and started crushing her skull that he fell back into the room and puked his guts out. Before long, he heard the water stop running and the men leave the garage.

"I'm the next one on that table," Bob thought. He was ready to die but not that way.

Bob went into the garage and began looking around. The garage floor was strewn with empty canvas bags, obviously their contents had been emptied into the luggage bags lined up along one wall. He was pretty much in a fog as he opened a closet door and saw what he would call a bazooka. He pulled it out of the closet and walked over to a window where outside he saw a group of men sitting around a table. He aimed it at them and pulled the trigger but nothing happened. He went back to the closet but couldn't find anything to load it with. He put the bazooka back in the closet reasoning it was no good to him if it wouldn't fire.

He continued his search coming across a leather bag on one of the work benches. For some reason it piqued his curiosity. Inside Bob found it to be full of surgical tools. Maybe this was what he was looking for but how to do it quick, slash your wrists or cut your own throat neither sounded easy to him. He emptied the bag onto the counter top and to his surprise four sticks of dynamite rolled out of the bottom of the bag. They were bound together and attached to a phone.

"This is more like it," Bob thought as a wave of nausea hit him and he lost consciousness. When he came to, he found himself lying on the floor with the dynamite still in his hands. He picked himself up off the floor and began playing with the buttons on the phone.

# Thirty-Six

HENEKIE WOKE UP to a ringing in his ears, but it took a few seconds to realize the ringing wasn't in his head; it was Lena's car phone. He could feel the stiffness and sore spots in his body as he sat up and answered it.

"Sir, you said to try this number if you didn't return last night."

"Where are you, Tommy?" he asked.

"I'm down by the main docks where the mail boats come in."

Henekie's head began to swim as soon as he sat up, but he knew he couldn't stay here much longer without someone checking the car out. Probably the heavy tinting on the windows was all that had saved him this long.

"Okay, Tommy, I'm headed your way. Wait for me in the parking area." It took all his effort to control the dizziness as he drove. Twice he had to pull over until the waves of nausea passed. When he finally got to the parking lot, he spotted Tommy walking around looking for him. Henekie pulled up and parked beside him. Before Tommy could say anything, Henekie told him to get a bag out of the trunk and get in the car.

"You don't look good, sir," was all Henekie would let Tommy say.

"Okay, here's the deal," he told Tommy as he changed into blue jeans and an old shirt. "I'm your old man, and I'm drunk. I'll have my arm around you. If I pass out, keep going. Don't stop until you dump me in the boat, and then get the hell out of here," Henekie told him as he rubbed some black stuff on his face and arms.

They made their way to the dock without too much trouble, but when they got there, they were met by an angry black man who was mad at Tommy for parking in his spot. "I called the harbor master," he expounded. "They're gonna haul your ass out of here." The man's boat had them blocked in, and even though Tommy tried to explain that he had to retrieve his drunken father, the man wouldn't budge.

Henekie quietly told Tommy, "There's a hundred-dollar bill in my shirt pocket. Tell him it's his if he lets you go."

The man immediately changed his tune when he saw the money and allowed Tommy to leave. They didn't wait around to hear the lecture. Once they were back under the old warehouse, Henekie had Tommy make a hammock so he could lie in the salt water. Henekie knew he had been fortunate in that he had been spared the full blast of the explosion, and other than a dull headache and some nicks and bruises, he surprised himself at how fast he healed. The next day he felt well enough to climb the stairs up to the compound above.

He first went to Julio's garage, where through a crack in the wall, he watched as some men in white coveralls striped a woman of her organs and put the parts in coolers. Although this operation piqued Henekie's curiosity and he reasoned it was probably what would happen to him if he was caught, it was not crucial to the information he needed.

As soon as the men left, he made his way into the garage, pulled the ladder down to the attic, and climbed up looking for the missile launcher he'd left there years before. It wasn't there. He quickly climbed down, let the stairs up, and turned to face a naked man.

Not only was Henekie startled, he was very apprehensive of what the man held in his hands. "Is that a bomb?" he managed to get out.

"Yeah, looks that way, but I can't figure how to set it off."

"Well, I'd appreciate it if you didn't set it off while I'm around," Henekie tried to sound calm. "Are you one of them?"

The naked man nodded toward the shower. "If you mean am I one of the guys who butchered the girl? No."

Bob thought he should recognize the man's voice but his head was so fucked up he wasn't sure the man was even real or even if the conversation was real.

"But why are you here?" Bob tried to comprehend.

"I left something when I used to hang out here years ago, but I can't find it." Henekie tried to sound truthful.

"Yeah, and what would that be?"

Henekie thought he'd stick with the truth. "A missile launcher."

"Oh, that's in the closet over there," Bob pointed.

Henekie walked over to closet and pulled out the launcher. He pulled down a lever and carefully extracted the missile.

"Well, why in fuck couldn't I figure that out?" Bob sounded disappointed.

"This fixation to kill yourself must really turn you on," Henekie pointed at the naked man's half-erect dick.

Bob looked embarrassed, "I think someone filled me full of drugs last night because I can't get it to go down, but if you were the next one to go on that table you'd be looking for a quicker way to die just like me."

"I'll be on the table with you if I get caught in here," Henekie told him.

"I don't know how to set this thing off, so I guess I'll hide it and see if someone else does."

Henekie also noted the transfer of packages from the canvas bags to the luggage and knew they would soon be shipped somewhere. "You should take some of that cocaine," Henekie told him. "It might make your life a little easier."

"That stuff has been trying to kill me since I came to these islands. It might get me, but I swear I won't go alone."

"I have to go back to my hiding place, but I'll swear to you one thing. If you go into that shower, you won't die slow, and you won't die alone, Henekie said.

They shook hands. "Maybe someday we'll meet in another place," Bob told him. He went off into another room, and Henekie got the hell out of there thinking that's one of the craziest son of a bitch I've ever met.

Bob remembered seeing a yellow handbag sitting on a table behind where he'd left the woman sleeping. He opened it to find it full of articles he'd never seen before but he knew some of the items were sex toys. "She obviously likes her sex hot," he thought. This should fit right in. He put the dynamite in under some of the items and closed the bag. He was about to explore some more but two men caught him sneaking around and tied him to a chair. He was too tired to fight back and soon fell asleep.

Henekie now knew what had caused the explosion at his shop. Their being only one missile left explained that, and Karla screaming the name Julio explained who did it. Lena was the one who could tie it all together, that was if she would still talk to him. Henekie was pretty sure they'd have cameras and "bugs" in her house; it didn't take him long to disarm them.

It took a bit of coaxing, but Henekie finally lured Lena into the garage. Their conversation was at first intense, but eventually Lena admitted that his trying to steal the money had worked out well. "They need my signature and the Greens' to get the money back, so that gained us a few days. However, I don't do well under torture so my signature is a foregone conclusion."

She looked him in the eye. “That goes for you too. I’m going to have to tell them what I know about you.”

“That’s okay. Embellish your story all you can. The only reason they haven’t asked you about me is because they were hoping to trap me into coming for you.” Henekie told her.

“I figure we’ve got about two more minutes before someone’s here to see why the power went out. What else do you know?”

“Jon Smyskin is coming tomorrow. Some of his staff got here yesterday, and oh yes, Mr. Green told me that this property was going to be made into the Colombian Embassy. Another thing you may not know is that Mark Bertand and Bob Green are one and the same. Incredible as it might sound, there have been rumors that he’s the Referee, and everything he does is just an act. Come to think of it, maybe he is the Referee. Maybe he had himself thrown in here to find out everything I know, get the money in his account, and is now back on their side of the fence,” Lena stopped talking seemingly lost in thought.

“I didn’t recognize Mr. Green when I saw him over there,” Henekie told her. “He didn’t exactly look like he was enjoying himself.”

Lena just shrugged, “Maybe that’s just part of the act. Maybe he’s like you, Henekie, a chameleon. How did you get in here, anyway? Makes it hard to know who’s who in this game and how do you pick the winner?”

Henekie smiled, “Stick with what you know. I’ll meet with you tomorrow evening after you’ve talked to Jon Smyskin. Come to the garage when your living room light blinks twice.” Henekie threw the breakers back on and disappeared.

Security was tight around the embassy grounds as Jon Smyskin’s helicopter landed. Everyone came out to meet him, except for Henekie. He made use of the opportunity to go up into the attic. He listened as Jon made his rounds praising some and scolding others. Jon had a long private meeting with a man he addressed as the doctor, and then he got around to Bob Green.

"I'm sorry they're keeping you tied up, but apparently you've been a bad boy." Jon sat down in a chair across from Bob. "You probably don't know who I am. My name is Jon Smyskin."

"Yes, the cartel man," Bob answered.

"Mr. Green, I'm a legitimate businessman in Colombia, and you are now on Colombian soil. You committed a serious crime and will be tried under our law."

"You seem a little upset that Lena and I stole your money," Bob told him calmly.

"That's not the only thing I'm upset about, Mr. Green. Were you on board my father's ship the night he died?"

"So that's what precipitated all this?"

"Yes, I was on the ship before it blew up, but then you already know that. I'd have been in that shower last night except you need me to get your money back, don't you?" Jon hesitated for a moment; he had expected to meet a very frightened man. "You realize you and your wife are in a very precarious situation."

"I know where I am," Bob told him. "I'm ready to die. So your only option is to deal with me on my terms, or I don't help you get your money back."

Jon handed him a paper and said, "Why don't you just sign this and we'll forget about you."

"I'll sign, Mr. Smyskin, and then you can kill me and get your revenge. But first, Lena and my wife have to be guaranteed that you won't kill them."

"We might consider a deal for your wife, but why Lena?" Jon wanted to know.

"Just to piss you off. Okay, here's the deal. My wife and Lena are to be seen alive at Horatio's party. Then they can come back here where I can see they are alive. Sir Harry is to be allowed to come here and take them to wherever you want, to have them sign your paper. Then Sir Harry will take them someplace safe. When that happens, a man named Novak will phone me and I'll sign your paper."

"You're sitting here, tied up in a chair, telling me what to do," Jon sounded a little amazed.

"If you want your money back without any complications, it shouldn't be too hard for an honest businessman from Colombia to set up."

Jon stood up, "Now I see why you've lived as long as you have, Mr. Green. I'll give you credit for having guts. We shall see how smart you are when your guts are in the shower and you're screaming to die."

Bob didn't back off, "I might be screaming, but I won't sign your fucking paper."

"Okay, maybe we can come up with something suitable for all concerned." Jon got up and left.

The doctor had been standing to one side. He grabbed Jon's arm once he was out of the room. "You're not going to listen to all that bullshit, are you?"

Jon turned to him, "No, but the U.S. banker says I should have all three of these people present in front of him when we sign the papers. Maybe I can use this to my advantage."

Up in the attic, Henekie listened to the conversation with great interest. He too thought Green had a lot of guts, or as Lena had mentioned, was this part of a grander scheme set up by a mastermind that put even Henekie himself to shame?

Jon stood in the main reception area of his bank in the Bahamas. He'd never been here before even though this bank generated billions of dollars for him. Lena had built it and run it. Now it was time to show who the real boss was. The bank was the largest employer in the Bahamas with over twelve hundred employees. The reception area only held about half of them; the rest would listen to his speech broadcast on loudspeakers installed throughout different floors of the building. The employees were generally in a good mood; it was Friday, which meant the rest of the weekend would be theirs.

Jon stepped in front of a small podium amid a round of applause. "I am sorry to report that over the last year, we have had over one billion dollars stolen from this bank. We find that the Internet systems and security systems here in Nassau are inadequate to handle the volume of business we do. Therefore we are moving the bank and all its businesses located here in Nassau, to Bogotá, Colombia. All employees will receive their termination notices today except for a few needed to finish up the business here. All employees will receive one month's compensation. I am sorry to have to tell you this news, and I thank you for your good work."

The doctor guided Jon out a side door and into a waiting car before the people listening let his words sink in. Word spread like wildfire; people spilled out into the streets, talking in groups. It was here that paid insurgents began sowing the seeds of discontent.

The next morning, Jon's speech was front-page news. Everyone knew the loss of a business this size would affect all of the Bahamas, not just Nassau. Again, there were agitators in the bars and on the streets stirring the people until by evening the city was in an ugly mood. One thing was ingrained into people's minds, both Jon Smyskin and the prime minister would be at the Crystal Palace that night.

"How do you know he'll rent a tux?" Tommy wanted to know.

Whenever he could, Henekie tutored Tommy. "It's all deduction. The rental shop you found is close to Novak's home, and he's too cheap to buy a suit. We know he will have to mingle with the guests so he'd stand out in a crowd if he didn't wear a tux." Henekie shrugged. "That's my deduction. Let's see if I'm right."

They went into the shop and talked to the man behind a desk. "I am renting a tux for my friend who doesn't have time to get over here. He's going to the same place as Mr. Novak. He says the same size will fit him. Do you think we could see Mr. Novak's suit?"

"Yes of course," the man said and showed them the suit. Henekie took the tux and put something in the pants pocket before handing it back.

"Perfect," Henekie told the man. "I'll take one the same size along with a pair of shoes."

"Who's the tux for?" Tommy asked after they left the shop.

"A naked man needs it," was all Henekie would say.

Novak was pretty satisfied he'd done everything possible to be ready for this evening. Already some of the dignitaries were arriving, these were people who had arranged private meetings before the main event started, and some just didn't want to wait in line. He made one last pass outside and then went to get dressed. The hotel always had dressing rooms set aside for its staff.

He was completely dressed and about to leave when he felt the package in his pocket. He fished out something wrapped in plastic and opened it. He recognized the necklace immediately; streams of memory passed through his mind as he remembered the tears that had been shed over this necklace, his own included as he pried the tiny piece of the necklace from a dead Mountie's hand. He looked around.

"How in hell did this get in here?" he asked himself. Novak opened the piece of paper with it. "When Sir Harry leaves with Mrs. Green and Lena, have someone give him the message that he is not to go to the embassy but directly to Smyskin's boat. Next, phone this number and ask to speak to the doctor. Tell him they are not to hurt Green and to take him with them to Jon Smyskin's yacht. I sent the necklace to show this is not a hoax. Beware, Mr. Novak, keep your troops around you as all hell is about to break loose." Novak knew that whoever sent him this message was sincere; the necklace was something that would not be given up lightly.

Novak had been hearing reports of trouble in the city center, and this evening he had to send some of his men to help out. Jon Smyskin certainly knew how to put a damper on a party. Novak did not take this warning lightly; there'd be no more of his men leave the hotel tonight no matter who the request came from. He checked the back side of the hotel and was told the helicopters were coming in on schedule. Then he made his way out front to watch the limos as they dropped off their passengers and then were whisked away to the parking lots. Across the street he noticed some protesters, but that was to be expected at an event like this.

He took a deep breath; so far so good, he thought as he went up to the surveillance room where he could get an overall view of the proceedings.

"Hear you've got some trouble up town," Wilbur Smith said to him as he entered the room.

"I imagine you'd be upset too if you were one of the people who just got laid off," Novak answered. "I've got a strange feeling Smyskin knew what he was doing when he picked the day before Horatio's party to make his announcement. After all, El Presidente was his father. I see Smyskin's supposed to escort Lena to the party tonight. I doubt either of them will show up."

"Well, looks like everything's under control up here," Wilbur told everyone in the room. "I'm going to go down and mingle."

Novak waited for him to leave the room. "When you see Sir Harry leave the hotel tonight, give me a call and make sure you know who he leaves with, would you?"

"Yes, sir," one of the men said, "but speak of the devil, you should see who just walked in." Novak went over to the screen.

"Who in hell is that with Sir Harry?" one of the men whistled. There wasn't a man in the place who hadn't stopped to watch her come into the ballroom.

"That's July Green," Novak hated that he sounded like he was bragging that he knew her. "Cut it out, you guys," he chided as they zoomed in on her low-cut dress.

"Holy shit, here comes another one." The screens moved back to the doorway where Lena stood draped on the arm of Jon Smyskin. Now Novak was worried. There had to be a good reason for him to bring Lena here.

Just then, Novak got a call from his sergeant in front of the hotel. "There's a crowd building out front, sir, and they're getting aggressive."

"I'll be right down," Novak told him.

As soon as Novak saw the size of the crowd forming across the street, he knew they could be in trouble. He phoned headquarters to see if they had put up roadblocks to stop people getting out to the hotel. Headquarters told him they had tried, but there were too many people headed out that way to be effective.

"Are the helicopters in the air?" Novak asked.

"All of them," was the answer.

"Okay, send one of them our way. I'll make sure the deck is clear for him. We have to get the prime minister out of here."

He went inside and was happy to see that the guests were still calm, obviously unaware of what was happening outside. The prime minister's chair beside Horatio at the head table was empty. Novak saw two of his men standing in front of the door off to one side of the main ballroom; he brushed by them and into the room. Inside, he saw the prime minister and Jon Smyskin in a heated discussion.

"Ah, good, I've caught the two of you together. Mr. Prime Minister, it is imperative that you leave here immediately."

"What's the problem, Novak?" The prime minister sounded annoyed.

"There is a mob forming outside, and I don't think we can hold them. I'm hoping if we send you and Mr. Smyskin out of here and let them know you're leaving, the crowd might back off," Novak told the two men. "Your helicopter will be landing in about ten minutes, sir."

He turned to Jon Smyskin, saying, "You'll have ten minutes after that to get your helicopter in and out, or you'll have to wait and take your turn with the rest of them. If you don't get out now, I can't guarantee either of your lives."

"Damn it, Smyskin, I knew this would happen," the prime minister said angrily.

"You'll have to continue your conversation later, sir," Novak told him. "Get yourself and your wife out back to the pool deck and take Horatio and his wife with you. If the crowd breaks through our line, we'll have to open fire on them, and neither of you want to be here if that happens."

The doctor took Jon's call. "Tell Julio to get his mother on the helicopter and get down here. I have to leave the hotel in the next fifteen minutes. There's a mob outside the hotel, and they're about to storm the place."

"Then your plan is working?" the doctor quietly asked.

"Too damned good," Jon confirmed.

"Hey, Julio, Jon wants you down at the hotel. Get your mother and go right now."

"I haven't got the entire luggage on board yet," Julio complained.

"Just do as you're told," the doctor told him. "We'll take the rest of it when the chopper comes back for me."

Julio went and got his mother and loaded her onto the helicopter. "Bring my bag with you when you come Julio," she told him.

"Ya, ya, I'll get it mother."

Julio had been hitting the coke pretty hard. Right now he couldn't remember where he'd put the doctor's bag. "But fuck it," he thought, "I know I put it in that room with him somewhere and that's all that matters. Anyway, this would be the last time he'd have to take orders from that asshole."

Novak stood on the pool deck watching the prime minister's helicopter leave and Smyskin's come in.

"Did you plan this?" Novak asked Jon.

Smyskin continued to look out into the night air. "Business is business, but to be at the top of your business, you have to have power. It takes power to bring a country to its knees, Mr. Novak, and the Bahamas had to be shown who is boss.You'll be surprised at how good this will be for my business."

Novak shrugged. "I guess it's good to have a goal in life."

Jon smiled, "I didn't make these decisions by myself. "You have to surround yourself with good people, don't you?"

Novak wasn't sure what the hell he meant by that. "Make sure you fly up over the front of the hotel so the crowd can see you leaving, and remember there are other choppers right behind you," he told Jon's pilot. Novak closed the door and watched them lift away. He hurried out to the front of the building to see if the crowd cooled off on hearing and seeing the main reason for their anger leaving.

Julio pulled the signaling device from his shirt pocket making sure no one saw him. His man had told him the higher he was, the better the signal would be, so he waited until they were up over the hotel.

"What are you laughing about, Julio?" his mother asked.

"I'm just happy to be here with you, Mother," he said as he pushed the button.

Novak's mouth opened in awe. The helicopter blew apart before his eyes. A cloud of dust appeared, and out of the cloud came four burning bodies all travelling straight sideways in different directions then plunged to the ground. Bits of debris seemed to scatter in the air before it began to descend. The part that fascinated Novak was that the rotor blades kept spinning and gaining altitude until they too succumbed to gravity and fell to earth.

Novak looked down to see where just seconds ago the braver ones in the crowd had begun making contact with the police line. Now everyone was scattering including his own men, trying to get out of the way of the hot steel raining down from the sky. People began rushing out of the hotel to see what had happened. Novak's instinct quickly told him that now his problem lay within.

He gathered some men and blocked the entrances then took the bullhorn and began telling the guests not to panic. "A helicopter has crashed outside. Please remain inside while we help the injured people, and then we shall begin letting you go in an orderly fashion."

He gave the bullhorn to one of his men and headed back outside. It was amazing; the crowd had evaporated. A few agitators were in the street trying to rally the troops, but Novak had his men put a stop to that. For the first time all night, he stopped and rested, leaning against a post by the front door, and then a call came over his radio.

"You said to call when Sir Harry left, Mr. Novak."

"Oh yes, I did," Novak answered.

"He just left with Mrs. Green, the woman called Lena, and our boss," the man in the surveillance room told him.

"How in hell did he get out of here?" Novak wanted to know.

"He took the patrol boat parked out back," the man told him. "Trust Sir Harry to look after himself." But now what; did he follow the instructions on the message or ignore them?

"You mean they were all on the helicopter," Wilbur Smith exclaimed on hearing who was involved in the crash. "Now what?"

"I think we should grab Lena and July and get them out of here," Sir Harry told him.

"Might take a while," Wilbur answered. "My helicopter is caught up in the queue, and it wouldn't look good if I tried to get priority."

Just then two security guards brought Lena and July out to where the two men were standing. "Things have gotten pretty unstable out front of the hotel," Sir Harry told them. "For security reasons, I want you ladies to come with us." Sir Harry led them to a boat docked nearby. "I confiscated this patrol boat. I'm sorry about the accommodations, but it was the best I could do for the moment."

The men helped the two women aboard, and Sir Harry guided the boat out into open water. The two women were staying calm and distant to one another.

Wilbur decided there wasn't going to be a catfight, so he joined Sir Harry up in the cockpit. "The girls seem to be staying out of each other's way, so I thought I'd come up and see what you were thinking," Wilbur told him.

"Out of tragedy rises opportunity. Since there are no Smyskins left, that leaves a billion dollars up for grabs, wouldn't you think?"

"Well, there is Lena and the U.S. government who might have some interest, not to mention the doctor," Wilbur warned.

"Look, said Sir Harry, "we know there is a banker being wined and dined on Smyskin's yacht, waiting for Lena and the Greens to sign the document releasing the money. We have two-thirds of the signers with us. The doctor has the other signer. He needs a bargaining chip to get out of the Bahamas because I don't think the Colombian government will help a man of his character. So if we guarantee his safe return to Colombia for Green, I think the doctor might be quite interested."

"I don't know," Wilbur sounded worried. "He's got the Miami mob there with him, and he is fucking crazy. Maybe he'll kill Green before we can get to him."

"No, the doctor won't do anything until Smyskin tells him to. Once he finds out that's not going to happen, he'll realize Green is the only bargaining chip he's got," Sir Harry surmised. "Let's go and take my boat out close to Smyskin's. We can negotiate from there."

Lena and July sat silently in the cabin. Finally, Lena broke the silence. "I think your husband is still alive, Mrs. Green."

"You've seen him, Lena?" There was a sense of urgency in July's voice.

"I haven't seen him for a couple of days, but I know someone who saw him very recently."

"Thank you," July answered, "that means a lot to me, but why was he where you were?"

"Let's just say he was forced into it. His chances of getting out of where he is are slim and none, but he's a very resourceful man, so who knows?"

"How can I get to him, Lena, he's my life?"

"Did you know you have a billion dollars in your American account, Mrs. Green?"

July almost laughed, "Did he try to buy his way out of trouble?"

"I'm not kidding, Mrs. Green. Your man and I stole the money from the Smyskin family and put it in your account."

"Why in hell's name would you do that?" July wondered.

"At the time, it was in desperation, now it's a bargaining chip." Lena saw Wilbur come into the cabin and signaled July to be quiet. "Don't sign anything until you know your husband is safe," she whispered.

Henekie was getting nervous; everything depended on Novak's call, and so far that hadn't happened. He had been hiding in the garage listening to what the doctor and the Miami guys were talking about, but if Novak didn't phone soon Smyskin would be back, and that would be the end of his plan.

Finally, the phone rang; Henekie listened as the doctor said, "Yes, Mr. Novak, this is the doctor. Okay, we won't do anything till we hear from Jon."

Henekie squared his shoulders and walked into the room carrying a bag in one hand and a tux in the other. “Hello, gentlemen,” he said. Everyone in the room looked startled.

“Who in hell are you?” the doctor asked.

“Jon didn’t tell you. He brought me over to dismantle Lena’s computers. I got an e-mail to bring Mr. Green a suit. I assume you are Mr. Green,” he said, looking at Bob, “being as you’re the only one in here naked.”

“Hello, Henekie,” a man leaning against the back wall said. “Must be ten years since the last time I saw you. The Sudan I think it was.”

“What are you doing here?” Henekie asked the man he recognized as a mercenary he’d worked with years before.

“I work for the Smyskins now.” The man turned to the doctor, “He’s probably all right. You always were a bit of a geek, weren’t you, Henekie? I’ll go outside and have a look around, just to make sure. Until we’re sure what you’re up to, Henekie, just sit down beside Mr. Green where we can keep an eye on you,” the man told him.

Henekie handed the tux to Bob. “Jon said for you to get dressed. You’re supposed to take him with you when you all go out to the boat,” Henekie told the doctor. The doctor nodded, and Bob began putting on the suit.

“I thought the deal was that my wife would come here where I could see she was all right,” Bob asked.

“Change of plans, Mr. Green, looks like I won’t be able to put you in the shower after all,” the doctor told him. Bob didn’t argue with that.

Henekie turned to the three men sitting together on a couch. “Jon told me you’re from Miami, right?” The men nodded. Henekie showed them the bag in his other hand. “I found this along with a bunch more cocaine over at Lena’s. I’d say it’s pretty high grade stuff, but maybe you could confirm what I think.”

Henekie reached in the briefcase and pulled out a plastic bag. He threw one to the doctor and one to the three men on the couch.

The doctor squinted his eyes, "Where did you say you found this?" he asked as he opened the bag.

Suddenly, there was a pop, and white powder covered the doctor, but Bob saw that his face was covered in blood, and both his arms were missing up to the elbows. Then Bob heard a bigger bang, and he looked over to see three men going over the back of the couch just before the room was consumed with white dust. Bob got to his feet trying to remember where the door was when he saw a patch of light appear in front of him.

Something grabbed him by the collar and the seat of his pants and threw him at the patch of light. His head hit something soft, and he heard a grunt as he felt himself land on someone. The air was clear outside the room, and he saw that he was on top of the same man who'd caught him and the girl trying to escape.

The man was trying to reach for his gun that had fallen on the floor. Bob punched him in the face and then caught hold of the man's arm as he tried to bring his pistol around. Bob wrestled with the man, and the gun went flying. Bob pummeled the man's face with his fist and then rolled away and picked up the revolver. It was then that he saw that the doctor had Henekie pinned to the wall. He had a knife in his teeth, and it was inches away from Henekie's throat.

Bob had no qualms; he took the revolver and shot the doctor just as the man on the floor jumped him, and again they wrestled for the gun. Bob felt the gun ripped out of his hands and then heard two shots, the man on top of him went limp and Bob crawled away.

He got to his feet ready to run, but Henekie waved for him to follow, "Come with me, you'll have the Colombian army to fight if you go that way." Bob didn't see much choice but to follow Henekie as he took him through a tunnel and then down a set of steps and finally into what looked like an underground cavern. A black boy appeared out of nowhere.

"Tommy, is that you?" Bob looked at the boy and then at his surroundings in amazement.

"The first time I saw this place I thought I was in heaven," Tommy told him, "but I'm real, and this place is real, Mr. Green."

Bob figured this had to be some kind of underground waterway and one hell of a place to hide.

"Is the boat loaded?" Henekie asked.

"Fueled up and ready to go," Tommy told him.

Bob was still having problems understanding how things worked as they went up through the locks and then out into the open water, but now that he felt the night air hit his face, he had a different set of questions.

"So have I just jumped out of the frying pan into the fire?" he asked Henekie.

"Probably, does my name mean anything to you, Mr. Green?"

"The man back there called you Henekie. The man who tried to kill me was called Henekie. Everyone blames everything on Henekie. Am I supposed to believe that you're the Henekie?"

"Do you remember a cold snowmobile ride with me on your ass, or a phone call telling you I had your daughter, or the night El Presidente's ship went down? I can go on, Mr. Green."

Bob was stunned. "You are the son of a bitch."

"Yes, Mr. Green. You see, you killed my best friend. You're the man I went to sleep hating and the man I woke up in the morning planning to kill. Funny us sitting together now, isn't it?"

"I heard you in the hospital that day. I was pretty well helpless. If ever there was a time to kill me, it was then, why didn't you?" Bob sounded like he needed to know.

"I couldn't kill my nemesis while he was lying in a coma, Mr. Green, or maybe I was scared I'd have nothing to get up for in the morning. You see, I was taken in by a pack of wolves and taught to kill to survive.

Then one day, the pack was gone, and I thought it was all your fault. As time went on and the farther I followed you, I began to realize you were just a symptom, not the cure. In a way, we were both caught up in something way over our heads, the only difference was that you wanted to get away from it, and I was trying to get my share. In the end, we both ended up here, Mr. Green. The goal is I want Lena and you want your wife. Are you with me?"

"You think they're in the same place?" Bob wasn't sure how that could happen.

"That's what I suspect," Henekie got up off the seat and moved up to the front of the boat. "Get Novak on the phone."

"I don't know his number," Bob told him.

"Yes, but your son does."

It seemed to Bob that Henekie knew an awful lot more than he should as his son came on the phone. Rikker was full of questions, but Bob couldn't answer them now.

"I'm sorry, Rikker, all I can tell you is I'm trying to find your mother. Please patch me through to Novak."

"Seems you spend a lot of time doing that," Rikker said as he put him through. Rikker's sarcasm did not go unnoticed by his father, but this was no time for a family squabble.

Novak sat up in the surveillance tower watching the last of the guests leave the ballroom in the Crystal Palace. Some of his men had gathered with him, congratulating one another on turning a disaster into an orderly exit of guests; many of whom still thought the helicopter crash was the reason they had to leave early. Novak was completely exhausted and looking for a quiet place to relax when his phone rang. He recognized the office number where Rikker had been monitoring his calls in order to keep some semblance to what he had to deal with.

"Job well done, Rikker," Novak spoke into the phone.

The answer Novak heard made him jump up off his chair. "This is Bob Green."

"You disappeared on us, Bob. Where are you?"

"I'm on a boat with a man whose main goal in life has been to kill me, but now we are both trying to find July and Lena."

"Sounds like the story of your life," Novak told him.

"Yes, it does, doesn't it? Here's Henekie, he wants to talk to you."

"Hello Novak, I need some information."

"I got your message, and I made the phone call, that's about all you're going to get from me," Novak answered.

"Green thanks you for the call. It's probably the only reason he's still alive. If you won't help me, maybe you'll help him," Henekie replied.

"What is it you want?"

"There are a few things you don't know, Novak. Lena and Mr. Green stole a billion dollars from the cartel's account and hid it in a U.S. account under the Greens' name. Smyskin knows where the money went and wants it back. Problem is, the United States won't give it back to Smyskin, so he has to go through Lena's bank and the Greens have to sign that her bank put the money in their account by mistake. Smyskin's going to have them all on the boat tonight to sign the papers and Sir Harry's delivering the ladies."

"For fuck's sake, Henekie, or whoever you are, you can come up with a better story than that. Sir Harry's had Mrs. Green all week, he's been protecting her from assholes like you," Novak stated.

"Okay, if you're so smart, why did Sir Harry bring her to Horatio's party?" Henekie spat into the phone. Novak didn't respond so Henekie continued on.

"I'll tell you why, because he had to prove to Smyskin that he really did have her. I'm sure he's getting well paid to keep her away from nosy guys like you, Novak." Novak had a funny feeling that what this guy was telling him was true. "Something went wrong with their plan, Novak.

Why did they take the patrol boat? Wilbur Smith was supposed to take the two women out to Smyskin's yacht in his helicopter."

"Okay, Smyskin's helicopter blew up killing everyone on board, which is probably what you planned. Anyway, I'm confirming it," Novak told Henekie.

"Did Sir Harry leave after or before the helicopter came down?" Henekie asked. This was not the response Novak had expected.

"After," Novak replied.

"So Sir Harry knew the Smyskins were dead. Why did he change his plan and take the patrol boat?" Henekie wondered out loud. There was still a lot of shit going on here.

"I suppose he wanted to protect the women."

"No, he wanted them for something," Henekie responded. "Sir Harry thinks he can get all the money for himself. That means he's headed for Lyford Cay where his yacht's tied up, but then you didn't even know he had a yacht, did you, Novak?"

Novak overlooked the cynicism. "If you go after Sir Harry, I'm going to try to stop you. I warn you, if you harm any of these people, I'll hunt you down until you're dead."

"For fuck's sake, Novak, why do you think Sir Harry took you under his wing and put you where you are? It's because he needed an over efficient, naive young man to do all his work for him. You're a source, Novak, a source for all the information he needs, so get your fucking head out of your ass and realize you're working for the man they call the Referee," then the phone went dead.

Novak's first reaction was one of anger to be talked to that way, but something Jon Smyskin had said stuck in the back of his mind: "You have to surround yourself with good men don't you."

"Do we have anything available to get us over to Lyford Cay?" Novak asked the men around him.

"No, sir. Everything is busy, and traffic still has the road tied up," one of the officers told him.

"Do we have a jeep of any kind around here?"

"I have one in the parking lot," another officer told him.

"All right, you three come with me." The next thing the officers knew, they were hanging on for dear life, as Novak honked his way through traffic over a steel fence and then through the golf course across the street.

Rikker Green listened into the phone conversation and decided that he too would head for Lyford Cay. There was little traffic to impede his motorcycle at this time of the morning, but seeing as he was not familiar with this area of Nassau it took him a little while to find the entrance. When he did find it, it was manned by a guard who didn't want to let him in. Rikker would not be deterred; he went back up the road then turned around and took a run at the entry, passing through a narrow walkway between the guardhouse and gate at a high rate of speed leaving the guard running for cover.

Once he was into the gated community, he slowed down then stopped on the channel bridge and thought he saw some lights at the other end of the channel. He followed the road until it came to a point where the channel and sea met. There was no sign of anything moving in the channel, but as he turned his bike around, he saw lights down by the water. The lights were behind a high brick wall that appeared to surround a house.

Rikker saw that the wall turned into a chain link fence as it got closer to the water. He decided to take a look and eased his motorcycle down along the brick wall and stopped his bike. He walked the last bit to peer around the wall and there they were; the patrol boat was tied up to a dock, but out farther were the lights of a much bigger boat.

Rikker was trying to work out some kind of plan when something hit the wall near his head. Instantly, he knew someone was shooting at him and dived for the ground as he heard the whine of bullets bouncing around him. He tried to crawl away on his belly, but when he looked back he saw two men closing in on him fast.

Just then, the lights of a vehicle swung around and pointed toward him. Rikker heard the sound of shots and knew the men behind him were shooting at the car lights and watched as the lights quickly retreated behind the front of the brick wall. The two men who had been looking for him seemed to fade back into the darkness, Rikker quickly turned and continued to ease his way back down to the fence.

Novak and his men were stopped on the channel bridge when they heard the shots. They couldn't locate where they came from until they reached the end of the street and went to turn around. The sound of bullets whining overhead encouaged them to quickly spin in behind a wall for cover. Novak thought he could sneak down along the wall, but there was too much background light, and a hail of bullets chased them back. Their pistols weren't much good at this range, and it was pretty evident that they were pinned down with no place to go. An orange glow began to appear from inside the wall, and then the crackling of wood burning told them that something substantial was burning inside.

"I'm going to try going down the outside of the wall again," he told the men and crouching low, he began making his way down toward the water. He drew no fire, and he made good time until he saw someone moving ahead of him. Whoever it was seemed to be stationary near where the wall ended. Novak pulled out his pistol and carefully made his way up behind the man. Novak was right behind him when he recognized him.

"Rikker, what the hell are you doing here?"

Rikker didn't even seem to be surprised. "About time you got here. They spotted me and pinned me down, but I'm pretty sure I saw Mother getting on that boat. They took her out to the yacht out there. Now the boat's back picking up the rest of them. They set everything inside on fire before they left," he reported.

"Do you think they're all gone?" Novak asked. He could see that the boat leaving the dock was a patrol boat, probably the one Sir Harry had used to leave the Crystal Palace.

"Yep, there's no one shooting at me anymore, and I watched them get on that boat."

Novak got on his phone, "Bring the jeep down here. They seem to have left."

Then he called the police dispatcher and finally got through. "I need a helicopter down to Lyford Cay and send any patrol boats that are available."

"Is this to do with the fire down there, sir?"

"Yes, and we need to check out a yacht that's leaving here."

"Sir Harry already informed us about all that. He said he had it under control and not to worry about it."

"I want a helicopter down here right now," Novak yelled into the phone.

The dispatcher sounded annoyed. "I'm sorry, sir, but you know how busy we've been. There's nothing available right now, maybe in an hour or so. We'll do our best, sir," and he was gone.

Novak put down his phone; slowly it was sinking in. Henekie was right; without Sir Harry and Horatio to back him up, he had lost all his power.

The Nassau police had always resented Horatio being made police chief, and Novak knew they resented him for moving in and covering up Horatio's inadequacies. Well, better he knew where he stood than making a fool of himself later.

The men had brought the jeep down to where the wire fence started. Now they were ramming the fence until it fell over, and they all went inside the compound. The prevailing breeze coming in off the water still didn't totally dispel the intense heat; they could see there was a long garage attached to the main house with at least six cars outlined in fire. It was pretty evident that this had been a pretty posh estate, but not much would be left now.

A palm tree between them and the burning buildings burst into flame scattering everyone until they understood what it was. The men gathered around Novak. "There's something sinister about this place. There aren't any fire trucks, no lights coming on in the houses down the street. No one is coming out to see what's going on. Who in hell lives here, Novak?" one of them asked.

Novak took a deep breath before he answered. "The people who live here don't know their neighbors and don't want to know them. The man who lives in this house is the same guy who owns that yacht out there and your boss Wilbur Smith is with him."

"Then why are we here?" the same man asked.

Novak was saved from answering right away by the ringing of his phone. He thought it would be the police dispatcher giving him an update, instead he heard a staticy voice.

"Are you over at that fire we can see on shore?" the voice asked.

Novak was taken off guard. "Yes," was all he answered.

"Well, stay there. I'm sending a package your way."

Novak had a hundred questions to ask, but Henekie was gone.

"Gentlemen, that call was to tell us we might just as well stay here and secure things until they send something our way. If we go back, I know they'll find something for us to do, so let's rest up here till someone comes and tells us different." They were all tired, and the men didn't argue; it was a beautiful beach and a beautiful night. There was nothing they could do about the fire but watch it burn, so the men began finding a comfortable place to bunk in.

Novak joined Rikker who continued to pace the beach.

"Look," he pointed, they left the boat. I can swim out to it." Rikker had no sooner waded into the water when they saw a flash of light. The patrol boat bucked and then began turning on its side.

"Might as well relax, Rikker," Novak told him. "Your dad and another man are out there on a boat. I have no idea what they're going to do. I just wouldn't want to be the guys on that yacht."

"He shouldn't have let her get there in the first place," Rikker answered angrily.

"I think you'd better sit down here beside me, and I'll tell you the story of your mother and father, Rikker. It's pretty obvious you have no idea how every time those two were torn apart, how hard your father had to fight to get back to her. Let's hope he can do it one more time."

# Thirty-Seven

"TORCH IT!" SIR Harry said into the phone.

"It's done," his man said back to him, "everything's on fire. This old timber is going up like a matchbox."

"Good, I want nothing left. Who do you think the people are out front?" Sir Harry asked.

"Don't know. They didn't shoot back so if it is the police, they aren't well armed."

"We're headed for the patrol boat now. We'll be aboard in a few minutes," his man told him.

Sir Harry turned to his captain and pointed to a chart. "Here's where we're going. About here, you'll see the lights of a ship. Call me and I'll tell you what to do from there. Until then, I'll be in the stateroom, and I don't want to be disturbed." Sir Harry started down the stairs with Wilbur Smith close at his heels.

"I thought we were taking what we had and getting the hell out, Harry? What's this we're still going out to Smyskin's yacht?"

"The trouble with you, Wilbur, is you think too small. Do you think I brought those two women along just so you could fuck them? They are our ticket to the billion. Smyskin's yacht is just sitting there, expecting us to come aboard. That's why I brought my men along. We hit them and hit them hard before they know what happened, Wilbur. I not only want the billion, I want his yacht too." Sir Harry stopped on the stairs, "You'd look pretty good in this yacht, wouldn't you, Wilbur?"

A look of comprehension came into Wilbur's eyes. "Okay, but what about the banker from the states? He'll know something is up."

Sir Harry turned and continued down the stairs. "You also worry too much, Wilbur. All he wants is the cash we promised him to make this deal work, and I've got that with me in a suitcase."

Sir Harry had kept Lena and July apart for the simple reason that he didn't want them messing each other up in a catfight and then having to present themselves in front of the American banker. He had them both brought into the stateroom and placed across the table from each other. "It's pretty obvious you two don't like each other, but I need you to behave yourselves until you do a little business for me. If you do as you're asked, then there'll be no consequences, and we'll all go on our way."

"So what is it, Harry? We go out to Smyskin's yacht, have a little party, fuck Smyskin and his brother, and everybody goes home happy," July asked sarcastically.

Lena laughed, "Good guess, but no cigar. Your husband put a billion dollars of Smyskin's money in your account in the states, and now you have to sign some papers so he can get it back.

" I'm sure you had nothing to do with this," July fired back.

"Sure, I helped him do it," Lena answered her.

"Ladies, ladies, this is exactly what I didn't want," Sir Harry warned them.

"For your information, both the Smyskins were killed last night, so that leaves you all off the hook, but in return, I want that money turned over to me." Both Lena and July sat quietly digesting this turn of events, so Sir Harry carried on. "Mr. Green has to sign too, so we are flying him out to meet us. Once the papers are signed, I'll take you wherever you want to go." The two women were not paying any attention to Sir Harry; their attention was on each other.

"So you and Bob stole a billion dollars and planned to run away together."

Lena lit a cigarette then she responded. "You don't like me much since I fucked your husband, do you?"

Everyone in the room expected July to go over the table after Lena, but she fooled them all by sitting back in her chair. "If that's what he wants, then he can fucking well have you."

Lena's response was also unexpected. "Oh, I'm not what he wants, July."

"He wasn't presented to me as your husband, not that that would have stopped me because I like men, and they enjoy me. Your husband was different. I once accused him of being gay because no matter what I did, I could never seduce him. After a while, I just decided he was too wrapped up in himself to let me in, but now that I've seen who my competition is, I understand why."

"Nice try, Lena, that makes me feel a lot better about you two stealing money together." It was obvious July didn't trust her. "Someone was trying to steal that money from me, July. I needed a foreign account to hide it in, and your husband happened to have one. Inadvertently, I think that account saved his life because the Smyskins needed him to get the money back." Lena took a drag from her cigarette giving July some time to take this all in.

"There's something else you should know. There is no way Harry here can let us go alive once we sign the paper. We will sign because you and Mr. Green won't be able to stand seeing each other tortured and I can't stand pain, so our only bargaining tool is to ask to make our demise quick," Lena said calmly.

"Now ladies, let's not be so morbid. Of course I'll let you go, just do as I ask, and everything will be all right."

July looked over at Sir Harry, "I can usually pick a man apart and put him back together pretty quickly, but you seem to have somehow gotten under my radar. How does a man like you end up here and is that 'Sir' like the rest of you, not real?"

Sir Harry chuckled, "You are right, July, not much of me that you see is real, but I'll tell you what is real. All I can remember before I was fourteen was never having enough to eat. It was the end of World War II, and Italy was in a shambles. Somehow my mother found enough money to put me on a train to Germany. The Americans were pouring money in, and there was lots of work. I got off the train in Germany with no food, no money, and didn't speak a word of German. Of course one of the stipulations to working there was that you had to speak some German.

Luckily, I met some Italian kids singing on the steps in front of their building. I could play the guitar a little bit, so soon we became friends. They gave me a crash course in German that night, and somehow I stumbled through an interview the next morning and by that afternoon was working on a factory floor.

Within a few months I was a foreman, and the next year I moved into the office. It was a large pharmaceutical company, and along the way a drug had been developed that could keep people going for long periods of time without rest. It was a derivative made from nose spray. The Nazis had used it at the end of the war to compensate for a shortage of labor, and of course it was highly illegal to use in most companies.

It just so happened that Japan had a chronic shortage of labor after the war. They came to our company to see if such a drug was available. I was sent to Japan to open a lab so the company could send me the legal ingredients, and I turned it into what the factory floors needed. Every morning, the workers would take their daily shot of stimulant and work long hours.

This lasted into the early sixties. The only way it was detected was from the odor it left on the workers' breath, and the Japanese were forced to ban it. I bought the lab and moved it to Hong Kong. There was still a market for the drug in North and South Korea and in Hong Kong. No one cared what was in anything as long as you made money and gave the right people some of it.

The South Korean market dried up in the early seventies, but by then I was making lots of drugs, mostly with an opium base and dealing with people both buying and selling all over Asia. I had a lavish lifestyle and everything I could possibly want until a member of the British Narcotics Division showed up at my back door one evening.

So I became a double agent, turning in all kinds of agents and dealers all across Asia and parts of Eastern Europe. When the British deemed it too hot for me to stay in Hong Kong, they gave me a new identity and pensioned me off in England. I had no intention of trying to live off a small pension, not after what I was used to, so I took my memoirs to a member of Parliament. He got my story published, and I became famous.

The crown and state wanted to reward me for my services, so suddenly my birth certificate was found in Hong Kong and I was knighted. The trouble was that I had now created a logistical nightmare for the Department of Foreign Affairs. Anyone in the drug business anywhere in the world knew there was a big reward on my head. Luckily right at that time, the CIA was looking for someone with enough experience to broker a deal between El Presidente, the main drug lord in Colombia, and the Drug Enforcement Agency in the United States. So the British gave me a body makeover that made me look twenty years younger and sent me off to the Bahamas."

The girls thought Sir Harry was going to stop there, but he

only hesitated and then continued on. "There was no other way the government could control the amount of cocaine coming into the States, so they wanted El Presidente to agree to a quota. In return, they would allow him relatively free access to the American market.

This worked well for quite a few years. The CIA was happy with my work and gave me all the money I needed to get a new government elected in the Bahamas. It won on an anti-corruption platform, but really it was just new corrupt politicians who were much more pro-American. Over time, I became the most powerful man in the Bahamas and the beauty of it was everyone thought I was some mythical character called the Referee, but all good things must come to an end.

Drug lords in South America became tired of the quotas and began shipping across the Mexican border. At first we tried to help the Americans, but they trained Hispanics to fight in their wars. When these guys came home, there wasn't much for them, so they joined the Mexican cartels, and soon the cartels had a trained army fighting for them. We gave up and got out. The cocaine was coming across the border like the snow you see drifting on the Canadian prairies.

It creates nothing but problems, and all the money needed to fix the problems is shipped back across the border. I don't know how much longer that can go on, but we didn't want to find out, so except for the Miami market, we moved our markets to Europe and the Middle East where quality brings top dollar.

This pissed my partner in the CIA right off. His cut was now getting very small, so he decided that if he could get rid of El Presidente, he could then move in and control the Colombian market. You know how the elaborate plan he hatched turned out, don't you, July? I had to come out of semiretirement to get a new CIA man and get El Presidente's son to leave Harvard and take over the family business in Colombia, but Harvard doesn't teach you how to fight in the trenches these days. They are more into the philosophy of 'trust me, I'll look after your money' theory that seems to be popular these days. Jon Smyskin just didn't have what it takes to survive in this business, so now Wilbur and I are getting out and taking whatever he left behind."

"I guess that tells me pretty well all I need to know, Sir Harry. You are capable of anything and that tells me Lena's right. We're a loose end you need to tie up," July told him.

Sir Harry looked at July. "You and your husband have been a thorn in my side for a long time. We arranged for you people to come to the farm on Andros because we needed the airstrip opened back up. We figured you'd last a couple of years and then be gone, but you wouldn't quit. We offered money. We even tried to starve you out, but for some reason you kept hanging on. Finally, we got you so desperate you went on a wild goose chase looking for money, and we were able to hang a false narcotics charge on your husband.

Then it wasn't me, but we think Waddell sanctioned a hit on your husband up in Canada. Somehow he survived and made his way back to the Bahamas. Again his luck held out because my CIA partner decided he needed him to help entice El Presidente out of Colombia.

Of course both you and Bob were expendable when the exercise was over, but somehow you were among the only ones that survived. I have a soft spot for you, July, and I thought your husband was pretty well fucked. I bought El Presidente's yacht and gave the proceeds to you because the stipulation was that you had to spend the money in the Bahamas. When I heard you wanted to buy the old Andros Hotel, I thought perfect, I can keep an eye on you there. I went to Gator and convinced him to sell the hotel to you. I remember telling him that he'd get a renovated hotel back in a couple of years, and the Greens would be the perfect ones to run it for him.

Instead you turned the place into one of the finest hotels in the islands and look at Lena here. All her life she gave men what they wanted, but given a chance, she turned that into what men needed and became a very rich woman.

No, I won't kill you, July, but your family is another matter. And I might as well tell you right now you cannot go back to your hotel because I promised it back to Old Man Gator.

Lena is a different situation. She has no family, but take away her beloved computers and rich men and force her to live like Jon Smyskin had planned for her, abject poverty. I'm pretty sure in time she'd take her own life."

At this point, the captain came in and whispered something in Sir Harry's ear.

"Excuse me," he said to the women and left the stateroom.

"Sorry to bother you, sir, but there's a Henekie on the phone. He says he's going to blow up the ship unless you talk to him."

Sir Harry had to stop and think for a moment. He fell back on his old MI5 training manual, 'Find your adversaries' weakness and build on it'. Trouble was, he was sure Henekie had read the same book.

"Hello, Henekie," Sir Harry said into the phone. "I thought Lena was just trying to scare us when she said you were still alive. Guess I should have paid more attention to her. What is it you want?"

"Hello Sir Harry, what I want is Lena."

"Well, you can have her when I'm done with her, and what the hell's this threat that you're going to blow us out of the water?"

"You remember that explosion in Nassau a while back they attributed to a missile? I have that same missile launcher aimed at your yacht. I suggest you stop your boat now because in about fifteen minutes, you'll be out in open water where it gets too rough for us to get a good shot," Henekie told Sir Harry. "If you keep going, I'm going to have to pull the trigger, Lena or no Lena.

Sir Harry looked over at the captain, "Have you got anything on radar?"

"Once in a while we get a blip of something out there, but it could be almost anything."

"Okay, stop the engines and turn out all the lights and curtain all the rooms off," Sir Harry told the captain and then went back to the phone.

"How in hell do I know you are really out there, Henekie? I think your bluffing."

"Well then, why did you just shut out your lights and stop," Henekie wanted to know.

"I've got cash on board, Henekie, lots of it. Take what you can and get out. If you figure you're going to take Lena out to Smyskin's yacht and get that money, you're crazy," Sir Harry's voice sounded a little strained.

"You are missing one piece of the puzzle, Harry old boy," a different voice came on the phone.

"Is that you, Green? How in hell did you get in on this?"

"The doctor's body parts quit working, so I decided to come out here and see what you were up to," Green answered.

"Interesting company you're keeping these days, Mr. Green, but then you both do like to stick your nose in other people's business, don't you?"

Henekie's voice came back. "I'll sweeten the pot, Sir Harry, you give me Lena and a million cash and I'll give you Green."

Sir Harry's mind was racing; he had got a concession out of Henekie, maybe he could make this work. "Okay, let me talk to Lena."

"I can put a boat over the side and see if we can sneak up on this guy," the captain said.

"No, you have no idea what this man is capable of. We'll negotiate our way out of this if possible."

Sir Harry made his way back into the stateroom and sat down

beside Lena. "Is there any way we can get that money without you being there?"

He'd obviously caught Lena off guard. "I don't know. Why?"

Sir Harry decided to level with her. "Someone wants to take you off this boat in exchange for Bob Green. You would like to get off this boat wouldn't you, Lena?" Anything was better than the situation she was in now.

"Well, there might be a way. That banker is not the owner of the bank, he is just a signing officer. I could appoint you as a signing officer of my bank. I think I can give you pretty good documentation, but we'll have to talk to the American banker."

Sir Harry led Lena up to the captain's deck and put her through to Smyskin's yacht on his ship to shore phone.

"Hope they are treating you well," she said to the banker when he came on the phone.

"Yes, yes, very well," the banker answered.

Sir Harry was happy to hear that he was in a good mood.

"We've had some problems in Nassau tonight. The airport has been closed, and most of the communications are out. As a consequence, it is not safe for me to travel," Lena told him.

"I have therefore given Sir Harry signing authority with my bank to act on my behalf. I hope this is all right with you." The American banker was hesitant to answer.

"I guess if you had a witness who is a commissioner of oaths in the United States, it might be acceptable."

Lena didn't miss a beat. "Yes, he witnessed my signature, and he will be available in person on your yacht. His name is Wilbur Smith, and he is the man in charge of the CIA for the Miami and Caribbean area."

The banker sounded very impressed.

"Sounds like you've been very thorough Miss Lena. Yes, that will be quite adequate."

"Perfect, Sir Harry and Mr. Smith will arrive at the yacht in about an hour." With that, she signed off.

Sir Harry did a little jig. "You are a clever little devil when your back is against the wall, Lena."

"I'll never feel safe as long as you're around," Lena leveled with Sir Harry.

I wouldn't worry too much about anyone bothering you again with Henekie behind you, but what he has in mind for you, I don't know," Sir Harry warned her.

Lena shrugged, "Can't be any worse than what you had planned for me, can it?"

Sir Harry didn't answer. He was already on the phone to Henekie. "All right, we have a deal. How do you want to handle the exchange?"

"I'll have my man bring Green over in a small boat," Henekie told him. "Don't forget the money. Put it in a suitcase that Lena can carry, and make sure she sees the money. We wouldn't want some kind of a bomb in there, would we, Sir Harry?" Henekie didn't wait for an answer. "When I get Lena back to my boat, I'll turn on a small green light on the bow, and you'll see me head away. Then it will be safe for you to continue on."

"All right, bring him over," Sir Harry told him.

Henekie darkened his face and hands before they got on the boat. "Before we go, Mr. Green, I have to tell you what's about to happen. You've got fifteen minutes or less to get off that boat once it gets underway. There's no way Sir Harry can be allowed to get away. He has too many friends for any of us to stay alive long if he does. I don't like to send a man into a bad situation without evening up the odds a bit."

He put a small round piece of metal in Green's hand. "See this lever? Keep your thumb on it. When it's released, you have five seconds to get something between you and the blast. Anything will do—a body, door, wall, anything that will stop the shrapnel. When you get on the yacht, they'll frisk you down, but it will be dark, and I'm betting they won't check your hands. If they do, you'll have to use this a little quicker than we planned, that's all. If I see the flash of that going off, I'm going to wait about twenty seconds and then let the yacht have it, so you and your wife had better be off by then. You've been in some tough spots before, Green, piece of cake, right?"

Henekie shook his hand, "Just don't accidentally take your thumb off that lever for God's sake."

Bob Green sat in the front of the boat, and Henekie sat at the back with the motor; they didn't talk again. When they reached Sir Harry's yacht, the exchange was quick; Bob and Lena's eyes met as they passed each other, but there was nothing to say. Bob climbed the stairs up on to the ship's deck and was immediately subjected to a body search. Henekie was right; they patted Bob down but didn't check his hands.

"All right, just wait here with us until they call for you."

Time was of the essence, but Bob knew he had to be patient. He looked at the starlit sky and felt the warm sea breeze on his face. "Not a bad night to die, I suppose," he thought.

Lena sat quietly in the front of the boat thinking that the man driving was of no consequence until she heard his voice.

"Hello Lena."

"You," she gasped recognizing the voice. "This is your entire fault, Henekie. You're the one who stole that money."

"I had to, Lena, I promised it to a man in return for my life. Now I'm saving yours because I finally realized you're more valuable than anything I'll ever come up with in my time. No one will ever bother you again, and in return you'll give me the money to do whatever I want to do."

"With your success rate at business, this will cost me a lot of money," but for some strange reason, Lena felt very safe right now.

When Henekie arrived at his larger boat, he helped Lena move to the back of the smaller boat and sat her down. “This is as far as you go with me, Lena. See that fire on shore? Novak's there waiting for you.”

“Are you expecting me to drive this boat all the way over there by myself?” Lena sounded about to panic.

“You can do it, Lena. I'll set the throttle at half speed, and all you have to do is turn this handle to steer it.”

Henekie went to the front of her boat and screwed in a pipe. A green light appeared on the top of it then he came back to her.

“Just keep that light between you and the fire. Novak will see you coming and help you out,” and then he jumped into the bigger boat and put the outboard in gear.

Lena left screaming, but he saw she was heading in the right direction.

Sir Harry and his captain scanned the water with their binoculars watching for a green light. “There it is,” the captain shouted. Sir Harry saw it too; he began to relax as they watched the light move across the water away from them.

“Okay, let's get this baby moving,” Sir Harry told the captain. He went outside to the back and hollered over the railing, “All right, bring Green up to the stateroom.”

Bob Green followed the men up some stairs down a narrow hallway to a heavy-looking wooden door. Of interest to him was that the bathrooms were situated along the hallway. The wood door opened, and Sir Harry invited him in. He held out his hand, but Bob paid no attention to him. All he saw was July sitting on one side of a large table. He sometimes forgot how beautiful she was until he saw her in person again. Those big blue eyes full of questions: are you all right, where have you been, or if she was really worried, where in hell have you been, you son of a bitch?

“All right, have a quick hug you two, then we have to get down to business," Bob heard Sir Harry say. It wouldn't have mattered what Sir Harry said. Bob and July were in each other's arms.

"I love you," July whispered in Bob's ear.

She expected to hear the same words of endearments from Bob, instead she heard, "Tell them you have to go to the bathroom."

"All right, that's enough," Sir Harry told them. "If you don't break it up, I'll have you put in separate rooms." Bob and July sat down across from Sir Harry.

"Tell me what happened to the doctor." Sir Harry wanted to know.

Bob started to tell him when July interrupted. "I have to go to the bathroom," she told them.

"Of course, my dear. They are just down the hallway," he pointed to the wooden door. July got up and headed for the door then Sir Harry seemed to have a second thought.

"Maybe you should escort her, Wilbur. We wouldn't want something to happen now that we're this close." Wilbur got up and followed July out the door shutting it after him.

Bob gave a sigh of relief that narrowed the odds a lot, and July was out of harm's way. Bob assessed the situation. Sir Harry was directly across from him. The only one armed was the guard, and he was sitting behind Sir Harry reading a newspaper. Now was the time; he pushed the table skidding Sir Harry and his chair into the guard, and they both went sprawling. Bob tossed the grenade into the two men and then flipped the table on top of them and stood on it. He felt the men struggle to lift the table then there was a deafening bang, the table lifted tossing Bob off and sent him rolling across the floor.

Bob didn't stop to see if he was hurt. The explosion from the grenade gave him a headache and he couldn't hear anything but his goal was to get to Smith before he knew what had happened. Bob threw open the wooden door; Wilbur was standing there about to come in.

"What's going on?" was all Wilbur got out before Bob punched him right between the eyes. Wilbur went down like a stone.

"Come on, July," he yelled. "We have to get out of here."

July came rushing out of the bathroom, and they headed up the hallway back the way Bob had been brought in. Bob wanted to get down to the lower deck before they jumped, but as they came out onto the upper deck stairs, Bob saw someone on the steel steps running up toward them.

"We're going to have to go over from up here," he told her. She didn't ask any questions. They climbed the railing; she grabbed his hand, and they jumped.

Henekie kept one eye on his watch and the other on the sea. We can't wait any longer, sir," Tommy warned him.

"All right, Tommy, make your run." Tommy turned the boat toward Sir Harry's yacht and opened her up. Henekie had pretty well given up on Bob, but just as they started their attack, he saw a flash of light and knew Bob had detonated the grenade.

Problem was he had little time to let Bob off the yacht. Henekie moved in far closer to the yacht than he wanted to before he fired. He watched as the missile went into the heart of his target. As they turned away, it was as if the whole top of the yacht lifted away. Even Henekie hadn't expected that much of a reaction. Tommy had the boat wide open as the sky above them filled with debris. Henekie could feel the heat from the explosion on the back of his neck; he knew they'd be lucky to get away. He couldn't see any hope for Bob Green at all.

Bob and July had simultaneously left the railing as the blast occurred. It flipped and tossed them through the turbulent air, and then they hit the water hard. It was as if a giant force was pushing them down. Bob struggled to fight his way up but July was limp beside him. All this time, she had never let go of him, and he wouldn't either, because, well, because that's the way it was.

It was Rikker who saw the green light first. "I think there's a boat headed our way," he yelled, bringing everyone to their feet. They were standing on the beach watching the green light bobble toward them when they saw the huge explosion behind it.

They stood in awe, forgetting about the approaching boat, until Lena appeared out of the darkness plowing through the sand and up onto shore scattering everyone.

Novak was the first to reach her. She was frozen to the steering handle and shouting verbal abuses which made him think she was all right. Novak released her hand and stood her up, but all her attention was on the burning yacht.

"The son of a bitch blew it up. He blew Sir Harry to kingdom come."

"Who did, Lena?" Novak wanted to know.

"Henekie. He got me off the boat." Novak put his hands on her shoulders trying to get her to focus.

"Where are the Greens?" he asked her.

She started to cry. Novak had never seen Lena cry before; when it came to emotion, it was like she hung a curtain of steel around herself.

"They were on the yacht," she told him. Novak looked down at her boat. The boat itself looked all right, but the motor had stalled, and the prop was definitely bent.

"Okay guys, I want you to take Lena to my place. She'll be safe there," he said as he handed her the keys. "Rikker and I are going to see if we can get this boat to run and go on out to the explosion. See if you can get someone out there as soon as you can."

The men helped Rikker and Novak get the boat down to the water then they loaded Lena into the jeep and left. To Novak's amazement, the motor still ran, but the prop was pretty wobbly, and they could only travel at a slow, agonizing speed. At times, they were sure they saw a bright light scanning the waters around the fire and hoped it was a rescue boat looking for survivors. When they finally got out to the wreck, it was daylight.

Novak and Rikker searched through the debris, quickly noticing that they were joining a search already underway by a number of fins protruding from the water. They found part of a body dressed in a white uniform and some unidentifiable body parts, but that was all. Within an hour, they were joined by a patrol boat, but they had heard of no reports of survivors.

Rikker finally broke down and cried on Novak's shoulder. "I never got a chance to say goodbye," he sobbed.

"They knew you loved them, and that's all that matters," was all Novak could think of to say. It was pretty obvious the Greens' luck had run out.

# EPILOGUE

NOVAK WATCHED AS Mindy and Rikker walked across the windswept cemetery. Grandma Green had died, and she'd always wanted Bob and July's name on the tombstone with hers. Their bodies had never been found, so the kids had agreed to this, although they knew their parents might resent the fact that they were buried here. They had made the islands their home, but this was in name only, so it was okay.

Novak had been forced to quit his job with the Bahamian government, but Interpol had insisted he stay on with them so he'd been allowed to stay in the islands which he too now considered home. Novak's luck had stayed with him; he wrote a book about his adventures. It became a best seller, and he had become very famous because of it.

He guessed that Horatio Norton had neutralized Old Man Gator because he never put a claim to the hotel on Andros. Mindy had taken it over and made it more successful than ever. It probably hadn't hurt that Novak spent a great deal of time there and a lot of people came so they could meet him and see the hotel he so often wrote about in his stories. He stayed there because he felt at home and he could keep an eye on Mindy.

Rikker was a different story. He worked at the hotel for a while, but that wasn't for him. He'd gotten a taste of the Interpol world, and Novak had to admit he was a natural at it. Sir Harry had always said the Greens liked to stick their noses in other people's business, and Rikker was no different. In fact he'd pretty well taken over Novak's job, but he didn't mind; it gave him time to pursue his other interests.

No one saw much of Lena anymore except for Novak. They still had their liaisons. It was from her that he learned that Henekie was in South America where he lived with a woman he'd met in Germany. One of her boys, which Henekie considered to be his own, ran the show for her here in the Bahamas.

"He's a computer wizard and smarter with money than I'll ever be," Lena told Novak.

Henekie apparently owned a prosperous town where everyone worked in a sugar mill that he also owned. One side of the mill, of course, produced enough cocaine for him to ship a planeload every month directly to Africa, where his other two sons looked after the distribution from there.

Some things don't change, Novak thought. The world had become smaller, and the Bahamas were no longer needed as a distribution center, but the white powder still sifted its way around the world.

There was one story that would haunt Novak until the day he died. He'd done everything he could to verify the story, but there was nothing he could find to back it up, and he found out the old man who told him the story told lots of them. Novak decided that it was his heart that made him want to believe it was true, not his head.

There had been an old black man at the Andros Hotel one night. He was from one of the southernmost Bahamian Islands and was telling stories about the islands that Novak loved to hear.

The old man had far too much to drink, and Novak was about to leave when he began one last story. "I got a little dock down there, where you's know I gas up a few boats, and I gots a little store up the dock that people can get some fishin' supplies or whatever they might needs when they's passin through.

I was closing up one night. It was just dark when I heard the sound of a big powerful engine pullin' in. This ain't you're usual fishin' boat, you understand. This was the kinda boat used for things we don't talk about. There was a man and a woman aboard. Thing that struck me funny was they was dressed in fine clothes just like they come from a fancy ball, but when I saw them up close, I could see they was beat up like they'd been in a fight.

This old boy didn't like the looks of things, but the man asked me if they could still get fuel, and I hoped to get rid of him by saying we only took cash. He handed me five hundred American and said, 'If that ain't enough, let me know.' Next he asked me if there's anyplace they could clean up and maybe buy some clothes. The woman rubbed her stomach and said, 'Yes, and maybe something to eat too.' I didn't usually say anything, but I knew they got money, so I told them, 'My sister's got the restaurant and store up at the end of the dock. I'm sure she's around there someplace. She'll help you out.' They headed on up the dock, and I didn't see them for a while, but that's okay. The locals come down on the dock to have a look at the boat and tell me the peoples are having something to eat.

I dozen't mind. I got lots of company and nothing too important to do anyway. After a while, the two peoples come down the dock looking like tourists, and I realize it's not the boat these boys want to see—it's that blonde. Man, she was some good-lookin' woman. She wasn't like most of these stuck-up white woman either. She started talkin' to those black boys just like she knew them all her life.

The man came up to me and asked if I knew anyone looking for a boat like this one. I says yes, I know such a man. He lives down in Aruba, but I know he'd pay big money for a boat like this. I writes down the name for the man, and then he asks where's the next place to the south he can get fuel. I shows him on my chart where he has to go, but I tells him it's a good eight hours away. 'You ain't gonna find that place at night,' I tells him. He says, 'No, the sea is very calm tonight. We have to go while the goin's good.' They get in the boat, and the man lights up the dash in front of him. Then he said, 'Don't worry about us. We'll just follow that star.' I looked up at the sky, but there were a million stars up there."

The old man dozed off; Novak reached over and shook him.

"Then what happened?" Novak desperately wanted to know.

"They idled their way out of the harbor, and then we heard that powerful engine open up, and they was gone."

But then there are lots of stories in the islands.

Watch for Bob's next book, "The Caine Train" as some of these same characters continue to move the white powder around a modern-day world.

CPSIA information can be obtained at www.ICGtesting.com
Printed in the USA
BVOW072105271112

306627BV00003B/5/P